One Day Of Magic

One day of magic, one girl and one boy.
One day of magic that filled us with joy.
Only one day of magic, but magic is done,
Just one day of magic, and now I have none.

One day of magic and it was so right.
One day of magic that turned into night.
Only one day of magic, but that day is gone.
Just one day of magic, and now I'm alone.

One day of magic was all that we had.
One day of magic, was it really so bad?
Only one day of magic, and now we're apart.
That one day magic has shattered my heart.

One day of magic that I shared with you.
One day of magic, I wish it were true!
Only one day of magic, the magic supreme,
But that one day of magic was only a dream.

Crossroads Part I: One Day Of Magic

Copyright © 2005-2006 by Larry J. Bristol

10-Digit ISBN 1-59113-903-1
13-Digit ISBN 978-1-59113-903-4

All rights reserved. No part of this book may be reproduced, stored in a retrieval system, or transmitted in any form or by any means, electronic or mechanical, including photocopying, recording, or by any information storage and retrieval system, without permission in writing from the author.

Printed in the United States of America

The characters and events depicted in this book are fictitious. Any similarity to real persons, living or dead, is coincidental and not intended by the author.

Booklocker.com, Inc.
2006

Illustrations and cover layout by Christina Cartwright, Digitell Design, http://www.digitelldesign.com

Crossroads

Larry J. Bristol

For Xylah Lee Gullett

Your little green frog will find you someday, and you will live happily ever after in a beautiful white castle resting on an island in the middle of the river that runs through the Five Lands.

"Darth" Zayde

Forward
(Author's Notes)

This is a work of pure fiction.

Well, nothing is all that pure these days, and this is certainly no exception to the rule. The story unfolds during the late 1960's and early 1970's in Bryan, a small town in central Texas about a hundred miles northwest of Houston. Many of the persons, places, and events in this story are based on actual persons, places, and events I remember from real life.

But let's not get carried away! First of all, my memory is simply not that good. In no way is this intended to be an autobiography, even an unauthorized one. While the main character of this story seemingly has my name, shares many of my interests, and certain parts of my history, it is important the reader note once again my first statement: *This is a work of pure fiction!* If you happen to be one of the privileged few with some personal relationship with the author, then congratulate yourself, but do not draw any conclusions about either my personality or history from the stories and accounts presented herein. Just remember one simple rule: *(Here's another clue for you all!) It ain't me, babe! No, no, no, it ain't me!*

Other than my own, few of the names used in this story are the names of real people. How does that standard disclaimer go? *"The characters depicted in this story are fictional, and do not represent any specific individual. Any similarity between these characters and any person, living or dead, is purely coincidental."* That about covers it. This especially applies to the character by the name of Lawrence Jackson Bristol!

So right about now, you might be asking yourself, "Self," you ask, "why did he use his own name?" That's a really good question that possibly deserves a better answer than simply, "Because!" The truth is I don't know. Part of it, perhaps, is I know more facts (and jokes!) about the name *Bristol* than any other name I could think of. So I kept the last name. I could have changed the first name, I suppose, but what would have been the point? For the record, my name is *not* Lawrence Jackson anyway; it is simply Larry Jack. Why would I want to change the guy's name to something like Leonard James Bristol? Mishuganah! (This is as good a time as any to point out the Glossary found in the back of this book!)

Many of the characters in the story are actually composites of various personalities I knew during my life, rather than any specific individual. Whenever there is an exception to this rule, the name of that individual has been mangled in an honest attempt to protect the identity of both the innocent and the guilty. Of course, every once in a while, the real name of a real person is mentioned in an incidental manner. Some are historical figures; some are personal acquaintances. It is my fervent hope these individuals will feel honored by the respect being given to them.

When it comes to places, almost all of the locations mentioned in the story are real places that actually exist, or *did* exist during the time in question. There is no denial, of course, a little artistic license has been taken in the description of some of them! Sometimes the real place was just not a perfect fit, and was rearranged slightly to better suit the story. Placing the lost continent of Atlantis in the middle of Lake Somerville is not all *that* much of a stretch, is it? Other times, it is simply my memory that is imperfect. The story is supposed to represent a time nearly forty years in the past, and since I have slept a time or two since then, my memory might be a little foggy here and there.

The dramatic events unfolding in this story never actually happened. There are, however, references to certain historical events that are quite real. Whenever such historical events are mentioned, I have taken great strides to ensure these events are represented accurately. That does not mean to say they are described with a completely unbiased interpretation. It's my story, and I'll tell it the way I want to! At least all of the dates are real and accurate. Even the phases of the moon are accurate! With a single (known) exception, song titles are not mentioned in the time-line of the story until after these songs were actually published. (It should be noted, however, this does not apply to chapter subtitles.) When athletic events are mentioned in the story, the teams, dates, and final scores given are historically accurate whenever possible, although partial scores and other play-by-play descriptions of such events are mostly fictionalized.

So what is the story all about? Since it's about the 60's and 70's, you probably think it's all about *Sex, Drugs, and Rock and Roll!* But I'll remind you the story takes place in Bryan, Texas, a small, conservative town that does not cotton to such things, at least not in public. The story is about a lot of things. I want to say it's a nostalgic recollection of the times, but like most other things these days, nostalgia is just not nearly as good as it used to be back when I was a kid.

Do you like romance? It's in there. It contains a bit of philosophy. Life and death, war and peace, religion and politics – nothing is held sacred! Perhaps you will even be offended by what you read. I hope so! Anyone who is offended by such things deserves their fate! Maybe it will cause you to think a little. Be careful not to strain yourself too much. At least you can be grateful there are no gratuitous, graphical depictions of violence where somebody's guts are spilled on the ground in sickeningly gory detail. Does anybody really like that sort of thing?

In addition, there are no gratuitous, graphical depictions of sexual frenzies where the only point is to over-stimulate your libido, raising both your body temperature and blood pressure. No, wait! OK, so maybe there *is* a little of that, but after all, everyone likes a little sex now and then! I can assure you that every bit of this is done tastefully, and is included only because it is relevant and pertinent to the story line, doncha know!

Now that I think about it, drugs and alcohol do receive some mention here and there. It might not be possible to tell a story of the 60's without at least mentioning such things. I have heard it said that those who can remember the 60's must not have *been* there. I agree completely, although frankly, I have no idea why.

A couple of the main characters also happen to form a folk-rock band, and then a rock band later in the story. Music, especially folk songs, protest songs, and rock and roll songs, was an integral part of the times, and any story that failed to mention such music could not possibly represent reality. Music is so important to this story that the subtitle to (almost) every chapter is the name of a popular song from the era. While it would be difficult (even inappropriate) to seek permission to include the lyrics to the many songs mentioned within, there is no denying that knowledge of those lyrics would enhance your understanding and enjoyment. I encourage you to seek that knowledge by acquiring the appropriate recordings, or simply by searching the various sites on the Internet that provide song lyrics for educational purposes.

So maybe the story *is* about *Sex, Drugs, and Rock and Roll*, after all?

Not really. Everyday, perhaps several times a day, as each of us walks along the

Forward

road of life, we come to crossroads. At these crossroads, we are presented with choices. We can turn left, turn right, or continue to go in the same direction as before. The cumulative effect of all these choices brings us to our final destination, wherever that may be, and determines the quality of our lives. Some of these crossroads can force us to make choices that are clearly significant, perhaps even monumental. Other crossroads may offer choices that seem to be quite ordinary and mundane at the time.

This story attempts to illustrate that *all* of these choices, even those that seem trivial, still have significance, for it is the accumulation of these choices that establishes the nature of the road on which we travel. These choices define our character, demonstrating for all who would see exactly who and what we are. Whether or not we reach the final destination we have chosen for ourselves may well depend on a choice we make that seems totally inconsequential at the time. When one considers that the journey of our lives is quite probably more important than its final destination, it should be clear every crossroads we encounter is truly important, whether or not we can see its importance at that time.

This story depicts the lives of some young people as they come to their crossroads, make their choices, and mature into adulthood. In particular, it describes one young man's desperate search for happiness, love, the meaning of life, the universe, and just about everything. The 60's and 70's were turbulent times, with changing norms and values. An astute observer will note, however, that other than technology, nothing of any importance has actually changed since those days. Just because the experimentation these young people do with sex, drugs, and alcohol does not happen to lead them into harm's way does not mean to imply I condone such activities, or encourage others to do the same. Nor should it be assumed I have any personal experience with such things. For the record, let me state I have absolutely *no recollection* of any time in which I personally participated in any illegal activities involving sex, drugs, or alcohol. Go figure! I also have no recollection of breakfast this morning!

Crossroads Part I:
One Day Of Magic

Prologue
Once upon a time...

Monday, September 10, 1973
Diary

Larry was bubbling with enthusiasm from the moment he woke. This was to be one of those proverbial red letter days, one he had been eagerly anticipating for weeks. The only negative he could think of was no one woke beside him to see and share his enthusiasm. Even *that* issue could not dampen his spirits this morning. Taking steps to address that issue was exactly what this day was all about!

All of the plans had been carefully laid. As long as he kept his wits about him, he could slip inside, do the "dirty deed" as it were, and be gone, without anyone knowing a thing about it. He chuckled to himself realizing this was not exactly true. Mrs. J would know, of course, but she was remarkably good at keeping secrets, especially from Mr. J and their daughter, Julia.

Isn't that strange? he thought turning on the shower to let the water warm up. *I've known them all this time and never given a second thought to the number of "J's" in our names – Lawrence Jackson Bristol, Julian Jacobson, Jessica Jacobson, and last, but not least, Julia Anne Jacobson.* He shook his head in wonder. The thought had entered his brain from nowhere, like a stray neutrino that appears briefly, performs the random mischief for which it was designed, then disappears back into the void, swallowed by a black hole. *That's all the universe is,* he chuckled stepping under the warm spray of water, *one huge black whole. Come to think of it, why does it have to be huge? Maybe it's actually a very tiny black whole!* He laughed out loud realizing relative terms like "huge" and "tiny" have no meaning when applied to the universe. "Huge compared to what?" he asked aloud grinning. He received no answer to this query; he had learned over the twenty-four years of his life not to expect one.

After drying himself, he continued his morning routine, brushing his teeth and shaving the light stubble that grew on his face. He never had much facial hair. Perhaps he had a little too much native American blood in his veins, a mixture of Cherokee and Choctaw, carefully blended with those White Anglo-Saxon Protestant genes. He wondered what his beard or mustache would look like if he could actually grow one. Studying his face in the mirror, his mind began to contemplate this great question. How would a brown beard look on his five foot eleven inch frame, beneath his brown hair and brown eyes? Would covering up his ordinary features somehow make him look more mysterious? With his hair in a Beatles style shag as it was, would a beard make him look more like Paul McCartney as well as sound like him?

After a moment, his mind returned from his journey and he answered his question with a resounding, "Probably not!" Once again he contemplated his face in the mirror. He suddenly stuck out his tongue at his own reflection, mildly amused when the image in the glass returned his taunt. "What's the matter, old Spectre?" he asked mockingly. "It's been almost exactly two years since you paid your little visit. Don't you want to come out and play again this morning, or are you now too busy eating those words you said to us?"

Receiving no answer (he had not expected one), he shook his head and stuck out his tongue once again. "You really need to stop talking to yourself, doncha know," he mused. "People will realize you've lost your mind completely!"

"Nonsense!" he answered. "Talking to yourself is completely normal, especially when you've spent as much time alone as we have. It only indicates a problem when you start carrying on complete conversations with yourself."

"I'm not so sure," he countered. "If I were you, I'd be more careful about that."

"Well, I *am* me, and I say you're wrong!" he said mockingly. "I happen to know you quite well! The clearest sign emotional problems need to be addressed is when you start giving yourself advice during those conversations!"

"Or when you start arguing with yourself," he countered. "That's a sure sign you've gone completely nuts!"

"No, it isn't!" he replied.

"Yes, it is!" he answered with a laugh. "Besides, I have it on very good authority you don't have to worry about losing your marbles as long as you still have enough wits to worry about whether you're losing your marbles. You see..."

"Mishuganah! Du bist eynss kranken hintl!" he interrupted. "If you'll kindly excuse me, I have things to go, places to see, and people to do this morning."

He headed into his closet and selected his clothing for the day. He needed something practical, yet something he would not mind getting dirty. He bounded down the stairs of his studio apartment, pleased to find, strangely enough, the kitchen was still in the same place he had left it the night before. Surely this was a good sign, and meant the day was off to a good start!

He began his search for breakfast with the refrigerator. Staring inside, however, did nothing to alter its contents. There were the things one would expect to find in the refrigerator of a twenty-four year old bachelor – two six packs of beer, each with three cans removed, some loose cans of soda, a box containing the remains of a half-eaten pizza, bowls of various shapes and sizes containing forgotten leftovers from equally forgotten meals, a half-gallon jug halfway filled with milk (not half empty; he was known by his friends as the eternal optimist), and a crisper drawer filled with what an imaginative person might easily describe as an active study in microbiology.

He collected the milk jug, then scanned his small pantry, quickly locating an unopened box of Grape Nuts Flakes, his favorite cereal. Grabbing a bowl out of the dishwasher, he briefly asked himself whether it had been run recently. After a shrug, he opened the cereal box and poured himself a generous serving. Something made him hesitate just before he poured on the milk. When he put his nose against the opening of the jug, its aroma caused him to pass on cereal that morning. Calmly placing the cereal bowl and milk into the refrigerator (hoping it might somehow be better tomorrow morning), he decided leftover pizza would make a perfect breakfast.

His excitement began to build while making the short drive from his apartment to the Jacobson house. He turned onto the now very familiar country lane leading to his destination, and found himself humming *On The Street Where You Live* as he drove along. When he pulled into the driveway, he once again urged himself to be careful, as it was absolutely vital the true purpose of today's quest remain a secret. One misstep, and she would know instantly what he was up to. Even his best friends, John and Sam, had no idea what he was planning. After all, the only way to keep something truly secret was to tell no one at all. So far, so good!

Jessica Jacobson was captivated by the bright smile greeting her when she opened her back door. "Good morning, Mrs. J!" Larry beamed. "How are you today?"

"Fine, Larry! Just fine. And yourself?" she answered. "You certainly seem to be in a good mood this morning."

With a small shrug and a sly smile, he answered, "Yes, ma'am. I've been looking forward to this, and I can hardly wait to get started!"

Jessica could sense the excitement in the young man, something she had seen in him many times. She also sensed his excitement was somehow different. This was going to be an unusual day! "Well, let's be patient, shall we? We can take all the time we need. Have a cup of coffee and tell me exactly what you're looking for."

Larry entered the house through the back door, like he had done so many times before. "I'm not really sure what I want, Mrs. J," he answered with another shrug. His smile beamed once again as he added, "but I'll certainly know it when I see it!"

When they arrived in the kitchen, she directed Larry to the table and poured their coffee. The enthusiasm of this young man was certainly contagious; she also felt a sense of excitement. He reminded her so much of her husband as a young man – free of worry, warm and tender, and so very romantic – things not too common among other young men she knew. Her husband, Julian, still had all of those characteristics. He was just more mature now, having carried the weight of supporting his family for years without a single complaint. While still a strong man, Jessica could see this burden had bent his back just a little. She smiled thinking he would vigorously deny that. This was merely one of the many reasons why she loved him so.

Placing a steaming coffee mug in front of him, she noted, "Most of the old stuff is in boxes in the attic. The personal items, especially the more recent ones, are in her bedroom." *How lucky Julia is to have found a young man so much like her father.*

"I want this to look like that old *This Is Your Life* television program," Larry explained. "Personal items will be best, the more personal, the better. I also want to have some family history to introduce it all. You know – things about how you and Mr. J met and got together. I'll tell about Julie as a baby, her early childhood, and finally about how she and I met. I want it all to be fun and light-hearted, but if I can embarrass her a little, that will be fun, also. Some of the stories I've been planning will probably be more embarrassing to me, unfortunately, but what the heck!"

"I hope she'll forgive us," *and especially me,* Jessica thought to herself, "for going through her personal things without her knowledge." *And I hope she'll forgive you if you embarrass her too much!*

"If this comes off like I hope, Mrs. J, she won't even realize we've done so." He laughed, "At least, not until she sees it along with everybody else! By then, I think she just might have forgiven us. If not, I'll disavow any knowledge, doncha know."

Jessica noted how he grinned like a Cheshire cat, and wondered just what he might have on that devious mind of his. "And leave me holding the bag, eh?" she giggled. "Just please try not to embarrass her too much. Remember this is her twenty-first birthday party. Not only will all her friends be there, but so will most of our family. And don't you forget Rabbi Tober is also coming, so try to keep it clean, OK?"

"Why, Mrs. J!" he feigned surprise. "Surely you know me better than that!"

"Yes, I know you very well, you devil!" she teased him.

They both laughed. "Well, OK, I'll try. Of course, this means I won't be able to use my best jokes. Would it be OK if I sneak in a few good ones? Rabbi Tober has heard me tell jokes before. I think he'll be disappointed if I keep it squeaky clean."

Jessica smiled as she shook her head in half-hearted dismay. "But don't forget you'll also have to answer to Mr. J for any serious indiscretions you commit."

"Oops," he gulped smiling. "I almost forgot. I guess I'd better behave myself."

While they finished their coffee, they talked more about the details of Julia's special birthday party. It would be held on their patio, the traditional location for her birthday parties. They had invited just about everyone she knew. They would start with dinner, followed by the traditional birthday cake and ice cream. Julia would open a few gifts, mostly gag items from her friends. More significant gifts would be given to her privately. Then Larry and John would entertain, a tradition for Julia's birthday parties. Once again this year, they would be joined by Riverside, the rock band they had started. And also this year, it was Larry's idea to conduct a special *This Is Your Life* segment in honor of Julia turning twenty-one.

"Let's start with the attic, if you don't mind, Mrs. J," he suggested, pulling the folding stairway from the ceiling and starting his climb. "I need to come up with some ideas about the early days for you and Mr. J. While we look, maybe you can tell me where you and he were born, how you got together, and that sort of thing."

Jessica followed hesitantly, anticipating the attic to be dusty and dirty, filled with bugs and spiders and other nasty creatures. Attics in central Texas are uncomfortably warm, even in early September. Reminding herself she was doing this for Julia, she tentatively climbed the stairs, diverting her fears by thinking it might be nice to remember the old days and tell Larry stories about those times.

Larry sensed her apprehension and saw it as a perfect opportunity to tease her. "If I scream, be sure to pull me out of here as quickly as possible. I would hate to come face to face with a black widow spider about six inches across, or even worse, a brown recluse of *any* size."

"If you see either of those," she choked, "you'd better not say a word unless you want me to faint outright."

"I'm hip!" he agreed. "So let's make a pact. If either of us faints, the other promises to drag them down the stairs to safety!"

"You're not helping things at all!" she grimaced. Reaching the top step, she sat on the floor near the opening. "I think the things of interest will be in the stack of boxes over there. Oy, I should have had Julian fetch them down yesterday."

"But then Julie would have seen them! You know how sharp she is about that sort of thing. She'd know instantly something is going on! We'll have to go through them and get everything packed back up and stored away before she gets home."

"That won't be until late this afternoon," Jessica sighed. "Fortunately, she has a full day of classes today."

Larry fetched the first box and after inspecting it carefully for the little nasties they had joked about earlier, opened it. The top item was an old photo album containing pictures of people Larry clearly did not recognize. "That's one of Julian's old family albums," Jessica explained. "I'm somewhat surprised he doesn't keep it in his study.

"There's a picture of his father and mother, Benjamin and Ruth Jacobson. It must have been taken in Amsterdam in the early twenties. That toddler his father is holding is Julian's older brother, Benjamin Jr., and if you look closely, you can see his mother is pregnant. This is probably the first picture ever taken of Julian!

Monday, September 10, 1973 – Diary   -17-

Amsterdam. That's where he was born, in 1923. His father was a successful diamond dealer in those days.

"Then things started getting a little dicey in Europe. It wasn't just bad in Germany. There were problems of various degree in all the surrounding countries. In the early 30's, when Julian was ten years old, his father sensed danger. He picked up the family and moved them to America, to New York City, leaving everything he owned behind, including his business and the rest of his family. There was a thriving Jewish community in New York where they could fit right in, and they were soon back on their feet again.

"When the war came to America in 1941, his brother Benjamin was among the very first to volunteer. He went into the Marines. Just look at this picture of him! He was so handsome in his uniform. Julian literally worshipped his older brother, and he joined the army himself a few weeks later. There he is, my handsome young man at eighteen – just a boy, really.

"Julian saw action in North Africa, then Italy, and the big push into Germany itself. You've heard him tell some of his war stories. But he still won't talk about those final days of the war, even to me. I think he saw things he would rather forget.

"Right after he enlisted, Benjamin married Mary, his high school sweetheart, like so many other couples were doing in those early days of the war. Before he shipped out, Mary was pregnant. Their daughter, Sarah, was born while he was out in the Pacific. She sent him pictures of her, but he never actually got to see his daughter, never got to hold her." Jessica could not hold back her tears adding, "He was killed on Guadalcanal. I never actually met Benjamin, myself, but I can feel Julian's pain whenever the subject of his brother comes up."

"I know you and Mr. J treasure family as much as anyone I've ever known," he said softly. "I think for my purposes, I should avoid this subject."

"That's probably a good idea," Jessica agreed. "Things quickly went from bad to worse. Julian's father died of a heart attack while reading the telegram bearing the news of Benjamin's death. Suddenly, Julian found himself the patriarch of the whole Jacobson family, responsible for his mother, his sister-in-law, and even his brother's infant child."

"What about you, Mrs. J?" he asked. "Where are your roots?"

Jessica stopped turning the pages in the current photo album. "There's another album here somewhere, with pictures of my family. They're not nearly so exotic as these, I'm afraid. I was born in New York City and grew up there. I won't tell you what year it was, although I'm sure you'll be able to figure it out if you try hard enough. But if you reveal it to anyone during all this, I'll skin you alive!"

Larry grinned. "Will it be OK if I say you're over twenty-one? Since Julie is going to be twenty-one, most people would suspect that." They both laughed, and Larry continued, "I've heard it said if you want to see what a girl will look like in twenty years, all you have to do is take a look at her mother. I hope in twenty years, I'm married to a lady as lovely as you."

Jessica blushed. "You silver-tongued devil!"

"I hope you mean me no evil!" he grinned. "I assume the *'silver-tongued'* part is intended as a compliment, meaning I say nice things. But the devil is the Prince of Lies, and I assure you I'm only saying what's on my mind and in my heart."

She smiled at him once again, then returned her attention to the photo album, mainly to change the subject. "Here's a picture of Julian and I together a few years after the war. It was taken in the summer of 1949." She removed the photo from the album and handed it to him, seeing he was intrigued by it.

"I would have bet this was a picture of Julie!" he said. "It occurs to me if I can look at you now and see an image of what Julie will look like in twenty years, then I must also be able to look at Julie and see an image of what her mother looked like twenty years ago. This photo proves it!"

"You *are* a devil, young man," she grinned before continuing to describe the photograph. "It was in the middle of summer. We were out on Coney Island, and so much in love it was disgusting! I think you know what I mean," she grinned. "Just moments before this picture was taken, Julian proposed to me. One of the happiest days of my life, I remember that day like it was yesterday – July 2, 1949."

"That was the day he proposed to you?" Larry asked. He seemed stunned by this information. He looked at the date written on the back, then turned once again to the front. In the photo, the face of a clock could clearly be seen in the background, and Jessica noted how fascinated he was by that clock. It showed the time to be 4:37 in the afternoon. *Why does he find that so significant?* He spoke before she could ask. "Mrs. J, I beg of you to let me borrow this photo! I promise I'll be very careful and return it unharmed! This is exactly the kind of thing I'm looking for!"

"Of course you can take it, Larry. What is it you find so interesting?"

"I... I can't tell you right now, Mrs. J," he struggled, "but it's very important, I think. Can I wait and explain it on her birthday?" They sat in silence a few moments, Jessica noting how Larry stared at the photo, obviously lost in thought. Eventually, he placed the photo into an envelope he had brought, and looked up. "So what happened next?" he asked, as if the photo now meant nothing to him.

"Well," she smiled, "Julian and I got married, of course! He was quite a catch! We got married the next spring, on March 20, 1950, and since you seem to like fairy tales so much, I'll tell you we lived happily ever after." Larry burst out loud with laughter at this jab. "You ought to think about getting married yourself," she continued with a grin, now showing him the wedding photos.

Larry snickered as he picked more photos, placing them into his envelope. "Do you have anyone in mind? I've never been very successful with girls, as you know."

"Oh, you could marry any girl you please," she said as a matter of fact.

"I know that," he grinned back at her, "but apparently, I've never pleased one."

"Old joke, Larry," she snickered.

One corner of his mouth turned up into a smirk as he shrugged. "Do you think I've been pleasing Julie? You know how much I want to marry her someday, if she'll only have me. But she still has another full year of school to go before she gets her degree. And besides, I promised Mr. J I'd seek his permission and blessing first. You wouldn't want me to break my promises, would you?"

"You'd better not!" she chuckled. Jessica was sure she knew all about Larry's plans. She prided herself on her ability to wrestle tiny bits of information from various sources, then put them together to form a coherent picture. She was seldom surprised about matters as important as this! For the last several weeks, she had been gathering tidbits from Julia, Larry, her husband, and some of their friends. Everything indicated Larry was going to propose to Julia this coming Valentine's Day, assuming he could get up the nerve. Jessica was not sure who was more excited about the prospect – herself or Julia!

"Mrs. J, tell me something, honestly," Larry asked seriously. "Do you really think I'm good enough for her? What could I do to prove myself worthy? I mean, don't you think there's some other man who'd make her much happier than I ever could?"

"Is this supposed to be a joke?" Jessica grinned. "You know as well as I no man could possibly make her any happier than she'll be the day she marries you!"

Jessica sensed Larry was extremely pleased by her answer. In fact, he seemed almost smug about it! When he smiled innocently and tried to move things along, she wondered if he was hiding something. "So how about some of Julie's baby pictures? I hope you have a picture of her naked on a bear skin rug!" he grinned.

"As a matter of fact, we do," Jessica laughed, setting aside her suspicions for the moment. "She's liable to kill you if you show this picture in public."

"I'll take my chances," he smiled. He gathered various photographs of Julia as a baby in the hospital, on the bear skin rug, her first day of school, and other events.

"We were still living in New York when Julia was born, of course. You know the date well – October 22, 1952. At about the same time, Mary, Julian's sister-in-law, lost her battle with cancer, and we legally adopted our niece, Sarah, then nearly ten years old." Larry gathered a few more photographs and absorbed vital information as Jessica described the early years of Julia's life before moving to Texas.

Turning to a new page, Larry asked, "Who are these people, Mrs. J?"

She could see Larry was intrigued by the photograph of a couple in their early thirties, posing behind a boy of perhaps ten. She wondered, *Is that a look of recognition on his face he's trying to disguise?* "That's one of Julian's old army buddies, David Udasel, his wife Barbara, and their son Richard. You might find this interesting. They were very instrumental in getting us to move to Texas!"

"Really? I'm very interesting in things like that! What's the story?"

"Well, let's see," she smiled, putting aside her earlier question. "That was taken in the summer of 1961. Julian and I came down from New York to visit the Udasels who lived here in Bryan."

"Did Julie come with you?"

"No. Julia stayed with her grandmother to attend a summer dance class."

"I see," Larry said looking slightly disappointed. "I was just wondering... Do you remember the night we first met how Julie was sure she'd seen me somewhere before? I thought maybe she saw me while visiting the Udasels."

Jessica smiled. "Nice shot but no cigar. Why is figuring that out so important?"

"Oh, it's not important, Mrs. J," he said dismissing the idea, even though she could clearly see otherwise. "Some people put a lot of stock in silly coincidences like that, but not me. I don't believe in fate, kismet, predestination, or any of those things."

"Of course not, dear," she said, trying not to chuckle.

Larry blushed and moved to change the subject. "So, how did the Udasels convince you to move to Bryan?"

"We had a great time during that visit," she replied, "and it sparked our interest to move away from the city so Julia could grow up in a simpler, more easygoing environment. The highlight of the trip was the afternoon we went to watch Dickie play in a Little League Baseball game. He was a pretty good pitcher, and his team won by something like one hundred to three," she giggled, "and in truth, the other team scored those three runs only after the coach put in a much younger backup pitcher to give him a little experience. I took this picture during the game. Little

Dickie has just thrown a pitch. You can see the batter swinging, but if you look closely, you can see he's missed, and the ball is about to go into the catcher's mitt!"

"That's a neat picture, Mrs. J!" Larry smiled. "And this baseball game made you guys want to move to Bryan?"

"I think it was probably several things, really," she said thoughtfully, "but that baseball game made a big impact. I remember when the game was over, both teams came out onto the field to shake hands, and as soon as the coaches let them, all the little boys ran as fast as their legs could go to get in line at the concession stand! I'd never heard so much delightful laughter as they ran away whooping and hollering! Apparently, win or lose, the coaches bought them all a snow cone after the game, and naturally, they all wanted to be first in line!

"I also remember seeing this little girl run up to a couple of Dickie's teammates, apparently expecting them to share their snow cones with her! After a mild argument and maybe a little skirmish, they must have given in, because I saw them later sitting side-by-side in the bleachers, sharing the two snow cones. How carefree and happy they all seemed! I decided right then I wanted Julia to live in a place just like that, and to have friends just like that!"

She noticed Larry almost choked on his words. "That's a sweet story, Mrs. J!" She asked herself, *Does he really think it's that sweet, or is he just happy we decided to move to Bryan?* He did not give her time to ponder that question. "May I borrow these pictures? I definitely want to include this story on her birthday."

"Of course you may!" she grinned. "I really wish we could have left New York sooner. It wasn't really a great place for either Sarah or Julia to grow up. When we got back home from that trip, Julian did some research, and before I knew it, we were making plans to move. It took two years before it actually happened, but we moved here in the summer of 1963. Julia was ten, about to start the sixth grade. By that time, Sarah had joined the Peace Corps and was living in Africa." She turned the last page of the album and looked into her young friend's face. "That seems to be the end of this photo album, Larry."

For the rest of the morning, they continued digging through other boxes, looking at photographs and other memorabilia. Larry seemed to be very pleased with the results. Not only was he gathering photographs of Julia's life story, he was learning a lot of intriguing information about her family and her life before he met her. He and Jessica carefully repacked everything they had studied, then descended the staircase. Jessica made them a light lunch and they engaged in small talk as they ate.

"I'll also need stuff about the years after you moved here," he said after lunch.

"This is going to be the tricky part," Jessica offered. "I assume you mostly want things about her, not Julian and myself, and that means we'll need to invade her privacy. If you take anything, there's a real danger she'll notice it's missing."

"That's a risk I'll have to take," Larry sighed. "Like I said, I think she'll forgive us if this comes off as planned. I want to avoid things that are extremely personal, like her diary, for example. As much as I'd love to read her diary, I know better. A Bread song by the name of *Diary* comes to mind, and the story frightens me. Even though that story doesn't apply to our situation, I think reading her diary would be tempting fate just a little bit too much!"

Jessica knew enough about his past to understand his concern. "I thought you didn't believe in things like fate," she teased, grinning as she saw his face turn red once more. After a pause, she announced, "Julia's been keeping a scrapbook ever

Monday, September 10, 1973 – Diary

since we moved to Bryan. I doubt it'll contain anything nearly as secret as her diary. Maybe you can find what you need there. And as busy as she is starting her final year in school, maybe she won't notice if one or two things are missing."

"That sounds perfect, Mrs. J! Can we take a look?"

Jessica led Larry into Julia's bedroom. She knew he had been there several times before. Most of those visits were completely innocent, of course, but she could sense a little apprehension in him as they entered, as other less innocent visits jumped into his memory. Larry surely knew Julia had told her much about those times, as well as other times in other places. Still, she thought it was sweet how it all seemed to make him just a little nervous to be there. *Yes, Julia has this one completely snared. What a lucky boy!* But she also knew Julia was a lucky girl to have found him.

Bringing her attention back to the matter at hand, Jessica located the scrapbook high on a shelf in the back of her daughter's closet. She and Larry sat on the edge of Julia's bed, examining its contents. Many of the things they found were completely expected – pressed flowers, some ticket stubs, valentines and other greeting cards – normal items a young girl might collect as memorabilia of her life. As they flipped randomly through the pages, Larry smiled brightly at each of the seven dried red roses they saw, each representing one of the last seven Valentine's Days.

But Jessica saw him nearly jump out of his skin when they turned to one of the earliest pages. On a page by itself was a carefully preserved program from *The Sound of Music*, a musical production performed by members of the A Capella Choir of Bryan's Stephen F. Austin High School in 1965. He tried to act nonchalant, but a slight tremble in his voice betrayed his keen interest. "What's this all about, Mrs. J?"

Jessica's smile broadened as she remembered the story. "Oh, it's just one of those silly things a young girl might keep. It was the during the second year after we moved. Julia was twelve, as I recall, in the seventh grade. Julian bought tickets for us to attend this play. Even though we loved living here, we were starting to miss some of the cultural advantages of the big city. We heard these kids were pretty good, and as it turned out, they really were!

"See the date? It was our fifteenth wedding anniversary – March 20, 1965 – and Julian took Julia and I to see this play. Julia wasn't excited about the idea when she first heard about it, but that all changed once we got there. It must have been her first big crush. Do you know the story? There's this telegraph delivery boy..."

"Yes," Larry interjected. "The telegraph delivery boy is named Rolfe."

"I think you're right," Jessica agreed. "Anyway, there's this darling little scene where he meets up with one of the Van Trapp daughters..."

"Liesl," Larry stated.

"Yes, that sounds right, also. How do you know so much about it?"

"I've seen the movie. I like musicals, just like you."

Jessica was a little skeptical about his answer, but continued. "So in the scene, the boy sings, *'You are sixteen going on seventeen...'* It's actually a duet, and in the second verse, the girl sings since he's *'seventeen going on eighteen,'* she'll depend on him to take care of her, and kisses him on the cheek. He ran off the stage with the wheels of his bicycle hardly touching the ground, letting out a *'Yippee!'* that almost brought the house down. It was just darling!"

Larry pondered this for a moment. "I don't think that's exactly how it goes in the movie," he stated, biting his lower lip. "So why is this program in her scrapbook?"

"I think Julia's first big crush was on that boy. All she talked about for days was that play and that boy. She was simply love sick! A few months later, of course, she found her first *real* boyfriend, and poor Rolfe got put out to pasture." She smiled as she remembered this time in her daughter's life so many years ago. "Obviously, she never forgot about him completely, and kept this program all these years."

"May I borrow this, Mrs. J? This is exactly the sort of thing I'm looking for!"

Jessica could once again sense there was more to this than could be seen on the surface, but she decided to let it go. She knew Larry well enough to know he would not easily reveal whatever he was thinking, at least not right then. She could find out soon enough. All she had to do was ask his friends a few subtle questions. "Of course, Larry. I know you'll take good care of it."

Larry held the program in his hands staring at it, shaking his head slightly. He was startled when he opened it. "What happened to the inside part? It's blank!"

"It was just a misprint, I suppose," she replied. "The ones Julian and I were given listed the characters in the play, and the names of the cast members. Unfortunately, we didn't keep ours, and we didn't discover Julia's was misprinted until we got home. By then, it was too late."

Larry collected a few other items Julia had placed in her scrapbook, especially information about her former boyfriends. "I think I have enough, Mrs. J," he announced finally. "If I can't tell her life story in an interesting and, I hope, humorous way from all of this, then I really shouldn't even try."

1966

Saturday, October 15, 1966
Turn On Your Radio

It was a typical Saturday, and that meant Larry was in a rush. Like most high school seniors, he lived for the weekends, even though his weekends were anything but typical. His version of a typical Saturday started earlier than most, jumping out of his bed around 7:20, well ahead of his parents. He would quickly shower and dress before creating his breakfast masterpiece, more often than not consisting of little more than a bowl of Grape Nuts Flakes, his favorite cereal. By 7:45, he was out the door, hopping into his car to make the short drive into downtown Bryan, making sure he arrived to work at the Carnegie Public Library no later than 8:00.

When he got off work at 5:00, he rushed to get home once again. "Hi, mom!" he called, stepping inside his back door, and going directly to his room without waiting for a response. There was no time for idle chitchat, for in less than two short hours, he was to meet his best friends, John and Sam, at the radio station. Showering off the dust and grime that always covered him after a full day of work in the library, he practiced his station breaks. In a bright, jaunty voice, he recited, "This is the voice of the greater Brazos Valley, KORA, 1240 on your AM dial." In a more mellow voice, he followed with, "You are listening to 98.3, KORA FM. It's 6:00 o'clock."

For dinner, he sometimes accompanied his parents to the dining hall at the Allen Military Academy, a private military school where both of them worked as teachers. Faculty members and their families were invited to have all their meals with the students. Only a few years earlier, the word *expected* would have been more appropriate than *invited*, but that changed after the construction of a new cafeteria-style dining hall replacing the family-style meal service Larry had experienced as a youngster. More often than not, once he was actually given the choice, he chose to eat his meals *anywhere* rather than at Allen. Sometimes his mom would cook a family dinner at home. Other times, he would use the money he earned at the library to buy himself a hamburger, a pizza, or something of a similar nature.

"Bye, mom!" he called as he stepped out his back door at 6:45. This particular Saturday night, he would have plenty of time, easily arriving at the radio station studios on Villa Maria Road well before 7:00, the time his friends agreed to meet. The friendship between Larry Bristol, Sam Kronkite, and John Myers was so phenomenal they were widely known by their peers simply as the *Three Musketeers*. Wherever you found one of them, you were sure to find the other two. They even formed a secret spy organization they called *Spectre*, loosely based on ideas obtained from James Bond movies and television spy programs such as *The Man from U.N.C.L.E.*, and *Get Smart*. Larry thought it was fun to play the Maxwell Smart character, while John filled in as the Chief, and Sam was perfect as Larry's sidekick, Agent 99. Both boys thought Sam even *looked* a lot like Barbara Feldon, the actress who played the role on the TV show.

The weekend was the primary time when Larry could pursue his music, one of his two great passions in life. Music had been a life-long obsession for him, starting when he was a small child singing in church. Then, in his early teens, he was given a guitar as a birthday gift, and his world changed. While his playing ability was truly never much more than average, he was at least a competent rhythm guitar player, able to accompany himself while singing.

Computers, his other passion, were a more recent addition, and he longed for the day when he could pursue that passion more directly. He had been introduced to them during the past summer, between his junior and senior years in high school. Good in math, he had been selected to participate in a summer study program sponsored by the National Science Foundation. This program was conducted at Texas A&M University in College Station, Texas, a mere five miles down the road from Bryan, making it easy for him to attend.

During the first day at this summer program, he was given a book on computer programming in Fortran IV, an account number allowing use of the facilities at the university Data Processing Center, and some free time. Fascinated by the machines, Larry spent the rest of the summer at the DPC learning to write computer programs, totally neglecting the higher mathematics the professors wanted to cover. Not too surprisingly, he flunked the final. He didn't even know there was going to *be* a final! On the other hand, he didn't really care very much about flunking, because he knew he had found his career. Not too many high school seniors are lucky enough to have such a clear picture of their future. To Larry, the summer had been a smashing success.

If only everything else could be so wonderful. During the short drive to the radio station, as he often did, Larry reflected on his life. His passion for music and computers merely gave him a temporarily escape from the unhappiness that permeated his life. This unhappiness bore down upon him constantly, especially when he tried to go to sleep at night, or any other time when his mind was not engaged in pursuit of those passions. No matter how much he might like computers, he thought of them as solitary items he could not truly share with anyone. While he could share his music with others, he could not share it with the special someone he wanted to find so badly. Tonight was a perfect example. He would spend Saturday night with his best friends at the radio station. At the end of the night, he would drive home alone, wishing things could be different. Quite simply, he was lonely.

While he was liked by just about everyone who knew him, he was not the most popular guy in school. He had a good circle of friends, both male and female, that he greatly cherished. But he had never had what one would call a sweetheart. He had never even had a steady girlfriend. He had never known what it was like to make that connection with somebody special. He could see others around him were enjoying such things, but not him, and he wanted to change that badly. Very badly! He could normally get a date if he tried hard enough, but he usually felt like he was just going through the motions. He was not especially interested in casual dating, taking out a different girl every weekend. What he really wanted was to find someone he could care about. More than anything, he wanted someone who would care about him, and think of him as someone special, to make that special connection he craved.

Larry had never considered himself to be part of the "in" crowd. He was just an average guy. You would not think of him as being ugly; nor would you think of him as being handsome. He had played Little League Baseball, and even had a go at playing school football, but at his best he was merely an average player, lacking any true athletic ability. His family was average. His parents were teachers in a private school. They lived in a modest house provided by that school. He drove an old 1960

Ford Falcon his father provided. Just about everything about him was average.

Unfortunately, he sometimes thought, he was *not* just average academically. He was one of those smart kids who learned readily, always got good grades, and seldom needed to study hard to get them. He was especially good at math, demonstrated by his selection for the NSF summer study program. These skills did not raise his popularity since many of the other kids tended to struggle with math. Even his interest in music seemed to hurt his image. He was a member of the school choir, but there were many who thought being in the choir was sissy. It was much more socially acceptable to be a member of the school band. But there were no guitars in a marching band, and that was the only instrument in which he had any interest.

With all these factors, it was somewhat natural for many of the other students, and even some of the teachers for that matter, to think of him as a nerd. He was not the kind who wore striped pants with legs too short, a plaid shirt sporting a pocket protector, and a slide rule hanging from a belt loop. He was just a little too smart for his own good, and was constantly looking for ways to break his nerd image. To his relief, the radio program seemed to be helping.

John's van was already in the parking lot when Larry arrived. He hopped out of his car and quickly went inside, finding John as expected, digging through the tape vault. "Hey, guy!" he greeted. "What are you looking for this time?"

"Nothing in particular. I'm just browsing. How's it hanging tonight, dude?"

"It never actually hangs these days," Larry chuckled. "How about yours?" John and Larry had met a few years earlier when they happened to land on the same Little League Baseball team. Though John had no real interest in organized sports, he was a decent player in most athletic games. He could easily hold his own in a pick-up game of basketball when he was interested, which was not very often. In baseball, he alternated between playing shortstop and third base.

"I guess I'd start worrying if all mine did was hang there," John grinned. John Myers was a typical teenager, one year younger than Larry, in his junior year of high school. He was considered to be a good looking guy, tall and lanky, with long sandy blond hair his parents forced him to keep just short enough to be, in their opinion, socially acceptable. While he was accepted by the "in" crowd, he was not an official member, mainly because his interests pointed elsewhere. He did not mind at all, especially since the "in" crowd was reluctant to accept Larry, his best friend.

John was something of a maverick, and felt right at home as part of the hippie generation. During the past summer, he even considered moving to California to join a commune. Larry talked him out of that, convincing him to wait at least until finishing high school, still two years away. John's views tended to be more liberal than Larry's, but they had no difficulty in seeing eye-to-eye when it came to most things. In particular, they shared a growing concern about the nation's involvement in Vietnam, although neither of them was particularly interested in taking any overt political action. What could two high school boys do about that, anyway?

"Get a grip on yourself, John," Larry suggested. "I do that a lot, and it helps me!"

"Har, har, har!" While John shared Larry's obsession with music, in many ways, he and Larry were complete opposites, like ying and yang. John was a gifted guitar player. In fact, it seemed like he could effortlessly play any stringed instrument handed to him. On the other hand, while his singing voice was adequate, it was unremarkable. At least their musical tastes were similar. They both enjoyed folk songs and folk-rock, such as those being performed by Peter, Paul and Mary, Simon and Garfunkel, and others. And they both loved rock and roll, especially the new musical styles being created by the Beatles and other musical groups.

John had no interest in math or science, and could not understand Larry's fascination with those so-called "thinking machines". He was not a bad student; in fact, he was quite intelligent. He just did not want to put out what little effort it would have taken to get better grades.

While the girls would not exactly swoon when he entered a room, John had no trouble getting dates. His main problem with the dating scene was that most of the girls he knew were not particularly interesting to him. They seemed to be concerned with latching onto some poor guy they considered a good catch, and the sooner they could do so, the better. They studied home economics, striving to become good wives and mothers. John was looking for a girl with different priorities.

"Has Sam gotten here yet?" John asked, subtly teasing his friend.

"I didn't see her car," Larry answered, ignoring the underlying suggestion, "but I'm sure she'll show up any minute. I'll go start pulling records for the show. You can keep searching for sound effects if you want."

"From the way you were talking, I figured you might start pulling something else! I'll meet you guys in the main studio in a few minutes," he grinned, returning his attention to the rack upon rack of tapes stored away in the sound vault.

Larry headed down the hall for the main control room, and met Sam just as she was arriving. "Hey, doll!" he smiled.

"Hi, good looking!" she answered, returning his smile. "Are you ready to go?" Sam Kronkite was bright and spirited, with a great sense of humor and a musical laugh. Larry and Susan (her real name though she asked her friends to call her Sam for some reason no one ever knew) were the same age, now seniors in high school, having been good friends since the third grade.

"I'm always ready!" he said with a twinkle in his eye. "Just say the word, Sam, and I'll go with you any time, any place." Sam was just the sort of girl Larry liked. He regularly asked her to go on dates with him, but she always declined politely, stating she was going steady with some college guy. It seemed to Larry this was the story of his life. Every girl he liked already had a steady boyfriend. He was always a day late and a dollar short.

"Down, boy!" she grinned. This was a regular game for them. She relished the attention Larry gave her, and they both knew it. "I meant are you ready to go to work!" Sam was, of course, a very popular and pretty girl, totally acceptable to the so-called "in" crowd, although she preferred to hang out with her best friends, Larry and John. When the boys began playing their guitars and singing together, practicing, and dreaming of a day when they might become stars, she recognized her friends' talents, and encouraged them to pursue their dreams of stardom. Since Sam played clarinet in the school band, she had a good understanding of music, and liked what she heard when the boys played.

Sam's father died years earlier, before she started the first grade, and her mother had been forced to act as a single parent in raising her young daughter. Sam had developed a strong and independent personality, and was completely capable of taking care of herself, even at those times when having a father around would have been beneficial. Her mother kept a keen interest in all of Sam's friends, especially the boys. She adored her daughter's two best friends, Larry and John. While neither of them could take the place of her missing father, they had filled in for years as surrogate brothers. Her mother always assumed those roles would change dramatically as they all grew older.

"One of these days, Sam," Larry smiled, "you're going to sorry you didn't take me up on any of these offers!" Even though it was not of a romantic nature, Larry and Sam had a very special relationship, far beyond what might be expected between friends, or even between a brother and sister. Some even thought they could read each others' minds. They were so much like identical twins in so many respects (other than their sexes) it was very confusing to those around them.

"You're probably right about that, sugar, but we both know we would only break each others' hearts in the end," she smiled.

Larry recognized this code phrase as a signal Sam was ready to end this game. "Perhaps we'd go out in a blaze of glory," he said with a crooked half smile, "but wouldn't it be a wonderful adventure for a while, Sam? Give it a little thought and get back to me when you see the error of your ways!"

Sam returned his grin and merely shook her head.

They arrived at the control room door and waved through the soundproof window to get the attention of Diggs, the station's chief engineer. He returned their wave and pressed a button to release the electronic lock, allowing them to enter the inner sanctum, into the actual sound studios used for live broadcasts. The only professional on the show, his real name was Steve Diggins. At first, the kids bastardized his name to "Digg Stevens", eventually evolving into the simple, cool sounding, yet somehow dignified nickname of "Diggs". He did all of the technical work during the Saturday night program – cuing the microphones, spinning the records, playing the appropriate commercial messages, and generally ensuring they all followed the rules and regulations established by the Federal Communications Commission, affectionately known as the FCC. But his main job on Saturday nights, according to station owner James Krueger, was "to keep those damn fool kids under control" so the station would not endanger its precious broadcasting license, begrudgingly granted by that same FCC.

It all began a few years earlier, when the station started broadcasting a live Saturday night program called the *Top Forty Showcase*. It was intended mainly as a way for a struggling small town radio station to save money. Rather than hiring a professional disk jockey for the Saturday night time slot, the station got a few local teenagers to host the program, always under the careful scrutiny of Diggs. In a nutshell, it was simply a lame dedication call-in program where the listeners called the station to request their favorite records, asking they be dedicated to someone or something. One group of teenagers manned the telephones, writing down the dedication requests, while another group read them on the air. From his control room, the chief engineer would turn on a microphone in the studio just long enough for some teenager to announce, "The next song goes out to Billy and Betty, Dick and Jane, Tom and Sally, and to the entire Stephen F. Austin Bronco football team!" then kill the microphone and spin the record.

A few months back, the group of teenagers who previously hosted the program invited Sam to join them. Their true intention was to quit the program, freeing up their Saturday nights for other activities. They knew if they got Sam involved, Larry and John would also come along, meaning their plan to abandon the program to her would work perfectly.

The *Three Musketeers* were actually quite happy to take over the show, thinking it could be a great deal of fun! Slowly, they began to change the format of the show to make it more interesting. They still did the same lame song dedications, but they also began coming to the station during the week to prerecord comedy bits and skits, some original, and some "borrowed" from any source they could find. John and Larry even recorded themselves singing and playing their guitars. These items became regular features of the program.

As the style of the program changed, the other teenagers in the area found it a lot more entertaining than it used to be. The *Three Musketeers* slowly developed an image of being pretty cool as more and more of their peers listened in. When the station owner noticed people were requesting Larry and John to do more of their songs (dedicated to Dick and Jane, of course), the trio was given more free reign over the show. It helped that potential sponsors, noticing the increased popularity of the show among the teenage population, were eager to buy commercial time.

A few minutes after this particular edition of the *Top Forty Showcase* had gone on the air, Sam introduced *Turn, Turn, Turn*, the latest hit from The Byrds, dedicated to so-and-so and such-and-such. When Diggs killed the studio microphone, John mentioned to Larry an interesting request he had received. "Hey, dude! I've been meaning to mention something to you. My little brother, Jimmy, is trying to impress his girlfriend. It seems her fourteenth birthday is coming up, and her parents are planning a party. He suggested she invite you and me to the party to entertain with some folk songs. Apparently, she loved the idea and begged her parents to approve."

"So did they?" Larry queried.

"Hey, you guys!" Sam inserted. "That's cool! Your first real gig!"

John did not answer Larry's question. "How about that, Larry! We won't get paid for it, but it really *is* like a real gig. At least we're invited to the party, and Jimmy tells me it's going to be quite a shindig."

"Maybe you'll meet some hot girls," Sam giggled.

Larry rolled his eyes at her and returned to practical matters. "How many songs do they want us to play? Do they only want folk music, or could we throw in some light rock, or even some of the comedy bits we've been working on? And what about requests? Do they have any special songs they want us to play?"

All John could answer was, "I don't know." "I don't know that, either." "Nothing that I know of."

Larry just shook his head. "John, John, John..." Finally, he grinned, "I guess none of that really matters, does it? You know as well as I do that we're going to do it. Hang on..." The Byrds finished their number, the microphone came on, and Larry introduced the next song. Diggs killed the microphone and spun the record. "We'll just have to wing it when we get there, I guess. So when is this party?"

"Next Saturday night," John responded, happy to finally have an answer to one of the questions. "I knew you'd want to do this. The party starts at 7:00, but we need to be there about 5:00 to get things set up."

"Yipes!" Larry exclaimed. "I'll have to leave the library early!"

"You guys are going to leave me all alone next week to run the whole program by myself?" Sam asked, pretending to pout. "Whatever shall I do?"

Larry smirked at her as he answered, "I guess you and Diggs will have to huddle together every night this week to work that out." He suspected Diggs might actually be Sam's mysterious college guy, and he wanted to see how she would react to this suggestion. He was disappointed when she merely shrugged. After a brief pause, he suggested, "I'll tell you what, Sam. John and I will prerecord a song and a comedy bit or two, like always, and you can play them as if we're doing them live. It's easy to be two places at once when you're on the radio. No one will ever have to know!"

The current record ended and it was John's turn. "Hey, Rocky!" he said impersonating Bullwinkle J. Moose, "Watch me pull a rabbit out of my hat."

"Again?" Larry said on cue using his imitation of Rocky the Flying Squirrel.

"Nothing up my sleeve," Bullwinkle continued. "Presto!" He hit a button to start the tape selected for this bit, and a lion roared. "Don't know my own strength."

"And now here's something you'll *really* like," Rocky finished on cue. After John announced the next song, Diggs killed the microphone, spun the record, and grinned at them through the soundproof window.

Back to thinking about the party, and back in his normal voice, Larry fired his next question, "Why do we need to be there at 5:00, John? We don't need any setup time. Do you really think it'll take two hours to open our guitar cases?" He suspected there was something John had not mentioned thus far.

"Well... err... no, of course not," John fumbled. "But we need to check out the acoustics, right? And make sure we're tuned together, and figure out what songs we'll play, and so forth."

"I think we'd better figure out what songs to play before we *get* there," Larry said flatly. With a slight scowl and one eyebrow raised, Larry stared at John as if to say, "And what else?"

There was a poignant pause before John's confession. "OK, OK. We need to be there early because the girl's parents want to meet us first."

"I knew it!" Larry practically shouted. "So they haven't actually approved of this at all, have they? They want to check us out first, and if we don't measure up to their standards, then what? *'Thanks for coming by. Here's your hat. What's your hurry? We'll get back to you! Y'all come back now.'* Isn't that it?"

"It's not like that at all," John pleaded. "Actually, Jimmy says they're ordering pizza and we're invited to have dinner with them. Perhaps they just want to make sure we're not weirdos or something."

"How do we know *they're* not weirdos?" Larry demanded.

"Look, Larry. Jimmy tells me they're very protective of their daughter," John tried. "They used to live in New York, and moved down here a couple of years ago to get away from all the troubles in the big city. They're... a little different from most people around here, and are cautious around people they don't know."

"Different? In what way?" Larry asked. "Are they from another galaxy?"

Sam laughed. "Yeah, that's it! They wear their underwear on the outside of their clothes, and even when indoors, if humans are around, they wear a hat to cover up the third eye on the backs of their heads."

Larry continued with, "And I suppose they walk around making *'BEEP! BEEP!'* noises, and are always asking if they can look in your ears, or some other orifice, with a weird instrument of some kind."

John suggested, "And for some reason nobody understands, there are no insects or birds living anywhere near their property!"

"No wonder your little brother likes this girl," Larry laughed. "He'd fit right in with such a family. I've been meaning to ask. Are you sure he's not adopted?"

The three of them enjoyed a good laugh. Finally, John got back to the true story. "It's not really a big thing. They're not all *that* different. It's just that... well... they're Jewish."

Larry was surprised by this information. "There aren't too many Jews around here, are there? Maybe down in Houston, I suppose, but not here in Bryan. In fact, I think I've only known one Jewish family in my whole life. You guys remember Dick Udasel, right? The best pitcher on our Little League team? He was Jewish."

"I didn't know that," Sam said.

"I don't think it actually shows," Larry shrugged. He paused as the others nodded their heads, before adding, "You know me well enough, John. This makes no difference at all. They could be Buddhists for all I care!"

"I guess I can understand they might feel a little isolated," Sam considered, "and maybe even a little wary of strangers. There are a lot of German immigrants and communities around here. It's not that any of them are Nazis, of course, but there are some prejudiced people around, and not all that hatred is aimed at Negroes."

"So you figure they just want to make sure we're not Nazis, is that it?" After a moment's reflection, Larry concluded, "OK, John, no problem. Tell them we'll show up at 5:00 and submit to inspection. Let's wear brown shirts with red armbands, and if you keep referring to me as *'Mien Fuhrer'*, I'm sure they'll like us."

"Now there's a plan!" Sam laughed. "And if they don't?"

"Zen ve haf vays of *making* zem like us," Larry suggested with a grin.

"Ja, und if zey don't, it's off to zee camps mit zem!" Sam snickered.

"Oh, bloody hell!" John laughed.

"'ey, guv'nor. That's *my* line, doncha know!" Larry inserted with a grin. "Pip pip, tally ho, and all that sort of rot."

"Limey bastard," John teased.

"Not for over a century," Larry laughed. He joked about his family history on many occasions. The family legend was that a few years after his great great grandfather immigrated to America, he was contacted by a solicitor back in Bristol, England. It seemed great great grandfather Bristol was to inherit a large estate, including an actual castle, and was also to receive a title of some sort. The solicitor was willing to pay first class steamship passage for the entire family if they would just come back and look at this inheritance! If they were not interested after looking it over, the solicitor even agreed to pay for their return passage out of his own pocket. Great great grandfather Bristol, however, refused to even go look. Family speculation was taxes and other fees would probably have gobbled everything up, if there was really anything to be gobbled in the first place. After all these years, no one now knew what, if anything, this inheritance was about. But that did not stop Larry's speculation. "Just think about this! You'd better treat me with a little respect, because I'm practically royalty."

"We treat you with as little respect as we can!" John whispered to Sam, drawing a giggle from her.

Undaunted, Larry continued, "My great great grandfather had an actual title. My great grandfather was his first and only son, my grandfather was his firstborn, and I'm the only male heir from my father. Now granted, my father had a couple of older brothers, but you know what? An assassination here, a little accident there, and before you know it, I'd become the Duke of Earl or the Earl of Sandwich or Prince of something! That's right! I'm the crowned prince, heir to the throne of all England!"

"So when did the evil witch come along and turn you into a frog?" Sam teased. The current record ended and Sam could not stop laughing as she announced the next song. Diggs wondered what the kids thought was so funny, and so did the listening audience. No one really cared, unless the station owner called and demanded to know what was going on. The owner's special red phone did not ring on this occasion, however.

"So," John began after they quit laughing, "are you going to take a date?"

Larry looked down, reflecting on the question and gathering his reply. "I don't think we should, John. If we really want to work as musicians, then we need to think of this as a professional gig, regardless of the fact we'll enjoy doing it." Seeing John's disappointment, he continued, "Besides, dates would just get in the way. How old is this girl, Jimmy's girlfriend? Fourteen, I think you said? Maybe she'll have some of her friends at the party and like Sam suggested, we can scope them out, perhaps finding a couple of hot new prospects. I have nothing against younger girls, doncha know. And now that I think about it, I believe I'd like to change that! I can see how I might *enjoy* getting something against a younger girl!"

"And just what is this something you want to get against them, you pervert?" Sam smirked keeping the mood light. "I know you too well, Larry Bristol. You just like girls, regardless of their age!"

"Thighs and breasts and all the rest!" Larry laughed. "And you had better say the same thing, John, or I'm going to become very, very worried about you."

John merely grinned and shook his head.

Saturday, October 22, 1966
I've Just Seen a Face

Larry was in an upbeat mood. He left work a little early, and rushed home to prepare himself for the party. This was going to be a fun evening! John and he had agreed on matching outfits – blue jeans and a shirt looking like it might have been cut from an American flag. For the very first time, they actually were requested to entertain at a party. It wasn't a professional gig since they were not getting paid, but they *were* getting a free pizza dinner out of it. And they had been invited to attend this party, something that would not have happened otherwise, since they did not know the guest of honor.

John arrived at Larry's house just before 5:00, driving because his little brother, Jimmy, age fourteen, did not have a driver's license. Jimmy provided directions to his girlfriend's house in Steep Hollow, a rural residential community a few miles outside the Bryan city limits. "What's your girlfriend's name?" Larry asked.

"Julia," Jimmy answered. "Julia Jacobson."

"You told them we were coming?" Larry confirmed. "They do expect us, right?"

"Yes, I told them," Jimmy replied. "Give me a break, OK?"

When the boys arrived at the house and turned into the driveway, Larry immediately concluded that while it was not exactly what one would call a country estate, it was obvious the Jacobson family had more financial resources than his own. The Jacobsons built this new home shortly after moving to Bryan, while Mr. Jacobson worked to establish his new business. Obviously, he was being successful.

Larry loved the idea of living in the country, even though he had no interest in agriculture. The Jacobson property impressed him as something he had often envisioned in a dream – a nice house, resting in the middle of a few acres of wooded, rolling countryside. He immediately felt at home as John drove slowly down the gravel driveway and parked the car in the shade of a large oak tree.

Jimmy was the first out of the car, and bounded straight for the front door, while John and Larry looked around the property and noted its natural beauty. The grass was recently cut, and the flower beds were well tended. These mostly contained native plants, many of which were still blooming even this late in October. Trees were in abundance, mostly the temperamental post oaks so common to the area. There was also a scattering of pin oaks, an occasional live oak or water oak, with a few cedars and lob lolly pines thrown in for good measure. The trees nearest the house had been carefully cleared of yaupon holly that always grew so pervasively around tree trunks. In Larry's mind, the best word, perhaps the only word, to describe this place was "homey".

After a moment, John and Larry headed for the front door. Jimmy was already inside, but the door was open wide in a note of welcome. Standing in the doorway was an attractive woman in her thirties, wearing a nice dress, looking like she had just stepped out of the <u>Lady's Home Journal</u>. Mrs. Jacobson introduced herself and welcomed the boys with a warm smile. "It's so nice of you to entertain for Julia's party. She's been looking forward to this ever since Jimmy suggested it. Julia has always loved music, but mostly all she has comes from her records and from the radio. This will be some of the first live music she's heard since we moved here. Live music is always the best music, don't you agree?"

They looked at each other thinking this was not exactly the sort of greeting they were expecting. She escorted them into the kitchen. There was little doubt this kitchen was the very heart of the house, where the family spent most of their time. It opened into a large family room with plenty of seating, and boasting a well equipped entertainment center. In one corner of the family room, a large grandfather clock stood majestically, adorning the room with a stately and elegant touch. On another wall was a massive rock fireplace. In front of that fireplace, a conversation pit contained a built-in sofa and love seat, and was seemingly filled to the brim with comfortable pillows.

As they stepped into the family room, Mr. Jacobson put down his newspaper, got up from his chair, and greeted the boys. "Good afternoon, boys, and welcome!" He was in his early forties, but hardly looked that old. He had a genuine and engaging smile further enhancing the welcome they had been given by his wife.

"Good afternoon, sir," Larry said, offering his hand. "Thank you for inviting us. My name is Larry Bristol."

Mr. Jacobson took the offer and shook Larry's hand with a firm yet friendly grip. "I'm glad to meet you, Larry. I'm Julian Jacobson and you've already met my wife, Jessica." He offered his hand to John, and repeated his name.

"John Myers, sir. I'm Jimmy's older brother. It's nice to meet you."

"Before I forget, there's one question I want to ask you boys," he stated seriously. "I understand you call your band the Drug Company. I'd like to know how you came to choose that name. I want it clearly understood I do not approve of drugs or teenage drinking."

John and Larry looked at each other sheepishly. "Yes, sir," Larry replied, "I understand. It's just a joke that comes from our last names. You know – Bristol and Myers – the drug company?"

"Tsk, tsk, tsk. Kids these days," Julian said as he shook his head.

"Are just like the kids of yesterday," Jessica reminded him with a smile.

"And the same as the kids of tomorrow?" Larry suggested hopefully.

John's eyes swiveled in their sockets as he tried to keep up with this conversation. Finally, Julian grinned at them, and the boys returned his smile. "OK, I'll accept that answer." He then changed the subject abruptly, "The party will be on the patio in the backyard. Let me know if you boys need anything."

"That will be fine," Larry answered. "Should we go ahead and start setting up? Is there anything in particular you want us to do?"

"Do whatever it is you kids like," Julian said. "This party is for Julia, not for me."

"And not for me, either," Jessica inserted. "But I hope you won't damage our eardrums with your loud music."

John and Larry smiled. "We do play electric guitars, but we've only brought acoustic ones today," John said, "and no microphones or anything. We figured to do some simple folk songs."

"But we just might throw in a couple of surprises along the way," Larry added with a twinkle in his eye.

"I'm sure it will be fine," Jessica agreed. "You have plenty of time. Let me fix you something to drink and maybe you can tell me a little about these surprises over dinner. The pizza is already here, on a table in the backyard. Julia is still getting ready and will join us a little later, Jimmy," she mentioned before departing to the kitchen to prepare the soft drinks. While she was gone, Larry admired the grandfather clock and thought about what nice people the Jacobsons seemed to be. When Jessica returned, she handed each of them a glass and motioned for them to go into the backyard.

With a soft drink in hand, Larry walked through the back door and onto a patio filling a large area in the backyard. His eyes were instantly drawn to a large willow tree adorning one side of the patio. Surrounding the tree was a low brick retaining wall providing comfortable casual seating. But it was the tree itself that captured his imagination, and he stared at it in silent disbelief. It seemed oddly familiar to him, as if he had sat under its branches many times in the past. But how could that be? He had never been here before!

"I love that old tree," Jessica said to him, noting the boy's stare. "That tree was the main reason I insisted we buy this property. Then I insisted the house be built right here so this tree would shade the whole backyard." She looked up at the tree as a gentle breeze whistled through its leaves and branches. "Listen! I sometimes think the tree is trying to tell me something."

"Maybe it is," Larry answered in a low voice. "Trees are living things with long lives. I sometimes think they see things we humans miss because we don't pay enough attention." As the wind whistled through the tree again, he noted, "I feel like it's saying something to me right now for some reason. I wish I knew what it was."

Jessica smiled at the boy. "It must also be talking to Julia at times, because she spends a lot of time sitting under it, when she's not *climbing* in it, that is. I wish it would tell her to be a little more careful so I wouldn't have to keep doctoring the little cuts and bruises she gets when she falls!"

Without saying a word, Larry flashed one of his patented, half smiles. One side of his mouth showed a big grin while the other side hardly moved at all. *So this girl is a tomboy*, he thought. He already knew he was going to like her.

Jessica herded the boys to an area where several tables had been arranged, inviting them to enjoy the pizza. When the boys dug in eagerly, she laughed, "Save a slice or two for the birthday girl!" The boys stopped in their tracks looking embarrassed. "Oh, don't worry. There's plenty of pizza. Help yourselves to all you want!"

Mr. and Mrs. Jacobson sat at a nearby table and began to eat some of the pizza themselves. Larry noted they were eating a simple cheese pizza, without so much as a single slice of pepperoni! At first, he was surprised by this, but then remembered John saying they had recently moved here from New York City. He recalled hearing good things about New York pizza. Maybe that was the style there!

Larry's mind wandered as he munched on his own slice of pizza, looking up at the old willow tree again. *What is it about this tree I find so familiar, so intriguing, and so inviting?* Because he was so distracted by the tree, he did not notice the small dachshund until it ran up to him. He woke from his daydream when the dog stood on its hind legs, placing its paws on Larry's leg, wagging its tail enthusiastically.

He looked down to see the dog looking back at him. "Well, hello there!" he smiled. He had a dog very much like this one a few years earlier, named Dan Dee. While fighting off the memory of the little dog he still missed so much, he scratched this one behind its ears and asked, "What's your name, boy?"

A soft voice from behind answered, "His name is Schotzy." Larry's thoughts were so engaged in the questions about the tree and the dog he had not noticed when the birthday girl came from the house and walked to the table where the boys were sitting. "Hello, Jimmy," she added sweetly. Larry blinked at the sudden intrusion into his world, and looked up to see the source of that voice. For the first time, he beheld the face of Julia Anne Jacobson. Her eyes captured his, and he stared into the infinity surrounded by deep green irises. A voice within that infinity called out to him and touched something deep inside, but he was too stunned to answer.

"This is Julia," Jimmy announced. "Julia, this is my brother John and his friend Larry."

John was quick with his introduction. "Hi, Julia. I'm John. Happy birthday!"

"Thanks, John! It's nice to meet you!" she said, then turned to look at Larry.

Breaking his stare from the depth of her eyes, he saw before him a skinny little girl of fourteen. Her bright smile revealed a mouth full of braces. There were a couple of small teenage-style blemishes on her forehead she had attempted to cover with some light make up. Her golden hair was shoulder length with a slight wave near the ends that brought it under her chin, framing her pretty face. She wore a solid navy blue skirt, a pale blue blouse, and a white sweater. For a girl of just fourteen, Larry thought Julia was really pretty. Based on the look of her mother, he knew she was going to grow up to be quite a fox!

He was oblivious to the passage of time. An eternity might have passed in that one instant. As he began to regain his senses, he realized everyone was looking at him expectantly. "Oh, I'm Larry. Larry Bristol. It's nice to meet you, Julia. Happy birthday!" To the others, hardly any time had passed at all. No one other than Larry had been aware that a huge gap had opened within the space-time continuum. He breathed a sigh of relief with the realization the others had not noticed.

"Thanks! It's nice to meet you, also! You must have a kind face," Julia said as her mother came to stand beside her. "Schotzy doesn't usually take to strangers."

"Dogs and kids always seem to like me," Larry smiled. "A few years ago, I had a dachshund who looked just like this one."

"Get down, Schotzy," Jessica said gently.

Larry reached down and picked up the dog and placed him in his lap. "It's OK, Mrs. Jacobson," he grinned. "I also like dogs and kids." Now in Larry's lap, Schotzy stood with his paws on Larry's chest, licking Larry's mouth and face, happily wagging his tail even faster. "See what I mean?" he laughed, gently struggling to keep the dog from licking the inside of his mouth.

"Oh, for goodness sake!" Jessica chuckled. "He certainly has taken to you! Don't let him take advantage of you, Larry. Put him down whenever you want."

After a few more seconds of doggy kisses, Larry set the dog back on the ground. Schotzy ran around Julia's legs, barking excitedly. She looked at Larry with a curious expression on her face. "Don't I know you from somewhere?" she asked.

Now Larry was the one looking puzzled. "Maybe, but I'm sure we've never met," he answered. In the privacy of his own thoughts, he was even more sure. *I certainly would not have forgotten meeting you!* He began to speculate about where she might have seen him. "Perhaps you've seen me around school. No, I don't think that could be the answer. I'm three years older. You go to Lamar like I did, but I would already have left and gone on to SFA before you started." He referred to Lamar Junior High, where he had attended the seventh through ninth grades, and where Julia went now, and to Stephen F. Austin High School, where he and John now attended.

"I doubt I've seen you in temple," Julia noted.

"I've been through Temple a few times, but I've never stopped there," Larry answered, oblivious to her reference. To Larry, Temple was the name of a town claiming to be square in the heart of Texas.

"I think she means what you'd call church," Jessica grinned, catching Larry's mistake. "Where do you go to church, Larry?"

He stumbled with his answer, "Oh! I go to the Church of Christ over on Twenty-Ninth Street."

"I doubt you saw him there, sugar," Jessica snickered. "Perhaps you've seen him somewhere around town."

"Yes, maybe at the library," Larry suggested. "I have a part-time job at the Carnegie Library downtown, in the children's section. I work a few hours after school and then most of the day Saturday. Have you been there?"

"No," Julia stated, "but I'm sure I've seen you somewhere before."

"Maybe you've seen him on the radio," Jimmy added, a little concern in his voice. He tended to be the jealous type, and was not happy Julia was paying so much attention to his older friend. When everyone looked at him curiously, he added, "John and Larry usually work at the radio station on Saturday nights."

John rolled his eyes and explained, "We usually help out with a teenage request show, where kids call in and request a song be dedicated to *'Bobby and Sally'*, *'George and Gracie'*, *'Ricky and Lucy'*, or maybe even *'Batman and Robin'*. That sort of thing."

Jimmy continued, "Yes, and they even sing on the air."

John looked at Jimmy with slight disdain, "It's actually on tape most of the time. Has it occurred to you, dummy, that she couldn't possibly have *seen* us on the radio?"

Rebuffed, Jimmy claimed, "Jeez, it was just a joke!"

Julia giggled at his distress. "I guess it doesn't really matter, but I'm sure I've seen you before. Maybe I'll remember later. Anyway, it's great to meet you, Larry. You too, John. Thanks for coming to my party! Jimmy says you guys are pretty good!"

"And he should know," John smiled. "He has good taste. He comes by it naturally since he's my little brother."

"I still say he must have been adopted," Larry added with a grin.

Julia giggled, and Larry heard music dancing in the air. "I'll decide for myself how good you guys are in a little while. Is there any pizza left? I'm starving!" She sat in a chair next to Jimmy and began to enjoy her dinner. They learned pizza was her favorite food, and she had specifically requested pizza for her birthday dinner. Larry noted she selected plain cheese pizza, like her parents.

His gaze returned to the willow tree, but his eyes kept oscillating between the tree and the girl, sensing a link between them. Julia finished eating, and began to help her mother clear up the remains. They continued the preparations, setting out napkins, cups, and all the other things one needs for a birthday party. The boys helped with additional tables and chairs, which Mrs. Jacobson and Julia quickly covered with birthday decorations.

It was just after 6:30 when everything was in readiness for the party. They were all standing around a large table as Mrs. Jacobson outlined the schedule of events they had planned. "If it's OK, I think it would be nice if you boys played a few songs as the guests start arriving. Around 7:30, we'll bring out the cake and ice cream, and Julia can open any gifts she receives. After that, we'll turn on the radio so you kids can dance if you want." Winking at Larry and John, she added, "Jimmy wants us to tune to your radio show for that part. Then you boys can play some more songs starting about 10:00 until the evening winds down. Does that sound OK?"

Since Larry seemed to be distracted by something, John answered, "It sounds just fine, Mrs. Jacobson. We'll get our guitars and start warming up, eh Larry?"

"Huh? Yeah! That sounds great." John and Larry returned to the car to get their instruments. "Did I just make a fool of myself?" he asked when they were alone.

"Not any more than usual, I guess," John grinned. Then seeing the curious expression on Larry's face, he answered more seriously, "No, I don't think so, but you do seem a little distracted. Is something bothering you?"

Larry pondered a moment before lying, "No, not really. I guess not."

As they fetched their instruments from the trunk of the car, Larry realized he had no idea what was happening to him. If he could not explain it to himself, how could he hope to explain it to John? What was the deal with that tree? And this skinny little girl child reached inside his very soul and touched... touched what? What was he feeling? *Sure, she's cute, but she's too young for me. Maybe in a couple of years, things will be different. Besides, it's déjà vu all over again, isn't it? She already has a steady boyfriend."* It would not be the last time he would have those thoughts.

John's voice interrupted his thoughts, "Come on then, Larry. If you're OK, let's go have some fun. If not, then you'd better start talking."

Larry looked at his friend with a lot of questions in his head, and very few answers. "I'm fine," he stated unconvincingly. John merely stared back at him.

"Really! I'm fine! Let's go! Break a leg, John!"

"May you break all your strings and cut your fingers!" John added with a grin.

The two-man band known as the Drug Company, comprised of Lawrence Jackson Bristol, age seventeen, and Jonathan Andrew Myers, age sixteen, by request of James Michael Myers, age fourteen, entertained at the fourteenth birthday party of Julia Anne Jacobson, only daughter and namesake of her father, Julian Absalom Jacobson, and the sunlight in the life of her mother, Jessica Anne Jacobson. The guests numbered about thirty, friends Julia knew from school, and in some cases their dates. As they arrived, the guests were surprised to find live music. John and Larry played several contemporary and classical songs, such as *The House Of The Rising Sun*, *Peggie Sue*, and *Unchained Melody*. They played *Daydream Believer*, a song popularized by The Monkees, a band thrown together by some TV executive to cash in on the popularity of rock and roll music, followed by *A Summer Song* recorded by Chad and Jeremy, and *(All I Have To Do Is) Dream* by the Everly Brothers. The kids grew more appreciative with each song, and the boys were happy to continue.

Given the choice, Larry would have sung all night, but the party needed to move on into the next phase. As the clock reached 7:30, they ended the session with *Good Morning Starshine* from the rock opera *Hair*, and Mrs. Jacobson signaled she was ready to bring out the birthday cake.

"Good evening, everyone!" Larry announced. "I'm Larry and this is John, and we are otherwise known as the Drug Company. We'll be playing..." He was interrupted by a round of light applause. "Thank you," he said, responding with a bow. After a moment, he held out his hand towards John, and the applause increased once again momentarily in appreciation. "Thank you, really!" he continued as the applause died down. "We'll be playing some more songs a little later this evening, and we hope you'll enjoy hearing them as much as we plan to enjoy playing them for you. If you only enjoy it half as much as we do, then we'll enjoy it twice as much as you!" Larry noted the joke bombed. It was probably a little too cerebral.

"But right now," he continued smoothly, "we've been given a special request. As some of you probably know, we thrive on special requests." There was a scattering of laughter from the kids who were familiar with the radio show. He smiled in acknowledgment. "This is a very special song. So special, in fact, we request each of you join with us in singing it. It's really a very easy song to sing, and it goes something like this. Come to think of it, it goes *exactly* like this:

Happy birthday to you.
Happy birthday to you.
Happy birthday, dear Julia.
Happy birthday to you!"

While they were singing, Mrs. Jacobson brought out a large birthday cake, adorned with fourteen burning candles, and sat it in front of her daughter. Julia made a wish and then blew out the candles with ease.

"What did you wish for?" Jimmy asked.

Julia laughed and told him, "If I tell, then it won't come true!"

She made the traditional first cut into her cake. Her mother placed pieces of cake on small plates, while her father scooped ice cream. As everyone enjoyed these treats, Julia opened a couple of gifts brought by her closest friends, including one from Jimmy, a copy of the *Revolver* album recently released by the Beatles. When she leaned over to kiss Jimmy on the cheek, Larry felt his heart skip a full beat.

The radio was switched on and tuned to KORA, "1240 on your AM radio dial," Larry mumbled to himself. He recognized the voice of Diggs, urging listeners to stay tuned for the *Top Forty Showcase*, coming up after a commercial break. He faintly heard the grandfather clock in the house chime eight times. The radio played a familiar theme from the *Rocky and Bullwinkle* show, followed by his own imitation of Rocky the Flying Squirrel, "And now it's time for the *Top Forty Showcase*."

The kids at the party listened intently as John's imitation of Bullwinkle J. Moose interrupted with, "Hey, Rocky! Watch me pull a rabbit out of my hat!"

"Again?" Rocky asked.

"Nothing up my sleeve," Bullwinkle continued. "Presto!" The sound of a large diesel locomotive was heard, its engines roaring, horns blasting, and bell ringing, followed by the familiar clickity clack of heavily loaded freight cars speeding past.

"Wrong hat?" Rocky asked.

"I think it must be a six and seven eights," Bullwinkle answered.

"Now here's something you'll *really* like," Rocky stated. "Take it away, Sam!"

"Thanks, Rocky. Thanks, Bullwinkle," Sam continued, the program now live. Some of the kids at the party looked at the boys questioning what they had just heard, even though they knew intellectually it had been on tape. "I'm sorry to inform you the Drug Company has passed into the great beyond and won't be with us tonight." She paused dramatically, then continued, "By *'the great beyond'* I mean simply they're doing a live performance elsewhere and aren't here in the studio. But they've left us a few goodies on tape we'll play from time to time during the evening. I hope your gig is going well!" She announced the first song along with its dedications, and Diggs spun the record.

An idea popped into Larry's head. "Can I use your phone for a minute, Mrs. Jacobson?" Jessica showed him a wall phone just inside the back door, then returned to the party where some of the kids were dancing to the music on the radio. "Sam! It's me. Can you get Diggs to pick up the line?" She motioned through the soundproof window to Diggs. When he joined, Larry continued, "Diggs, I want to announce the next song over the phone! Can we do that?"

"No problem, chief. Just stay on the line, and I'll get it all set. Two seconds after the current song finishes, you'll be on the air. You'd better not be up to anything or you-know-who will come down on you like a ton of bricks!"

"Diggs!" Larry said feigning innocence. "You know me well enough by now!"

"Exactly! So keep it clean, OK? Just wait on the line," he instructed.

"What are you up to?" Sam asked. "And how's the party going?"

"Honestly! I'm not up to anything!" Larry laughed. "I'm just going to make a dedication for the birthday girl, and confuse the hell out of the kids at the party who don't seem to know what's live and what's on tape! Take over after my message and do the dedications normally. Everything is going fine. I'll tell you all about it later."

The song ended and Larry counted silently to himself, *one thousand one, one thousand two*. "Hey, guys! This is Larry from the Drug Company, and I just wanted to let you know the news of our demise is greatly exaggerated. It's now 8:10 on Saturday, October 22, 1966, and I'm just as alive as ever. At least, I was last time I checked." After a brief pause, he continued, "I want everyone to join me in wishing a happy birthday to Julia Jacobson!" Looking out the window into the backyard, he could see the surprise on everyones' faces, including John's. Thinking quickly, he added, "Happy birthday, Julia, from Jimmy, John, Sam, and me. Back to you, Sam!"

After Sam completed the dedications for the song, and Diggs spun the record, he sneaked out the door and quietly rejoined the kids at the party. John soon spotted him and signaled a thumbs up. Julia smiled brightly when she saw Larry. He decided he'd do just about anything to see her smile again.

Linda Livingston had heard Larry and John sing many times before. A year older than Julia, she was a sophomore in high school, and was also a member of the school choir. Though she had heard them sing choir songs, she had never heard the boys play and sing on their own. She and her friend, Helen Hightower, were admiring their performance tonight, including the one on the radio, and found they were developing a new interest. They maneuvered themselves into close proximity, hoping to gain their attention.

It was not long before John noticed. Larry was still distracted by something and had not yet noticed the two girls hovering nearby. When he had the opportunity, John made a subtle signal to Larry indicating they were being watched.

Happy to forget the strange questions swirling in his mind, Larry actually made the first move. Considering his shyness around girls, this was quite unusual. He turned around, pretending to see Linda for the first time, and greeted her brightly. "Hi, Linda! I didn't know you'd be here tonight."

"Hi, Larry," she replied. "Julia and I are old friends. We met about a year ago at school. Since we're both crazy about the Beatles, we sometimes share our record collections. I'm surprised to see you, too! Where did you meet Julia?"

"I just met her today, actually," he answered. "Jimmy, that's John's little brother, talked her into inviting us to come play tonight."

Pretending to hear his name mentioned, John turned to join the conversation. "Hi, Linda!" Both boys looked over to Linda's friend whom neither had met before.

Taking the cue, Linda introduced her friend. "This is Helen Hightower. She's also in our private little 'record club' with Julia. Helen, meet Larry and John."

The boys said, "Hi!" so simultaneously it could have been rehearsed. (It was!)

Helen jumped at the chance to stroke the male egos. "You guys are really good! You can sing for me anytime you want!"

John and Larry exchanged a grin, delivering a secret message this could easily be arranged. In the same message, they agreed how to divide the spoils. John would take Helen, and Linda went to Larry. If things did not work out, maybe they could swap later. "I think I remember seeing you at school a time or two," John told Helen.

"I've seen you a few times, also," Helen smiled. They entered into a private conversation intent to discover shared interests.

Larry took the opportunity to get in a little private time with Linda. "So, what did *you* think of our performance?" he asked, fishing for another compliment.

"You guys *are* good," she agreed. She knew she was stroking Larry's ego, but it was true, anyway, and besides, she enjoyed stoking boys' egos. "I've heard you sing in choir before, but I didn't know you also played the guitar."

"Not even on the radio?" Larry asked, trying to boost his status even further.

Linda looked surprised. "You guys have made a record?"

"A tape, actually," he explained, "We've also played live on the show a few times."

"Wow!" she cooed. "Maybe I should listen more often."

Larry pounced on the opening. "Why don't you let me take you to the station sometime? You can hear us play, and can see how a radio station works! I'll even put you in front of a microphone to announce a song. Are you busy next Saturday?"

"No, I'm not busy," she replied. "It sounds like fun."

"Great," Larry said, simultaneously thinking, *It worked!* "The show starts at 8:00, and we'll need to be there no later than 7:30. If it's OK, I'll pick you up at 7:00. We can get something to eat first, or take it to the station with us. Do we have a date?"

"Sure!" she smiled.

So far, so good! he thought, and decided to press his luck. "John and I've been talking about the big game next Friday night," he lied. He knew John could not care less about school sports. "Maybe you and Helen would like to come along with us?"

"Well, I can't speak for Helen," she giggled, "but I'll go with you."

"That's swell! I'll pick you up at 7:00 on Friday, also," Larry suggested. "It sounds like a great weekend to me. Would you like to dance?"

"Sure! Do you know what the next song is going to be?"

"Of course!" he grinned. "I'm psychic, doncha know."

Linda looked at him skeptically. "Psychic? Then what am I thinking right now?"

Larry held his fingers to his forehead and closed his eyes as if in deep concentration. "You're thinking someone around here is full of crap." When Linda giggled, he opened his eyes, pointed at Jimmy, and whispered, "I think it's him."

Now Linda laughed even more. "I think you may be right," she whispered.

Linda and Larry began dancing when the next song started. John and Helen joined in, as did most of the other kids at the party. There were several fast songs in a row, but finally, a slow dance came along. He opened his arms in an offer for Linda to join him.

Linda had been hoping for a slow dance. She slipped her left arm around Larry's neck as he put his right hand around her waist. Their other hands clasped as they began to sway to the gentle beat of the dance number. After a few moments, Linda released his hand and slipped her other arm around his neck. His free arm quickly went around her waist, and she snuggled close to him while they danced. For a few moments, he forgot about everything else, including those strange thoughts invading his mind earlier.

She did not let go of his neck when the song ended. She smiled sweetly and looked sheepishly into his eyes. He could not possibly have missed that signal. She offered no resistance when he leaned his head forward and kissed her gently on the mouth. As their heads parted, they smiled at each other, and Larry noticed they were standing under the spreading arms of the old willow tree.

Another song began, but they decided to sit this one out, moving to the refreshment table for a cool glass of punch, joined by John and Helen. After a little light conversation, the girls excused themselves and departed to the ladies' room to compare notes, leaving John and Larry alone for a few moments, to compare their own notes.

"How are you doing?" John asked.

"Not bad," Larry answered. "Not bad at all! We have a date for the game Friday night, and she's coming to the station Saturday. I even got a kiss! How about you?"

Saturday, October 22, 1966 – I've Just Seen a Face

"Brilliant minds work in similar channels," John answered.

"You asked her to the football game?" Larry asked in amazement.

"I knew you'd ask Linda! I assumed you'd suggest to her we were going to the game, and maybe she and Helen would like to come along. I sometimes know you better than you know yourself." He looked at his friend and they exchanged smiles. As far as they were concerned, this party was already a brilliant success.

Linda and Helen exchanged their notes in the powder room, agreed to leave the arrangements as they were, and returned just in time to hear Sam announce a song by the Drug Company the boys had recorded earlier that week. They had worked extra hard on this recording, and were very proud of the result. They just hoped others would appreciate it. The song was their rendition of the Beatles hit *And I Love Her*.

When he tried (and he naturally did), Larry sounded very much like Paul McCartney. With his family roots in Bristol, England, he did not find the Liverpool accent difficult to duplicate. The song was also a natural fit for their style, especially when Larry produced an arrangement matching their capabilities. Larry played rhythm guitar, John played lead guitar, and they sang the song in two part harmony instead of three. A casual listener, however, could easily mistake their rendition with the original.

When the recording ended, the kids at the party showed their appreciation to the extent Larry and John were embarrassed, especially by the gushing of Linda and Helen. Several people approached them privately to express their congratulations. Later, they learned several listeners had called the radio station requesting it be played again. It proved to be the turning point in their singing careers.

At 10:00, the radio was turned off and the boys returned to their instruments to provide more live entertainment. They started with several recent songs by Simon and Garfunkel, including *Cloudy*, *A Poem Written on the Underground Wall*, and of course, *Scarborough Fair/Canticle*. Larry and John both enjoyed doing songs by Simon and Garfunkel, but they were especially important to Larry.

Earlier in that year, Larry and an older friend named Glen, along with both mothers, had driven down to Houston. Glen was entering the navy, and had to catch a flight out of Hobby airport. On their way through town, they stopped at the H & H Music store where Larry purchased a guitar music book entitled <u>Songs by Paul Simon</u>. It soon became one of his most cherished possessions! Wandering through Hobby airport, turning the pages in this book, and paying more attention to the songs than where he was going, he accidentally bumped into someone. Preparing to apologize, he looked up into the face of Paul Simon, who also happened to be waiting for a flight. Larry's eyes popped out of their sockets, while his mouth hung open in shock. Without saying a word, he handed over the song book, which soon boasted a cherished autograph. To Larry's greater amazement, Art Garfunkel suddenly appeared through a side door, also signed the book, and with few words, both musicians disappeared back through the same door, leaving Larry in a stupor, but with a special memento, and quite a story!

The boys decided at the last minute to add an unplanned song. Mr. and Mrs. Jacobson had mentioned seeing the hit play *Oliver!* in New York, so they added the song *Where is Love?* by Lionel Bart. Larry found the lyrics personally meaningful, and worked out a special arrangement he and John could do. He sang solo, while both accompanied on guitar. The song was not exactly in the same genre as their other songs, but the boys hoped it would be appreciated by the older Jacobsons, and at least tolerated by the younger crowd. It nearly turned out to be a disaster.

John played an introduction, and Larry began singing, *"Where is love? Does it fall from skies above?"* Matching his actions to the words of the song, Larry looked skyward. *"Is it underneath the willow tree that I've been dreaming of?"*

His eyes caught a glimpse of the willow tree he found so fascinating. He nearly choked on the words when he realized he *had* seen this tree in his dreams, and this was why it seemed to be speaking to him all night! He closed his eyes in accord with the song. He thought about his earlier dance with Linda, but when a pair of beautiful green eyes appeared to look back at him, his eyes snapped back open in alarm. He remembered how musical were the first words he had heard her speak. Only, hadn't she spoken them to someone else? And it wasn't even Linda's voice, was it?

Moisture was forming in his eyes, but there was nothing to do but continue the song, fighting the growing tightness he could feel in his throat. He tried to relax during the brief musical interlude before the final verse, a prayer that come tomorrow, he would first see the face of someone who would love him. He thought to himself, *Don't I say this prayer every night?* His eyes overflowed, and his voice could not carry the final words to the song.

It was to be the last time Larry would ever sing that song in public. After that night, he could not bear to hear that song, or even think about it. That night, those words reached deeply into his very soul. They had not affected him so strongly before, and he was not sure why it was so different this time. Years later, he would realize his prayer, expressed in the final verse, had been answered this night. He had seen her face.

One should be careful when they pray. Receiving an answer to your prayer may not be what you really want. It might not make you happy after all.

There was a long pause when the song ended. Mrs. Jacobson, sensing both the emotion of the moment, and the distress felt by this young singer, called out, "Bravo!" announcing even the singer in New York had not sung the song with such feeling. She handed Larry a birthday napkin. "It's especially moving to see how well you acted out that emotion," she said, hoping to explain away the tears flowing down his cheeks and save him from embarrassment. Slowly, the kids at the party began to show their appreciation. Larry dried his eyes with the napkin, smiled and thanked her, but the gratitude was expressed more by his eyes than by his words.

Recovering as quickly as he could, Larry glanced at John and chuckled, "Whew! That was a lot harder than I thought it would be. Let's lighten the mood a little. Let's do a folk song, John!"

John took the cue and began to introduce another song, this one lifted almost verbatim from an album made by the Chad Mitchell Trio. "One very exciting area of folk idiom and folk music to us has always been... the hatchet murders in Massachusetts." There were some startled looks and a few snickers from the audience as he continued, "I think that this quaint bit of suburban living can best be explained through the use of our poet laureate, Larry Bristol."

With as much dignity as he could get into his voice, Larry spoke the introduction:

> *Elizabeth Borden took an ax*
> *And gave her mother forty whacks.*
> *And when the job was nicely done*
> *She gave her father forty-one!*

He immediately launched into the song, joined at the appropriate points by John's harmony. It would have brought the house down had they been inside. The kids laughed throughout the song. Mr. and Mrs. Jacobson, former New Yorkers, were especially delighted with the phrase, "*Massachusetts is a far cry from New York!*"

This was the last song they planned for their performance, but the audience would not let them stop, insisting, "Just one more song, please!" Since many of these requests came from Julia, the guest of honor, they happily obliged. Someone eventually asked them to repeat *And I Love Her*, the song played on the radio.

The final song was *If I Fell*, another Beatles song Larry had adapted for them. He smiled each time his eyes would meet Linda's during the song. Unconsciously, the smile faded when his eyes met Julia's. They sang the last line "...*If I fell in love with you,*" John played a short guitar riff, and the concert ended. The audience showed their appreciation one last time. It had been a smashing success.

The radio was turned on once again. The boys mingled with the guests, accepting congratulations as gracefully as they could. Before long, they rejoined Linda and Helen and started dancing. Slowly, the party ended as those few guests with cars began to leave, and parents arrived to pick up the others. With midnight approaching, only the three couples, Larry and Linda, John and Helen, and Jimmy and Julia remained, still dancing. When the next song ended, Mrs. Jacobson turned down the music, subtly indicating it was time to wrap things up.

Linda and Helen excused themselves once again, while Jimmy and Julia went to get one last cup of punch. Mrs. Jacobson thanked the boys for their performance. She had enjoyed it immensely, and was absolutely sure Julia was quite pleased. "I can also tell you," she added with a wink, "that even Mr. Jacobson enjoyed it, although he'd never admit to that, of course. I'd have to say you were a real hit!"

"Thanks, Mrs. Jacobson," Larry said humbly. "Actually, it's been our pleasure." John nodded his agreement.

"And I hope you continue to have good luck with those girls," she whispered with a giggle. She turned away to join her husband before the boys could react. All they could do was look at each other and smile. In silence, they agreed Julia's mother was a classy lady. They really liked her.

Julia came back with Jimmy in tow. "I want to thank you so much for coming and playing for my party. Thank you, John," she said as she hugged him. "And thank you, Larry," she said giving him a hug, as well. Larry experienced another gap in the space-time continuum no one else noticed. She concluded by saying, "I think this has been the best birthday party I've ever had!"

The boys were almost speechless, mumbling things about how the pleasure was all theirs, and they were happy to do it, and they would do it again next year if she wanted them to, and so forth. She giggled at their embarrassment, then suggested to Jimmy they needed to say goodnight.

Linda and Helen returned, and Larry and John asked hopefully if they needed a ride home. "No, we're spending the night," Helen announced. "We girls are going to have a slumber party, listen to Julia's new record, and talk all night!"

"What are you going to talk about?" John snickered.

The girls giggled, and Linda answered, "We'll think of something." She moved to stand close to Larry and put her arms around his neck. Giggling, she whispered, "I wish you could stay!" He looked into her eyes, but since he could think of nothing to say, he just kissed her gently, as John and Helen exchanged a goodnight kiss, also.

The boys carried their guitars to John's car, placed them carefully in the trunk, and got in the front seat to wait for Jimmy. Presently, Julia and Jimmy appeared near the front door. When Jimmy turned to kiss his girlfriend goodnight, Larry subconsciously looked away. *Why do I not want to see that? Why do I care?* It was not to be the last time he would ask himself such questions.

Larry and John were discussing their performance when Jimmy climbed into the back seat of John's car. They messed up one song when Larry forgot the third verse and went straight into the chorus, while John continued to play the main melody. Another was damaged when John forgot to play his guitar solo at the right moment. But other than those two gaffs, which they had successfully managed to cover, they thought the performance had gone rather well. They asked Jimmy his opinion.

"Oh, I thought it was *quite* a performance," Jimmy answered bitterly.

John and Larry stared at each other. Jimmy did not seem to be in a good mood ever since he had gotten to the car. "What's eating you?" John asked.

Jimmy's lips grew thin as he responded. "I don't particularly like the idea of someone trying to score points with my girlfriend while claiming to be my friend."

"What are you talking about?" John asked. "Who was hitting on your girlfriend?"

"He knows," Jimmy said, nodding his head at Larry.

"What?" John asked, turning a puzzled look at Larry.

Larry shrugged at John and turned to look at Jimmy directly. "I was a little busy with Linda, or did you notice? Are you saying you think I was hitting on Julia?"

Jimmy scowled at him. "Yes! All that talk about where she might have seen you before, and that birthday dedication on the radio. And it surely looked to me like you enjoyed that hug she gave you *way* too much!"

Larry was stunned, wondering if Jimmy was right. *Was I trying to score points with this girl without even realizing it? No, that's just not my style.* "Jimmy," he said calmly, "it was Julia who brought up the subject of seeing me somewhere before. I made a fool of myself with that 'temple' thing, you know that."

"And dear old brother John was helpful to point out my mistake about 'seeing' you on the radio," Jimmy threw out.

"She thought it was cute!" John protested.

"You embarrassed me, and you know it," Jimmy insisted.

John didn't know what to say, and looked to Larry for help. "Neither of us meant to embarrass you," Larry said trying to calm things down. "I think your girl was just teasing with us, including you. She strikes me as a girl with a great sense of humor."

"Just the way you like them!" Jimmy spat.

Larry was not distracted. "Yes, you're right. A sense of humor is something I demand in a girl. Linda has a great sense of humor, and that's why I spent so much time with her. Did you notice? Now, I won't deny enjoying that hug Julia gave me. It was warm and genuine, and it felt good. But to tell the truth, I think I would have enjoyed a hug from her mother just as much. She's a classy lady!"

"So now you like older girls as well, I see," John teased. He was in too good of a mood to let the others get him down.

Ignoring him, Larry continued, "I wasn't hitting on your girl. I won't deny I like her. She seems like a really sweet girl, and you should be very proud to be with her! But you should be more careful, because she might not like the jealous type. Maybe when she gets a little older, if you decide you no longer want her, then send her my way! But for now, I'm interested in Linda, and I'm not trying to steal your girl."

Jimmy did not appear to be convinced, so Larry continued. "I'll make you a solemn promise, OK? I promise I won't make a move for your girlfriend, Julia, until you tell me you're no longer interested in her." Both Jimmy and John took notice of this statement. They knew Larry did not make promises lightly. At the time, Larry had no reason to think he would ever regret it. "I don't go hitting on another guy's girlfriend. That's a fool's errand! If the girl really wants to be with him, then you're not going to get anywhere that way, and most likely, they'll both get mad at you. And if she doesn't want to be with him, then it's a lot smarter to wait and let things run their course, and make sure you're around to help pick up the pieces when their relationship falls apart.

"Look, Jimmy, you're my friend. I can see you're really fond of this girl, and if you've been paying attention, then you'd know she likes you as well. I can see that, even if you can't. Think about this! She kissed *you* goodnight, not me."

John had to jump in, "You were too busy kissing Linda!"

"I'm not like you guys," Jimmy pleaded. "You guys can get any girl you please. It's not easy for me to get a girl like her."

Larry saw the perfect opening for his little joke, but was not in the mood for joking. "Maybe your brother can, but I can't. I have a lot of trouble finding a girl who likes me, and when I do, I've even more trouble keeping her. Let me give you some advice, from someone who's older and maybe a little wiser. You can take it or leave it as you wish. I know you've heard the old adage: *If you love something, let it go. If it loves you, it will come back to you.*"

"...and if it doesn't come back, you can hunt it down..." John added. He was in a good mood whether the others were or not! Larry hushed him with a glance.

"The surest way to loose a girlfriend is to try to possess her," Larry continued. "Trust me on this, my young friend. I have a lot of experience loosing girlfriends! The very best part of having a girlfriend isn't because you want to be with her. The best part is when she wants to be with you! Give her the freedom to be with whoever she wants, then pray like hell she'll want to be with you. That's a treasure beyond any price."

They rode along in silence for a while, thinking about the advice Larry had delivered. He was not sure himself from where that advice had come, but he realized it applied to him as much as it did to Jimmy. After a while, Jimmy apologized for accusing Larry of betraying their friendship. It was never mentioned again.

Sunday, October 23, 1966
Slumber Party

Julia slipped her new album onto the stereo and started the automatic switching mechanism. The girls had changed out of their party clothes, and were lounging in the family room near the entertainment center. Linda and Julia wore simple white teeshirts, panties, and cotton socks, while Helen wore satin pajamas. Mr. and Mrs. Jacobson retired to their bedroom and closed the door, seeking both solitude, and relief from the constant noise of the girls' giggling and the rock and roll music.

"When they sang, *'If I fell in love with you'*, I thought I would just die!" Julia squealed.

"Me, too!" Helen agreed.

"I *did* die, but Larry gave me mouth-to-mouth resuscitation," Linda giggled.

"I got some from John, too!" Helen snickered.

Julia laughed, "You girls are lucky! I think they're just dreamy!"

"You'd better include yourself in that," Linda said. "I saw that goodnight kiss you gave Jimmy. Do either of you still have your tonsils?" she laughed.

Julia laughed, "I wouldn't know what to do if he stuck his tongue in my mouth."

Linda cooed, "The best thing to do is stick *your* tongue back into *his* mouth!" She grabbed Schotzy and smothered him with mock wet kisses as the others giggled.

"Did Larry stick his tongue in your mouth?" Helen asked excitedly.

"It's called a 'French kiss' guys," Linda suggested, "and no, Larry didn't stick his tongue in my mouth. Not this time, anyway, but I hope that will change on Friday."

Julia snickered as she asked, "Did he ask you out?"

"They asked both of us out," Helen inserted gleefully. "What I mean is John asked me out, and Larry asked her out."

"A double date?" Julia asked.

Linda grinned dreamily as she answered, "Not exactly. Larry is picking me up on Friday and we'll meet John and Helen at the football game. He's also taking me to the radio station on Saturday night!"

Helen piped in, "And John is taking me there, also."

"Wow!" Julia said. "I wish Jimmy could drive, so we wouldn't have to get one of our parents to take us somewhere." Then, with some exasperation in her voice, "Oh, but what difference would it make? My parents already told me they won't let me go on a car date until I'm fifteen."

"Hey, Julia," Helen said. "Maybe John would be willing to let Jimmy and you come along with us on Saturday. After all, they are brothers!"

"Do you think so?" Julia asked excitedly. "Maybe mom and dad would let me go if it was like a double date!"

"You better ask John, first," Linda grinned. "Some guys wouldn't like their little brother hanging around. It all depends on what John has on his mind! Maybe he plans to take you out parking, and wants to keep the back seat free!" she giggled.

"Hubba, hubba!" Helen laughed.

"You girls are scaring me," Julia snickered. "I'm not ready for that sort of thing."

"First you let him put his tongue in your mouth," Linda winked, "and then he puts his finger into your belly button. Only it's not *really* your belly button! But that's

OK, 'cause it's not really his *finger*, either!" Helen rolled over on her back pretending to moan, laughing with delight. Schotzy came over to lick her face.

Julia snickered, but looked a little apprehensive. "Have you ever, you know, done it? With a boy?" she asked.

Helen was quick to respond. "I wouldn't want to do it with anything else!" she giggled. "I haven't done it yet, but I might be ready if I found the right boy."

Linda teased, "One who wears pants, right?"

"At first," Helen giggled, "but he won't wear them all night! What about you?"

Julia giggled, "I haven't, either. I'm not sure Jimmy would even know what to do if I showed it to him! He's just a little boy most of the time, but I guess that's all I really want right now. What about you, Linda?"

Linda smiled knowingly. "That's for me to know, and you to find out!"

"Oh, come on," Helen and Julia chided.

"That's sort of private," Linda began. Then, seeing the look of anticipation on her friends' faces, she added, "OK, yes, but only once." She actually had more experience than that, but did not want the other girls to know too much.

"Who was he?" Helen demanded gleefully. "Anyone we know?"

"I'll never tell!" she grinned. "Don't even try to get me to tell you, because that's a secret I'm not going to reveal!"

"Did it hurt?" Julia asked.

"No. Not at all!"

"What was it like?" Helen asked.

Linda smiled, remembering how it had been the first time. "It was OK, I guess. I mean, it was very exciting, and it felt really good for a moment. It feels a lot better than when you play with it yourself! But there really wasn't much to it. To tell you the truth, it was over before I even got started. I could sure tell *he* liked it, though!"

"Weren't you scared?" Julia asked. "That you might get pregnant or something?"

"A little," Linda said, "but my mom and I had talked before, and she told me to make sure the boy wore a rubber. They're not completely safe, she told me, but it's better than nothing!" Linda saw Julia was still a little apprehensive, and continued seriously, "Look, Julia, if you're worried about this sort of thing, talk it over with your mom. She seems pretty cool to me. Otherwise, my advise would be, if in doubt, keep it out!"

The girls screamed with laughter. The subject matter changed to records, school, clothes, horses, and all the other things young girls like to talk about, returning on occasion to their favorite subject – boys! Eventually, they settled down, started listening to the music a little more than talking, and slowly they each fell off into a dreamy sleep.

Friday, October 28, 1966
Poli High

Larry pulled into Linda's driveway and stopped. It was a dreary evening, with low hanging clouds heavy with moisture. The leading edge of a cold front was expected to pass through the area during the evening, dropping temperatures into the low forties. The weather promised to make for a sloppy field, not good news for the SFA

Bronco football squad. Their team was built on speed and agility that would be hindered by such conditions, unlike the ponderous size of the Conroe Tigers, their arch-rivals and opponents for tonight's game.

Not that this meant much to Larry. He had been looking forward to this evening all week. He had a date with Linda Livingston, a very pretty and popular girl! It seemed his stock had risen sharply this last week. The kids at school had been more friendly than usual, and a few had even gone out of their way to greet him. He assumed people were hearing about his and John's performance at Julia's birthday party. He figured the spreading news about the party had been started by Linda, and he felt maybe, just maybe, his life was starting to change. Maybe his plan was going to work after all!

The doorbell was answered by Linda's mother, a pleasant woman who's slightly plump facial features served to enhance her jovial smile. Larry barely managed to introduce himself and the purpose of his visit before he was ushered in to meet Linda's father, a hard looking man in his late thirties – nothing like Larry expected. He merely grunted as Larry was introduced, remaining in his chair and not so much as offering his hand.

"This is one of the young men who sang at that party Linda went to last Saturday," Mrs. Livingston explained to her husband, trying to break the silence of the moment. "He sings in the choir with Linda, and even has his own radio program!"

"Well, it's not just my program," Larry corrected. "Sam, John, and I are the hosts, and other kids work the show when they want to."

"But he's the *star* of the show," Mrs. Livingston gushed. Mr. Livingston grunted again without looking up from the television screen.

Before he could protest about his sudden rise to stardom and fame, Linda entered the room from the hallway. She flashed a warm smile, greeting Larry with a simple, "Hi!" She was wearing a plaid skirt, a plain white blouse, loafers and knee high socks – the kind of outfit that complimented her image as an energetic young girl in prep school. Larry was pleased with her appearance and commented about how nice she looked. She returned the compliment, then suggested they should get moving so they could get to the stadium in time to see everything.

"Have her home by midnight," were the first and only words Mr. Livingston spoke.

"Yes, sir," Larry replied. He started to add a flippant comment about her turning into a pumpkin, but decided discretion was the better policy. "Goodnight to you, sir, and to you also, Mrs. Livingston. I'll take good care of her."

"I'm sure you will, young man," she said. "You two be good, and have fun!"

Larry bit his tongue to keep from demanding she make up her mind, and Linda, practically reading his mind, grinned at him. "Goodnight, mom," she said over her shoulder, closing the door softly behind her. He escorted her to the passenger side and opened the car door for her. It was a little corny, even in those days, but Larry had been brought up to be polite to a lady. She smiled for him and slid into the seat. He closed the door and trotted around to get into the driver's seat.

Linda was already sitting in the middle. "I'm glad you don't have bucket seats. I like to sit close to my date. How about you?"

"I like that, too!" he smiled. "I guess that's one of the advantages of having an old piece of junk like this." Larry's car was a 1960 Ford Falcon with no frills at all; it was just simple transportation, with a heater, a radio, and nothing else. Larry's father told him that was all he needed, and truth be told, Larry agreed. Still, he sometimes wished he had something a little more stylish to make a better impression on a date.

"It's cute," Linda said. "I think it suits you."

He was not quite sure what she meant by that, but decided not to press the subject. He turned the ignition and the car started right up. He was grateful, at least, the car was dependable. Maybe that was what she meant.

"Would you like to get something to eat before going to the game?" he asked. "You sounded like you are eager to get there."

Linda looked at her date and smiled. "No. I mean yes, I'd like to get something to eat," she giggled. "I just wanted to get out of the house as quickly as I could."

"Why is that?" he asked innocently.

She looked at him wondering if his eyes had been closed. "I wanted to get away from my mom and dad," she said bluntly.

"Don't you get along with them?" he asked. "Your mom is pleasant enough. I guess your dad might be a little tired after a hard day's work?"

Linda tilted her head and looked at him, wondering if he was really so naive. "My mom is wonderful. My only complaint is she always wants me to do things her way so I won't 'end up like her' as she puts it. She wants to relive her life through me. My dad, well, he isn't a very happy man. Don't get me wrong, I love them dearly and they take good care of me. I just don't always like to be around them."

"It's not really any of my business, Linda. Is the Dan Dee Dog OK with you?"

"Fine. I'm not really very hungry, anyway," she answered. "I don't mind sharing these little problems with you, Larry. It's not like they're big family secrets no one outside the family knows. Why don't we forget about it and just have a good time?"

She grinned as he flashed his patented, crooked half smile. "Sounds good to me!"

They arrived at the Dan Dee Dog drive-in restaurant and ordered a light meal. One of the more popular items on the menu was a corn dog, a wiener on a stick, dipped in cornbread batter and deep fried. It was the item that gave the place its name. It was also the favorite item for Larry's family. It's vague resemblance to a dachshund provided the inspiration for the name of the dog he once had.

Larry and Linda talked about the game, how the weather would affect it, and how it was going to get chilly before the game was over. A light drizzle had already started, and the wind was dying down in anticipation of a shift in direction.

When they finished eating, Larry drove to the football stadium and found a parking space. He got out of the car, planning to run around to open the passenger door for her. But she slid under the steering wheel and exited through the driver's door, surprising him with a good look at her silky smooth legs. He admired the view discretely, smiled, but felt a little embarrassed. She relished his admiration and smiled back brightly.

"I brought a wool blanket we can sit on," he said, suddenly worrying about how those rough wooden bleachers might damage those beautiful legs. "If it gets too cold later, we can wrap it around us for warmth."

"Sounds cozy," she remarked with another smile. "Helen asked me to look for her and John when we got here."

"Yeah, that's what John said, also," Larry lied. He and John were great friends, but when it came to girls, neither of them wanted to see what the other was up to in real time. They would, of course, compare notes later.

As they walked to the gate, Linda slipped her arm around his waist. He relished the attention. It had been too long since a girl was this nice to him, and he enjoyed the feeling. For him, it was like he was being given food desperately needed for a starving ego. For her, it was just the natural way to show a boy she liked him.

They arrived at the gate and Larry bought two admission tickets. He and Linda walked up the ramp, arms still around each others' waists, and looked for the best seats. They were soon spotted by Helen, who motioned for them to come to the spot where she and John had saved a couple of seats. They had to release their holds on each other in order to maneuver through the crowded bleachers, but eventually they arrived, and greeted their friends. Larry spread out their blanket and motioned for Linda to sit next to Helen. The girls sat in the middle, with John and Larry flanked to either side.

Larry smiled across at John and raised his eyebrows in greeting. John got Larry's signal things were going well, and returned it. The girls giggled and whispered secrets while John and Larry carried on their unspoken, yet effective, conversation.

Various friends wandered by during the game to greet the foursome and silently express their approval of the new "arrangements". The girls urged everyone to listen to the radio program Saturday night. John and Larry grinned slyly at this suggestion, saying they had a few tricks up their sleeves for tomorrow's show.

Halftime came and was gone. Late in the third quarter, the wind shifted with a vengeance as the anticipated cold front passed through town, abruptly dropping the temperature, forcing everyone to don their jackets, or for some, heavy coats. Larry lifted a portion of the blanket so he and Linda could get under it, capturing their own warmth, and get a break from the wind. To his delight, Linda snuggled up close to him, once again putting her arms around his waist, and resting her head on his chest and shoulder. Deeply, he breathed in the fragrance of her hair and frolicked within the warmth of her embrace, his ego feasting on the nourishment he needed so badly.

Near the end of the game, trailing 14-7, the Broncos mounted their best drive of the night, scoring what appeared to be the tying touchdown with only twelve seconds remaining on the clock. The coach asked for a time out and requested a conference with the officials, baffling most of the people in the stands. But Larry knew the situation, and explained it to those sitting nearby. "It's all about something they call penetrations. If a game ends in a tie, the team with the most penetrations is declared the winner. The coach is asking the officials who leads in penetrations. If we do, then they'll go for the tie; if not, then we'll undoubtedly go for two."

Upon learning they were trailing in penetrations, the Broncos sent the regular offensive team onto the field to attempt a two point conversion. The outcome of the game, in fact the outcome of the entire season, would rest on this one play, because the winner of this game would advance into the state tournament, while the losing school would forget about football for another year, and start thinking about its basketball team. The ball was snapped, and the Bronco quarterback ran a bootleg to the left, looking to pass. Spotting his tight end all alone in the back of the end zone, he prepared to make the easy pass that would seal the victory. But as he tried to plant his feet for the pass, the slippery sod and mud betrayed him, and he fell to the ground. The play, the game, and the season were over. The Broncos lost 14-13.

The foursome looked at each other in disbelief. Finally, Helen broke the silence.

Friday, October 28, 1966 – Poli High   -51-

"Oh, well. *Que será será.*"

John, Larry, and Linda, a small subsection of the Stephen F. Austin High School A Capella choir, sang in unison, "*Whatever will be, will be. The future's not ours to see. Que será será.*"

They all broke into a laugh and began to gather their things to leave. Noting it was only about 10:30, Helen suggested they go someplace together. Linda responded she and Larry already had other plans, pointing out they would all be getting together tomorrow night at the radio station. Neither Larry nor John objected, so the two couples soon went their separate ways.

"Tell me about these plans we have," Larry asked when they were alone near his car, hoping he had not forgotten something important.

"I don't know," she giggled. "I just wanted to spend some time alone with you."

Larry looked at her and smiled. "Your carriage awaits thee, ma lady. What's your pleasure?" This time, he simply opened the driver's door. Linda slid into the front seat, once more providing him with a nice view of her legs, and he quickly followed.

She sat close to him and pondered her reply. After a moment's reflection, she suggested, "Why don't we go to my house, listen to some records, and just talk a while. My folks won't mind, and they won't bother us."

It wasn't exactly what he wanted, but he agreed. Even though things were obviously going well, this was, after all, their first date. He drove back to her house and they entered the living room. Her mom passed through just long enough to greet them, and made some hot chocolate before discretely returning to her bedroom.

Linda put the *Revolver* album she had already borrowed from Julia onto the stereo, and turned the volume low so not to disturb her parents. She motioned for Larry to stretch out in a large bean bag chair, and then settled down beside him.

The bean bag chair was wonderfully soft and comfortable, warm and intimate. Without saying a word, Linda wrapped her arms around Larry's neck, pressed her warm body against his, and kissed him firmly on the mouth. He put his arms around her waist and returned the kiss. During the third kiss, as the stereo played *Eleanor Rigby*, their tongues met and danced together.

Neither of them did any talking, but the communication was powerful. Larry was hungry for affection, starving in fact, and he feasted on the banquet Linda presented. He was determined, however, to be a perfect gentleman, because he wanted to return to this banquet again and again, and feared if he pushed things a little too far, he might not get that chance. Without an actual menu to guide him, he reasoned it was better to fill up on the delicious appetizers already being served, rather than risk requesting a main course item that might not actually be available on that menu.

When side one of the record ended, Linda got up, deftly turned the album over, and quickly returned to his arms. His hands caressed her back and her shoulders, but he refused to let them roam to those intimate places he longed to touch. They kissed each others' lips, cheeks, and ears. She moaned slightly when he kissed her neck. He could remember feeling such excitement only once before, and Linda's rising temperature told Larry she was just as excited as he.

He wanted this moment to last for eternity. But alas, time moves too quickly when one experiences joy. The record ended all too soon, and a small clock chimed to signal the arrival of midnight. "I should go," he sighed between kisses. It was, he realized, a kind of code talk. Whenever there was something he knew was the right thing to do, but the last thing in the universe he actually wanted to do, he encoded it in this manner.

Linda sighed and responded, "I should let you go." They smiled at each other in their mutual understanding of the implied meaning.

Slowly, after a few more kisses, they disengaged from their embrace and Larry stood to leave. "See you tomorrow?" he asked pointlessly.

"I'll be watching for you," she replied.

He walked to the door, but stopped and turned back to her, allowing her to fall into his arms again. Finally, reluctantly, sadly, Larry released her, whispered, "Goodnight," and stepped through the front door. She watched him, lost in thought as he walked to his car, waved to him as he opened the door and got in, and slowly closed the front door as his car disappeared down the street.

Larry drove home in the now pouring rain, reflecting on the events of the evening. Linda was someone very special, exactly what he needed. Girls seemed to like him before, but things had a nasty habit of blowing up in his face. *Will this last more than a couple of weeks?* he wondered. He hoped things would be different this time.

He was fighting a vicious circle, and even though he was keenly aware of it, he seemed powerless to break out of its horrific pattern. First, he would meet someone new, or as in this case, maybe someone he already knew would show a little interest in him she had not shown before. They would start seeing each other. Things would be going along just great, and he would start to have special feelings for the girl. He wanted to have a special girlfriend so badly! Then, out of the blue, she would tell him it was all a mistake, that they were finished. Once again, his heart would be broken. After a while, he would recover, and then the circle would start all over again. But each time the cycle turned, he got a little more desperate than he had been the last time, making it a little more difficult to find someone new, and a lot more difficult to keep her when he did.

Typically, the break up would be punctuated with the statement she "really wanted to be *just-friends*". Oh, how he despised that phrase! "But we *are* friends!" he would say. He would want to cry out, "Isn't that the way things are supposed to start? Why can't we be special friends? I just want you to want me. I want you. I just need you to need me! I need you!" But it never mattered.

He also despised it when someone said one could never have too many friends. *They're wrong!* he insisted. *It's easy to have just one friend too many. I always have one friend too many! I would give my soul to reduce the count of my just-friends by one.* He concluded the word "just" had nothing to do with justice, and should never be used in the same sentence as the word "friends".

He arrived home and went to his room. Assuming the rest of his family was asleep, he was careful not to wake them. Settling into his bed, he thought about the fact he was happy for the first time in... *How long has it been?* he wondered. *Will it last for a while this time?* He remembered the prayer from that song. *I found her underneath that willow tree! Is this finally the girl I've been looking for?*

Lying in his bed, he looked up at the ceiling and daydreamed. He was surprised to find what appeared to be a pair of mysterious green eyes staring back at him, making him uncomfortable. He rubbed his eyes, but found this vision would not go away. Even with his eyes closed, those other eyes continued to stare at him, beckoning to him. "God, help me!" he cried aloud. The apparition departed, leaving only the tears it had brought. He hoped his outburst had not awaken anyone. Relieved from the image of those green eyes staring at him, he finally fell asleep, but his dreams were troubled, and not for the last time.

Saturday, October 29, 1966
Count Larry

The children's reading room at the Carnegie Public Library was decorated in colors of orange and black, with pictures of various ghosts, goblins, witches, and other spooky characters. It was the day for the special Halloween program.

Larry thought it was great fun to have Sam around at work. They both got part-time jobs at Bryan's Carnegie Public Library during the summer, and kept those jobs after the school year began. He worked both after school and on Saturdays, while Sam worked only on Saturdays. They were always clowning around in the library, being careful to avoid the evil eye of the librarian, old "Hard Hearted" Hannah.

Mrs. Amelia "Hard Hearted" Hannah was the librarian for the children's section. It would be impossible for anyone to seriously consider her to be "hard hearted" because it was obvious she truly loved to be around the children of all ages who came to her library. On Saturday mornings, there was always a special children's program, where she would read stories, show movies, or conduct little skits. Larry and Sam were responsible for just about everything to do with the program, of course, but they didn't mind. In truth, they both loved children almost as much as old Mrs. Hannah did. Larry would never have admitted to this, of course, because it was not considered cool to actually like the little rug rats. Sometimes all he had to do was run the movie projector. Other times, he might have to play an evil troll in a play. He and Sam would prepare the "sets" (such as they were), and provide all of the sound effects. Secretly, Sam and Larry enjoyed every moment of it.

He arrived for work at 8:00 o'clock, as usual. He was not, however, dressed as usual. Today, he was wearing an old fashioned formal suit with a large, dark cape. An outfit like this might have been worn a hundred years ago by a nobleman from eastern Europe, a Count. Makeup darkened the features of his face, and drops of fake blood oozed from the corners of his mouth, just where the fake fangs protruded from his lips. His persona was Count Larry, Master of the Undead, the essence of evil and dread. He climbed the stairs to the children's section, flared his cape, and greeted Mrs. Hannah with an evil laugh, "Ha, 'ah, 'ah! Gooood evening!"

She tried to suppress a slight grin as she made a nonchalant reply, "It's morning. Who are you supposed to be, anyway?"

"Ha, 'ah, 'ah! I am Count Larry, master vampire and ruler of the undead!"

"The sun has been up some time. Shouldn't you be in your coffin?" she queried.

"Not any longer! Ha, 'ah, 'ah! I have the power to mask the sun. Now I shall unleash my terror upon all who oppose me. Today, I shall achieve my destiny and rule the world!"

"Oh, please," she said suppressing a laugh. "There will time for all that nonsense later. Help me get things ready for the program. You know what needs to be done." Mrs. Hannah was not particularly tolerant of teenage "nonsense" as she called it, but she had grown to like this young man. If he would just be a bit more serious, he would make something of himself one of these days.

Larry merely smiled. "Yes, ma'am," he said, getting to work. The Halloween program was the second most important one of the year, second only to Christmas. Something suddenly occurred to him he had not considered before – everyone did not celebrate Christmas. Was the same true for Halloween?

Sam arrived moments later, dressed as a witch. Spectacular makeup gave her a pointed chin and a grotesque nose, complete with warts. She failed to notice Larry sneak up behind her. "Gooood evening," he said using his best Bela Lugosi voice.

"Shit!" she cried, started.

Mrs. Hannah chastised her with, "I will not tolerate such foul language around here, young lady!" She thought Susan was a lovely girl, but perhaps a little more undisciplined than most.

"I'm sorry, Mrs. Hannah," Sam apologized as Larry died laughing. "He surprised me." Sam gave him an evil stare, as if to say, "I'll get you back!"

Larry flared his cape, flashed his fangs, announcing, "I vant to drink your bluhd."

"Hee, hee, hee, hee!" she cackled in her witch's voice. "If you so much as touch me, I'll turn you into a newt!"

Mrs. Hannah had enough. "OK, you two. Cut out the nonsense and get to work."

Sam and Larry grinned at each other and then went about their duties. He began arranging the chairs in front of the stage. How he loved going on that stage! It was seldom used, and about all he ever did was walk across it to access one of the storage rooms in the back. But his mind always wandered while he was up there, and he dreamed of taking bows before cheering crowds. What little stage experience he actually had was the result of his participation in the school choir, and he relished each and every moment.

The chairs varied in size from those needed by a young adult, all the way down to those perfect for a small toddler. Today, because they anticipated a large audience, there probably would not be enough chairs to go around, and many of the children would sit on the floor. But as always, everyone would have a good view, no matter where they sat.

The program started at 9:00. Mrs. Hannah first read a ghost story from one of the new book acquisitions, while Larry and Sam made appropriate sound effects. When she finished the story, she pointed out to the children they could check this book out, take it home, and read all of the other wonderful stories it contained. Since Larry was hidden from her view, he got Sam's attention and silently mouthed the words, "I pity that poor book!" Sam had to hide her face as she giggled in agreement.

Shortly, Larry ran the projector to show a few "spooky" cartoons. He continued to make faces at Sam, hoping Mrs. Hannah would scold her when she laughed for no apparent reason. But as usual, she managed to hide her mirth. The film ended, and the children were allowed to pillage the bookshelves, and to play Trick or Treat with Larry and Sam, who passed out small pieces of candy while doing their best to scare the wits out of the children. Larry would open his eyes wide, flare his cape, and brandish his fangs. More than once, a tiny child would squeal with mock fear and run away for mommy. Larry especially loved it when that happened.

By 11:00, things were starting to settle back into what passed for normality. Most of the children had departed. Those who remained huddled against their mothers while the ladies chatted with Mrs. Hannah. From the condition of the shelves, Larry knew the afternoon would be spent trying to restore order. Sam would first spend her time trying to file the cards for each of the books that had been checked out, then would join him. Since neither was eager to tackle these chores that always followed the Saturday morning programs, they continued to entertain the children still hanging around, and would continue to do so until Mrs. Hannah finally ordered them to get back to work.

Julia and her mother came to downtown Bryan to do some shopping. They normally would go to the Townshire Shopping Center, but a newspaper supplement had tempted them into the downtown area that day. Potts' Jewelry was having a big sale, and never having been there before, Mrs. Jacobson wanted to have a look at their merchandise.

Jessica looked at the bracelets and watches. While she did not find anything she was ready to purchase immediately, there was a beautiful man's gold watch that would make a lovely gift for Julian. She examined it closely, asking several questions, and finally decided she would discreetly grill Julian to see if he would like to have a new watch like that. Julia briefly admired the engagement rings, dreaming about the day when a knight in shining armor would come for her. But ultimately, it was the assortment of stud earrings that captured her attention.

"Do you see anything you like?" Jessica asked, sneaking up behind her.

At first, Julia was embarrassed by this sudden intrusion into her daydreams. But since it was her mother, she quickly relaxed. "I like just about all of them, especially the pair that looks like little stars." She pointed out the pair that caught her attention.

Jessica smiled. "Would you like to get your ears pierced, Julia?" she asked.

"Could I?" Julia asked excitedly.

"If you think you're ready," Jessica said. She could see her little girl was growing up. Jessica was almost jealous of the fact so many adventures lay ahead for her lovely young daughter. "Now, I don't want to force you, but if you're ready, I'll buy you those star earrings you like so much."

Julia hugged her mother and responded joyfully, "Oh, thank you, mom!" Then, with a little trepidation, "Will it hurt much?"

"Not too much," Jessica reassured her. "You probably won't even notice, but you'll have to be careful to keep them clean, and make sure they don't get infected."

Julia smiled and said, "Then let's do it!" As long as she had her mom's support, Julia could face anything at all, no matter how ghastly it might appear to be.

The store owner, Mrs. Mary Potts, took Julia and her mother into a small room. She wanted to do this job herself to ensure it was done correctly. She was aware of the Jacobsons and their growing affluence in the community, and wanted to impress them with personal service, hoping they would return to do more business in the future. She cleaned the girl's earlobe carefully, then made the simple incision. Jessica was right, and Julia hardly felt a thing. A tiny drop of blood was quickly cleaned away, and a sterile stud was inserted into the small hole. She completed the other ear just as efficiently.

Mrs. Potts explained, "You shouldn't wear your new earrings for a couple of days, Julia, not until your ears have healed completely. Keep the incision as clean as possible, and don't remove these studs. You don't want the holes to grow back closed, do you?" She smiled at the young girl and handed her a small mirror.

Julia looked at the temporary studs, nothing more than small shiny balls. They were not as pretty as the little stars she had picked, but they would do for a little while. "Do you think Jimmy will notice?" she asked no one in particular.

"Of course he will," replied Mrs. Potts with a smile.

"If he knows what's good for him," Jessica snickered. "Who knows, Julia? Some boys will notice such things, and some won't. There's nothing you can do about it either way. It's just their nature."

Julia looked back in the mirror and daydreamed. "I hope so. I want a boy who'll notice such things." The older women looked at each other and smiled in agreement.

After completing the transaction, Jessica and Julia left the store and decided to walk around the downtown area they had not visited before. One of the larger stores was Ellison's Pharmacy. It did not sound interesting to Julia, but Jessica noted it had an old fashioned soda fountain, and urged her daughter inside. She sat them at the counter rather than in one of the booths. This place brought back fond memories from her youth. She noticed the drink menu listed cherry lime aid, something she had not tasted in years, and immediately ordered two of them.

Julia protested briefly, but on her mom's assurance she would like it, decided to give it a try. Her mom was usually right about such things. She watched as the soda jerk squeezed the juice from fresh limes, mixed in a simple syrup, added some cherry flavoring, filled the glass with carbonated water, stirred briefly to mix it all together, and topped it off with a fresh cherry. They were served the concoctions, and after her first tentative sip, Julia realized her mom was right yet again. It was delicious!

After finishing their sodas, Jessica searched the shelves for small bottles of alcohol and hydrogen peroxide, to make sure Julia could keep her newly pierced ears clean. Julia wandered around the store, stopping to look at some small music boxes. She loved music boxes, and had started building a little collection. She found a pretty little one with a mechanical ballerina on top next to the lid. When she wound it, the box played a beautiful tune while the ballerina danced! She thought about it for a moment and then decided to return it to the shelf. Her mom had already done enough for her that day.

Her attention was soon drawn to some small children in Halloween costumes who were laughing and playing outside the store. There seemed to be a lot of them, and she wondered what it was all about. Looking through the big glass windows in the front of Ellison's Pharmacy, she saw other children coming out of a large building across the street. The sign in front of the building read, "Carnegie Public Library".

Jessica paid for the alcohol, hydrogen peroxide, a small package of cotton balls, and a tiny music box with a mechanical ballerina. She quickly secreted this item away into her shopping bag, then walked up beside her daughter and asked, "What are you looking at?"

Julia indicated the building across the street. "It's the library, mom. Do you think Jimmy's friend Larry might be working there today?"

"Why don't we go see," Jessica suggested.

They left the store and waited on the curb for the traffic signal to change. Directly across the street was the Palace Theater. A lot of her friends had mentioned going there to see movies and to hold hands with their boyfriends. Julia decided she wanted Jimmy to take her there sometime.

As they walked towards the library, Jessica removed the music box from her bag and handed it to Julia. "Mom! You shouldn't have! You've already done so much!"

Jessica hugged her daughter. "I know I'm going to spoil you, but I just can't help it. I love you so much!"

"I love you, too, mom," Julia smiled.

Next to the theater was a small park, the grounds for the public library. Julia's mind wandered, daydreaming about a time when she might walk through such a park, hand-in-hand with her boyfriend. At last, they reached the library's massive doors and pulled them open. They entered the vestibule containing a few furniture items, but the principle features, other than another set of large doors opening into the main library, were the two flights of stairs flanking either side of the room. A small sign near the bottom of one staircase indicated the children's section was upstairs.

"Didn't he say he worked in the children's library?" Jessica asked.

"I think so," Julia replied. They were both startled by the squeal from a small girl who came bounding down the stairs laughing and holding onto a cherished candy treat. They heard an evil sounding laugh coming from somewhere high above them.

"Are you sure you want to do this?" Jessica asked her daughter with a smile.

Julia nodded. "There's no reason to back out now, is there?"

Larry laughed to himself, having dispatched the last of the little girls in the children's section. When he heard more footsteps on the stairs, he assumed some brave soul was coming back for more candy. He hid himself behind the door at the top of the stairs, a door that was never closed to deny access to the children who came seeking books.

Noting two soft footsteps had reached the top of the stairs and tentatively entered the room, he came out from his hiding place, intent on surprising the new arrivals. "Gooood evening!" he said as he opened his eyes wide in an evil stare, spread his arms to flare his cape, and bared his horrible fangs.

Startled by the voice behind them, Jessica and Julia turned to see this apparition and almost screamed. Recognition spread across their faces, as well as Larry's, and they all started laughing, bringing a reproachful "Shh!" from Mrs. Hannah, to which Larry immediately apologized. He motioned for Julia and Jessica to follow him.

"Mrs. Hannah," he began, "I want you to meet some friends of mine. This is Mrs. Jacobson and her daughter, Julia."

"I'm Jessica," she said pleasantly. "We're sorry to disturb your library, but it was quite a shock at first."

"It's nice to meet you, Mrs. Jacobson. Jessica," she corrected. "Welcome to the children's library. I'm Amelia Hannah. By now, no doubt someone has referred to me as 'Hard Hearted' Hannah," she said, giving Larry a reproachful look. "Don't you have something you should be doing right now, young man?"

Julia snickered. Larry remembered how much he had enjoyed hearing her laugh. "Yes, ma'am," he replied, then backed away towards the bookshelves. He spotted Sam and mouthed silently, "Amelia?" when Mrs. Hannah wasn't looking. It was the first time either of them had heard Mrs. Hannah's first name. Both Sam and Julia covered their mouths to hide their giggles.

Julia followed Larry towards Sam. They were soon hidden between the shelves, invisible to "Hard Hearted" Amelia Hannah. He sighed, and the girls giggled again.

"Hi, Julia! I'm Sam. I hear you had quite a birthday bash last Saturday."

Julia immediately liked Sam. "Nice to meet you! Yes, Larry and John put on a good show. It was really special." Then she put it together. "Oh, you're the third member of the radio show, aren't you!"

"Yep," Sam replied casually. "Be sure to listen tonight. The Count here promises there will be a lot of special 'things' on the show!" Larry bowed gracefully. "That is, if he can keep his hands off his date long enough!"

"Sam!" Larry protested. "Have a little sensitivity, will you? You mustn't corrupt the ears of this sweet young thing!" As he said that, he noticed her ears. "There's something different about you. You had your hair down the other night. It was pretty, but I also like the way you have it in a ponytail today. And did you just get your ears pierced or something?"

Julia blushed as she answered, "Yes. Mom let me get them pierced and she bought me a nice pair of little star-shaped earrings. I can't wear them for a few days, though. She also bought me this." She held up the little music box with the dancing ballerina.

"Pretty," Larry said.

"I collect music boxes," Julia said with a smile. "I don't know why mom is being so nice to me today, but I'm not going to make her stop!"

"Good idea!" Sam advised. "Let them give you everything they want to."

Then Julia responded to an earlier suggestion. "Oh, and I'll have a ringside seat for tonight's show! Jimmy begged John to bring us to the show tonight."

Sam and Larry exchanged a glance, surprised John had not mentioned this little fact. "That's great!" Sam said. "We'll put you two to work doing something."

"Don't put me on the air," Julia pleaded. "I'd choke and say something stupid."

"Sounds like she'd be perfect, doesn't it?" Larry grinned. "The more stupid we get, the more popular the show becomes!"

Sam looked directly at Larry and noted, "That's why I keep you around. When it comes to being stupid, you're a natural."

"Why thanks..." Larry pretended to do a double take. "Hey! Wait a minute!"

Both girls laughed at him, bringing another "Shh!" from Mrs. Hannah. "I should get back to work, I guess," he sighed. "If I don't get this mess straightened out by the end of the day, I'll probably have to work all night!"

"But if you did," Sam teased, "you could spend some private time with Ms. Amelia. From what John tells me, you like older women."

"Not *that* old!" he shuddered, drawing a snicker from both girls.

"I'm looking forward to this," Julia said. "It'll be fun having you and Linda, John and Helen, and Jimmy and me together again. Will your boyfriend be there, Sam?"

"No," Sam replied. "He's off at college, and won't be in town this weekend."

"Oh, I'm sorry," Julia said sincerely.

"It's OK," Sam stated. "I ought to be used to it by now."

Noting her mother was looking for her, Julia injected, "It looks like mom is ready to go. I'll see you both tonight!"

"Later," Sam and Larry replied. "And if you don't take care of those ears," he added in his Count voice, "I'll have plenty of your bluhd to drink. Ha, 'ah, 'ah!"

Julia grinned at him as she waved goodbye. Larry waved to Mrs. Jacobson, and watched intently as Julia disappeared through the door and down the staircase.

Sam had not missed the intensity in his eyes as he watched Julia and her mother depart. She decided to tease him to draw some information. "I see you're already

Saturday, October 29, 1966 – Count Larry

getting a new one lined up. And after only one date with Linda. Tsk, tsk, tsk! Which one of the Jacobsons is it you want? The younger one or the older one?"

"Huh?" Larry responded brilliantly. When he realized what she meant, he tried to brush it off, "Oh, hell, Sam. Julia's too young for me. Besides, that's Jimmy's girlfriend. Her mother is a classy lady, but give me a break, OK?"

Sam smiled, but all she said was, "Uh huh," and returned to work. Larry wondered what Sam meant. *What did she see in my eyes, and what is it about this girl child who draws my attention so?* It would not be the last time he asked himself this question.

The speaker in the lobby of the station played a familiar theme from the *Rocky and Bullwinkle* program. This was normally followed by Larry's imitation of Rocky the Flying Squirrel, but things were to be a little different tonight. Instead, listeners heard the voice of Count Larry greeting them with, "Gooood evening. Ha, 'ah, 'ah!" All night long, loud rolling thunder sounded whenever the Count laughed. "This is Count Larry, and it's time for the *Top Forty Showcase*. Ve are going to have a monstrously good time, but vatch out! If you don't vant me to drink your bluhd then you had better be careful. Ha, 'ah, 'ah! I'll be on the prowl all night long."

John's imitation of Bullwinkle interrupted with, "Hey, Count! Watch me pull a rabbit out of my hat!"

"Again?" the Count asked.

"Nothing up my sleeve," Bullwinkle continued. "Presto!" The sound of a jet plane with its engines blasting at takeoff came through the speaker.

The Count asked, "Vhat vent wrong?"

"There's no doubt about it. I need to get a new hat," Bullwinkle answered.

"Vatch it, moose. You might end up in a crypt before this night is over. Now let's all go up to the lab and see vhat the doctor is cooking on the slab. There's sure to be something there you vill really like," the Count announced. "Take it avay, Sam, unless you vant me to come bite your neck first! Ha, 'ah, 'ah!" The sound of thunder rolled through the radio waves, followed by Sam announcing the first song.

Larry and Linda were squeezed together in one small sound booth, while John and Helen occupied the other. Larry always thought this was one of the best things about bringing a date to the station – squeezing them into one of the small sound booths. It did not matter its glass panels did nothing to hide whatever activities occurred inside. The important thing was that nice tight squeeze. If that thought had been spoken aloud, Linda would have agreed.

John also liked the close confinement of the sound booth. He and Helen had gotten along very well the previous night, even though the football game provided little entertainment value for either of them. It turned out Helen felt the same way about such things. She had only gone to the game because John asked her. Football did not fall within her field of interests. John did, however, so she tolerated the football game.

Jimmy and Julia were in one of the smaller side studios, positioned at a desk with two multi-line telephones. Their job was to answer the request lines, write down the dedications, and carry them to whoever was doing the next live announcement. At first, this job rotated between Sam, John, and Larry. Later, they would coerce Helen and Linda into taking turns under the spotlight. Jimmy and Julia declined to be on the air, but Sam was sure they could be convinced to try it later, after they saw how easy it was.

Sam sat at a table in the main studio and made the first announcement. This was the normal arrangement, ever since the boys started introducing the show using the Rocky and Bullwinkle bit. She wondered how long they planned to keep this up, as the "joke" was very predictable. Tonight had been different. Normally, the only fun part would be the wild sound effect John found buried somewhere in the station's sound vault.

Sam announced the first song using her normal voice, the record spun, and they all looked at each other with a sigh of relief. When the microphone was closed, Larry, John, and their dates exited from the sound booths and entered the main studio. The opening bit had come off well, they agreed, and they hoped to keep things hopping for the next two hours and fifty-seven minutes.

They divided the show into four segments of forty-five minutes each. A commercial break separated each segment, and there was a brief station identification each hour. Each segment began with a special production performed by the kids. The Rocky and Bullwinkle bit opened the first. The second segment, starting about 8:45, opened with a song by the Drug Company. This was occasionally done live, but most of the time, it was prerecorded. The third segment opened at 9:30 with a comedy bit, typically some sort of skit performed live by whoever could be coerced into joining. The final segment at 10:15 was opened by another song by the Drug Company.

Jimmy brought out the dedications requested for the second song and returned to the small studio without saying a word. The regulars had stressed to each newcomer the critical rule there was to be no talking in the main studio. Apparently, Jimmy did not catch on this only applied while they were on the air. Larry asked John not to tease him too badly, embarrassing him in front of his girlfriend. John had agreed, but realized it was not going to be easy if Jimmy kept leaving himself so open.

The first set of notes included one request to dedicate a song to Sam and The Count, and another requested a dedication to Sam and Bullwinkle. They laughed at what this seemed to imply, and discussed whether or not they should correct the mistaken impression some listeners had about their relationships. Larry thought they should, but John wanted to leave it alone. If Linda and Helen had a vote, they would have agreed with Larry, but they kept quiet. Sam casted the deciding vote – let them think whatever they want. It might be good for the image of the show for people to think there was some sort of triangular relationship going on. They would discuss it more later and think of ways to exploit this angle.

The microphone went live and Larry announced the next song including the personal dedications. "How about this, Sam? Someone wants it dedicated to you and the Count!" With the Count's voice, he delivered a hearty, "Ha, 'ah, 'ah!" accompanied by an appropriate thunderclap. Then back to his normal voice, "And here's someone else who wants it dedicated to you and Bullwinkle. What do you say we just ignore that one. After all, what would a fine fox like you want with a stupid moose?" He signaled Diggs to kill the mike, and the record spun as they all had a good laugh. Through the glass panel, they could see Jimmy and Julia were also snickering in the side studio.

Larry could see Linda was not overly thrilled about the joke. He put his arms around her waist, squeezed her close, and using a Boris Badenov voice suggested,

"You stay away from Moose, also, Natasha, or I weel contact Fearless Leader!"

"Borees!" Linda replied as Natasha Fatale, "I deedn't know you cared!"

John leaped into the conversation, "Hey, she's good! Let's put Boris and Natasha into a bit later in the show."

"Oh, I don't know," Linda giggled. "I'm not sure I'm ready for that!"

Escorting her back into one of the sound booths, Larry said, "Come weeth me, Natasha. I am geevingk you parsonal instroction."

"I knew it," Sam said shaking her head and laughing. "We're not even ten minutes into the show, and already Larry is starting to molest his date."

The remainder of the first segment was uneventful, with standard requests and dedications, and the typical barbs exchanged among the three hosts. The first break began at 8:45, as scheduled. It was concluded by a commercial from the local Dr. Pepper Bottling Company, a first-time sponsor of the show.

There had been so many requests for a repeat of the song from the previous week, Larry and John decided to replay the Beatles song *And I Love Her*. Only this time, they did it live. They played a simple guitar introduction, and Larry sang the song in his imitation Paul McCartney voice, much to the delight of the listening audience and the others in the studio.

The third segment opened with a comedy bit featuring Boris Badenov and Natasha Fatale that Larry, Linda, John, and Helen recorded earlier in the evening.

"Vhat do you vant thees time, Badenov?" John said imitating Fearless Leader.

"Bwah-ha-ha!" Larry said as Boris Badenov. "I haf discovered a vay to eliminate moose and squirrel once and for all!"

"Vunderful, Borees!" Linda said as Natasha Fatale. "What are ve goink to do?"

"Is easy!" Boris replied. "Some dolphins have asked moose and squirrel to doink zem a favor. In return, dolphins haf agreed to make moose and squirrel invincible!"

"You nincompoop! Vhat is spashial about dolphins?" asked Fearless Leader.

"Zay haf great powers, Fearless Leader," Boris replied.

"Vhat are zay vantink from moose and squirrel?" Natasha asked.

"Zee dolphins vant moose and squirrel to go to land of Slob-achia and bring zem spashial sea gulls," Boris said. "Zee sea guls vill make zee dolphins immortal!"

"Badenov, you nincompoop!" yelled Fearless Leader. "What good is making moose and squirrel invincible ? Und thees are not dolphins! Zay are porpoises!"

"Porpoises, smorpoises," Badenov answered. "Vhat difference is it makink! Dolphins vill make whoever is bringink thees gulls to zem invincible! All ve haf to do is steal sea gulls from moose and squirrel and carry zem to dolphins ourselves!"

"Und zee dolphins vill be makink us invincible?" Natasha asked.

"Of course, Natasha!" Boris answered.

"Vhat is your plan, Badenov?" Fearless Leader asked.

"Is easy!" Boris replied. "All ve haf to do is vait until moose and squirrel are leavink Slob-achia, zen ve steal the sea gulls und carry zem to dolphins ourselves!"

"Porpoises," Fearless Leader corrected.

"Porpoises, smorpoises," Boris said disgustedly.

"You had better make sure thees time, Badenov," Fearless leader explained, "or you vill be goink to concentration camp!"

"Vhat could go wrong?" Boris asked.

Helen, as the announcer, now explained, "So our heroes travel to the land of Slobachia to find the sea gulls." We hear soft calls of sea gulls in the background as the story continues.

"Hey, Rocky," Bullwinkle asked, "what do the dolphins want with the sea gulls?"

"They're porpoises, not dolphins, Bullwinkle," Rocky explained. "They want the sea gulls so they can become immortal."

"That's nice," Bullwinkle said.

"Yes," Rocky agreed, "and in return, they'll make us invincible so those spies will no longer be able to bother us."

The announcer now explained, "But as our heroes are crossing the border, they encounter Boris and Natasha, disguised as merchants selling hats for sea gulls."

"Sea gull hats," Natasha called. "Get hats for your sea gulls here."

"Hey, Rocky," Bullwinkle said. "Maybe we should get the sea gulls some hats. That will make them look nice when we give them to the dolphins."

"Porpoises," Rocky corrected. "I don't know, Bullwinkle," he said suspiciously. "Don't you think it's a coincidence someone is here to sell hats for the sea gulls?"

"See how nice thees hats vill make your sea gulls look?" Natasha asked. "Step into our dressink room and try zem on for sizes!"

"Lulled into a false sense of security," the announcer proclaimed, "our heroes enter the dressing room so the sea gulls can try on some hats. But once inside, Boris springs his trap and our heroes are hopelessly entangled in a net. Boris and Natasha snatch up the sea gulls and run off to deliver them to the dolphins."

"That's *porpoises*," Rocky corrected.

"I meant to say porpoises," explained the announcer. "So Boris and Natasha are walking down the path that leads to the porpoises, when suddenly they encounter a majestic lion sleeping right in the middle of the path."

"Vait, Borees!" Natasha exclaimed. "Vatch out for zee lion!"

"Vhat kind of lion is it?" Boris asked.

"How should I know zat?" Natasha replied. "But it is huge and has huge claws! Und see how stately it looks with that long mane!"

"If it is asleep, Natasha, zen ve haf nothink to vorry about," Boris said. "Ve vill simply step over it very quietly und continue on our way."

"But when they stepped over the lion," the announcer explained, "it suddenly awoke and growled, baring its huge fangs. Terrified, Boris and Natasha dropped the sea gulls and ran for their lives, the lion in hot pursuit. Our heroes, having freed themselves from the net, appear again, collect the sea gulls, and continue down the path to the dolphins."

"*Porpoises!*" Rocky insisted.

"I'm *sorry!*" the announcer replied.

"What just happened, Rocky?" Bullwinkle asked.

"Isn't it obvious, Bullwinkle?" Rocky explained. "They violated a very important rule. One must never carry gulls across a stately lion for immortal porpoises!"

To open the final segment, Larry and John played another Beatles song. The response they got from *If I Fell* at Julia's birthday party convinced them they should

Saturday, October 29, 1966 – Count Larry -63-

play it again. Somewhat uncharacteristically, they played it live, also. It began with Larry singing an opening bridge. John joined in with harmony for the rest of the song, and of course, played some nice guitar parts in Larry's arrangement.

Just like when Larry sang this at Julia's birthday party, he felt distracted. He smiled at Linda as he sang, thinking maybe she was just the girl he had been looking for. Just as before, however, something caused his smile to fade when his eyes caught a glimpse of Julia and Jimmy. Those green eyes seemed to reach out and grab his attention, making it difficult for him to look away from her.

"And that's a wrap, guys," Sam said relaxing. "Good show tonight!"

"I thought so as well, Sam," Larry agreed. Turning towards the newcomers, "I want to thank all of our guest stars once again. Did you girls have a good time?"

"Yeah," Jimmy said, "but it was a lot more hectic than I thought it'd be."

"I don't think he was asking you, little brother," John said sarcastically.

John and Larry looked at each other and shook their heads while the girls snickered. Julia was the first to answer, "I had a *great* time! But I didn't expect it to be so much work!" It was not easy to run the show at the fast pace and high energy levels Sam, John, and Larry were trying to maintain. This was the difference between their show and those other teenage request and dedication shows they thought were so lame.

"It's not as easy as most people think," Sam agreed. Linda and Helen nodded their head in agreement. "So, are you going to come back and work the show again?"

"I will!" Julia answered enthusiastically.

"Me, too," Linda agreed, smiling at Larry. Helen concurred.

"That's great!" Sam told them. "You can come back and work with me anytime. You can drag those guys along if you must." Sam believed Julia really did enjoy it and would come back to the show whether Jimmy came or not, but she suspected Linda and Helen would fall by the wayside without their respective interests in Larry and John. As usual, she was absolutely correct in this assessment.

"So what do we do now?" Julia asked.

"We have to return all the records we played to the storage bins," Sam began. "I'll take care of that, since Diggs is very particular about getting them filed correctly. Larry and John have to straighten up the sound booths, return the sound effect tapes to the vault, and catalog the new tapes they recorded. The rest of you take care of cleaning up the studios we used. We have to get everything back like it was before we can leave, and we're supposed to leave as soon as we're done. You don't have to go home, but you can't stay here! So hop to it!"

Larry and John saluted smartly and headed off to the booths. Sam returned the salute and walked to the control room door. Diggs hit a button releasing the electronic door lock, granting her admission. The rest of the kids gathered bits of used note paper, discarded empty soft drink cans, and restored the main studio to its original condition.

When the kids walked out of the main door to the radio station at 11:20, they were greeted by a blast of a cold north wind. The rains from the passing cold front had departed during the show, leaving clear skies, and temperatures predicted to plunge as low as thirty-five degrees overnight. This was somewhat lower than normal, even for this late in October, and caught them all by surprise.

Jimmy and Julia made a dash to John's car and its supposed warmth. Reaching the car door, they yelled a hasty, "Goodnight, guys!" and piled in. John and Helen huddled together for warmth, walked casually to the car, and slid into the front seat, turning to wave at the others. John started his car and pulled out of the parking area onto the street, headed in the general direction of Julia's house.

"Goodnight, Larry," Sam said casually. "It's been very nice to meet you, Linda."

"Nice to meet you, too," Linda replied.

"Are you sure you'll be OK?" Larry asked. "We both know the engine in your old car gets cantankerous when the weather turns a little cold. I'll wait until you get it started and you signal everything is fine before we leave."

"Thanks, Larry. I'll be fine," she said without a lot of confidence. She added with a little smile, "Always the perfect gentleman, aren't you, Larry? Tell me, Linda, is he always the perfect gentleman with you?"

Linda giggled, "So far, anyway."

"Too bad," Sam giggled in return.

"OK, you two," Larry ordered. "Let's get it moving. Maybe I happen to have some ungentlemanly things on my mind tonight, and all this chitchat is slowing things down and cramping my style. That clock keeps ticking away, and we don't have that much time to spare as it is!"

"Yes, sir!" Linda giggled, practically running for the car.

"You've got a live one, Larry," Sam whispered. "I hope you can handle her!"

Larry scowled in mock disgust, then smiled. "Goodnight, Sam," he said before turning to follow Linda.

"Goodnight, Larry!" Sam laughed. She reached her car, got in, and cranked the engine, which sputtered, coughed, and then died. The second attempt was not much better. But on the third try, the engine engaged cleanly and began to run smoothly. She turned on her headlights, put the car into gear, and turned towards the exit, honking at Larry and Linda as she drove past.

Larry and Linda were left alone, standing next to his car. He opened the door for her as he had done before, and she slid into the front seat. He was mildly disappointed; because it was dark, the view of her legs was not nearly as good as it had been previously. He moved onto the seat beside her, and she edged close to him, as before. He pushed the key into the ignition and started the engine. The radio came on, and they heard Diggs announce a station break at the bottom of the hour.

"Where would you like to go?" he asked. "We only have about thirty minutes."

"Why don't we sit here and talk for a while," she suggested with a smile.

Larry returned her smile. "The car will warm up faster if we're moving."

"I'm not cold," she said softly, snuggling closer to him and placing her arms around his neck. "How about you?"

"No," he agreed. He slipped his arms around her waist and drew her even closer to him. "I'm not cold any more!" He looked into her smiling eyes, returned that smile, and then kissed her gently, but firmly on the lips.

Their tongues met for the second kiss, and they continued to kiss each other again and again, each kiss growing a little longer, stronger, and a little more passionate. He remembered the joy he felt the previous evening, and how delightful it was to hold her, to kiss her. And now once again, he felt like he was seated at a banquet prepared for a starving man. He reminded himself how desperately he wanted, no *needed* to be able to return again and again to this banquet table. He craved the attention and the affection. He reminded himself to make a conscientious effort to keep his hands from wandering, to avoid those intimate places calling so strongly.

Linda moved to kiss Larry on the neck. He responded by kissing hers, and then moved up to nibble gently on her ear. "Ummm," she whispered. "That tickles. You aren't really the perfect gentleman all the time, are you?"

"If we'd left before Sam got her car started," he answered, ignoring the real question, "then she might have been stranded here. It'll be well after midnight before Diggs could leave the control room to assist." He looked at her and smiled.

"I see," she said with a grin, turning her head so she faced the front of the car.

Larry reached over to her chin and gently turned her head back so she was facing him again. He leaned forward and kissed her gently but squarely on the mouth. As they resumed kissing, he moved his hand down to caress her neck and then her shoulder. He relaxed, allowed his mind to enjoy the pleasure of the moment. He marveled at how wonderful it felt to have her in his arms, at how powerful his need was to hold and kiss her, and at how delightfully soft and warm her shoulder felt.

A soft moan escaped Linda's mouth, bringing Larry's attention back from his woolgathering. He realized his hand was no longer on her shoulder like he thought. It had continued to move downward as if it had a mind of its own. Through her soft cotton shirt, below what he assumed was a similarly soft cotton bra, he was actually caressing not a shoulder, but a delightfully soft and warm breast.

His first reaction was to pull his hand away, but Linda intercepted this movement, and placed her own hand over his, holding it in place. She looked deeply into his eyes and smiled tenderly. Larry nervously looked at her smile, then at his hand, and then back into her eyes. He had been to "second base" before, but it had never been so casual, so natural, and so delightful. They kissed again. He squeezed her breast gently, and she rewarded him with yet another soft moan.

"After these commercial messages, we'll return with news at the top of the hour," Diggs said over the radio.

Time is too swift for those who fear, Larry thought sadly. "I have to get you home fast or your father will kill me!"

Linda teased him. "And maybe not because I'm getting home a few minutes late!"

He looked at her, saw her smile, and laughed. "I guess that all depends on whether you plan to tell him about this or not." Reluctantly, he moved his hand to the steering wheel.

"I'll think about it," she grinned. She released her embrace enough so Larry could drive. He put the car in gear and hurriedly left the radio station towards her home. Fortunately, it was not too far, and they just might be able to get there before the clock struck midnight.

As John drove towards Steep Hollow, the kids were a little too cold to talk much. Helen sat close to him and put her head on his shoulder as he drove. In the back seat, Julia sat by the passenger door and Jimmy sat nearby on the "hump".

John broke the silence. "By the way, Helen, I'm not sure where Larry and I will be practicing tomorrow. We can't go to my house or Larry's house this week, and Sam told me tonight we can't use hers tomorrow, either. I'll have to let you know. We may have to skip practice this week."

"I can ask my folks," Helen volunteered. "I doubt Linda will offer her house."

"Maybe you could all come out to my house," Julia offered.

John glanced at her in the rear view mirror. "You'd better ask them first, Julia. They might not like having a crowd of teenagers on a Sunday afternoon. There's me and Larry, and we'll be bringing Helen and Linda. And Sam usually joins us."

"Don't forget about me and Jimmy!" Julia added.

"Now I get it," John laughed. "You're just wanting me to bring Jimmy!"

Julia giggled. "Right! But I'll also enjoy listening to you guys sing some more."

"Well, you ask them first," John said. "Including you two, that would make... seven teenagers! That's an awful lot to ask of them!"

"I *will* ask," she said, "and I think they'll say it's OK."

The car got quiet because of the chill. When the car warmed up, Julia asked a question to start a conversation. "Is the radio show always that much fun, John?"

"That's the way things go almost every week," he replied. "Whether you think it's fun or not might depend on who you're with," he said looking at Helen and grinning.

"I wish I could be as brave as you guys," Julia continued. "Don't you get nervous when you talk on the radio?"

"I did at first," John laughed, "but I just keep remembering something Mr. Austin, the choir director, tells us before a choir concert. He says to imagine everyone in the audience is naked! It makes them all a lot less intimidating, and helps you relax."

"Is that why you stared at me so often tonight?" Helen asked with a giggle.

"Of course," John grinned. "I was thinking about you being naked so I wouldn't be nervous! Why else would I do that?"

Julia giggled, then asked, "What about Sam?"

"I sometimes like to think about Sam being naked..." he said.

Julia giggled again, but Helen punched her elbow squarely into John's ribs. "Ouch! OK, OK, OK! I know what she meant," he said to Helen. He thought for a moment before replying, "Sam is such an enigma most of the time I really don't know what goes on in her head. She might be shivering in fear for all I know. I doubt she'd ever let me or anyone else even know."

"I think she's nice," Julia said simply.

"She's a jewel," John concurred, "but she keeps her thoughts mostly to herself. Sam and Larry have been friends a lot longer, so he'd know more about her than I do. Maybe you should save your questions for him."

"And what about Larry?" Julia asked. "It all seems to come naturally to him. It must be nice to be so outgoing. I wish I was more like him instead of being so shy!"

John laughed out loud. "Larry? He's probably the most shy and insecure person you could ever meet!"

"What?" the others said almost in unison. Helen continued, "Why do you say he's shy? That's about the *last* thing I'd ever say about him!"

"It's all an act, actually," John explained. "He puts on a brave face so people won't see how shy he really is. He calls it *bravado*. I think he's far too worried about what other people might think of him. He always acts like a clown so people will laugh with him. According to him, if he didn't do that, they'd all just laugh *at* him. And girls actually terrify him! I guess that's because he hasn't had what you'd call a great deal of success, and maybe his shyness is the reason why. It's great to see he and Linda getting along. He needs someone to build up his confidence."

"I'd never think that," Jimmy said. "He seems so confident, so self-assured."

"No," John said simply, "he's not. The strange part is he thinks people don't like him. Granted, he's not the most popular guy around, but I really couldn't tell you why! When you get right down to it, I don't know anybody who doesn't like him. He's fun to hang around with, and you couldn't ask for a better friend. He seems to know when you need something, and is always willing to help. When you're feeling down, he'll go out of his way to make you feel better, even though he's probably hurting more himself. And he always seems to notice those little things most other people overlook." Julia thought about how Larry noticed her new earrings that morning. So far, no one else had. John added sincerely, "I'm very proud to call him my friend."

"I hope he thinks of *me* as a friend," Julia said.

"I'm sure he does," John stated.

They arrived at Julia's house and John parked his car as close to the front door as possible. Jimmy and Julia hopped out, dashed for the door, and disappeared.

Putting his arm around Helen's shoulder, John said softly, "It's good to be rid of the kid for a few minutes. How shall we take advantage of this opportunity?"

Helen rewarded him with a kiss. "Is that what you have in mind?" she asked.

"It's a start," he said, kissing her again.

She slipped her arms around his neck and kissed him warmly. She broke the kiss for a moment and giggled, "Maybe you should wait until Jimmy gets back. I have a feeling he could use some pointers from an older and more experienced brother."

John chuckled, "Let him learn it the hard way, like I had to." They tightened their embrace and continued kissing.

John was considering his next move when Jimmy opened the car door and jumped into the backseat. "They said yes," he announced.

Perturbed at the interruption, John asked, "Who said yes, and to what?"

"The Jacobsons," he explained. "It's OK to come here tomorrow afternoon."

"Cool," John laughed. "I hope they know what they've gotten themselves in for!" He turned the car around and headed back for the road. Julia, still standing in the front door, waved at them. John honked the horn as they waved back. "Did you remember to kiss her goodnight, little brother?"

Jimmy hesitated, then answered, "That's my business, not yours!"

That hesitation was all the answer John needed. He glanced at Helen and saw her grin. She put her head on his shoulder and they rode in silence back to town and dropped off Jimmy. "Why don't we go to my house," Helen suggested, "We can park the car in the driveway, and just sit and get better acquainted, like we did last night?"

"An excellent suggestion," John smiled.

Larry and Linda pulled into her driveway just as the radio network announcer began reading the news. They had made it with seconds to spare. As Larry started to reach for the door, Linda stopped him. "We don't have to go in just yet."

"I thought you had to be home by midnight," he said, a little surprised.

"So?" she smiled. "I'm home, aren't I?"

Larry smiled back. "I don't think that's exactly what your father had in mind!"

"No, I suppose not," she giggled, "but I can't go in just yet, anyway. The light in the garage is on." Seeing the confusion in his face, she continued, "It's a signal my mom uses. When I come home from a date, if she doesn't want me to come inside just yet, she turns on the light in the garage."

"I don't understand," Larry said. "Why wouldn't she want you to come inside?"

Linda's expression changed while she looked at him. "Sometimes, my father will... well, he sometimes drinks a little too much..."

"You don't have to tell me this, Linda," he said sincerely.

"No, it's OK. Sometimes he drinks a little too much, and sometimes this makes him a little... angry. Mom can handle him, and he'll eventually go to bed and sleep it off. She's afraid of what he might say to me or to my date in this condition, and so we arranged this little signal. When he's settled down, she'll turn off the light."

Larry was not familiar with this sort of thing, so he did not know what to say. His father was a "tea-totaler" who never consumed alcohol. "What if she goes to bed and forgets to turn off the light?" he asked.

Linda snuggled up close to him and grinned, "In that case, then you get to have your arms around me and kiss me all night long!"

He returned her grin as his mind contemplated this scenario. Without saying a word, he put his hands on her shoulders and drew her close so he could kiss her once more. She slipped her left arm around his waist and placed her right hand on his hip, draping her arm across his lap. After a few moments of continued kissing, she slowly slid her hand down to rest on his leg. This was a new sensation for Larry and it thrilled him. The reaction of his body was powerful and immediate. He hoped Linda would not see the bulge he feared was surely obvious.

To his dismay, they both soon noticed the garage light had been extinguished. It was time for Linda to go inside. They looked into each others' eyes and exchanged an understanding their dialog would continue. Reluctantly, they released their embrace. He opened the door, they slid out of the seat, and walked in no hurry to the front door.

"I'll see you tomorrow afternoon about 2:00," he said as they reach the doorstep. "I don't know where we'll be going yet, but I'm sure we'll find someplace."

"Sounds fine," she said simply. "Goodnight, Larry!"

"Goodnight," he said. She kissed him warmly, then disappeared behind the door.

He waited for the door to close completely, then returned to his car, his mind troubled by something he did not quite understand. He tried to ignore those thoughts, reflecting instead on how exciting the evening had been, and how much he was looking forward to continuing that dialog with Linda. He returned home and slept peacefully, gratefully untroubled by the apparition of the previous night.

Sunday, October 30, 1966
Truth Or Dare

Larry arrived at Linda's doorway just after 2:00 o'clock. Mrs. Livingston greeted him as she had done before and invited him into the living room. "I'll let her know you're here," she said with a smile and disappeared down the hallway.

"Good afternoon, sir," Larry said to Mr. Livingston. Linda's father did not look up from the television where he was watching the Dallas Cowboys demolishing the Pittsburgh Steelers. The final score was to be 52-21, and the game was already well out of hand. "How's the game going?" he asked, trying to be friendly.

"What's it to you?" Mr. Livingston replied without looking up.

Larry kept silent for the few moments remaining before Mrs. Livingston returned with Linda. "Hello, Larry," Linda said sweetly.

He remembered a line of that song he had song from *Oliver!* and wondered if this greeting was really meant only for him. "Hi," he said meekly, flashing a bright smile. Linda looked great in a soft knit blouse and tight bluejeans. Looking at her mother, he said, "We'll be going to the Jacobson's house, Mrs. Livingston. They've invited John and I to practice out there. I hope they know what they've let themselves in for!"

Mrs. Livingston smiled at him. "I'm sure they do."

"Since it's a school night," he asked, "what time should I have Linda home?"

Without looking up from the television, Mr. Livingston answered before anyone else could, "Ten o'clock should be fine. Isn't that right, mother?"

"Yes," Mrs. Livingston agreed. "Ten o'clock should be fine. Have a good time."

"Thank you," he said. "Thank you, sir. I promise to take very good care of her."

"I'm sure you will," Mr. Livingston said, looking Larry squarely in the eye. Then looking at Linda, he said, "Have a good time, sugar."

Surprised, Linda barely managed to say, "Thanks, daddy." Mr. Livingston returned his attention to the game. Linda and her mother exchanged a glance and a shrug. "We'd better get going. You don't need to wait up, mom. He'll get me home on time."

They walked outside and Linda closed the front door. She immediately turned to Larry, put her arms around his neck and kissed him warmly. "I expect to get a big hello kiss from my boyfriend when he picks me up," she smiled.

Larry returned her smile. "That sounds like an excellent policy. Next time, I'll kiss you inside, before we walk out the door."

"If your *cajones* are big enough to do that, mister, I'll be impressed!"

"You just watch. They might surprise you," he grinned. For some reason, it did not embarrass him to joke about parts of the male anatomy with Linda.

They walked to the car and he opened the driver's door for Linda like he had done before. As she slid under the steering wheel, he was disappointed her bluejeans did not allow a good look at her legs. He got into the seat beside her and started the car. She moved in close, placed her head on his shoulder, and rested her arm on his right leg. He found that exciting, and decided the best course was to relax and drive normally, keeping both hands on the steering wheel. As they drove to the Jacobson's house, they made small talk. She occasionally shifted her hand slightly, caressing his leg. He ate it all up hungrily.

On arrival, they saw John's and Sam's cars were already parked in the driveway. Larry parked nearby and they climbed out. Linda waited for him to fetch his guitar and music cases from the trunk, then they walked casually to the front door.

Julia and Schotzy greeted them almost instantly. "Hi, guys! The others are already here. Come on in!" She turned and escorted them towards the family room. With the two girls walking in front of him, Larry noted Linda's jeans were much tighter than Julia's, and the way she filled them drew his attention powerfully.

Thoughts about the delights hidden under those jeans brought a smile to his face.

"Hello, Linda. Hello, Larry," Mrs. Jacobson said as they walked past the kitchen.

"Hi, Mrs. Jacobson," Larry replied, disappointed his attention had been snapped. "Thanks for having us this afternoon. I hope you can put up with seven teenagers!"

She smiled. "We'll manage. Actually, you're doing us a favor. One disadvantage of living in the country is all of Julia's friends are too far away, and most of them are too young to drive. So by coming to see her out here, you save us the trouble of driving her into town and then going back to pick her up."

"I hadn't thought of that," Larry stated. "Well, I appreciate your hospitality. I promise we'll try to behave ourselves."

His smile told her his gratitude was genuine. "Go on into the family room. The others are cozying up to the fire." It wasn't a particularly cold day, but sitting in the conversation pit and watching the fire was a relaxing way to spend a fall afternoon.

They entered the family room and greeted the others. Julia rejoined Jimmy on the built-in sofa. Sam was lounging on some large pillows spread near the fireplace. John and Helen were sitting on the hearth. John was already picking a few notes on his guitar. "Come on in," he suggested. "We saved the love seat for you guys."

Linda walked down the steps into the conversation pit, sat on the built-in love seat and looked back for Larry to join her. He did, then opened his case to fetch his guitar. Schotzy jumped up onto the love seat and laid down next to Larry. After a few chords and some minor adjustments, the boys got down to some serious practice.

They liked to warm up by playing some familiar songs. Today, they elected to start with a general medley of Beatles songs, since the girls seemed to like them the most. They began with some of the earlier songs, like *I Saw Her Standing There*, *Please Please Me*, and *Twist and Shout*. For practice, it did not matter to the boys that having only two guitars, no bass, and no drums meant the sound was somewhat empty. They especially missed having the harmonica so important in songs like *Love Me Do*. The girls were appreciative anyway. The boys sometimes experimented with some new ideas during such practice sessions, attempting to adapt songs to a two-man band. Larry seemed to have a knack for doing this, and generally did all of the song arrangements for their band.

He insisted, however, learning to play the music of other bands was not good enough. "Even if we duplicate the music perfectly," he would say, "then all we're doing is copying their music, their style. Who's going to pay anything for that? If we're to be successful, then we're going to have to develop our own style, create our own music."

John agreed completely. He was happy when Larry came up with a unique arrangement for a song, and was eager to help with suggestions about lead guitar parts. He also knew Larry was trying to write some poetry they could hopefully use as lyrics for some original songs. That was to remain a carefully guarded secret until they could unveil such a song. There was to be no song debut this afternoon!

But Larry had put together a simple arrangement of *Do You Want To Know a Secret* they decided to play next. They simultaneously struck a single chord, as Larry began singing the slow introduction. He smiled and tried to stare into Linda's eyes during the song, but for the most part, she would just giggle and look away. In his counter part, every time John sang "Ooh", Helen grinned at him and puckered her lids into the same syllable. When they finished, everyone agreed it was the best song they had played so far that afternoon.

They continued with a few more Beatles songs, these a little more recent, playing *A Hard Day's Night*, *I Should Have Known Better*, and *I'm Happy Just to Dance With You*. They decided to skip *If I Fell*, one of the songs they played at Julia's birthday party, but at the girl's insistence, they replayed *And I Love Her*. John liked the guitar part he played in that song, and also enjoyed seeing the attention Larry got because of the similarity in his voice to Paul McCartney. The girls provided the expected "ooh's" and "ah's", practically gushing their appreciation, and agreed Larry sounded just like the famous Beatle.

Then the boys switched gears to play some songs by Simon and Garfunkel. The simple but beautiful song *April Come She Will* gave Larry a chance to show off a different voice imitation, and John a chance to play some nifty guitar parts. Similarly, they enjoyed the songs *Cloudy* and *The Dangling Conversation*. Finally, they played *The 59th Street Bridge Song (Feelin' Groovy)* drawing a good reaction from the girls. Larry brought out his autographed copy of the Paul Simon music book, to which the girls reacted almost as strongly as they had to the singing.

As a joke, the boys played an old rock and roll song called *Hey School Girl*. Sam was the only one who remembered hearing it. "Who did that song?" she asked.

John and Larry grinned at each other. "Believe it or not, it was done by a group that called themselves Tom and Jerry at the time, although they changed their name later. As I understand it, now they don't even acknowledge they ever *did* this song!"

"What did they change their name to?" Linda asked.

"We've been doing their songs for the last thirty minutes or so," Larry grinned.

"You're kidding!" Linda exclaimed.

Larry and John just laughed, and started playing another song. They switched among various other bands and song styles. They enjoyed playing for an audience, even a small one. It was a great practice session.

At about 6:00, Mrs. Jacobson disappeared into the kitchen. When the boys wrapped up their last song, she came into the family room and announced there were cold cuts, bread, condiments, chips, and soft drinks on the kitchen table.

"Oh, Mrs. Jacobson," Larry said, "You didn't need to do all that!"

She smiled and said, "I'm happy to do it. Besides, I have to believe you boys must be getting hungry by now." She noticed Jimmy, Julia, and Sam had already moved into the kitchen and were helping themselves. "For that matter, so are the girls!"

"I just feel bad you're going to so much trouble," Larry continued.

"Don't worry about it, Larry," she smiled. "I have to do something to make sure you'll come back again, now don't I?"

"You're just too nice to us, Mrs. Jacobson," Larry grinned. He took Linda by the hand and helped her out of the love seat, and they walked into the kitchen, following John and Helen. "Come on, Schotzy," he called.

The kids fixed themselves sandwiches and returned to the conversation pit. Mr. and Mrs. Jacobson also made sandwiches and sat at the kitchen table to eat. Sam decided to join the Jacobsons, leaving the three couples on their own.

"How long have you known these boys?" Jessica asked to make conversation.

"I've known Larry since the third grade," she answered. "I'm not really sure what it was, but we just naturally became friends and have been ever since. I met John later when he and Larry started playing on the same baseball team."

"I'm a little surprised you're not more than just friends," Jessica stated casually.

Sam smiled. "Don't let Larry hear you say that! If there is any phrase he hates to hear, *'just-friends'* would have to be the one."

Jessica looked at her intently. "From the way you said that, I get the impression he must have heard that phrase a lot more than he'd like."

"Yes, ma'am," Sam agreed looking a little sad.

"So why haven't you done something about that?" Jessica asked. "Oh, I'm sorry, dear. I don't mean to pry into things that aren't any of my business."

"Of course not," Mr. Jacobson added sarcastically. Jessica gave him a dirty look guaranteed to keep him quiet for a few minutes.

"It's OK," Sam said. "For some reason, it just never worked out that way. Larry and I have a very special friendship neither of us wants to jeopardize. He's asked me out several times, and I have to admit I'm always tempted. But in the end, I don't want to risk our friendship, and I know he feels the same way." There was an obvious moment of contemplation before she finished, "Besides, eventually I would break his heart." Sam looked down at the food in her plate and just pushed it away.

Jessica knew there was more to this story than had been told, but decided not to press for any more details. "I'm sorry, Sam. I can tell I'm prying. Forgive me. If you ever need a friend, just need someone you can talk to, I'll be here."

Without looking up, Sam said, "Thanks. I appreciate that." She brightened and said, "Besides, I already have a boyfriend! He's away at college. I don't get to see him as much as I'd like, but that just makes it more special when I *can* see him."

Jessica smiled warmly. "Good for you!"

Sam soon excused herself and returned to the pillows she had been lounging on near the fire. The other kids finished their meal and were starting to tell stories and laugh among themselves. Jimmy was being particularly vocal, talking about the pranks he and some friends were planning for Halloween, tomorrow night. "We're going to scare the willies out of the little kids who come for Trick or Treat! We have weird music, strange lights, and even have some firecrackers left over from the Fourth of July!"

"You'd better be careful, little buddy," Larry cautioned. "Some of those little kids might remember what you did to them and get you back when they grow up."

Picking up on the reference to "little buddy", Helen started talking about the *Gilligan's Island* television program. "I wonder what it'd be like to be stranded on a desert island."

"I think," Linda grinned at Larry, "it'd depend on who you're stranded with."

Sam laughed at the obvious suggestion and added, "And whether they're capable of taking care of the things that are important, right Linda?"

Larry scowled at Sam as if to say, "And you don't think I would be?"

"If you were going to be stranded on a desert island," Julia asked looking at the ceiling, "who would you want to be stranded with?"

"Hey!" Sam suggested. "That sounds like a good question. Why don't we go around the room and get everyone to answer it." The girls agreed this was a great idea. They especially wanted to hear what the boys would say.

Larry disagreed. "It sounds a little too much like that old *Truth or Dare* game to me. I haven't played that one in years, and I don't think I'm ready to go back now."

"Oh, come on, Larry," Sam teased. "Don't you want anyone to know your innermost desires? Your deepest secrets?"

"Not particularly," he said.

"Well, we do!" Linda giggled. "Come on, Larry. I dare you to tell us!"

"And there's proof Larry is right," John added. "This sounds exactly like you girls want to play *Truth or Dare*."

"Then it's settled!" Sam declared with a laugh. "We'll go around the room and everyone will have to answer this question: If you were stranded on a desert island, who would you want to be stranded with, and why?"

Helen decided to stipulate a rule for the game. "And it can't be anyone currently in the room. You can't simply pick your own girlfriend or boyfriend. That also applies to you, Sam, even though your boyfriend isn't here!"

"It should be someone famous," Julia said, "someone we'd all know."

"This is stupid," Larry said.

"If you don't play along, you'll be sorry!" Linda assured him. The other girls giggled when Larry obviously gave in to her demand.

"I think we should go by age," Sam added thoughtfully, "youngest to the oldest."

"Girls first," Jimmy demanded. Larry and John looked at him with disgust, since this suggestion made it obvious the game would pit the boys against the girls. All Jimmy had actually wanted to do was to postpone his own turn.

"Agreed!" Sam accepted with delight. "OK, girls. Let's show these guys we'd make better choices than they would! You get to go first, Julia. Are you ready?"

"Yes," Julia began, "I already know who I'd pick. If I was going to be stranded on a desert island, I'd want to be with Paul McCartney, because he's so dreamy!"

"Ooh!" the girls agreed. The boys just looked at each other.

Jessica grinned at her daughter and asked, "And just what do you think you and Mr. McCartney would be doing on this desert island?"

"He would sing to me," she answered, blushing.

"And what would you do at night?" Linda asked with a wink.

Julia's blush became stronger. She covered her face with her hands and giggled.

Sam decided to tease the younger girl even more. "Are you sure it's really Paul McCartney you want to be stranded with, or do you really want to be stranded with someone who sounds like him?" She made a show of winking at Larry.

Julia giggled more strongly from behind her hands. Linda could not hide the fact she did not particularly care for this suggestion. Jimmy glared at Larry.

Larry simply shrugged. He glanced over at Julia, and saw she was looking back at him through the fingers covering her bright red face. He wondered why he found her green eyes so intriguing. He gave a slight smile and lowered his own eyes so he would not be caught staring. "OK, I think you've embarrassed poor Julia enough."

Anxious to change the subject, Linda agreed, "Yes, let's move on. But it suddenly occurs to me we need to add another rule. You can't repeat an earlier answer. So Paul McCartney has been taken, and Helen couldn't also choose him, for example."

"I agree," Sam said, "but it needs to be more general than that. *All* of the Beatles are now off limits. Maybe we should include all rock singers."

"But I've already made my choice!" Helen complained. "I picked John Lennon."

"I don't think it's allowed," Sam said. "How are we going to know whether you picked him before Julia announced her choice or after?" The girls agreed this was a good rule, while the boys looked at each other and shook their heads.

"Then give me a moment to pick someone else," Helen requested. She thought about a new television program she was watching this fall and decided one of the characters on that show was an even better choice than John Lennon. "For me, I'd want adventure. So my choice is James T. Kirk, Captain of the Star Ship Enterprise. It doesn't really matter whether we're stranded on a desert island or a desert planet."

Linda and Julia concurred with Helen's choice. The girls had been watching *Star Trek* diligently and agreed being stranded with the swashbuckling captain of the Enterprise would be very exciting.

"I've never heard of him," Larry said. "I don't think that's a valid choice."

Sam was not familiar with *Star Trek* either, but defended Helen as a teammate. "It's not like you have to know who they're talking about, but it has to be someone you *could* know about. If you'd been watching this program, then you'd know who he is."

Jessica decided to act as referee. "Sam is right. You don't have to pick someone everyone knows. That might not be easy with all the many different interests you kids have. You have to pick someone everyone has a reasonable chance to know."

"It seems to me," Larry grimaced, "the rules are being made up as we go along."

Jessica smiled at him. "No, the rules are just being refined as necessary. Now, Helen, you haven't finished your answer. You have to tell us *why* you'd want to be stranded with this James T. Kirk."

Helen, Julia, and Linda all laughed. Linda voiced the answer, "Do you really want her to tell, Mrs. Jacobson? The answer is obvious. Can we just assume that?"

Jessica interpreted this to mean James T. Kirk exhibited a lot of sex appeal. "Maybe we should," she agreed grinning at Helen, and winking at Linda. "If there are no objections, then we'll move on. I think you're next, Linda."

Linda smiled. She was ready to give her answer. "My choice is a little different than the previous ones. Since I'm not allowed to picked anyone in the room, I decided to pick someone who *reminds* me of someone in the room. If I was stranded on a desert island, I'd want to be stranded with Roger Miller. It's because I think he's cute, I like the way he sings, and he makes me laugh. That's the kind of guy I'd like to be stranded with." She put her arms around Larry's neck and grinned.

The other girls squealed with delight. "Ooh-la-la!"

It was Larry's turn to blush. Linda had found a way to violate the rules without cheating. She named someone famous, but her real choice was clear. There was nothing he could do but smile, and take whatever verbal abuse was now going to be thrown at him.

And there was plenty of it. "So I understand he'd sing to you during the day," Sam offered. "It must be during the night he'd make you laugh? Now why is that?" Eventually, they eased up and it was time to move on.

Sam was the next older girl. "I'm surprised no one stole my choice before my turn. If I was stranded on a desert island, I'd want to be stranded with Bond, James Bond, Mister Double-Oh-Seven himself! Do I really need to explain why?" She picked up a section of the newspaper laying nearby and fanned herself with it.

"No," Jessica grinned. "I think we all understand that well enough! You girls are worrying me with all these sexy men you're selecting!"

Recovering from his embarrassment, Larry tried to turn the tables. He knew there was nothing he could say about James Bond that would embarrass Sam, so he took another approach. "I'm not surprised you'd select some secret agent type, Sam, but I thought you'd pick agent 86, otherwise known as Maxwell Smart. After all, you look just like his faithful sidekick, agent 99." Sam bore a striking resemblance to Barbara Feldon, the actress who played that role on the program.

"Wow!" Jimmy added. "She *does* look like agent 99!"

"Thank you, Jimmy," Sam replied, sticking her tongue out at Larry and throwing her newspaper fan at him. "Actually, it was a difficult choice between James Bond, Maxwell Smart, and Napoleon Solo. On the other hand, if I was going to pick someone from *The Man from U.N.C.L.E.*, it would have been Illya Kuryakin. He's the cutest." Larry could see there was no way to embarrass Sam in all this.

"Why don't we move on," Jessica suggested. "That takes care of the girls..."

"Not so fast!" Larry interrupted. "We haven't heard from you, Mrs. Jacobson!" This brought a round of giggles from the girls, and smiles from John, Jimmy, and even Mr. Jacobson, listening to the game while pretending to read his newspaper.

"But I'm not a part of your game," Jessica said with surprise.

"Of course you are!" Larry insisted. "You've been participating from the very beginning. So come on and tell us. If you were stranded on a desert island, who would you want to be with, and why?"

"I've already chosen," she tried. "I married the guy I'd want to be stranded with!"

"Buzz!" Larry grinned. "The rules have already been established. You can't pick someone who is currently in the room!"

"I shouldn't have to play by the same rules. I'm married," Jessica pleaded.

"That's not fair, mom," Julia giggled. "You have to pick someone else, just like the rest of us."

Jessica looked at her daughter with a frown that quickly turned into a smile. "OK, then. Since the rules don't allow me to give you my first choice, I'll give you my second. If I was to be stranded on a desert island, I'd choose to be stranded with my daughter Sarah, her husband Joseph, and their new baby daughter, Ruth. As for the reason, there are lots of them. For one thing, if we were stranded, Julian and Julia would surely come looking for us, and when they found us, we could all be together, like I wish we were right now."

"Aw, mom," Julia said. "I wish we could, also."

Even though this choice did not qualify under the established rules, Larry decided to let it go. He had learned something he did not already know, and wanted to hear more. "We didn't know Julia had a sister. Tell us about Sarah!"

Jessica smiled. "Sarah is actually my niece, Julia's cousin, the daughter of Julian's older brother Benjamin, who was killed during the war. After Sarah's mother died, Sarah came to live with us, and we formally adopted her later."

"Where is she now?" Larry asked.

"She's in Africa," Jessica said sadly. "She left home to go to college in Israel before we moved to Texas. After graduation, she joined the Peace Corps and went to work with some people in Africa. She met Joseph there, who was also in the Peace Corps, and they were married just over a year ago. And she just had a baby girl."

"How long has it been since you've seen her?" Larry asked.

"Over six years," Jessica answered sadly. "We have some photographs, but haven't seen her. We've never met her husband, and of course, haven't yet seen the baby."

"Well, congratulations on becoming a grandmother!" Larry said brightly. "I hope you'll be able to see them all soon!" The other kids voiced their agreement.

"Thank you, Larry. Thank you all!" she said fighting back a tear. "Now let's get on with this game before I start crying. It's not a pretty sight!" She grinned as best she could. Larry returned a warm smile.

"OK," Sam said. "It's the boys' turn. Let's see if these guys can come up with anything as good as the choices *we* made!" The girls taunted the boys in agreement.

"All right, guys!" Larry urged. "Let's show these girls we can make even better choices than they can! Go for it, Jimmy!"

"Well, first of all," Jimmy began, "I don't think any of the choices the girls made are very practical. If I were stranded on a desert island, my first thought would be survival. I'd want to be surrounded by people who have experienced being stranded like that. So I'd pick the passengers and crew of the S.S. Minnow – Gilligan, the Skipper, Mr. and Mrs. Howell, Ginger, the Professor, and Mary Ann."

A blanket of silence fell over the room. *Brilliant,* Larry thought sarcastically, *just fucking brilliant.* At first, Larry just stared at Jimmy in disbelief, and then turned to look at John. John looked back and shrugged. The girls started laughing.

"A very practical choice," Jessica said, trying not to laugh. Jimmy was embarrassed, but really did not understand why they thought his answer was funny.

"You're next, John," Jessica stated, trying to save Jimmy from any more ridicule.

"Go, John, Go!" Larry urged.

John had decided to stay with the television theme, but wanted to go for both fun and practicality. "My choice is Samantha Stephens, for a lot of reasons. First of all, she certainly wouldn't be boring! There are all kinds of adventures she could conjure up for us to experience. And if we got tired of being stranded, she could simply wiggle her nose, and whisk us back to civilization. What could be better than that?"

"I wonder how long it'd be before she turned you into a newt," Sam giggled.

"Who'd notice?" Helen suggested, drawing a round of giggles from the other girls.

John looked at Helen pretending his feelings were hurt. "What a mean thing to say! If an evil witch turned me into a toad, wouldn't you kiss me to break the spell?"

"Yuck!" she said in mock disgust. "I wouldn't want to get warts!" This brought another round of giggles from the girls. Finally, Helen relented and leaned over to give John a little kiss.

Larry sat shaking his head. He really expected something better out of John.

Sam knew Larry would be the key player for the boys' team. She wanted to make a preemptive strike against him to see if she could get him rattled. "OK, Mr. Smartypants. We're all waiting. Let's hear your answer. If you were stranded on a desert island, who would you want to be stranded with, and why? And you'd better make it good, because your team has fallen a long way behind!" The other girls voiced their agreement.

Larry had not thought of a good answer yet, and so stalled for time. "Other than the people in this room, there really *isn't* anyone I'd want to be stranded with. The important thing isn't who I want to be with, but who would want to be stranded with me." Looking at Linda and hoping for support, he announced, "So my choice is to be stranded with the person who would most like to be stranded with me!"

"Foul!" Sam declared. "You haven't picked anyone. The point of this game is to reveal little secrets about your innermost desires. You're trying to avoid that by selecting someone who wants to be with you, instead of who you want to be with."

"But that *is* my innermost desire," Larry argued.

Jessica stepped in to act as referee. "And your choice is a very wise one, Larry. But I have to agree with Sam. The point of the game is to reveal little secrets about yourself. None of us is ever going to be stranded on a desert island with a Paul McCartney or a Captain Kirk, or any of the other people who have been mentioned. So make the assumption whoever you choose is going to *like* being stranded with you, and give us a name."

"Yeah," the girls agreed, giggling. "Tell us about your dreams!"

He figured he would never get away with that answer, but it was worth a try. Now he was stuck, however, as he still did not have any good ideas. He thought Jimmy's and John's choices had been particularly lame, and he did not think Mr. Jacobson was likely to save the situation. Unless he came up with a really dynamite answer, he could see the girls were going to win this little "game" by default.

He looked around the room, searching for an inspiration. Suddenly, he found it on the pages of the newspaper Sam threw at him. A sly smile came to his mouth. "OK, OK, if you really must know. If I were to be stranded on a desert island, and I could choose to be stranded with anyone I wanted, and that person would be happy to be stranded with me, and I can't choose anyone currently in this room..."

"Get on with it!" Sam demanded.

"Such impatience!" he exclaimed. He looked around and paused dramatically. "So, as I was saying, I'd choose to be stranded on a desert island with..." He made another dramatic pause, and then announced his choice, "Virginia Pip-a-Lee-Ne!"

"Who the hell is that?" Sam asked. "Sorry... I mean who's that, Larry?"

John suggested, "She's one of those hot, seductive Italian movie stars, right?"

"I've never heard of her," Sam said. None of the others had ever heard of her, either. "This is another foul! You can't just pull a name out of the air and claim this is the girl you want to be stranded with. It has to be someone we actually know."

"Are you claiming," he said pointedly, "you actually know James Bond, or Paul McCartney, or Roger Miller, or any of the other people you girls have chosen? With the exception of Mrs. Jacobson, of course."

"No," Sam insisted, "but at least everyone has heard of them before. As far as I'm concerned, all you did was make up a name no one has ever heard of."

"I can't help it you've never heard of her," he stated simply. "I can assure you Virginia Pip-a-Lee-Ne is a very famous person. If you were keeping up with things in the world, you'd know who I'm talking about."

"Nonsense! You have to pick someone we know about!" Sam insisted.

Jessica acted as referee once again. "Larry, I think she has a point. You say this person is famous, but no one seems to have ever heard of her. Now if you can supply some evidence this is a real person who we might actually have heard of, then we'd have to accept your answer. But if you can't do so..."

"There's a story about her in today's newspaper," he said with a shrug. "Would that be evidence enough?"

"Yes," Jessica agreed. "If that's the case, then your answer would be acceptable."

"Who is this Virginia Pip-a-Lee-Ne!" Sam demanded.

"Well," he said, picking up the newspaper. "I don't actually know a lot about her, but there's a story about her in today's paper. I didn't have a chance to read the story, but the headline alone was enough to convince me I'd want to be stranded with her on a desert island. My choice would definitely be Virginia Pip-a-Lee-Ne!"

"Show us the newspaper!" Sam insisted.

Larry folded the newspaper so the headline of the story was highlighted. "Here you are," he said calmly. The headline read, *2000 Workers To Lay Virginia Pipeline*. "What sort of guy wouldn't want to be stranded with a girl like that!" he added. This was just the sort of prank Larry loved. No one had seen it coming. It was perfect.

"I'll kill him!" Sam declared. "Let me at him, girls. I swear I'm gonna kill him!" she said grimly, even though she could not stop herself from grinning.

Linda fell over on her back and started laughing hysterically. Julia blushed and started giggling. John and Helen looked at each other and grinned before they also started laughing. Jimmy just looked baffled.

For her part, Jessica also blushed slightly but covered her mouth with her hand to keep the others from seeing her laugh. As soon as she could, she announced, "It appears we have to accept Larry's answer."

When he first saw the headline, Mr. Jacobson chuckled, but quickly recovered and forced himself to appear like he made no reaction at all. To him, the best part was Larry's joke had put an end to this game, meaning he would not need to come up with his own answer!

Once the laughter died down, Larry and John picked up their guitars again for just a little more practice. This was their time to do experimental things. Sometimes they would experiment with some original melodies, anticipating the creation of some original lyrics. Sometimes they would try an oddball arrangement to a familiar song, like maybe singing a rock song in country style; if they were in a really odd mood, they might try doing a country song in rock style. Tonight, they decided to keep things simple and just sing some different words, sometimes funny words, to familiar songs. Everyone giggled at Larry as he sang, *"I'm in the nude for love..."* But the highlight of the evening was the rewording of the Beatles song, *I Saw Her Standing There*:

> *Well she was just eighty-two,*
> *You know what to do,*
> *And the way she looked*
> *Was way beyond repair.*
> *So how could I dance with grandmother,*
> *Oh, when she starched my underwear?*

The boys were growing tired and the tips of their fingers were getting sore from pressing against the steel guitar strings. They decided they had played all the songs they cared to play for the day, and began to pack up their guitars and music. The girls picked up the plates and cups remaining and carried them to kitchen. When everything was packed and cleaned, the kids headed for the front door.

"It's been fun," Mrs. Jacobson said. "I hope you'll come back and do this again."

"Thanks, Mrs. Jacobson," Larry replied. "I hope we haven't been too much of a bother for you and Mr. Jacobson."

"Not at all!" she assured him. "We both enjoyed it. And like I said earlier, you saved us the trouble of driving Julia into town so she could see her friends. Feel free to come back anytime. You can make this your regular practice place if you want."

"Yes, please," Julia urged.

"Well," Larry said. "I appreciate that, but we don't want to be such a bother. We usually go to my house or to John's, and sometimes to Sam's. Maybe we could add this into the rotation and come back from time to time, if you really don't mind."

"Suit yourself," Jessica said, "but you're welcome anytime."

"If you don't come here," Julia asked, "will someone please come and get me? I don't want to miss out on all the fun!"

John grinned at her, replying, "No way! I don't need my little brother hanging around all the time and cramping my style!"

Helen grinned at him and said, "I still think you should be giving him the benefit of your so-called style. Not to mention your experience and wisdom!"

"I don't need to learn anything from him!" Jimmy insisted.

"You tell him, little buddy," Larry teased.

"I have an idea, Larry," Linda giggled. "Maybe *you* should give Julia and him a ride, so he can learn from *your* style, experience and wisdom."

"What experience and wisdom is that?" Larry asked before thinking.

"I'll show you later," Linda giggled.

In unison, the other girls once again said, "Ooh-la-la!"

Trying not to blush, Larry attempted to ignore them. "I'll tell you what, Julia. I'll make you a promise. If that slug John won't pick you up, then you just call on me."

John was quick to jump on that offer. "It's a deal! And Julia, Larry has never broken a promise in his entire life!"

"That's not actually true, John," Larry added, almost as if he were admitting an original sin. "I have broken promises. I just try very hard not to."

"Well," Julia smiled, "just so long as *somebody* comes for me."

Larry and Linda were the first to the door. "Goodnight, Julia," Larry said. "Goodnight, Mrs. Jacobson. And please tell Mr. Jacobson goodnight for me. I'll see the rest of you guys later!" The other kids exchanged goodnight wishes in unison.

Larry and Linda headed for his car, John and Helen headed for theirs, and Sam headed for hers. Jimmy held back, determined to collect on the goodnight kiss he had neglected the previous night. Sensing his intentions, Jessica smiled and excused herself to the kitchen, leaving Jimmy and Julia alone on the door step.

Larry opened the car door for Linda and she slid under the steering wheel as before. Before he could follow, he looked back to the door step and saw Jimmy lean over and kiss Julia goodnight. Larry's hesitation was slight, but enough that Linda noticed and asked, "Are you getting in?"

"Huh? Oh! Sorry. My mind drifted for a second." He sat behind the steering wheel and closed the door, as Linda snuggled up next to him. He smiled at her, but the smile faded briefly when he heard John honk his horn, and caught a glimpse of

Jimmy running to get into his brother's car.

"You *are* distracted," Linda said. "What's the matter?"

"Oh, it's nothing," he said distantly. Then he turned his full attention to Linda, gave her a huge grin, and asked, "And where shall I take ma lady this evening? It's only a few minutes after 8:00; we have nearly two hours to spend together!"

"How about some desert island?" she suggested with a smile.

"I've never been much of a fan of Roger Miller," he grinned, "but I'll drop you off there if that's what you want." Linda giggled as Larry started the car and headed out of the driveway onto the country lane. Popular rock music played over the radio.

A big problem with small college towns like Bryan and College Station is there are not a lot of things for high school kids to do. There are movie theaters, but the show times on Sunday nights are not designed for teenagers who need to be home early on a school night. There were no nightclubs where they could go dance. Such clubs catered more for the college crowd, and since they served alcohol, teenagers were generally not even allowed to enter. There were activities such as bowling and miniature golf, but none of these offered much to a young couple eager to become better acquainted.

Linda made the suggestion. "It really is a beautiful night, and we're already out in the country. Why don't we find a nice quiet spot and just sit for a while. We can listen to the radio, talk, look at the stars and just get to know each other better."

There would be no argument from Larry! He turned down the next side road and looked for a spot providing privacy and a nice view, but not too close to any of the houses in the area. They soon found a likely spot. He parked the car and turned off the headlights. Without the light pollution, a canopy of stars opened in the clear skies of a brisk, but not cold, autumn evening.

"Oh, how beautiful!" Linda said looking up at the stars.

"Just like you," he said, wanting to get more of her attention. His arm was already around her waist. He nuzzled her neck and kissed her ear, drawing a giggle, a smile, and a short kiss.

"This weekend has been really special, hasn't it?" she asked rhetorically.

"Yes. I've been looking for someone like you."

"So what are you going to do now that you've found me?" she giggled.

"I'm sure we'll think of something," he answered smoothly. This was unfamiliar territory to Larry. He had taken a girl "parking" before, but Linda was nothing like the girls he had experienced previously. She encouraged him. She enticed him. She thrilled him. But best of all, she liked him!

It would not be easy to convince him other girls liked him. In previous encounters, things seemed to change much too quickly. He would think a girl liked him, but it never seemed to last. Everything changed in a blink of the eye. One minute she liked him; the next minute she didn't. He was desperate to understand why. In less lucid moments, he imagined a great female conspiracy existed to persecute him individually. Their purpose was to see how much pain they could inflict on him, how often they could break his heart, to see how much he could bear before it destroyed him utterly.

In reality, he assumed there was just something wrong about him. Maybe what he wanted in a relationship was not the same as what girls wanted. But how could that be? All he wanted was to have someone who would care about him, someone who would think he was special. Wasn't that what girls wanted, also?

His best guess was his emotions moved more quickly than others. When a girl liked him, he responded by liking her twice as much. Inevitably, he wanted the relationship to be more than she did, and she would break up with him, perhaps because she felt she was being trapped into a relationship she was not ready to accept. He often wished he could be more like John. It seemed to Larry like his friend could turn his emotions on or off at will, and never seemed to get hurt, never seemed to have his heart broken.

He was determined to change all this. This time, he would let Linda take the lead in their relationship. It would be Linda who would decide what it was to become. He would remain passive, trying not to let his emotions run away from him.

For her part, Linda could think of a lot of things Larry could do with her. She had experienced an intimate relationship before, and discovered how exciting it was. She enjoyed the attention being an attractive female brought her. She enjoyed the excitement she felt when a boy pursued her, kissed her, and ran his hands over her body. Being a little older than her previous boyfriends, she anticipated Larry would be even more interesting in this regard.

She wrapped her arms around Larry's neck and kissed him. Their embrace began as it had the two nights before, and just like those times, grew closer and stronger the more they kissed. They could not seem to kiss each other enough, yet both of them wanted to give this their best try.

After several minutes of hot, passionately wet kisses, they broke for a moment to catch their breaths. They laughed when they noticed the stars were no longer visible because the car windows were completely fogged. "Everybody always talks about the weather," he said, "but no one ever does anything about it. Perhaps we've discovered the way!"

"I doubt we could get a patent on this discovery," Linda laughed.

"Yeah, but think about it!" he chuckled. "If we could get that patent, can you imagine how rich we'd become?"

"No doubt about it!" Linda snickered. She slid away from him, moving closer to the window. At first, he was afraid something had gone wrong. But she held out her arms and beckoned, "Don't you want to get out from under that steering wheel?"

Larry eagerly moved to the middle of the seat, placing his hands on her shoulders, and drawing her face to his. They resumed kissing, Linda leaning against the passenger door. Moments later, she twisted her body to the front, causing Larry to lie against the back of the seat. Lying on the outside of the seat, she pressed her body against his. He found this even more exciting than the beanbag chair in her living room.

She took his free hand, kissed it, and placed it on her right breast. Even through her shirt and bra, he could feel her nipple was erect. It certainly was not the only thing erect, he realized. When they resumed kissing, Larry gently caressed her breast and nipple, and longed for more. Unable to control this desire, he reached down, moved his hand under her blouse, and returned it to her breast, now shielded only by her soft cotton bra.

Linda rewarded this act of bravery with a soft moan, and rolled her body so she was almost directly on top of him. While this forced him to remove his hand from her breast, it freed his right arm. Both arms went around her waist, and she was now lying completely on top of him, her legs straddling his. Both his hands went under her shirt and up her back, finding the hooks holding her bra in place. At first, this presented him with a puzzle, but he quickly realized the solution was a simple matter of applied mathematics. Rather than trying to pull them apart, he pushed the ends of the straps together, and was rewarded when they disconnected effortlessly. Linda lifted her chest, and with his help, removed her shirt. Larry had won the privilege of sliding the bra straps from her shoulders, and removing it completely.

He stared at a pair of soft, warm breasts, nipples fully erect and inviting, and was more excited than he had ever been in his life. Linda smiled warmly at him, inviting him to enjoy himself. Returning her smile, he raised his head and softly kissed her lips, trying to express his gratitude. He kissed her cheeks, then her chin, then her neck, as he slowly worked his way downward. She lifted her chest higher to grant him more access. Eventually, his lips kissed the top of one breast, then the other, and moved on until they finally reached her luscious and inviting nipples.

While his tongue massaged her breasts, Linda cupped her hands behind his neck and kissed the top of his head, expressing her delight. His hands slid down her back, finding the gentle curve of her waist, and continuing until they rested on her bottom cheeks, albeit on the outside of her tight fitting bluejeans. He cupped his hands to those cheeks and squeezed them gently.

She slid herself down his body. Their faces were realigned so they could resume their passionate kissing. He was no longer able to kiss her breasts, but found he was just as excited by the movement of her tongue against his. A further reward arrived when she wiggled her hips, thrusting her pelvis against his, moaning with pleasure.

The radio rudely announced it was 9:45. Linda stopped wiggling, and raised her head to look Larry in the eyes. "Damn!" she said sadly. "Just as things were really getting interesting!" Larry's heart was pounding in his chest, and he was having a little trouble speaking. She could tell by the look in his eyes she owned him; at that moment he would do anything she asked. This was one of the things she liked the most about this game – the power she obtained. She grinned at him and kissed him passionately. "What do you say we continue this conversion later?" she teased.

He managed to laugh. "I suppose by later you mean next week?" They already had a date for Friday, and would also be returning to the radio station Saturday.

"I'm afraid so," she grinned. "You can wait that long, can't you, big boy?"

He smiled in spite of his disappointment and frustration. "If I must, I must."

"You'll just have to get a good grip on yourself," she teased.

"Oh, thanks!" he laughed, surprised at how easy it was to talk with her.

"I'll have to do the same thing," she giggled.

"Girls do that?"

"Of course, silly," she laughed. How naive he was about certain things!

"How?" he asked without thinking.

"Would you like to watch?" she giggled.

"No!" he said, but quickly reconsidered. "Maybe I would! Could I?"

"You better start driving, or you won't get me home by ten!"

He started the car and drove out of their hiding spot while she slipped her bra and shirt back on. They reached the paved road, turning towards town. He hoped to find the garage light on when they got to Linda's driveway so he could spend more time exploring, if only a few more minutes. To his disappointment, the garage was dark.

He opened the car door and helped Linda as she slid out. They walked hand-in-hand to the front door and embraced, kissing happily. But all too soon, she had to go inside. They said goodnight, and kissed each other one last time. She reluctantly opened the front door and went inside, then watched as he walked back to his car and started home.

Monday, October 31, 1966
Trick Or Treat

Halloween had always been a special day to Larry. As a small boy, he liked it almost as much as Christmas. Now that he was growing older, he found he liked Halloween just as much, and for the same reasons. He loved to see the wonder and delight in the faces of the small children. It was a little odd for a teenager to care about such things, especially one who had no younger brothers or sisters, but that did not matter to Larry. Maybe he just missed those days when life seemed to be so much simpler. Maybe he liked to reminisce about the days in his own childhood he remembered had been happy.

How long has it been since I felt truly happy? He recalled the last summer he had played Little League Baseball. He was twelve. His team, coached by his father, had gone undefeated the entire season. Then they were demolished in a first round playoff game by a team from College Station with a first rate pitcher of questionable age. That summer was the last time he could remember feeling happy. *Did my life turn on that one event?* No. He knew his life had turned at the *end* of that summer, when he started the seventh grade, and discovered girls. Unfortunately, he also discovered loneliness. His love life, if one could actually call such a thing "living," had been one disaster after another. It became an obsession to him to find the cause and fix it.

But surely that was now changing! He had an exciting new girlfriend and his popularity had never seemed higher. He was convinced his problem had been caused by his tendency to get ahead of the game. He would simply start having feelings about a girl more quickly than she liked him, and the imbalance caused the relationship to fly apart.

Now that he understood it, he could control it. He would let Linda set the pace of their relationship. He was crazy about her, but would hide those feelings as best he could and allow her to catch up with him. Wasn't it working? What wonderful times they were sharing together! He could see they were already close and became a little closer each time they got together. This time, things would be different!

That Monday would be an ordinary school day for the most part. Some of the less social elements, "hoods" as they were known, bragged about how they were going to pull various pranks that night, like throwing rotten eggs and stealing the Trick or Treat candy from some of the younger kids. Larry hoped they would get caught if they really tried to do that. Other kids were giggling about how they planned to scare the little ones with various tricks. But most of the kids were planning to have a simple night at home, helping their parents distribute candy to the hoard of small children who would wander through the neighborhoods in search of treats that would undoubtedly cause an upset stomach in the morning, and perhaps an unhappy visit to a dentist in a few weeks.

Monday, October 31, 1966 – Trick Or Treat

For Larry, the highlight of the school day was choir. This would be the only time when he and Linda would be in the same place. She was already in the room when he arrived, and smiled and waved at him as he entered. He returned her smile, but there was no time for anything else. The bell rang and Mr. Austin insisted everyone take their places. This meant Linda sat among other girls in the soprano section, while Larry sat among the tenors and baritones along with John. Larry's voice did not truly fit into either category, so he sometimes switched parts from song to song depending on what seemed to be needed.

Mr. Jim Austin had been the choir director for several years, teaching voice in both high school and junior high. His crowning achievement was the Stephen F. Austin High School A Capella Choir. It consistently won choir competitions at various levels, and was a matter of community pride. It not only performed the traditional choir concerts at various school functions, but also organized special musical events.

Larry's first exposure to these events had been in the seventh grade when the high school choir produced the musical *Show Boat* by Rogers and Hammerstein. He was given a non-speaking bit part, in which he wore black face makeup and pretended to be a Negro boy sneaking aboard the paddle boat named *The Cotton Blossom* to watch the shows. In 1961, no black students attended Stephen F. Austin. This "role" as he liked to call it, was Larry's first real exposure to the theater, and it would be a huge influence on his life.

Mr. Austin encouraged students to pursue musical interests outside of choir. He was one of the few adults following the *Top Forty Showcase* radio show. When another choir member mentioned hearing Larry and John on the radio, Mr. Austin started taping the show, so he could skim through at his leisure to hear the boys sing. He was impressed with their audacity as much as anything; the boys simply did not have the musical talent to propel them into opera, or even Broadway. But he could not deny they demonstrated enough talent for popular entertainment purposes. He had offered them constructive criticism on several occasions, and the boys listened to his advice carefully.

When the choir period ended, Linda and Larry went their separate ways, having only enough time to exchange a quick "Hi!" and a smile. As they left the music room, John teased Larry about how Linda seemed to be attracting so much of his interest. He was looking forward to exchanging notes with Larry about how their dates had gone, but that would have to wait until later in the evening.

The school day ended, and Larry went to his part time job at the library. He worked only an hour and a half everyday except Thursdays, when the library stayed open until 8:30. A full day Saturday meant eighteen and a half work hours a week. He needed every penny, especially since he hoped to take Linda out each weekend.

These weekday afternoons were not particularly busy. Only a few of the older children would come to the library during the week. For the most part, all he had to do was restock the shelves with the books being returned. Sometimes, he worked on some posters or other decorations, especially once Mrs. Hannah discovered he could draw the Snoopy character from the *Peanuts* cartoon strip. When Sam found out, she immediately gave him the nickname "Snoopy". He really didn't mind that too much; he thought Snoopy was pretty cool for a dog.

At 5:00 o'clock, Larry rushed home to get into his costume. John, Sam, and he traditionally got together on Halloween night, in costume, to make the rounds visiting various friends. It gave them the chance to continue playing the Trick or

Treat game, even though they were too old for such nonsense. He once again assumed the role of Count Larry, Master of the Undead, the essence of evil and dread. He assumed Sam would wear her witch costume again, but had no idea what John was preparing.

He applied the theatrical makeup to bring Count Larry to life (or "undead" as it were), and inserted his fangs. These were no ordinary plastic teeth, but a special costume item used in theatrical productions containing vampires. He had probably spent too much money to acquire them, but Larry thought they were worth it, and would not listen to arguments to the contrary. The fangs were comfortable to wear, but the most important thing was they looked real! He quickly donned the rest of his costume and departed. He and John were to meet at Sam's house, and the trio would proceed from there.

Sam greeted him with a cackle, "Hee, hee, hee, hee! Double Bubble toil and trouble!" She was, as he had guessed, dressed in her witch costume once again.

He thought the makeup was quite spectacular and again complimented her on it. "That's a really nice costume, Sam. Of course, I always thought you were pretty much a natural in such a role, right Mrs. K?"

Sam's mother grinned with agreement, "Yes, Larry, I often think so."

"That's one of the reasons I go by the name Sam," she said, "as in Samantha."

"You look more like agent 99," Larry teased. "You better not let Helen hear you say that. She may decide you and John have something going on the side." Then, as if it was an afterthought, he asked, "Do you?"

"What do you think, Larry?" she answered defiantly.

John arrived dressed as Captain Hook. It was a really nice costume, with a fancy hat and coat, frilly sleeves, a sword, and of course, a metal hook for his left hand. Sam and Larry teased he was dressed as the wrong captain; he should have dressed as James T. Kirk, Captain of the Star Ship Enterprise!

"Then why aren't you dressed as Roger Miller?" John countered.

"Ah!" Larry laughed, "because she said she wanted to be stranded with someone *like* Roger Miller. I could have dressed up as myself!"

"I'll never understand what you kids are talking about," Mrs. Kronkite said throwing up her hands in frustration.

"Larry's new girlfriend said he reminded her of Roger Miller," Sam explained.

"You see, Susan?" Mrs. Kronkite teased. "I told you if you kept rejecting him he'd eventually find someone else. Good for you, Larry! I hope this girl is smart enough to treat you like you deserve to be treated."

"I'd rather have mercy than justice, Mrs. K," he grinned.

"So where did you guys go last night?" John asked. "I need an update on the entire weekend. Did you get any?"

"Did he get any *what*?" Sam demanded. "Is that all you guys ever think about?"

The boys looked innocently at each other, then back to Sam as if to say, "Well, yes! What else *is* there to think about?" Larry laughed at Sam, then said to John, "That's a private matter between me and the young lady in question. A true gentleman doesn't talk about such things in public." Then in a whisper, he added, "I'll tell you all about it later. How did *you* do?"

"Probably about the same as you," John grinned. "Third base?"

Larry held a finger to his lips saying "Shh!" then grinned, nodding his head.

Sam crossed her arms and glared at them. "How would you like it if girls talked about you guys behind your backs like that?"

He stared indignantly and winked at Mr. Kronkite. "You're claiming you don't?"

"Well, of course we do," Sam said defiantly. "But that's OK because we're girls, and we do so to exchange information, not just to be gross like you guys."

"Well, that's all we're doing," Larry said innocently. "We just want to make sure what we're doing is correct and efficient, maximizing the enjoyment for both ourselves and for our partners. Isn't that right, John?"

"Of course!" he agreed. "I don't understand why you say we're gross. We only talk about such things for the benefit of you ladies."

"What a load of bull shit!" Sam said. They all laughed, especially after Mrs. Kronkite threatened to wash her mouth out with soap.

"We won't be late, mom," Sam said as she gave her mother a hug.

The kids headed for John's car. "Be careful, and keep an eye out for all those little ghosts and goblins out there," Mrs. Kronkite reminded them.

Since John was driving, their first stop was Helen's house. There were several children moving up and down the street, but Helen's house was currently not under siege. They arrived at the door, rang the doorbell, and in high pitched voices yelled, "Trick or Treat!"

Helen recognized them immediately when she came to the door. "Aren't you guys a little old for this sort of thing?" she giggled, inviting them in.

"You're only as old as you feel. Ha, 'ah, 'ah!" Larry announced with glee. Halloween made him feel like a young kid again.

Mrs. Hightower came to investigate the commotion. Count Larry greeted her by raising his cape and brandishing his fangs. "I have come to drink your bluhd!"

"My goodness," she exclaimed, "and I have so little to spare! I recognize Captain John over there. I assume you're Larry, and this horrible witch must be Sam."

"Hi, Mrs. Hightower," John said. "But first, we must be given a treat, or my crew will board your vessel and steal all of your treasure!"

"Of course," she laughed. Helen grabbed the large bowl containing the candy treats they were giving to the children and handed them each a few pieces of candy.

Satisfied, they followed her into the family room to meet Mr. Hightower. He was a pleasant man who laughed at the sight of these characters invading his abode. Helen introduced her parents and her little brother, perhaps nine years old, sitting on the floor busily sorting out the candy he had already collected.

"That's quite a haul," Larry grinned as he sat down in front of the small boy.

"Who are you supposed to be?" the boy asked.

"I am Count Larry!" he responded. "Master of the Undead! The essence of evil and dread! Ha, 'ah, 'ah!"

"Oh, brother," the boy laughed. "Aren't you a little old for this?"

"I am over three hundred and fifty years old," he grinned. "Ha, 'ah, 'ah! I live by drinking the bluhd of the living, turning them into creatures of darkness like myself!"

"Can you turn yourself into a bat?" the boy asked.

"Ha, 'ah, 'ah! Of course!" Larry responded.

"Then go ahead and do it," said the boy with a snicker, "and see if you can fly someplace where anyone cares!"

Larry shook his head at the audacity of this child. "Say! I don't see any Tootsie Rolls in your stash. Didn't you get any Tootsie Rolls?"

"Not this year," the boy answered with a frown, "and that's my favorite!"

"Mine, too," Larry agreed. "This is where it helps to be Master of the Undead, the essence of evil and dread. Observe!" He showed the boy his empty hands, and then reached into the air as if catching a small creature flying by. When he opened his hand, it contained two miniature Tootsie Rolls. "Ha, 'ah, 'ah! One for you, and one for me, for I am Count Larry, Master of the Undead, the essence of evil and dread! Ha, 'ah, 'ah!" The boy laughed and happily took the Tootsie Roll being offered. Larry unwrapped the other one and popped it into his mouth with a grin.

"OK, Count," Sam interrupted. "It's time to move on if that's OK with you."

Larry got up, and winked at the boy. He shook hands with Mr. and Mrs. Hightower, saying how happy he was to meet them, and followed Sam to the front door, with John and Helen bringing up the rear. As Sam and Larry stepped onto the porch, they turned to see John put his hook behind Helen's neck, draw her to him, and kiss her warmly. Sam and Larry looked at each other, grinned, and nodded their heads in agreement.

Seeing a group of small children approaching the house, Sam and Larry went into their act. "Hee, hee, hee, hee!" she cackled. "Looks like we'll have something tender for dinner tonight!"

"Ha, 'ah, 'ah!" came the Count's response. "And I will get to drink the bluhd!" The children let out horrible screams, but managed to run past them to reach the supposed safety of the front door, yelling, "Trick or Treat!"

Sam and Larry slid into the car seat, joined shortly by John. He expected them to tease him, but they didn't say a word. Instead, they talked about the costumes the children wore, how nice the Hightower's were, and about Larry's magic trick.

The next stop was Linda's house. There was already a crowd of children at the front door when they arrived, so they parked the car nearby and approached unseen. When the children moved to the next house, the kids stealthily made their way to the front door, rang the bell and yelled in high pitched voices, "Trick or Treat!"

Mrs. Livingston answered the door, but did not recognize Larry at first. She was surprised to see such large children, but decided to give them some candy anyway. When Count Larry announced, "I have come to drink your bluhd! Ha, 'ah, 'ah!" she recognized his voice and giggled. Linda heard his voice also, and ran to the door.

"Hi! Aren't you a little old to be doing this?" she laughed, inviting him to come inside. She saw Larry was accompanied by John and Sam, and invited them in, also. "Mom, this is John Myers and Sam Kronkite."

"So pleased to meet you kids," Mrs. Livingston said. "Linda has told me so much about how much fun she had this weekend."

"Thanks," Sam said smiling. "It's nice to meet you."

Mr. Livingston stopped watching television and stood up to greet them. Seeing he had done so, Linda introduced him. "Guys, this is my father. Daddy, I want you to meet Sam Kronkite and John Myers. You've already met Larry."

Mr. Livingston shook hands with John and Larry, and smiled at Sam. "Nice to meet you," he said. He sat in his chair and returned his attention to the television.

"So why are you here?" Linda asked.

"Arrrrh, me matey! We came to raid the candy bowl!" John said. "Now give us a treat or we shall board this ship and take whatever treasure we can find!"

"He sounds serious," Mrs. Livingston giggled. "Here's your candy. Oh, please don't harm us, kind sir!"

"You go for your treat, and I'll go for mine. I want to drink your bluhd!" Larry said to Linda, lifting his cape and brandishing his fangs. He walked up to her, first kissing her on the lips, and then biting her gently on the neck. In a whisper, he added, "I told you I had the cajones to kiss you in front of your father."

"Hmm," she whispered giggling. "Maybe I'll want to check that out for myself."

The thought of her doing that excited Larry. He shot a quick glance at Mr. Livingston, still sitting in his chair watching television, apparently oblivious to the activity around him. Larry smiled at Linda, and then at her mother.

Sam announced it was time for them to move on. She and John said goodnight to the Livingstons and headed for the car. Larry and Linda stepped outside the door and lingered for a moment. They exchanged another kiss before Larry headed for the car. About halfway there, he turned and waved to her. She returned his wave and smiled before going back inside.

Larry got into the front seat of the car. Sitting between the boys, Sam just looked ahead through the windshield and said nothing. Casually, John said, "I'm really looking forward to hearing your report about this weekend."

Still staring out the windshield, Sam added, "I'd like to hear this report, also."

"Indeed," John agreed. "I think we'll have to hear a full minute by minute report before we let him get away from us."

"Oh, come on, guys!" Larry pleaded.

John and Sam giggled at him, but after a moment, Sam said seriously, "I'm happy to see this, Larry. I hope things continue to work out for you two."

"Me, too, my friend," John agreed. "Me, too."

Nothing more was said about this subject, as the threesome moved through their other planned stops, briefly visiting various friends from school. It was still early when they completed their rounds.

"You know," Larry said suddenly, "we've overlooked someone. Don't you guys think we should run out to spook Julia?"

"Why, of course," Sam agreed. "We certainly should!"

"Are you going to make me go pick up Jimmy?" John asked.

"Only if you want to," Sam said. "As far as I'm concerned, he's on his own. Let's go play Trick or Treat with our new friend, Julia!"

"I agree," Larry added with a smile. "Let's go, John!"

"Fine with me," John grinned.

When they arrived at the Jacobson house, the lights told them the family was still up. The porch light was not illuminated, however, the traditional signal the household was expecting and welcoming visits from children playing Trick or Treat. Since they were not really looking for candy, they decided to chance it anyway.

John parked the car in the driveway and they got out. They walked quietly to the front door, and rang the doorbell. They could hear Schotzy as he barked at the intrusion. In a few moments, the porch light came on and Mr. Jacobson opened the front door. The kids yelled "Trick or Treat!" and looked at him hopefully.

"What in the world are you supposed to be?" Julian laughed. "Jessica! Julia! Come see what madness infects these Texas kids when they chew loco weed!" Schotzy jumped up and placed his paws on Larry's leg, wagging his tail, delighted to see his newest friend.

When Jessica saw who it was, and how they were dressed, she laughed merrily. "You kids get in here and let me get a good look at you!" she insisted. They walked into the foyer a little sheepishly and submitted to inspection. Jessica and Julia had seen the costumes worn by Larry and Sam in the library on Saturday, and were also impressed by John's Captain Hook costume.

Larry did his introduction bit. "I am Count Larry, Master of the Undead, the essence of evil and dread! I have come to drink your bluhd."

"Hee, hee, hee, hee!" Sam began. "Double Bubble, toil and trouble! I will cast an evil spell and turn you into a newt."

"Arrrh, me mateys!" John added. "I am the evil Captain Hook. My gang of pirates have come to board your ship and steal away your treasures!"

Mr. Jacobson shook his head and tried not to laugh. Jessica and Julia were laughing hysterically. "When Julia and I went downtown Saturday," Jessica explained, "we stopped at the public library and saw Larry and Sam wearing these costumes. The Count came up behind me and gave me quite a scare. They were hamming it up for the children. You should have been there, too, John. Your Captain Hook costume is just wonderful."

"Thank you, ma lady," he said with a bow.

"So why are you here?" Julia asked.

"Well, why are *any* of us here, really?" Larry answered. "I mean, isn't that the question about what life is all about? There are many who believe we're here to..."

"No," Julia grinned. "I don't mean that. I mean, why are *you* guys here?"

"Oh, I see!" Larry replied. "I have to admit I was surprised by your question. Matters of philosophy aren't really something young people like to talk a lot about these days, do they? Come to think of it, I don't suppose young people have ever..."

"No, no!" she laughed. "I mean what are you *doing* here?"

"Apparently," he said looking around, "we're talking philosophy. I'm impressed you're interested in such an intellectual subject, Julia. Most people our age..."

"No, no, no!" she giggled. "I mean what *brought* you here tonight?"

Larry looked at her as if mystified. "Why, John's car, of course."

"That's not what I meant either," Julia said in frustration.

The others laughed. "That's enough, you creep!" Sam said to Larry. "Can't you see you're confusing this poor girl?"

"Turnabout is fair play," Larry insisted. "Girls confuse me!"

"Just like they do me," Mr. Jacobson chuckled. "I hate to tell you this, boys, but that will never change."

Mrs. Jacobson looked at him with satisfaction, before returning to Julia's original question. "You kids must have something on your mind to drive all the way out here this evening. What is that?" she asked, daring Larry to make a flippant answer.

Larry just grinned. John answered, "We've come to demand a tribute! Give us a treat or we shall board your vessel and steal your precious cargo!"

"Oh, please," Sam said with mock disgust. "The game is supposed to be you give us a treat, or we perform some trick on you, like paper your house or something."

"Oh, we know about Trick or Treat, all right," Jessica stated. "We've found out here in the country, we don't get many callers. Most of the people who live here take their children into town. It's just too far to walk between the houses. So we don't actually have any candy, I'm afraid."

"Mr. Jacobson," Larry asked sincerely, "could we borrow about twenty rolls of toilet paper? I promise we'll return it to you!"

Julia giggled. "Mom, perhaps we can appease them with some hot chocolate?"

Jessica smiled. "An excellent suggestion. I think I'd like some myself! How about it kids? Will you spare our house for a tribute of hot chocolate?"

The kids looked at each other and decided to accept the offer. They all followed Jessica into the kitchen, and sat around the table while Jessica began preparing the drink. "So, why *did* you come out here?" Julia tried again.

Larry had picked up Schotzy and was petting him softly, but seemed to be distracted by something, so Sam decided to answer. "We came to play Trick or Treat at the house of a friend. Since we're too old to actually go around the neighborhood and beg for candy, we started doing this as soon as one of us could drive. Come to think of it, I guess this is only the third year! Anyway, we go around visiting friends on Halloween, wishing we could be little kids again."

"That's sweet," Jessica said. "I'm glad you decided to include Julia."

"Yeah, thanks guys!" Julia said sincerely.

"I'm ashamed to tell you," Sam said, "we almost forgot our newest friend. It was Larry who suggested we come see you, right Larry?"

"Huh? Oh. Yeah, I guess so." Larry had looked into Julia's deep green eyes again, and was once more confused. "We went to see Helen and Linda earlier." He hoped thinking about Linda would help to clear some of the fog in his mind.

"So you just can't stay away from them for twenty-four hours," Jessica laughed, bringing the hot chocolate to the table.

"Mrs. Jacobson," Sam began, "these boys are just disgusting. You ought to hear what they talk about to each other!"

"I can just imagine," she grinned. "Sort of like the things you girls talk about, right? I can still remember being a teenage girl, Sam."

"I thought you still were, dear," Mr. Jacobson suggested.

Jessica shook her head as the girls giggled. "The best thing about teenage boys," she grinned, "is they never actually grow up. Or is that the worse thing? I never seem to be able to keep that straight."

The boys, including Mr. Jacobson, looked at each other and shrugged. Jessica, Julia, and Sam dominated the conversation, while the men looked mystified. Larry had the additional mystery of why he wanted to stare into Julia's green eyes.

When they finished the hot chocolate, Sam announced once again it was time for them to move on. The kids thanked Jessica for the treat, said their goodnight and headed for the car.

As they started back to town, Sam noticed Larry was strangely quiet. "Is something bothering you, Larry?" she asked.

"I don't know, Sam," he said truthfully. "It's just that every time..." John turned onto a small gravel road that intersected the country lane. Larry recognized it from the night before. He thought about the events of last night, and forced himself to forget about the confusion he was feeling. "It's nothing."

"Anyone want a smoke?" John suggested.

"Actually," Sam answered, "I thought you'd never ask!"

When John parked the car, Larry was happy to note it was not the same location he and Linda had used the previous night. John reached under his seat, brought out a small plastic bag, removed one of the joints he had prepared previously, and handed it to Sam. "Ladies first," he grinned.

Sam fetched a lighter from her purse and drew a deep breath before passing it. Similarly, Larry took a deep draw and passed the joint over to John. After exhaling, he asked, "So John, when are you going to tell us about you and Helen?"

John took a drag from the joint and held it in his lungs. "Right after you tell us about you and Linda," he laughed, exhaling. "Where did you two go after the game Friday night?" The joint was passed back to Sam.

"We just went to her house," Larry answered. "We sat in her living room, talked, and listened to the *Revolver* album."

"Did you two make out?" John asked. "Did you get to second base?"

"Can't you guys be a little less gross?" Sam asked, passing the joint back to Larry.

"Don't you like baseball?" Larry laughed. He took another hit from the joint and passed it back across. "No, John. We made out in her living room, but nothing else happened Friday night. After Sam drove away from the studio Saturday night, we made out some more in the parking lot. She thinks I'm a good kisser, Sam!"

John took a hit and passed the joint to Sam. She grinned at Larry, saying, "I actually don't doubt that at all." She pulled from the cigarette and passed it on.

"Maybe you should try him for yourself, Sam," John teased.

"I'll leave that for you, John," she replied, knowing that would keep him quiet for a few seconds, anyway. "So keep going. What happened in the parking lot?"

"Baseball!" Larry grinned. "I stole second base." Larry was starting to feel the effect from the marijuana. It helped him to relax.

"My man!" John said with a laugh, taking his next draw from the cigarette. "So what happened last night?" Sam put a roach clip on the joint before her next hit.

"Well," Larry said trying to be dramatic, "after we left Julia's house, we found a nice secluded spot on this same gravel road and got, shall I say, better acquainted. I took a big lead off of second base. If the game hadn't been called on account of darkness, I'd have reached third for sure."

After passing the roach to Larry, Sam crossed her arms and looked disgusted. "I wish you guys would just talk plain English. What does it mean to take *'a big lead off of second base'*?" she asked.

"He got her bra off," John said bluntly. "Game *'called on account of darkness'* means they ran out of time. Do you know what *'third base'* is?"

"Yes," Sam said disgustedly.

"So how did you and Helen do, John?" Larry asked. He sucked as much smoke as he could off the roach and held his breath.

"Pretty close to the same," John responded. "All three nights, we went back to her house and parked in the driveway. Unfortunately, we always stopped at second base. We'll have to move to a new ball park before we can do any advanced base running."

he laughed, accepting the remains of the joint.

"I bet you guys will stop talking this baseball stuff if either of you ever manages to actually score," Sam giggled. John passed the last little bit of the roach to her and she sucked in the last of the smoke.

"You could shut my mouth any time you want, Sam," Larry teased.

"In your dreams," she grinned. John and Larry launched into an A Capella version of the Everly Brothers hit *(All I Have To Do Is) Dream*. Sitting between them, Sam extended her elbows outward rapidly, jabbing each of them in the ribs, ending the song, and starting a round of laughter.

"Time for another?" John offered.

"I'm game," Larry said, "but no more after that. The last thing I want to do is get stoned. I have a hard time driving like that."

"Same here," Sam agreed. She accepted the second joint from John and lit it. There was not a lot of conversation as they passed it around. When they had smoked it down to a very small roach, Sam returned to an earlier thought. "Earlier, I asked if something was bothering you, Larry. I can tell something still is. What gives?"

"I don't want to tell you," he giggled, feeling a little high and a lot more relaxed. "You guys will just tease me."

"We're gonna tease you no matter what," John laughed, "so you might as well give us something good to tease you about."

"Oh, come on, John," Sam laughed. "Can't you see this is serious?" She accented the final word by snickering.

"See what I mean?" Larry laughed.

Sam stopped herself from laughing and said, "Come on, handsome. Tell us your troubles and we'll resolve them for you."

Larry hesitated, but since he was feeling good and knew he was among friends, his tongue was a little freer to speak about the things he was concealing. "It's really funny," he chuckled, "but anytime I get around Julia, I have the strangest thoughts."

"Already looking for a little on the side, eh?" John teased.

"It's not like that," Larry said as seriously as he could. "I mean, here I am, starting to get involved in a hot relationship with Linda... And she's definitely the fanciest girl I've ever been with... And yet every time I see Julia..."

"I'll tell my little brother on you," John laughed.

"That ought to scare him!" Sam teased.

"I wonder which one would be scared the most," John continued.

Larry was starting to wish he had not told them about this. "Come on, guys! I'm certainly not going to drop Linda so I can chase after Julia. She's just a little girl!"

"But she's going to grow up to be a big girl someday," Sam grinned, "and I don't think it's going to take much longer. I've been watching you. I saw how you looked at her in the library Saturday morning, during the show, again yesterday afternoon, and now tonight. You have a crush on her, and you might as well face up to it!"

"No way, Sam!" Larry insisted. "I'm interested in Linda."

"And don't forget your promise to Jimmy!" John teased.

"What promise is that?" Sam asked.

"After Julia's birthday party," John continued. "Jimmy thought Larry had been hitting on Julia all night..."

Monday, October 31, 1966 – Trick Or Treat

"Were you?" Sam snickered.

"No!" Larry insisted. "I spent the entire night hitting on Linda!"

"You know how jealous Jimmy is," John offered. "So after the party, he jumps on Larry about it. My friend here made a solemn promise to my little brother he won't make a move on Julia as long as Jimmy wants her."

"And now you're sorry about that promise, aren't you?" Sam teased.

"No!" he insisted. "Give me a break! Jeez, I'm sorry I ever said a word."

Sam thought Larry had been joking about all this, but now saw he was actually serious. "I'm sorry, Larry. I can see this is really bothering you. What do you think it's all about?"

Larry sighed. "I don't know, Sam. I really don't understand any of it. All I know is I've finally found someone who wants to be my girlfriend, and I really want to be with her. I don't understand why I also have to be so attracted to this little girl."

Sam pondered for a moment. "Well, which one of these girls do you really want? You're going to have to make a choice sooner or later."

Larry knew that to be the case. "I want to be with Linda," he decided.

"Then fine!" Sam urged. "Go be with Linda, and put Julia out of your mind."

"Sound advice, Sam," John agreed. Then laughing, he added, "And if you don't, I really *will* tell my little brother on you!"

Larry also agreed it was sound advice. "OK, guys," he laughed. "Julia is officially out of my head. Jimmy can sleep soundly! Please, John. Don't even mention this conversation to him. I want to keep him as a friend."

"All the conversations we share are strictly confidential," John assured him.

"Absolutely!" Sam agreed.

"Like the *Three Musketeers!*" Larry laughed.

"All for one and one for all!" John and Sam joined the laughter.

John started the car and drove back to Sam's house. During the ride, the conversation was light and happy. Larry and Sam poured out of John's car and waved as he drove off.

"Goodnight, Sam," Larry said, walking to his car.

"Are you really OK?" she asked him.

He looked back at Sam, and she saw there was still trouble in his eyes. "I guess so, Sam," he said softly. "Sam, how do you go about putting someone out of your mind when you don't even know why they're there in the first place?"

Sam walked over to Larry and gave him a hug. "I guess the first thing you have to do is figure out the answer to *that* question. After that, putting her out of your mind should be easy. Or not. I guess that'll depend on what that answer is, Larry."

He looked into the distance for a moment, then back to Sam, and nodded his head in agreement. "Goodnight, Sam-I-Am. Thanks."

"Goodnight, Larry. You're welcome! And good luck."

Tuesday, November 1, 1966
Green Eyes And Sam

Larry was tired at school. Driving home the night before, he had laughed to himself about the "Sam-I-Am" reference. It was a pet name he sometimes used for Susan, even more intimate than just plain Sam. The name came from <u>Green Eggs and Ham</u>, one of the most popular books in the children's library, written by the famous Dr. Seuss.

He reconsidered the parting words he and Sam had exchanged. He needed to get Julia out of his head, but those green eyes kept staring at him, calling to him. He sat through class after class, hardly paying any attention to his teachers, obsessed with a different idea forming in his head. Every now and then, he would scribble a few notes to himself. His last class before lunch was choir. The sight of Linda helped make this idea fade, so he decided not to mention it to John. *It's a silly idea anyway.* By the end of choir practice, he had decided to forget all about it.

Sam sat next to him in the school cafeteria. "Hi, dude! How's the day going?"

"Hi," he smiled, happy to see her. "I'm fine. You?"

"Same as always," she grinned. "Just trying to decide whether to eat this joke they call lunch, or wait until I get home."

The school cafeteria served hot lunches. Most of the time, it was pretty good, but the kids still made jokes about it, claiming the school system went around the countryside every night to scrape up all the road kill so there would be something called meat in the school lunches. Skunk, armadillo, possum, and squirrel were the top contenders. The choicest parts, of course, would already have been claimed by the turkey vultures, but after all, kids are used to getting leftovers.

Most days, Larry brought a sack lunch from home, going to the cafeteria mostly to socialize, and to get something cold to drink. "Here, Sam. You can have this boiled egg if you want it."

"If it's not green on the inside," Sam laughed, then saw Larry instantly lose his smile. "I'm sorry. I didn't mean to imply your mom's a bad cook."

"It's not that, Sam. I've been thinking about what we talked about last night."

"That's good. Have you come to any conclusions?"

"Yes and no. Do you remember I called you Sam-I-Am last night?"

"Yes."

"Well, that got me thinking about that Dr. Seuss story. And, well, you do know that Julia has green eyes, right?"

"I hadn't really noticed, I guess," she answered.

"All day long, I've had this poem in my head. I was going to forget about it, but your reference to green eggs just reminded me. I'm not so sure anymore."

"How much is done? Could I see it?"

"Just a few notes and scribbles, but I do have a name for it – *Green Eyes And Sam*. Kind of catchy, don't you think?"

Sam saw the pain of confusion in Larry's eyes. She wanted to give him a hug, but was afraid it might cause those big brown eyes of his to overflow. Even if not, it was sure to embarrass him, sitting as they were in the school cafeteria. "Everything will be alright," she assured him. "Just figure out what you really want, then go for it."

"I know, Sam. I really do want to be with Linda. She's exactly what I've been needing for so long. She's good to me and good for me. But there's something about Julia I don't understand. I wish it would either go away, or I could figure out what it is."

"Why don't you finish your poem? Maybe it'll help you understand."

For the remainder of the school day, Larry thought about his poem and it began to take shape. By the time the bell signaled the end of his last class, it was finished.

I saw a green eyed monster
Beneath a willow tree.
Those green eyes try to seek me out,
They try to capture me.
Oh Sam-I-Am! Oh Sam-I-Am!
I saw a green eyed monster, Sam!

Do you see them over here?
Do you see them over there?
Yes, I see them here and there!
I think I see them everywhere!
They frighten me, those green eyes, Sam!
I want those green eyes, Sam-I-Am!

Do green eyed monsters have black art
To steal your soul and then your heart?
I did not think so at the start,
Now everything is torn apart!
Save me from those green eyes, Sam!
I need those green eyes, Sam-I-Am!

This monster bit you, so it seems.
Do you see them in your dreams?
Yes, they seem to hold my dreams,
And even in my waking schemes!
I cannot shake those greens eyes, Sam!
Do I love them, Sam-I-Am?

Then seek those green eyes that you love
And tell them what your dreams are of!
I cannot do so, don't you see?
I fear that this can never be.
Oh, Sam-I-Am! Oh, Sam-I-Am!
Help me forget those green eyes, Sam.

Oh, Sam-I-Am! Oh, Sam-I-Am!
I must forget those green eyes, Sam!

Friday, November 4, 1966
Only The Good Die Young

Larry had been waiting all week for Friday night to arrive, hoping it would provide him some answers. It was another brisk fall evening, but just light jacket weather, not cold enough to cause any discomfort. He rang Linda's door bell with high expectations. Her mom answered the door, like always, and welcomed him into the living room. Her father sat in his easy chair watching television, as always.

"Good evening, sir," Larry said, trying to be friendly.

Mr. Livingston actually looked up from his program and glared at Larry. "You again, eh?" he said without expression.

"Yes, sir," Larry smiled.

Mr. Livingston returned his attention to the television as Linda entered the room. "Hello, Larry," she said sweetly, standing beside him. She was wearing a brightly colored blouse, a full skirt in a solid dark green, white bobby socks and loafers.

Larry thought she looked adorable. He placed his hands on her shoulders, pulled her face to his and kissed her. "Hi, sugar! I've missed seeing you this week."

"You've seen me every day in choir," she teased.

"But I couldn't kiss you in choir," he grinned. He wondered if Mr. Livingston, who was sitting to his back, had reacted to any of this. Behind Linda, he could see Mrs. Livingston was smiling at them. "Are you ready to go?" he asked quietly.

"Yes," she smiled. "Goodnight, mom."

"Goodnight, dear," her mother said. "You two have fun."

"Take care of him," her father said. "He might actually be worth something."

Linda looked at her father with an expression of surprise. "That's exactly what I plan to do! I'm going to take really good care of him. Goodnight, daddy." She gave Larry a big smile and motioned him towards the door.

Outside, Linda placed her arms around Larry's neck and demanded, "Now give me a proper kiss, or I just might decide to stay home for the night." He smiled and kissed her again. Perhaps it was not all that proper, but it was certainly longer and much more interesting. "That's much better," she said, temporarily satisfied.

They walked to the car and once again, he opened the driver's door for her. She hiked her skirt a little as she sat down, sliding to the middle seat. It was designed to give Larry a good look at her smooth legs. His only disappointment was the view stopped short. He moved in beside her and smiled as she cuddled up to him.

Once he started the car and prepared to back out of the driveway, Larry breathed a sigh of relief and said a little prayer of thanks. He had several superstitions. One of them had to do with the number three. He noticed there was a pattern surrounding this number. His troubles with girls started after the third kiss, or after three hours, or after three dates. He and Linda had been out three times last weekend, and he feared things would turn sour when he picked her up tonight. There were still plenty of future "*three's*" to worry about, but at least, he felt safe for a little while.

"How do you feel about a pizza dinner?" he asked her. Most of the time, a dinner date consisted of a trip to a burger joint, and Larry was trying to send the message this date was to be a little more upscale. She smiled at him and indicated pizza would be very nice. Message understood.

The local Pizza Hut was considered by most kids to be the best in town. There were already several cars in the parking lot. Larry did not recognize any of them individually, but noting how new and fancy many of them were, this was obviously the place for the "in" crowd to be tonight.

He parked his old car in a discrete location, so as not to draw a lot of attention to it, got out of the car and held the door for Linda. When she slid out of the seat, her skirt hiked up a little higher than before, showing a brief glimpse of her white cotton panties. In the language used by the boys at school, it was a "squirrel shot". Since it was not accidental, she grinned, noting he had tried not to stare, but failed miserably.

She put her arm around Larry's waist as they headed to the door, and he happily responded in kind. Inside, the jukebox was loudly playing popular songs, and about three quarters of the tables and booths were occupied. Several of the kids saw them enter, and a few even acknowledged them, mostly friends of Linda. They placed their order at the counter then slid into an empty booth. He felt comfortable with her, even here, surrounded by kids who might normally look down on him and call him a nerd. His life seemed to be improving ever since he and Linda got together.

Sally Sutherland and Roger Warner approached the booth where they were sitting. Sally was the same age as Linda, a sophomore, one of the Bronco cheerleaders. Roger was a junior, an athlete on the football, baseball, and track teams. To Larry, they were about as "in" as anyone could be. "Hi, Linda!" Sally announced. "Hi, Larry!" He was a little surprised Sally even knew his name.

"Hi, guys!" Linda said in response. "Would you like to sit with us?"

"Sure!" Sally said, scooting into the seat.

Roger slid in behind Sally and looked at Larry, who tried to make conversation. "That was a tough break last week! We were all proud of how you guys kept fighting though everything including the weather seemed to be against you."

"That's the way it breaks sometimes," Roger said simply.

"At least," Larry continued, "the coach was smart enough to check with the ref about penetrations. If it had been the other way around, I doubt the Conroe coach would have been as sharp."

Roger nodded his head, impressed Larry understood the need for the two point conversion. "A lot of Monday morning quarterbacks though he'd made a mistake."

"So what are you two guys doing tonight?" Sally grinned.

Linda return her grin. "That depends on whether Larry plays his cards correctly!"

Trying to appear nonchalant, Larry smiled at the girls. "Our plans are fairly simple. After dinner, we're going to a movie, and we'll see how it goes from there." He turned to look at Roger, who gave him a sly smile and a wink.

Sally giggled, "I think you just might be in good hands, Linda."

"His hands were pretty good last weekend," Linda agreed with a grin.

Larry smiled and tried to act innocent. Mostly, he tried not to blush. Fortunately, with the darkness in the restaurant, no one could have seen it anyway. An even luckier break was he heard their number called over the loudspeaker, so excused himself to pick up their order.

Returning to the table with pizza in hand, it seemed to Larry like everyone in the restaurant was looking at him. While it made him self-conscious, he was not nervous. It seemed he had won their approval and they were accepting him. What a difference a single week can make! He placed the pizza on the table and returned to his seat next to Linda. "Go ahead and join us, if you want," he offered to Sally and

Roger. "As long as you're willing to share yours with us, that is!"

"Thanks," Roger smiled. "We ordered the same kind of pizza ourselves!"

The four of them shared the pizza and some small talk. After a few moments, Roger got up and returned with a second pizza and the conversation continued. Since Sally and Roger did not know a lot about Larry, he seemed to be the main topic of conversation.

"Tomorrow night, Linda and I are going to the radio station," he explained. "You guys know Sam Kronkite and Mike Myers, right? The three of us produce the *Top Forty Showcase* radio show. We're trying to turn it into something interesting, and not just one of those lame dedication call-in programs."

"Really?" Roger asked. "I haven't listened to it for quite a while. Last time I checked, it was pretty lame, all right."

"We're trying to change that," Larry said. "I suppose parts of it are still pretty lame, but we're working on it."

"You ought to hear them," Linda suggested. "Larry and John even play guitars and sing on the air from time to time. They're pretty good!"

Larry looked uncomfortable and tried to play it down. "We have a band. Mostly, we play folk music, but sometimes we do rock songs, especially if we can adapt it for a two-man band. John's a really good guitar player. I just try to keep up."

"Don't let him kid you," Linda interjected. "He sounds just like Paul McCartney."

"Really?" Sally smiled. "We'll have to check this out, won't we Roger?"

"Sure thing, babe," he responded. "Does your band have a name?"

"Yes," Larry laughed. "We call ourselves the Drug Company."

"I can dig it!" Sally responded. "What kind of drugs are you guys into?"

Larry smiled sheepishly and pretended to ignore her question. "It's just a joke. My name is Bristol, and his is Myers. So we're Bristol-Myers – the drug company."

"Good name," Roger chuckled. "We'll be listening tomorrow night. You ready to blow this joint, Sally?"

Larry tried to keep a straight face, but could not stop himself from snickering at that comment, remembering a line from a comedy record by "Brother" Dave Gardner. Roger and Sally slid out of the booth. "You guys take it easy. Maybe we'll catch up with you later," Sally said pleasantly.

"Maybe so," Larry said. As Roger and Sally walked out of the restaurant, their arms around each others' waists, they shouted greetings and waved to other members of the "in" crowd.

Larry and Linda smiled to each other. "Shall we?" he asked.

"I'm ready whenever you are," she answered. He did not pick up on the double meaning she intended this to convey. He was too busy thinking about how nice it felt to be accepted by his peers. They departed with their arms around each others' waists. The other kids waved to them as they passed. He felt like he was on top of the world!

They reached Larry's car and he opened the door for her as usual. Once again, Linda hiked up her skirt a little as she slid onto the seat. Larry noted the view was better while she was getting out of the car than while she was getting in, but he enjoyed it for all it was worth before seating himself behind the steering wheel. He was eager to get to their next stop, anticipating a repeat of the earlier view. She cozied up to him and put her hand on his right leg as they drove downtown.

He found a parking spot about a blocks away from the Palace Theater, hopped out of the car and held the door for Linda, hoping for a nice show. He was not disappointed. She made sure her skirt "caught" on the seat cushion as she slid under the steering wheel, giving him a full view of her panties, her legs spread slightly for effect. "Oops," she smiled at him, pulling her skirt back down. Larry was not *that* naive! He realized she had deliberately provided him with this view, making it all the more exciting!

They put their arms around each others' waists once again and walked casually past the library and the small park, to the ticket office in front of the theater. He purchased two tickets and they entered the lobby. After getting some popcorn and sodas, he escorted Linda into the theater itself. They paused for a moment, allowing their eyes to adjust, then located an empty area not quite halfway down the aisle.

They watched previews of upcoming movies, an advertisement for a local dry cleaner, another for the snack bar, then more previews. They laughed at the antics of Wile E. Coyote and the Road Runner, then settled back to enjoy the main feature, *Fireball 500,* starring Frankie Avalon, Fabian, and Annette Funicello.

Larry simply wanted to hold her hand during the movie, but Linda picked up his hand and held it so his arm was around her shoulders. She rested her head on his shoulder, and placed her other hand on his knee, which Larry covered with his own. He had to admit this was a lot better than merely holding her hand.

During the movie, Linda moved so his hand came to rest on her breast. She covered his with her own hand to make it less obvious. She moved her other hand from his knee so it touched the inside of Larry's thigh. He had never received such treatment and was thrilled. Linda smiled to herself, enjoying the power coming with the knowledge she completely owned him once again.

The movie ended a few minutes after 10:00 o'clock. He could not have told anyone the story line of the movie if his life depended on it, but he would have described it as the best movie he had ever attended. They disengaged from their embrace as the lights came up, looked at each other and smiled. She leaned over and kissed him softly, but opened her mouth and ran her tongue over his.

She stood up and Larry faithfully followed. She reached the aisle and waited for him. She put her arm around his waist and he responded in kind. "I need to visit the little girls' room," she whispered to him as they reached the lobby.

"OK. I'll meet you back here in a minute."

Linda soon rejoined him, and they departed for the car. Their conversation consisted of small talk, recounting the highlights, such as there were, of the movie. He opened the car door and waited for Linda to slide in, which she did as before. Larry really did like looking at those legs! He climbed into the driver's seat, backed out of the parking place, and started driving with no destination in mind.

"What would you like to do now, sugar?" he asked. It was only about 10:20.

She cozied up to him as closely as possible, and looked into his eyes. "I think I'd like to continue that conversation we started last week," she said with a sweet smile.

He looked at her and smiled. Maybe he just wanted to make sure she was serious. "I think I'd like that, also," he said softly. She rested her head on his shoulder while he drove to the same gravel road and parked in the same location as Sunday night.

Once again, the canopy of stars was beautiful when the light pollution from the headlights was removed, but neither of them would see them for a while. She moved over to the passenger door and beckoned him to follow. As he did, she positioned him with his back against the car seat and lay next to him, kissing him with abandon. Even if he wanted to resist, a few kisses like that would have forced him to abandon all such hope. Even *he* knew she owned him, but did not care in the slightest.

He carefully removed her blouse while she removed his shirt. Her bra came off as smoothly as it had the previous weekend. When she lay on top of him, his arms pulled at her skirt and lifted it so his hands could caress the soft cotton panties covering her smooth bottom. Soon, he tried to remove her skirt, but was clumsy at it, so she helped him. She unbuckled his belt and jeans, and while she pulled, he lifted his hips so she could remove them. She lay back on top of him, stranding his hips as before. His soldier stood at attention, restrained from his mission only by his briefs and her panties. The warmth emanating from her body was exceeded only by his own. She rubbed her body against him and repeatedly pressed her pelvis against his until he thought he could bear it no longer. She then removed his briefs while he eagerly worked on her panties.

His eyes feasted on the incredible banquet arrayed before him. Her smile was brighter than the sun as she wiggled and moved her hands over her body to draw his attention to every detail she wanted to show him. His eyes became round as saucers when she revealed her special flower, beckoning for him to dip his stinger and gather a golden drop of honey. He moved towards this goal, but she resisted him, even as her eyes beckoned him forward.

Suddenly, it dawned on him what she was waiting for. He reached into his glove compartment, removed a small package and opened it. It surprised him when Linda took the prophylactic from his hand, and carefully unrolled it onto his member. She lay on top of him, once again straddling his hips. She leaned forward and kissed him even more passionately than before. He was filled with intrigue, watching as she reached between their legs and guided him into her welcoming vagina. She pressed herself against him, wiggling her hips. What little control he had over his mind deserted him, as every movement brought an intense pleasure beyond anything he had ever imagined. He gave himself to this pleasure completely, praying it would last forever!

It didn't even last a full minute. Quickly reaching his climax, he yelled, "Sweet Jesus!" Linda felt the throbbing of his organ and knew he was exploding with ecstasy. She pumped him for all she was worth, not only for her own pleasure, but for his.

Slowly, his throbbing subsided, and Linda began to relax. She wished he could have lasted a little longer, but knew from his clumsiness it had been the first time for him. Actually, he had not been too bad! She smiled to herself, knowing he would become better and better as he gained experience. And she would happily provide him that experience! She raised her head and smiled warmly, looking into his eyes. "Did you enjoy that, sugar?" she asked rhetorically.

He felt like his eyes were bulging from their sockets, and he was still trying to catch his breath. The only response he could manage was a weak, "Uh huh." He brought his hands to her face, cupped her cheeks in his palms, and kissed her with as much warmth, tenderness, and love as he could muster. She smiled at him sweetly and rested her head on his chest. There was a slight whimper in his throat as he sighed. He ran his hands through her hair, stroking it in wonder. He knew she owned him completely. He could deny her nothing.

After a few moments, she sat up and searched her purse, withdrawing a package of cigarettes. "I sometimes like to smoke after sex. How about you?" she asked.

"I do now!" he managed to laugh. "Actually, I don't care for tobacco. Would you be interested in something a little different?"

Linda was intrigued. It had not occurred to her Larry might offer something she had never tried before. Maybe the name of his band was not merely a joke after all! "What are you talking about?" she asked curiously.

"Would you like to smoke some grass?" he asked carefully.

"Do you know where you can get some?" she asked.

"I think I could get my hands on some," he smiled. "Interested?"

Even though her smile was enough, she answered anyway. "I've never tried it. What's it like?"

"It's like smoking tobacco as far as that goes, but before long, you start to feel a buzz coming on, and it just gets stronger and stronger the more you smoke. If you smoke too much, you'll get stoned. I'm told it's like getting drunk, but not unpleasant, and there's no hangover in the morning."

"It sounds like it might be fun!"

"I think it is!" He reached under the seat and produced a plastic bag with some green stuff in it. To her, it looked like oregano. He removed a joint he had prepared earlier and handed it to her. "Ladies first," he said with a grin.

"Maybe you should show me how the first time," she suggested with a giggle, handing it back to him.

He smiled at her as he lit the joint and took a deep drag. Exhaling, he said, "You just draw it into your lungs like you would a cigarette. It can be a little harsh at first, so be careful. Hold the smoke as long as you can, then exhale slowly." He handed her the joint and looked at her expectantly.

Linda thought about it briefly, but decided to give it a try. She took a tentative puff, held the smoke in her lungs, and coughed as she exhaled. "It tastes funny."

"That was just a little puff," he said. "Go ahead and try it again!"

Linda took a bigger draw and repeated the process. She barely coughed the second time. "All I do with a cigarette is puff on it," she explained. "I don't actually draw much smoke into my lungs."

"It's OK. You'll get the hang of it before you know it," he said. He took another drag and held the smoke. He could already feel the warm, relaxing effect. He handed it back to Linda and encouraged her to try it again.

Her third draw was more effective. She held the smoke in her lungs, exhaled, then smiled. "I'm starting to feel it. I see why you call it a buzz! It's nice!"

He smiled, took another hit, then handed it back to her. "Wow!" he laughed. "Sometime we're going to have to smoke *before* sex!"

She giggled at this idea, and took another drag. She could feel the warm buzz making her body tingle. "I'm game!" she said.

Larry took back the joint and pulled on it again. "This stuff is too good to waste," he said, adding a roach clip. "This will allow us to smoke it right down to nothing!" She took another drag, but was having a little difficulty. "Be careful you don't burn those luscious lips! Let me show you." He placed the roach close to his mouth and sucked. She saw how the smoke went into his mouth not only from the end of the joint, but from the sides as well. She took it from him and repeated his action. They passed it back and forth several more times. Even after Linda thought there was not enough left to smoke, he kept sucking on it and passing it back to her. Finally, there was little more than a small scrap of paper stuck in the jaws of the roach clip.

"What do you think?" he asked, hoping she was liking it.

"I like it!" she smiled. "And it'll just get stronger if we smoked more?"

Taking the hint, he grinned at her and fetched the other joint he had already prepared. This time when he handed it to her and said, "Ladies first," she took it from him with a smile and reached for the lighter.

They enjoyed the second joint immensely, laughing at silly little things as they got high together. They had an especially good laugh suddenly noticing they were still naked. They might have done something to take advantage of that, but unfortunately, they also noticed it was nearly midnight. Time is too short for those that laugh.

Larry carefully returned his stash to its hiding place. They played a little game of slap and tickle as they redressed. She snuggled up close to Larry and put her head on his shoulder when he started the car and headed home.

It was midnight when they pulled into her driveway. Once again, Larry was sorry to see the garage light was off. In spite of this, he sat in the seat for a moment looking into her eyes. "This has been the best night I've ever had in my life!"

"Me, too," she said honestly, smiling warmly.

He returned her smile. He wanted to say more, but recalled he had promised himself he would let Linda set the pace of their relationship. He got out of the car, and held the door for her. She slid over to the driver's seat and with a smile that almost turned night into day, she pulled up her skirt and purposely showed him her panties. She continued to smile at him as she rubbed between her legs suggestively. "If you keep up the good work, you can have more of this tomorrow! Interested?"

"You know it!" he laughed.

She giggled, pulled down her skirt and got out of the car. He took her in his arms and kissed her with abandon. "Down, lover boy. You have to wait until tomorrow."

"It *is* tomorrow!" he insisted, laughing. She just shook her head and grinned. He walked her to front door and held her in his arms again. "OK, I'll be a good boy for now, but I'll hold you to your promise!"

"I hope so," she said kissing him once again. She stepped inside the front door, partially closed it, and watched as he walked back to his car. She went to her room, undressed, and crawled into bed. Almost immediately, her hand went between her legs to finish the job Larry had only started. *Oh, yes,* she thought, *with a little more practice, he's going to be just about perfect!*

As Larry drove home, he reflected on the thought that for the first time in his life, he would *not* have to finish by hand the job his date had started. He had finally scored a home run! It occurred to him such things really should be kept private. He did not want to spoil Linda's reputation by talking publicly about what they had done together. He knew he could trust John and Sam to keep a secret, but maybe he should not tell them about this at all. Maybe the best policy was for a gentleman not to talk about such things, forcing other people to guess at what he and Linda knew.

He got into his bed thinking this had been the best day in his life, and tomorrow promised to be as good, if not better. Life really was worth living after all. Almost immediately, he fell into an untroubled sleep, dreaming of a bright and happy future.

Saturday, November 5, 1966
Glad All Over

At 8:00 o'clock, Larry arrived at the library for work as usual. He greeted Mrs. Hannah politely and set about performing his duties. The Saturday following Halloween was not expected to be a particularly busy day, although there would still be a regular Saturday morning program. He began by collecting the books from the overnight return, and placing them on the desk so they could be checked back in.

Sam arrived moments later, and greeted Mrs. Hannah and Larry. She saw he was in a good mood, but was not joking and teasing as he usually did. He merely smiled at her when she greeted him and returned to his work. Sam set about her duties also, which included matching each book with the card filed when the book was checked out. Shortly, Larry would collect those books, arranging them on the cart he used to carry them back to their proper positions on the shelves.

After the books were processed, Larry began arranging the chairs for the Saturday morning program. Today's program was a simple nature film, showing the wonders of the wild kingdom of plants and animals. When she completed her initial duties, Sam began to help Larry arrange the chairs, still marveling at how different he seemed to be acting this morning.

At 9:00, Mrs. Hannah introduced the film to the children who had gathered. When she finished, Larry started the projector and the movie unfolded its message. An hour later, the movie ended, and the children, many of whom were stimulated by the film, began rummaging the shelves for books about wild animals. Larry rewound the film, removed it from the projector, and packaged it for shipment back to the rental service. Sam helped Mrs. Hannah process all of the books being checked out.

Eventually, the scene settled back to normal, or what passed for normal following the Saturday morning program. The chairs were in disarray, but this was minor compared to the damage inflicted on the bookshelves. Larry would take care of the chairs as soon as the crowd thinned out, then he and Sam would spend the afternoon restoring order to the bookshelves. Just after noon, Mrs. Hannah announced she was taking her lunch break. Normally, she brought a sack lunch from home, and would retire to her office for lunch, but today she decided to go for a hot lunch. For one hour, she left the children's library in the capable hands of Larry and Sam.

"What's with you today," Sam whispered, not disturbing the few children present.

"What do you mean?" Larry whispered in response.

"You seem different. I can tell you're in a good mood, but you're not clowning around like you usually do."

"I guess I'm in a better mood than I've been in a long time," he said calmly.

"How come?" she asked curiously.

"I had a good time last night! Linda and I had a really good date."

"Oh!" she grinned. "So you played a little more baseball, did you?" Noting how Larry simply smiled, she decided to continue along this line. "Last week you said you got a long lead off of second base. What happened? Did you get to third base?"

"That's sort of personal, don't you think, Sam?" he asked quietly. "Would you want your boyfriend to go around telling everyone how far he's gotten with you?"

"No, I guess not," Sam smiled. She knew instantly Larry had gone far beyond third base, and had scored his first run. In one way, she was delighted for him. She had observed most boys began to mature more quickly after gaining this experience. In another way, she was sad to think Larry was sure to lose part of that naive innocence she thought made him so sweet. For a moment, she even wished she had been the one to introduce him to the joy of sex, but that thought quickly faded when she realized the full implications such action would include.

She wondered if Larry would tell John about it. He was another guy, after all, and maybe guys would share such secrets with each other. Girls who were close friends might share such a secret, but not always. After a little consideration, Sam concluded Larry probably would *not* tell John. She and Larry had been very close friends for many years, and if he would not even tell her, then he probably would not tell John, either. But she knew it would be good for John to know. In this way, John could observe and understand what was so different about his slightly older friend. After all, this would also happen to him someday, quite probably in the near future.

The best part about all this, Sam decided, was Larry no longer seemed to be troubled by that green eyed monster. Maybe he was finally going to have some peace and a little happiness he so badly needed, and so richly deserved.

Larry arrived at Linda's doorstep precisely at 7:00, already excited simply by the chance for a repeat performance of the fireworks from the previous night. Mrs. Livingston answered the door, as normal, and invited Larry into the living room. Also as normal, Mr. Livingston sat in his easy chair watching television, and did not look up when Larry entered the room.

"I think she's nearly ready," Mrs. Livingston smiled. "I'll go hurry her along."

"Thank you, Mrs. Livingston," Larry said politely. She disappeared down the hallway, and he was once again confronted by the silent countenance of Linda's father. He hoped she would hurry, not only because her father worried him, but because he knew time was going to be a precious commodity that night. They would have only a brief thirty to forty minutes of privacy after the show before she was expected home. And those brief moments were immensely important!

He wondered if that could be changed. "Mr. Livingston?" he said just as Linda and her mother entered the living room, "I wonder if I could ask a favor of you." Mr. Livingston looked up from his television and stared at him blankly, without uttering a word or making a sound. Larry realized it was too late to turn back. "When the show is over and we put everything back where it goes, it'll be almost 11:30. That only leaves us a few minutes to relax and enjoy ourselves. Could I persuade you to let Linda stay out a little later, perhaps until 1:00 o'clock?"

Mr. Livingston stood up and looked squarely into Larry's face. "I'll give you this, boy, you have spunk. Just what exactly do you hope to do with my daughter with this extra time?" He turned his glance to Linda and asked, "Well? I'm waiting."

Linda's eyes were open wide like saucers. She opened her mouth to speak but no sound came from her mouth. Larry jumped to her rescue. "We'd get better acquainted, sir. We're so busy with the show we hardly even get a chance to talk. And with all the other kids there, it's not easy to talk about, uh..." He stumbled trying to think of a way to complete that sentence.

"About personal things, daddy," Linda said. "About us."

Suddenly, Larry noticed her father's stone face actually cracked into a slight smile. He turned his stare back to Larry and said, "You can keep her until 12:30."

Larry sighed with relief. "Thank you, sir!" he said nervously.

"You're not like those other wimps who come calling on her," he said. "You got balls! I appreciate that." The smile disappeared and once again, he glared at Larry intensely. "You just be really careful how you use them. You hear me, boy?"

"Yes, sir!" Larry gulped. "I'll be *very* careful!"

Mr. Livingston returned to his chair and his television. Mrs. Livingston ushered the couple to the front door. "You kids have a good time," she said nervously.

"Goodnight, mom," Linda said. As she was closing the door, she looked at her father and said, "Thank you, daddy! Goodnight."

Larry and Linda stood on the doorstep for a moment and stared at each other. It was Linda who finally broke the silence. "Damn! You really *do* have balls!"

Larry laughed, shaking away his nervousness. "I thought you already knew that!"

She answered with a giggle, "Yes, but I didn't notice how *big* they were. I'll have to pay more attention tonight!" He reached down and gently squeezed his crotch.

"You do that," he smiled. "Hey! I'm supposed to be getting a big hello kiss right now!" Linda returned his smile, put her arms around his neck and planted a warm and wet kiss on his lips. "That's better!" he said as they headed for the car. He was only slightly disappointed to note Linda was wearing bluejeans. It meant he would not get to see her legs when she got into the car. But he knew later in the evening, he would get to see not only her legs, but a lot of other interesting things as well!

Larry and Linda stopped to pick up dinner before going to the radio station. Sam was already present when they arrived. Jimmy and Julia, tagging along with John and Helen, arrived a few minutes late, also stopping on the way to pick up dinner.

"Hi, guys!" John announced as the foursome entered the main studio.

"Glad you could make it," Sam teased. "We were thinking we were on our own!"

"Would I do that to you?" John grinned.

"Maybe," Sam said as she put her hands on her hips. "You'd better eat those burgers and get yourself ready to do the opening. You'll find Larry in the tape vault, looking for a new sound effect, and trying to figure out how he's going to do the voices of both Rocky and Bullwinkle!"

"I'll go rescue him," John laughed. "Come on, Helen. Let's go see what mischief Larry and Linda are getting themselves into!"

"And Diggs tells me the request line is already ringing," Sam said to Jimmy and Julia. "Could I persuade you guys to get into the side studio and start taking calls?"

"We're on our way!" Julia said, saluting smartly, and dragging Jimmy in the right direction. They departed for the side studio and got to work as they ate their dinner. Sam returned to the control room to complete the task of pulling records and stacking them near the turntables so Diggs had easy access to them.

After working out the opening for the show, yet another goofy bit featuring the voices of Larry and John imitating Rocky the Flying Squirrel and Bullwinkle the Moose, the boys and their dates returned to the main studio, and entered the sound booths. It was nearly show time!

At precisely 8:00 o'clock, Diggs turned on the microphone in the sound booth so Larry could do the station identification required by the FCC. "You are listening to KORA in Bryan, Texas, 1240 on your AM radio dial," he announced. This approved format was followed by an ad lib, "Have you ever wondered how we know what you are listening to? We *always* know! This proves big brother really *is* watching your every move. Don't you find that just a little worrisome?" After a pause, he started a tape, playing the theme song from the *Rocky and Bullwinkle* cartoon show, and switched to his imitation of Rocky the Flying Squirrel. "And now..."

"Hey, Rocky!" John said as Bullwinkle. "Watch me pull a rabbit out of my hat!"

"Again?" Rocky exclaimed, sounding exasperated.

"Nothing up my sleeve," Bullwinkle continued. "Presto!" He started his own tape, producing the sound of a cricket chirping loudly.

"Wrong hat again?" Rocky asked.

Bullwinkle replied, "Maybe the cricket ate the rabbit?"

"Or maybe that's the sound of the listening audience expressing their appreciation for the way we open the *Top Forty Showcase*," Rocky answered. "And now here's something we're sure you'll *really* like!" Diggs killed the microphones and turned the show over to Sam. She gave the dedications to the first song, and everyone relaxed. Another edition of the *Top Forty Showcase* was on the air!

The foursome stepped from the sound booths and grinned at each other. Those grins disappeared when Diggs spoke over the intercom, asking Larry to come into the control room. Through the soundproof glass, the kids could see Diggs holding the handset of the red telephone to his ear, the direct line from the station owner.

"What's up?" he asked innocently stepping into the control room. Diggs merely shook his head and handed him the telephone. "Hello?" he said timidly.

"That wasn't an approved station identification, young man," Mr. Krueger stated.

"I don't understand," Larry said meekly. "What did I do wrong?"

"That *'big brother'* comment was completely unacceptable," Mr. Krueger replied. "The FCC might monitor what goes out over the air waves, but they certainly don't monitor what people are listening to."

"Of course not," he said. "It was just a joke. They couldn't do that, could they?"

"I don't know and I don't care!" Mr. Krueger said. "All I care about is maintaining a professional image at all times. Do I make myself clear?"

"Yes, sir," Larry said timidly. "I'm sorry, sir. I won't do that again."

"You'd better not," Mr. Krueger said forcefully. "There are plenty of young people who would be happy to replace you. Now, let me talk back to Mr. Diggins."

"Yes, sir," Larry said, "and goodnight, sir."

Larry handed the telephone back to Diggs and walked back into the main studio. There were concerned looks on each face when he stepped inside. "What was that all about?" Sam asked.

"The station identification bit," Larry replied, shaking his head. "Apparently, big brother really *is* listening!"

"Oh, brother!" Sam said, shaking her head.

"Yeah, well just forget about it," he said trying to calm everyone down. Larry, John, and Sam exchanged a look among themselves while the others looked mystified. The truth was even Larry, John, and Sam were mystified!

Jimmy and Julia stepped into the main studio to deliver the dedication notes, and to find out what the excitement was all about. "What's the deal?" Julia asked.

"It's nothing," Larry assured her. "Apparently, our illustrious station owner doesn't want us to mention *'big brother'* is watching." Suddenly, a smile came to his face. "Are those the earrings you told us about last week? They're very pretty!"

"Why, yes," Julia said with a smile, showing off her new star-shaped earrings to everyone in the room. "Thanks for noticing them, Larry!"

"You're very welcome," he grinned to her. Then he turned to John and changed the subject. "John, we need to get our song ready for the next segment."

"Goodnight, guys!" Larry announced as he and Linda strolled out of the radio station with their arms around each others' waists. Without actually waiting for a reply, he escorted Linda to his car and opened the door for her. They scooted into the front seat and quickly drove out of the parking lot. It was only about 11:20. Even with the extra thirty minutes they had been granted, Larry did not want to waste a moment. Besides, he realized John would be driving down the same country road to take Julia home, and wanted to get far enough ahead so they would not observe his car when he turned onto that familiar gravel road.

Pulling into their private parking spot, Linda giggled at him. "You certainly didn't waste any time getting here! Have you got something on your mind?"

Larry grinned at her, feeling a little embarrassed. "Who? Me?"

"Yes, you," she snickered, as she threw her arms around his neck. "Why have you brought a sweet and innocent little girl like me out here in the woods all alone. Are you going to eat me?"

"That's not a bad idea," he laughed. "I'll give that some thought." He understood the concept of oral sex. While he had no experience, the idea intrigued him. But then again, so did the idea of repeating the activities of the previous night. "Would you like to share a smoke?"

"Sure!" she said. "We both learned something new last night, didn't we?"

He grinned at her as he fetched his stash. It made him a little nervous to have someone watch him roll a joint, but he managed to get it done without too much of a problem. "Ladies first," he said as he offered it.

"Why, thank you, Sir Galahad," she giggled as he held his lighter for her. She pulled her first drag and offered it back to him. They shared the smoke, mixed in a little small talk, played some slap and tickle, and laughed. When they finished, they were feeling warm, relaxed, and just a little high.

Linda scooted over to the passenger door like she had done the previous night and beckoned him to join her. With no hesitation, he slid over to her and they immediately began to kiss and pet each other. He was happy to learn it was no less exciting than it had been the night before.

In fact, it was even more exciting. He reached second base, and laughed to himself about how silly that baseball talk suddenly seemed. She suggested they move into the back seat where they would have a little more room. He would have agreed to anything she suggested, even if she had wanted to climb up onto the roof of the car.

When she opened the car door, the dome light came on. Suddenly feeling like they were on stage under a spotlight, they jumped out as quickly as possible to close the door and turn off that light! They laughed and made a game out of seeing how fast they could open the back door, jump into the car, and get that door closed again. It was to become one of their favorite games, and they would practice it now and then, even when they were in town, or in Linda's driveway.

He lay on the backseat and she climbed on top. They both seemed to like this arrangement. He liked her on top because it gave his hands freedom to explore. She liked the feeling of dominance it gave her. To her, one of the very best things about sex, besides the physical pleasure, was the amount of control she gained over her partner. Larry was the perfect companion in this regard. He was inexperienced and very eager to learn how to please her. She could manipulate him like a puppet.

He kissed her neck and shoulders. She moved upwards so he could kiss her breasts. When he unbuckled her bluejeans, she moved a little higher, so he was kissing her torso. As she moved a little higher, her pants moved a little lower, and so did his kisses.

She found herself getting more and more excited as this game progressed. Since she was becoming pressed against the window, he slid himself downward so the game could continue. Soon he was kissing her panty line, and after a moment, he moved downward even further. His lips kissed her soft white cotton panties, while his hands caressed her cheeks. He had never heard of pheromones, but if he had understood them, he would also have understood why this game was so exciting!

The warmth pouring from Linda's skin told him he was on the right track. So did the soft moan she emitted when he moved his hands to her waistband and slowly pulled her panties down. He kissed her tummy, brushing his lips across the soft pubic hair. Soon, he found a second pair of lips and kissed them, amazed that they seemed to be kissing him back! He loved this game, and her reaction made it clear she was in complete agreement the game should continue!

He gently lifted her body to slide out from beneath her. He turned her so she was lying comfortably on the seat, and completed the process of removing her bluejeans and her panties. He kissed her toes, then moved slowly upward to her shin, her knee, and her thigh. He was eager to return to that second set of lips. When she invited him to do so by spreading her legs, his lips found their target and kissed gently. Just like the lips at her mouth had done when he kissed them, these other lips parted, inviting a French kiss.

He responded instinctively, rewarded when Linda instantly gasped and arched her back. He allowed himself to explore, and based on her reactions, quickly learned which places were the best to kiss as her excitement rose further and further. He discovered he was also stimulated just by having an excited woman before him. As she reached her climax, Larry almost did so himself from the sheer excitement of it!

Forcing himself to relax, he moved upward, and his kisses also moved higher. Their faces met and Linda kissed his mouth enthusiastically and passionately. He managed to break away from her kisses long enough to look into her eyes and smile. She returned his smile, then closed her eyes and whispered, "Do it!" He had no desire to argue.

Saturday, November 19, 1966
This Is My Song

It was an ordinary Saturday night. Once again, the gang was preparing to produce the *Top Forty Showcase* radio program. This was to be a special night, however, as the boys announced there would be a special treat when they began the second segment. No one, including Sam, knew what sort of treat they were talking about, and they refused to give any further hints. Everyone would just have to wait.

The boys were not the only ones with something up their sleeves that night. While

Saturday, November 19, 1966 – This is My Song

sitting with Linda in the sound booth during the opening, Larry noticed something unusual. She was wearing a set of pierced earrings in the shape of five-pointed stars. "Where did you get those earrings?" he asked. "Did you borrow them from someone?"

"No," she grinned. "I bought them this afternoon at a jewelry store downtown. Do you like them?" Linda asked casually.

"Well, yes, as a matter of fact, I do!" he replied, mystified.

When John and Helen stepped out of the other sound booth and joined them, Larry noticed Helen was wearing an identical pair of earrings. "Helen has earrings just like them! Did you girls pick them out together or something?" he asked.

"Do they look familiar to you?" Linda asked with a giggle.

Sam walked over to join them as if it were all scripted. Larry immediately noticed that she also was wearing identical earrings. "Apparently, this is a very popular style this year," he said, shaking his head in wonder.

"They certainly are!" Julia said as she walked up wearing hers as well.

"It didn't take him nearly as long to notice as I thought, girls," Sam laughed.

"Notice what?" John asked, dumbfounded.

"They've all decided to wear matching earrings, John," Larry explained. "I guess they wanted to see how long it would take for someone to notice."

Looking from ear to ear, John and Jimmy now caught on. "What a coincidence!" Jimmy announced. "Did you know you were getting earrings like Julia's?"

Linda and Helen looked at each other and started giggling. Sam winked at Julia and smiled. Julia put her hands on her hips and stared at Jimmy like he must have lost his mind. It was John who broke the silence, "I think they wanted to see how long it'd be before old eagle eyes noticed, little brother."

"And did I pass the test to your satisfaction?" Larry asked, turning his face towards Linda and giving her a big grin.

"This time," she laughed.

After the commercial break between the first and second segments, the show continued in its usual manner with a song recorded by the Drug Company. When the tape began, Larry made a special announcement. "We're going to do something a little different tonight. Normally, we perform our version of a song written and produced by someone else. Tonight, we're going to perform an original song, one written by yours truly. I call it *Green Eyes And Sam*, and I hope you'll find it entertaining." It was the public debut of Larry's first original song. The simple song, based loosely on the book by Dr. Seuss would be requested by audiences for years to come.

Larry and John stepped out of the main studio with their dates, knowing there were bound to be a few comments when the song ended. "I love it!" Linda announced. "Did you write it for me? As observant as you are, I'm surprised you hadn't noticed I have blue eyes, not green ones!"

"Well," Larry blushed, "it wouldn't exactly have worked right if I had called it *Blue Eyes And Sam* now would it? To tell the truth, Linda, it's not really about you. It's not about anyone. It's just a play on words, but I'm very glad you like it!"

Saturday, November 26, 1966
(All I Have To Do Is) Dream

John's family was visiting relatives for the holidays, so he and Jimmy would not attend the show that Saturday. On Tuesday night, the boys taped the opening, their two songs, and a comedy bit. Neither of them were happy with the comedy bit, however, and they agreed to let Sam decide whether it would be used or not. Since Julia did not have a ride to the radio station, and she enjoyed doing the show even if Jimmy was not present, Larry agreed to provide her with transportation.

Julia still haunted his mind occasionally. The only time he could be assured the image of her green eyes would not disturb him was when his mind was completely occupied by Linda. Since Linda would be with him that night, Larry did not expect any problems with this arrangement.

He arrived at Linda's house at 7:00 as normal. Picking her up was no longer much of a strain for Larry, although he was still worried Mr. Livingston would change his mind about allowing Linda to stay out a little later on Saturday nights. They immediately drove to Julia's house. As they passed their favorite gravel road, Linda nudged him and grinned. He realized bringing Julia back home after the show would not cut down on the precious time he and Linda would have together since Julia's house was close to their favorite parking spot.

He parked the car in Julia's driveway and hopped out. "I'll be right back!" He immediately turned back to Linda and asked, "Do you want to come with me?"

Linda laughed. "Always the perfect gentleman! Don't you think she can find us? Do you want me to protect you from that little green eyed monster?"

Larry did a double take. *Does Linda know about my thoughts about Julia? How could she?* He quickly realized she was just teasing him about his song and relaxed. Casually, he asked, "Does Julia have green eyes? I hardly think she's much of a monster. I can take care of myself. Besides, I thought she was your friend!"

"She's my friend as long as she doesn't try to get her hooks on you!"

Larry forced himself to smile. "She's just a little girl, and she already has Jimmy. What would she want with me?"

"She may be just a little girl, but I'm pretty sure she's old enough to recognize the difference between you and Jimmy," she smiled. She intended it as a compliment.

He recognized it as such, but the concept still disturbed him. "I'll be right back." He closed the car door and headed up the walk to Julia's porch. Schotzy greeted him just as he always did. Julia greeted him halfway up the walk.

"Hi, Julia," he responded. He also greeted Mrs. Jacobson standing in the doorway. "Hello, Mrs. Jacobson. How are you this evening?"

"I'm just fine, Larry," she said. "Thanks for coming to get her."

"Happy to," he said truthfully. "I'll have her home as soon as the show is over."

"Hi, Linda!" Mrs. Jacobson called to the car. Linda smiled and waved back. Turning back to Larry and Julia, she told them, "You kids have a good time. Come on, Schotzy!" she said, calling the dog back to the house.

After exchanging goodnight wishes, Larry escorted Julia to the car. He opened the passenger door and held it as she climbed in. The girls were already engaged in conversation by the time he climbed behind the steering wheel. All the way to the station, the girls chatted and giggled; Larry could not get a word in edgewise. He

Saturday, November 26, 1966 – (All I Have To Do Is) Dream

would have been thoroughly depressed except Linda placed her hand on his thigh as he drove, telling him she knew he was still there.

Sam picked up Helen to bring her to the show. The Hightower's had some relatives visiting from Lafayette, Louisiana, during the holidays. Helen's cousin, Joey, one year younger, was fascinated by the stories Helen told about working on the radio program. Joey wanted to try it for herself. If it had not been for her interest, Helen would have stayed home since John was not going to be there.

The speaker in the main studio played the familiar theme song from the *Rocky and Bullwinkle* cartoon show. "And now..." Larry said as Rocky.

"Hey, Rocky!" John said as Bullwinkle. "Watch me pull a rabbit out of my hat!"

"Not again!" Rocky said with a sound of disappointment in his voice.

"Nothing up my sleeve!" said Bullwinkle. "Presto!" The noise of a turkey gobbler sounded through the speaker.

"Wrong hat again?" Rocky asked.

"No doubt about it, Rock," Bullwinkle said. "This must be a Pilgrim hat."

"And now here's something you'll *really* like," Rocky continued.

"Thanks, Rocky!" Sam began. "We're a little short handed tonight since part of the crew is out of town for the holidays. Hey there, John and Jimmy! I hope you turkeys didn't get eaten the other day!"

"What a mean thing to say, Sam!" Larry interrupted.

"But they *are* a couple of turkeys!" Sam laughed.

"I didn't mean that," he grinned. "Hey, you turkeys! Never mind what she said! The rest of us hope you *did* get eaten!" There were snickers from the other girls.

Sam could not believe Larry said that on the air, and hoped the reference was too vague for the station owner to notice. She continued, "As you can obviously tell, Larry and I are here live. We also have some of our regulars, Linda, Helen, and Julia, and a newcomer named Joey. Don't forget the Drug Company will be along later in the show! Without further ado, let's start down the hits!" She introduced the first song and its dedications, and the *Top Forty Showcase* was on the air.

Larry did the introduction for the second song. "I got a message for you guys in radio land – eat your hearts out! I'm the only guy here with five gorgeous babes!"

"Just do the dedication," Sam giggled.

"Anything you say, doll!" he laughed, then read the dedication list. Diggs killed the microphone and spun the record.

Suddenly feeling an inspiration, Larry said, "I have an idea for a joke I want to try. Can I get you girls into the sound booth?"

"One at a time, or all at once?" Sam laughed.

"Now there's an interesting thought," he grinned. He gazed into the distance smiling, pretending to be lost in a fantasy.

"Hey!" Linda said, nudging him. The other girls giggled.

"Oops!" he said pretending to return into the real world. "I realize the sound booth is just a little too small for all of us at once, but I'm willing to make the sacrifice if you girls are!" When they rolled their eyes at him, he suggested, "One at a time, then?" When they also seemed to be declining that invitation, he continued with mock disappointment, "OK, then, maybe we should just use the recording studio down the hall. Anyway, this sort of thing is exactly what I have in mind for the joke."

"We can't *all* go, Larry," Sam said. "Someone has to run the show!"

"I haven't forgotten," he said, sticking out his tongue. "You and Joey can keep things moving for a while, can't you Sam? I'll take Linda, Julia, and Helen for now. Later, you two can come with me so I can record your lines, and then I'll piece it all together." After Sam reluctantly gave her approval, he urged the others to follow.

He led the girls down the short hallway to the recording studio. He mounted a blank tape onto the recorder and positioned some microphones. "I need to get a sound level from each of you. Just say something intelligent like, 'Testing 1, 2, 3,' when I point at you. Don't be nervous. There's no one here but you and me!"

"Should we try to imagine the audience is naked?" Julia giggled.

Larry laughed out loud. "Where the hell did you hear about that? Oh, never mind. Yes, Julia, you can imagine the audience is naked. For that matter, you can imagine anyone you want is naked if it'll help."

"If I did that, I don't think I'd be able to remember my lines," Linda grinned. Julia and Helen giggled as Larry smiled innocently. "What's the big joke, Larry?" she asked.

"I'm not going to tell you," he grinned. "I'm just going to ask you some questions and record your answers. In a bit, I'll have you read one line I'll write down. After I get everything I need, I'll go through an edit process and piece the joke together."

"So we won't even know what it's all about?" Helen asked.

"That's right," he said. "You won't know until it gets played on the air."

"What if we don't like it?" Linda asked.

"I think you will. If you must know, the joke is on me. If you don't like it, then I guess you'll just have to kill me."

"It's a deal, but you'd better be right about this!" Linda laughed, joined by giggles from Helen and Julia.

He tested the sound levels and everything was ready to go. He started the tape, then turned his attention to the girls.

"What are we going to do?" Helen asked.

"Let's get some of the easy things out of the way first, just to help you relax. I need you girls to make some sound effects for me. Let's start with some laughter."

"What are we supposed to laugh at?" Linda asked. He made a silly face, collecting a small giggle from them. He scooted his chair up close to Linda and goosed her. She jumped as expected, and looked at him sternly. "We'll talk about this later, you creep!" she said, adding a smile. The other girls laughed.

"You know you're the only girl for me," he said.

"I'd *better* be!" Linda glared. The girls laughed heartily.

"OK, girls, all together now! I want some enthusiasm from you. When I hold up my hand, tell me which one it is – left or right. OK?"

He held up his right hand. "Right!" they said.

"More enthusiasm!" he demanded, holding up his left hand.

"Left!" they responded more enthusiastically.

"Better! Now even more!" he demanded, lifting his right hand once again.

"Right!" they responded, followed by a hardy laugh.

"Again!" he insisted, again holding up his left hand.

Saturday, November 26, 1966 – (All I Have To Do Is) Dream

"Left!" they exclaimed, followed by more laughter. He switched hands. "Right!" they yelled. Then he held up both hands. There was a mixture of responses, "Left! I mean right! I mean..." followed by laughter. He smiled at them, and the laughter settled down to a few snickers and giggles.

"You see? It's not so hard, is it?" He pretended to see something on Julia's shoulder. "Julia, would you like me to get that bug off your shoulder?"

"Yuck!" she shouted, swiping her hands over her shoulder. When she realized he was just kidding, she giggled once again.

"Helen," he asked, "would you like me to remove the bug from *your* shoulder?"

"Oh, sure!" she replied. "Like I should believe you?"

"OK, girls. Pretend Ringo Starr just walked in. What do you say about that?"

"Ooh!" they screamed.

"And he's followed by George Harrison!" he said.

"Oooh!" they screamed more enthusiastically.

"And now here's John Lennon and Paul McCartney!" he shouted.

"Ooooh!" they drooled.

"And look! Paul just swept Julia into his arms. What's he doing? Oh, wow! What a big wet kiss that was!" he laughed.

"Ooh-la-la!" they giggled as Julia blushed.

"Perfect! Just perfect! OK, now I need you to use your imagination a little bit. Put this image in your mind. You're outside in a beautiful meadow, and a man walks up to you with a magnificent white stallion. You girls do like horses, right?"

"Yes!" they all agreed.

"OK," he continued. "The owner of the horse has agreed to let you ride him, but only for one hour each. What do you have to say?"

"I get him for the first hour!" Linda said.

"I'm next!" Julia shouted.

"Then me!" Helen added.

"Wow!" he laughed. "You girls are wonderful! The owner says you can exercise him a little longer, but he needs a heavier load to work up a good sweat!"

Linda suggested, "Let's all ride him together!" receiving enthusiastic approval.

"That was fantastic!" he shouted. "OK, girls. Now settle down. I just need to ask you a few very simple questions. I'll ask the question, and then point to one of you. Don't worry about getting the answer right, just give me your first impression, OK?"

"OK," they agreed.

"What's the square root of fifty-eight thousand eighty-one?" he pointed at Linda.

"How the hell should I know?" she said.

"Could it be two hundred forty-one?" he laughed.

"I'm not sure," she answered.

"That's close enough. Helen, where did Amelia Earhart crash her airplane?"

"Somewhere in the Pacific, I would guess."

He grinned. "Perfect! Now, when someone has amnesia, what's the first thing they'd probably say when they wake up?" he asked, and pointed to Julia.

"Where am I?" she said.

"What if they were alone?" he shot back, still pointing to her.

"Is there anybody else here?" she responded.

"Great!" he said. "Now, do you girls remember when we were at Julia's house a couple of weeks ago, and we played that stupid *Truth or Dare* game? When I point to you, I want you to simply state who it was you wanted to be stranded with."

He pointed to Linda, who replied with a grin, "I said I wanted to be stranded with Roger Miller, but you know I really wanted to be stranded with someone else!" The girls giggled appreciatively.

Next he pointed to Julia. "I wanted to be stranded with Paul McCartney."

When he pointed at Helen, she said, "I wanted to be stranded with Captain Kirk."

"That's good, but this time, I want you to put some emphasis on the word '*wanted*', OK?" he said, and pointed to Helen.

"I *wanted* to be stranded with Captain Kirk," she said.

Then he pointed at Julia. "I *wanted* to be stranded with Paul McCartney."

"Perfect!" he grinned. "Now here comes a tough part. I want you to think about those choices once again, but also think about me. Try to think of how I might remind you of that person, OK? Linda, how might I remind you of Roger Miller?"

"I already told you!" she smiled. "I think you're cute, I like the way you sing, and you make me laugh."

He pointed at Julia. "At least you *sound* a little like Paul McCartney," she giggled.

Next, he pointed at Helen. "Sometimes I think you *act* like Captain Kirk," she laughed. "You certainly are bossy enough!"

"Oh, thanks a bunch, Helen!" he grinned. "OK, we're almost done. I'm going to write your line on a piece of paper. Don't look at it until I point to you. When I do, open it up and read it aloud." He wrote one short sentence each on three pieces of paper, folded them in half, and handed one to each of the three girls. "Are you ready? Be sure to put some feeling into it!"

First he pointed at Linda. She opened the paper and read, "Look, girls. I know he's my boyfriend, but since we may be here for a while, I'm willing to share him with you." She looked at Larry and added, "And just what's this supposed to mean?" The other girls laughed, and so did Larry.

"It's just part of the joke," he said. "Don't worry about it!" She glared at him doubtfully, drawing another round of giggles from the other girls.

When he pointed at Julia, she read, "Who's dream do you think this is?"

Helen opened her paper and read, "So you're the only guy here?"

"That's all there is, girls," he smiled. "I have everything I need. Give yourselves a round of applause! You girls were great!"

The girls cheered, more relieved it was over than anything else. As they returned to the main studio, they tried to get him to reveal the joke, but he steadfastly refused.

"How did it go?" Sam asked. "Did he make a grab for anybody?"

"Only Linda," he grinned, "and only once. I was a perfect gentleman!"

"Well," Linda teased, "nobody's perfect." The other girls giggled at the fake look of disappointment Larry put on his face.

The rest of the first segment was uneventful, containing just the ordinary songs, dedications, and a few barbs thrown back and forth between Sam and Larry. After the 8:45 commercial break, the prerecorded song by the Drug Company was played.

Saturday, November 26, 1966 – (All I Have To Do Is) Dream

The song had been difficult for them, but when the recording sounded OK, they elected to use it on the show. It was called *Patterns* written by Paul Simon, and originally performed by Simon and Garfunkel. When the song ended, Diggs cued the microphone in the main studio. He could see the girls were clapping and cheering, and he thought it would make a nice touch. Sam saw the microphone had been made live, and prompted Helen to announce the next song. When she completed that, Diggs killed the microphone, spun the record, and grinned at Larry.

"Thanks, man," he said to Diggs and walked out of the control room. When he entered the main studio, the girls applauded again. He used his hands to thank them, and called for them to settle down. "Thanks, guys. Can I get you girls to take over the song announcements for a little while? I still need to take Sam and Joey into the back room and have my way with them!" he said with an evil grin.

Joey objected she hardly knew him. Linda had other grounds for her objection. Sam held up her hand to silence them. "Not in his wildest dreams, girls, not even in his wildest dreams!" The girls all laughed.

Larry, Sam, and Joey retired to the recording studio. Sam sat silently as Larry repeated some of the routine with Joey, asking her a few questions and recording her comments. When he had the material he wanted, Joey was allowed to return to the main studio.

"So, what's the joke, Larry?" Sam asked.

He looked at her and grinned. "You actually delivered one of the punchlines while we were in the main studio, Sam. It's too bad I didn't have the recorder going in there! The girls gave me some great material to work with, so all I have to do is fill in the sound effects, and a few lines from you and me to carry the story."

First, he played the tape of the comedy bit he and John had recorded on Tuesday night. She agreed it was lame, and hoped his new idea was better. When he briefed her on the concept for the new joke, she agreed it could be hysterical if they could put it together. Then he played back the tape of the material collected from the other girls, pointing out the lines he planned to use. "Do you think we can get away with the mild sexual innuendo?" he asked.

"Probably," she agreed. "But if that red phone rings, you're on your own." Referring to *Mission Impossible*, one of her favorite shows for the new television season, she added, "If anything goes wrong, Mr. Briggs, I will disavow any knowledge of your actions!"

He laughed at the reference. "Then let's get to it!" They created a new tape containing a mixture of their own lines, some music, some special sound effects, and of course, selected material collected from the other girls. When it was done, they played it back one last time and agreed it was ready.

"Don't let on you know the joke," he suggested. "I told them no one would know until it was played. It'll go out after the 9:30 break, in the usual joke spot." He carried the tape to Diggs and told him it when it was to be played. The remainder of the second segment finished without a hitch.

The regular commercial break at 9:30 signaled the beginning of the third segment. The listening audience was used to hearing a comedy bit at this time. At first, they thought they were going to be disappointed. Without any introduction, Diggs started the tape. It began with part of a song John and Larry had recorded a few weeks earlier:

Drea-ea-ea-ea-eam, dream, dream, dream,
When I want you in my arms...

The song faded into the background. In the foreground, the sound of ocean surf became clearer, accented by the cries of sea gulls flying overhead and arguing over some tidbit of food. Then voices could be heard coming from the beach.

[Julia]	Where am I?
[Linda]	I'm not sure.
[Helen]	Somewhere in the Pacific, I would guess.
[Joey]	How did we get here?
[Sam]	We're on a desert island. I think we must have been stranded here!
[Joey]	I wish I could have been stranded with my boyfriend.
[Julia]	I *wanted* to be stranded with Paul McCartney.
[Helen]	I *wanted* to be stranded with Captain Kirk.
[Linda]	I said I wanted to be stranded with Roger Miller, but you know I really wanted to be stranded with someone else!
[Sam]	And I wanted to be stranded with James Bond, but I don't think this is our dream. It must be someone else's dream.
[Julia]	Who's dream do you think this is?
[Sam]	I don't know. Let's look around. Maybe we can figure this out if we can find any clues.

The sound of the ocean surf and the sea gulls got stronger, and one could hear the sounds of footsteps walking around in the sand.

[Larry]	Hello, girls!
[Sam]	What are *you* doing here?
[Larry]	Hey! Why shouldn't I be here? It's my dream, after all.
[Sam]	I might have known you were behind all this.
[Julia]	Is there anybody else here?
[Larry]	You mean like Jimmy or John or some mysterious college guy no one knows anything about?
[All girls]	Right!
[Larry]	Nope. There's only you girls and me! It's my dream, after all.
[Helen]	What are we going to do?
[Joey]	What are you going to do with us?
[Larry]	I don't know about you girls, but I'm going to enjoy this! My suggestion is you all try to do the same. After all, we may be here for a long, long time.
[Sam]	I'm afraid he's right girls, especially since it's his dream, after all.
[Joey]	His eyes are the same color as my boyfriend's.
[Julia]	At least you *sound* a little like Paul McCartney.
[Helen]	Sometimes I think you *act* like Captain Kirk.
[Linda]	I already told you! I think you're cute, I like the way you sing, and you make me laugh.
[Sam]	You're more like Maxwell Smart than 007, Larry.
[Larry]	That's OK, Sam. I think you look more like Agent 99 than...
[Sam]	Hey! This may just be one of your weird dreams, but you *still* can't say *that* name on the radio, OK?
[Larry]	Yeah. Bummer, isn't it?
[Helen]	So you're the only guy here?

Saturday, November 26, 1966 – (All I Have To Do Is) Dream   -117-

[Larry]	That's right! This is going to be just great!
[Joey]	One guy and five girls?
[Linda]	Look, girls. I know he's my boyfriend, but since we may be here for a while, I'm willing to share him with you.
[Larry]	Wow! What a great girl!
[All girls]	Ooh-la-la!
[Larry]	And what a great dream this is!
[Linda]	I get him for the first hour!
[Julia]	I'm next!
[Helen]	Then me!
[Joey]	Hey, don't forget me! I don't want to loose my turn!
[Sam]	Don't look at me. Not even in your dreams, Larry!
[Larry]	Aw, come on, Sam!
[Linda]	Let's all ride him together!
[All girls]	Ooh!

The sounds of the ocean surf and sea gulls suddenly vanish.

[Sam]	Hey, Larry! Wake up! It's time for you to announce the next song!
[Larry]	What?
[Sam]	Wake up! You fell asleep on the sofa. Wake up!
[Larry]	What happened?
[Sam]	You fell asleep on the sofa. It's time to announce the next song!
[Larry]	I wasn't asleep!
[Sam]	Yes, you were.
[Larry]	How do you know? Was I snoring?
[Sam]	No. But from the look of things down there... [other girls giggling]
[Sam]	...I would say you've been having one of *those* dreams! [other girls laugh]
[Larry]	Huh? Oh. Oops!
[Sam]	You must have been having some dream!
[Larry]	Yeah, I was. You were there, along with Helen and Julia. Even Joey was there. And Linda, of course.
[Linda]	I'd *better* be!
[Larry]	We were all stranded on a desert island, and you girls were trying to figure out how you were going to share me.
[Helen]	Oh, sure!
[Julia]	Yuck!
[Joey]	I hardly even know you!
[Linda]	We'll talk about this later, you creep!

We hear the sound of footsteps as the girls go stomping off.

[Larry]	What about you, Sam?
[Sam]	Not even in your wildest dreams, big boy!
[Larry]	But...
[Sam]	Forget it! Here! Just read this!

The tape ended and Diggs cued the microphone in the main studio. The sound of laughter nearly drowned out Larry's voice as he read the announcement. "The next song is dedicated to Rick and Susie, Tom and Malinda, Roger and Sally. Maybe I should dedicate it to myself while I'm at it." Diggs killed the microphone and spun the Beatles hit, *I'm Only Sleeping*, the perfect selection to follow the comedy bit.

The remainder of the show went like clockwork. There were the ordinary songs, special dedications, and after the 10:15 commercial break, of course, came the second song prerecorded by the Drug Company. Due to popular demand, the second song was a repeat of their original song, *Green Eyes And Sam*.

At the end of the show, Diggs cued the microphone in the main studio, where everyone was whooping it up and applauding. Sam began the announcements to close the show. "Hey, gang! I hope you all enjoyed tonight's show as much as we enjoyed bringing it to you. I want to thank Joey for helping us tonight, even though she was too chicken to go on the air live!" Larry and the others taunted her with chicken clucking and laughter. "I also want to thank our guest stars!"

"I'm Linda!"

"Helen!"

"I'm Julia!"

Sam noticed Diggs was using a hand signal to stretch for time. "Have you got anything to add, Larry?" Sam asked. She knew it could be dangerous to hand him an open microphone asking for an ad lib, but he was usually careful about what he said.

Larry also saw the signal from Diggs. "Why, yes I do, Sam. This is a special holiday weekend, and I want to extend a caution to all our friends out there in the heavy holiday traffic, doncha know."

"That's right, Larry," Sam added. "We should advise everyone to drive carefully!"

"Absolutely!" he agreed. "In fact, my advice would be for everyone to get away from the traffic as much as possible. If you're driving on city streets, go out to the country. When you get to a nice quiet country road, pull over and park the car."

"Well, that sounds a little extreme," Sam added, knowing he was up to something.

"Please be careful this holiday season," he advised. "Don't drive around too much, guys. Park those cars out on some isolated country road. Remember, girls! He's doing it for safety reasons. Now don't forget parking can also cause accidents, so be careful, and be sure to use..."

"I think that's quite enough," Sam laughed. "Say goodnight, Larry."

Obligingly, he said, "Goodnight, Larry!"

"Goodnight, everybody!" Sam said, as the others joined in. Diggs killed the microphone and went to a commercial message.

"Great show, guys!" Diggs announced over the loudspeaker. "Shall we take bets on how long it'll be before the red phone rings?"

"Was it that bad?" Larry asked.

"We'll know soon enough," Diggs snickered. But the phone did not ring that night. The kids filed the records, cleaned up the studio, and logged the new tapes. At about 11:25, they completed their work and stepped out of the station, waving at Diggs.

"Thanks for helping us, Joey," Larry said sincerely. "I hope you had a good time. It's too bad you couldn't have met Helen's boyfriend John while you were in town."

"Thanks, Larry," she said sweetly. "I had a great time. It was nice to meet you, and hopefully I'll get to meet John next time. It was nice to meet all of you!" Sam, Helen, and Joey piled into Sam's car. She had no trouble getting it started, and the girls were soon waving as they drove out of the parking lot.

Saturday, November 26, 1966 – (All I Have To Do Is) Dream

The others walked to Larry's car. He went to the passenger side first and opened the door for Julia. "I'm not helpless!" she giggled as she hopped into the front seat.

"Sir Galahad here has to open the door for everyone," Linda laughed.

"And don't tell me you don't appreciate it, because I know better," he grinned as he walked back to the driver's side. As he opened the door for Linda, he was almost grateful she was wearing bluejeans. It occurred to him Julia might see him staring at Linda's legs.

"Thank you, Sir Galahad," Linda teased as she slid under the steering wheel.

"Think nothing of it, ma lady," he responded with a grin.

The girls talked to each other and giggled all the way to Julia's house. Once again, Larry could not get in a word. So he listened to the girls banter, sometimes trying to understand what it was they were talking about. For the most part, he gave up and daydreamed about what he and Linda would be doing after they dropped off Julia.

Larry parked the car in Julia's driveway and hopped out. Julia already had the door open when he got to the passenger side, but he held it for her as she got out. "You guys can come in for a while if you want to," she said to them.

"Thanks, Julia," Linda said, "but we have other plans. Some other time, OK?"

"OK. Goodnight, Linda," she smiled. "Goodnight, Larry."

"I'll walk you to the door," he announced.

Larry and Julia walked up the path to the door step and Julia opened her front door. "Goodnight, Larry," she said once again.

Seeing her look at him with those big, beautiful green eyes, Larry felt more awkward than he had ever felt in his entire life. He forced a smile, told her goodnight, and turned away. The sound of the door closing softly behind him sounded to Larry more like the thud of a huge castle door being slammed shut. He walked briskly back to the car and sat under the steering wheel.

"No goodnight kiss?" Linda teased.

The look he gave her for the first instant was full of mixed signals, but he quickly recovered from the confusion running rampant within his brain. "Should I go back?" he grinned. "Or perhaps you'd like to try to make up for it." Linda smiled and shook her head. He turned the car down the country lane that led back to town. They only went a short distance before he turned down a familiar gravel road to a quiet secluded spot that had become their favorite. Very quickly, Larry's confusion left him as he concentrated on enjoying the incredibly delightful feast before him.

Sunday, November 27, 1966
Turning Japanese

Since John was not expected to return until late in the afternoon, the usual Sunday afternoon practice session was canceled. Larry spent this Sunday afternoon at home. He spent some of his time trying to create some song lyrics, but gave up due to a lack of inspiration. He ended up just watching a professional football game on television. His favorite team, the Dallas Cowboys, had played on Thursday, defeating the Cleveland Browns 26-14. This left him little to watch than the Houston Oilers, who lost their fifth straight game, this time to the Buffalo Bills by a score of 20-42.

John called around 6:00. "I heard you had a good show last night," he chuckled.

"Were they talking about it all the way over in Georgia?" Larry laughed.

"No," John said, "I got a full report from Helen. Did you think I'd call you first?"

"I should have known," Larry laughed. "If you're interested, I'll swing by and pick you up. We'll get Sam and discuss how long it'll be before the smoke clears."

Catching the underlying message, John agreed. "I'll give Sam a call while you're on the way over here and make sure she's decent."

"Killjoy!" Larry laughed.

"You know," John said a little more seriously, "one of these days she's going to get tired of that sort of comment. She's going to haul off and knock the crap out of you! I hope I live long enough to see it!"

"I hope you do, too, John," Larry laughed, "because I think you'll have to live a long, long life. You still don't understand the kind of friendship we have, do you?"

"I wish I did," John said. "I think I wish I had a friend like that myself!"

"Hey! You got me!" Larry protested with a laugh.

"She's a lot prettier," John chuckled. "See you in a minute."

Larry hung up the phone and announced to his family he was going to see John and Sam. Since he had no homework to do, there was no objection, as long as he did not stay out too late.

John came out his front door as soon as Larry arrived, waving to his folks. "Sam likes your idea about blowing some smoke," he chuckled.

Larry chuckled at the notion there would be any doubt about it. "I'm going to have to replenish my supplies pretty soon."

"Are you smoking more lately, but enjoying it less?" John asked, referring to a television commercial for one of the major tobacco companies.

"Yes and no," Larry grinned. "Me and Linda have been smoking more lately, but we both seem to enjoy it more and more."

"Do you guys smoke after sex?" John asked laughing, fishing for information. Larry had not been very forthcoming lately about how things were progressing.

Larry had a serious expression on his face. "I've never thought to look!" He joined in when John laughed.

When they arrived at Sam's house, she came running to meet them. "Hi, guys!"

"Hang on," John said getting out of the car. "Don't you want to take your usual position in the front seat? Or are you worried about what this guy might do?"

Sam grinned at him, then slid into the middle of the front seat. When John completed the boy-girl-boy sandwich, Larry backed out of the driveway, and headed towards their favorite outdoor smoking room. "Hey, girl," Larry winked. Sam understood the reason her friend was in such a good mood and was happy for him.

John fetched Larry's stash and squeezed three cigarettes out of it. "You *are* running low," John stated. "Have you and Linda been getting stoned or something?"

"Nope," he replied. "But you know how it goes. A little toke here, and a little toke there. Here a toke, there a toke, everywhere a toke, toke..."

"Been working on a new song, I see," Sam laughed. John handed her the first joint as was their custom. There was an unspoken rule, however, that nothing would be lit as long as the car was moving. "So I take it you and Linda are still getting along OK. Have you been playing any more baseball? Which one of the girls took your bat in her hand when you left the station last night?" Sam saw the change in his expression. "I'm sorry, Larry. Still troubled by the little green eyed monster?"

He just shook his head slightly. "It's not a problem when I'm with Linda. She has this tendency to keep my thoughts focused on something else," he grinned. "But other times... Can we change the subject? John, I haven't heard your report in a while. How are you and Helen getting along?"

"We're OK, I guess," John said simply. "But since you won't talk about you and Linda, I don't see why I should tell you about me and Helen."

"I've been observing our friend here, John," Sam smiled, "and I think I should warn you he and Linda are beyond the baseball diamond, and have retired to the locker room."

"You don't know that, Sam," Larry said simply.

"Are you going to deny it?" Sam dared.

"Look, guys," he tried, "this is sort of private, doncha know."

"See what I mean, John," Sam grinned. "If he wasn't getting it, he'd tell you he was taking a lead off of third base, or making a suicide bunt or something."

"What's a suicide bunt?" John asked, smirking at Sam.

"How the hell should I know?" she laughed. "But you know I'm right about this, don't you? The fact he's closed up that clam shell of his is all the proof I need. I guarantee you he and Linda have been humping each others' brains out all month!" Larry tried to protest, but Sam was not going to allow it. "Look, Sir Galahad, I appreciate your chivalry and I'm sure Linda does, too. I wouldn't want Donald to go around blabbing about our private matters in public. But John and I don't count as 'public'. We're your friends! You know we're not going to spread it around town and spoil your reputations. So why don't you come clean with us and tell us how much fun you've been having so we can both share it with you?"

Larry pulled off the country lane onto the familiar gravel road. He drove past their normal smoking spot and parked the car where he and Linda had been spending so much time. "OK, but this is just between us *Spectre* agents, alright? No one else can ever know you know anything about it!" They exchanged their "secret" handshake and laughed. Now that the car was stopped, Sam lit up the joint and drew a deep hit.

"So get on with it," John grinned as Sam passed him the joint. He took a pull from it and passed it over to Larry.

Larry sucked on the joint and held his breath before returning it to Sam. "OK, Sam's right. We've been carrying on like a couple of rabbits. This is our spot," he said pointing outside. "We've been out here every Friday and Saturday night for the last four weeks, and sometimes on Sundays. We've done it with me on top, with her on top, and a few times when I'm not really sure *who* was on top! Last night we did it seventy times! That's a sixty-nine in the back seat and once again in the front!"

"Now you're talking!" John said.

"But I've decided I like doing seventy-seven the best!" Larry announced. John and Sam looked at each other, and shrugged. Seeing their confusion, he played with it a bit longer. "Do you know why seventy-seven is better than sixty-nine?"

John and Sam looked at each other once again. "No," Sam replied. "Why?"

"Because you get ate more," he said simply. John and Sam groaned at the bad pun, but snickered nevertheless. "You know, John, sex is nothing like I thought it would be. It's fun and exciting and all that, but there's so much more. I don't know how to explain it."

There was a slight pause as they continued to pass the cigarette around. "I'm glad to hear you say that, Larry," Sam smiled. "It's not just a physical thing, is it?"

"No way," he agreed. "I think the best part of all is the incredible closeness I feel with her. I mean, having friends like you guys is really special, but this... It's like we're just one person. We can share everything. It's just so... intimate!"

"Yes," Sam agreed, smiling at Larry.

"If I might be so bold, you seem to know what he's talking about," John said.

Sam turned her head and smiled at John equally. "Yes, John, I understand him completely. Actually, I wasn't sure guys felt that way about it. Maybe not all of you guys feel the same way, but that's what it's like for me."

Larry looked at Sam and asked, "I just realized you mentioned the name Donald. Is that the name of your boyfriend, Sam? Who is he? For that matter, *where* is he?"

Sam looked off into the distance as small tears formed in her eyes. "Yes, his name is Donald, but please don't ask me for more right now."

Larry wondered why she would not talk about him, but was not about to pressure her for more. "I'm sorry. I don't mean to bum you out." Noting they had finished the first one, he said, "Fire up another reefer, John, and let's get this girl into a better mood." He marveled at how his relationship with Sam was just as close and intimate as his relationship with Linda, as if they had been sharing their bodies for years.

"I envy you guys," John said as he lit the second joint. He took a draw and passed it. "I don't think Helen and I are going to share this closeness, at least not anytime soon. We seem to be stuck on second base."

"It'll happen, John," Larry assured him. "Maybe not next week, and maybe not even with Helen. But sooner or later, you're going to be with just the right girl at just the right time. Be ready when it happens. It'll be the best adventure of your life! You know what? I envy you! This is something you can still look forward to!"

"Now that just sounds plain stupid, Larry!" John laughed.

"You're right, especially since it seems to get better each time!" he laughed.

"And that's just rubbing it in," Sam grinned.

"OK, I'll shut up," he smiled. It was his turn for the joint. He accepted it with great delight before passing it on. By the time they had finished the second joint, each of the threesome was getting pretty silly. But since there was only enough grass for one more joint, they decided to go for the gusto and fire that one up as well.

"Maybe you should bring Helen out here and get her stoned," Larry giggled. "A little weed always makes me get horny."

"Everything makes you horny, you pervert," Sam laughed. "Maybe we ought to switch seats, John. Now that he's dipped his stinger into one honey pot, he might decide all girls are fair game!"

"Not in *your* wildest dreams, sugar!" Larry teased.

"It doesn't make me any hornier," John laughed. "At least, I don't think so. I can't imagine *being* any hornier than I already am!"

"I doesn't make me any hornier, either," Sam agreed. "But it *does* make me hungry! What do you guys say we go get some tater tots in a bit."

"I'm hip," Larry agreed, adding with a laugh, "Tater tots make me horny, also!"

"Shit!" Sam giggled. "It's a good thing I didn't suggest pizza, or we'd be cleaning

Sunday, November 27, 1966 – Turning Japanese

man goo off the windshield! Get a grip on yourself, will you?"

"If I get horny enough," Larry giggled, "I'll *have* to!"

"Don't you stop doing that once you start getting tang?" John asked laughing.

"It hasn't slowed me down at all," Larry laughed. "In fact..."

"You guys are gross!" Sam giggled.

"Oh, get off your high horse, sweetie," Larry teased. "Since we're being so open and honest around here, tell us just how often you... Well, the first thing you can do is give us a name! What do you girls call it?"

"I prefer the name 'jilling off', but there are lot's of other names, just like you guys have a lot of names for your little hobby."

"That's cute," Larry said. "Jack and Jill went up the hill..."

"Jeez," John said. "Would you guys laugh if I told you I didn't even know girls did that sort of thing?"

"Yes!" Larry laughed.

"No," Sam said simultaneously. First, she looked at Larry and said, "I'll bet you didn't know either before Linda mentioned it, now did you? Maybe she even showed you! You'd like that, I bet! Some girls do it just as often as boys. Maybe even more."

"No shit?" John asked.

"No shit!" she answered.

They had smoked the third joint down to a roach, and concentrated on finishing the job. They were completely silly and agreed they needed to sober up a little before driving back to town. Since it was only a little after 8:30, they had plenty of time. But those tater tots seemed to be beckoning!

Soon, Larry drove back into town, heading straight for the Buccaneer. They specialized in great burgers and, very importantly at this particular moment, family sized orders of french fries and tater tots. He parked the car near the back, walked casually to the window to place the order, and waited for the few moments it would take to prepare.

When he returned to the car, Sam and John were laughing hysterically over the number of different names they could remember for masturbation. They had been through the obvious ones, like *jacking off, jilling off,* and *jerking off,* and it was starting to turn into something of a contest. The boys decided to challenge Sam. They would each give a name boys used, and Sam would provide a name used by girls. The first team failing to come up a new name lost the game.

[Larry]	Flogging your dong
[John]	Choking the chicken
[Sam]	Fingerbating
[Larry]	Beating your meat
[John]	Wanking
[Sam]	Beating around the bush
[Larry]	Cranking the shank
[John]	Pulling your pud
[Sam]	Gagging the clam
[Larry]	Pocket pool
[John]	Buffing the banana

[Sam]	Buffing the muffin
[Larry]	Shaking the snake
[John]	Having a Roy
[Sam]	Two finger taco tango
[Larry]	Firming your worm
[John]	Hand to gland combat
[Sam]	Pushing the button
[Larry]	Doodle your noodle
[John]	Draining the dragon
[Sam]	Pampering the pussy
[Larry]	Blowing your load
[John]	Bleeding your weed
[Sam]	Brushing the beaver
[Larry]	Squeezing the burrito
[John]	Punishing the Bishop
[Sam]	Parting the Red Sea
[Larry]	Jerkin' your gherkin
[John]	Slapping the salami
[Sam]	Rowing the little man in the boat
[Larry]	Greasing the weasel
[John]	Shifting into first gear
[Sam]	Playing tag in the foxhole
[Larry]	Beef strokin' off
[John]	Floggin' the dolphin
[Sam]	Digging for clams
[Larry]	Milking the one-titted cow
[John]	Tenderizing the tube steak
[Sam]	Playing the clitar
[Larry]	Shpritsn der schmekel
[John]	Squeezing the squid
[Sam]	Playing the pink oboe
[Larry]	Turning Japanese

"Turning Japanese?" Sam giggled. "I don't get it. What in hell does that mean?"

"Would you like me to demonstrate?" Larry chuckled, winking at John.

"No, thank you!" Sam laughed. "That won't be necessary! OK, I get all of the other expressions, but not this one. Just explain it to me without being too graphic, if you don't mind!"

"What do you think, John?" Larry grinned. "Should we let her in on the joke?"

"We may as well," John snickered. "OK, Sam, imagine Larry and I are having a date with Rosie Palm and her four sisters. Do you have this picture in your mind?"

"Oh, please! Do I have to?" Sam giggled.

"If you want to learn," Larry said, fighting desperately to keep a straight face. "It keeps getting better and better. The ultimate moment is *coming*, so to speak."

"Get on with it!" Sam snickered.

Larry and John contorted their faces, squinting their eyes as if in a moment of pure ecstasy. With a thick Japanese accent, they delivered a loud chorus, "Ah, so!"

Sam fell over in hysterics, and the boys joined her laughter. They probably could have gone on for hours, but the game was called on account of the fact none of them could keep a straight face anymore, and they were laughing so hard they had trouble understanding what was being said. The people in the next car thought these fool kids must be losing their minds. It was good both cars had the windows rolled up!

Saturday, December 10, 1966
I Get A Kick Out Of You

The gang was slightly shorthanded for the radio program that night. Julia decided to stay home with her parents to celebrate Chanukah. Jimmy decided he would go to the radio station stag, even when John indicated he would rather have the chance to spend more time alone with Helen, without his kid brother looking down their necks.

At 8:00 o'clock, the speaker in the main studio played the familiar theme from the Rocky and Bullwinkle cartoon as the *Top Forty Showcase* program began. Larry and Linda were intimately squeezed into one of the sound booths, while John and Helen occupied the other. "And now..." Larry said imitating Rocky the flying squirrel.

"Hey, Rocky!" John said as Bullwinkle. "Watch me pull a rabbit out of my hat!"

Larry had a sudden inspiration and varied from the script. Still using the Rocky voice imitation, he fired back an unexpected ad lib. "Out of your *what*, Bullwinkle?"

John continued as if on cue. "See? Nothing up my sleeve," he said as Bullwinkle. He then realized Larry had changed the script and looked through the glass panels to see Larry grinning. He caught the joke and started laughing, having completely lost control of the Bullwinkle character.

Larry began a tirade of ad libs, still in character, still using his Rocky imitation. "Every week, it's the same old thing. *'Watch me pull a rabbit out of my hat!'* And every week, you have the wrong hat. Don't you think we've all had enough of this?"

John still had not regained control of himself. He and Helen were just sitting in the booth laughing on the air. So Larry continued, "I shouldn't have to work under such conditions. Look at me! I'm a *star!* I have my own television show. Why should I have to put up with a stupid moose who can't keep track of his own hat?"

"Bwah-ha-ha-ha!" he said next, switching to the voice of Boris Badenov. "Moose and squirrel have finally cracked. We must contact Fearless Leader!"

Linda joined the fun with her imitation of Natasha Fatale, "Yes, Borees!"

"And that's another thing," Larry said, returning to his Rocky imitation. "Why do I have these inept spy types following me around all the time? Why would a spy have any interest in a flying squirrel and his stupid moose sidekick?"

"I don't know, Rocky," John giggled as Bullwinkle, trying to recover.

"Shut up, you stupid moose!" Rocky said. "I've had it. I'm a star! A star like me should be surrounded by starlets and beautiful show girls, not by a couple of incompetent spies and a stupid moose!"

"I weel be your showgirl," Linda offered as Natasha.

"Defecting, Natasha?" Boris interrupted. "What weel Fearless Leader think?"

"I'm not afraid of Fearless Leader," Natasha said.

"Forget it," Rocky continued. "I need starlets and showgirls, not a retired spy. The worst thing of all is this high pitched voice I have! Do you realize how old I am? My voice should have changed years ago. I need a *real* woman, not some cartoon floozy. Say, where is that Sam chick? Now *there's* a real woman!"

Larry signaled to Diggs to cue the microphone in the main studio. The radio audience heard Sam and Jimmy laughing. Seeing the microphone was on, Sam recovered enough to respond, "What do you want, Rocky?"

Larry continued his tirade, "Hey, Sam! How about it? What do you say we grab a couple of bottles of mooseberry juice, then go out behind the station and have a go! I'll put a smile on your face you won't be able to wipe off for a week. Flying squirrels have a lot of interesting tricks up their sleeves! Not like a stupid moose who can't even pull a rabbit out of his hat."

"Oh, Rocky!" Sam gushed, playing along. "I didn't know you cared!" She handed the list of dedications to Jimmy. The audience heard some footsteps and a couple of doors opening and closing, as Sam and Rocky supposedly left the building.

When Jimmy looked dumbfounded, Sam urged him to go ahead with the first song dedication. "Uh, OK, gang. It looks like I've been put in charge. The first song is dedicated to Bill and Nancy, Tom and Wanda, and Roger and Sally." He added with a giggle, "And I think I should add a special dedication to Sam and Rocky!"

Diggs killed the microphones and spun the first record. When everything was settled, he grinned at Larry, but shook his head, and pointed a finger at him accusingly. Almost immediately, the expression on his face changed as he reached to answer the red telephone, and signaled for Larry to come into the control room.

The rest of the gang watched anxiously as Diggs talked on the phone. Larry stood in the control room waiting. After a few moments, Diggs gave the handset to Larry. They could not hear the conversation, of course, but they could easily read Larry's lips, since about the only words he was saying were, "Yes, sir," and "No, sir."

When the current song ended, Helen read the next dedication, with some clear tension in her voice. Diggs routinely killed the microphone and spun the next record. The kids saw Larry tap Diggs on the shoulder and then point, first to the hand set and then to the main studio. Sensing his request, Diggs patched the telephone conversation onto the speaker in the main studio so the rest of the kids could hear.

"...thought you knew better," Mr. Krueger said.

"Sir, yes, sir," Larry said. "I'm sorry, sir."

"That's just not good enough, young man," Mr. Krueger insisted. "You can apologize to me all you want, but who's going to apologize to the listeners? And what about the parents of those listeners? Who's going to apologize to them?"

"I will, sir," Larry suggested. "I understand your concern, and to be perfectly frank, I agree with it. I'll be happy to make a public apology if that'll help."

James Krueger thought about that for a second. "Do you really expect me to let you back on the air after this?"

"I just wasn't thinking about that aspect of it, sir," Larry pleaded. "Frankly, I was more concerned about the sexual implications, and it just didn't occur to me the reference to *'mooseberry juice'* implied the use of alcohol and was promoting teenage drinking. I know I have this tendency to push against your limits, but I really do try to be careful. I'd never intentionally violate your rules."

After a pause, Mr. Krueger relented slightly. "I'll let you back on the air, but with one condition. You must make a sincere public apology indicating neither this station nor you personally condone the use of alcohol by teenagers."

"I understand, except for the personal part. Is that really important?"

"Absolutely!" Mr. Krueger insisted. "I want it to come from you *personally*. A lot of young people look up to you and respect your opinions, and much of that respect is the result of your involvement with this radio station. I don't want it to sound like you were forced into making this apology. I want everyone to know this apology comes from you personally, and that you fully support it. And you'd *better* make it sound sincere!"

"Yes, sir," Larry agreed. "I'm really sorry. Does it have to be a formal sounding statement, or would it be OK if I made this apology as part of a casual conversation between Sam and myself?"

"That'd be fine," the owner agreed. "In fact, that might make it sound more sincere, even if you don't really mean it."

"Oh, but I do mean it, sir," Larry continued. "I don't normally like voice-overs, but would it be OK if the conversation is conducted while a record is playing?"

"What song?" Mr. Krueger asked, wondering if Larry was up to something.

"Nothing in particular. Just whatever comes up next." He looked at the top of the record stack. "There's a Beatles song coming up called *Girl*. Would that be OK?"

"How does it go?" Mr. Krueger asked.

"Is there anybody going to listen to my story, all about the girl who came to stay."

"OK," Mr. Krueger agreed. "That'll be fine. Make your apology. And watch yourself in the future!"

"I will, sir. Goodbye." Larry handed the telephone back to Diggs and walked out of the control room, returning to the main studio. Diggs killed the speaker in the studio, and while Larry walked back, the kids saw Diggs talk briefly with the station owner and then hang up the red telephone.

Because two turntables were used alternatively for the program, the record on the top of the stack was not actually the next song to be played. When Diggs cued the microphone, Linda made the normal announcement of the dedications. He killed the microphone and spun the next record. Larry had a moment to relax and reflect.

"What are you doing to do?" Sam asked.

Larry looked at her sadly. "Exactly what he demanded, Sam. I'll do the dedication as normal, but we'll leave the microphone active. No, wait. I don't want any of the requested dedications at all. During the song, I'll make the public apology. I want you with me, Sam, but everyone else is to leave the studio. Or I guess you and I could go into one of the sound booths."

"Let's do it that way, Larry," she said. "It'd be less trouble for the others."

Larry and Sam went into the sound booth to wait for the next song. Now isolated from the others, Sam asked, "Are you up to something, Larry?"

He looked at her, smiled, and Sam saw a twinkle in his eye. "Do you really think my reference to *'mooseberry juice'* will influence anybody to drink alcohol?"

"Of course not," Sam agreed. "But Larry, if you don't sound sincere, he's not going to let you come back!"

"That's not a problem. I'll sound sincere, because everything I say will *be* sincere," he assured her. "But there'll be a double message. You'll get it. So will Diggs. John and Linda will get it. I don't know about the others. A lot of the kids listening out there will hear it and get a real kick out of it, but their parents won't get it at all, and neither will old Mister Stuffyshirt! Whatever you do, Sam, please don't laugh. If he gets suspicious, he'll kick me out of here with no questions asked."

"Then why take the chance, Larry?" Sam wondered.

"I don't know, Sam," he said honestly, smiling. "It just seems to be the right thing to do at this particular moment in time."

The record ended and Diggs cued the microphone in the sound booth for Larry to introduce the next song. "The next song has a special dedication from me to Sam, my dear friend. Sam, I want to make a public apology to you. You and I have known each other for a long time, and are very good friends. We tease each other constantly and don't think anything about it. I know we're teasing, and you know it, but people listening to this program may not understand that. Some of the things we say could be interpreted incorrectly if one doesn't understand these things are just part of a joke. I want to apologize to you for the things I implied earlier this evening. When I suggested you might go out behind the station to have some fun with me, I implied you might be less than the very nice and sweet girl I know you to be. I was just joking, of course. You knew it was a joke, but some of the listeners might not have known. I went too far with this joke, and may have damaged your reputation. I apologize most humbly and sincerely. I hope you will forgive me."

"Oh, Larry," Sam said, realizing this apology was completely sincere, "no apology is necessary. Of course I forgive you."

"I appreciate that, Sam," Larry said, signaling Diggs to start the record. "This song just happened to be the next on the list, but in some ways, it's very appropriate. You're a very special girl to me, just like the one described in this song."

He began speaking again during the second verse. Diggs adjusted the volume of the record so his voice was dominant, with the music in the background. "I also want to apologize to all our listeners for something else. Earlier this evening, I made a statement implying I thought it acceptable for young people to drink alcohol. I want to state for the record neither I nor this radio station condone teenage drinking."

He timed his speech so that as the Beatles sang, *"Ah, girl,"* he was saying, "Personally, I don't drink alcohol." Again, the Beatles sang, *"Girl,"* as he stated, "I don't condone the use of alcohol." In the recording, just after the words "girl" at the end of each verse, there is a sound of someone sucking heavily on a cigarette.

During the bridge, Larry continued his apology. "I want to urge all of our listeners to think carefully before drinking alcohol. Alcohol is the number one cause of accidents and traffic fatalities. Alcohol abuse has serious health implications. So I urge all our listeners to do like I do, and abstain from the use of alcohol."

He continued during the next verse. As the Beatles sang, *"Ah, girl,"* he stated, "Alcohol is bad for your health." As they sang, *"Girl,"* he urged listeners, "Please do not drink alcohol." When the song finished, Sam read the next set of dedications and Diggs spun the record. Larry and Sam looked out of the booth to see Diggs grinning from the control room, shaking his head. In the main studio, John was doubled over in hysterics. Linda, Helen, and Jimmy were giggling and whispering to each other.

As Larry and Sam exited the sound booth and returned to the main studio, the kids once again saw Diggs answer the red telephone. Larry immediately asked everyone to straighten up and act naturally. Knowing they were anxious about the telephone call, Diggs patched the conversation onto the speaker in the main studio.

"What did you think, Mr. Diggins?" Mr. Krueger asked.

"He sounded sincere to me, sir," he said, trying not to snicker.

"Yes, I thought so, too," Mr. Krueger continued. "I thought the apology to Sam was a particularly nice touch. Tell me what they're doing right now."

Diggs looked at the kids, all of whom were gathered in the main studio looking at him anxiously. "They're looking at me talking to you on the telephone, sir."

"No one is laughing? No one thinks this is all some big joke?" the owner asked.

"No, sir. I think you underestimate these kids, sir," Diggs said. "They're young and inexperienced, but they have a vitality and enthusiasm that just can't be denied."

"I can see that," the owner said, "but that can get them and us into a lot of trouble with the FCC if we don't keep them under control."

"Yes, sir," Diggs agreed. "But I think they've learned their lesson for now."

"I hope so, Mr. Diggins," he said. "I hope so."

Diggs hung up the phone and killed the speaker in the studio. He gave a big grin and an enthusiastic "thumbs up" before returning his attention to operations.

"You are absolutely nuts!" Sam said.

"You are absolutely right!" Larry agreed with a smile.

"Why did you take such a chance, Larry?" John asked. "You could have gotten us *all* thrown out of here!"

"I know, John," he said sincerely, "and I apologize for that. I wish I could have consulted with you guys first, to let you know what I was thinking, but there just wasn't enough time. There were three reasons I did it. First of all, I admit I was being selfish. As you well know, I've worked very hard to build up my reputation, to make other kids think of me as someone cool. I was afraid I'd throw that all away if I did it straight, exactly the way he demanded." John and Sam indicated they understood this reason.

"Secondly, I was thinking about *our* image. I hope our friends will realize we don't condone the double standards set up by the establishment, whatever that is, concerning drugs and alcohol. I hope the message they got was if they used either drugs or alcohol, they should do so in a sensible manner." John and Sam agreed with that, also.

"Finally, I was thinking about the program. I knew it was going to be obvious to everyone I was being forced into making that apology, no matter how sincere I tried to make it sound. I wanted to divert attention away from that, so nobody got mad at us, the program, the station, *or* its owner."

"So you were actually doing him a favor?" Sam asked with a grin.

"Of course!" Larry said with a twinkle in his eye.

The rest of the program went without incident. The number of calls into the request lines that night was the highest in history. Many of the callers did not request a dedication, but called just to offer support to the gang for taking a stand.

Tuesday, December 20, 1966
You Can't Do That

It was the last day of school before the Christmas break. Julia waited for the school bus to arrive to take her home. It was Jimmy's custom to wait with her before riding his bicycle home. "What are you doing for Christmas?" he asked innocently.

"Nothing," she answered. "We don't celebrate Christmas, remember?" It bothered her Jimmy did not seem to understand this. What was worse, he was not even interested in hearing about her family's celebration of Chanukah that had run for eight days starting on December 8 that year.

In fact, a lot of things about Jimmy were bothering her. They used to have a lot of fun running through the meadows near her house, climbing trees, listening to records, and playing board games. She still enjoyed doing these things. But somehow, it was not as much fun to do them with Jimmy as it used to be. He had changed. His jokes seemed silly to her, and were not nearly as funny as they once were. He also seemed so awkward when he tried to kiss her.

Her mom told her it was all normal. It actually wasn't Jimmy who was changing. *She* was the one changing. Jimmy was just a boy, not quite ready to grow into a young man, as boys did not mature as quickly as girls. Julia was starting to change into a young woman, and as she did, she would leave boys her own age, like Jimmy, behind. Her mom explained this difference in maturity was the reason she was becoming more interested in older boys like Larry and Jimmy's brother John.

But the worst thing about Jimmy was how jealous he got of everyone who tried to talk to her. Jimmy would even compete with his own brother if John paid any attention to her at all. And she had seen flashes of anger in Jimmy's eyes when Larry teased her.

It did not stop with the older boys. Greg Dunstan, a boy who lived not too far from Julia in the Steep Hollow community, rode the same bus to and from school. Even though a year younger than Julia, he had a crush on the pretty little blond-haired girl he saw twice a day. Jimmy, of course, was suspicious of Greg, even to the point he accused Julia of cheating on him with Greg as they rode the school bus together. Nothing Julia could say would convince him there was no hanky panky going on behind his back.

Greg walked up to Julia and Jimmy and greeted them. "Are you guys going anywhere during the holidays?" he asked innocently.

"She doesn't celebrate the holidays," Jimmy responded roughly.

"Yes, I do," Julia corrected. "I just don't celebrate Christmas."

"Whatever," Jimmy sulked.

"You don't celebrate Christmas?" Greg asked.

"No," Julia answered. "I'm not a Christian like you are. I'm Jewish."

"Oh," Greg said. "I didn't think about that. But you have a holiday called Han-a-caw, or something, right?"

"It's called Chanukah," she corrected mildly. "There are a lot of differences, of course, but we spend time with our families, and we give each other gifts, just like Christians do."

"That sounds neat," Greg said.

Julia smiled at him. "If you want to learn more about it, I'll explain it all to you during the ride home."

"Sure," Greg agreed. "I'd like to hear all about it!"

"No, you don't," Jimmy said with his nostrils flaring. "Julia is *my* girl, and I want you to stay away from her!"

Greg looked sheepish, but Julia came to his defense. "What do you mean by that? You don't own me, Jimmy. I'm not your girl in that sense. I can talk to him if I want to! If Greg wants to hear about Chanukah, then I'll be happy to tell him about it!"

Jimmy repeated his demand, "You stay away from her, Greg, or you'll regret it!"

"I'm not afraid of you," Greg said, gaining some courage.

Jimmy was angry because Greg had defied him. What made it even worse, Julia had also defied him. Using both hands, he reached out and shoved Greg, knocking him to the ground. At first, Greg was stunned, but he quickly regained his feet and was ready to fight, even though Jimmy was a year older and somewhat bigger than he.

A nearby teacher quickly intervened. "What's going on here?" she demanded. When neither of them said anything, she asked Julia if she had seen what happened.

"Yes, ma'am," Julia replied. "Greg wanted to talk to me on the way home, and Jimmy told him to stay away. When Greg refused, Jimmy pushed him down."

"Is that right, boys?" the teacher demanded.

"Yes, ma'am," Greg said. Jimmy just glared at Greg.

"I think you boys better shake hands and forget about this," the teacher said, "or would you rather have me take you to the principal and let him straighten this out?"

"No, ma'am," Greg said.

The teacher looked at Jimmy and waited. Finally, he gave in, "No, ma'am."

Greg offered his hand, and Jimmy shook it begrudgingly. The teacher suggested the boys go home and cool off. The school bus arrived and students began to climb aboard. Greg gathered his belongings and got in line with the other kids.

"I'll talk to you later," Jimmy said to Julia.

"Don't bother," Julia responded. "I'm through talking with you." She got in line behind Greg, who politely let her go in front of him. Once they got on the bus, Julia made a point of sitting with Greg, and made sure Jimmy saw she had done so. Jimmy watched silently as the bus departed.

"I'm through with him," Julia told her mother after explaining what had happened. She was both angry and sad, and there were tears in her eyes.

Jessica smiled at her daughter and tried to comfort her. "If it's any help, Julia, I've seen this coming for some time. You're growing up, and you've outgrown Jimmy."

"Why do boys have to be so stupid, mom?" she asked.

Jessica laughed at the question. "Girls can be just as stupid. What I'll never understand is why boys can still be stupid even when they grow up and turn into men! If you figure that one out, you explain it to me, OK?"

"It's a deal," Julia laughed. "Who needs them anyway!"

"Well, I do, for one," Jessica smiled. "And so do you."

Julia looked at her mom and giggled, "I guess you're right. But how do you stand it? Don't they finally grow up and stop being so stupid?"

"Not really," Jessica grinned. "When they grow up, I suppose they seem to be stupid less often, but it never stops completely. Every once in a while, however, they'll say or do something absolutely wonderful. And every time they do, you'll forgive them for all of the other stupid things they've said and done."

"What sort of thing will they do?" Julia asked dreamily.

Jessica looked at her daughter and laughed. "You'll never know what to expect. You fix yourself up perfectly, spending hours doing your hair, putting your makeup on just right, and wearing some beautiful new dress, and they hardly even notice. And then, one day you'll be all slouchy, but they'll mention how shiny your hair looks. Those silly little things like that seem to make it all worth while."

"Maybe they'll notice you're wearing new earrings or something?" Julia asked.

"Yes, that's the sort of thing." After a little reflection, she looked at her daughter and asked, "Has someone noticed you wearing some new earrings?"

"It was just an example," Julia answered, but the blush on her face told Jessica there was more to this story than her daughter was telling.

"Do you have a replacement?" Jessica asked. "Will Greg be your next boyfriend?"

"No!" Julia answered, a little too forcefully. "Wouldn't that be jumping out of the frying pan and right back into the fire? Greg is even younger than Jimmy! I think I'd like someone a little older next time."

"Not too much older, OK, sweetheart?" Jessica said simply. "Older boys are going to be interested in things you might not be ready for just yet. So far, you've only been on dates where a parent went along. We allowed you and Jimmy to go to the radio station in John's car, but we probably shouldn't have, really. Don't forget you're not allowed to go out alone with a boy in his own car. Not for another year."

"I know," Julia said sadly. "I wish I were a year older, like Linda and Helen, and had a boyfriend like the ones they have!"

"You like Larry and John, don't you?" Jessica asked.

"I sure do!" she agreed.

Jessica giggled, "They're just so dreamy, aren't they?"

"Oh, mom," Julia giggled back. "Don't tease me about that."

"OK, sugar," Jessica agreed, "I won't. They do seem to be nice boys. Maybe they're a little rowdy, but they're nice boys nevertheless. One of these days, you'll have a boyfriend like that, I promise."

"How can you be so sure?" Julia asked.

"I know a little about boys," she smiled, "and I know what they like. It won't be too long before you're going to start turning their heads so far you just might break some necks! Not to mention all the hearts you're going to break!"

"But I don't want to break anyone's heart," Julia said.

"You won't be able to prevent it, sugar," Jessica told her. "You should never do it on purpose, of course, but you'll break them, anyway."

The telephone rang and Jessica answered. After a moment, she turned to her daughter and said, "It's for you, Julia. It's Jimmy."

Julia looked sad for a moment, then announced, "Tell him I don't want to talk to him. I never want to talk to him again."

Jessica pursed her lips before replying, "Sweetheart, if that's what you really want, you should tell him so yourself. Don't ask another to deal with your dirty laundry."

"Please, mom?" Julia begged.

"No, bubee," Jessica smiled. "You have to tell him yourself."

Julia wanted to try again, but knowing she would never win this battle, she took the phone from her mom and brought it to her ear. "I'm sorry, Jimmy. I don't want to talk to you anymore. I just can't deal with your jealousy anymore." "It's not that I don't forgive you, Jimmy, but we've talked about this before." "I think it's time we stopped seeing each other." "No, I'm not going to change my mind." "I'm sorry, but it's over. Goodbye, Jimmy." Julia hung up the phone and looked at her mother.

"I guess that's the first one that gets broken," Jessica said a little sadly.

Tears formed in Julia's eyes. "What else could I do, mom?" she asked, pleading for an answer that would make her feel better.

Jessica gave her daughter a hug and answered, "Nothing, sweetheart. Like I said, sometimes you won't be able to prevent it, no matter how much you might want to. Whenever you know you must break someone's heart, do it just like that. Don't try to sugarcoat it. Don't try to hint at it. Just explain it to them, clearly, concisely, and even bluntly if you have to. Have a little mercy and do it sooner, rather than later, so they can get over it and get on with their lives. In the long run, they'll appreciate it."

Sunday, December 25, 1966
That Spirit Of Christmas

Christmas arrived like so many other times in central Texas – bright and sunny. Temperatures dipped into the mid-forties overnight, but this afternoon promised to be especially pleasant, with a cloudless sky, an afternoon high in the upper sixties, and only a slight breeze.

Any thought of snow was preposterous! Snow might come to Bryan once every ten years or so, whether they needed it or not, and even then only during the "hard winter" during those three or four weeks in late January and early February. Larry had only seen snow twice in his life. The first time was on Valentine's Day in 1959. A freak storm had passed through Bryan during the night and blanketed the ground with snow almost two inches deep! It was such a strange event all the schools were closed for a day. Larry's grandparents, who lived in the Rio Grande Valley of south Texas, jumped in their car and made the three hundred fifty mile drive north to Bryan just to see it for themselves! The other time he had seen snow was in the summer of 1961 when his family visited an uncle living in Portland, Oregon. They made an excursion to nearby Mt. Hood, where Larry climbed the dusty slopes far enough to find patches of snow surviving because they were sheltered from the sun by rock outcroppings.

Early on Christmas afternoons, Larry had a tradition of visiting his closest friends to wish them Christmas cheer, and to deliver small gifts. Linda would not be included this afternoon. She and her parents had gone out of town to visit relatives, and would not be returning until Wednesday. He had delivered her Christmas present earlier in the week, before she departed.

It was not the weather making Larry anxious this afternoon. He was concerned about how the final stop he planned was going to be received.

John answered the door when Larry rang the bell. "Merry Christmas!" they both shouted as they patted each others' backs. Guys found it difficult to actually hug each other in those days, even friends as close as they. John ushered Larry into the living room, where Jimmy and his father were watching a college football game. From the kitchen, Mrs. Myers stuck her head into the room to say, "Merry Christmas, Larry!"

"Merry Christmas, Mrs. M! You too, Mr. M, Jimmy!"

Mr. Myers acknowledged Larry. "Want to watch the game with us?"

"Oh, no thanks, sir," Larry smiled. "I only have a few minutes. Santa's helper has to make several stops this afternoon, doncha know." He noticed Jimmy had not looked up from the game, and was not reacting to the big plays like his father was. "How are you doing today, Jimmy?"

Jimmy's reply was flat. "Fine," he said without looking up from the game, and not reacting when one team intercepted a pass and returned it for a touchdown.

John responded to Larry's questioning look. "He's not been happy all week. He and Julia got into some kind of argument, and she hasn't spoken to him since." Jimmy got up, stormed into his bedroom and slammed the door behind him.

Mr. Myers looked up at the two older boys. "John, can't you feel a little sensitivity for your kid brother? She was his first real girlfriend, and he's really hurting. Don't you remember how it was when you broke up with your first girlfriend?"

John scowled slightly as he answered, "Yeah, I do. And I swore to myself I'd never let that happen to me again. If a girl wants to be with me, then fine, I'll be with her, but if she wants to dump me, then I'll just move on to the next one."

Larry looked sadly at his friend, and noted, "I envy you don't get hurt like I do when things go wrong, John. But you can never experience the true joy of victory unless you're willing to risk the agony of defeat."

John's father gave Larry a look of approval, "That's right, Larry."

"Well," Larry said wanting to change the subject, "I still have some Christmas spirit I need to spread!" He reached into the large bag he was carrying and handed John a package. "Merry Christmas, my friend!"

"Thanks," John said. He reached under the family Christmas tree and brought out the only package remaining and handed it to Larry. "And merry Christmas to you!"

The boys opened their packages simultaneously and let out a howl of laughter. They had given each other the same gift – a guitar music book containing songs by The Beach Boys including their most popular hits of the year, *Sloop John B, Good Vibrations*, and *Wouldn't It Be Nice*. John managed to stop laughing only long enough to say they should learn to play these songs twice as fast as usual.

Their mirth died down after a few moments. "I have a small gift for Jimmy, also. Do you think he'll talk to me?" John only shrugged.

Larry walked down the hallway, stopped at Jimmy's door, drew a deep breath, and then knocked. Jimmy responded with, "Go away, John!"

"It's me, Jimmy," Larry said calmly. "Can I come in?"

Jimmy sighed before answering, "I guess so."

Larry opened the door and peeked inside the room. Jimmy was laying on top of his bed on his stomach. He did not look up as Larry entered, so Larry closed the door behind him. Sitting on the end of Jimmy's bed, he reached into his bag for a small package, and said without much enthusiasm, "I have something for you."

When Jimmy turned to look at him, Larry could see his eyes were red and damp. Larry knew all too well what it meant. After all, he had often done the same thing. He felt sympathy for his young friend, but knew there was nothing he could say or do that would possibly be of any help. The only cure for a broken heart was time, but time is too long for those who grieve. "Would you like to tell me about it?" he asked. "Sometimes it helps to just get it off your chest. I should know. I've had more experience with this sort of thing than you could possibly understand."

Jimmy dried his eyes with a pillow case. "Why? All I want to know is why?"

Larry looked down and sighed. "The eternal question," he said, not really meaning to say it aloud. He looked directly into Jimmy's eyes. "My life would be so much simpler if I only knew the answer to that one question, Jimmy. I've asked it myself more times than I want to count. The best answer I've ever heard was simply, *Because.* Maybe, in truth, there's no answer at all." He waited a few moments before asking, "How did it happen?"

"I should have paid more attention to your advice," Jimmy sniffed. "I was jealous, jealous of everyone who so much as spoke to her. I was jealous of you, John, and even Sam! I couldn't help myself. I just want to be with her so much!" Jimmy closed his eyes as the tears streaked his cheeks. "What am I going to do?"

Larry had asked himself that question on many occasions. "You're going to survive. You're going to pull yourself up by your bootstraps, brush yourself off, and move on. That's all you can do." Jimmy looked at him with such intensity it made Larry hurt. "I'm sure by now someone has told you there are plenty of other fish in the ocean and so forth. I'm not going to tell you that. It's all bullshit! Right now, the ocean could be so full of fish they were overflowing onto the shore, and it would make no difference at all. When there's only one fish that matters, who cares how many others there might be?"

Larry felt tears forming in his own eyes. "I believe every one of us has someone out there who is our perfect soul mate. There's one for me, and there's one for you. Maybe you thought you'd found yours. I've thought I've found mine many times." Larry paused when Jimmy put down his head, sobbing for a moment.

When Jimmy regained some composure, Larry continued. "But you know what, Jimmy? I've always been wrong! It'll take some time before you realize it, but you will in time. You think Julia was your soul mate. But what does that really mean?"

"It means she's the perfect girl for me, the one I want to spend my life with."

"Yes," Larry nodded. "But the perfect girl for me will also think I'm the perfect guy for her. If she doesn't want me, then she's not perfect! Like I told you once before, the important thing is not that you want to be with her, but she wants to be with you. So if Julia was really the perfect girl for you, then she'd think you're the perfect boy for her, and she'd want to be with you, am I right?"

Jimmy looked bewildered. "Yes," he agreed, "she would."

Larry asked him a direct question, "Could you ever get so mad at your perfect girl you'd send her away, possibly forever?"

"Of course not!" Jimmy answered.

"Of course not," Larry agreed. "But she got that mad at you, didn't she? So ask yourself this question – is Julia really the perfect girl for you?"

Jimmy's eyes filled with tears again. "I guess not."

Larry smiled to himself. That was the first critical step, the realization the girl you wanted so badly was not so perfect after all. "The truth is, Jimmy, no one is absolutely perfect. It's not physically possible. If you think about it, you change from moment to moment. One moment, you might want to be silly, and the next moment, you might want to be serious. The perfect girl would have to change her mood from moment to moment, and somehow perfectly match her mood to yours."

The second part was to restore hope. "If she's not really the perfect girl for you, then she's not your soul mate, is she? But everyone has that perfect soul mate out there somewhere, including you. Don't you see what that means, Jimmy? It means your perfect soul mate is still out there, looking for *her* soul mate. She's hoping her soul mate will come and find her! And her soul mate is you!

"I know it's not easy right now, but in a little while, after a few days or even a few weeks, you'll see I'm speaking the truth. You will survive." Larry repeated his earlier statement, this time as an imperative. "Pull yourself up by your bootstraps, brush yourself off, and move on. She's still out there, somewhere. Go find her!"

Jimmy suddenly felt a kinship with Larry he had never felt before. "I'll try, Larry. I want to be with Julia so much! Why doesn't she want to be with me?"

"Because," Larry answered with a shrug and half a smile. "Because."

After a moment of silence, Larry handed Jimmy the small package. He looked at it for a moment, then opened it gingerly. It was a plastic model kit of a 1967 Chevy. "Do you remember when you, me, and John went down to the Chevy dealership a few months ago? We all liked the new models, but you were the most excited. You swore to us you'd be the first to own one. Looks like you were right!"

Jimmy managed a small laugh. "Thanks, Larry."

"You're very welcome, Jimmy. Merry Christmas!" Larry walked out of the room, and was ready to close the door behind him, but Jimmy was already up and moving.

As he returned to the living room to watch the football game with his father, Jimmy turned to Larry and said, "Thanks for everything, Larry."

Larry just smiled. "See you later!"

John followed Larry outside to his car. "What did you say to him?"

"Just the truth, John," Larry grinned. "Just the truth. Do you think Jimmy will want to keep doing the radio program with us now?"

"I doubt it," John replied. "He told me he only did it because it was a way he and Julia could spend more time together."

"That's what I figured," Larry said thoughtfully. "I wonder if Julia will want to keep coming." John smiled but made no comment. "See you later, John," Larry said as he started his car. "Merry Christmas!" He waved and backed out of the driveway.

"Hello, Mrs. K," Larry greeted Sam's mother at the door. "Merry Christmas!"

"Merry Christmas to you, Larry," she said warmly. "Susan will be right out. Would you like a Christmas cookie? I just took a batch out of the oven."

"They smell just wonderful!" Larry said following her to the kitchen.

Gayle Kronkite was delighted. She loved the attention she received from her daughter's friends, especially the boys. Since her husband passed away, she seldom got much attention from males, except the boys who came to see her daughter, Susan.

Sam bounded into the kitchen wearing the bright smile Larry liked so much.

"Merry Christmas, Larry!" she grinned grabbing a cookie. "Mom's trying to make us all fat!"

"And she'll do it," he chuckled, "if she keeps baking cookies every time I come over! Thanks, Mrs. K." He reached into his bag and drew out a package, handing it to Sam's mother. "This is for you. Merry Christmas!"

Gayle was truly surprised. "Oh, you shouldn't have gotten anything for me. Save your money for all those girlfriends you must be collecting!"

"But you and Sam *are* my girlfriends!" he grinned. He knew Mrs. Kronkite was lonely, and he often wished he knew a single gentleman about her age. He fetched another package from his bag. "Speaking of girlfriends, this one is for you, Sam." The smile Sam gave him cheered Larry. She always seemed able to do that.

Gayle Kronkite opened the package, finding a ceramic cookie jar shaped like an old steam locomotive. "Oh, how sweet," she said, giving Larry a hug. "If you two don't eat them all up, I'll have some cookies to put in it!"

Sam opened the small package Larry had handed her. Inside was a crystal figurine in the shape of a unicorn. Sam gazed at it with a bit of wonder. When she held it up, she noted how it sparkled in the sunlight.

"The way it sparkles reminds me of your smile, Sam," Larry stated. The little unicorn was light and delicate, and definitely held a feminine charm. Sam was a little taller than the other girls, and Larry knew she sometimes felt clumsy, like maybe she was a little less feminine than she was in reality. He knew the real reason she was a little taller than other girls was because she had long, shapely legs. Everything about Sam was very feminine!

The little unicorn touched her in a way he did not expect. Sam gazed at Larry with a bit of wonder. *Can he actually read my mind the way he sometimes teases?* Without saying a word, she cupped Larry's cheek in her hand and kissed him on the mouth. As she withdrew, he reached out and held her neck. "Whoa there, big boy!" she grinned. "My boyfriend might understand the first course, but not seconds!"

Larry was disappointed, but managed a laugh. "It's the story of my life. One of these days, I'm going to chase that guy away so I can have you for myself!"

Sam just smiled at him while her mother giggled. She escorted Larry into the living room and sat him on the couch. She reached under the tree, found a package, and handed it to him with a smile. "We didn't forget you," she said, winking to her mother who was being included in the gift.

Looking at the package, and based on its weight, Larry could see it was a book of some kind, or maybe more than one. He figured it must be a music book. But when the wrapping paper was removed, he saw it was a collection of children's books by Doctor Seuss. He looked at Sam with a smile on his face and a question in his mind.

She smiled back at him and answered the unspoken question. "You think you're so clever, making fun of old Mrs. Hannah and all those kids on Saturday mornings, pretending to be the typical teenager. But I see how you look at those kids when no one is watching. It's as plain as the nose on your face. Someday, you're going to need something to read to your *own* children, and I want you to have the very best."

Larry was touched deeply. He stood up and hugged her, and then hugged Mrs. Kronkite. "Oh, Sam, I don't know what to say."

"How about saying Merry Christmas?" Sam replied.

"Yes," he agreed with a smile. "Merry Christmas!" After a moment of reflection, he changed the subject. "Did you know that Jimmy and Julia have broken up?"

"I'm not surprised," she said. "I could see that relationship wasn't going to last."

"Why do you say that?" he asked.

"Because, silly," Sam chuckled, "he's just a little boy. Julia may be only fourteen, but she's growing up fast, and she's getting interested in older guys. Like you!"

Larry was genuinely surprised. "Oh, come on, Sam. She's just a little girl. Besides, what interest would she possibly have in someone like me?"

"She's not going to be just a little girl for long!" she laughed. "The worst thing I see about them breaking up is she might not come to the radio station anymore."

"I thought about that," he said.

Sam studied her friend's eyes and saw the sadness in them. "You don't like the idea of not seeing her again, do you?"

"It doesn't matter to me," he said at first. "I'm with Linda!" He then lowered his head and added softly, "Well, it shouldn't matter, anyway. Oh, hell, Sam! Regardless of who's with whom, Julia is still my friend. You're absolutely right. I don't like the idea of not seeing her again!"

"I doubt we'll see much more of Jimmy, either," Sam noted. "But I'll bet Julia would keep coming to the station if someone asked her to."

"Probably," he said softly. "She did seem to be very enthusiastic about it, ever since that first program."

"So why don't *you* ask her?" Sam suggested with a slight grin. "Don't try to fool me, Larry. I saw the way you looked at her when she came to the library after the Halloween program. And I've noticed other things, too. You still have a thing for that little green eyed monster!"

He sighed. "OK, Sam, I'll admit I like her. There's something about her I find fascinating. She's just a cute little girl right now, but I can see she's going to become quite a knock-out when she gets a little older!"

"I thought so," Sam said pleased with herself.

"But, you need to understand some things," he added. "First of all, I'm with Linda. But even if I wasn't, I made a promise, Sam, a solemn promise to Jimmy. He thought I was flirting with her at the birthday party. Maybe, I was; I don't know. But I promised him I wouldn't make any move for Julia as long as he wanted her. I just came from there, Sam. I can assure you, he still wants her!"

"So then ask her as your friend!" Sam said. "I'm not saying you need to dump Linda and chase after Julia. But if she's really your friend, and if she still fascinates you in other ways, then for heaven's sake, *do* something about it!"

"I don't want to do anything that might be misinterpreted, Sam," he argued.

"OK," Sam said softly. "Then *I'll* ask her to come back to the show."

"You'd do that for me, Sam?" he asked.

"I'd do anything for you, Larry," she answered sincerely. "You're my friend! Someone has to help you find the mother of those children you're going to read those books to," she added with a laugh.

He laughed, also. "Well, I think it's a little early to start thinking about that sort of thing. Unless *you're* volunteering, that is!" he said, reaching out to grab her.

"I'll leave the room so you two can be alone," Mrs. Kronkite snickered.

"You pervert!" Sam screamed, slapping his hands. "Julia is my friend, also. Isn't that reason enough for me to ask her to keep coming back to the show?"

When the mirth settled down, Larry announced he needed to go. "Guess where I'm going next?" he asked.

Sam was astonished at the obvious answer. "You're going to play Santa Claus at the Jacobson house? Maybe I should rethink some things. You've even got bigger cajones than *I* thought!"

"I may not have them for very much longer," he chuckled. "I suppose it depends on how Mr. Jacobson reacts to this visit! Merry Christmas, Sam! Merry Christmas to you, Mrs. K!" He was in a good mood when he got into his car and backed out of the driveway. One more stop to go.

As Larry pulled his car into the Jacobsons' driveway, he felt a knot forming in his stomach. He had given a lot of thought to this visit, but finally decided, *Damn the torpedoes! It's the right thing to do.* That did not cure his anxiety, but it braced his courage, and he was determined to carry it through.

He stopped his car and got out quietly. Walking to the front door, he suddenly realized unlike the others, the Jacobsons would not be expecting him. *If it would be done, then let it be done quickly!* he decided, and reached to ring the doorbell.

He smiled when he heard Schotzy barking. A moment later, Mr. Jacobson answered the door. "Hello, Larry! Come on in. Julia is in the back. I'll take you."

"Thank you, sir," he replied. They walked through the house without a word, and exited onto the patio, with Schotzy following.

"Julia," Julian called. "You have a visitor."

Julia was sitting on a branch about halfway up the willow tree. The tree looked somewhat bare in its "winter" foliage, but Larry did not even notice the tree. It was the first time he had seen Julia in her tomboy mode, and it fascinated him. Various thoughts flashed through his mind. He found himself fighting the urge to climb up that tree and join her! Fighting to clear his mind of those thoughts, he said quickly, "Actually, Mr. Jacobson, I've come to see *all* of you. Is Mrs. Jacobson around?"

With a look of surprise, Julian replied, "Why, yes. She's inside. Would you like me to ask her to join us?"

"If it's not too much trouble, sir," Larry said politely. Julian left to fetch Jessica, and Julia waved as she started climbing down the tree. "Don't fall!" he teased. "I won't be able to catch you."

She moved deftly from branch to branch, quickly reached the ground, and ran up to face him. "You were saying?" she laughed. He merely grinned at her. Julian returned with Jessica just in time to hear Julia ask, "Why are you here?"

Larry looked very serious. "Well, why are *any* of us here? I mean, isn't this the ultimate question of life and everything? There are those who think..."

Julia laughed. "No, no, no! Not that again! I mean why are *you* here?"

"Everybody's got to be somewhere!" he replied. "Oh, I see what you mean. I wondered why you wanted to discuss philosophy and the meaning of life. I mean, it's sort of unusual for young people today to question such things, and..."

Julia laughed again. "Stop! I mean what *brought* you here today?"

Larry glanced at her parents, then back to her. "My car, of course."

Julian and Jessica exchanged a smile. They had gotten used to Larry's dry wit, and wondered just how long he planned to keep this joke going. They also wondered why he wanted to see all of them, and not just Julia.

Starting to feel exasperated, Julia demanded, "What are you *doing* here?"

"It appears," he replied with a grin, "that I'm discussing philosophy with you and your parents. It really makes no difference to me, but if that's what you want..."

"You creep!" Julia exclaimed laughing. "Why did you get in your car and drive out here to see us today?"

Julian laughed aloud and asked, "Is this going to take long, Larry? Jessie, could I ask you to bring me a cup of coffee? I'm already getting dehydrated from this!"

"Why don't I get us all some," Jessica suggested. "Would you like some coffee, Larry?" He nodded in the affirmative. "And you, Julia?" When she also nodded, Jessica returned to the house to prepare the coffee. The rest of them took seats around the patio table under the branches of the willow tree.

"I still can't get over this tree," Larry commented. "It looks so sad right now. No wonder we call it a *'weeping willow'* sometimes." When there was no response from either Julia or her father, he changed the subject. "I went by John's house earlier this afternoon. John's father was watching one of the bowl games on TV. Do you like to watch football, Mr. Jacobson?"

Julian gazed at him with a puzzled look. *Surely this boy has not driven all the way out here to ask me that!* "Sometimes, but I prefer professional football. My team is the New York Giants, and they don't appear on the local station very often, except when they're playing your Dallas Cowboys, that is. You're aware the Cowboys will be playing the Green Bay Packers for the NFL championship next Sunday, right?"

"I don't know much about professional football, but I should have known your team would be from New York," Larry replied. "Do you miss living in New York?"

Julian decided the boy was stalling for time. "There are some things about New York I miss, but on the whole, I'm very happy we moved down here. For one thing, there's no way we'd be sitting outside this late in December if we were in New York."

"Yes," Larry agreed. "It is a beautiful day, isn't it?"

Jessica returned from the house with a small tray containing a carafe of coffee, a creamer and sugar bowl, along with four cups and spoons. Larry jumped from his seat as she approached the table.

"No need to get up, Larry," she urged. "I can handle it." She sat the tray on the table and began to pour coffee into the four cups.

Larry blushed. "Force of habit, I guess. I was taught to stand when a lady..."

Jessica smiled. "Why thank you, sir! And how do you take your coffee?"

Larry was not sure what she meant. He seldom drank coffee, and was not familiar with the proper etiquette. When Julian said he would take his black as always, Larry decided imitation was the safest course. "I'll take mine black, also," he said.

Jessica and Julia exchanged a grin. "I'll take lots of cream and three sugars, please," Julia giggled. She only drank coffee on occasion, and she always doctored it to be more like a milkshake than coffee.

When everyone was served, the Jacobsons all looked at Larry expectantly. When he did not appear to be forthcoming, Jessica smiled at him and posed the question, "Well, Larry, what do you have on your mind today?"

He could not think of a flippant answer to the direct question she had posed. At least, there was not one he wanted to share aloud. So he was caught in the net, and knew it was time for him to come clean. He looked at Mrs. Jacobson with an appreciation of her ability to force him to come to the point. With a great deal of hesitation, he began, "Well... you see, it's like this. Uh... Well... That is..."

"Oh, get on with it!" Julia laughed.

"Just relax, boy," Julian grinned. "We're not likely to kill you. Are we, Jessica?"

"Only if he keeps stalling," Jessica giggled.

Larry blushed with embarrassment. "I know, I know. It's just that, well, I'm not too sure how to approach this subject." He paused to gather his courage, then stated, "OK, I know in your religion, you don't recognize Christmas as a holiday..."

"That's right," Julian stated bluntly. "Frankly, I'm a little surprised to see you here today. Shouldn't you be at mass, or something?"

"No, sir," Larry replied looking flustered. "Actually, mass is a Catholic thing. I'm not Catholic, doncha know."

"In your church, then," Julian suggested.

Larry was getting more worried. "Well, yes sir. I mean, no sir. I mean... Wow, this is harder than I thought it'd be!" When the others just looked at him, he gathered his courage and continued, "Look, this may be a surprise to you, but the way I've been taught, Christmas isn't a religious holiday to me, either!"

Julian was genuinely surprised by this remark. "What? Are you not Christian?" He looked at Jessica for some confirmation.

"Yes, sir," Larry responded. "I am a Christian, but... well, there are a lot of different kinds of Christians. Well, that's not exactly what I mean either, but I guess it's as close as I can get to explaining this to you."

"We're listening," Jessica assured him. "Go ahead."

Larry took a deep breath. "Well, all this Christmas stuff is really just something that the Catholics invented. As I understand it, some Pope decided they needed to have a Christian holiday to compete with the pagan holiday of the winter solstice, and so they declared a special mass on December 25 to celebrate the birth of Jesus. As far as I know, there's no actual evidence to indicate He was born on this day at all. It seems more likely it was sometime in the spring rather than in the dead of winter."

Julian noted, "Believe it or not, Larry, I've heard this before. What's your point?"

"I was taught," he continued, "that we... I mean, Christians should celebrate the birth of Jesus not just once a year, but on every day of the year. In fact, in my religion, there are no religious holidays at all! Unless you want to count Sundays, I guess. We treat every Sunday as a holiday, but don't observe any of the other so called Christian holidays. Christmas, Easter, you name them, they aren't religious holidays to me. I pay about as much attention to them as I do Ground Hog Day!"

The Jacobsons looked stunned as he continued, "Look, to me, Christmas is a day when friends and families get together just to celebrate being together. We give each other gifts, and to me, the best thing about Christmas is the spirit of giving. I like to give gifts to the people who are special to me, and well, I can't think of any reason why that shouldn't include the three of you!" Following that comment, he reached into the bag he carried with him and brought out a nicely wrapped box and handed it to Mr. Jacobson. Another was given to Mrs. Jacobson, and a third was placed in front of Julia. Then he looked at each of them and in turn said, "Merry Christmas!" Then to all, he said, "Please accept these small gifts in celebration of friendship."

Mr. Jacobson was speechless. Jessica's voice cracked a little as she expressed her feelings, "Thank you, Larry. I think this is the sweetest thing anyone has done for us since we moved here." Julia just looked at Larry in wonder.

"Well, open them up!" he urged. "The best part of giving a gift is seeing the expression on people's faces when they open it!" His face was aglow with a beaming smile. "Why don't you go first, Mr. Jacobson?"

Julian looked at his wife, who nodded at him to proceed. He removed the wrapping paper and found a cardboard box. He reached inside the box and removed a bottle of Mogan David wine. Larry beamed with excitement. "I hope you like it. I couldn't buy it myself, of course, so I convinced an older guy I know to buy it for me. I told him I wanted something kosher, and he came back with this. I hope it's OK?"

Julian smiled at his wife, and responded, "It's just fine. Thank you very much."

Larry was relieved. He was confident of the other gifts, but had been unsure of that one. "Go ahead, Mrs. Jacobson," he suggested, turning his attention to the next gift.

"Why don't you call me Jessica?" she smiled.

Larry blushed. "Oh, I couldn't do that! Would it be OK if I called you Mrs. J?"

She smiled as she answered, "That'd be just fine, Larry." Looking at the package, she asked, "Now what could this be?" The package was about twelve inches square, but only a quarter of an inch thick.

"It's a pony!" Larry whispered to Julia.

Julia giggled, but Jessica laughed out loud. "Then I guess I'd better hurry and let it out before the poor thing suffocates!" She tore back the wrapping paper to reveal the jacket of a record album, the soundtrack to *Oliver!* "Oh, thank you so much, Larry! I can't wait to play this!"

"If you would be so kind, Mrs. J, please wait until I'm gone before you play that track." He pointed to the song he had sung a few weeks ago in nearly the same spot he was sitting. He forced a smile when she looked up at him. Jessica understood he might still be embarrassed by that song. She returned his smile in agreement.

"Now, it's your turn," Larry said to Julia with a genuine smile.

Julia returned his smile and pulled the wrapping paper from the box. There was an unmarked cardboard box underneath. As she opened that box, she exclaimed, "Oh, how pretty! Look, mom! It's a music box!" She carefully removed it from the packaging, wound it up, and opened the lid. It played the old Beatles song *From Me To You*. Julia's eyes smiled as broadly as her mouth. "Oh, thank you, Larry. This is so sweet!" She leaned over and hugged him.

Time stood still once again. Larry blushed and mumbled it was nothing, and he hoped they would all enjoy the gifts, and that sort of thing.

Julian stood up from the table. "I have some things I really should be doing right now." Turning to Larry, he added, "Thank you for your thoughtful gifts, Larry. I never thought I would say something like this, but well... Merry Christmas to you." With that, he turned and walked into the house.

"Wow!" Julia said simply after he disappeared.

"Indeed!" Jessica added with a giggle in her voice.

They looked at each other, and then back to a somewhat mystified Larry. No one said anything for a few moments. Larry broke the silence with, "I really missed doing the radio show last night."

"Me, too," Julia agreed. "I need to get used to not doing it. I guess I won't be going up to the station any more, unfortunately."

"You can if you want to," Larry stated simply, without any further explanation. When Julia started to protest, he added, "You can come anytime you like, Julia. I've already been by to see John this afternoon. I've spoken with Jimmy. I know the situation. Look, Julia, I still want to be your friend, and I hope you still want to be mine. John and Sam feel the same way. We'd like you to stay on the show. If you want to, of course."

Julia looked sad. "But Jimmy..."

"Jimmy wasn't part of the show before you came along," he interrupted, "and John tells me he isn't interested in coming back. On the other hand, John, Sam, and I all want *you* to stay, and we think that's what you want, also. If you do, then you're welcome to join us. We'll be like the *Four Musketeers!*"

Julia looked a little surprised at first, but then smiled at him. "But I can't drive. I don't have a way to get there," she hinted.

"Linda and I will pick you up Saturday, if you want, Julie," he said.

"That sounds great!" She then realized he had mispronounced her name. "You called me *'Julie'*. My name is Julia."

"Oh, I'm sorry," he replied. "I guess I like to think of you as *'Julie'* for some reason. I won't do it again," he said with a pronounced sadness in his voice. He was not sure why he suddenly felt so sad.

"It's OK," she said. "I kinda like it. You can call me *'Julie'* if you want to."

Larry was relieved. He wasn't sure why it was important to him, but he really did want to call her "Julie" for some unknown reason. He smiled, but all he could think to say was, "I should go." He realized he had just used the code talk. Leaving was the last thing in the world he wanted to do. "Bye, Julie. I'll see you Saturday."

"Yes," she said simply. "Bye, Larry."

He said goodbye to Jessica, walked around the house, turning back once to wave at them, got in his car, and started home.

Julia and Jessica watched Larry walk away. They smiled at him, returned his wave, and saw him disappear around the corner of the house. They heard his car start and listened to the sound of the engine fade as he turned it around, drove out the driveway, and departed down the country lane.

"Mom," Julia said breaking the silence. "Can I talk to you about something?"

Jessica smiled. "You like that boy, don't you, sugar?"

"Yes," Julia said softly. "I really do."

"The problem with being a girl," Jessica began, "is we don't get to choose what boy comes calling. All we can do is encourage the ones we like. The problem boys have is they take a chance of rejection every time they call on a girl. It's a funny game." She saw the worried look on her daughter's face and added with a giggle, "But it's a lot of fun to play!"

Julia giggled as well. She then reflected, "I think Larry might be the main reason why I broke up with Jimmy. I accused Jimmy of being jealous, and he was, but the more I think about it, maybe I'm just as guilty. I'm jealous of Linda. To me, she has everything! She's pretty, popular, and has a really nice boyfriend! She's told me over and over about how wonderfully he treats her. I want to have the same things."

Jessica smiled. "You already have all those things, Julia. You're pretty..."

"Oh, mom," she said. "Now you're just talking like my mother. How can I be pretty with all this metal in my mouth?"

"It'll all come out soon enough," Jessica reassured her, "and you'll be even prettier than you are now. You're already just as pretty and popular as Linda. Jimmy was a nice boy. You'll find a new boyfriend soon enough."

"I guess so," Julia agreed slowly. "But he was just a little boy! He's not like Larry and the older boys. Do you think he likes me?"

Jessica could not keep from laughing. "Larry? Of course he likes you! Why do you think he came here today?"

"Did you know," Julia asked, "Larry was the only one who noticed I had my ears pierced? He spotted it that day in the library, just after it was done. Jimmy never said anything about it."

"Some boys," Jessica said wistfully, "are just more observant about things. I guess that's how he learned you like music boxes, as well. Your father is that way. I just realized Larry reminds me a lot of your father. I didn't actually know your father at Larry's age, but I can see they're alike in many ways."

"Daddy was like that?" she asked.

"Oh, yes, Julia! He was just *dreamy!*" she laughed. "In many ways, he still is. Your father has always been a very romantic man, with a great sense of humor. He only acts like the stern father because he loves you, and wants to protect you."

"I know he loves me," Julia said, "and I love him. I love both of you, mom!"

"And I love you, sugar," Jessica responded.

Julian walked into the kitchen and glanced at the bottle of wine. "Do you think you can do something with this? Can you cook something with it?" he asked Jessica.

"Don't you want to drink it, Jules?" she teased.

"Get serious, Jessie," he replied. "You know my tastes in wine."

Jessica just grinned. "I can probably figure out something to do with it. It's the thought that counts, Jules."

"Yes," he agreed. "The boy's heart is in the right place, but this stuff is *ghastly!*"

"Don't you dare let him know that, and don't let Julia hear you say it, either! She has a more than casual interest in that boy."

"I would think after all these years," he pouted, "you'd know me better than that!" Then, a little more seriously, "She has a thing for him, does she? How bad is it?"

"No worse than you might expect," she grinned, "and anyway, he has another interest right now." Jessica put the bottle of wine away, and she and Julian retired to their bedroom. "It was sweet of him to get us anything," she said as she prepared for bed. "The record he bought me is something we can both enjoy, and Julia, of course, is thrilled to have another music box for her collection."

Julian simply grunted as he pulled back the covers and slid into bed. Jessica slid in on the other side and snuggled up beside him. "Our little girl is growing up," she said with only a little sadness. "Oh, the adventures she's going to have!"

"Not all of them will be pleasant," Julian added.

"No, but isn't that the way life is supposed to be?"

"All we can do is prepare her as best we can, but in the end, we can only place her into God's hands and pray He will take care of her."

"One of these days, some boy is going to come to you and ask you to place her into *his* hands. Are you going to be ready for that?"

"Probably not," he grinned. "I just hope it's some nice Jewish boy."

"And if it isn't? What if a boy like Larry were to come to you in a few years and ask you for her hand. What would you do then?"

"Well, whoever he is, I hope he has better taste in wine!" When she did not react to his joke, he looked at her. One glance told him her question was serious. "I don't know, Jessie. I'd rather not think about that right now. I know I'm getting old, but I still have a few years before this happens, don't I?"

Jessica laughed at him. "You? Old? You'll never get old! You're only as old as you let yourself be." She kissed him warmly. "But I think I should warn you not to wait too long. Time has a way of slipping past without you noticing."

"I know, my love, I know." When he returned her kiss, Jessica rolled over on top of him and stroked his chest. They kissed again, caressing each other like so many other times over the years. When they made love, it was as fresh and wonderful as that first time, so long ago in that secret place they found in Central Park.

Wednesday, December 28, 1966
You've Got To Hide Your Love Away

The Livingstons had left to visit some relatives for the holidays on last Wednesday, the first day school had been closed. They were expected to return this afternoon. Larry asked Linda to call him when they got home so they could get together that evening. When 6:00 o'clock rolled around, he was concerned, and decided to try calling her.

Mrs. Livingston answered, "Hello!"

"Hello, Mrs. Livingston," he said, a little surprised to find they were home. "This is Larry. May I speak to Linda?"

"Of course," she replied. "Just a moment."

He waited patiently for Linda to come to the phone. "Hello?"

"Hi, sugar, it's me!" he said brightly. "Did you have a good trip?"

"It was OK."

"When did you get home?"

"About 4:00, I think."

"Oh," he said, feeling a little confused. "I was hoping you'd let me know."

"I'm sorry. I forgot. I guess I'm a little tired from the trip."

"That's OK," he said sincerely. "I've missed you, and I'd really like to see you tonight! Are you too tired to go out?"

"No, I'm not too tired," she said a little flatly. "I missed you, too."

"About 7:00 then?" he asked hopefully.

"Sure," she replied. "See you at 7:00. Bye!"

He thought Linda sounded a little odd. Maybe she really was just tired from the trip. He decided he would not keep her out too late. After some rest, she would probably be her old self again.

At 7:00, he was at her front door, welcomed enthusiastically by her mother. Mr. Livingston had already retired, exhausted from the long drive. Larry waited alone in the living room while Mrs. Livingston went to fetch Linda. She came to the living room wearing blue jeans and a new sweat shirt, greeting him with a hug and a kiss.

"Hi, sugar. If you're hungry, let's grab a bite and decide what to do this evening."

"Fine," she smiled. "Don't wait up, mom! I'll be home by midnight."

Larry opened the door for her as usual, and she snuggled against him as they headed to the Buccaneer. "You sounded tired on the phone. Are you OK?"

"I'm fine," she said. "Maybe I *am* a little tired."

"If you want me to take you back home after we eat, it'll be OK. I've missed you, but I can wait until tomorrow night to spend more time with you. I have to work until 8:30 on Thursdays, but better late than never, right?"

"No, I'm not that tired. Actually, I've been thinking about you all day long as we drove home. Let's eat, and then get down to some serious monkey business!" She grinned at him and placed her hand on his thigh.

After dinner, they drove out to their favorite parking spot and began to engage in their favorite activities. After sharing a smoke, they got down to some serious necking and some enthusiastic sexual exercises. As they basked in the afterglow, they snuggled together while Larry attempted to prepare another joint for them to share. "I missed you a lot more than I thought!" he laughed.

"I missed you, too," she agreed.

"What would you like to do tomorrow night?" he asked casually.

Linda smiled at him as she answered, "How about doing the same thing we did tonight? I happen to know you like doing that."

"You like it, too," he grinned. "I was thinking maybe we could have a pizza and then do a little bowling. You seemed to enjoy that last time, and we haven't gone bowling for a couple weeks." Then he remembered he was expected to work on Thursday nights. "Oh, rats! I forgot tomorrow is Thursday and I have to work until 8:30. What do you say we wait on the bowling until Friday?"

Linda's smile was weak. "I'm sorry. I have other plans for Friday night."

"Oh," he said, a little stunned. He quickly realized these plans of hers could mean anything. "Some sort of family thing?" he suggested hopefully.

"No," she said softly. "Someone else asked me out, and I said yes."

Now he was *truly* stunned. "I see," he said, trying to appear casual.

"You're upset," she said. "I'm sorry, Larry. I didn't figure you'd mind too much since we're not actually going steady or anything."

"We aren't?" he asked. "I mean... Linda, I know we never talked about it, but I just kinda assumed... Well, what I mean is, I figured our relationship was special."

"It *is* special," she smiled. "I always have fun when I'm with you. You do everything just right so I get my cookies every time."

"You do everything just right so I get *my* cookies every time," he snickered. He paused a moment thinking about the implications of her going out with someone else. "OK, I guess I just assumed too much about our relationship. I'll try not to be jealous you're going out with another guy, but I hope it'll be the last time. I'd like to go steady with you. After that date is over, will you go steady with me?" He caught her attention so she was looking in his eyes. "I love you, Linda," he said sweetly.

"Oh, don't say that, Larry," she said with a slight grin.

"Why not?" he asked smiling. "You know it's true. I *do* love you!"

Linda looked at him cautiously. "No, you don't love me. I don't want you to love me. Can't we just have a good time without getting so serious?"

"I don't understand," he said looking confused. "You don't want me to love you?"

"That's right," she said looking him directly in the eyes. "I'm not ready for that sort of thing. I just want to have a good time. Can't we just have fun? Can't we just have sex and smoke pot and enjoy everything without having to bring love into it?"

Larry was astounded. She was expressing an attitude a lot of guys had. He never thought he would hear this from a girl! "I can't help how I feel, Linda. These last two months have been the best time of my life! I want it to keep going!"

"That's what I want, also," she said. "At first, I had to teach you how to please me. But now, you are doing things, wonderful things, that really turn me on! Do you know how many times I got off while we were doing it tonight?"

"I wasn't counting," he said sadly. "To me, we were making love."

"Love has nothing to do with it," she said strongly. "I'm not ready for love. I don't want to settle down with just one guy, even a hot stud like you. I want to experience everything life has to offer! Don't you?"

"Of course I do," he said. "One of the things I want to experience is the joy of knowing there's someone who wants me, someone who needs me, someone who loves me. Don't you want that?"

"No," she said, "at least, not yet. I'm only fifteen years old, Larry. There'll be plenty of time in my life for love. Right now, I just want to have fun."

"I love you, Linda," he tried again.

"I'm sorry, but I don't feel that way," she said. "I like you, I like being with you, and I like fooling around with you. But I'm not ready for a serious relationship. It's not just you. I don't want a serious relationship with anybody! To tell you the truth, Larry, I don't even want to go steady with just one guy, even a great guy like you!"

"But..." he tried.

"No, Larry," she said pointedly. "I think you'd better take me home."

He stared at her for a moment in disbelief, but realized his old nemesis had caught up with him again. It was a surprise to him, but he realized his feelings for her had advanced way out in front of her feelings for him. Slowly, he slid back underneath the steering wheel and started the car. This time, Linda did not slide next to him.

He drove her home in silence, trying desperately to think of something to say. The truth was everything had already been said. There was nothing more he *could* say. Their relationship was not what he thought it was! To him, he and Linda were lovers. He was ready to start planning a future together. That was obviously not what she was thinking.

As they neared her house, he asked her, "Where do we go from here, Linda?"

She did not respond until they got to her driveway. "I don't know," she said sadly. "I'd be happy to keep seeing you, but I don't think it'll ever be the same. Do you?"

He parked in the driveway and got out of the car, this time walking to open the passenger side door for her. He escorted her to her front door and looked into her eyes, trying to fight back his tears. "I still love you, Linda, even if you don't love me."

Standing in her doorway, she looked at him sadly. "I'm so sorry, Larry," she said softly. "Believe it or not, I never meant to hurt you. I thought you understood. I think the best thing would be to end it now, before either of us gets hurt any worse." She looked into his eyes one last time, and said, "Goodbye, Larry." With that, she turned away from him and closed the front door behind her.

Thursday, December 29, 1966
Yesterday

John's car was already in the station parking lot when Larry arrived around 8:45. He fetched his guitar from the trunk and entered through the main door. Through the glass panels in the main control room, Diggs waved at him and smiled as he walked past. Larry waved back, but found he could not bring himself to smile. He walked down the corridor and came to the back entrance to the smaller recording studio.

John greeted him as he entered. "Hi, guy!" he said cheerfully.

"Hi, John," Larry said without enthusiasm. "I appreciate you coming tonight."

It was quite obvious to John Larry was unhappy. He decided not to press that matter immediately. "I have most of the equipment already set up. All we have to do is load a blank tape onto the recorder and adjust the sound level."

"I appreciate that," Larry said dully. "If possible, I'd like to do this in one take."

Larry and John had originally planned to do this song live, and had practiced it many times. Making the recording in one take was not unreasonable. Still, John was mystified by the sudden change in plans. "One take, eh? What made you change your mind about doing it live?"

"I'm not sure I could do this song if anyone is watching, John."

"Does that include me?" John asked smiling, in spite of his growing concern.

"I can trust you, John," Larry said flatly without looking at him.

"Yes, Larry," John said simply. "You can trust me. I'm glad you know that. Would you mind telling me what this is all about?"

For the first time since he arrived, Larry looked John in the face. John saw his facial expression was empty, yet there was a telltale redness in his eyes. He had none of that sparkle he usually exhibited, no trace of twinkle in his eyes. "I find this song hits a little too close to home. Linda doesn't want to see me anymore."

"What happened?" John asked.

"I don't know," he said truthfully. "I said something wrong, just like in the song!"

John shook his head in dismay. "What did you say to her?"

"Just three little words," Larry stared at the floor. "I love you."

John saw tears were now streaming down his friend's cheeks. He tried to think of something to say, but could not come up with anything appropriate.

"It's the story of my life, John," Larry continued. "I find someone I like, and everything seems to be going along just great. Then out of the blue, it all goes to pieces, usually at the point where it does the most damage. Just like this time. Just as I was beginning to feel my luck had finally changed."

"I find this hard to understand, Larry," John said. "You told her you love her and she doesn't want to see you anymore? What precisely did she say?"

Larry looked at him with despair in his eyes. "She said all she wanted was to have a good time, and didn't want to get involved in a serious relationship. We've had some great times together, but she was not in love with me, and didn't want me to be in love with her. She said that would spoil everything. She broke all of the dates we had arranged, and told me to go away."

John looked stunned. "Are you sure? Maybe she was just feeling... I don't know! Maybe it's one of those female things I can never understand."

Larry nodded his head. "I'm very sure. I don't think I'll ever understand females, but I'm quite sure she isn't *on the rag* right now, John. You know how you always call me the eternal optimist? I've tried and tried to come up with some explanation, *any* explanation offering any hope at all. But I can think of nothing." He looked at John hopefully, but John was silent, unable to think of any explanation other than the obvious one. "I won't make a fool out of myself this time, John. I tried to convince her to stay, but she refuses. I'll follow the advice I gave Jimmy, and move on."

Larry fetched his guitar from its case and indicated to John he wanted to get started. John retrieved his guitar and they made sure they were in tune with each other. They played a few bars together and got the sound levels adjusted. When everything was ready, John nodded to Larry, and started the tape recorder. The short guitar introduction was followed by Larry's solo voice as he sang the Beatles classic *Yesterday*. A steady stream of tears flowed from Larry's eyes during the entire song, but his voice never wavered, never faltered. The rendition was an absolute and undeniable expression of pure emotion, of a heart shattered beyond repair.

After a few moments of silence, John stopped the recorder. He looked at Larry, who was trying to dry his eyes, and waited. When Larry looked at John, they silently agreed, baring any technical problems, there would be no need for a second take.

"You listen to it, John," Larry pleaded. "I'm going to the can. If it's OK, then we're done. I hope so. I'm not sure if I could do it again."

As Larry got up to leave the studio, John said softly, "Go ahead, Larry. I'll meet you in the lobby and let you know." He rewound the tape, and listened to the song from beginning to end. He rewound it again and sat in silence for a moment. He flashed a signal to Diggs, "Can you listen to this song and give me your opinion?"

"Sure," Diggs said. "I have at least five minutes before I need to do anything." Diggs patched his headset into the appropriate channel, and John pressed the button to start the playback. When the song ended, Diggs switched back to the intercom. "Damn! You guys have a real winner there! I like that one even better than the original. Was that Larry's arrangement? That string quartet the Beatles used was beautiful, but there's something really moving in what you guys did. Larry was really in fine voice, and your guitar was even better than all those strings!"

All John said was, "Thanks, Diggs. We'll play it on the air Saturday night." He rewound the tape one last time, and cataloged the recording in the log. He packed both guitars and carried them out to the lobby.

Larry was standing at the front door looking out when John arrived. "OK, John?"

"Yes. It's much better than OK. Would you like to hear it?"

"I'll hear it Saturday. There's no way I could do that song live."

"I understand," John said.

Larry noticed John was carrying both guitars. "I'm sorry, John. I didn't mean to make you do everything yourself. I'm not thinking very clearly, I guess."

"It's OK," John said reassuringly.

Larry took his guitar from John. "Thanks. I'll see you Saturday."

Saturday, December 31, 1966
Alone Again (Naturally)

Larry drove into Julia's driveway a little after 7:00. The only evidence something was different was Sam was in the front seat, not Linda. When it occurred to him he had promised to pick Julia up to take her to the station, he knew he had to do something. First, he doubted the Jacobsons would let their daughter go to the station with him alone. Secondly, in his state of mind, he was not sure how he would react when he saw those green eyes of hers. Finally, there was the matter of the promise he had given Jimmy. Larry begged Sam until she agreed to ride with him.

"I'll be right back," he told Sam after parking the car. As he was closing the door, he stopped and asked hopefully, "Unless you'd like to come with me?"

Sam smiled as she asked, "Are you afraid?"

"Yes," he said seriously. Slowly, his face changed into a slight smile as he shrugged and headed to the front door. Sam understood the pain he was going through, but she was helpless to do anything to ease that pain.

Julia did not meet him on the sidewalk like she had done a few weeks back. He walked all the way to the front door and rang the bell. Mrs. Jacobson greeted him warmly, "Hello, Larry. Julia's almost ready."

"Thanks, Mrs. J. We're not in a rush. Did Julie tell you we have extended hours tonight? Since it's New Year's Eve, we're going to be on the air an extra hour, until midnight. We'll ring in the new year before ending the show. She'll be a little later than usual, if that's OK."

"Yes," she replied. "She told me. I like that bright yellow shirt you're wearing!"

"Thanks, Mrs. J," he said simply.

There were some traditions in which one wore yellow on New Year's Eve to show one is searching for their true love. Jessica concluded Larry was probably unaware of the tradition. "Is that Sam in the car with you?"

"Yes, ma'am," he said sadly.

Julia came to the entryway before Jessica could pursue. "Hi!" she said brightly.

"Hi, Julie," he said with as much enthusiasm as he could muster.

Julia smiled warmly at him, enjoying the sound of her new nickname. "Are you going to wait up for me, mom?"

"If you want me to, sugar," Jessica replied. She turned to Larry and added, "If you kids want to come here after the show, you can have some traditional Yankee style New Year's food. No black-eyed peas, but plenty of bagels, cabbage, and herring!"

"It sounds nice, Mrs. J," Larry said flatly. "I'll pass that along to the others and see what they think."

"Give me a call a little later, Julia," she instructed, "and let me know whether to stay up and wait. Have a good time, kids!"

"I will, mom," Julia agreed. She and Larry walked through the front door and headed towards the car. "Is that Sam in the car?"

"Yes," he said without explanation. He did not know whether knowledge of the breakup was wide spread yet. His blood suddenly ran cold when he thought what Linda might tell her friends, particularly Julia, about the relationship they had shared. He quickly concluded there was nothing he could do about it, and since he was not ashamed of what he had done, there was no reason to worry about it, either.

Saturday, December 31, 1966 – Alone Again (Naturally)

They reached the car and Larry opened the passenger door for Julia to get in. Sam surprised him by jumping out of the car. "Why don't you take the middle, Julia?" she suggested with a smile. "Larry likes to have a pretty girl sitting close to him."

Julia giggled and asked, "So why didn't *you* scoot over then?" But she didn't wait for a response. She slid into the middle seat, grinning at Sam who climbed in behind her. Sam winked at Larry, who shook his head and closed the door.

Larry walked to the other side and climbed behind the wheel. Julia smiled at him sweetly as he did so. He forced himself to return her smile, but said nothing, grateful Julia did not snuggle up to him the way Linda always had. On the other hand, maybe he wished she would! At that moment, he really hated that promise to Jimmy!

Sam and Julia did most of the talking on the way to the station, while Larry simply drove the car and tried to look natural. Inevitably, the subject he wanted to avoid came up. "Where's Linda tonight?" Julia asked him. "Is she still out of town?"

"No," Larry answered flatly. "I'm not sure what she's doing."

Julia looked baffled, then turned her head towards Sam, looking for an explanation. "Larry and Linda are not..." Sam started.

"We broke up," Larry said without emotion.

"What happened?" Julia asked with surprise. She thought Larry and Linda were about the most perfect couple she knew. Linda always spoke so highly of Larry, and it was clear Larry was crazy about Linda. Julia, in fact, was quite jealous of their relationship, wishing she had a boyfriend like Larry. Suddenly, it dawned on her with Linda out of the way, she just might have that chance!

"I'd rather not talk about it," he said.

"I'm sorry," Julia said sincerely. "I didn't mean to pry."

He looked at her with a sad expression. "I'll be OK, Julie. I'm just confused right now." For Sam's benefit, he added, "I'm confused about a *lot* of things."

The opening bit for the show was performed live by Sam and John. Larry had no enthusiasm to do anything, especially anything to do with comedy. When finished, they turned the microphone over to Larry to read the first set of dedications. When he did so without enthusiasm, Sam privately suggested to Larry he just stay off the air that night.

When the commercial break between the first and second segments began, Larry disappeared into the men's room and stayed there. The second segment was to be opened by the recording of *Yesterday*, and Larry was not sure how he was going to react to it. He sat out the song in one of the stalls, grateful he had the sense to get away from the others. While artistically, he thought the recording was the best rendition of the song he had ever done, his reaction to hearing it was much the same as it had been on Thursday night when he and John recorded it. He did not want anyone to see him in that condition. The problem, of course, was *he* could look in the mirror and see *himself* in that condition.

A few minutes after the song ended, he washed his face, collected his wits, and returned to the main studio. Sam could easily see the signs of damage on his face, and tried to comfort him as best she could. "Your song was beautiful, Larry. I understand how difficult it must have been for you, but the results are fabulous. Hang in there, my friend. Things will get better."

"I know they will, Sam," he replied softly, forcing a brave smile. "I have nowhere to go from here but up."

Larry, of course, was not the only one feeling sad that night. This was Julia's first trip back to the radio station since her breakup with Jimmy, and it brought back memories she wanted to forget. Seeing how sad Larry was only seemed to make matters worse for her.

For the opening of the third segment, they decided to play a tape of *The Ballad Of Lizzie Borden* by the Chad Mitchell Trio the boys had made a few weeks earlier. While it was playing, Larry realized they had played this song at Julia's birthday party, which reminded him of where he and Linda had first gotten together. He decided to spend the rest of the song in the men's room once again.

While trying to recover, his thoughts turned back to the night of Julia's birthday, and he remembered just before *The Ballad Of Lizzie Borden*, he had sung *Where Is Love?* from *Oliver!* Obviously, Linda was not the source of that *"sweet hello"* meant only for him. *What about that prayer? Where is she? If only my eyes could see her face!*

It seemed like Larry had barely returned from the men's room before the fourth show segment was to begin. Once again, they had chosen to dip into the archives to play a song Larry and John had taped sometime earlier. It was the Beatles classic *You've Got To Hide Your Love Away*, a very appropriate song for the occasion. Larry reminded himself he must not let his feelings get ahead of the next girl he would find. *Whoever and whenever that might be,* he thought sadly.

Because of the extended hours for the New Year's Eve show, there was a fifth segment. Since there had been so many requests for it, they elected to play the tape of *Green Eyes And Sam*. Once again, Larry disappeared discretely, realizing he no longer had Linda to distract his attention from the true inspiration for that song. *Will those green eyes now drive me completely insane?* he wondered.

"Where's Larry?" Sam asked, gathering the entire troop into the main studio so they could count down the final seconds and welcome in the new year.

"He was here just a minute ago," Julia said.

"I haven't seen him for a few minutes," John said. "Maybe he went to the can. Do you want me to go look for him?"

"No," she said. "He'll show up. There just isn't time." It occurred to Sam Larry might want to spend most of his time alone. If that were so, then there was no point in looking for him. If not, he would be along any moment.

The final song ended, and Diggs cued the microphone in the main studio. "It's almost midnight, gang!" Sam announced. "We want to thank you for listening tonight. In just a moment, we'll count down the final seconds of 1966! In the meantime, I want to thank our guest stars for helping us out tonight."

"I'm Helen!" she announced.

"And I'm Julia!" she said enthusiastically.

"John, Larry, and I want to thank you for making us part of your New Year's Eve celebrations! Here it comes, guys!" They all joined in and counted down the final seconds. "Ten... Nine... Eight... Seven... Six... Five... Four... Three... Two... One... Happy New Year, everybody!"

Diggs started a recording of Guy Lombardo's *Auld Lang Syne* playing it underneath the whoops and hollers of the kids in the main studio. He slowly faded

Saturday, December 31, 1966 – Alone Again (Naturally)

the studio microphones, leaving just the recording, then signaled the microphones were dead.

Larry wanted to be alone with his thoughts. When he thought no one was watching, he sneaked out of the studio and walked out the front door into the cold night air. Nothing these kids did escaped the watchful eye of Diggs, however, who noted Larry's departure. Diggs had observed Larry's usual girlfriend was not with him, and Larry had been unusually quiet the whole night. His conclusion was the relationship had faltered. Now he understood the source of all that emotion in the recording of *Yesterday* Larry and John had made. He felt sorry for his young friend.

Larry stood alone in the cold, brisk air. He was tempted to fetch his stash from the car and fire up a smoke, but concluded that would not be a very smart thing to do. Who knew who might happen to drive by and see him there?

He stood under the light of a three quarter moon and reflected on the past year. 1966 had been a year with a lot of highs and lows. He had discovered computers, and recognized this would become his career. He had raised his popularity a great deal, primarily by his music and by his participation in the *Top Forty Showcase* radio program. He had experienced sex for the first time. Many boys his age would have been thrilled by such accomplishments.

But as the year drew to a close, Larry felt empty. *What am I going to do?* he wondered to himself, hoping one of those stars up there in the sky would provide him an answer. It was not one of the stars, but a voice within his brain providing the answer he sought. *You're going to survive,* it told him. *You're going to pull yourself up by your bootstraps, brush yourself off, and move on. That's all you can do.* The realization of the truth, of course, did not reduce his pain. It intensified it. Linda was obviously not the girl he had been looking for all his life. The tears flowing down his face were caused more by the thought he now had to start his search all over again, rather than the pain of loosing her.

On top of it all, there was this strange attraction to that little green eyed girl inside, and the problem of a promise he had made. From the speaker in the lobby, he heard the others in the studio as they counted down the clock to welcome the new year. "Ten... Nine... Eight..." they called. Larry tried to pull on those bootstraps, but found he did not have the strength to lift himself up. "Seven... Six... Five... Four..." they counted. He tried to brush himself off, especially the tears flowing so freely from his eyes, but they were not cooperating. "Three... Two... One... Happy New Year, everybody!"

There were a few superstitions Larry subscribed to. One of them had to do with New Year's Eve. Whatever he was doing at the stroke of midnight as the new year began was something he would repeat over and over again during the coming year. Based on that superstition, Larry expected 1967 was going to be a year filled with more heartache, loneliness, and tears. *How is that going to be so different from all the previous years?* he asked himself.

1967

Sunday, January 1, 1967
The End Of The World

"That's a wrap, guys," Sam announced. "Great show! What do you say we get everything cleaned up and get out of here?" John went off to file the tapes while Helen and Julia started picking up the note paper. Sam was going to look for Larry, but decided to stop by the control room first to ask Diggs if he had seen him.

"He stepped outside," Diggs replied. "I think he wanted to be alone for a minute."

She met him at the front door just as he was stepping onto the landing. "Hi, Sam," he said nonchalantly. "Show over?"

"You know damn well it is!" she flashed. "Where were you for the countdown?"

"You did just fine. You certainly didn't need me. No one needs me." Sam started to speak, but he held up his hand to silence her. "I needed to be alone for a little while, Sam. I didn't want anyone to see me at that particular moment. OK?"

Sam softened her mood. "I'm sorry, Larry. You seemed to be doing so well, I forgot..." Seeing the redness in his eyes, she suggested, "Why don't you go to the men's room and wash your face. If anyone asks, I'll tell them you got sick at your stomach and have been in there for the last few minutes."

"Thanks, Sam," he said. "You're the best!" They went inside and Larry turned down the hallway towards the men's room. Sam returned to the control room to file away the records played that night. After washing his face, Larry joined John to help finish the task of logging the tapes they had used, filing them back into their permanent storage locations. Soon, all of the cleanup tasks were completed. As they walked past the control room on their way to the door, the kids all mouthed a "Happy New Year!" to Diggs, who grinned and mouthed the same wish back to them.

They decided to decline the invitation of Mrs. Jacobson to go back to Julia's house to begin New Year's Day celebrations. Julia called home earlier to let her mom know she was off the hook for the early morning gathering. The gang already planned to meet at Julia's house later that afternoon for a guitar rehearsal.

John and Helen waved goodnight and headed for his car yelling, "Happy New Year, everybody!" Larry, Sam, and Julia returned the wish and headed for Larry's car. When he opened the door, Sam again insisted Julia take the middle position.

They drove first to Julia's house. The simple truth was it would have been more convenient to take Sam home first, but Larry wanted to avoid that. First, he was not sure how Julia's parents would react. More importantly, Larry was not sure how *he* would react. When they arrived at Julia's house, Larry hopped out to open the passenger door for the girls as he normally did.

Sam beat him to it. She opened the door herself and jumped out of the car, allowing Julia to follow. "Goodnight, Julia! I hope you have a very happy new year!" she said giving Julia a friendly hug.

Julia returned the hug. "Thanks, Sam! I hope you do, also."

While he escorted Julia to the front door, Larry looked back to see Sam grinning at him, apparently daring him to do the same. When they reached the landing, he offered, "Goodnight, Julie. May you have a very happy new year!"

"You, too, Larry," she said sweetly, giving him a hug. He saw an expectant, almost hopeful look in her eyes, but was in no condition to interpret its meaning. He returned her hug, but when that ended, he looked sadly into her eyes and repeated, "Goodnight." Julia went inside, turning back to watch Larry return to his car. She waited until the car had started down the driveway before closing the door and heading for her room.

Julia could not see the tears flowing from Larry's eyes as he walked back to his car, but they were clearly visible to Sam. She watched them as he climbed back into the car and started the engine. She noted how carefully he turned the car around and drove down the driveway returning to the country lane taking them back to town. "Would you like to talk a little while, Larry? I could use a smoke, anyway."

He thought about her suggestion for only a moment. "Yes, Sam. I think I'd like both." He drove the short distance up the lane and turned onto the gravel road, stopping at the spot where Sam, John, and he had smoked once before, rather than the spot where he and Linda had spent so much time together. After parking the car, Larry retrieved the materials, and handed a joint to Sam. "Ladies first," he said without emotion, more out of habit than anything else.

Sam smiled as she took the marijuana and proceeded to light it. She took a light draw and immediately passed it to Larry. "I think you need this a lot more than me."

"I'm OK," he tried to assure her, unconvincingly.

"Can you explain something to me?" she asked. "You and I both know you're very interested in Julia. So why don't you go after her?"

Larry pulled on the joint and passed it back to her. "I've already explained this to you at least once. I really don't understand what it is about her that draws me so. But anyone can plainly see I'm just too old for her right now."

"Which is it, Larry? Are you too old for her, or is she too young for you?"

He looked at her and smiled weakly. "I'm not surprised you'd recognize the difference. No, Sam, I said it exactly the way I meant it. She's not too young for me, at least not as far as I'm concerned. I think she's very special, and I'd really like us to get together. But I'm too old for her."

"Why do you say that?" Sam asked. "I don't think *she* thinks you're too old for her. I think she'd be thrilled if you paid a little attention to her."

"Can you imagine what her parents would say if I asked them for permission to take her out on a date? They don't want her to start dating for at least another year."

"They let Jimmy take her out on a double date with John and Helen."

"Yes, and I think that even surprised her! But they were very insistent John take her directly to the station, and then bring her directly home after the program."

"So you believe her *parents* think you're too old for her," Sam said pointedly.

"Perhaps you're right," he agreed. "I'm not at all sure how they'd react to me."

"So why not try and *see* their reaction?" Sam asked. "What have you got to lose?"

"Because I made a promise. You know how I feel about promises."

"That promise to Jimmy? What exactly did you promise him?" She was hoping to find a loophole so he could pursue the interest she could see so obviously.

He sighed before responding. "I promised I wouldn't make a move for his girlfriend, Julia, until he told me he was no longer interested in her."

"Ah, ha!" Sam said. "You're off the hook! She isn't his girlfriend any longer!"

"But he still wants her to be, Sam," he said. "He'd take her back without hesitation. I know you're trying to help me, but using a silly technicality like that would be a violation of his trust. You know that just as well as I do."

She knew he was right. "But, Larry, all is fair in love and war!"

"But this is neither of those," he insisted. "I'm in love with *Linda!* That's the real cause of my problem! If Linda isn't ready for my love after everything we've shared together, then why do you think a girl who's even younger would be any better?"

"So what are you going to do?" Sam asked.

He thought about his answer for quite a few seconds. "I've had my heart broken before, Sam, and I survived. I guess I ought to be used to it by now. I'm going to try to get myself back together. Then I'll start looking for my dream girl again. One of these days, I'm going to find her. If I didn't believe that..."

Sam did not want to think about what he would do if he truly lost all hope. "And what about Julia? Hasn't she been in your dreams?"

He had to think about that question for a while, also. "Yes, she's been in my dreams, but I don't understand what those dreams mean. I'll certainly keep my eye on her, Sam. Maybe I'll figure it all out someday. Maybe not. When she gets a little older, and I'm freed from the promise I gave Jimmy, maybe I'll make a move for her. Doesn't that sound like the sensible thing to do?"

Sam considered his options. "No, Larry, it doesn't. I think you should make your move for her right now. You have the perfect opportunity. She doesn't have another boyfriend, and I'll give you my personal guarantee she's interested in you!"

"And what about my promise to Jimmy?" he asked sadly.

"Screw Jimmy!" she said.

"If you think it would help him forget her," he snickered, "then go ahead. I'll leave that decision to you. Personally, I'm not qualified."

Sam just shook her head sadly. "Someday, you're going to regret this decision."

"You may be right, Sam," he said. "If that's the case, then maybe you can help me correct it. For now, all I ask is you respect my reasons."

There was a moment of silence between them. Noting they had finished the first joint, he asked Sam if she wanted another. "I guess not. Maybe I'm not in the mood."

"Me, either. I should take you home." Sam recognized the code phrase. He really needed some company, but she was soon encouraged by the way he overcame his despair. "Unless you've finally come to your senses. Are you ready to dump this Donald character and be *my* girl?" he asked with a faint grin, and even fainter hope.

She returned his grin, thinking this was more like the Larry she knew so well. "I'd just end up breaking your heart."

"You already have," he chuckled as he started the engine. He then added seriously, "Sam, every girl I've ever loved has broken my heart. It occurs to me every girl I ever *will* love will break my heart. Except maybe one – the last one, and then only if I'm lucky enough to die before she does."

Sam laughed, but recognized the sad truth to this bit of philosophy. He drove her home and leaped out of the car in order to open the passenger door for her. She just shook her head and smiled. As they walked to her front door, she turned to him and said, "Happy New Year, Sir Galahad, my dear friend. I hope you will finally find happiness this year."

"Thank you, sweet thing," he replied. "Happy New Year to you, also. Somehow, I don't think 1967 is going to be my year. But they say hope springs eternal."

Sam put her arms around his neck and hugged him warmly. When he returned the hug, she kissed him on the cheek. They stood there for several moments because neither of them really wanted to release that hug right away. Eventually, Sam looked him in the eye and said, "I have to go in. Goodnight, Larry."

Larry returned to his car and started the short drive home. He had not slept much for several days, and nothing would change tonight. As he drove home, a song popped into his head, *The End of the World*. Somehow, it just seemed appropriate.

"Good morning, mom, and happy new year!" Julia said entering the kitchen.

Jessica smiled at her daughter, a little surprised to see her up so early. "Happy new year to you, too, sugar," she replied. "Would you like some breakfast?"

"Sure," Julia said enthusiastically. "I'll help you make it!"

"Thanks!" Jessica smiled. "It'll just be the two of us. Your dad is probably going to sleep in this morning. He celebrated a little more than he intended last night."

Julia giggled, "Did he drink that bottle of wine Larry gave him?"

"No," Jessica laughed, "I think it had more to do with the bottle of scotch he bought for himself yesterday. Would you like some coffee this morning?"

Julia thought about that question for a moment. "Yes, I would! I think I'll even cut down on the milk and sugar this time."

Jessica smiled and poured her daughter a cup of coffee, then freshened her own. Julia added some non-dairy creamer, one sugar cube, and stirred. She frowned a little when she took her first sip. "It's a little bitter, but I guess I could get used to it."

"You will if you want to," Jessica assured her. She and her daughter laughed with each other as they shared the simple pleasure of preparing breakfast – bagels, cream cheese, lochs, and capers. As they sat down to eat, Jessica turned the conversation to the events of the previous night. "What's the story with Larry and Sam?"

"Larry and Linda broke up," Julia said simply. "That's why Linda wasn't with him. I'm not sure why Sam was riding with him. Maybe she's his new girlfriend."

"They broke up?" Jessica asked, surprised. Julia nodded in confirmation. "That's quite a shock! I thought they were getting along so well together!"

"So did I, mom! The last time we talked, Linda was going on and on about how great he was treating her, what a nice Christmas present he'd given her, and how much she was looking forward to spending more time with him over the holidays."

"Did he talk about it last night?" Jessica asked.

"I didn't hear him say a word about her all night," Julia answered. "I got the feeling John and Sam were talking about her after the song *Yesterday*, but I didn't quite catch the meaning. Apparently, Larry and John originally planned to sing it live, but Larry changed his mind. They recorded it Thursday, the day after he and Linda broke up. All I caught was they recorded it on one take, because he couldn't have sung it live."

"Did he act any differently last night?" Jessica asked, probing for information.

Julia thought before answering. "Yes, he *was* different. He didn't joke and cut up like he usually does. He might have been sick, because he spent most of his time in the restroom. I don't think he even teased me about anything all night long! And he looked really sad when he walked me to the door and told me goodnight."

Jessica saw some disappointment in her daughter's eyes with that last comment and decided to pursue that angle for a while. "He walked you to the door?" she grinned. "What else did he do?"

"Nothing," Julia answered sadly. "Sam even forced me into the middle of the car seat so I was sitting beside him all the way there and all the way home. I think she was trying to push us together! I guess he walked me to the door just to be polite. I've heard both Sam and Linda tease him about being a perfect gentleman, calling him *Sir Galahad*. When I wished him goodnight, I gave him a hug. He hugged me back, but that was all there was."

"No kiss, eh?" Jessica smiled. When Julia did not return her smile, she added, "I imagine he's very hurt and confused about things right now, sugar. From what you have told me, it sounds like Linda broke up with *him*, not the other way around."

Julia looked confused. "Why would she do that?"

Jessica just smiled and suggested, "Why don't you give Linda a call in a little while to wish her a happy new year, and see if she wants to tell you anything."

They finished their breakfast and cleaned up what few dishes there were. Julia went back to her room to finish getting dressed. The gang, or what was left of it, would be coming to her house that afternoon. She wanted to talk to Linda, but her mom suggested she wait until noon before calling.

Promptly at noon, Julia dialed the number for the Livingston's house and asked to speak to Linda. "Happy New Year!" she greeted as Linda got on the line.

"Thanks, Julia. Happy new year to you, also."

"How was your trip?" Julia asked, hoping Linda would address the subject first.

"Fine."

Julia thought it must be obvious to Linda she wanted to talk about her breakup with Larry, but Linda apparently did not want to talk about that subject. "Did you listen to the show last night?" she asked. "What did you think?"

"Yes, I listened," Linda answered flatly. "It was a very good show."

"Did you hear their version of *Yesterday*? What did you think?" Julia asked.

"I heard it," Linda answered without further comment.

Julia tried a different approach. "Will you be coming over to my house with the rest of the gang this afternoon?"

Linda paused before answering. "I don't think that would be a good idea."

There was a long pause in the conversation. Julia could see Linda was not going to volunteer any information, so she posed a direct question. "What's happened between you and Larry?"

"I don't want to make you angry, Julia," Linda said, "but that's our business, and not anyone else's. All you need to know is it's over between us."

"But why, Linda?" Julia asked. "When we talked just the other day, you told me everything was *great* between you two. Maybe it's not any of my business, but I really do want to know. I consider both of you to be my friends. I *need* to know." When Linda continued to remain silent, Julia begged, "Please?"

"It's just one of those things," Linda provided hesitantly. "We were looking for different things. He's looking for a longterm relationship. I just want to have fun."

"I don't understand," Julia said honestly. "Weren't you having fun?"

"Yes, we were having fun together. That was exactly what I wanted! That was *all*

I wanted! But he told me he loved me. I think he wanted us to start planning for a future together. I'm only interested in the present, not the future."

Julia was very puzzled by this comment. "Couldn't you have both?" she asked innocently. Linda did not answer. After a few moments, Julia gave up, deciding she could probably get an explanation from her mom. "OK, Linda, I guess it's not any of my business. I'm sorry. Are we still friends?"

"Of course we are," Linda replied. "I'm sorry, too."

Larry was the first to arrive, much to the delight of Schotzy, just before 2:00 o'clock. Mrs. Jacobson greeted him at the front door, "Happy New Year, Larry!"

"Thanks, Mrs. J," he said politely. "I hope you have a happy new year, also." He looked down at the dog and added with little enthusiasm, "Hi there, boy!"

Jessica could see the sadness in his eyes, especially since the redness did so little to hide it. He looked very tired and very miserable. She smiled warmly, "Thanks, Larry. Come on in out of the cold. Would you like to get a head start on some of the goodies? Have you ever eaten herring?"

"No, ma'am," he said a little too politely. "I mean I've never eaten herring. Perhaps I should go ahead to be out of their way when the rest of the gang gets here."

She could see how utterly miserable he was. Hoping to cheer him up a little, she chuckled, "You're too late. Julia and Julian have already started!"

"Hello, Larry," Julian greeted him. "Happy new year to you!"

Larry forced a smile. "Thanks, Mr. J. Happy new year to you, also." He looked at Julia and quietly added, "Hi, Julie."

Julia smiled at him. "Dig in!"

"Let me put these things down," he said, indicating his guitar and music case, "and I'll be right with you." He carried the items into the family room and placed them next to the hearth. The door bell rang again as he returned to the kitchen.

Mrs. Jacobson greeted John and Helen and escorted them to the kitchen. John was exuberant at the sight of the goodies. "Wow! What a layout, Mrs. J! It looks great!"

Jessica smiled at him. For one thing, she was pleased he appreciated the food. Additionally, she liked the nickname Larry had chosen for her, and was pleased the other kids were also picking up on it.

Sam arrived a few moments later, and another round of greetings was exchanged. Soon, all of them moved to the family room to eat the traditional foods and to talk. John and Helen took their usual place on the hearth, while Sam lounged on some large pillows. Julia sat on the sofa; Julian and Jessica positioned themselves on the love seat.

Larry was left with the choice of standing or joining Julia on the sofa. Jessica noted he chose the sofa, but positioned himself at the opposite end. He only picked at his plate, mostly sneaking food to Schotzy, who was, as usual, snuggled up as close to Larry as he could get. She also noticed that while the conversation was almost as lively as usual, one of the players was uncharacteristically quiet. Other than to compliment Jessica on the food, Larry said little unless spoken to directly.

When everyone finished eating, Jessica began to gather the dishes. Julia made a point of getting Larry's dishes herself, and smiling sweetly as she did. He thanked her and forced himself to return her smile. While Jessica and Julia were in the kitchen, John fetched his guitar and began to tune it. "Are you ready to get started,

Larry?"

Larry hardly made a move. He looked at John, and then at Sam, and said, "I really don't think I'm much in the mood for singing just yet, John."

John looked at him sadly. "I understand. Maybe you'll be ready in a little while?"

"Maybe. I'm sorry." He looked through the windows into the back yard, then stood and headed to the back door. "I think I'd like to take a little walk."

"Would you mind if I tagged along?" John asked.

"Not at all, John," Larry said. "I think I'd like that."

The boys walked to the back door and left without another word, the dog following closely. When Jessica and Julia returned, Julian told them, "The boys went for a walk. I don't think Larry is feeling well."

John followed Larry outside and stood silently while Larry looked up into the branches of the old willow tree. It was not hard to guess Larry was remembering the night he and Linda had first gotten together. After a moment, he looked back down to the ground and shook his head, as if trying to clear it of those thoughts. He started walking in no particular direction, leaving the patio, and heading out into the pasture behind the Jacobson house. Essentially, the dog was in the lead. John walked along in silence, knowing Larry would speak when he felt like it.

The dog led them through the tall, dry grass along a path wandering down to a good sized stock tank. Larry stopped on reaching the tank and stared into the murky waters. He reached down to pick up a small flat stone, and threw it with a spin onto the surface of the water. The stone skipped across the surface several times before sinking. "What am I going to do, John?" he asked as he picked up another stone and skipped it across the tank.

John picked up his own stone and skipped it on the water before speaking. "I hope you're going to follow your own advice, the same advice you gave Jimmy. Pick yourself up, brush yourself off, and get on with living."

"Good advice," Larry agreed. "How's Jimmy doing, by the way?"

"Better than you are, but only barely. What is it about the holidays that causes so many couples to fall apart?"

"That's a good question, John," Larry said picking up another stone. "I'll have to give that some thought. It looks like I'll have plenty of spare time on my hands. Are you and Helen getting along OK?"

"We're fine," John responded softly. He saw Larry's eyes were ladened with tears as he skipped another stone across the water. "Would you listen to some advice?"

"Of course," Larry said, looking around for another stone.

"Why don't you go back to the house and show some interest in that little green eyed monster who's been bothering you ever since the night you met her?"

Larry looked John in the face. "You, too, eh? That's what Sam wants me to do."

"So how about it?" John asked sincerely.

"You know the answer better than Sam does, John," Larry said calmly.

"Fuck that promise!" John insisted.

Larry actually managed to laugh at the suggestion. "At least that's better than Sam's idea. She wanted me to fuck Jimmy!"

John stared at his friend for a moment and then laughed. "I'd tell you to go ahead, but I don't think I could stand to hear all the bragging he'd do if he somehow managed to get himself laid before I did!"

Both boys laughed at the thought. "Speaking of getting laid, are you and Helen making any progress these days?"

"Still stuck on second base," John grinned. "Other than that, everything is fine."

"In many ways," Larry said sadly, "I wish I was still stuck there, also. Maybe I wouldn't hurt so much. I know a lot of guys who'd kill for the kind of relationship Linda was offering. All the sex I wanted, with no strings attached. No commitment. No attachment. Just great sex!"

"Is that all it was, Larry?" John asked.

"I guess so," he answered. "She didn't want me to love her. She just wanted to have a good time. My being in love with her was just getting in the way."

"You make it sound like she was just some sort of slut, or something," John said. "I don't think you mean that!"

"No," he agreed. "She's not. I don't really think she'll do it with just anybody. On the other hand, she did it with *me*, so maybe she *will* do it with anybody." He sighed heavily. "I've heard of love without sex, and I know most guys would like to have sex without love. Imagine my surprise when I found a girl who wanted that!"

John did not comment. Larry skipped another stone across the tank. Once more, he looked directly at John, "Love is wonderful even without sex, and yes, I've now learned sex is wonderful even without love. But I don't want just one or the other, John – I want both. Next time a girl is ready to have sex with me, I'm going to make sure she's in love with me first!" As John looked at his friend, a grin slowly widened across his face. Seeing that grin, Larry thought about what he had just said, and slowly began to chuckle. "You're right, John. I *am* full of shit!"

"Feeling better?" John smiled.

"Yeah, a little. I know I'll get over her eventually. I always do, right John? It's the same old story. Larry meets girl. Larry's emotions get ahead of girl's. Girl dumps Larry. And just when Larry thought he was beginning to figure it all out."

"I understand," John said. "You just got surprised. For what it's worth, I thought she was in love with you, too."

"I wish I could be more like you, John," Larry sighed. "If this sort of thing had happened to you, you'd already have blown it off and started looking for a new girl. I wish I wouldn't get myself hurt so badly all the time."

John smiled, "On the other hand, you can't feel the thrill of victory unless you're willing to risk the agony of defeat."

Larry looked at John with a slight grin. "That sounds like a good philosophy. Who said that? Anybody who would really know about such things?"

"A friend of mine. Just a really good friend." After a brief pause, he asked, "Are you ready to go back?"

Larry skipped one more stone across the water and sighed. "Sure. Let's go."

"I know Larry isn't feeling well," Jessica said to Julian as the boys walked off the patio and headed out into the pasture.

"Do you know what the problem is?" Julian asked.

"Linda broke up with him earlier this week, Jules."

"Oh," Julian said, looking out into the pasture. He saw a signal from Jessica indicating she wanted to talk to the girls, and he should make himself scarce. "I should have guessed it was something like that. I think I'll step outside and wait for them."

"Poor boy," Jessica said to no one in particular once Julian closed the back door. "What a terrible way to have to start the new year! Does anyone know why Linda decided to break up with him?"

Helen offered an opinion. "I spoke to Linda on Friday, and she told me they had broken up. She said he wanted something she wasn't ready to give."

"Oh, I see," Jessica said.

"I think you're jumping to a wrong conclusion, Mrs. J," Sam said quietly.

"Why do you say that, Sam?" Jessica asked.

"I can guess what you're thinking," Sam replied. "Let me say I'm very sure Linda was quite willing to give him *that*, and had done so on more than one occasion."

Jessica looked at Sam and saw how much more mature she was than the other girls. She realized Sam probably knew what she was talking about, but wanted a little more information. "How do you know that, Sam?"

"Would you believe a little bird told me?" Sam offered, attempting to get away with an imitation of Maxwell Smart.

"I think she's right about that," Julia said just before Jessica pursued the subject a little further. Julia looked at Helen and asked, "Do you remember the slumber party after my birthday? We talked about some things, especially about boys, and Linda told us a little about her experiences."

"Yeah," Helen said. "I'd almost forgotten about that."

"I see," Jessica said. She would pursue that conversation with her daughter later, in private, just to make sure Julia was not confused about anything. She returned her attention to Sam. "You've known Larry the longest. What do you think happened?"

"It's not unusual for him to get hurt," Sam shrugged sadly. "He just never seems to have very good luck when it comes to his relationships with girls."

"Why is that, Sam?" Jessica asked. "It strikes me most girls would *want* to get their clutches on that boy. He's cute, sweet, sings nicely, and is a lot of fun to be with. At least, that's the way he seems to and old fogy like me!"

"He's all of those things and more," Sam agreed. "And you're not *that* old, Mrs. J," she laughed. Jessica grinned in return.

"I really like Larry," Julia said. "I'd like to find a boyfriend just like him." Jessica smiled at her daughter knowing the "just like him" part was unnecessary.

Helen was a little less enthusiastic. "I like Larry well enough," she said, then giggled, "but I think I'll stick with John if you don't mind."

"I don't mind at all, dear," Jessica chuckled. "So what *is* the problem with him?" she asked, looking at Sam for information.

"We've been good friends for a long time. We're very close. I doubt most people would understand the kind of relationship we have. I'm not even sure *I* do!" Sam grinned. More seriously, she added, "Larry and I talk openly about a lot of very personal things. I'd never reveal any of those secrets without his permission, of course, but I don't think he'd mind if I told you what *he* thinks his problem is."

"Go on," Jessica urged.

"I think most people would try to blame their problems on someone else. Not Larry. He thinks *he* is the cause of all his problems. He told me once he's not interested in *'moving from girl to girl like a bee moves from flower to flower'* the way a lot of guys do. Those are his own words, by the way. What he wants more than anything is a steady girlfriend. He wants a meaningful relationship.

"But according to him, he has some sort of character flaw. He thinks maybe he's more emotional than other guys. When he gets into a new relationship, his feelings always get ahead of the girl's. He wants her to be his steady girlfriend before she's ready to go steady with him. When the girl senses that, she reacts negatively, thinking maybe he wants to pin her down, possess her, or something. So she gets scared and dumps him. At least, that's his theory."

"Interesting. And what do *you* think?" Jessica asked.

"There may be something to what he says," Sam answered, "but personally I think he's just had a long string of bad luck. He and Linda were together about two months. I think that may be the longest he's ever kept a girlfriend. He wants a relationship to last a little longer than that. Who can blame him?"

Julia chimed in saying, "That matches what Linda said to me when I spoke to her a little earlier. She said she broke up with him because he was looking for a longterm relationship, and she just wanted to have fun."

Jessica nodded in understanding. "Perhaps that's what she meant when she spoke to you, Helen. Perhaps he wanted some kind of longterm commitment, and she wasn't ready to make one." After a pause, she added, "Or it's possible she only *thought* he wanted some kind of longterm commitment."

"That would be my guess," Sam nodded in agreement.

Jessica saw the boys and Schotzy had returned from the pasture and were chatting with Julian on the patio. "What's done is done," she announced. As the boys headed towards the back door, she cautioned the girls to act naturally, and not to let on they had been talking about Larry.

When the boys returned, they immediately began their practice session. Sam helped by going through their music books to suggest songs. She was careful to avoid love songs, knowing any one of them could destroy the tenuous control Larry was exercising over his emotions. Julia and Helen listened appreciatively, as did Mr. and Mrs. Jacobson.

For warm up, Sam picked out some Beatles songs for them. She started with some songs from the *With the Beatles* album recorded in 1963, including *Not a Second Time*. Not only did she want to make sure Larry would not react negatively to it, but she also wanted to plant the seed in his mind, even though she doubted it would be necessary, that he should not consider going back to Linda even if she changed her mind. She followed that with *Money* just because she liked the song.

Next, Sam picked *A Hard Day's Night*. She knew John appreciated having a song like that early in the session to loosen up his fingers so he could get serious with the guitar parts. She moved on to the *Beatles For Sale* album from 1964 to pick up *Eight Days a Week* and *Everybody's Trying to be My Baby*, hoping they would improve Larry's mood. She really took a chance by suggesting they play *I'll Follow the Sun*, a song about moving on after the end of a relationship. She was happy when Larry's reaction was positive.

By this time, John and Larry were working loosely, and the girls received a rare privilege of witnessing the creative process at work. When Sam mentioned seeing Patrick McGoohan on the *Secret Agent Man* television program, originally titled *Danger Man* when aired on the BBC, John started playing the guitar riff from the theme song written by P. F. Sloan, and recorded by Johnny Rivers.

"Hey, John," Larry said. "Check this out! See if you can time that riff to match this." He started playing the chords to the *James Bond* theme song. John started playing the *Secret Agent Man* riff over those chords, and after a few attempts, the boys had worked it out, much to the delight of Sam. "Let's put it all together!" Larry urged. They started at the beginning, and after the newly arranged guitar introduction, Larry started singing the song. Afterward, Larry and John decided they would work on it a little more, and planned to record it for an upcoming show.

After the boys played a few Paul Simon songs, Larry played a chord pattern and hummed a tune nobody recognized. When John asked him what he was playing, he just shrugged and suggested they move on to play something else.

Eventually, they grew tired and decided to call it a day. It was obvious to all Larry was feeling much better than when he arrived, acting much more like his old self again. After packing his guitar and music, he announced he needed to leave. "Thanks, guys!" he said sincerely. "I appreciate your friendship more than words could ever express."

"Happy new year, Larry!" Sam said. Larry looked at Sam and smiled, but he merely shrugged and made no direct response to her.

Instead, he turned to the Jacobsons. "Thank you for allowing us into your home, and sharing your traditional New Year's Day foods."

"You're very welcome," Jessica said. "I hope you have a very happy new year." He smiled to her, but once again merely shrugged.

"Bye, Helen," he said with a faint smile. That smile faded a little when he turned to look at Julia. He forced the smile to return as he said, "Bye, Julie." Without waiting for a reply, he quickly turned and headed for the door. After rubbing the dog's head, in the blink of an eye, he was gone.

After John and Helen exchanged goodnight wishes with everyone and departed, Sam was also preparing to leave, but Jessica intercepted her. "Can you wait a moment, Sam? I have something I want to send to your mother." Jessica began to prepare a plate of food for Sam to take home with her.

"It isn't necessary, Mrs. J," Sam said, "but thanks."

"Your mom might enjoy some of this," Jessica replied. "I'll walk you to your car."

"Thanks!" Sam said. "Goodnight, Mr. J! Goodnight, Julia! Happy new year!"

While the others expressed their goodnight wishes, Jessica led Sam outside and closed the door behind them. Walking to Sam's car, Jessica confessed her ulterior motives. "Actually, Sam, I just wanted to have a private word with you."

"I figured that, Mrs. J," Sam responded. "How can I help you?"

"It's about you and Larry," Jessica said.

"I figured that, also," Sam replied.

"If it's none of my business, then just say so, OK?" Jessica began. "There are some things I'd like to understand. It's a little more than just idle curiosity."

"I'll try, Mrs. J," Sam said sincerely. "I understand why you're interested."

"You seem to know Larry very well," Jessica noted.

"Yes, we've been friends for a very long time."

"He's hurting pretty badly right now, isn't he?"

"Yes, ma'am. I'd say Linda has broken his heart worse than it's ever been broken before. Some of this I picked up from what John told me, but my understanding is she broke up with him because he told her he loves her. Can you imagine? Breaking up with a sweet guy like Larry just because he says he loves you?"

Jessica saw tears forming in Sam's eyes. "No, I have to admit that's something I can't imagine. Would you say Larry would be a good 'catch' for a girl?"

Sam laughed at the metaphor and answered in kind. "I think if a girl found him wiggling on the end of her line, she'd be crazy to throw him back in the water."

"Then why," Jessica smiled, planting the hook now that the bait had been taken, "have *you* not reeled him in for yourself?"

The expressions passing across Sam's face told Jessica almost as much as her words. Sam was surprised by the question and did not have a ready answer. She faltered with her first attempt. "Because! Just because." Maybe Larry would have been able to make that answer stick, but the look on Jessica's face told Sam she would have to do better. "Because, Mrs. J, I'd break his heart, and I love him too much to do that!"

Jessica saw the tears, and put her arms around the younger girl. "It's OK, dear."

"He told me something just last night I'll never forget," Sam said as the tears began to flow. "He told me every girl he has ever loved has broken his heart, and it occurred to him every girl he ever *will* love will break his heart. Except maybe the last one, and then only if he's lucky enough to die before she does."

Jessica considered those words. "Perhaps he's right about that," she said thoughtfully. "Could you not prove him wrong if you wanted to?"

"No!" Sam insisted as the dam in her eyes burst. "I could *not* prove him wrong! I would break his heart far worse than Linda, worse than anyone has or ever will. No matter how much I might want to, I cannot give him what he truly wants, what he truly deserves. It would just be impossible. Please, don't ask me to explain!"

Jessica saw Sam was keeping a deep secret but knew this was not the time to pursue it. She had gotten the information she needed. Larry was exactly the kind of boy he appeared to be. The person who knew him best obviously loved him dearly. "I'm sorry to pry into your personal life. I hope you understand I needed to know."

"Yes, ma'am," Sam said drying her eyes. "I understand more than you think. You *do* need to know, but unfortunately, it may be a long time before it really matters."

Jessica decided to let that comment pass also, and after wishing Sam a goodnight, she walked back to the house. Sam got in her car and drove home.

Jessica knocked on her daughter's door before entering. "I thought I'd check to see if you were OK, sugar," she said as she came into Julia's room.

Julia was lying face down on her bed, thinking about the events of the last two days. She dried the small tears in her eyes before answering. "I'm fine, mom."

"That's good," Jessica said warmly as she sat on the edge of her daughter's bed. "I was concerned you might be a little confused about things."

"I *am* confused," Julia admitted. "She told me she just wanted to have fun, but by her own words, they *were* having fun. Why would she just throw it all away?"

Jessica brushed her daughter's hair and smiled. "Sometimes, it's not easy to understand certain things, sweetheart. To you, Linda had it all. She's a very popular and pretty girl, and she had a really nice boyfriend. I know those are exactly the things you want to have. Somehow, I guess, they just weren't enough for Linda."

"What more could she want?" Julia asked.

Jessica shook her head before responding, "It's hard to say. Perhaps she just wants to be free. She is, after all, only fifteen. Girls should get to know a lot of different boys before they commit themselves to just one. Maybe she found herself falling in love with him and broke it off while she still could."

"But what if the first boy you meet just happens to be the right one?" Julia asked.

"I don't know the answer to that, sweetheart," Jessica said. "How would you know he's the right one unless you have others to compare against?"

Julia contemplated that question before speaking. "I don't know. I hope I don't find the right boy until I have enough experience to *know* he's the right one. I wouldn't want to pass him by just because I wasn't sure!"

"Is that what you think Linda has done?" Jessica asked.

"I guess no one will ever know," Julia answered.

Jessica was impressed by Julia's answer, and decided her daughter was ready to think about something more serious. "I want you to think about something else for a moment, sugar. Linda is experimenting in a dangerous area. I think you know what I mean. So far, the only harm would seem to be she broke Larry's heart. She didn't understand he was developing some very strong feelings for her, feelings she was not ready to return to him. Maybe they were both lucky it was nothing worse than that."

"Mom, tell me something honestly. Do you think it's absolutely necessary for one to wait until after marriage to have sex?"

Jessica was so proud of her relationship with Julia. "What do you think, sugar?"

"I don't know, mom. That's why I'm asking you!"

"Well," Jessica began, "I think you're going to have to figure out the answer for yourself. Some people would give you an absolute answer, but I really think it depends on the individuals. There are certainly some very serious things to consider first, especially since the consequences might affect a tender and innocent new life.

"But it would be hard for me to find fault with two people who are truly in love with each other expressing their love in that manner. Maybe that's the key – it needs to be two people who are truly in love with each other, and not just one person in love with another. If it's not mutual, one or the other or maybe both of them are likely to get hurt. Unfortunately, that hurt can be very, very painful to more than just the two of them."

"I think I understand," Julia said.

"Yes, sweetheart," Jessica said, "I think you do."

"I love you, mom," Julia said warmly.

"And I love you, Julia," she said. "Goodnight, and sweet dreams!"

Sunday, January 8, 1967
Tomorrow Never Knows

Julia saw Sam's car pull into the driveway. "Sam's here! Bye, mom! Bye dad! See you later!" When she heard them respond, she stepped through the front door, quickly ran to Sam's car, and piled in. "Hi, Sam!" she said enthusiastically.

"Hi, Julia," Sam replied. "Cold enough for you?"

"You call this cold?" Julia snickered. It was something of a game she and the other kids played, comparing the weather in Texas to that up north.

"I call it cold," Sam giggled, turning the car around. "What do *you* call it?"

"A little chilly," Julia grinned. "Maybe!"

"If you're thinking of joining the polar bear club," Sam snickered, "I'll take you over to Lake Somerville this afternoon. You can convince me it's not cold; just take off your clothes and jump in." Julia giggled. "I'd bet you'd also convince the boys it isn't cold. They might take off their clothes and jump in with you!"

"And if *they* did," Julia giggled again, "perhaps it'd it be enough to convince you and Helen it isn't cold, and you'd do the same!"

"That'd be quite a sight! I wonder if we'd get arrested, or sent to the loony bin?"

"That'd probably depend on what the boys were doing," Julia giggled once again, "and whether we were screaming in fear or from delight!"

"Oh, you're a naughty girl!" Sam giggled. "That settles it! Let's go pick them up and head for the lake!"

"Don't you *dare* tell them what I said!" Julia exclaimed. "Besides, John would go for Helen, Larry would go for you, and I wouldn't have anyone to keep me warm."

"I wouldn't be so sure if I were you! Besides, you said it isn't cold anyway!"

"Well, it's still chilly enough to make certain things pucker up like little raisins!"

"Certain things on the boys would shrivel so small we might not be able to find them!" Sam giggled.

"*Now* who's being naughty?" Julia grinned.

"I'm older and wiser than you," Sam grinned, pointing her nose in the air. "When you get to be my age, you start getting more desperate."

"You're so full of shit!" Julia giggled.

"Where did you get such a potty mouth?" Sam laughed.

"From hanging out with *you* guys, where else?" Julia grinned.

"I hoped we wouldn't corrupt you, but now I see the damage is done," Sam snickered. "Whatever you do, when your parents find out, be sure to blame it all on the boys. I'd like your mother to keep thinking of me as a nice girl."

"You still have her fooled for now," Julia giggled, "but I already know better, and knowing my mom like I do, it won't take her long to figure it out, either!"

"Rats!" Sam laughed. "If you blow my cover, I'll have to kill you!"

"I have *all* of you guys figured out." Julia smiled.

"Oh, really?" Sam grinned. Julia nodded her head and smirked. "OK, then show me. What have you figured out about John?"

"John is a sweetheart of a guy," Julia said, "who simply worships his friends, Larry and Sam. He would probably do anything either of you asked him to do."

"He probably would," Sam smiled. "What have you figured out about Larry?"

"Larry is a sweetheart of a guy, too," Julia grinned, "who simply worships his friends, John and Sam. He would probably do anything either of you asked him."

Sam laughed out loud. "There's only one thing wrong with that analysis. Larry has this tendency to do those things *before* you ask him!"

"And then there's Sam," Julia continued. "Sam is a sweetheart of a girl," she grinned warmly, "who simply worships her friends, Larry and John. There's no doubt in my mind she would do anything either of them needed her to do."

Sam looked at Julia and grinned. "Maybe you have us figured out better than I thought. They don't call us the *Three Musketeers* for nothing! Larry, John, and I are friends, and like you say, friends will do whatever they have to do to help each other." Almost under her breath, Sam added another sentence to that description, "Although sometimes they refuse that help, even when they need it so desperately."

"What do mean by that?" Julia asked.

"Oh, nothing," Sam said casually, then changed the subject. "Julia, I know I'm speaking for the guys when I tell you we also think of *you* as a special friend. We're going to have to change our nickname to the *Four Musketeers* pretty soon."

Julia and Sam exchanged a glance and a smile. "I'm honored to be your friend, Sam," she said. "Just like I'm honored to be Larry's friend and John's friend."

"All for one, and one for all!" Sam giggled.

Larry greeted John and Helen with as much enthusiasm as he could muster, which was pitifully little. "Hi, guys. Come on in and we'll get started."

"Thanks, Larry," Helen smiled happily, stepping inside. "I'll go see if your mom needs a hand with anything. Is she in the kitchen?" When Larry nodded his head, she kissed John on the cheek and departed.

"Hey, dude!" John smiled. "How's it hanging today?"

"I'm OK, John," he replied without a lot of feeling.

"Just OK?" John asked.

"I feel numb," Larry replied. "I consider that a blessing. At least, I don't hurt."

"I hear you. Are we going to work here in the living room?" he asked, wanting to change the subject. He knew his friend was still hurting a lot more than he was showing, and it distressed him to see it.

"Yeah," Larry said, nodding his head slowly. "Find yourself a spot and get settled. I'll fetch my guitar so we can get started whenever you're ready." John sat on the sofa, leaving plenty of room for Helen, removed his guitar from its case, and began to tune up. Larry returned, pulled a chair from the dining room table, taking a position nearby. Within seconds, they were tuned, and started to warm up.

Sam and Julia arrived while they were exercising. "Hi, guys!" Sam said brightly.

"Hi, Sam. Hi, Julie," Larry replied, trying to appear like everything was normal.

"Hi, Larry," Julia said sweetly. The brightness of her smile caused a shiver to run down his spine. He had to force his eyes away. Those green circles surrounding infinity were simply more than he could bear. After a moment, she greeted John as well. "Hi, John. How are you and Helen getting along these days?"

"Hi, Julia. We're doing fine. Here she comes now!"

Helen returned ahead of Larry's mom. "Hi, Julia! Hi, Sam!" she greeted.

"Hello, girls," Lena added, also stepping into the room. "I came to take drink orders. Would you rather have something hot or something cold?"

"Hi, Mrs. B," Sam grinned. "I'd rather have something hot, myself, but since Julia has been telling me it's only slightly chilly today, she'll probably want something cold! Later on, she wants to run over to Somerville for a quick swim."

"Sam!" Julia giggled. "Ignore her! I'd like something hot, also. Can I help?"

"I want something hot," Helen agreed. "I'll get yours while I'm at it, John. Would you like me to get something hot for you?"

Larry closed his eyes and shook his head, trying not to react in any manner at all.

John lightly chuckled, and would have managed not to laugh except he saw Larry shaking his head, and broke down. In turn, this got Larry snickering. "I'm quite sure he'd rather you get something hot for him," Larry said, trying not to laugh.

Helen smiled at Larry, and tried not to look mystified. "Come along, girls," Sam giggled. "Let's help Mrs. B with the drinks and leave these two perverts to stew in their own juices."

While the girls headed to the kitchen, Julia looked back and smiled. Something in her smile raised Larry's spirits, and John noticed. "Man, I can see it in your eyes! You want her! Why don't you go for it? Can't you see she digs you, too?"

Larry sat for several seconds, silently considering his options. "I want to, John," he said finally. "I really do! But I'm too old for her, and there's still that promise."

"Oh, man!" John replied. "I wish you'd forget that damn promise!"

"How can I, John?" he said, shaking his head. "You know how I feel about that sort of thing. He's my friend. I understand how he feels. He needs to find someone new and move on, just like I do. How could I use his misfortune for my own benefit? How would you feel if you broke up with Helen and I started dating her?"

"I wouldn't like it," John agreed, "but I'd forgive you. You're my friend, Larry, and I'd give you anything you need."

"I know you would, John," Larry said, "just like I'd give you anything. More than anything else, what I need right now is time to get over Linda. When I can think straight again, maybe I'll give some thought to breaking that promise. Or maybe Jimmy will get over Julia first and release me. Either way, I need time. OK?"

"OK, dude," John said sadly.

The girls returned with mugs of hot chocolate, and the boys settled down to practice. When the afternoon was over, Larry wished his friends goodnight. As he watched them depart, he hoped time was on his side as much as his friends were.

Saturday, January 14, 1967
I'm Into Something Good

It was an ordinary Saturday. Larry arrived at the library on time, greeted Mrs. Hannah and Sam, and ran the projector for the children's program. The afternoon would be spent straightening out the damage inflicted on the bookshelves.

Sam took her lunch break at noon, as usual. At 1:00 o'clock, Larry walked out of the library through the main doors. It was a cold, clear day, and he decided to go for a hot lunch. On Bryan Avenue, the next street over from Main, and a few blocks away from the library, was a lunch room frequented by many people working in the downtown area. It was called *Tony's*, but Larry gave it the nickname *Tony's Ptomaine Palace*. It wasn't because the food was bad. In fact, the food was much better than you might expect based on the appearance of the place. It was just one of those teenage things.

He was not paying a lot of attention as he walked down the street, his head hanging low for two reasons. First, the cold north wind he was walking into threatened to bite his ears off. Second, he still hurting inside and did not feel like making eye contact with anybody. Just as he walked past a clothing store on Main Street, three girls popped out the door. He stepped right into one of them, knocking the packages from her hands. "I'm so sorry," he said, bending over to pick up the

Saturday, January 14, 1967 – I'm Into Something Good   -171-

packages. When he stood to return them, he stared into the face of Sally Sutherland, one of the junior class cheerleaders.

"Hi, Larry!" she said brightly taking back her packages. "It's been a while. Wasn't it at the Pizza Hut? You and Linda shared a booth with Roger and me."

"Uh, yes," Larry said feeling confused. "That's right!"

"You know Betty and Sharon, right?" she asked, indicating the other two girls.

Betty Simpson and Sharon Cushing were also cheerleaders, and Betty was a member of the A Capella Choir. "Yes! Hello ladies. Doing some shopping, I see?" He wanted to kick himself in the head for his dazzling and brilliant conversation.

"We each got some money for Christmas," Sally said, "so we waited to take advantage of the after-Christmas sales. How about you?"

"I have a part time job at the library on Saturdays. I'm on my lunch break."

"Where were you headed?" Sally asked.

"I was going to *Tony's Ptomaine Palace*, but maybe it's too cold to walk that far."

Sally laughed at the nickname. "I've ever been there. How about you guys?"

"Not me!" Betty snickered.

Sharon grinned at Sally and replied, "It certainly sounds appetizing, doesn't it?"

He smiled at them. "It's really not all that bad, but I think I'll turn around and just grab a burger at Ellison's. Are you guys hungry? You're welcome to join me."

"I could eat a few fries," Sally grinned. "Why don't we join him?"

"Why not?" suggested Betty. "Let's go."

The foursome headed back up Main Street, making idle chit chat, and entered into Ellison's Drug Store. The lunch crowd was already gone, and several booths were available. Larry led them to an empty booth and suggested they take a seat. Sally slid into one side, while Betty and Sharon took the other. His main question answered, Larry slid into the seat next to Sally.

"I might have guessed you worked in the library," Sharon giggled.

Her meaning was not lost on Larry. "It's even worse than you think, babe! I work upstairs in the children's section!" he said, snickering defiantly.

Sharon and Betty exchanged a grin, but Larry noticed Sally did not join their little game. The waitress came and the girls each ordered a soft drink and agreed to split an order of fries. Larry ordered a cheeseburger, fries, and a lime aid.

"How did you come to work at the library?" Sally asked, honestly interested.

"My mom is the head librarian at Allen Academy. She and Mrs. Richardson, the head librarian here at Carnegie, were talking one day. Mrs. Richardson happened to mention they had a job opening, and my mom volunteered me!" He chuckled, "I didn't mind all that much. It pays better than most other part time jobs around here."

"You must keep pretty busy," Sally continued, "with two jobs!"

He was not sure what she meant at first, until it occurred to him she was talking about the radio program. "Oh, the radio stuff! Yeah, that keeps me busy, but we don't get paid for it. We do it just for fun."

"What radio stuff?" Betty asked. "Are you the one Mr. Austin keeps talking about?"

"Yeah," he smiled. "John, Sam, and I run the *Top Forty Showcase* program every Saturday night. Sam also works at the library."

"You should listen to the program," Sally told the others. "I used to think it was just some stupid dedication program, but they're making it a lot more interesting. Larry and John play guitars and sing every now and then. They also do comedy skits, and all sorts of things. It's fun!"

"Well, we have a *few* fans, anyway," he smiled. He noted the other girls were not making quite so much fun of him now. The waitress brought their food and placed four checks on the table.

"What time does it come on?" Betty asked.

"Saturday night at 8:00," Sally answered, looking to Larry for confirmation. He nodded his head and she continued, "I'm not sure how late it goes."

"11:00 o'clock, most of the time," he answered.

"How did you get started doing that?" Sharon asked.

He was pleased to note Sharon was treating him like a real person. She had been the toughest "nut to crack," so to speak. Sally accepted him the night she and Roger met at the Pizza Hut, and Betty knew him from choir. "Sam asked me. She got invited by the previous hosts, and we've sort of inherited the show. One of these days, we'll pass it on to the next group, I guess."

"It sounds like Sam has taken Linda's place," Betty asked a little indelicately.

He looked down at his plate for a moment, then forced himself to smile. "No, Sam is one of my very best friends, but we're not dating." With a laugh, he announced, "Right now, ladies, I'm unattached, so if any of you want to claim me..."

The girls laughed along with him. "What would you want with one of us?" Sally giggled. "You can probably have any girl you please!"

"Of course I can!" he grinned. "Unfortunately, I haven't pleased one yet!" The girls laughed with him once again. At least, Larry hoped this was true, that they were not merely laughing *at* him. They continued to joke around while Larry ate his lunch.

"I really need to run," Sharon announced, picking up the check nearest her.

"Why don't you let me treat?" he offered. "After all, I invited you to join me."

"Thanks, but you don't have to. My only problem is figuring out the tip."

"Please," he repeated. "Figuring the tip is easy. If you want to leave a standard twelve per cent tip, just take a tenth of the total, and add another fifth of that."

"Huh?" Sharon asked.

"Let me show you," he suggested, taking the check from her hand. "The fries are on your check, and it comes to $1.25. To compute a twelve percent tip, you just take a tenth, twelve and a half cents, then another fifth of that, two and a half cents, and add it up. Your tip is fifteen cents." He gathered all the other tickets and chuckled, "But now I have *all* of the tickets, so none of you need worry about computing the tip, anyway!"

"OK, then thanks, Mr. Wizard," Sharon giggled. "If you want to spend your money so badly, help yourself!"

He thought she meant it as a joke, but was still a little sorry he had gotten carried away and demonstrated his skills with arithmetic. He often thought this was one of the main reasons why he was treated as an outcast. "Well, after all," he said flashing his smile, "I'm a wealthy man of means, with two part time jobs!"

The girls giggled. "If you don't mind, Sharon," Betty asked, "could I catch a ride?"

"No problem," Sharon said. "How about you, Sally?"

Saturday, January 14, 1967 – I'm Into Something Good

"I brought my own car. I'll see you guys later!" Sharon and Betty bid their farewells, walked out of Ellison's and headed down the street to Sharon's car.

Still sitting on the same side of the booth as Sally, Larry felt a little awkward. "I'll let you out when you're ready to go," he offered.

"I'm in no hurry. Keep your seat. Thanks again for buying our fries and drinks."

"I was happy to," he said honestly. "It's a lot more fun being with you girls than eating all alone down at *Tony's Ptomaine Palace.*"

Sally grinned in agreement. "I was sorry to hear you and Linda broke up. Have you heard who Linda is seeing now?"

"I'm afraid not," he shrugged. "I don't usually keep up with the latest gossip."

"She's dating Roger," Sally said. "I think Roger decided she was a better prospect than me that night we shared a booth at the Pizza Hut."

"A better prospect for what?" he asked, not thinking this could prove indelicate.

"Never mind," she smiled as she looked at him.

Larry recovered quickly from his *feaux pas*. "He must be crazy, Sally. When I heard you two were no longer together, I figured you'd dumped *him!"*

"It was inevitable. Like most guys, he thinks he's God's gift to women, and we should all lay down and worship at his feet!"

"Temper, temper!" he teased. "Well, who cares, right? I imagine half the football team and all of the baseball guys are already chasing after to you!"

"You're sweet, but no. They seem to be avoiding me. Maybe Roger told them some nasty things about me or something."

He liked Sally, and wondered if there might be a chance to improve his social status. *Would Sally consider going out with me?* His nervousness was apparent when he suggested, "Sally, if you're interested, I'd be happy to take you to the radio station sometime and show you how everything works. You might think it's fun."

She smiled at him and answered, "I think I'd like that, Larry!"

Cautiously, he tried something more specific, "How about next Saturday night?"

"OK," she said with a sweet smile. "What should I wear?"

"Wear something emphasizing how pretty you are," he grinned. "Even though no one can see you over the radio, I'll see you in the studio. I'll pick you up at 7:00 if that's OK." She agreed and they had a date. "I wish I didn't have to go back to work. I'd like to talk with you some more!"

"Me, too! Thanks again for buying my drink!" She leaned over and kissed him on the cheek then stood to leave. "I'll see you next Saturday!"

She turned and walked out of the store as he watched. *Wow!* he thought. *I got a date with a cheerleader! Who'd a ever thunk it?* He totaled the four tickets in his head, added an appropriate tip, and returned to the library in a really good mood.

Near the end of the day, Sam got a chance to talk to Larry without Mrs. Hannah eavesdropping. "You've been acting like the cat that swallowed the canary all afternoon long! What gives?"

"You know Sally Sutherland, right?" he asked. "I bumped into half of the cheer leading squad including Sally, Betty, and Sharon when I went for lunch. I mean that *literally.* I bumped into her and knocked some packages out of her hands. So I invited them to join me for lunch."

"Join you?" Sam grinned. "How come? Where you coming apart?"

"Cute," Larry replied rolling his eyes. "They sat with me over at Ellison's while I ate lunch, sharing some fries."

"You're much too easily impressed," Sam said, knowing there had to be more to this story. "Three cheerleaders sat with you while you ate lunch. Did reporters come take pictures? Will this be on the front page of tomorrow's Bryan Daily Buzzard?"

"No, smartypants," he sneered, "but after Betty and Sharon left, I got better acquainted with Sally. Guess who's coming to the station with me next weekend?"

"Besides me and Julia?" she asked, returning his sneer. That dash of reality came as a surprise. He had not thought about the driving arrangements, and Sam saw the sudden change in his expression. "I suppose you'll be begging me all week long to bail you out of this jam, right?"

"Please?" he asked pitifully.

"I really ought to let you cook in your own juices. I would just love to hear you explain to Sally you also have to pick up this other girl and take her home. For that matter, I'd like to hear you explain it to Julia! She's the one you ought to be chasing after, and you know that as well as I do!"

"Oh, Sam! Julie is a dear sweet little girl. One of these days, I'll probably be panting every time I see her, but right now, I'm just too old for her. That's not even counting my promise to Jimmy! Please don't keep after me. My life is hard enough as it is, OK?"

"One of these days, you're going to regret this!" She sighed, then agreed to bail him out. "I'll pick her up, assuming she still wants to come after hearing this news."

"She doesn't do the show because she likes me, Sam," he insisted. "She likes being with *all* of us. I think she's becoming a really good friend."

"I happen to know you already care about her, and we both know she has a crush on you. You're crazy if you don't do something about it!"

Larry just looked at her sadly. If only he could get out of that damn promise!

Larry picked up Sam and then drove to get Julia, the same as he had done the previous two weeks. Like before, Sam put Julia in the middle seat. Even though Julia seemed to appreciate it, Sam did it more to aggravate Larry than anything else. They met John and Helen at the station, producing another episode of the *Top Forty Showcase* program.

Driving home after the show, Sam brought up the change in arrangements for the next week. "I'll be the one picking you up next week, Julia. *Don Juan* here has a hot date, and having two other girls in the car with him might cramp his style too much."

"Give me break, will you, Sam?" Larry asked.

Julia giggled, though disappointed to hear this news. "Anyone I might know?"

"You might," Sam answered. "Larry is moving up the social ladder. He has a date with none other than Sally Sutherland, one of the junior class cheerleaders!"

"Ooh!" Julia teased, "A cheerleader! I don't think I've ever met her, but I've heard Linda and Helen mention her name. I understand she's very pretty!"

"She's pretty if you like that sort of thing," Sam said to tease Larry a bit more. "I guess girls like us just aren't good enough for him anymore."

"Come on, you guys!" he pleaded. "It's just one date, OK? I happened to be in the right place at the right time. She used to go steady with Roger Warner..."

"Hey, that's Linda's new boyfriend!" Julia said without thinking.

"So I'm told," he frowned. "Since he decided to chase Linda, good old Larry is getting a shot at his leftovers."

"Don't be so bitter, Larry," Sam said.

"I'm just saying you shouldn't make such a big deal out of it," he insisted. "One date doesn't mean very much, now does it?"

"You have to have a first date with someone before you can have the second and the third," Julia said, smiling at him.

"I guess so," he smiled back. *Oh, how I wish I was having my first date with you!* He decided to have a chat with Jimmy to see how he was getting along. *Maybe Jimmy will release me from that damn promise!*

Sam could read Larry's mind and decided not to tease him anymore. She knew what he wanted. She wished he was not so obstinate about keeping that promise. On the other hand, she realized his honesty and trustworthiness were two of the things she appreciated the most. She should be complimenting, rather than teasing him.

They arrived at Julia's house, and while Larry was walking around the car, Sam opened the door to let her out. "Goodnight! We'll see you tomorrow afternoon."

"Oh!" Julia added. "I almost forgot. I won't be going with you tomorrow."

Larry looked at Sam, expecting her to read his mind, *Didn't I tell you?* He looked at Julia and asked, "Is there a problem, Julie?"

"I have a school project due on Monday I have to finish."

"I see," Larry said. "Next week, then?"

"If you guys still want me," she said a little sadly.

"Of course we do," Larry and Sam said in unison. Sam added, "We all have other things to do from time to time. I'll pick you up next Saturday at the usual time."

"Thanks, Sam," Julia said hopping out of the car. "You really don't have to walk me to the door, Larry. I can find it on my own."

"I don't mind, Julie. It's just something I like to do." He walked to her front door, wishing this had been a date. "Goodnight," he said as she reached for the doorknob.

"Goodnight, Larry," she said. "I'll see you next week, I guess."

Damn! Larry swore to himself walking back to his car. He knew she was unhappy about his upcoming date with Sally, and this would hurt his chances with her even if Jimmy *did* release him.

"I thought that went rather well," Sam said sincerely when Larry got into the car.

"Do you?" he said sarcastically. He did not think it went well at all, and thought Sam was still teasing him. He started the engine and began to turn the car around.

"Yes, I do," she repeated. "Come on, Larry! Lighten up a bit! How did you expect her to react?"

"I don't know, Sam, but I didn't expect her to start avoiding me."

"What makes you think she's avoiding you?"

"Why else would she suddenly decide to skip guitar practice tomorrow?"

Sam looked at him and sighed. "I'm surprised at you, Larry. You aren't usually so self-centered. Have you already forgotten who's house we're going to? Have you forgotten who'll be there besides you, me, John, and Helen? Did it occur to you she might be trying to avoid someone else?"

Larry suddenly felt stupid. "I guess you're right. I don't know what I thought. I haven't been thinking very clearly at all lately. Damn it, Sam! I don't know what's wrong with me!"

They pulled out of the Jacobson's driveway and onto the country lane heading back towards town. "It's OK, Larry," Sam said trying to sooth his feelings. "I know you're still hurting from Linda, and you're just trying to find a way to get over her. I'm sure Julia understands that, too."

Not far down the country lane, Larry turned off onto the familiar gravel road and stopped in the familiar place. "I wonder how much she really understands, Sam. I doubt she understands why I don't ask her out," he said sadly. He needed a smoke, and assumed Sam would want to share.

"Would you like me to tell her?" Sam asked accepting the joint from Larry.

"Maybe," he said at first, followed immediately with, "Oh, I don't know. I've already admitted I'm not thinking straight. Give me your honest opinion, Sam. What do you think I should do?"

Sam lit the joint, took her first pull and handed it to Larry. "To be honest, Larry, I'm not sure. I wish you'd break your promise to Jimmy, but I understand how you feel about that. I guess I even admire you for it. If Julia were to ask me why you don't ask her out, I'd certainly tell her the truth. On the other hand, I'm not sure it'd be a good idea to volunteer that information."

"Do you think that might cause even more problems?" he asked.

"Yes," she nodded, "like having to explain to her why you made such a promise in the first place." Larry nodded his head in understanding, then sighed heavily. "Why don't you talk to Jimmy and see if he'll release you from that damn promise?"

"I plan to do that, although I'll have to proceed rather delicately with that, as well. I can't just ask him to release me without giving him an explanation why."

"You may be right about that. In the meantime, just go about your business and see what happens. Be patient! Sometimes, things have a way of working out all by themselves," she said trying to give Larry some encouragement. She knew he was still very confused and very hurt.

"And sometimes, they don't," he said. It was an uncharacteristically pessimistic statement demonstrating just how confused and hurt he truly was.

Sunday, January 15, 1967
What Becomes Of The Brokenhearted

It was John's turn to host the weekly guitar practice. The crowd was to be smaller than usual since Julia would not attend. Even though the need for such an arrangement was not in place today, Larry decided to pick up Sam as a courtesy. He was sure he would want to talk privately with Sam before this day was out.

After a few hours of serious practice, mixed as always with equal amounts of horseplay, the gang was ready for a change. John's suggestion, "I'm hungry. Anybody want pizza?" was greeted with an enthusiastic response. The gang debated briefly over the style and quantity, but after quickly coming to agreement, the order was called in.

Larry jumped on an opportunity. "You guys stay and relax. I'll go pick it up."

John tried to protest, "Hey! I'm the host this week. I should be the one to go!"

"Yes, you *are* the host, so I expect you to *pay!*" Larry grinned. "But why don't you just hang out with Helen. Sam can chaperon, and Jimmy can come with me."

"That's a great suggestion!" Sam agreed, understanding what Larry had in mind. "You guys take off, and I'll make sure they don't get too frisky while you're gone."

"Don't you think having my parents in the next room is enough?" John laughed.

"I don't know, John. I'm not sure having your parents in the next room would stop *me!*" Turning to Sam, he added, "Actually, I don't want you to prevent them getting frisky. Just catch everything on film; we can watch it later and critique!"

"Roger!" Sam laughed.

Helen and John blushed when they looked at each other. Giggling with delight at his brother's embarrassment, Jimmy hopped up and decreed, "Let's go!" Larry nodded at him, and the two boys headed for the door, stopping long enough only to demand tribute from John to pay for the pizza.

"I haven't had a chance to talk with you for a while, Jimmy," Larry said as they got into his car. "How are you getting along?"

"What do you mean?" Jimmy asked.

"The last time we talked, you weren't feeling very well," Larry smiled. "I was wondering if you were feeling any better."

"Oh, I see," Jimmy sighed. "I guess so."

"Good!" Larry said hopefully. "Have you found someone new yet?"

"No," Jimmy said sadly, "I'm not feeling *that* much better! I still think about her all the time, trying to think how to get her back. Have you got any suggestions?"

"I'm afraid not, Jimmy," Larry said, disappointed.

"You told me you had a lot of experience with this sort of thing," Jimmy continued. "Have you ever gotten back with someone after breaking up with her?"

"No. I used to try, but I don't anymore. All I ever did was make a complete fool of myself." Larry looked at his young friend and saw the sadness in his face. His continuation was honest advice, even if it was a bit self-serving. "I've learned the best thing to do is forget the past and look to the future."

"How can you do that?" Jimmy asked sincerely. "How can you simply forget about the best thing you've ever known in your entire life?"

"That's not what I meant, Jimmy. You want to remember all of the good times, the wonderful things you've shared with someone who was special to you. Those are precious memories you'll cherish, that will bring you joy the rest of your life."

"I don't think I'll ever be able feel joy again, especially when I think about her," Jimmy said. "Not unless I can get her back! Don't you want Linda back?"

"No," Larry replied honestly.

"You don't care about her anymore?" Jimmy asked.

"It's not that, Jimmy. I still care about her very much. I still love her. I always *will* love her. Love does not end just because a relationship does."

"Then how can you say you don't want her back?" Jimmy asked.

"Linda and I shared something very special, very wonderful, but I don't want her back. All of the good times I had with Linda are becoming memories I'll always cherish. But, Jimmy, my relationship with Linda *is* over. I want to have that kind of relationship again, but it won't be with Linda. Do you remember what I told you about looking for the perfect girl? Linda obviously isn't the perfect girl for me, so I've started searching again. Maybe next time, I'll find her. Even if I don't, perhaps I'll find a relationship that's better, and hopefully, one that will last a lot longer."

"I wish I could be so philosophical," Jimmy sighed.

"It's not philosophy," Larry smiled. "It's practicality. You'll learn to be the same in time. I know you've heard the old saying you can never go back home again. In cases like this, *'home'* refers to a love that has been lost. Once that happens, all you can do is move on to the next one, and hope it's the one that will be permanent."

"But you said love never ends!" Jimmy protested.

"That's right, Jimmy," he agreed. "Love never ends. For the rest of my life, I'll love Linda. You'll always feel the same about Julia you do right now. But relationships do end. My relationship with Linda is over, and since it'll never come back, I'm looking for a new relationship, someone else I can love. I advise you to think about your relationship with Julia in the same way."

"I'll try, Larry," Jimmy said sadly. "I wish I could be more like you. I don't know how I'll ever be able to think of Julia that way."

"It'll just take time, Jimmy," he said sadly. Not only was he disappointed to learn Jimmy still wanted Julia, but this conversation had reopened some of his own wounds.

The boys arrived at the pizza parlor and picked up their order. On the way home, Larry told Jimmy about bumping into Sally and making a date with her. "It's just that easy," he told Jimmy, encouraging him to find a new girlfriend. "When you least expect it, an opportunity can come out of the blue. Be alert and take advantage. Don't ever let a chance get away from you!" Larry felt a knife cut through his heart as he uttered that last sentence, and thought about how it applied to himself.

"I think I understand," Jimmy said.

"Good!" Larry said enthusiastically. "It won't be long before some girl notices a good looking guy like you is all alone. Let me know when it happens, OK?"

"OK," Jimmy said with as much of a laugh as he could muster.

They got back to the house and pulled into the driveway. Jimmy hopped out and ran inside, carrying the pizza. Larry lingered a moment to collect his thoughts, to discreetly wipe the excess moisture in his eyes, and to curse that damn promise.

"How did it go, Larry?" Sam asked when they backed out of John's driveway.

Even though it had been a couple of hours since he had returned with the pizza, the meaning of her question was perfectly clear. "No dice," Larry said simply.

Sam looked at him sadly and asked, "So he's still carrying a torch for her?"

"Yep," he said. He was very confused, and in that state, he tended to get quiet.

Sam shook her head. "Don't worry, Larry. He'll get over her soon. How long can he carry that torch without any encouragement from her?"

He thought for a moment before replying, "Sam, do you remember when we were in the seventh grade, and I had a crush on a girl named Judy?" Sam nodded her head to indicate she remembered. "I carried that torch for more than a year, almost to the end of the eighth grade. I had no encouragement, hardly ever saw her, never got to talk to her, and never so much as held her hand. So how long do *you* think it might take?"

Sam stared out of the passenger side window, feeling Larry's pain and confusion as if she was an empath. "Eventually, you know you're going to have to break that damn promise, even if it means you lose Jimmy as a friend."

Larry shook his head in disagreement. "Sam, if I only knew what about Julie calls me so, I might be ready to break it right now, at this very moment. The trouble is I don't know; I can't break a promise, tossing away a friend, when I don't know why!"

"I guess I understand," Sam said quietly. "But what if Julia just happens to be the answer to all your dreams? What if she's the perfect girl you've been searching for?"

It was his turn to think seriously. "I don't know. Maybe I should have learned my lesson about such things, but I'll make another solemn promise, Sam, only it's a promise I'll make to myself. I *promise* I won't let Julie get away from me forever without discovering the answer to that question!"

Saturday, January 21, 1967
The Ides Of Texas

Larry arrived at Sally's house promptly at 7:00. Her father answered the door. "Good evening, sir. My name is Larry Bristol. I'm here to see Sally."

Mr. Sutherland was somewhat surprised by Larry's demeanor. He was more used to the arrogant and sulking attitudes most of his daughter's dates typically expressed. This one was different, and he immediately liked this newcomer. "Good evening, Larry," he said stepping aside in welcome. "It's nice to meet you. Come on in."

The Sutherland house was decorated in a soft spoken elegance that impressed Larry. "Thank you," he said walking into the tiled entryway.

"This is Sally's mother, Wendy," he said. "Wendy, this is Larry Bristol."

Mrs. Sutherland greeted him with a warm smile. "Hello, Larry. It's nice to meet you. Sally has told us so many things about you this week."

"I deny everything!" Larry said with a bright smile.

Mrs. Sutherland smiled. "Everything she told us was very complimentary!"

"And you actually believed her?" Larry grinned.

The Sutherlands chuckled. Sally had warned them this boy had an unusual sense of humor, and they were beginning to understand. They were impressed with his simple charm and self-effacing style. "I'll go check on her while you men get better acquainted," Mrs. Sutherland said. She turned and disappeared through a doorway.

"Tell me about yourself," Mr. Sutherland asked.

The request was delivered in such a friendly and relaxed manner Larry did not feel threatened in the slightest. "There's not much to tell, sir. I'm a senior, planning to go to A&M after graduation. I have a part time job at the Carnegie library, and for fun, I help do a radio program on Saturday night. That's where Sally and I are going. If you listen to it, you might get to hear your daughter on the radio tonight!"

"We might just do that! I understand you're an honor student, and rather good in math. What do you plan to study when you get to college?"

Larry blushed slightly, "Computers. I got the opportunity to learn about them last summer, and I was hooked. I plan to make a career in the computer industry."

"It sounds like you have your life pretty well planned out," Mr. Sutherland said. "That's impressive for a young man your age."

"Thank you, sir," Larry said as he blushed once again. "I have certain parts of my life planned, I suppose. The rest is totally up in the air, I'm afraid."

Mr. Sutherland smiled in understanding. "From what Sally told me, I thought you might be planning a career in music."

"Not likely," Larry chuckled. "I love music. I might even be good enough to sing for my supper, but I'll never be lucky enough to get that big break one needs to become a successful musician."

"On the other hand," Mr. Sutherland continued, "it's a very lucky man who loves his work so much it doesn't seem like a job to him."

"Yes, sir," Larry agreed. "I've heard that said. Fortunately, that's the way I feel about computers. It's more like play than work! Maybe if I was extremely lucky, I could get rich with a career in music, but not only is that unlikely, it'd never be very secure. On the other hand, while I doubt I'll ever get rich working in computers, at least I'm very sure I can manage to make myself comfortable."

"Very sensible," Mr. Sutherland agreed. "Ah! Here's Sally!"

"Hi, Larry!" Sally said brightly.

Larry really liked how pretty this girl was when she smiled that way. "Hi, Sally! It's a shame people won't be able to see you over the radio. You look fantastic!"

"Why, thank you!" she smiled, turning around so he could appreciate her from all sides. She was dressed in a simple skirt and blouse, bobby socks, and sneakers, looking like the prototypical cheerleader. "You look nice yourself!"

"Thanks," he said with a blush.

"It's been a pleasure to meet you, Larry," Mr. Sutherland smiled. "Please have her back by 1:00."

"Yes, sir," Larry agreed. "It's been a pleasure to meet both of you."

"You kids have a good time!" Mrs. Sutherland added.

Sally said goodnight to her parents, then she and Larry walked out the door and closed it behind them. He escorted her to the car, and as always, opened the passenger door for her. After she slid into the seat, he closed the door and walked around to get in on the driver's side. Hiding his disappointment she had not met him in the middle, he asked, "What would you like to have for dinner?"

"Do we have much time before we have to be there?" she asked.

"As much time as we need," he replied, not quite truthfully. It was only a few minutes after 7:00, but they really should reach the station no later than 7:30. "We can pick up something and take it with us if you'd like."

"Let's do that!" she said enthusiastically. "I'm eager to see all the sights up there!"

And I'm eager to show you! He reminded himself to behave. This was their first date, and she was a very classy girl. To have a chance for a second date, he needed to be a gentleman. Of course, he was always a gentleman until encouraged to be otherwise. "What would you say to a burger and fries from the Buccaneer? We can take them with us, and if I get an extra order of fries for the gang, we might even get to eat in peace!"

Sally laughed at the concept. "Sounds fine!" she said with a sweet smile.

They made small talk as he drove to the burger stand and parked under the canopy. After a few moments, they made their selections from a menu painted on a large billboard. He went to the window, placed their order, then returned to the car.

He started explaining how the station operated and how they ran the show. "We don't have to handle any of the technical details. The chief engineer, Diggs, takes care of all that. He turns the microphones on and off as needed, spins the records and plays the tapes. Come to think of it, I guess he does just about everything there is except for the actual program content."

"The content?" Sally asked.

"Yes," he smiled. "We pick the songs to play, make all the announcements, and write all of the comedy material."

"You write those yourself?" she asked. "I thought you got them from a script."

"Well, someone has to *write* that script!" he chuckled. "John, Sam, and I usually do that during the week, but sometimes we'll write it during the middle of the show."

"Is everything done live?" she asked, impressed at how much control the kids had.

"Not everything," he confessed. "Most of the songs John and I do are prerecorded. The comedy skits are usually live, but not always. All of the song dedications are done live." He heard the announcement for their order. "That's us! I'll be right back." He hopped out of the car, went to the window, and paid for their order. When he returned, he was delighted to discover Sally had moved over into the middle of the seat.

"Hi, guys!" Larry announced when he and Sally entered the main studio. "This is Sally Sutherland. I think most of you already know her. Sally, meet John Myers and Helen Hightower. That's Julia Jacobson, and this is Sam."

"Hi, everybody!" she said brightly. "It's nice to meet you, Julia! I already know everyone else."

"It's nice to meet you, too, Sally," Julia said with a genuine smile. Not only was Sally a very pretty girl, she had a naturally outgoing personality, the main reason she was popular enough to be selected as a cheerleader. Julia could not help but like Sally, even though she was just a little envious of her at the moment.

"We brought some extra fries," Larry grinned, "so we could eat our dinner in peace. I'll get some drinks from the machine in the lobby. What would you like, Sally?"

"Whatever you have is fine with me," she answered sweetly.

"Anyone else want something while I'm out there?" he asked. When everyone declined the offer, Larry departed for the lobby, leaving Sally alone with the others.

"Did Larry tell you about how things go?" Sam asked.

"Some," she giggled, "but not enough so I know what you want me to do!"

"That figures," Sam laughed. "As usual, he leaves all the details to someone else!" Sally nodded her head and grinned as if this sort of thing was typical for her, as well. "There are two main jobs, especially for rookies like yourself. One is to answer the telephone and take requests and dedications. The other is to announce the dedications over the air. You can do either one, or a little of each. Whatever you want is fine."

"I'd like to watch a while before going on the air," Sally said a little nervously.

"That's normal," Sam said. "Julia has been doing this about three months. She'll go on the air sometimes now, but we still have a hard time getting her to. Most of the time, I just stick a piece of paper in front of her and turn on the microphone!"

"Hey!" Julia laughed, "I'm not *that* bad, am I?"

Sally laughed along, "She can do all my parts for a while, until I learn the ropes."

"If I must," Julia said, warming up to Sally even more.

As Larry returned with the drinks, he heard Sally ask, "What do the guys do?"

"They're typical guys," Sam laughed, "which means they don't do very much unless they really want to in the first place. Just be careful not to let them trap you in one of the sound booths!"

"Don't listen to her," Larry laughed. "She's just jealous because that's where all the fun stuff happens, and no one ever invites *her* in there!"

Sally looked at Sam and saw the twinkle in her eyes. "When lover boy here gets a girl into one of those sound booths, he turns into Octopus Man!" Sam giggled, winking at Sally. "Just remember, Larry, it has glass walls, and everyone can see where your hands go. And Sally, everyone will also be able to see you slap the crap out of him. I'm personally looking forward to that!"

"I'm deeply hurt, Sam," Larry said with mock dismay. "I thought you were my friend. How about telling Sally the truth for a change. You've been in one of those booths with me. Have I ever groped you in there?"

"Well... No, not really," Sam confessed with a smile. She loved to tease Larry about such things, but really did not want to give Sally, or any other girl, the wrong impression about him. Larry was a very special friend, and Sam would happily help him get laid, or at least, not interfere in the process.

"And what about you two?" Larry asked Julia and Helen.

Helen giggled her answer, "I've been in one of those booths with John, but not with you. Of course, I've seen you in there with Linda."

"And?" Larry looked her in the eye, smiling.

"I never heard her complain," Helen giggled.

Larry shifted his gaze to Julia. "How about it, Julie?" he asked.

"I've never been in a booth with you, either," Julia answered with a sweet smile. She knew Larry well enough to tease with him. "Was that an invitation?"

He was delighted with her response, and smiled broadly at her, trying to conceal his wish to answer her question seriously. "One of these days, sweet thing, I just might do that! What would your answer be then, I wonder?"

Sally decided it was time to take the initiative. "Well, tonight you're *my* date, so if anyone is going into that booth with you tonight, it'd better be *me!*"

"That's the spirit!" he laughed. "Are you ready now, or do you want to eat first?"

The whole gang had a good laugh. Larry and Sally sat down at the table and ate their hamburgers. The rest shared the extra fries Larry brought them, and casually completed the few tasks remaining to prepare for the show.

Precisely at 8:00 o'clock, Diggs pushed the button to start the prerecorded introduction to the *Top Forty Showcase* program. Ever since the now infamous ad lib Larry had done during the Rocky and Bullwinkle bit, they no longer used it to open the program. Tonight, the show was introduced using the special arrangement of the title song from the *Secret Agent Man* television program Larry and John had been working on for the last three weeks. Over the next few months, this song would be requested over and over again by listeners to the program.

That night, the other songs Larry and John performed on tape were ones they had learned to play from the Beach Boys song books they exchanged at Christmas. *Sloop John B* and *Wouldn't It Be Nice* had both been big hits recently, and were still on the charts. Larry could not help but think of Julia whenever he sang that second song. It would indeed be nice if she was just a little bit older!

For humor, they lifted another song from the Chad Mitchell Trio called *The Ides of Texas*. There was no doubt it was the highlight of the evening. Most of the listeners thought the song was making fun of the goofy scandal involving Billie Sol Estes. To Larry and John, it was a political protest against President Lyndon Johnson. John played an instrumental introduction, and started speaking over the music:

[John]	Some of America's most beautiful ballads come from the land of the sagebrush and sun: the Great Southwest.
[Larry]	What's a sagebrush, John?
[John]	I don't know, it must be something that grows out in west Texas.
[Larry]	Like cactus?
[John]	Something like that, I suppose.
[Larry]	I've never seen a cactus, doncha know.
[John]	I have! One of my neighbors has a cactus garden.
[Larry]	How do they keep the cactus alive?
[John]	They water the crap out of everything nearby, so by comparison, the cactus thinks it's in an arid area.
[Larry]	That makes sense.
[John]	It does?
[Larry]	How would I know?
[John]	Are you ready to do the song?
[Larry]	OK!

The show ended, and after exchanging their goodnight wishes, the gang members went to their respective cars in groups of two – John and Helen, Sam and Julia, Larry and Sally. John headed for the Dairy Queen, the traditional stop he and Helen made on their way home after the program. "It's a shame Larry and Linda broke up," Helen said. "I miss having her with us at the station and when you guys practice your music."

"Yeah," John smiled, "but Sally sure seems nice, doesn't she?"

"Yes," she grinned. "I'm glad he found someone. I could tell he was really hurt."

"I've heard his side of it, but not Linda's. Has she told you what happened?"

"Not a lot," she answered, "just enough to know my original idea was wrong."

"What was that?" he asked.

"Well, you know how he's always teasing the girls about sex," she smiled. "At first, I thought maybe he wasn't just teasing."

"I see," John said, wondering what Helen knew about the relationship between Larry and Linda.

"But Linda told me that wasn't the case. She said he wasn't any more pushy in that regard than any other guy."

"Do you think I'm pushy?" he asked, trying to appear casual.

"You're a sweet guy," she grinned at him.

"No more pushy than any other guy?" he asked, a little more confidently.

"No," she chuckled.

John pulled the car into the drive-in window, stopped at the order station, and pushed the button. He looked at her, smiled, and asked yet another question, "Am I pushy enough? I mean, I wouldn't want you to be disappointed because I didn't do everything you wanted me to!"

A voice came over the speaker at the order station, "May I take your order?"

"I'll have the usual," Helen answered with a grin.

John placed the order, then pulled forward to the window. As they waited for their order to be filled, he looked at Helen with a wistful smile, but said nothing. He paid for their drinks when they arrived, and drove on, now headed for Helen's house.

Helen put her head on John's shoulder as he drove. "I really do like you. I like you a lot! You know that, don't you, John?"

"I know that," he answered softly. "I hope you know I care about you, as well!"

"I do," she said. "It's just that... Well, John, it's just I'm not sure I'm ready for that just yet. Do you understand?"

"I understand," John said, trying not to look disappointed.

"I can't think of anyone I'd rather do it with than you. Are you mad at me?"

"No, I'm not mad," he said sincerely. "Maybe a little disappointed, but not mad."

"I understand," she said softly.

They arrived at her house and parked in the driveway. It was their custom to sit in the car and make out until midnight, when Helen's curfew required she go inside. These make out sessions tended to get hot and heavy, and they quickly reached the second base position. This was as far as Helen had ever allowed things to go. John broke away from a kiss for a moment and looked at his left hand, as it gently caressed her breast from the outside of her blouse, assuming once again this was as far as things would go that night.

Helen saw the look of disappointment in John's eyes, and decided to take things a little further. She placed her hand over his, and looking into his eyes with a soft smile, she gently moved his hand down her body, and slipped it underneath her sweatshirt. After a few more kisses, they were looking into each others' eyes once again, as John rubbed across her back silently asking a simple question.

When her smile gave him her answer, he attempted to unhook her bra strap, but found it mystifying. Fortunately, he remembered Larry telling him how this barrier could be easily defeated, and soon disengaged the little hooks. They both took a deep breath, trying not to gasp as he brought his hand forward to fondle her nipple, now freed from its prison. They exchanged a warm smile as John took that long lead off of second base while an imaginary crowd cheered.

"You certainly are being quiet tonight, Julia," Sam said when they were about halfway home. Neither of them had said a word since leaving the station.

"Am I?" Julia asked wistfully. "Sorry. I guess I was just thinking."

"Unless it's none of my business, what were you thinking about?"

Julia paused before answering. "Sally certainly is a pretty girl, isn't she?"

Sam laughed, "If you like that kind of thing."

"Boys seem to," Julia said, looking out the window.

It was not hard for Sam to read what Julia had on her mind. "Yes, boys are certainly attracted to pretty girls like Sally." She paused for a moment to make sure what she wanted to say before continuing. "Larry's the same as other boys in that regard. He isn't immune to being attracted to a pretty girl like Sally. But he's a lot different than other boys in many other respects."

Julia was glad Sam had mentioned his name first. Now she felt like she could talk about him without appearing to be too interested. "How is he different?"

"Most boys his age are just looking to have a good time with as many girls as they can. Larry isn't like that. He just wants one girl, and he thought he'd found that. Right now, he's very hurt, very confused, and very lonely. When a pretty girl like Sally pays a little bit of attention to him..."

"Anyone can see she likes him, but I doubt he's the only boy she's interested in."

"I agree," Sam said. "He's a smart guy, and I'm sure he knows that, also. But he's very vulnerable right now. I'd hate to see him get hurt again."

"Me, too," Julia agreed.

"He confuses you, doesn't he?" Sam asked.

Julia looked carefully at Sam before replying. "Yes. I guess I shouldn't try to hide from you I have a crush on him."

"I know, Julia," Sam said softly. "If it makes you feel any better, I happen to know you're a big part of his confusion, also."

"What do you mean by that?" Julia asked.

"I've known him for a long time," Sam said, looking Julia in the eye. "It'd be very difficult for him to keep many secrets from me. It's no secret to me he's taken notice of you, but he's confused by you. He's confused by a lot of things right now. Maybe there are so many things going on in his life he doesn't know which way to go, where to look, who to turn to."

"And then along comes Sally..." Julia began.

"...distracting his attention away from other paths that might bring him closer to finding the answers to all those questions in his head," Sam completed.

Julia contemplated the ideas expressed in this conversation. "You seem to be suggesting a girl interested in him should learn to be patient."

Sam was impressed by this younger girl's insight. Apparently, Julia had a very mature and very wise teacher. "I know as long as Larry has hope, he'll chase after his dreams until he either finds them, or dies from the effort. That chase may lead him through some strange territory, and it might be years before he finds the right path, but he *will* find that path somehow, someday."

Julia nodded her head in understanding. "Thanks, Sam," she said sincerely. "Larry is lucky to have a friend like you. *I'm* lucky to have a friend like you, also."

Sam smiled as she replied, "Thank you, Julia! I think that's about the nicest thing anyone has ever said to me." Sam decided it was time to change the subject. "Are you coming to listen to the guys practice tomorrow? It's at *my* house this time!"

"If I can get a ride," Julia answered with a laugh.

Sam grinned back at her. "Well, I seem to recall Sir Galahad promised you'd always have a ride if you wanted it, so if I were you, I'd count on someone coming to pick you up tomorrow at the usual time. I don't know who it might be right now, but one thing you can count on is Larry *always* keeps his promises!" Sam laughed as she remembered hearing him make a promise to himself last Sunday night. She decided if he did not keep that one, she would kill him personally!

Larry followed slightly behind Sally as they walked to the car, waiting to see which door she would go to. He was pleased when she walked to the driver's side. Opening the door for her, he asked, "Did you have a good time in there, Sally?"

"Yes, I did!" she smiled, slipping under the steering wheel and moving into the middle seat. "To be honest, Larry, it was a lot more fun than I expected it to be! Or maybe it was the company that made it so much fun."

"I'm glad," he said truthfully. Sally was much more graceful in her movements than Linda. While he was disappointed his view was not nearly as spectacular, he was still impressed. "We have plenty of time remaining. What would you like to do now?"

"Even though I've known you for a couple of years," she smiled, "it occurs to me I hardly know anything about you. Why don't we just go talk for a little while and get better acquainted?"

"I'd like that," he said returning her smile. "Do you have any particular place in mind? I know a nice quiet spot out in the country. It sits on a hilltop and has a great view of the stars and the moon. Interested?"

"It sounds romantic," she said continuing to smile at him. Larry returned her smile but said nothing. When she leaned against him and placed her head on his shoulder, he headed to the little gravel road in Steep Hollow he had frequented. As he drove, he reminded himself this was his first date with Sally, and there was no reason for him to think she had any special interest in him.

He parked the car and turned off the lights. "What do you think of the view?"

"It's lovely," she said, looking up into his face.

He smiled as he put his arm around her shoulder. She smiled back as she snuggled up to him and continued to look into his face. It was a welcome invitation he had not expected. Hypnotized by her bright eyes and sweet smile, slowly and carefully, he leaned over and kissed her softly, halfway expecting her to put up her hand to stop him, or worse. Instead, her response was soft and warm.

Once again, he reminded himself this was their first date, and he must not assume too much. He decided a little romance would be therapeutic for his soul, helping to reduce the pain he still felt from the breakup with Linda. But by no means was he going to allow his feelings to leap ahead!

They kissed for a while, then talked and laughed together, and then kissed a little while more. She laughed at his jokes, and even threw a punchline back at him from time to time. But time is too short for those that laugh, and all too soon, it was time for him to take her home.

They arrived at Sally's house a few minutes before 1:00. "I hope you've had as much fun tonight as I have, Sally," he said as they remained in the car for a moment.

"I was thinking the same thing," she said with a chuckle.

"Would you go out with me again?" he asked hopefully. "Would you like to go to a movie with me next Friday night?"

"I'm sorry, Larry," she said sweetly, "but I already have plans for Friday. It's basketball season, and I'm a cheerleader."

"I forgot," he said. He was slightly discouraged, but quickly noted this was a completely honest response, and hopefully was not just a convenient way to blow him off. So he tried again, "Then how about Saturday? We could go back to the station if you want, or I could take a night off so we could go to that movie instead."

"I'd like that," she said. "Maybe we could do both."

"Maybe so," he smiled. "Shall I pick you up at the same time next Saturday?"

"Sure," she said, still looking warmly into his eyes. Larry felt Sally draw him like a magnet. *Or is it more like a moth to a flame?* he wondered. Either way, he could not stop himself from moving to kiss her again. Her response was as before – warm and tender – exactly what he needed it to be. "I should go in now," she said when the kiss was completed.

He nodded in understanding, wondering if she was using his code talk. He decided to forget such ideas. If she liked him, it would show over time, and if not, he was determined his feelings for a girl would never again get ahead of her feelings for him.

He smiled at her, then opened the car door and climbed outside. He turned back to offer his hand to help her, which she accepted with a smile and climbed out of the car to stand beside him. He held onto her hand even though providing her with a little help to get out of the car was no longer an issue. She did not try to take her hand away, and they walked hand-in-hand to her front door.

At her door, Sally faced him and said, "It's been a wonderful evening, Larry." With her hand still in his right one, he reached with his left to take her other. As they smiled into each others' eyes, he drew her towards him by gently pulling her hands behind his back. Their goodnight kiss, the first with full body contact, was warm and exciting. Even better, it was lingering.

But all good things must end. "Goodnight, Sally," he whispered.

"Goodnight," she said softly. She let go of his hands and turned to open the door. She returned his smile while slowly and softly closing the door behind her.

Sunday, January 22, 1967
White Rabbit

Julia was anxiously watching for Larry's car to pull into her driveway. He had promised she would always have a ride to both the radio station and the Sunday afternoon guitar practices as long as she needed and wanted one, but she was not completely sure she could count on it. Sam was confident, but Julia had only known Larry for three months. In fact, it was exactly three months ago today they had first met. He had also met one of her best friends that night, and the two of them had been together most of that time. *If only I hadn't been with Jimmy at the time,* she thought, *maybe it would have been me.* But she quickly realized if she had not been with Jimmy, then he would not have convinced her to invite his brother, John, to come to her birthday party, and so she would never have met Larry in the first place.

How strange and subtle are the events in our lives, she thought. Even now, the events seemed so strange. She was no longer with Jimmy, and Larry was no longer with Linda. She liked him, and thought he liked her. She hoped so. Yet there seemed to be something keeping them apart, especially now that Sally had entered the picture.

What was it that Sam had said? Larry was a "one girl" type of guy. Sally was not likely to want that, so whatever relationship they had was probably going to be short lived. There was nothing she could do anyway – boys did the chasing when they found a girl they liked. When a girl liked a boy, all she could do was encourage him to chase after her. Sam was right. Patience was the key.

Julia saw a car turn into her driveway, but since it was not Larry's, she almost ignored it. Then she realized it was John's car, and looked more closely. As it approached, she could see John and Helen sitting in the front seat. When it stopped, one of the back doors opened, and she was a little surprised and very excited to see Larry hop out, and head towards her front door.

"He's here, mom!" Julia called. Jessica heard the announcement from the family room, and started walking to the foyer to greet him. Jessica had taught Julia it was "improper" for a girl to greet a gentleman caller herself. It was an old fashioned concept, and they all knew it, but it was still standard practice at the Jacobson house for one of the parents to answer the door at such times, even though this was not an actual date.

Julia strategically retreated into the kitchen. The doorbell rang just as Jessica entered the foyer. Schotzy barked and jumped for the doorknob as if he could open the door himself to greet his friend. Jessica paused momentarily so it would not appear anyone was waiting at the front door, and after a reasonable delay, opened it to greet the caller. "Hello, Larry! How are you today?"

"Hi, Mrs. J," he replied brightly. "I'm just fine, and thanks for asking." He reached down to pay some attention to the dog. "Hi, old fellow! How are you doing today?" Returning his attention to Jessica, he asked, "How are the rest of the Jacobsons doing?"

Jessica could not help but think about how different he seemed now than he did just three weeks ago. Perhaps this new girl was already helping him get over Linda. "We're doing very well. Come on in for a moment, Larry. Julia will be right out."

"Thanks," he said with a smile as he entered the foyer, closely followed by the dog. "I really hate these three or four weeks of winter we have, don't you?" he grinned, making a little smalltalk, and teasing Jessica about the difference in climate between central Texas and New York City.

"You should be ashamed of yourself for complaining," Jessica teased back. "How quickly you seem to forget those nine months of summer we have every year!"

He shrugged and continued to grin. When Julia entered the room, he immediately greeted her, "Hi, Julie! I'm glad to see Sam got you home safely!"

"No thanks to you!" she giggled. "Did Sally get home safely?"

"Of course!" he said, trying to look like a guilty person pretending to be innocent. "She was with me. What could possibly have happened to her?"

Julia exchanged a glance and a grin with her mother. "Of course," they both said in unison, then laughed. "We'd better get going. The B.S. is getting a little deep in here, and I would hate for mom to spend the whole afternoon scrubbing the walls!"

Larry just grinned. "Your carriage awaits thee, ma lady," he announced with a bow. "Have a good afternoon, Mrs. J! Bye, Schotzy!"

"Thanks," Jessica said. "You kids have fun." With that, she returned to the family room to join her husband, and the kids headed for the car.

Like always, Larry opened the car door for her, and Julia hopped in. Before closing the door, however, he noticed Julia had moved to the other side of the car, and was looking back at him with a grin. "Are you getting in?" He merely shook his head, got in the car, and closed the door behind him.

"Hi, Julia," Helen said from the front seat.

"Hi, guys!" Julia said. "I have to admit I'm a little surprised to see all of you."

"Just saving some gas," John laughed. He turned the car around and headed out the driveway and back onto the country lane. On the ride out to Julia's house, John had purposely avoided the subject of Larry's big date with Sally. He waited until Julia had joined them so he could maximize the ribbing. "So, Larry, you haven't told us about how things went with Sally after the show last night."

Larry saw John grinning at him via the rear view mirror. "It went just fine, John," he said, glaring back at him with a bit of menace in his voice.

"I want details," John snickered. "Where did you go? What did you do?"

Larry scowled at John in the mirror. He noticed Helen and Julia were both looking at him and waiting for his answer. "We just drove around for a little while and talked. Sally said even though she'd known me for quite a while, she really didn't know much about me. I agreed, so we just wanted to get better acquainted."

"That's hard to do while driving," John teased. "You parked for a while, right?"

Larry rolled his eyes and frowned at the mirror, as if to tell John he was going to get him back for this. "Yes, for a little while."

"Did you get to second base?" John asked with a laugh.

"Uh, John," Larry said continuing to frown, "that's not really... I think I've already told you a gentleman doesn't go around talking about such things."

"Wow!" John laughed. "A home run on the first date? I *am* impressed!"

"Why do you think that?" he shouted. "I said I wasn't going to talk about it!"

"If nothing happened, all you have to do is say nothing happened," John teased.

Larry shook his head. Helen had turned around in her seat and was grinning at him. Julia was also looking at him, but the smile on her faced seemed a little unnatural. "John, I'll neither confirm nor deny anything that may have happened."

Helen joined the teasing. "If nothing happened, all you have to do is deny it."

"No, I won't confirm or deny anything of the sort!"

"Larry," Julia said calmly, "if a gentleman doesn't talk about such things, you shouldn't say anything. But if there's nothing to tell, what's wrong with denying it?"

He looked at Julia and realized she had provided him with his escape mechanism. "Tell me something, Julie. Suppose I deny it. Now suppose next week, someone asks me a similar question, and I deny it again. Suppose this happens over and over. But then one day, someone asks me the same question and I *don't* deny it. Suppose I refused to talk about it again. What conclusion would you make?"

"I'd conclude you were hiding something," Julia grinned.

"Exactly," he smiled, "so after denying it, any future refusal to talk about it would be pointless. You'd know something had happened. Since a gentleman shouldn't talk about these things, how do I avoid telling someone there's anything to hide? I suppose I could lie about it..."

"...but you don't like to lie about anything," Julia continued, now showing a more natural smile. She could already see where Larry was going with this.

"Exactly!" he said brightly. "The only other choice is not to talk at all, whether there's anything to tell or not! If anything happened last night, then it's a private matter between Sally and me. You can come to your own conclusion. I won't confirm or deny it."

"What a load of crap!" John said.

"He's got you, John," Helen snickered while Julia giggled in agreement.

Larry grinned at John's face in the rear view mirror, but could see John was actually a little upset by this turn of events. After all, the guys had been sharing information about such things for some time. With a twinkle in his eye, he continued the story. "Of course, that gentleman thing doesn't count among good friends. A gentleman doesn't want to soil the reputation of his girlfriends by having intimate details passed around as gossip. But if you guys promise to keep it a secret, I'll tell you what *really* happened last night!"

Julia had seen that twinkle in his eye and knew Larry was up to something. "I promise," she giggled. John and Helen also promised to keep the secret.

Larry leaned forward in his seat and motioned for Julia to do the same. When all of their heads were close together, Larry told the story in a whisper. "John, you know that place we go sometimes to... uh... have a smoke? Sally and I went there. There's a beautiful view of the countryside, and when the skies are clear like last night, the stars and the moon make it very romantic." He decided to tease his friend a little. "Has John ever taken you there, Helen?"

Helen blushed and giggled. "It doesn't sound familiar," she grinned at John.

"You should suggest it to him," he winked. "It has a great view of the stars and a little lake. Very romantic!" He grinned at Julia who was giggling at John's distress.

"Get on with what happened last night," John said, now with a scowl of his own.

"Oh. Ah!" Larry said as if he had forgotten. "So there we were, sitting under the canopy of stars. We kissed a little, then talked a bit. She laughed at my jokes, and then we kissed a little more."

When Larry paused, John urged him to continue, "And?"

"And that's it!" he smiled. "We had a few laughs, shared a few kisses, and then I took her home. Game called on account of darkness, eh, John?"

"Nothing else?" John asked again.

"I will neither confirm nor deny..." he started to say, but started snickering before he could finish the sentence. Julia and Helen laughed along with him. John shook his head then joined the laughter.

They arrived at Sam's house. As soon as the car was stopped, Larry opened his door and hopped out, planning to run to the other side to open Julia's door. But as he was about to close the door behind him, he noticed Julia had slipped across the seat and was already climbing out of the car on his side.

He smiled at Julia as he held the door for her, thinking about what a little sweetheart she was, wishing he could have been with her last night. He was grateful the story of his date with Sally had gone the way it had. Since Julia did not seem to be upset, maybe the damage was minimal. *If only I could get Jimmy to release me from that damn promise!*

The girls went to the front door and knocked while the boys fetched their instruments and music books from the trunk. Sam greeted them happily, welcoming them inside. Sam hugged Helen and Julia, then turned them over to her mother who greeted them the same way. Sam also hugged John and Larry, kissing them on the cheek, before passing them off to her mother.

"Hi, Mrs. K!" Larry said. "Thanks for letting us disturb your Sunday once again."

"You're always welcome here," Gayle replied. "Come on in and get yourself settled. I made some cookies this morning, and they're already in that beautiful cookie jar you gave me. I'll make you all some hot cocoa whenever you're ready."

"You're the best, Mrs. K!" Larry said, giving her another hug. "Why don't you convince Sam to run off with me so you can be my mother-in-law!"

"I thought you were only interested in cheerleaders now," she teased.

"Oh, please," Larry sighed followed with a laugh. "Not that again!"

John saw a look of confusion on Sam's face and recounted the conversation from the ride over. Sam laughed, and nodded her understanding to Larry. "You blew it, Larry," she grinned. "I was ready to run off with you, but then you turned to Sally. I'll just have to stay with Donald."

"I'll keep working on her, Larry," Gayle laughed.

"Mother!" Sam protested. "I thought you *liked* Donald!"

"Of course," she winked, "but I'll always hope you'll end up with the very best!"

"And I thought the B.S. was getting deep at *my* house," Julia laughed.

The kids settled down in the living room. John and Larry were eager to start practicing. They got their guitars out of their cases right away, and began to tune up.

As the clock approached 7:00, the kids began to wrap things up. It had been an excellent practice session, and Larry felt as happy and relaxed as he had in a long time. He still hurt from the breakup with Linda, but realized the worst was over. The one date with Sally had somehow brought him back into reality. He was glad there would be another date, but he also knew a longterm, exclusive relationship with her was not in the offing. He would enjoy whatever time she granted him, helping him forget Linda, and being seen with her would enhance his social standing.

It also seemed the relationship with Sally would not damage his future chances with Julia. He was very grateful of that fact. Someday, hopefully soon, he would be released from his promise, and would get his chance to be with her, to find out exactly what it was about her that called to him so strongly. For now, he just needed to be patient. Patience was the key concept he was trying to introduce into his character, particularly when it came to his relationships with girls. *Be patient!* he would remind himself over and over in the future. *Don't let your feelings get so far ahead of hers you frighten her away. Wait for her to come to you!* He hoped this philosophy would lessen his chances of being hurt so badly in the future.

"Goodnight, Mrs. K!" the kids called, headed out the door. "Goodnight, Sam!"

"Goodnight, all," Gayle said cheerfully. "Be careful driving home!"

Larry got to the car first, opened the back door for Julia, and stood back smiling. Julia returned his smile as she slipped into the back seat, and moved over to make room, not *quite* all the way to the far door. Helen slid under the steering wheel to sit in the middle beside John. In the backseat, both passengers wished they could do the same, but neither of them made the move. Julia's restraint was because the boy should initiate such things. Larry's restraint was a promise he refused to break.

As they drove towards Steep Hollow, John decided to take a new initiative. "Do you girls like to smoke?" He had not introduced Helen to his little hobby, and thought it might be a good time. He laughed when he heard Larry choking.

"I'm not much of a smoker," Helen replied. "I've only tried it once or twice."

"I've never smoked at all," Julia said.

"I think you'd better clarify what you're talking about," Larry said calmly. John brought the subject up, and Larry wanted to stay out of it.

"I suppose you're right. I'm not talking about tobacco, girls."

Helen caught on quickly. "There's something to the name of your band after all?"

"Not really," John said, "but we do smoke a little grass now and then."

Julia should not have been so surprised. "You guys smoke marijuana?"

"On occasion," Larry confessed. It scared him a little to admit this to her, but he realized it was a small part of his life. The perfect girl would understand and accept it, whether she chose to join or not. It occurred to him it was important to see how she would react. "Have you ever tried it, Julie?"

"No!" she said emphatically. "My parents don't approve of drugs!"

"I didn't plan to offer any to *them*," John said.

Larry thought this was not the ideal response, and decided to get involved to soften it up a little. "I think what John means is everyone has to make up their own mind about such things. Your parents don't approve. I accept that and respect it. This wasn't part of their generation and they don't understand it. But it's part of ours, and sooner or later, everyone has to make their *own* choice. Personally, I think one should have a good understanding of any subject before they make a decision."

"So you think I should try it?" Julia asked, doubtfully.

"That's completely up to you, Julie. I'm not going to try to convince you one way or another. I was a little hesitant before I tried it the first time, but then I realized all of the things we've been told about it simply weren't true. It doesn't make you go crazy, and it doesn't make you want other drugs. Maybe it can be the first step for some, who move on to other things, but that wasn't the case for me, at least."

"How long have you been smoking?" Julia asked.

"About a year, I think. Isn't that right, John?" He nodded in agreement. "I found it to be relaxing and pleasant, especially if I don't smoke too much at once."

"If you do," John explained, "you get pretty stupid. It's called getting *stoned*. I understand it's a lot like getting drunk. The funny thing is, I can't compare, because I've never drank enough alcohol to get drunk!"

"Yeah, alcohol is too hard to get!" Larry laughed.

The girls laughed at his joke, but were still a little tentative. Helen was very curious, however, and asked, "Would I be acting weird when I got home? Would my folks be able to tell what I'd been doing?"

"Not unless you smoke too much," John assured her. "No one will know but us."

Helen thought for a moment. "What do you think? I'm willing to try if you are."

"Will we still be in control?" Julia asked. "Is this how you convince girls to..."

"We only *wish* it could be as easy as that!" Larry laughed. "No, Julie, you'll still be in control. It won't make you do anything if you don't already want to. I promise you'll be safe. You're my friend, and I'd never do anything that would harm you."

Julia heard the word "promise" and remembered Sam explaining how significant that word was to Larry. She knew she would be safe, so it was just a matter of deciding whether or not to go against the wishes of her parents. She remembered how her mother told her she had to make her own decision about when it would be right to have a sexual relationship, and decided the same thing should apply in matters such as this. "OK, I'll try it, too. But you'll have to show me what to do."

Larry could almost see the wheels turning as she thought. When she announced her decision, he smiled, realizing she had made this decision on her own, even though she knew her parents would not approve. He realized it would not be long before he could no longer think of her as a little girl. How he longed for that day!

John turned off of the country lane onto the gravel road, and stopped in the familiar place they knew as their "smoking room," not too far from Larry's favorite romantic spot. He retrieved the necessary materials, and proceeded to roll a joint. He handed it to Helen out of habit, saying, "Ladies first!"

"Since this is their first time," Larry chuckled, "we can't be so chivalrous, John."

The girls giggled nervously, and Helen handed it back to John. "It'll seem a little harsh at first," John said. "You want to draw the smoke into your lungs and hold it as much as you can. It'll probably make you cough until you get used to it." He lit the joint, drew his first toke, and handed it to Helen. She took a tentative puff, coughed a little, and tried to hand it back to John. "Pass it to Larry!"

Larry took the joint and showed it to Julia, hoping to show her there was nothing frightening about it. "Watch me," he said, and drew a small toke. He looked at her and smiled as he held his breath, then offered the joint to her.

Julia took it from him, hesitated, but decided she would go through with it. She imitated what Larry had done, drawing a small amount of the smoke into her lungs and holding her breath. But the harsh smoke made her cough. Larry quickly took the joint from her fingers and passed it to John. "Are you OK?"

"I think so," Julia said, still feeling the harshness in her throat.

"You did fine," he assured her. "You'll get accustomed to it and then it won't make you cough."

John had already drawn his next and once again passed it to Helen. She drew a slightly larger amount than before. She held her breath and managed to pass it to Larry before coughing. Larry took another small draw and held it out for Julia. She repeated her previous attempt and held her breath much longer than before. When she attempted to give the joint back to Larry, he told her to pass it to John.

Now they had completed their little circle, and future movement from person to person proceeded smoothly. After another circuit was completed, John attached a clip to the remainder. It was a little earlier than normal, but he wanted to show Helen how they would smoke the joint all the way down to the end. When he passed it to Helen, she duplicated his technique.

"We don't stop like they do with tobacco," Larry explained. "We try to smoke it down completely. Ideally, there'll be nothing left but a little bit of paper. We use a clip to hold it so we don't burn either our fingers or our lips. Watch how I draw the smoke without even putting it to my lips."

He demonstrated the technique as Julia watched. "I think I can do that," she said. She sucked the smoke around the joint and passed the remains to John. She held her breath without coughing this time. When she blew out the smoke, she started giggling. "Now I understand the joke you made when you apologized for the mooseberry juice!"

Larry laughed with her. "How do you feel?" He already knew the answer.

"I feel funny, but I like it. It's sort of like my whole body is buzzing."

"Me, too," Helen giggled.

"We have reached the state of buzz!" Larry laughed, feeling a little buzzy himself. John agreed, and after his last draw, passed the joint around the circle one last time.

When he examined it, Larry decided there really was not enough for both of them. He offered the remainder to Julia, who told him to go ahead. He drew what he thought might be the last, but decided to pass it to her anyway. She managed to get a little smoke, then passed it to John, who disposed of what little evidence remained.

"So what happens now?" Helen giggled.

"We just relax and have fun," John said. "You'll be amazed at how much funnier Larry's jokes are after having a smoke!"

The girls laughed. Larry countered with, "I don't need my audience to be high for my jokes to be funny, John, but it certainly helps yours!" The girls laughed a little harder. They teased each other back and forth for a few moments. The boys were pleased the girls seemed to be enjoying this new experience.

John began to prepare a second joint. "If we share another, it'll get even better." When he had it ready, he handed it to Helen. "Now that you're experienced druggies, we can be chivalrous again. Ladies first!" he insisted, offering her a light.

Helen giggled as she lit the cigarette and drew the first toke. She held her breath like a pro and passed it to Larry. He immediately handed it to Julia, saying, "Ladies first!" Julia smiled and took her toke, then handed it back to Larry. They continued in the new order until the second joint was a memory, and their buzz was stronger.

"Are we really druggies now?" Julia laughed, but was truthfully a little concerned.

"Not in the sense you're thinking," Larry assured her. "You could decide you never want to smoke again, and nothing bad will happen to you. There'll be no withdrawal symptoms. Or you can be like me, and decide you like it enough you want to try it again from time to time. The truth is you can decide to quit any time you want. I don't see how anyone can call that addiction. Personally, I don't even think marijuana is truly a drug in that sense, unless you agree alcohol is also a drug."

The kids sat in the car, joked with each other, and enjoyed the warm and relaxing feeling. John and Helen played a little slap and tickle, and giggled with each other. Larry and Julia giggled along with them, but true to his word, none of them did anything they were not already prepared to do previously. Larry was tempted to play a little slap and tickle with Julia, but since he would have resisted that temptation before smoking, he continued to resist even though he suspected she might welcome it.

Before long, the buzz began to fade. The girls wanted to have a little more, but the boys said it was time to slow down. "As you are right now," Larry said, "no one would think anything more than you're in a really good mood. But if you continue, you'll start to get stupid. The last thing I want to do is take you home stoned!"

"Killjoy," Helen giggled.

"Yeah," Julia agreed. "You introduce us to something we like, then won't let us have any more. What kind of friends are you, anyway?"

"The best kind," Larry smiled.

Julia looked in his eyes and agreed. "Yes," she said with a warm smile, "I think you may be the best friends I could ever hope for!" She leaned over and gave Larry a hug, thinking maybe it was not improper for a girl to hug to a dear friend. After all, she had seen Sam hug both John and Larry, and knew their relationships were not romantic.

Larry returned her hug, fighting desperately to resist the urge to bring his lips to meet hers. When the hug ended, he hoped she had not noticed how his heart was pounding inside his chest.

John started the car and completed the drive to Julia's house, arriving before her 10:00 o'clock curfew. Larry got out of the car, smiled as Julia followed him, and walked her to the door as was his custom. "Now that we're alone, Julie, tell me what you *really* think about what we just did."

"I really did like it, Larry," she smiled.

"Will you promise me you'll always let me be around whenever you smoke?"

"Would you be willing to make the same promise to me?" she asked sweetly.

His heart screamed, *Yes!* Ignoring it as much as possible, he grinned at her and thought about how much he wished that could always be the case. "It might be a little difficult to keep that promise."

"Then why would you ask it of me? Do you think that's fair?"

Larry smiled in appreciation. "I suppose not, but I have more experience with this than you. I just don't want to see it cause you any trouble."

"What kind of trouble?" she asked. "You said it was safe."

"It's safe as long as you don't abuse it," he said calmly. He looked at the ground and wondered if he could find a way to say what was on his mind. "I told you it wouldn't cause you to do anything you weren't already prepared to do. While that's true, it might lower your inhibitions. You might decide you're prepared to do something you weren't prepared to do previously. I just want to protect you – to know you're OK."

"I can take care of myself," she said sweetly, looking into his eyes. "Will it make you happy if I promise I'll be careful?"

He looked into her eyes and saw this was the best he could hope for. He smiled at her. "Goodnight, Julie. I'll see you next Saturday."

He was about to turn to leave, but Julia hugged him again. "Goodnight, Larry, and thanks. Thanks for being so wonderful."

"I'm just an ordinary guy," he said returning her hug, "but you're very welcome." When they released each other, Julia opened her door and stepped inside. She watched him walk to the car, waved as he crawled into the back seat, then softly closed her door.

Friday, January 27, 1967
I Am A Rock

Larry decided to attend the basketball game. Not only would it give him something to do, but he could sit in the stands, watching Sally and the other cheerleaders go through their routines, and think. It was an exciting contest, the Broncos defeating their arch rivals from Conroe by a last second field goal.

During the game, Sally saw Larry sitting in the stands, and waved to him. He smiled and waved back to her, but otherwise did not interfere with her duties. When the game was over, she motioned for him to come down to the floor of the gymnasium. "Hi, Larry!" she said when he arrived. "You girls all know Larry, right?" she asked, making sure the other cheerleaders noticed him. They all knew him by name, but other than Sharon and Betty, did not know much more about him, other than the nice things Sally had told them about her trip to the radio station the previous Saturday.

"Hi, ladies," he said politely. "You did a great job. I have to confess I paid more attention to you than to the game. Who won, by the way?"

"Don't let him fool you, girls," Betty laughed. "I've known this character three years now, and if you aren't careful, he'll charm the pants right off of you!"

"Only in my dreams, I suspect," Larry chuckled. Betty had not intended it quite the way it came out, but the girls laughed at his response to such an obvious opening.

"Are you here alone?" Sally asked.

"No," he answered smoothly, "I'm here with you, aren't I?"

Sally laughed at his impertinence. "I meant, did you *come* alone?" she corrected.

"Gee, that's a little personal, don't you think?" he smirked.

"Didn't I warn you?" Betty laughed. "Come on girls. Let's leave Sally to stew in her own juices."

The other cheerleaders giggled and left for the girls' locker room, leaving Larry and Sally alone. "It's nice to see you, Larry," she said sweetly. "Will you wait for me while I go clean up and change?"

"If you want me to," he said sincerely.

"Then I'll be back in a jiffy! Keep an eye out for my little brother, will you? He'll probably be out of the boys' locker room before I get back."

"Sure!" he replied. He sat on the lowest row of seats as Sally ran off to the girls' locker room to clean up. He chuckled to himself, realizing he never knew she even had a younger brother. It now dawned on him she was obviously related to Frank Sutherland, the sophomore who played briefly during the game.

The other students and fans departed quickly, leaving only a few stragglers waiting for someone after the game. This included the girlfriends of the players, and a couple of college age guys waiting for some of the cheerleaders. It occurred to Larry he was in some pretty exclusive company. That thought did a lot to boost his ego!

After a few minutes, several of the players began coming out of the boys' locker room. Frank Sutherland walked up to him. "Are you Larry?"

"Yes. Sally asked me to watch for you. Nice game!"

"Thanks!" Frank said simply. "I didn't get much play time tonight. I'm just happy to be on the team! Maybe next year I'll be able to contribute more." He sat down next to Larry to wait for his sister. As an explanation, he added, "I'm not old enough to drive, so Sally usually gives me a ride to the home games, unless she has a date or something."

"Makes sense," Larry agreed.

"You work at the radio station on Saturday nights?" he asked. "Sally told me about how much fun she had last weekend."

"Yes," Larry answered. "I'm glad to know she really did have fun. I think it's fun, but I don't imagine everyone would agree. Do you listen to the show?"

"Most of the time," Frank answered. "You guys are pretty funny! And I like to listen to the songs you and that other guy sing."

"John," he said, putting a name to the other voice. "I appreciate the compliment."

Larry saw Sally come out of the locker room and start toward them, so he stood up to greet her. She walked up to Larry and kissed him. "I see you guys have met. There's a post-game party over at Sharon's house. Would you like to come along?"

"I don't want to intrude without an invitation." Larry replied.

"I just invited you, silly!" she giggled.

Larry smiled, a little amazed at how he seemed to have gained so much acceptance from what he had always considered to be a closed society, the so-called "in" crowd. "Sounds like fun!"

"Why don't we all go together?" she suggested. "I'll drive my car, and bring you back here after the party."

"If you want," he agreed, "or I could drive and bring you back."

"You'd better let her drive," Frank snickered. "That's about all she thinks about since she got her license and dad bought her a car."

"It's settled," she laughed. "Come on you guys, or I'll leave without you." She turned and headed towards the main entrance to the gym, without looking to see if the boys were coming. Frank merely shrugged, grinned at Larry, and began to follow. Larry decided it would be smart to do the same.

She led them to a brand new 1967 Chevy Camero. She grinned as she sat behind the wheel, inserted the key, and started the engine. "Are you guys coming?"

"Not yet," Larry whispered to Frank, "but I'm definitely *breathing* a lot harder."

Frank laughed in appreciation of the joke. "I'll get in the back. You can ride shotgun." Larry nodded and opened the door. Frank tilted the seat forward and climbed in the back. Larry followed, sitting in the front seat next to Sally. He barely managed to get the door closed before she pulled the shift into reverse, backed out of the parking spot, shifted into drive, and stepped on the accelerator.

It was quite a ride! Sally laughed with delight as she drove. Being used to the way his sister drove, Frank laughed along with her, hanging on for dear life. Larry was apprehensive at first, but started to relax a little by the time they arrived at Sharon's house. When they pulled to a stop, he wanted to get out and kiss the ground, but decided that would not be the appropriate thing to do. Frank simply laughed and urged Larry to hurry up and let him out of the back sat.

"What did you think of that?" Sally asked with a grin on her face.

Larry grinned back, but was not sure what he should say. All he managed to produce was the single word, "Interesting!" Sally just giggled, took Larry by the hand, and escorted him to the front door.

Frank had beaten them. He rang the bell and was greeted by Sharon. "Come on in, guys. The party's already in full swing!" In the dining room, some kids were dancing to music coming from a stereo. In the living and family rooms, couples were sitting on furniture or the floor, most of them heavily engaged in exchanging spit. In the kitchen, some guys were standing around hoisting a few cans of beer. Sharon's parents were nowhere to be seen. Larry decided it would be better not to inquire about that.

"Will you get us some beer?" Sally smiled. "I'll meet you by the fireplace."

Larry nodded and departed for the kitchen. "Who's hiding the beer?" he asked one of the guys. He hardly finished the question before he was handed two cold cans. "Thanks!" he grinned to hide his confusion, and returned to the family room.

Sally was sitting on the hearth in front of a warm fire. She smiled at him and indicated he should sit beside her. He sat down, opened one can of beer, handing it to her before opening the other can for himself, trying to appear relaxed and natural, as if he did this all of the time. Sensing his nervousness, Sally snuggled up to him, put her arms around his neck, and kissed him, letting him know as far as she was concerned, he was as welcome as anyone present.

It helped. Before long, Larry relaxed and engaged in conversation with various other party guests. He knew practically everyone at the party, and all of them were acquainted with him, but none of them were exactly what one would call close friends. He was surprised at how open they seemed to be to him, genuinely eager to learn about this newcomer to their circle – the "inner" circle to Larry's eyes.

As the party progressed, the enthusiastic noise first characterizing it began to dwindle a little. Most of the unattached males grabbed a few cans of beer and departed for places unknown, primarily leaving couples, many of whom were absorbed in activities of their own, not showing much interest in whatever might be happening around them.

Larry and Sally were engaging in a bit of this activity themselves when they noticed everything had gotten a lot quieter. When they looked around to see what was happening, Sharon walked up to Larry carrying a guitar. "How about a song, Larry," she asked nicely. The others, including Sally and even one or two of the previously engaged couples joined in with this request.

"Do you play?" he asked Sharon.

"No way!" she laughed. "It belongs to my older brother who's away at college. Come to think of it, I don't think he plays either!"

Larry was a little embarrassed, but he accepted the guitar. It was badly in need of tuning, and he spent a few moments adjusting it, trying to think of a song he could play and sing without the support he was used to getting from John. He decided on a Beatles song called *We Can Work It Out* that he and John were about to use on the radio program. It would not be the same without John's guitar and his voice in harmony, but it should be OK as a solo number.

Encouraged by the positive response he received, Larry decided to try a Paul Simon song called *I Am A Rock* he and John had also been working on recently. The original version used an electric guitar and organ, but Larry was creating an arrangement suitable for acoustic guitar. He even practiced some of the lead guitar parts that made the music interesting, so was fairly sure he could play it solo with reasonable success, even without John's expertise.

The words to the song reflected an attitude he had at one time hoped to acquire, although he knew it could never be so simple as that. *How can one expect to feel the joy of victory unless they're willing to risk the agony of defeat?* Still, he was striving to make himself a little less vulnerable to the heartache he had experienced so many times in the past. Maybe one really could be a rock protected inside a fortress, even if only for some of the time.

After that song, he decided to lighten the mood a little. As a joke, he sang a rather bizarre song called *They're Coming To Take Me Away* popularized by Lenny Welch last year. The kids loved it, and Larry loved the attention they gave him. He decided he would tell John about this one so they could do a fancier arrangement sometime.

He was ready to quit after just these three numbers, but Sally and Sharon begged for just one more. So he sang the Beatles classic *And I Love Her* and it worked wonderfully, even without John's lead guitar and solo parts.

After watching the movie, John and Helen drove once again through the drive-in window at the Dairy Queen to get a cold drink. Since they still had over an hour before Helen's curfew, John decided to make her a different offer. "Would you like to go back to that place we went Sunday night and share another smoke with me?"

"Sure!" she smiled. Helen had enjoyed the experience very much, and was hoping John would make this offer. She also enjoyed the new experience they had shared the previous Saturday night, and even though she was not ready to go "all the way", she was eager to feel his hands on her body again.

He returned her smile and started driving towards Steep Hollow, and the little gravel road where he and his friends liked to smoke. When they arrived, John parked the car, turned off the headlights, and reached under the seat to collect his stash. He rolled one joint and handed it to her. "Ladies first," he smiled as he held out a cigarette lighter.

"Thanks!" They shared the smoke without a lot of conversation, just a little additional instruction for her, and some mild teasing. When it was finished, they snuggled up to each other and started their make out session. The mild high she had gotten from the marijuana made her feel very relaxed, and making out was somehow more exciting than it had been previously. It was not long before John was once again taking a very long lead off of second base.

She encouraged this action by helping him slip off her sweatshirt and bra, giving him a clear field to explore. She did not stop him when his hand moved down, exploring the warmth he found between her legs. She even matched his action by exploring the exciting warm lump she suddenly found between his.

But she had not abandoned all her inhibitions. When John wanted to unbuckle her jeans, she stopped him by taking his hands into her own, and returning them to her breasts. "No, John. Please don't. I'm not ready for that."

"Please, Helen," he asked.

The look in his eyes told her how desperately he wanted to keep going. "Oh, John," she pleaded, "I'm not ready to go all the way."

"We don't have to go all the way. But I don't want to stop here. I just want..."

Helen knew John was trustworthy. If he said they didn't have to go all the way, she knew he meant it. It was clearly important to him they go a little further, and the truth was she wanted to go further, also. Her main problem was she was not sure whether or not she could trust *herself* to stop. "Promise me you'll stop when I tell you to," she said softly, looking in his eyes.

"I promise!" he said.

Perhaps it was something she saw in his eyes that caused her to relent. She put her hands on his cheeks and kissed him warmly. His hands returned to her bluejeans and soon had then unbuckled. As he pulled down her zipper, she reached down to unbuckle his jeans and pull down his zipper as well.

She raised herself off the seat so he could pull down her jeans, allowing his hands to continue their search for the source of the warmth between her legs. Her excitement rose as he found it and began to rub tenderly. She also found the warm lump between his legs and began to explore it gingerly. Soon, each of them had a hand beneath their undergarments, attacking the excited sensitive organs, engorged with blood and throbbing as they kissed, engaging in mutual masturbation.

His excitement soon rose to a uncontrollable level and he exploded. Helen smiled as she observed him experience the pleasure of an orgasm, and was delighted to realize she had delivered that pleasure. She gently removed his hand from her own underwear, brought it to her mouth, and kissed it warmly. John responded in kind, taking her hands into his, and kissing them lovingly.

But time will not stand still for anyone, and it was now time for Helen to go home. Even though they had not gone "all the way", they both recognized the wonderful joy sexual intimacy delivered. Their goodnight kisses took on a new meaning. They had shared a whole new experience, one they planned to repeat and improve on.

John was in a thoughtful state of mind as he drove himself home. He understood why Larry had seemed to change so much after he and Linda began to share such things. Maybe it really *was* too personal to talk about in public. *Besides*, he thought, *how could I describe this? We got to third base, that's for sure, but there was more to it than that! Was this a long lead off of third base?* He giggled to himself considering the term Sam had once used – making a suicide bunt. It was perfect!

The big question on his mind was whether he should tell Larry and Sam. Larry had been reluctant, and John now understood. But in the end, Larry shared the experience with his friends. John decided to wait and see how things progressed. After all, Helen had not actually done anything he could not have done himself. On the other hand, her doing it was far better than anything he had ever experienced!

And then there was the matter of the scent he found on his hands. *God, what a wonderful smell that is!* He realized it was making him feel just as excited as he always felt when returning home from a date. He laughed out loud thinking how he now understood why Larry said getting tang had not slowed him down at all when it came to getting a good grip on himself!

Around midnight, as the party was winding down fairly seriously, Sally announced she was ready to leave. Midnight was Frank's curfew, and she was supposed to get him home by then. Larry assumed it must not be a very strict curfew, because it would have been impossible to get him home in time, even if they went there directly.

Frank dashed to the car, whooping and hollering, and hopped into the back seat. Larry and Sally walked calmly with their arms around each others' waists. He escorted Sally to the driver's door and opened it for her. She looked at him with that bright smile of hers and offered him the keys. "Would you like to drive?" she asked.

Larry was astonished. "Uh, well... sure! If you want me to!"

Sally just laughed and pushed the keys into his hand. "Get in!" she insisted. Without saying a word, Larry climbed behind the wheel and acquainted himself with the controls and instruments. Sally walked around the car and climbed into the passenger seat using the door Frank had left open, and closed it behind her.

"Oh, shit!" Larry said when he realized what had happened. "I'm sorry."

"Sorry for what?" Sally grinned. "Let's get going, shall we?"

Larry just shook his head and grinned. He put the keys into the ignition, started the engine, and listened to it purr for a moment. *What a sweet sound that is!* He moved the shift into drive, and pulled away from the curb, a little tentative at first. He was not used to driving a car belonging to someone else, and especially not one with a high performance engine such as this. But after a few stop signs, followed by hot starts, and going through some curves in the road, he began to gain confidence. It was an exhilarating experience! Sally urged him on, directing him where to turn, leading him to drive down some of the more interesting streets she knew. It was definitely not the quickest way back to his own car!

But this was not the best time to just drive around. Frank really did need to get home sometime. Besides, Larry would rather have spent the time making out with Sally, like he had done back at the party. After a few minutes of excitement, never quite as exciting as when Sally drove, Larry set a course back to the school gymnasium and his own car.

"This is quite a car!" he said to her as they approached the school. "One of these days, I hope I can afford something like this!"

"I'm sure you will," Sally said with a smile.

"I'll have to find a job that pays better than the one I have!" he laughed. "Even if I did, I suspect I'd need to hang onto the money for college. My parents are going to pay for my tuition and books, but everything else is to be my responsibility."

"Where are you planning to go?" she asked.

"A&M," he said. "I guess I'm lucky, because that's one of the best places in the state I could go to study computers, except maybe Rice. I couldn't afford to go there under *any* circumstances!" he laughed. He looked at Sally and said sincerely, "Thank you for letting me drive your car, Sally. It's been quite an experience!"

"You're welcome!" she said sweetly. "I thought you might enjoy it."

"When are you going to let *me* drive it?" Frank asked from the back seat.

She grinned at Larry as she answered, "About ten years after you get your license. Maybe by then you can keep it between the stripes!"

Saturday, January 28, 1967
Paranoia Blues

They arrived back at the school just after midnight, and turned down the street towards Larry's car. "Uh, oh," he said without explanation.

"What is it?" Sally asked.

"We're not the only ones interested in my old car," he replied, and pointed up the street. There was another car stopped on the street directly behind his. This one was black and white and covered with flashing lights. Larry drove just past the police car and pulled into the parking space beyond. Sally could see a look of concern on his face when he opened the door, illuminating the dome light. "Good morning, officer," he said as he stood outside the door. "That's my car. Is there a problem?"

"No. We just noticed it's been sitting here all night and were wondering if something was wrong with the car or perhaps with its owner." When Larry walked up to him, the policeman asked, "Have you got any ID with you?"

"Certainly," he said, reaching for his wallet. "I'm Larry Bristol. I went to a party after the ballgame with some friends, and we left my old car here so we could ride in that fancy new one." As he removed his driver's license from his wallet, he read the officer's name plate. "Here's my ID, Sargent Mallory," he said as calmly as possible.

Sally was out of the car by this time, and asked, "What's wrong?"

"It's nothing," he said nonchalantly. "These officers noticed my car has been parked here for a while, and were concerned about its safety and that of its owner."

"It all checks out," the second policeman said. "I ran the tags, and the car is registered to a C. L. Bristol at the same address as on his driver's license."

"Yes, sir," Larry said, "the car is registered to my father."

Sargent Mallory's face had a grin, but not a particularly friendly one. "I can smell a bit of beer of your breath, mister. Have you had anything to drink this evening?"

"I won't lie to you, sir," Larry said. "I drank two beers earlier this evening. The last one was well over an hour ago."

"Where did you get them?" the sargent asked.

"At that party I told you about," Larry answered.

"Don't play games with me, mister!" Mallory said. "Where was this party?"

"It was at my friend's house," Sally answered angrily. "Perhaps you've heard of her – Sharon Gilbert?"

"Yes, I know of her," Mallory said, looking a little disappointed. "It's a good thing you came along here when you did, I suppose. The car was locked, but we were just about to force it open to see what's inside. You wouldn't mind if we looked inside, would you, Mr. Bristol?"

"No, sir," Larry answered as calmly as he could.

"Is that really necessary?" Sally asked.

"And who are you, miss?" Mallory asked. "Maybe you and your other friend in the back seat should show me your IDs as well."

"I'm Sally Sutherland and that's my brother, Frank," she said, huffily. "My license is in my purse, if you just have to see it. I don't understand why you're making such a big deal out of this. Larry explained to you what we're doing."

"It's OK, Sally," Larry said, trying to calm her down. "They're just doing their job." He turned to the sargent and said, "I really do appreciate your concern for us."

"I recognize those two, Sarge," the other officer said. "Miss Sutherland is one of the school cheerleaders, and the other boy is her brother, one of the basketball players. Their father is William R. Sutherland, attorney at law."

"I see," Mallory said, frowning. After a pause, he said, "OK, you kids. Get on home." As he returned Larry's license to him, Sargent Mallory looked Larry right in the eye and said in a low, menacing voice, "You're getting off lucky this time, mister. But now I know who you are. I also know about your little rock and roll band, and I've heard you on that radio program with those other punk kids. I'm going to keep my eye you, on *all* of you. My bet is I'd find all kinds of interesting things in that car, now wouldn't I? You'd better keep your nose clean, because next time we meet, you just might not be so lucky as to have those two along with you!"

"Thank you for your concern and advice," Larry said calmly, returning his license to his wallet. Sargent Mallory turned sharply, walked back to his car, and drove off. Larry suddenly realized in spite of the cold temperature, he was sweating profusely.

"What a bastard!" Sally said. "I'm going to tell my father about this!" She then noticed Larry was visibly distressed. "What's wrong, Larry?"

"Thank God he didn't search my car," he said nervously, "or you'd be telling your father quite a lot more than you realize!"

"Why?" she asked. "What's in there?"

"Can't you guess?" he answered with a question.

"Holy smoke!" she said. When Larry gave her a startled look, she spotted the pun and all three of them started laughing nervously. When she recovered, she continued, "I thought all of that Drug Company stuff was just a joke!"

"Not completely," he grinned. "I thought you knew that. Do you remember when we shared a booth at the Pizza Hut in October? When you were leaving, Roger asked if you were *'ready to blow this joint'*. I assumed you guys were going for a smoke yourself, and you both knew I'd have a smoke from time to time, as well."

Sally started giggling. "It never dawned on me!" she said.

"I never realized you were that naive, sis," Frank grinned. "Do you remember

Saturday, January 28, 1967 – Paranoia Blues

when he made that apology on the radio about drinking alcohol while playing that Beatles song? I laughed my ass off. I knew he was a smoker right then!"

"Jesus!" she laughed. "I guess I'm naive at that!" She looked at Larry and grinned, "Are you going to be alright, Larry? You must have had quite a scare!"

"I'm fine. At least I will be when my heart starts beating again," he laughed. "I think I'd better find a new *hidey-hole* for my stash. And from what Mallory just said, I'd better warn some of my friends to do the same. He just might make a point of searching our cars in the near future!"

"One thing about hanging out with you, Larry," Sally grinned as she put her arms around his neck. "It's never boring!"

He smiled at her, put his arms around her waist, and drew her close. "You have this tendency to make my heart beat a little faster yourself, Sally." They grinned at each other and kissed enthusiastically. "Like right now!" he said chuckling.

"I need to get Bubba home. See you tomorrow?" she asked.

"Absolutely! Goodnight, sweet thing." Sally reached up and kissed him on the cheek and whispered her goodnight to him. She turned away, walked to her car, and slipped behind the wheel as Frank climbed into the passenger seat. "Goodnight, Frank!" Larry called as he was closing the door. Frank waved to him through the window while Sally started the engine, backed out the parking spot, and drove away.

It was only a few blocks from the school to Larry's house, but it seemed like the longest drive he had ever made. Paranoia is a terrible thing. He watched for Sargent Mallory to reappear from every side street, from behind every hedge and tree as he drove home. First thing in the morning, even before he drove to work at the library, he would find a new place for his stash, and tell John and Sam to do the same!

Larry got up early that Saturday morning. He had some little "chores" to be completed before he left for work at the library. First, he completely emptied the ashtray to make sure there were no telltale remains. Next, he removed the materials he normally kept under the seat, hiding them in a discrete location in his garage. From now on, if he wanted to carry some weed in his car, he would prepare one or two cigarettes ahead of time, and carry only this small amount. Before he would even do that, he first had to locate a good hiding place inside his car. That would require a little more thought, so for now, the car was to be squeaky clean.

After a quick breakfast, he said goodbye to his parents and drove to work, arriving a few minutes early, hoping Sam would also be early that morning so he could warn her about Sargent Mallory as soon as possible. Later that morning, he planned to make a telephone call warning John. Or maybe Sam could make that call while he and Mrs. Hannah were busy with the children's program.

Sam arrived for work right on time, but since Mrs. Hannah was already present, Larry could not talk to her immediately. As he performed his regular Saturday morning activities, he made enough eye contact with Sam to signal he wanted to talk. When he went to the storage room to fetch the movie projector, Sam volunteered to go with him to help carry the power cords and the other miscellaneous items required.

"What's up, Snoopy?" she asked once they were alone in the store room. The posters stored away in the room reminded her of the nickname she gave Larry after he displayed his talent for drawing the famous dog from the cartoon strip. She also knew they would only have a few seconds alone, so brevity was a necessity.

"If you're holding anything in your car, anything at all, you need to get rid of it ASAP! This morning – right now, if possible!"

"Why?" she said, reaching for the power cords she was supposed to be carrying.

"I'll explain as soon as I can. Just do it, Sam!" He lifted the heavy film projector and began to carry it out of the store room.

"I hear you, agent Forty-Two!" she giggled. The look on his face, however, convinced her he was very serious. She nodded her head to indicate she understood.

When they walked back into the main room, Larry carried on a conversation as if nothing had happened. He spoke in a low voice, as required in the library, but anyone who listened could hear everything. "I went to the basketball game last night, Sam. Very exciting! Our team pulled out a victory with a great shot as the clock ran out."

"Great!" she pretended interest. "Maybe we have a better team than I thought."

"Maybe. I met Sally after the game and we went to a victory celebration over at Sharon's house. It was quite a shindig! I'd never made the connection between Sally and her brother Frank."

"Really?" she said with a giggle. "You're moving up in the world, I see."

"You should see Sally's new car!" he said lifting the projector onto the top of the card file they used as a projection stand. "It's a bright yellow Chevy Camero."

"Be a little quieter, please," Mrs. Hannah said from behind the main desk.

"Yes, ma'am," he said, lowering his voice a little. He looked back at Sam and continued the story. "We drove her car to the party and left mine at school. After the party, when we got back to my car, the police were looking it over. They were concerned about it being parked there so late, with no one around and all."

"Oh!" Sam said, starting to see the connection. "What happened?"

"Nothing," he said nonchalantly. "Sargent Mallory was very professional. He told me he was interested in my personal safety, and he liked to keep a close watch on kids to help us stay out of trouble. He specifically mentioned those of us on the radio show, Sam. He must think we're special or something. It's very reassuring."

"That's very thoughtful of him," Sam said gaining a better picture of the situation.

"You kids should be thankful such dedicated officers are watching out for your safety," Mrs. Hannah suggested.

"Yes, ma'am," Larry agreed. "He was even nice enough to offer to inspect my car to see if there was anything dangerous that might lead to an accident. Since it was dark at the time, he couldn't do it then, but he assured me he'd get a chance in the near future."

"That was *very* nice of him," Sam said, now with a more complete understanding.

"It certainly was," he agreed.

"Mrs. Hannah, all this talk about cars and safety has got me thinking," Sam began. "I'm not sure if I remembered to lock my car when I got out of it this morning. Would you mind if I ran out and checked? It would only take me a moment."

"Go ahead, dear," Mrs. Hannah agreed.

"Thanks," Sam said. "I'll be right back." She looked at Larry as she headed for the stairs. She generally kept all of her things at home rather than in her car, but there were probably one or two roaches in the ashtray she needed to dispose of.

When Sam returned from her car, Larry was arranging the chairs in front of the movie screen. "It's a good thing I checked," she told Mrs. Hannah, just loud enough for Larry to hear. "It *was* unlocked, but I took care of it. Everything is fine now!"

"Very good," Mrs. Hannah said. "Why don't you help Larry arrange the chairs."

"Yes, ma'am, and thank you for letting me go check on it." She picked up two of the smaller chairs and moved them into position, discretely winking at Larry in the process. Their attention now focused on John. They needed a way to alert him to the situation as quickly as they could.

It was nearly 9:00 o'clock, however, and Mrs. Hannah always insisted the full staff be present and working during the children's program. Getting word to John would have to wait until the program was over, and the majority of the children had departed. It would be at least 10:00, and probably more like 10:30 before either of them could break away to make the telephone call.

At about 10:20, Sam thought the mayhem had died down enough, and requested to take her morning break. She walked briskly down Main Street towards the Palace Theater. The public telephones in the lobby provided the quickest access. Since there would not be a lot of movie goers on a Saturday morning, she hoped to be able to speak plainly, without being overheard.

"Hello, Mrs. M! This is Sam. May I speak to John, please?"

"Hello, Sam," Mrs. Myers responded. "He's being lazy this morning, as usual, but I think he got up a few minutes ago. Let me check."

Sam waited as Mrs. Myers put down the receiver and walked down the hallway to her son's room, returning a few minutes later. "I'm sorry, Sam. He seems to be in the shower at the moment. Do you want me to have him call you when he gets out?"

"I'm at work, Mrs. M, so he won't be able to reach me, but I have an important message for him."

"Let me get a piece of paper and I'll write it down," Mrs. Myers said.

"No, that won't be necessary. Just tell him I called and I need to reach him as soon as possible. It's about the radio program tonight. Tell him I'll call back in a few minutes. Just make sure he stays home until I reach him, OK?"

"OK, dear," she said. "I'll tell him."

"Thanks!" Sam said. "I'll call back in a few minutes."

She hung up the phone and worried. The longer the wait, the less time she would have to answer his questions before she had to go back to the library. She looked at her watch. It was 10:25, meaning she had already been gone five minutes. She would wait five more minutes before calling again. This would still leave her about five minutes to give him the message and get back to work on time.

At 10:30, she dialed John's number again. "He's still in the shower, I'm afraid," Mrs. Myers announced. "You know how people like to take a long soaking shower sometimes. If it's urgent, I'll make him get out and come to the phone."

"No, it's not that urgent," Sam said, trying not to alarm her. "Just tell him to hang around the house for a while. Larry will call him in a few more minutes, OK?"

"I'll tell him," Mrs. Myers said.

Sam hung up the phone and looked at her watch. It was 10:32, and she had to get back to the library, or Mrs. Hannah would ask her why she was late. That wouldn't matter too much, but the delay would prevent Larry from requesting his own break.

She returned to the library and climbed the staircase to the children's reading room. Larry saw her return and looked at her with a question on his face. All she could do was shake her head to indicate she had not completed her mission. Surely that would be good enough – Larry would place the call since she had failed reach him. Still, it would be better if she could let him know John would soon be waiting for that call.

"Mrs. Hannah, what would be the chances of having a shower installed in the library?" she giggled. "After these Saturday morning programs, I always feel like taking a nice long, hot shower!"

"Me, too!" Larry said with an enthusiastic grin.

"That is not very likely," Mrs. Hannah responded, giving Larry a reproachful glare, "but I agree with you. That would be very nice at times."

"May I take my morning break now, Mrs. Hannah?" Larry asked.

"Go ahead, Larry," she agreed. "It looks like you will have plenty to do when you get back, however, so don't dally too long."

"Yes, ma'am. And thanks for the shower idea, Sam," he winked. "It'll give me something to think about while I'm on my break."

"The clock is running, young man," Mrs. Hannah said.

Larry smiled as he headed for the stairs and the front door. When he reached the pay phones at the Palace, he immediately placed a call. John was apparently waiting by the phone, and answered it after only one ring. "Hello?" he said.

Larry breathed a sign of relief. "It's me, John. Now listen carefully." He explained the events of the previous night, urged John to take immediate action, and not to leave his house until doing so.

"That's pretty scary," John said after hearing the whole story.

"He certainly got *my* attention," Larry laughed. "There was something about the way he said things that convinced me he means business. I may even send him a *'Thank You'* card, especially if anyone gets pulled over for an inspection!"

"I'm hip!" John chuckled. "See you guys tonight."

"Later!" Larry said and hung up the phone. He returned to work so he could restore some sense of order to the bookshelves, something always needing a lot of attention after the Saturday morning program. He smiled at Sam when he reached the top of the stairs to let her know his mission had been accomplished. They both breathed a sigh of relief, then worked diligently for the rest of the day.

Larry arrived at Sally's house at 7:00 o'clock sharp. "Good evening, Mr. Sutherland," he said when Sally's father answered the door.

"Hello, Larry," Mr. Sutherland said. "Come on in. Sally will be right out."

"Thank you, sir," he said, stepping inside.

"Sally tells me you had a little excitement last night," Mr. Sutherland said.

"Yes, sir," Larry nodded nonchalantly. "It was quite a game!"

"That's not what I meant," Mr. Sutherland grinned.

"The party?" Larry asked, returning his smile and still playing coy. Mr. Sutherland looked at him and merely shook his head. "Oh, that!" Larry grinned. "It was nothing. Just a policemen doing his job."

"Sally said he was rather rude," Mr. Sutherland observed. "What did *you* think?"

Larry wondered if his interest was personal or professional. "No, sir. I didn't think he was rude. Maybe a little more aggressive than I liked, but not rude."

"Did he have reason to be aggressive?" Mr. Sutherland asked.

"None that I can think of," Larry replied.

"That's good," Mr. Sutherland nodded. "I know Sargent Mallory. He's been a diligent police officer for many years. I happen to know he has some personal issues right now, but I'd be very surprised to learn he'd done anything improper. You'll let me know if that changes, won't you?"

"Yes, sir," Larry said, relieved to know Sally had not told the entire story. "I'm sure he was just doing his job. If I didn't think so, I'd do something about it."

"Good for you!" Mr. Sutherland was saying as Sally walked in.

"Hi, Larry!" she smiled. "Has your heart started beating again?"

"A little," he snickered. "Would you make it beat faster, like you did last night?"

"I think I should close my ears to the rest of this conversation," Mr. Sutherland chuckled. "You kids have a good time tonight."

"Goodnight, sir," Larry called after him. He looked back at Sally and grinned when he saw she was giggling. "Shall we go?"

"I'm ready whenever you are!" she said. He doubted she meant that in any way other than the obvious one. They walked to his car, Sally went to the driver's side and waited for him to open the door. She sat on the seat discretely and scooted over to the middle, giving him a nice, albeit modest, view of her knees and legs.

"Are you hungry?" he asked as he backed out of the driveway. "Would you like to get something to take with us again, or would you rather have a private dinner before we go to the station?"

"That was a nice hamburger we had last week. I wouldn't mind if we went back there again, but this time let's eat before we go to the station."

"Whatever ma lady desires," he smiled. They made light conversation driving to the Buccaneer, parked, and began to scan the menu board. After deciding on their selections, he went to the window, placed their order, and returned to the car.

"What do you have in mind after the show," she asked.

"I'm flexible," he grinned. "When I asked you to go to a movie, you mentioned maybe we could do both things tonight. Would you like to go to a movie later?"

"We could," she giggled, "but actually I was hoping we could go back to that nice place you showed me last week and continue our conversation."

"Tempting," he said, rubbing his chin as if considering. "Let me think a moment. Would I like to drive to the country and sit in a parked car with a beautiful girl?"

Sally nudged him sharply in the ribs. "Don't go getting any ideas!" she giggled. "I just meant it was a nice place, and it's fun to be with you. You're a lot more fun than I originally thought you'd be!"

He smiled. "That sounds like a compliment. What did you *think* I'd be like?"

"Oh, I don't know," she said. "You always seemed a little..."

"Strange?" he suggested.

"Not really. You're just different than most other guys I know." She saw how he frowned a little at that, and added, "I don't mean it in a bad way. You're actually a lot nicer than most of them."

"A little awkward, then?" he suggested.

"Maybe," she giggled, "but mostly, you just seem to be a little bashful."

"Like a nerd?" he suggested, hoping she would disagree.

"I've never thought of you as a nerd!" she said quickly. "Some of the girls used to, but not anymore. Linda told us a lot of nice things about you, and I've confirmed it to them. And a lot of people have been listening to you on the radio. I don't think you should worry about anyone thinking you're a nerd!"

"That's good to know. I guess Linda doesn't say nice things about me anymore."

Sally smiled at him. "Actually, she *still* says nice things about you. In fact, many of us are wondering why she broke up with you! What's your opinion?"

He looked a little sad to be reminded. "You'll have to ask her. My guess is she just didn't want a longterm relationship with me. Maybe she did us both a favor."

"You wanted a longterm relationship?" Sally asked.

"Yeah," he said sadly.

"Larry," she said softly, "you do know I'm not looking for a longterm, exclusive relationship either, right?"

"Sally, what does a longterm relationship mean to you?"

"Oh, I don't know," she answered truthfully. "I guess it means something that lasts for years, and leads to getting married or something."

"My relationship with Linda was the longest one I've experienced my whole life," he said sadly. "It lasted just over two months. To me, a longterm relationship is simply one that lasts long enough to really get to know someone."

"I see," she said, surprised to learn this little tidbit.

"Sally, there's nothing I'd like better than a longterm, exclusive relationship, but I know developing such a relationship takes time. Maybe I wanted that kind of relationship with Linda before she was ready for it. Perhaps I just assumed too much. But I'm not likely to repeat that mistake with you or anyone else."

"I'm glad to hear that," she smiled.

Larry heard their number announced over the loudspeaker, and hopped out to get their dinner. He hoped the topic of conversation would change when he returned. "I hope you're hungry. There seems to be a lot more food here than I expected!"

"Then we'd better chow down," she giggled. "If there are any leftovers, we can take them to those vultures at the station. They certainly made short order of those fries you brought them last week!"

"You ought to see them when they have the *munchies!*" he laughed.

"Like after a smoke?" she asked with a giggle.

"Exactly!" he said. Realizing he was giving away too much information, he spoke again. "A few of them might have smoked once or twice. I wouldn't know much about that."

"A gentleman doesn't discuss such things?" she chuckled.

"Have you put a bug on me?" he grinned.

Sally looked at him and returned his grin. "It's just something I heard Linda say about you when I asked her some rather personal questions."

"I think I should take the fifth," he smiled.

"So you drink the heavy stuff, too, is that it?" she teased.

He just shook his head and grinned. "I'd better shut up. I might have known a lawyer's daughter could get information from me with a bunch of sneaky questions."

Sally giggled and decided to let Larry off the hook for now. She had learned everything she wanted to know, anyway, and the rest was just fishing. They engaged in idle smalltalk as they ate their dinner, and then headed for the radio station.

Julia waved goodbye to her mom and hopped into the car. "Hi, Sam!"

"Hi, Julia," Sam smiled as she also waved. "How are you tonight?"

"Just fine," Julia replied. "How about you?"

"Fine," Sam replied. "How was school this week?"

"Oh, the same as always, I suppose," Julia grinned. "Why do you ask?"

"Good," Sam grinned. "After I became a doper, I didn't enjoy school at all!"

"What are you talking about?" Julia asked innocently.

"I heard about the little adventure you and Helen had with the boys after practice last Sunday," Sam grinned. "Do you actually think those clowns could keep anything a secret from me?"

"I suppose not," Julia giggled. "I gather you join them from time to time?"

"Who do you think got them started?" Sam laughed. "Did you enjoy it, Julia?"

"Yes!" she smiled. "It made me feel all warm and relaxed."

"Just don't smoke too much, or even too often," Sam said with a reassuring smile. "And be very careful. Right now, it seems one of our local constables is on the warpath trying to catch us, and since you're part of the radio show, you might be a target yourself. We've decided to never carry anything on us, or even in our cars."

"What happened?" Julia asked.

"Nothing, fortunately, but we're going to be very careful, and I urge you to do the same." Sam wanted to lighten the mood. "Don't worry about it too much. Like I said, just don't smoke too much or too often. I'm sure the boys mentioned you get really goofy if you smoke too much. You don't want to smoke it all the time, either. It makes you feel so good you might forget how good *other* things make you feel!"

"They didn't mention that part," Julia said, "but I think I can see what you mean. It made me feel a little... Does it make you want to fool around, Sam? I mean, with guys. You know what I mean."

"Yes, I know what you mean," Sam laughed. She thought about her answer for a moment before proceeding. "It doesn't make me want to fool around any more than I normally do. But let's say I was with a great guy, and I already wanted to fool around with him, anyway. I'm quite sure it would make me more agreeable, and maybe even a bit more aggressive!"

"It sounds like you've had some experience with this," Julia giggled.

"Why, Julia!" Sam snorted. "Are you suggesting I'm not a nice girl?"

"Not at all, Sam!" Julia said before she realized Sam was just teasing with her.

"Then I guess you don't know me very well," Sam said, continuing to tease. Realizing she was confusing the younger girl, she added a serious comment. "I don't consider myself to be a bad girl, although I'm definitely not pure as the freshly fallen snow. How about you? Are you still cherry?"

"I will neither confirm nor deny it!" Julia giggled.

"I wonder who *you've* been talking to!" Sam laughed. "I should say gentlewomen don't talk about such things in public. Is that it?"

"Maybe," Julia grinned. "But that doesn't really count between friends, does it?"

"Your call," Sam smiled.

"I've never done it," Julia confessed. "I think people should be in love first."

"I agree completely," Sam stated seriously, then threw in the sort of twist expected of her, "One of the best times I ever had was when my boyfriend and I shared a room with another couple. The four of us were so much in love it was disgusting!"

"Sam!" Julia exclaimed before she looked at her friend's face to see her laughing.

After the show, the kids went their separate ways. John and Helen split for places unknown, Sam drove Julia home, and Larry and Sally followed at a discrete distance so they would not be noticed when Larry turned off the country lane onto the gravel road leading to his favorite parking place.

Just like she had done the previous week, Sally snuggled up to Larry as they sat in his car. They talked for a little while, and she laughed appropriately at his jokes. Then they kissed for a little while, and laughed some more when they noticed the windows had fogged up on the inside. Their make-out sessions were interesting and exciting, but not extreme. He carefully avoided any aggressively suggestive moves.

But the hands on the clock never stand still when one is having fun, and before they knew it, it was time for Larry to take Sally back home. They kissed a few more times while standing on her doorstep. "John and I, and the rest of the gang, usually get together on Sunday afternoons for guitar practice. If you're not doing anything, would you like to come with me tomorrow?"

"Sure!" Sally said. "What time?"

"We usually start about 2:00. I need to pick up something on the way, and practice will be at Julie's house tomorrow, out in Steep Hollow. To get all that done, I should pick you up around 1:00. How does that sound?"

"It sounds fine. I'll be ready! Goodnight, Larry," she said, putting her arms around his neck preparing for a goodnight kiss.

Larry collected on the offer. "Goodnight, Sally. I'll see you tomorrow!"

Sunday, January 29, 1967
I Fought The Law

"Hi, Larry!" Sally said sweetly when she answered the door.

Larry smiled at her as he stepped into the foyer. "Hi!" he greeted.

Sally's brother Frank also stepped into the foyer. "Would you mind if Frank comes along with us?" she asked sweetly. "He's a little bored this afternoon and he'd like to hear you guys play some more."

"No problem at all!" Larry said with a genuine smile. Frank had not interfered with anything Friday night, and Larry did not figure he would represent any problem this time, either. "The Jacobsons have a big house. I'm sure they won't mind an extra body coming along."

"If you're sure it's OK," Sally said.

"I'm sure," he replied. "You're welcome to come along, Frank!"

"You're sweet," she smiled. "As a reward, I'll let you drive my car again. We're going out on a country road, right? You can open it up a little bit if you want to!"

"I'm not going to pass up an opportunity like that!" he grinned. "I promise I won't kill any of us. I won't kill you, anyway," he said, winking at Sally.

"I'm not sure I like the sound of this," Frank chuckled.

"You'll be OK," she assured him. "You're no more likely to get killed with him than you would be if *I* were driving!"

"Now I'm *really* worried!" Frank laughed.

"As well you should be," Larry snickered. "If you're smart, you'll bucket your seat belt. Does your car even have seat belts, Sally?"

"I'm not sure," she replied. "I've never looked!"

"Tsk! Tsk! Tsk! One of these days, they'll probably be required, doncha know."

Larry first moved his own car out of the driveway and parked it at the curb. He was halfway back to Sally's car when he remembered something he just might be needing later! He went back and got his guitar, then rejoined Sally and Frank waiting patiently in her car. He put the guitar in the trunk, climbed behind the wheel, readjusted the seat position and mirrors, and fired up the engine. He carefully backed out of the driveway, and turned in the direction they needed to go. After pulling the shift into "drive", he punched it. The tires squealed as the vehicle accelerated, drawing laughter from Sally.

"OK, Frank," he grinned. "Just for you, I'll try to keep all four tires on the road!"

"Thanks," Frank said breathlessly.

Larry and Sally winked at each other and smiled. The rest of the drive within town was more sensible. Larry punched it again, however, once they got out of the city limits and onto the highway. He quickly accelerated to a hundred miles per hour, then lifted his foot to let the vehicle coast back down to the posted speed limit.

"Where are we going?" Sally asked. "I thought Julia lived in Steep Hollow?"

"That's right," he said, "but I wanted to run out to Snook to pick up some of those great kolaches. I hope you don't mind a little side trip!"

"You're driving," she said with a shrug and a smile.

They pulled up to the bakery and Larry hopped out. "I won't be but a minute. Would either of you like anything special?"

"I love those cream cheese kolaches!" Sally said.

"Umm, me too!" he grinned. "I'll get a couple of extra ones we can eat on the way!" He ran inside the bakery, purchased three dozen kolaches put into a box, six additional cheese kolaches placed into a paper bag, and a mysterious third item put in its own bag.

It was just after 1:30 when he returned to the car and the threesome headed back to town, munching on those cheese kolaches. As he was approaching the College Station city limits, he asked, "Do you mind if I go the long way? It'll take a little longer, but if I stay on FM 60 through College Station, then out on Harvey Road, I can cut over to Steep Hollow without going back through Bryan at all."

"Stay on the highway as much as you can," she said. "I'd rather take a longer way to get there, just so we can go faster!"

"That makes sense," he said, then added with a grin, "I think!"

Sally looked over at him and smiled. They took the long way to Steep Hollow, mostly traveling roads with very little traffic. Larry punched the accelerator on several occasions, especially as they were coming out of curves. It was a thrilling time for a bunch of teenagers out for a Sunday afternoon joyride.

"This thing is a monster!" he said turning into the Jacobson's driveway. "Why does a sweet little girl like you need a car like this? I'll tell you what I'll do. I'll speak to your father and explain this car is too much for you. Maybe he'll swap me even!"

"No way!" she laughed. "If you don't behave, I'll never let you drive it again!"

"I'll behave," he said meekly as he parked the car in his usual spot. He noted none of the others had arrived, yet it was already a few minutes after 2:00. He laughed to himself thinking about how the others were going to react when they saw this car parked in his usual space.

He hopped out of the car and trotted around to the passenger side to open Sally's door. She grinned at him appreciatively and climbed out. They were about to slam the door when Frank yelled, "Hey!" from the backseat.

"Do we have to let him out?" Sally asked.

"He's your brother," Larry shrugged, "and it's your car. You decide."

"We'd better," she giggled. "He has the kolaches!" They opened the door all the way and let Frank begin to extricate himself, carrying the box and the extra bag.

"I was wondering who it was," Jessica shouted to them from the porch. "Did you get a new car?"

"I wish, Mrs. J!" Larry shouted back. "Hi there, Schotzy!" he said, greeting the dog who ran up barking and wagging his tail. "This is Sally and Frank," he said to the dog. "Sally, Frank, this is Julia's dog, Schotzy."

Sally squatted to pet him. "Hi, boy!" He sniffed her hand and wagged his tail.

When Frank paid no particular attention to him, the dog returned to Larry and stood up on his hind legs begging for attention. "You'll have to wait until we get inside," Larry said as he fetched his guitar from the trunk. "Come on, Sally. I'll introduce you to some of the nicest people you'll ever meet."

They walked up to the front door, Schotzy leading and barking happily. "Hi, Mrs. J! I want you to meet Sally Sutherland and her brother, Frank. This is Mrs. Jacobson, Julia's mom. I hope you don't mind I brought them with me, Mrs. J!"

"Of course not, Larry," Jessica said. "It's nice to meet you, Sally. I've heard nice things about you from Julia. It's nice to meet you, also, Frank. The other kids call me Mrs. J, but you can call me Jessica if you'd like."

"It's nice of you to have us, Mrs. Jacobson," Sally said. "I mean, Mrs. J. I like that nickname. Who came up with it?"

"Who do you think?" Larry grinned.

"I should have known," she snickered.

"Come on in," Jessica smiled. "I'll introduce you to Julian, my husband. It probably won't come as a surprise the other kids call him Mr. J."

"We brought you some of those kolaches from Snook I've been telling you about," Larry smiled. "You won't have to bear the full burden of feeding the whole crew this time."

"You didn't have to do that," Jessica grinned, "but you've been talking about them so much, I can hardly wait to try them!" She took the box and the extra paper bag from Frank and headed for the kitchen to place them on the counter. Then they followed her into into the family room.

"Hi, Larry!" Julia greeted him, followed by a slightly less enthusiastic, but still friendly, "Hi, Sally."

"Julian," Jessica said, "this is Sally Sutherland and her brother Frank."

"Nice to meet you both," Julian said with a smile. "I understand you're one of the school cheerleaders, Sally. I can see why!" He then offered his hand to Frank. "And I understand you're a star basketball player."

"Not a star," Frank said. "I'm not even a starter yet, but I hope to be next year."

"Oh, Julie," Larry said almost as an afterthought, "I don't think you've met Sally's brother Frank. Frank, this is Julia."

"Nice to meet you, Julia," Frank smiled.

"Nice to meet you, too, Frank," Julia said, returning his smile.

"Don't get too close to him, Julia," Sally teased. "He bites!"

"Give me a break, will you, sis?" Frank pleaded.

"I mean he *bites*!" Sally laughed, "as in *'he bites the big one'*. He sucks!"

Julia looked back at Frank and giggled, "I'll keep that in mind."

"The others must be running a little late," Larry said. "I also brought something for Schotzy. It's deer season, and they're making a lot of deer sausage in Snook. I managed to get him part of a leg bone, doncha know. Is it OK if I give it to him now?"

"Sure," Jessica said. "Why don't you go out back? I'll watch for the others."

"I think it's neat even while living up there in Yankee Land, you bought a Texas dog," Larry chuckled. "It must have been an omen of the future!"

"I didn't know dachshunds were from Texas," Julia said, puzzled. "I thought they came from Germany."

"Oh, no," Larry said. "A lot of people think they're from Germany, but they're not. They're from right here in Texas. There's a saying we use down here in Texas about dachshunds. Haven't you heard us saying, *'Get a long little doggy'*? Dachshunds are definitely Texas dogs!"

"I should have seen that one coming a mile off," Julia laughed. The others just groaned and shook their heads. Most of them, however, made a mental note to tell the same joke next time they saw someone with a dachshund!

Larry went to the kitchen and fetched the extra paper bag. "I've got something for you, Schotzy! How would you like to chew on *this?*" he asked, pulling the bone from the bag. Schotzy barked and ran in a tight little circle, chasing his tail, like he always did when excited. The other kids followed as Larry led him to the back door and onto the patio. He bent down to let Schotzy have his treat. "Here you go, boy!"

"That was sweet of you," Julia said, watching her dog romp away with the bone in his mouth. He found a nice sunny location, and settled down to gnaw happily.

"Only the best for my friends," he said. He laughed and offered a correction. "Well, at least, only the best I can *afford!*"

"From the looks of that," Sally said pointing at the dog, "I'd say the best things in life don't have to cost very much!"

"That's my philosophy," Larry agreed. "On the other hand, I don't think it applies to cars! Did you see that monster we drove up in, Julie?"

"Yes! Where did you get that?"

"It's Sally's. She let me drive it today instead of my old clunker. One of these days, I'm going to get me a car like that!"

"I thought you had it all arranged with my dad to trade even?" Sally teased.

"Over my dead body!" Frank injected. "If anyone gets that car, it'll be me!"

"We'll see, Bubba," Sally grinned. "First you have to learn how to drive."

They heard a horn from the front of the house. "That's John!" Larry said. "Let's go see what he thinks. I wish I could have seen his face when he saw that car!"

Rather than going through the house, the kids walked around on the outside. When they got to the front, Larry was disappointed to see John seemed agitated, and had not even noticed the fancy car sitting in his usual parking spot. "My man!" Larry called. "What's shaking?"

"We are!" John said. "You won't believe what just happened to us!"

Julia and Sally went to check on Helen, who seemed frightened and visibly shaken. The boys went into a separate conversation. "What happened?" Larry asked, concerned about his friends.

"I got pulled over by that cop you warned us about! Man, I wasn't speeding or anything! He pulled me over, claiming I hadn't used my turn signal to change lanes. First he wanted to check my license and registration, and then he demanded I let him search my car!"

"Oh, shit!" Larry said. "Did you let him?"

"Did I have a choice?" John asked.

"Yes!" Larry said. "All you had to do was say no."

"He told me they'd get a warrant, if necessary," John said, "or I could let them search voluntarily. Since I was clean, I told them to go ahead and search."

"Thank God for that!" Larry said.

"Yeah," John continued, "but it was still a nightmare! There we were, standing on the side of the road while these goons go through my car with a fine-toothed comb. They took everything out of the glove compartment and emptied the trunk. They even removed the seats! All this time, people are driving by and staring at us like we're some sort of criminals or something. It was embarrassing! Not only for me, but think about poor Helen! They even made her empty her purse!"

"Damn!" Larry said.

"And when they couldn't find anything," John continued, "the bastards just drove off and left us there with all that stuff lying on the ground. They wouldn't even help me put the seats back in the car!"

Larry and John stood looking at each other as if they were in shock. Frank stood nearby shaking his head. The girls were trying to console Helen, who was still shaking and crying from the experience. "Can I use your phone, Julia?" Sally asked. "I want to call my daddy and tell him about this."

"Sure," Julia said. "Come on, Helen. Let's go inside and sit down. I'll get you something to drink." The girls walked to the house to sit Helen down, explain what had transpired to the Jacobsons, and to make a phone call. Meanwhile, the boys stood around outside, wondering what, if anything, they were going to do.

About ten minutes later, Sam arrived, also visibly shaken. She told them about the experience she had just had, almost identical in nature. On her way there, she was pulled over for some minor traffic violation, and forced to submit to a search. She was also left standing beside the road with parts of her car lying on the ground. A kindly older gentleman stopped and helped put her car back together.

Larry practically carried the tearful Sam inside, where they joined the other girls. "This is unbelievable!" Sally said as she got off the phone. "They can do this sort of thing any time they want! All they need is something called *'probable cause'*, which apparently can be anything from you waving a gun around to simply looking cross-eyed. They can stop you and search you and your vehicle at will. They don't even have to put things back the way they found them! They can leave all your stuff lying on the side of the road for you to deal with on your own, without so much as saying, *'sorry for the inconvenience'*. It's unbelievable!" She saw Larry helping Sam inside and asked, "What happened to her?"

"The same damn thing!" Larry said forcefully. "The bastard also did it to her!"

"Calm down, Larry," Mr. Jacobson urged. "It won't do any good to get yourself riled up. I understand this is upsetting, but there must be a reasonable explanation."

"It's bad enough to do this to a guy like John, but what reasonable explanation could there possibly be for leaving a teenage girl like Sam all alone with her car in pieces all over the roadside?" he asked angrily. "How would you feel if it had been Julie out there standing on the side of the road?" No one had any answer to offer. Sally called her father once again to tell him about this latest incident.

Something suddenly struck Larry like a bolt of lightning. "That prick told me he'd heard me on the radio program with *'those other punk kids'* he called them, and that he was going to keep his eye on us. This wasn't just a coincidence. They had it all planned to stop each of us! The only reason they didn't stop me was because I was in a different car, traveled at a different time than normal, and took a different route that didn't even go through Bryan at all!"

"Why would the police single you kids out like that?" Mr. Jacobson asked. "Have you been doing something I should know about?"

Larry stared at him angrily. After a moment, he relaxed a little, but still answered forcefully, "Mr. J, I'm sure we've done things you'd rather we didn't do. All kids do things their parents don't like from time to time. But we haven't done anything to justify this kind of treatment! Obviously, they were trying to catch us with something really bad – probably drugs of some kind. But they didn't find any, did they? They wouldn't have found any in my car, either. It's bad enough they have to hassle John and I, but what *really* makes me angry is the way they've treated Helen and Sam! There's just *no excuse* for that, I don't care *who* they are or who they *think* they are. The last time I checked, this *isn't* Nazi Germany, but I'm starting to wonder if that's really true anymore!"

The silence resulting from that tirade was deafening. The faces of Julian and Jessica were marked with a mixture of shock, revulsion, anger, and fear. The others simply stood staring at each other. The silence was broken when Sally came back into the room and announced, "Daddy wants to talk to you, Larry." He looked back at her as if he hadn't heard. "He's waiting, and he wants to talk to *you*."

Larry stepped into the kitchen and picked up the telephone. "Hello?"

"Are you ready to do something about it now, Larry?" Mr. Sutherland asked calmly. "I should probably tell you while I was talking with Sally just now, I noticed the police pulled up outside, looking intently over your car parked at the curb. At least they knew better than to open the doors or trunk without your permission or a warrant. But I imagine they'll be watching for your return."

"What *can* I do about it, Mr. Sutherland?" he asked.

"First of all," he told Larry, "you keep your nose squeaky clean! If I find out they have a reason for this, then I'll throw you kids to the wolves in a New York minute."

"And then what?" Larry asked.

"And then," Mr. Sutherland continued, "you go down to Police Headquarters first thing in the morning and file a formal complaint you and your friends are being harassed by Sargent Mallory without due cause."

"What good will that do?" Larry asked.

"They'll be forced to investigate," Mr. Sutherland said. "If proper procedures haven't been followed, they'll take disciplinary action against all involved."

"So one group of policemen will investigate something some other group of policemen has done?" Larry asked angrily. "Big damn deal! Isn't that like asking the fox to investigate why so many chickens are missing from the hen house?"

"It's not that way at all, Larry," Mr. Sutherland assured him.

"I'd rather stay as far away from those bastards as I can," Larry said.

"I understand how you feel," Mr. Sutherland said, "but you mustn't let the actions of a few cause you to loose faith in the others. The vast majority of police officers are trying to protect you and all the rest of us from harm. They have a very difficult job, made even *more* difficult when one of them behaves improperly. This sort of thing will continue until you and others come forward to complain, so the bad ones can be stopped. Someday, you may need help, and the police may be the only ones you can turn to. Don't you want to help keep them as good as they possibly can be?"

"I'd rather take my chances with someone I can trust," Larry said bitterly.

"You're just angry right now," Mr. Sutherland said. "Look, calm yourself down and give it some thought. If you change your mind, then you know where to find me. I can't help you if you aren't willing to help yourself."

"I appreciate your concern, Mr. Sutherland," Larry said. "I'll think about it. Would you like me to bring your son and daughter home right now?"

"That's not necessary," he said. "Try to relax and enjoy yourselves. Keep your nose clean, and come talk to me when you calm down."

"OK," Larry said. "I'll think about it." He hung up the phone, rejoined the others, and answered their questions as best he could.

After all the excitement, neither Larry nor John felt like singing that afternoon. Since it was a little too chilly to spend much time outside, the kids mostly sat around in the family room, listening to records, talking, and playing a few board games.

Around 5:00, the kids decided to leave, letting the Jacobsons have a little peace and quiet. It couldn't be easy to put up with seven teenagers for so long, even though the Jacobsons assured them they were welcome. But Helen and especially Sam, still unhappy about the earlier experience, wanted to get home before dark.

John assured Helen nothing would happen. He and Larry were more concerned about Sam, traveling alone. "I'll follow you home, Sam," Larry suggested.

"I'll be fine," Sam tried to assure him.

"Then would you mind if I followed you for my own protection?" Larry asked with a smile. "Personally, I don't feel particularly safe."

Sam smiled and thanked him. "Go ahead and follow me, so I can protect you."

John and Helen got into their car, waved nervously, and started home. Sam got into her car and waited for Larry and the others to follow. "Maybe I should let you drive," Larry said to Sally as they reached her car. "With all the excitement earlier, I'm sure they'll be looking for me to be driving when we get back to town."

"You're going to have to drive sometime, Larry," Sally stated sensibly. "I really don't think you'll have any trouble, not until you get back to your own car, anyway."

"I'll drive!" Frank offered, grinning at his sister, Julia, and the Jacobsons.

"That settles it," Larry grinned. "I'll drive. Otherwise, I walk! The last thing I want is to be sitting in a car with an unlicensed driver!"

"Now you're talking," Sally giggled. Larry opened the passenger door for her, and together, they practically shoved Frank into the backseat. "Goodnight," Sally said to the Jacobsons. "Thanks for letting us impose on you this afternoon."

"It was no imposition," Jessica said sincerely. "You're welcome back anytime."

"Goodnight, Mrs. J," Larry smiled. "You too, Mr. J." There was a worried look on his face when he turned to Julia. "Goodnight, Julie."

"Goodnight, Larry," Julia said sweetly noting the look on his face. "Goodnight, Sally. You, too, Frank."

Larry closed the passenger door and trotted to the driver's side while the Jacobsons headed back to their house. Julia stopped and looked back at him one more time, smiled, and waved goodbye. Larry started the car and followed Sam out the driveway.

They reached Sam's house without incident. Sam smiled and waved them on. Larry continued on, now driving even more carefully than before, especially as they approached Sally's house. Everything was quiet when he turned onto her street and pulled into her driveway.

He got out of the car and hurried to the passenger side to open Sally's door for her. She smiled sweetly at him, appreciating his courtesy, but thinking how unusual it was for a boy to be so gallant these days. "Why don't you come inside for a while, unless you also want to get home before dark," she suggested.

Larry hesitated at first, but then realized it would be unmanly for him to admit he was more than a little afraid of the drive home. "I'd like that, if you're sure it'll be OK with your folks." While Larry fetched his guitar out of the trunk, Frank went on ahead. Sally led the way, escorting Larry through the back door.

"Hi, mom," Sally said when they stepped into the kitchen.

"Hi, dear," her mom replied. "Hello, Larry. I hear you've had an exciting day."

"Well, not yet," he said nervously, "but a couple of my friends have."

Mr. Sutherland heard the voices and came into the kitchen. "Are you feeling any better, Larry?"

"I'm fine," he said. Seeing the doubtful look on Mr. Sutherland's face, he corrected with, "Well, I'm a little apprehensive about the drive home, but since I don't have anything I should be worried about..." He let his voice trail off rather than completing the sentence.

"That's good," Mr. Sutherland smiled. "How did your guitar practice go?"

Larry managed a nervous laugh. "We never got around to that. I don't guess we were in the mood."

"Do you feel like playing now?" Sally asked brightly. "I don't think mom and dad have ever heard you sing!"

Larry blushed bashfully. He was always a little leery of such command performances, fearing Sally might have given her parents higher expectations about his abilities than he could possibly match. Without John, his crutch on the guitar, Larry was especially uncomfortable he might not live up to expectations.

"You two go have a seat in the living room," Mrs. Sutherland urged, "and I'll make us all something to drink. I'd love to hear you play and sing. Both Sally and

Frank have told us how good you are!"

"Well," Larry said shyly, "I try to keep up, but John is the real guitar player. I can barely manage to play a few chords."

"He's just being modest," Sally smiled. "Just wait until you hear him sing! I think he sounds just like Paul McCartney when he wants to!"

"I'll have to take your word for that, dear," Mrs. Sutherland said. "I'm afraid I don't know who Paul McCartney is!"

Larry and Sally smiled at each other. "That's OK, Mrs. Sutherland," Larry said. "I think you'll know who he is one of these days." Sally led Larry into the living room and had him sit on the sofa. First she sat next to him on the left, but as he got his guitar out of its case, he urged her to move to his right. Not only would this allow him to look at her as he played, but from the right, she would not run the risk of bumping into the fret board on the neck of the guitar.

Mr. and Mrs. Sutherland soon joined them carrying glasses filled with icy cold soda. After a little warm up, Larry announced, "This is one of the more popular songs from last year called *Red Rubber Ball*. It was performed by a group called The Crykle, but the most important thing to me is it was written by Paul Simon and Bruce Woodley. Simon is one of my favorite composers. The song also reflects my feelings about an old girlfriend." Even though Larry still cared for Linda, and knew he always would, he was determined he would no longer shed any tears over her.

Mr. and Mrs. Sutherland were duly impressed and expressed their appreciation. When he heard the singing, Frank came out of his room to join them. "I told you he was good," Sally said, beaming with pride.

"I sound better when I have John with me," Larry said trying to be modest.

"And I'm sure you do," Mr. Sutherland said. "I've heard a few people around town talking about your band. You're starting to get quite a reputation around here."

"We'll never get anywhere unless we start doing our own music," Larry said with a slight frown. "Why would anyone want to listen to us when they can just as easily listen to the original?"

"That's a good point," Mr. Sutherland agreed, "but you have to start somewhere."

"Sing that song you wrote!" Sally injected. "It's a little funny, but I think it's cute, and so does everyone else I know."

Larry laughed at her description of his song, but agreed to do it. "It's called *Green Eyes And Sam*. The lyrics are sort of based on the children's book by Dr. Seuss, but it's about a little green eyed monster I know." He knew Sally's eyes were a deep blue, and he doubted she had ever noticed the actual green eyes fascinating him so much. After singing the song, he continued with the Beatles song *And I Love Her* so the Sutherlands could hear his imitation of Paul McCartney, even though they would not appreciate the similarity in his voice.

He was ready to call it a night, but Sally insisted on just one more song. So for his encore, Larry played one of his favorite Paul Simon songs, *Homeward Bound*. He would miss John's guitar playing for this song, but he decided he wanted to sing this song bad enough to take the chance. "And home is where I really ought to be going right now," he said with a smile after he had finished.

"You're really very good, Larry," Mr. Sutherland smiled, as he and his wife applauded. "No wonder I've been hearing good things."

"I appreciate you saying that, sir," he said. "I'll be sure to pass that information along to John next time I see him. I hope he and Helen got home alright."

"I'm sure they did," Mr. Sutherland said. "If you have any trouble, you tell them I've advised you not to allow a search of your car, and to file a formal complaint."

"And what if I've decided not to do that?" Larry asked.

"Whether you do or not, it's still true I've *advised* you to do so," Mr. Sutherland said with a grin. "I still think you should, but even if you don't, it might make them stop and think for a moment."

"I see," Larry smiled putting his guitar into its case and closing the latches. "Personally, I hope it's all over, and I won't be seeing or hearing from them at all."

"Me, too," Mr. Sutherland agreed. "Come along, mother. Let's leave these young people alone for a few minutes, shall we?" Mrs. Sutherland smiled at her husband, said her goodnight to Larry, and they departed.

"Goodnight, Larry," Frank said as he also departed.

Larry responded in kind, and found himself alone with Sally, standing in her living room. "Being around you is certainly exciting!" she said smiling warmly.

"I don't know about you," he said walking toward the front door, "but I could use a little less of that kind of excitement." They stepped onto the front porch. He sat his guitar down so he could put both of his arms around her. She put her arms around his neck and kissed him more warmly than she ever had. "However, I could *always* use a little more of *that* kind of excitement!" he said breathlessly.

"You're sweet," she said beaming her beautiful smile at him.

"Has this scared you away?" he asked. "Are you still willing to hang with me?"

"Of course I am, silly," she said keeping her arms around his neck hugging him.

"Would you like to come to the station with me again next Saturday?" he asked.

"I'm sorry, Larry, but I already have a date for next Saturday." She saw the disappointment in his face, and worried he might be thinking she really *was* afraid to be with him, she volunteered some information. "Last Friday was the last game of the season. There won't be any more basketball games."

Larry snapped at the bait. "How about Friday? Will you go out with me Friday?"

"OK!" she smiled, glad she had dropped the hint.

"Great! I'll pick you up around 7:00. We'll get some dinner, then go to a movie."

"It sounds fine." She hugged his neck, then kissed him. "See you Friday!"

Larry held out for one more kiss before he let her go. "Goodnight."

"Goodnight," she said stepping back inside the door. She stood watching as he picked up his guitar, then waved to him when he walked to his car. He stored the guitar in his trunk, waved back to Sally, then got in the car and started home.

He did not reach the end of the block before a paranoia attack set in on him. For the second time in as many days, he watched for Sargent Mallory to reappear from every side street, from behind every hedge and tree as he drove home.

Friday, February 3, 1967
Candy Man

After the frightening events of the previous weekend, the kids decided they would no longer carry contraband material in their cars. Their smoking room, outside the sargent's jurisdiction, was reasonably safe. The challenge would be safe transportation of smoking materials to that location.

Larry's casual comment, "Too bad we have to transport anything at all," prompted a discussion. They knew the land was owned by the father of a mutual friend. The boys had once experimented with rockets (the serious kind, not simple fireworks), and had used this as their launch site. Realizing the owner seldom came to inspect his property, the idea of storing their material on site became the obvious solution.

Monday after school, John drove out to the site to scout around, and found a perfect hiding place. Wednesday evening, an unusual time for them to get together, they relocated everything without incident. In future, they would rarely have contraband on their persons or in their cars.

Larry arrived at Sally's door promptly at 7:00, feeling on top of the world. The other kids accepted him dating the pretty and popular cheerleader as if completely natural, defeating the nerd image plaguing him in the past. After dinner, they enjoyed their first movie together, holding hands throughout. Sally even leaned her head onto his shoulder much of the time. Afterward, they drove to their favorite location in the country to talk, exchange a little spit, and just to be alone together.

"I must be an idiot, Sally!" Larry said suddenly. "With all the excitement, it never actually dawned on me to ask if you'd share a smoke with me!"

"Well, I was beginning to wonder if you'd ever ask," she giggled.

"I'd be very pleased to. Since our little adventure last week, I'm changing my security arrangements, but I can get my hands on a small quantity of shit if you don't mind waiting a moment."

"I hope this is the same sort of shit I'm thinking about," she giggled, "or I may have to take back the part I said about you not being strange."

"You'll like this. It's quality shit! I have papers and everything, doncha know!"

"Now you're scaring the shit out of me," she giggled again.

"Wait here a moment," he said, getting out of the car. He returned shortly with two joints. "What do you think of *this* shit?"

"Looks like good shit to me," she grinned.

"What kind of shit do you think it is?" he asked, carrying the conversation too far.

"Now you're *really* scaring me!" she laughed. "How many different kinds of shit do you know of?"

"Who gives a shit?" he snickered, handing her a joint and a lighter. "Ladies first!"

"Ooh!" she cooed. "How gallant!" She lit the reefer and took a puff.

"You've done this before," he grinned when she passed it back to him.

"First time in my life!" She giggled when he looked at her suspiciously. "Really! I swear it is!"

"Yeah. Me, too. First time I've shared a smoke with *you*, that is."

"That's what I meant," she confessed.

They smoked until it was getting too small. Before Larry could do so, Sally produced an alligator clip from her purse, causing him to shake his head and grin at her. They finished the first and proceeded to the second, both of them achieving a nice buzz. They continued to talk as before, Sally now laughing even more strongly at Larry's jokes.

They also kissed some more. Sally was a little more aggressive than she had been previously, casually moving Larry's hand to second base. "I sometimes get a little frisky when I smoke," she giggled, "especially if I'm with a great guy like you I can trust. I hope you don't mind."

"I don't mind," he laughed, "especially when I'm with a great girl like you! But to be honest, I'm offended you think you can trust me, Sally. Don't you think I'm just a little bit dangerous?"

"You're probably the most dangerous guy I've ever dated," she grinned, "so I'll have to be extra careful. Just don't go getting any ideas! I won't go all the way!"

Larry returned her grin. Her comment brought a mixed reaction from him. On one hand, he felt complimented she saw him as a serious threat to her "virtue". On the other, he was disappointed she was on her guard, and he was unlikely to get past second base. He decided to relax and enjoy what he had. His wish for more would probably be granted in his dreams.

After a while, she asked, "Can we go get some tater tots or something?"

"Munchies attack? No problem!" he chuckled. He was disappointed the make out session was over, but headed for the Buccaneer and the best tater tots in town. Sharing a large order of tots and a Dr. Pepper, and still feeling a little buzz, they teased each other, laughing at silly things, and playing slap and tickle. Time is too short for those that laugh, however, and soon it was time to take her home.

After a goodnight kiss, he asked, "Will you go to the Valentine's dance with me next Saturday night?"

"I'm sorry, Larry," she said sweetly, "but I already have a date for the dance."

"I guess I waited too long to ask, didn't I?" he said, showing his disappointment. "Then would you go out with me next Friday night?"

"I can't, Larry," she said softly. "I already have a date that night, also."

"I see," he said sadly. "I knew my luck was going to run out sooner or later."

"It's not like that," she assured him. "I want to go out with you again. It's just that someone beat you to it this time."

Already with two strikes against him, he decided to risk the third, needing to know whether his adventures with Sally were over for good. "Then will you go out with me the following Saturday?"

"Of course I will," she smiled. She did not like to make dates that far in advance, but saw in his eyes this was important to him, probably more than it should be.

"Great," he smiled. "I'll pick you up at 7:00, as usual."

"OK," she smiled, kissing him one more time. "Goodnight, Larry!"

"Goodnight, Sally," he said softly. She smiled and slowly closed the door.

Larry felt a little numb walking to his car. Reality had reared its ugly head once again. Intellectually, he knew from the beginning no exclusive relationship was likely to develop between he and Sally. But that hadn't diminished his hope; he *needed* such a relationship. Casual dating, all he could expect from Sally, might help him get over Linda, but it was not going to make him happy in the long run. Realizing he would have to look elsewhere, the first image in his mind was a pair of bright green eyes staring at him from the depths of infinity. To continue the metaphor from earlier in the evening, that image scared the shit out of him.

Saturday, February 4, 1967
I'll Follow The Sun

Larry was first to arrive at the station, and went about the activities needed to complete the setup for that night's program. It bothered him he was alone that night, but knew he was well on the road to recovery, in spite of the fact Sally was not a prospect to fill the void in his life. "Hi, girls!" he greeted Sam and Julia who arrived a few minutes later. "You both look great tonight!"

"Why are you in such a good mood?" Sam asked.

"No particular reason," he said with a smile.

The biggest surprise came when John arrived. "Hi, John! Where's Helen?"

"I'm not sure," he replied nonchalantly. "It's just the *Four Musketeers* tonight!"

Larry, Sam, and Julia exchanged a glance, raising their eyelids as if posing a question. It was Sam who voiced that question, "What gives?"

"She doesn't want to hang out with me anymore," John replied with a shrug.

"When did this happen?" Julia asked. "She didn't say anything Thursday night."

"Last night. She was fine when I picked her up. We headed for the Buccaneer before going to a movie. On the way, we saw a car pulled over by a policeman for some reason. It was our friend, Mallory. When Helen saw him, she freaked out!"

"What do you mean?" Larry asked.

"She just *freaked!*" John said, not really explaining. Seeing the puzzled looks on their faces, he explained things a little more clearly. "I think last Sunday affected her more than any of us realized. She was really frightened, and seeing him again must have brought all of those memories back. She started shaking and crying, and there was nothing I could do to get her to stop."

"So what did you do?" Larry pressed.

"When we got to the Buccaneer, we just sat in the car, and I tried to console her, but she just kept getting worse! She finally said she wanted me to take her home. When we got back to her house, we sat on the sofa and talked. Her mom tried to console her, but nothing helped, and her father stood there staring at me like I was some kind of criminal. Man, it was embarrassing!

"She eventually told us seeing Mallory again brought all those memories flooding back, and it frightened her to think he was going to stop us again. She couldn't bear to think about going through that again. She's now afraid to ride in my car!"

Larry shook his head angrily. "That bastard! Not only does he go out of his way to humiliate us, but he's even interfering with our relationships!"

"Not any more, he isn't," John said with a blank look on his face. "It's no big deal, guys. You know me. If Helen is afraid to be with me, I'll find someone else."

Like always, John was putting on a stoic face as if he did not care in the least, but Larry could see this was nothing but a sham. His friend was not at all like the rock he assumed him to be, and Larry could see he was deeply hurt. In reaching for the joy of victory, John risked the agony of defeat, and lost. He was now harvesting the bitter fruits of that gamble, a harvest with which Larry was intimately familiar.

"Let's go work on some sound effects, shall we, John?" Larry asked softly.

"Sure thing, buddy," John replied. "Let's go."

Saturday, February 4, 1967 – I'll Follow The Sun

"I don't know whether to feel worse for John or for Helen," Julia said.

"I feel bad for both," Sam sighed. "I thought they'd be together for a long time."

"Me, too," Julia agreed. "I'll call her to talk about it. Maybe it's temporary."

"I doubt it," Sam said sadly. "It sounds to me like whenever she sees John, she'll always remember what happened last Sunday. I'm afraid their relationship is dead."

"You're probably right," Julia sighed. "What a shame!"

"I know it's no consolation, John," Larry said, "but it seems we're both without girlfriends again."

"Did you and Sally break up, too?" John asked.

"Not in that sense," he explained. "There's nothing there, John. She's willing to go out on dates with me. I could go for her, but it's pretty clear nothing is ever going to develop on her side. She has lots of guys chasing her, and she's certainly not willing to give them up for the likes of me. Rather than letting myself get hurt again, I'm going to back off while I still can."

"So you won't be seeing her again?" John asked.

"I'll probably still see her from time to time," Larry replied. "She's out with someone else tonight, and is booked up next weekend both Friday and Saturday. I was hoping to take her to the Valentine's Day dance, but someone beat me to it. We made a date for two weeks from tonight, but I don't know if I'll ask her out again after that. There's not much point in chasing after a lost cause."

"I hear you," John agreed. "If a girl doesn't want you, then to hell with her!"

"Don't be bitter," Larry said. "I can see right through you, my friend. You and Helen had a good thing going. That incident Sunday must have been really traumatic! Give her a little time to get over it."

"It's over, Larry," John said sadly. "I'll be moving on."

"I wish I had your strength, John," Larry said softly. "I know you're hurting just as badly as I was when Linda dumped me, but you manage to hide it. My heart is always right out there on my shirt sleeve, where everyone can see it."

John and Larry looked in each others' eyes, and silently exchanged the knowledge of the sadness and disappointment in their lives. They briefly hugged each other, patting themselves on the back the way men do when they hug, and then got down to work on the sound effects they needed for the program.

Saturday, February 11, 1967
Save The Last Dance For Me

Larry was depressed driving to the radio station. He figured the *Top Forty Showcase* program was destined to be uneventful that night because so many of the former regulars would not be present. Linda, of course, would not be coming back. Sally had helped him get over the worst, but she was going to the Valentine's Day dance with someone else, and would not be coming to the station that night. Now that John's relationship with Helen was over, she was also unlikely to ever return.

But the most depressing thing to Larry was Julia would not be present. She called Sam earlier in the week to give her the news. Julia was also going to the Valentine's

Day dance! Of all people, Frank Sutherland called her on Monday asking her to go with him. Since he could not yet drive, his father was to chauffeur them. The Jacobsons were happy to allow her to go with this arrangement.

Sam, John, and Larry, the original *Three Musketeers*, would do the program alone.

"Good evening, Mr. Jacobson," Frank said. "I'm here to take Julia to the dance."

"Good evening, Frank," Julian smiled. "Step inside. Julia will be ready shortly."

Jessica greeted Frank when he stepped inside. "You look very handsome tonight, Frank. Julia is very excited about going to the dance. Thank you for asking her."

"I'm very happy to take her to the dance," Frank smiled.

Julian saw Mr. Sutherland standing beside the car and waved to him, inviting him to come inside as well. Bill smiled and stepped forward, meeting Julian on the front step. "Bill Sutherland," he said introducing himself.

"Julian Jacobson," he replied as they exchanged a handshake. "Call me Julian."

"Nice to meet you," Bill replied. "Call me Bill. Nice evening, isn't it?"

"Yes," Julian agreed. "Thanks for driving the kids to the dance!"

"My pleasure," Bill smiled. "Frank's still a little too young to get his driver's license, but I told him I'd be happy to act as chauffeur whenever he has a date. It works out great this way, because I get to see the type of girl he likes! Most of the time, a boy's father doesn't get that opportunity."

"I guess you're right," Julian smiled. "A girl's father *always* has that opportunity."

"Yes," Bill agreed, "we have an older daughter as well. The disadvantage to a girl's father is when he isn't impressed with the boy who comes calling, like the one taking *her* to the dance tonight! Oh, well. I guess he's no worse than the others."

"I understand," Julian laughed. "You don't have to worry about that where Frank is concerned. He seems to be a fine young man. We've met your daughter as well! She's a lovely girl."

"Thanks," Bill replied. "Oh! I just put two and two together! This is where she came when they had the excitement with the police, isn't it? Now there's a young man I appreciate. Too bad *he* isn't taking her to the dance. Anyway, I'm looking forward to meeting your daughter. Frank tells me she's very pretty and very sweet."

"We think so," Julian smiled, "but parents *always* think that about their little girl!"

"I suppose you're right!" Bill smiled.

"Would you like to step inside?" Julian asked.

"Perhaps next time, assuming there is one," Bill grinned. "I'd rather keep a very low profile, not cramping the boy's style. I think he's embarrassed to have me or his mom drive when he has a date."

"Ah!" Julian smiled. "I understand. But in this case, remind him Julia isn't old enough to go out on a date at all unless some adult is along. Maybe that will make him feel better about it."

"She's fourteen?" Bill asked. "We didn't let his sister go alone on a date until she was fifteen."

"That's what we're thinking," Julian nodded. "That happens next October."

"Well, stick to your guns, Julian," Bill chuckled. "Kids these days seem to have a way of getting you to back down whenever you try to draw the line."

"Amen to that!" Julian grinned. Frank and Julia stepped out of the front door,

Saturday, February 11, 1967 – Save The Last Dance For Me

followed by Jessica. "Jessica, this is Bill Sutherland. Bill, this is my wife, Jessica."

"It's so nice to meet you, Bill," Jessica smiled as she offered her hand.

"Very nice to meet you, Jessica," Bill replied, shaking her hand gently.

"And this is our daughter, Julia," Jessica continued.

"Hello, Mr. Sutherland," Julia smiled. "Thank you for taking us to the dance!"

Bill smiled. "You're welcome! It's nice to meet you, Julia. Are we ready to go?"

"Whenever you are, dad," Frank said.

"Then why don't you escort this lovely young lady to the car and wait for me," Bill smiled to his son. "I won't be but a moment." Frank and Julia departed for the car, where Frank politely opened the door and held it for her. They climbed into the back seat and waited. "It's nice to meet you both. My wife, Wendy, and I are chaperons for the dance. She went on her own. Frank thinks it's bad enough *one* of us has to drive him. He'd be absolutely *mortified* if both of us came along!"

"It's been a pleasure, Bill," Julian smiled, and offered his hand once again.

"Did Frank think to ask?" Bill chuckled. "What time should Julia be home?"

"No, I guess he forgot," Jessica grinned. "When she goes to the radio station with her friends, we have her come home as soon as the program is over. It ends at 11:00; she's usually home by 11:30."

"11:30 it is!" Bill answered. "Once again, it's been a pleasure to meet you. I'll say goodnight to you now. I don't think Frank would appreciate it if I came to front door with him when we get back."

"Probably not," Julian chuckled. "Goodnight, Bill."

"Goodnight," Jessica echoed.

Bill Sutherland smiled to them, then turned and walked smartly to his car. He got into the front seat, and acted as chauffeur, silently driving his son and his date to the Valentine's Day dance.

Tuesday, February 14, 1967
The Rose

Julia hopped off the school bus and ran for the house to get out of the cold wind. "Hi, mom! I'm home!" she shouted, bursting through the font door.

"Hi, sweetheart!" her mom called from the kitchen. "I was about to make some hot chocolate. Would you like some?"

"Sure!" Julia shouted back. "Let me put away my things and I'll be right there!"

Jessica already had the chocolate ready. She poured two cups, added a marshmallow to each, and sat them on the kitchen table. In the middle of the table sat a slim vase containing a single long stemmed red rose. She positioned herself opposite the rose, wanting to see Julia's face when she entered the room.

Julia hung up her coat and dropped her books on her bed. She also had a white paper bag filled with the valentines she had received at school. Most notable were the one from Jimmy, begging her to forgive him, and the one from Greg. She was not sure how to discourage the younger boy who seemed to have a big crush on her.

Julia almost froze in her tracks when she entered the kitchen and saw the beautiful red rose sitting on the table. "Where did that come from?" she asked, assuming her father had given it to her mother.

"It was delivered about an hour ago," Jessica smiled. "It was addressed to you, but there was no card attached. It seems you have a secret admirer!"

"What?" Julia asked. "No card?"

"None. Before he got away, I asked the delivery boy if the card had gotten lost. He assured me there hadn't been a card. There were also two envelopes for you in the mail. Maybe one of them will offer an explanation."

Julia looked at the rose and lightly stroked the stem with her fingertips. "It's beautiful!" She leaned over the table, bringing the rose to her face to sniff its aroma. "And it smells wonderful!"

"Yes," Jessica smiled. "I'm so jealous!"

"Oh, mom," she giggled. Then looking accusingly, "Did you get this for me?"

"No, bubee," Jessica replied, "I promise I didn't. I've already asked your father, and he also denies it, but he told me he has gifts for us when he gets home tonight."

"Then who could have sent it?" Julia asked as she examined it closely, perhaps hoping to find a secret message revealing the sender. "Where are those envelopes?"

Julia examined the two envelopes her mother handed her. One of them did not have a return address. The other indicated the sender was Frank Sutherland. She decided to open it first. The card contained a simple, standard Valentine's Day message, with a hand-written note. "Happy Valentine's Day! I hope you enjoyed going to the dance with me as much as I enjoyed taking you. Yours, Frank."

"No clue there," Jessica said. "Surely he'd have taken credit if he had sent it."

"I suppose you're right, mom. Perhaps the other one will provide the answer." She opened the other card and read the sweet but standard message. It was signed, "Your friend, Larry."

"That was sweet," Jessica said, "but no clue. I guess he didn't send it, either."

"I guess not," Julia said flatly.

"There's no doubt it's from some boy who really likes you," Jessica giggled. "A red rose means *'I love you'* in case you didn't know. Could it be from Jimmy?"

Julia thought about that possibility. "I don't think so, mom. He already gave me a nice valentine," she said, removing it from the paper bag and handing it to her mother. "If he had sent it, he would have included a card and taken credit for it."

Jessica agreed. "What about that sweet little boy who rides the bus? Greg?"

"He gave me this one on the way home," she replied, handing her mother the other special valentine. "Can you help me discourage him? I don't want a boyfriend even younger than Jimmy, and I don't want to hurt his feelings."

"Sometimes that can't be helped, sugar." After a pause, she asked, "Is there anyone else you can think of? Perhaps some boy at school who's been paying you a little more attention than usual?"

"No," Julia said after thinking for a moment. "No one I've noticed, anyway."

"Maybe it's from one of those boys at temple?" Jessica asked.

"I doubt it," Julia snickered. "They're either too young or too old to notice me!"

"Don't kid yourself," Jessica grinned.

"You don't suppose it could be from someone who's trying to throw us off the trail," Julia thought aloud. Then she shook her head and looked a little sad.

"Who are you thinking about?" Jessica asked.

"He already has a girlfriend, anyway," Julia said sadly.

"Oh," Jessica said, realizing she was thinking of Larry. "That would seem to be unlikely, sugar. If he had sent the rose, would he have sent the card as well, and not mentioned the rose?" Jessica did not understand why Larry had not pursued Julia after his break up with Linda. It was obvious he was interested, but something held him back. And when the pretty little cheerleader stepped in and turned his head, Julia dropped off his radar. Jessica still noticed him looking at Julia as if he longed to be with her, but surely she was mistaken about that.

"I guess not," Julia agreed unhappily.

"Well, I'd have to say whoever sent it has a pretty big crush on you!"

"Yeah, I guess so!" Julia said with a bright smile. "I'll have to keep my eyes open. Surely he'll reveal himself pretty soon, don't you think?"

Jessica returned her smile. "I'm sure of it!" she said brightly.

Saturday, February 18, 1967
My Last Date (With You)

Larry was not a happy camper on his way to pick up Sally. It seemed to him the universe was going out of its way to punish him. On one hand, it occurred to him this sort of thing had happened his entire life. On the other, he could think of nothing he had done to deserve such cruelty.

It started a week ago when Sam told him they would not be picking up Julia because she was going to the Valentine's Day dance with Frank. What bothered him the most was he had been the one who introduced Frank and Julia in the first place. Some other boy got to take her out while Larry languished in misery, waiting for Jimmy to release him from that damned promise. No big deal, right? It was, after all, only one date.

Insult was added to the injury. This week, Sally asked a favor. Frank was taking Julia out again, coming to the radio station. "Since that's where we're going," Sally asked sweetly, "would you mind terribly if Frank and Julia rode along with us? It would save my mom or dad a drive out to Steep Hollow twice that night."

How could he refuse such a request? How could he say, "No! I don't want to help Frank take my Julie on a date! *I'm* the one who should be taking her out!" Was that what it was all about? *Do I really want her to be my date?* He knew the answer was yes, he *did* want her to be his date, but he could not explain why it meant so much to him.

It did not matter what Larry wanted. Julia was going to be Frank's date that night. He could either be a gentleman about it or not, but those were his only two choices.

"Hi, Larry!" Sally smiled when she answered the door.

"Hi, doll," he replied. As unhappy as he was, Sally's bright smile had a way of cheering him, even though it was short lived. Seeing Frank instantly reminded him of the situation. "Hi, Frank. You guys ready to get going?"

"Hi, Larry," Frank smiled. "Thanks for letting me and Julia ride with you tonight. Mom and Dad would have given us a lift, but I'd much rather not have them along. I'm sure you understand!"

"Yeah, I understand," Larry said simply. "Let's go pick her up. On the way out there, we can decide what we want to do about dinner."

Sally suggested, "After we pick up Julia, why don't we run by the Buccaneer and grab something to take with us."

"Sounds good to me," Frank added.

"I guess that settles it," Larry smiled. "I doubt Julie will have any objection."

Larry opened the passenger side door and Sally slipped onto the seat. Frank hopped into the back while Larry walked around to the driver's side. Perhaps he was too distracted by other thoughts, but was surprised Sally had moved into the center to sit close to him. He chastised himself for not paying attention. He was on a date with a very nice, popular, and beautiful girl – a cheerleader! He should be happy!

"They're here!" Julia announced.

"OK, sweetheart," Julian answered, smiling at her enthusiasm. "Make yourself scarce for a moment or two. I'll answer the door."

"Yes, daddy," Julia giggled. She and her mom retreated down the hallway.

A moment later, the doorbell rang. "Good evening, Frank," Julian smiled.

"Good evening, Mr. Jacobson," Frank replied politely. "Thank you for allowing me to take Julia to the radio station tonight."

"You're welcome, Frank," Julian replied. "She'll be out in a moment."

"Thank you, sir," Frank said stepping inside.

Julian glanced at the car and saw Larry and Sally sitting in the front seat, watching the activities at the front door. He acknowledged their presence with a wave. "Frank, I just want to remind you I think Julia is too young to be going on unchaperoned dates like this. We're allowing it under the condition you go straight to the radio station, and return immediately when the program is over."

"Is it OK if we swing by the Buccaneer to pick up something to eat?" Frank asked.

"Yes, that'll be fine." As Julia and her mother entered the foyer, Julian added, "Now, I'm sure we can trust you and Julia to behave yourselves, but your father asked me to have you keep an eye on Larry and Sally so they don't get into any mischief!"

"I'll do my best," Frank chuckled.

"That could be a more difficult task than you realize!" Jessica grinned.

"Good evening, Mrs. Jacobson. Hi, Julia," he said, saving his best smile for her.

"Hi," Julia said sweetly.

"Off you go," Julian grinned. "Tell Larry I said to drive carefully, and to bring you straight home after the program."

"We will," Julia giggled. "Goodnight, daddy! Goodnight, mom!"

"Goodnight, bubee," Jessica said. "You two have a good time."

Frank escorted Julia to the car. "Hi, Julia!" Sally said brightly as Julia slipped into the middle of the seat, greeting both Larry and Sally. "I'll remind you to watch out for my little brother. He still bites!"

"Oh, he's not so bad," Julia grinned.

"Hi, Julie," Larry said softly. He started the car and began to turn it around.

"We planned to go by the Buccaneer on the way," Frank explained. "We'll pick up something to eat and take it to the station with us."

"Be sure to get something extra for those vultures up there!" Sally giggled.

The drive to the Buccaneer was a steady stream of idle chit-chat among the foursome, although Larry was a minor participant. His attention to the conversation was distracted as he watched Frank and Julia in his rear view mirror. On more than one occasion, he found himself wishing he and Frank could change places. But he realized it was just foolish thinking. Once again, he reminded himself, *I'm on a date with a very nice, popular, and beautiful girl – a cheerleader. I should be happy!*

After the program, Larry drove straight to Julia's house. He and Sally watched Frank and Julia walk hand-in-hand to her front door. When they reached her doorstep, she put her arms around his neck, and kissed him goodnight. Noting a pained expression on his face, Sally asked, "Is something bothering you, Larry?"

"Oh, no," he lied. "Maybe I should cut down on those tater tots."

Frank practically ran down the walkway to the car, and jumped in, obviously happy and excited. Sally noticed Larry tried to appear relaxed and normal as he drove, but was obviously bothered by something. At the Sutherland house, Frank rushed to get out of the car. "Goodnight, Larry. Thanks again for carrying me and Julia along. I really appreciate it!"

"No problem," Larry said with a forced smile as he climbed out of the seat.

Sally followed him, taking his hand as they strolled slowly to the front door. "It's been a really nice evening, Larry, just like always."

"I'm glad you enjoyed it, Sally," he smiled upon reaching the door. "You're a very special and wonderful girl." He put his hands on her cheeks, drawing her to him to kiss her goodnight.

"Goodnight," she whispered following the kiss. "You're pretty special yourself!"

"I'm just an ordinary guy," he said softly. "Goodnight, Sally."

From the doorway, she watched him turn away and walk slowly to his car, get in, and back out the driveway. She wondered what was bothering him. He seemed so distracted, so out of touch with everything going on around him. It then occurred to her for the first time, he had not asked her out again at the end of their date.

Larry knew in his heart rather than goodnight, this was closer to goodbye. It would be the last time he would ask Sally out. He knew if he took her to the radio station he would have to endure seeing Frank and Julia together again. It was possible, even likely, Frank and Julia would want to double date no matter *where* Larry might be taking Sally. He could not take that risk. *There is nothing I can do to prevent Frank and Julia from dating, but I'll be damned if I'm going to do anything to help or encourage it!*

In spite of this lack of encouragement from Larry, Frank was to become a regular member of the radio program. His mother or father would pick Julia up each Saturday night, bring them to the station, and then take her home. Larry would go to the radio station alone, see Frank and Julia together, and silently wish things could be different.

Saturday, April 29, 1967
The Senior Prom

"Oh, my!" Mrs. Kronkite gushed. "Please come in and let me see how handsome you are!" Before her stood a familiar young man of seventeen, all decked out in a black tuxedo, complete with a white shirt with ruffles, fancy satin cumberbun, and a black bow tie, looking like he had just stepped out of a James Bond movie.

"Thanks, Mrs. K," Larry said with a suave smile, trying also to act like he had just stepped out of a James Bond movie. "My mom thought I looked OK since I was all cleaned up for a change."

"Don't you try to fool me, young man," she grinned. "I imagine your mother was talking a hundred miles and hour, taking as many pictures as she could before she let you out of the house!"

"I think she took one or two," he smiled, trying to act nonchalant. "It's not like it's a big thing. So I got a little dressed up! What's the big deal?"

The "big deal" was the Senior Prom for the Stephen F. Austin High School graduating class of 1967. The evening would consist of dinner at a fancy restaurant, a formal dance in the ballroom of a local hotel, followed by less formal events as the seniors celebrated their upcoming graduation. It was a rite of passage, where seniors were converted from juvenile school children into responsible and respectable young adults. A typical comment by seniors hearing this description was, "Yeah, right!"

Larry had mixed feelings about the whole affair. He had not been dating very regularly during the last half of the school year, especially since he was reluctant to ask Sally out. There just was not anyone he thought was special enough to take to what was being promoted as such a special event. There were only two girls he though that special. One of them was seeing someone else, someone he himself had introduced her to. The other was his date for the evening.

With only a couple of weeks to go before the momentous event, Larry decided to ignore the whole thing, working on the radio program, as usual. When he mentioned his plans to John and Sam, he was surprised to learn Sam had made the same decision since her mysterious boyfriend would not be around to take her to the prom.

He realized instinctively this was not the way things were supposed to be. Regardless of the fact he thought the whole idea behind this event was rather stupid, it was still something special, something that would occur only once in a lifetime. Events occurring only once a lifetime should not be so casually cast aside, as if they had no meaning at all. That was the basis for his argument with Sam.

"Look at this way," he told her, "neither of us is ever going to have to worry about another Senior Prom in our entire lives. It's not like it really means anything, but I think we should go, especially you. This sort of thing means more to girls than guys." When she threatened to clobber him for that last comment, he realized his thinking was wrong. "OK, the truth is it means something to both, though guys probably don't know what."

In the end, he had a strong argument and made it stick. Susan Kronkite, his best friend, was to be his date for the 1967 Senior Prom. It was their first actual date together, and quite probably would be their last. In spite of all the reasons they could find to forget this crazy notion, they eventually agreed the idea made sense.

"I'll go see what's keeping her," Gayle said excitedly. "I happen to know she's

Saturday, April 29, 1967 – The Senior Prom

been ready for over an hour!" He returned her bright smile with his on. She disappeared down the hallway, leaving him standing alone in the living room. During this moment, a girl's father would normally grill the boy who had come with the obvious intent of raping his daughter. His role was to deliver a message instilling a certain "fear of God" into the boy's head. Not having a father to deliver such a message, Sam usually performed this function herself, something she undoubtedly was quite good at it!

Admiring a small crystalline figurine of a unicorn displayed on a bookshelf in the living room, he did not immediately notice Gayle's return. He recalled the look in her eye the moment Sam opened her Christmas present just four months ago. Gayle cleared her throat, making a not-so-subtle announcement of her return. He turned to look at her, and saw her beaming with more pride than he had ever seen in her before. She directed her attention to the hallway, intentionally drawing Larry's eyes in that direction so Sam could make her entrance.

She was dressed in a beautiful formal cocktail gown of shocking pink nylon chiffon, with a gathered waistband in shimmering pink satin. The full skirt had an attached crinoline and pink acetate liner, and when she turned a full circle for his inspection, he saw the back was adorned by a dramatic satin bow. "My God, Sam," he whispered. "No, wait a second. I should definitely call you *Susan* tonight! You are simply beautiful!" Never taking his eyes off of her, he stepped forward and offered her the white pasteboard box containing a orchid corsage made to match the color of her gown. Now he understood what color "cerise" actually was!

"Thank you, most kind sir," she said with a dazzling smile, accepting the corsage. "You're very handsome yourself!" The last sentence ended with a giggle. "Sorry. I'm not giggling at you, but at how silly I sound. You really are handsome tonight."

"Thanks," he giggled. "Does this mean you don't want me to call you Susan?"

"Let's stick to Sam, OK?" she grinned as Gayle pinned the corsage to the dress.

"Let me look at you two," Gayle gushed when the corsage was safely attached. Sam stood next to Larry so her mother could admire the attractive young couple all dressed up in their finest. "Oh, I just have to make some pictures of this! You two stand right there while I get my camera!"

Larry and Sam looked at each other and smiled. "What do you have to say now?" he asked. "Are you glad I insisted we do this?"

"Yes, I'm glad," she confessed with a snicker. She leaned over and kissed him on the cheek just as her mother returned.

"Oh, do that again!" Gayle begged. "I want to make a picture!"

"If we're going to go through with this, then let's do it right!" Sam said to Larry.

"I agree," he smiled. He put his arms around her waist, drew her close to him, and kissed her on the mouth. Gayle captured the moment with her camera, then insisted they do it again just in case the first picture didn't turn out. They laughed, but happily repeated their performance, and then posed for several other pictures.

After a few more special moments, drawing a few tears from Gayle, the couple agreed it was time to get this fabulous evening started. Gayle reluctantly bid them goodnight, and watched from the front door as Larry escorted Susan to the car. Rather than his usual car, he had borrowed the much nicer family car this evening. He proudly opened the passenger door, and Sam slipped into the seat, being careful not to wrinkle the cerise colored chiffon. Keeping to their announced intention of "doing this right", she slid into the middle of the seat, and sat next to Larry as they drove to the restaurant.

He wanted to take Sam to a restaurant called "The Texan", but found it impossible to get a reservation. The Texan was the premiere restaurant in town, run by the Stelljes family, and was booked completely solid that night. He made arrangements at another nice restaurant, one serving Italian food. Not as elegant as the Texan, it was still filled with couples dressed in formal wear, bound for the prom.

After dinner, as they were driving to the hotel where the dance would be held, they tuned the radio to 1240 on the AM band, and listened to John and the gang introducing the *Top Forty Showcase*, bemoaning how they were shorthanded because Larry and Sam abandoned them in favor of going to the Senior Prom. Larry and Sam looked at each other and laughed, each thinking they should make a little side trip on the way.

Julia was the first to see them enter the main studio. "Ooh la la!" she squealed. "Are we being visited by royalty?"

"Yes!" Larry laughed. "Haven't I told you how great great grandfather Bristol was the Duke of Earl, and I'm the crown prince, heir to the throne of England?"

"I don't think so," Julia laughed.

"And Sam is the beautiful Princess of Slob-aria!" he continued.

"Gee, thanks!" Sam said. "At least you got the 'beautiful' part right."

"Sam, I may be stupid but I'm not blind," he smiled sincerely. "You really are a beautiful princess!" She looked at him and smiled, but decided not to respond.

"That's a beautiful dress!" Julia exclaimed.

"It certainly is, Sam!" John agreed. "Both of you guys look fabulous! But I have to admit I'm surprised to see you. Did you come to your senses at the last minute, forget that stupid dance, and come to work the show with us?"

"Guess again," Larry grinned. "We heard you guys on the radio and thought we'd stop on the way and tease you about being couped up in here all night!"

"Hold on," John said as the current record ended. They waited as the microphone went live, Frank read the dedications, Diggs spun the next selection, then killed the microphone. "We won't be couped up as late as you guys! When the show is over, Frank's dad will take him and Julia home, and I'll go get some sleep."

"You're just jealous because they're going to a dance and an all-night party you didn't get invited to!" Julia teased.

"Who cares?" John tried.

"You will next year!" Larry grinned.

"Not likely," John grinned back at him.

"Sure you will," Julia said. "Maybe you don't think it means anything, but I'm *already* looking forward to my Senior Prom, and it's still three whole years away!"

"Good for you!" Sam grinned. She looked at Larry and could see the wheels turning in his head. *Might he be the lucky one who will take her to that prom?* She could also see the hope in his eyes the answer to that question would be yes. "Well, come on, my handsome prince," Sam said to him with a bright smile. "We'd better get going and let these people take care of show business."

"I'm no handsome prince, but you're beautiful as a princess tonight!" he smiled.

"I'm only a princess for the evening," Sam laughed. "This Cinderella wants to get to the ball before midnight rolls around and she turns into a pumpkin!"

Saturday, April 29, 1967 – The Senior Prom

"Maybe at the stroke of midnight," Larry snickered, "I should get you to dance with this guy I know by the name of Peter Peter..."

"You pervert!" Sam laughed.

"See you guys later," Larry grinned to the gang.

"Have a good time," Julia giggled.

"Thanks, Julie!" Returning his attention to Sam, he asked, "Your carriage awaits thee, my Princess! Shall I carry you, or would you prefer to walk?"

"It's too bad I'm not wearing my witch's outfit," Sam smirked. "That way, I could turn you back into the frog you really are, and I could carry *you*!"

"Don't you think I could find another princess to kiss me and break the spell?" Larry snickered as they headed for the door.

"Goodnight, guys!" John said as Larry and Sam departed.

Outside the radio station, Larry and Sam got back into his car to continue on their way to the dance. Backing out of the parking space, they listened to Julia announce the dedications for the next record, adding, "And a special dedication goes to my good friends, the handsome Prince Larry and the beautiful Princess Sam, who stopped by to see us, and are now on their way to the prom. I hope you have a wonderful time, guys!"

Larry and Sam looked at each other and smiled. While deep inside, both of them wished they could be with someone else that evening, each decided to put those wishes on hold for a little while. Tonight, they would smile for each other, hold hands, dance together, and enjoy each others' company. Each of them, from time to time over the years, had wanted to do that. Tonight, it would not be just a fairy tale.

Sunday, April 30, 1967
Love The One You're With

After the dance, Larry and Sam went to a party at Sharon Cushing's house. Many of their friends from the senior class were at this party along with their dates. The dates of the senior girls tended to be college guys, mostly students attending nearby Texas A&M University. The dates of the senior guys tended to be underclassmen, many of whom Larry or Sam also knew from school.

This party was a little more elegant than the one Larry attended with Sally and Frank following the basketball game back in January. For one thing, everyone was in formal evening attire. Sharon's parents were also present this time, although they made an effort to keep a low profile, allowing the kids a free hand to celebrate as they wanted. There was a magnificent spread on the kitchen table, as well as an ample supply of beverages, including beer, wine, and even hard liquor. The Cushings were not strict about alcohol, and merely asked everyone to drink responsibly. As a precaution, however, Mr. Cushing collected car keys as the kids entered; he would return them when someone wanted to leave, after confirming they were capable of driving.

The large dining room had been converted into a dance floor. Other couples disappeared onto the patio and the backyard, where various alcoves offered enough privacy they could make out. Some were adventurous enough to engage in more intimate activities, not even caring if others watched. The less adventurous gathered into various sized groups to joke and to play games, including a rousing game of "spin the bottle" organized in the middle of the living room.

Larry and Sam, like most couples, spent a little time in each of the activities, with the exception of the more intimate. They enjoyed the food and drink, danced, sat around and joked with other couples, and even joined the "spin the bottle" game. Naturally, Sharon fetched her brother's guitar and asked Larry to play a few songs.

It was intended to be an all-night party. At about 5:00, however, Larry and Sam, like most couples, decided to end the party in favor of breakfast. They went to the Dutch Kettle, a small diner-like restaurant not too far from Sam's house. A few other customers were present, but no one was surprised to see a young couple dressed in formal attire that morning. Everyone knew it had been prom night.

Sandra Gilmore, a friend also celebrating with her boyfriend were already seated, and waved at Larry and Sam when they entered. "Hi, guys! This is my boyfriend, Gary. These are my friends, Larry and Sam. Why don't you guys join us?"

"Thanks, Sandra," Larry smiled. "It's nice to meet you, Gary."

"Same here," he replied. "I saw you at the party. Who is the graduating senior?"

"Both," Larry grinned. Doing his Maxwell Smart imitation, he added, "Would you believe we met in a Siberian prison and have been secretly married for the last ten years?"

"No," he grinned.

"Would you believe this is our first date?" Sam asked, using her own imitation.

"I don't think so," Gary grinned again. Sandra nodded her head in agreement.

"You both loose!" Sam laughed. "We've known each other since we were in the third grade, almost ten years ago. Elementary school is worse than any Siberian prison! But we're not secretly married. After all, this really *is* our first date!"

"You're kidding!" Sandra said. "I figured you'd been an item for a long time!"

"We've been the best of friends," Larry explained, "and I've been begging her to go out with me since we were nine years old. This is the first time she's accepted. Her real boyfriend, the man of her dreams, lives... Well, I don't really know where he lives, but anyway, I guess she finally got desperate enough to go out with me."

"What about the girl of *your* dreams," Sandra grinned. "Where does she live?"

"I guess I don't know that, either," Larry laughed. "One thing for sure is she doesn't live within the city limits of dear old Bryan, Texas!"

Sam looked at Larry and grinned. *How subtly he can tell you the absolute truth and make it sound like a lie, or tell a whopper of a lie and make you swear it was pure gospel.* She put her hand on his cheek, turned his head towards her, and kissed him warmly. "I know where the girl of your dreams lives, you faker, and if you aren't careful, I'll call her up and tell her about it!"

Larry snickered, "Tonight, *you're* the girl of my dreams. Will you call yourself?"

"I live *inside* the city limits of Bryan!" she laughed. "Or have you forgotten?"

The other three enjoyed a laugh at Larry's expense, mystifying the waitress who arrived to take their orders. After she left, the conversation continued in a slightly more serious vein. "What are you guys doing after graduation?" Sandra asked.

"I'm going to relax for the summer," Sam explained, "but I'll be right back cracking the books next fall. I'm going for a business degree at A&M."

"There shall be no wick for the rested," Larry said. "I plan to start summer school about a week after getting my diploma, and get a part time job at the computer center. What about you?"

"Gary's going to TCU," she replied, "and I'm going to start there next fall. You said, *'no wick for the rested'*. Isn't that supposed to be *'no rest for the wicked'*?"

"Haven't you heard the story about the ladies who were supposed to stay up all night to greet King Arthur when he returned to Camelot?" Gary and Sandra shook their heads at him. Sam, seeing the twinkle in his eyes, put her elbows on the table and held her head as she shook it, chuckling to herself. "Well, you see there were these four damsels who were supposed to keep an all-night vigil waiting for King Arthur to return. They were supposed to light some lamps to illuminate his way when approached the castle.

"Now one of the girls was very diligent, and waited patiently in the dark for the King to return, keeping herself awake all night even though she was very, very tired. But the other girls were lazy. They lit their lamps long before the King arrived, and went off to sleep so they'd be well rested. In the wee hours of the morning, a trumpet call announced the King's return, and the girls jumped up to light his way.

"The diligent girl prepared to light her lamp by pulling the wick out of the oil slightly, and lighting it with a flint. But the other girls' lamps had gone out during the night, and their wicks had all burnt up while they were resting. They saw the diligent girl had brought some spare wicks, and asked to borrow them, so they could also light the way for the King.

"But the diligent girl just shook her head and scolded them. *'No! No! There shall be no wick for the rested!'* she told them. So you see, the moral of the story..." The waitress was once again mystified by the groans she heard coming from her customers when she delivered their breakfasts.

The eastern sky was aglow in colors of red, orange, and purple when Larry pulled the car into Sam's driveway. He opened the door, stepped out, and held the door for her as Sam followed closely behind. Arm-in-arm, they strolled to her front door, admiring the colors of the sunrise, but too tired to make any comment.

"This has been wonderful," Sam said softly once they reached the porch. "I'm so glad you talked me into going, Larry."

"I'm glad I did, too!" he smiled. "It has truly been a night to remember. I'm glad I shared it with someone as special as you."

"You're so sweet. I think you're pretty special yourself."

"Thanks, Sam," he said bashfully. "And I finally got to take you out on a date!"

"And you didn't even try to get into my pants!" she giggled.

"Who says I didn't?" he laughed. "Why do you think I've been so sweet to you! I've been trying to get into your pants all night long, but you won't give me a chance!" When Sam looked at him with a disgusted smile on her face, he smiled back at her and asked a little more seriously, "Did you really expect me to, Sam?"

"No. Not really."

He took her into his arms and looked deeply into her eyes. "Sam, we've known each other for a long time. A lot of people wonder why we haven't been dating the whole time. Maybe sometimes, I wonder about that myself."

"I know the feeling," she said sincerely, "but we both know the answer."

"I know," he sighed. "But there's something important I want to say to you, Sam. Perhaps if I had said this a long time ago, then just maybe you'd never have noticed

Donald, and perhaps I'd never have noticed Julia. I suppose none of that really matters now, but I still want to say this. You're my best friend in the whole world, and I wouldn't change that for anything in the entire universe. I love you, Sam!"

"I love you, too," she said softly. "We could have been together if that was what we really wanted. I think fate must have other plans for us. Maybe I'm supposed to be with Donald. Maybe you're supposed to be with Julia. Maybe there are things to come that will surprise us both. What's the line you always say from that song?"

"It goes like this," he said, then began to sing. *"Que será, será, Whatever will be, will be. The future's not ours to see, Que será, será."*

"Yes," she smiled. "Larry, I can't wait to see what the future holds for us!"

"Some of it may be unpleasant, but as long as I have a friend like you, Sam, I know I'll be able to face anything the universe wants to throw at me!"

"And so can I," she agreed, "just as long as I have a friend like you!"

They kissed each other as warmly as any couple has ever kissed. Their kiss lingered for several seconds, well beyond the amount of time either of them would have expected. Perhaps it was because they knew this might be the last time they would be together as a couple, rather than as exceptionally good friends.

"Goodnight, Larry," Sam said to him as the kiss ended.

"Good morning, Sam," he corrected. "It's the beginning of the first day in the rest of our lives. I hope you'll always be happy."

"May your path lead you to a happiness that will last forever," she said.

They kissed one more time, not lingering quite as long as the first. Then, reluctantly, Sam opened the front door and stepped inside. She watched as Larry turned, walked back to his car, and started the drive home.

Thursday, May 25, 1967
Pomp And Circumstance

When the ceremony completed, Larry went searching through the crowd to find his parents. On his way, he encountered Mrs. Kronkite looking for Sam, and begged her to stay with him as they searched. He soon spotted his parents chatting with Sam. Larry and Gayle maneuvered their way through the crowd to join them.

"There he is!" Sam pointed. "It looks like he's found mom. Over here, Larry!"

"Whew! Now I know how a salmon feels!" Larry grinned. "Why do you suppose everyone else is going in *that* direction?"

"An educated man like you should already know the answer," Larry's father said. "Congratulations, son! We're very proud of you!"

While Larry thanked his parents for their support in getting him through school, Gayle gave her daughter a hug. "Congratulations, sweetheart!"

"Thanks," she said, then turned to her dearest friend. "Congratulations, Larry!"

"Congratulations to you, too, Sam," he replied, offering her a hug. They laughed merrily together for a moment as they embraced. "We finally did it!"

John stepped out of the crowd. "You did? Why am I always the last to know?"

Sam looked at Larry and asked, "Are you going to deck him, or shall I?"

"Be my guest!" Larry laughed. "Mom, dad, you remember Sam's mom, right?"

"Of course," Lena said. "It's good to see you again, Gayle."

"It's nice to see you again," Gayle smiled. "Isn't it wonderful to see these children growing into fine young men and women?"

"It certainly is!" Lena replied.

"I'm sure you're going to want copies of the pictures I took on prom night. They came out perfectly! He was so handsome!"

"Please!" Lena said, returning that smile. "It may be the last time I get to see him all dressed up for years! He told me how beautiful Sam was. I'm looking forward to seeing those pictures."

Sam, John, and Larry looked at each other and made gagging noises, until they were interrupted by the arrival of Julia and her parents. "Congratulations, Sam!" Julia said as she gave her friend a hug. She turned to Larry, hugged him just as warmly and repeated the greeting, "Congratulations, Larry!"

Larry stood in stunned silence for a moment, trying to recover from yet another gap in the space-time continuum. Jessica hugged each of the graduates and congratulated them, quickly followed by congratulations from Julian. Larry happily accepted a handshake, while Sam waved it off and gave Julian a warm hug instead.

He came to his senses long enough to introduce his parents. "Mom, dad, you've already met Julie. These are her parents, Mr. and Mrs. Jacobson."

"Call me Jessica," she smiled.

"I've heard a lot about you, Jessica," Lena said. "Call me Lena, and this is Josh."

"Nice to meet you, Jessica," Josh said politely.

"And please call me Julian," he added, offering his hand.

"Josh Bristol," he smiled. "It's very nice to meet you, Julian."

Sam stepped in and introduced her mother to the Jacobsons. When all of the parents were on a first name basis, and talking about how wonderful it was Larry and Sam had graduated, the kids resumed their conversation. John was in a particularly festive mood. "I can't believe I just watched all those people matriculate right here in public! It was unimaginable! It's bad enough to see Larry doing it, but I've seen him matriculate many times before. I'd never have thought I'd watch Sam doing it. What does it feel like to matriculate in public?"

"I see John's been studying the dictionary like you do," Sam snickered.

Larry rolled his eyes and shook his head. "You should have been with us at dinner, John. You could have watched me masticate!" Julia giggled brightly, and she tried to cover her face which was turning bright red, much to Larry's delight. He pressed the issue just to tease her even more. "Imagine that! First I masticate in public, and then matriculate, all on the same night! No doubt Mallory will be looking for me again!"

"I'm just happy you aren't the president of the debate club," Sam giggled. "Can you imagine what John would be saying if you were a Master Debater?"

The parents had not been paying much attention, but could not help but notice the kids were laughing. "What are you kids giggling so much about?" Jessica asked.

"Just childish foolishness," Larry replied with a grin. She returned his smile, nodded her head knowingly, and returned her attention to the adult conversation. Once they were being ignored again, Larry grinned at his friends. "What brought you and your parents out here tonight, Julie?"

"Our car," she replied smoothly, with a sweet smile. Larry grinned at her, closed his eyes, and shook his head slowly, while Sam and John broke into laughter.

He considered his next question carefully. "Why did you and your parents come to the graduation ceremonies this evening?"

"So I could watch two of my best friends matriculate!" she chuckled.

Her answer was the perfect accent to John's joke. While John and Sam giggled, Larry smiled brightly and gazed into the green eyes of this little girl, this horrible monster who had been disturbing his sleep for the last several months. His appreciation of her intelligence, sense of humor, and style rose even higher than before. When he first met her, something about her had reached into his very soul and shaken it. Just in case there had been any doubts, she shook it again, proving to him it had not been an accident. "I'm honored," he said sincerely.

"And I was honored this afternoon," she replied. "Did you think no one noticed you sitting up there in the top of the gymnasium during my ninth grade 'graduation' ceremonies? Why didn't you come down and say something when it was over?"

"I figured everyone would be too busy congratulating you," he said, embarrassed he had been caught. "I needed to be there, anyway, and I didn't want to interfere."

"Don't be silly! You wouldn't have been interfering!" she assured him.

The conversation among the adults reached a lull, so Julian took the opportunity to bring the kids into the circle. "So what do our graduates have planned now? What are you going to do with that diploma you worked so hard to acquire?"

"I'm going to celebrate all summer!" Sam laughed. "Then it'll be back to the books next fall, when I start working on a business degree out at A&M. By the way, Mrs. B, I want to thank you again for your efforts in helping A&M go coed."

"I'm afraid I didn't do very much," Lena said. "I'm glad you girls now have the opportunity to study there. I know the boys are glad about that, also!"

"Amen to that!" Larry grinned. "As for myself, Mr. J, there shall be no rest for the wicked. I'll be registering for summer classes first thing in the morning! It's not that I really want to get a jump on the degree plan, but I have to be registered before I can apply for a part time job at the computer center. A friend of mine, a PhD in the Industrial Engineering department, promised to get me a job there!"

The topic of the conversation changed as Jessica picked up on Sam's comment. "Lena, what does Sam mean about you helping the school go coeducational?"

"Oh, it wasn't much," Lena said. "That was almost ten years ago. Another lady named Barbara Tittle and I tried to enroll in A&M. When we were refused admission because we were women, we sued for illegal discrimination. We won in district court, but the school appealed, and the appellate court overturned the earlier ruling. The Texas Supreme Court upheld the reversal, and the U.S. Supreme Court refused to hear the case. So, the bottom line is nothing happened."

"Yeah, but she helped get the ball rolling," Sam added. "A&M slowly started accepting a few more women over time, as exceptions rather than the rule. Last year, they finally opened the doors for all women."

"Why, that's wonderful!" Jessica said. "Whether you think you deserve it or not, I'd say congratulations are in order! You stuck to your guns and fought an injustice. My people know what happens when people don't take a stand and fight injustice."

"Well, thanks," Lena said. "I guess we did our best. Only now, it might turn out to be a problem for him!"

"Why is that?" Julian asked.

"There are some people who are very unhappy A&M is now coeducational," Larry said, "especially the 'old army' types who graduated a hundred years ago, back when dinosaurs still roamed the earth. A lot of them are now professors and administrators out there, and they have very long memories."

"You think some might discriminate against you because your mother sued the university?" Julian asked.

"I don't know. It's possible, but I like to think people are better than that. All I know is I plan to keep a low profile, especially around the ROTC people. Can you imagine what they'd do to me if I was in the Corps of Cadets and they found out about this? Thank God that's no longer compulsory!"

"It just occurred to me," Sam giggled. "You inherited that feisty attitude from your mother's side!"

"Maybe," Larry grinned, "or maybe *she* inherited it from *me*!"

"What are you going to do at the computer center?" Julian asked, impressed by the industriousness of his young friend. "Will you be programming the computers?"

"I wish! I'll be doing odd jobs, like loading blank paper into the printers, or mounting tapes. Maybe I'll even get to be the main system operator now and then!"

"Mounting tapes, did you say?" John smirked. "I'm not surprised you'd try to get a job mounting *something*, but tapes? That sounds more kinky than I'd expect!"

"Get your mind out of the gutter, John," Julian said, chastising even as he smiled.

"He's such a juvenile," Larry said with mock disgust, drawing a giggle from both Sam and Julia. *Why is the sound of her laughter like music to my ears? What could I do to hear her laugh again?*

Thursday, June 8, 1967
I'm Free

John's birthday in early June was always the first big event of the summer, and the gang, now including Julia Jacobson, always got together on this day to celebrate. Not only was it their friend's birthday, but because it always fell just after the end of a school year, his birthday doubled as a celebration for the beginning of summer.

One topic of interest that day was Larry's new job at the computer center. He explained his job title was "gopher", which meant whenever anyone needed anything, it was his responsibility to "go for" it.

The hottest topic of conversation was the latest war. It was the fourth day in what would come to be known as the "Six Day War", and everyone had an opinion. Most people agreed the war had been started by Egypt on May 22 when they placed a blockade at the Straights of Tiran, cutting off Israel's only supply route to Asia and stopping the flow of oil from their supplier, Iran. Israel was further provoked by inflammatory statements from Gamal Abdel Nassar, President of Egypt. Mobilization of forces by Egypt, Syria, and Jordan along the Israeli borders created an intolerable situation. Waiting for an Arab invasion would place Israel at a strategic disadvantage. On June 5, Israel launched a preemptive strike against Egyptian forces in the Sinai.

Israel assured King Hussein he would not be attacked unless Jordon struck first. Not truly prepared for war, Jordan was reluctant to join the conflict. When Jordanian radar picked up a flight of planes flying from Egypt to Israel, the Egyptians assured them these were their planes making an attack. Convinced Egypt was well on the way to victory, Jordan was lured into entering the war, and started shelling West Jerusalem. The Israelis quickly launched a counterattack. As it turned out, the planes on radar had actually been elements of an Israeli air strike returning home after virtually destroying the Egyptian Air Force on the ground. One does not simply say, "Oops! Can we start again?" in such situations. Once one gets themselves into a war, it is almost impossible to get back out. Why is that lesson is so difficult for some to remember?

In the north, Syrian forces, also deprived of air support by Israel's preemptive strike, were content to remain in fortified positions along the Golan Heights, firing artillery shells into Israeli territory. While more action was still to come on that front, it appeared to everyone the outcome of the war was already decided. A heavily outnumbered and totally surrounded Israel would emerge with a stunning victory that would have ramifications throughout the region for decades.

The birthday party at the Myer's house was attended by the usual gang, consisting of John, Sam, Larry, and Julia. Julia was joined by Frank, to no one's surprise but to Larry's continued dismay. There was a wonderful surprise, however, when Jimmy arrived and introduced Nora Norman, his new girlfriend. Larry waited for the first opportunity, finally managing to catch Jimmy alone in the kitchen for a little private conversation. "Hey, Jimmy! Nora is a real doll! Where did you meet her?"

"We both have jobs at the swimming pool in Sue Haswell Park," Jimmy smiled.

"That's great!" Larry smiled. "I've been meaning to check up on you, to see how you were getting along. I guess this means you're finally over that previous relationship? I'm really glad to see it!"

"Yeah," Jimmy agreed. "You told me I'd find someone else. I should have believed you. If I'd started looking sooner, I might have found Nora sooner!"

"Maybe," Larry grinned. "But don't rush. Let things develop at their own pace."

"I will," Jimmy assured him. "I'm not going to be a jealous fool this time. I've learned my lesson."

"Good!" Larry smiled once again. "No lingering doubts? Can I tell Frank he can relax now that you don't want your old girlfriend back?" he asked with a chuckle.

Larry was trying to appear casual, but was hanging on Jimmy's reply like it was a matter of national security. "I think you can safely make that assumption. Hey! I just remembered that promise you made you wouldn't make a move for Julia as long as I still wanted her. You're off the hook. Feel free to make your move! I'll even help you beat up old Frank if you want me to!"

"That won't be necessary," Larry chuckled. "I think maybe I'm still a little too old for her. I'm used to girls I can take out on a real date without having to bring mom or dad along, doncha know!"

Sam happened into the kitchen just in time to hear the last part of Larry's reply and Jimmy's laugh. "What are you boys talking about?" she asked, knowing exactly what they were talking about. "If you guys know any good jokes I haven't already heard, especially dirty ones, you'd better come clean before I slug you!"

"Just guy stuff," Jimmy replied with a grin. "Girls wouldn't understand."

Sam saw how Larry winced at Jimmy's comment. Under normal circumstances, such a comment was sure to earn Jimmy a painful punch on the arm, and then she would not relent until she knew every detail! "You'd better get back to Nora before she thinks you've forgotten about her," Larry suggested.

"Good thinking," Jimmy grinned. "See you guys later!"

In this case, Sam was willing to let Jimmy off the hook. She waited until he left the kitchen before starting to grill Larry. "So what do you think of Jimmy's new girlfriend?" she asked casually.

"She's cute," Larry replied simply. "What do you think of her?"

She was waiting for him to mention the other news, the news about Jimmy releasing him from that promise, but Larry apparently wanted to play it coy. "I agree. What were you talking about just as I came into the room. It sounded like you were complaining about having mom or dad with you when going out on a date. What was that all about?"

"Exactly," he agreed. "Taking young girls on dates is a real drag."

"What in the world caused that subject to come up?" she asked with a grin.

"Cut it out, Sam," he begged.

"Who brought up the subject of that promise?" Sam grinned even brighter.

"He did," Larry said, his face a mixture of both joy and sadness. "Even though it's John's birthday, Sam, it looks like I might be getting the best present!"

"You're free, Larry!" she said brightly. "You're finally released from that damned promise! I'm so happy for you!"

"I just wish it had come sooner," he shrugged, "like maybe before Frank entered the picture." Looking out the kitchen window at nothing in particular, he sighed. "Well, better late than never. At least now, should an opportunity actually present itself, I have a free hand to act."

"But you still think you're too old for her," she noted. "I just heard you say so."

"Yeah," he agreed, "I guess so, but you know what, Sam? I don't think I really care about that anymore. Even if I had to take my mom and dad along every time Julie and I went anywhere together, it'd be worth it. I want to know what it is about that little girl that holds my attention so strongly."

"So what are you going to do?" she asked.

"What can I do?" he shrugged again. "I'm going to keep my eyes open and wait. One of these days, I'll get that opportunity, Sam. She and Frank seem to be on solid ground right now, but that can't last forever." Almost as an afterthought, he looked at Sam and begged the question, "Can it?"

Sunday, July 2, 1967
Pleasant Valley Sunday

The second big event of the summer was Larry's birthday, and once again, the gang got together to celebrate. Not only did they celebrate their friend's birthday, but with it, of course, they mixed in Fourth of July celebrations. One of Larry's favorite jokes was that the whole country celebrated his birthday, but they always seemed to be two days late for some reason.

Trying to appear as if it meant nothing to him, Larry insisted since this was a Sunday afternoon, he and John should have a normal guitar practice, just like any other Sunday afternoon. Maybe the rest of the country would celebrate two days late, but his friends would never do so. Larry's birthday was the second of July, not the third or the fourth, and the party should not be late! Even though birthdays are just silly little things, they knew Larry looked forward to having his friends and family make a fuss over him, even if it was only once a year. Or maybe it was *because* it was only once a year.

Larry was turning eighteen today, making this one of those "special" birthdays. It was hardly lost on anyone this birthday was something like a rite of passage. He had just recently graduated from high school, and even though he was already attending college classes and working in a job at the university computer center, this milestone was too significant to ignore completely.

The usual suspects gathered at Larry's house. John brought a girl named Alicia Adams, his date from the previous evening. Julia and Frank were there together, of course, as were Jimmy and Nora. There was no one Sam wanted to escort her to the party, and even if there had been, she preferred to come alone, just so Larry would not feel like he was the only one without a date.

The Drug Company was enjoying increasing popularity, being invited to more and more of the better parties. At first, these parties were mainly given by their friends, sometimes newfound friends; they increasingly found themselves being asked to perform by people they did not know very well. Their popularity rose both from the word of mouth advertising from each successful gig, and from the free advertising they got because of their appearances on the *Top Forty Showcase* radio program.

John and Larry were diligent to maintain their practice schedule and were always eager to add new songs into their repertoire, especially the popular songs of the day. Larry would work out a special arrangement suitable for their two-man folk-rock style, and their "fans" would simply eat it all up. They found plenty of good material from the Beatles songs that year, including *All You Need Is Love* and *Penny Lane*. Perhaps the most popular of their songs was the acoustic guitar arrangement Larry put together for the Doors hit *Light My Fire*. They were not adverse to electric guitar, but they agreed amplified guitars were better suited to a full four or five man rock group than for a two-man folk-rock band.

That evening, just as dusk began to settle onto the central Texas countryside, the gang moved out to Julia's house in the country to get in a little early celebration with some Fourth of July fireworks. The gang had pooled their resources and purchased a nice assortment. The guys, of course, attempted to assume complete control of the more significant items. After Sam protested she was just as capable of handling these as the boys, they relented, allowing the girls to set off as many of the big ones as they wanted. Together, they produced a spectacular amateur fireworks display, much to the delight of themselves, the Jacobsons, and a few nearby neighbors who happened to take notice of the aerial displays.

After the fireworks display, the gang retired to a private location just up the road from the Jacobson house for a different type of firework, more concerned with the generation of smoke than flashes of light and loud sounds. The gang enjoyed these just as much as the earlier ones, if not more.

Saturday, August 26, 1967
Lil' Red Riding Hood

The final big event of each summer was Sam's birthday. Like the other events, the gang always made it special. Not only were they celebrating their friend's birthday, but it was a celebration in remembrance of the summer they had just enjoyed together, one last big blowout before the end of summer and the inevitable start of the school year.

The new school year was to be special in its own right. John would be entering his senior year in high school. Julia would be a sophomore, meaning she would leave Lamar Jr. High behind, moving up the ladder into Stephen F. Austin. The transition from junior to senior high was something all students looked to with eagerness. Not to be outdone, of course, Larry and Sam were taking an even bigger step up that ladder into Texas A&M University. No one was keen to mention, especially not Larry, he had actually taken this step back at the start of summer, and had already completed two whole courses, six semester hours, towards his degree.

But the most special part of the event was Sam's birthday. She was only a few weeks younger than Larry, and was also celebrating a very special birthday this year, turning eighteen, the age most people consider a huge milestone, the age at which a girl turns into a young lady! While this was probably true, Sam threatened to slug anyone who teased her about it. As a result, the gang kept the teasing to a minimum, mainly because it turned out she was not merely threatening at all, and John and Larry both had bruises on their arms to prove it.

The usual suspects gathered once more that evening to celebrate this event. Larry learned Sam's mysterious boyfriend was not going to make an appearance, and elected to be Sam's escort himself. John was bringing a girl by the name of Daisy Drummond, a nice girl he would take out from time to time. Jimmy was bringing Nora, and Julia, of course, would be accompanied by Frank.

The only unusual thing about this event was its location. Sam didn't really want to have a party at all, insisting the evening be conducted business-as-usual. All she wanted was for the gang to gather at the radio station to produce another *Top Forty Showcase*, just like any other Saturday night.

When the program resumed after the first break, Diggs played the recording Larry and John made for this spot. It began with a dedication the boys made to their friend on her birthday. The song, *Lil' Red Riding Hood*, was recently popularized by Sam the Sham and the Pharaohs. To embarrass her further, Larry made her stand in the middle of the studio as he pretended to be the big bad wolf drooling to get her in his clutches. She laughed at his antics.

Julia and the boys had carefully arranged the schedule so Sam was to read the next set of dedications after the tape, and Larry's antics were primarily intended to distract her. "Hey, Sam!" John said interrupting while she was on the air, "we have a *special* dedication for this next song." Sam looked up from her notes, clearly surprised, as interrupting someone on the air was against one of their longstanding rules. At that moment, Julia stepped into the studio carrying the birthday cake with eighteen burning candles, and they all sang *Happy Birthday* in unison.

Sam simply sat back and grinned at her friends, shaking her head. Larry took over the microphone and explained to the listening audience, "As you may have guessed, today is Sam's birthday, and we just presented her with a birthday cake. Blow out the candles, make a wish, and make the first cut, Sam. Whether you want any or not, the rest of us are hungry! I wish we could invite everyone out there to come join us in the studio, but that would be against the rules, I'm afraid. Be sure to wish Sam a happy birthday when you call in your requests tonight!"

Sunday, October 15, 1967
It's Not Unusual

To Jessica, Larry seemed more depressed than usual as the boys conducted their guitar practice. When they took a break, she knew the perfect subject to either cheer him up, or uncover the cause of his unhappiness. "I hear you've got a new girlfriend," Jessica smiled. "I'd like to hear about her. Her name is Susan, right?"

Larry's face went blank, as he stared at her in silence. He looked around the room, and saw the others were also waiting to hear about this mystery girl who had suddenly appeared out of nowhere. "There really isn't much to say, Mrs. J," he said sadly. "Especially since she's not my girlfriend."

John and Sam exchanged a glance, confirming with each other they saw the cause of Larry's mood. "It looked like she was last night," Sam said. "What happened?"

Larry shook his head. "She never *was* my girlfriend. I did it to myself again."

"I'm lost," Jessica said. "Would you mind starting from the beginning?"

"I guess not, Mrs. J. It's not a long story, I'm afraid," he said sadly. "How did it begin? Well, I met her about sixteen years ago, I guess."

"What?" Sam said. "If you've known her that long, how come I've never heard of her? I've known you about ten years myself!"

"She moved away long before we met, Sam," he answered. "It's like this. When my parents first moved to Bryan to teach at Allen Academy, they made friends with the other teachers there, especially with a couple named Hank and Jo Tollworth. My mom and Jo got to be very close. I guess I was about four years old at the time. The Tollworth's had a baby girl named Susan."

"You met her as a baby?" Sam asked.

"Yeah, but don't worry!" he chuckled. "It isn't going to be one of those stupid *'love at first sight'* stories. As you well know, I don't believe in that. A couple of years later, just before I started first grade, the Tollworth's moved away. It was a tearful parting for mom and Jo. You should see some of the pictures we have of that day!"

"It's a shame when good friends have to part," Jessica said. "There were some friends like that when Julian, Julia, and I moved away from New York."

"Yes," Larry agreed. "I worry about the day when one or all of us will move away from here. I don't want to part with my friends! There are never enough in the first place, doncha know?"

"I know," Jessica smiled. "So go on with the story. What happened next?"

"Well, nothing much happened for a long time. Over the years, we lost touch with them, but last summer, someone told my mom the Tollworth's were living in Dallas, so she started looking for them. About a month ago, she decided to call every Tollworth listed in the Dallas telephone book. She hit pay dirt on the very first call."

"That's nice," Jessica said. "I expect it was pretty exciting for your mom!"

"It surely was!" he nodded. "They talked on the phone for hours, it seemed, laughing over old stories, and catching up on what everyone had been doing all these years. They have an older son named Hanky, a couple of years older than me. Get this, John, he's a rock and roll singer up in Dallas, and even has a record! I understand he's studying to become an opera singer!"

"No shit?" John said excitedly. "Sorry! I mean, really?"

"Indeed!" Larry laughed at John's *feaux pas*. "It's a pretty corny song, but it's better than the nothing we've done!"

"You're getting sidetracked, Larry," Jessica chuckled. "So what about the girl?"

Larry would rather have talked about the brother than the girl right then, but he knew he would have to finish this story sooner or later. "I was coming to that. It's a little too expensive to talk much by long distance, so mom started planning to drive to Dallas for a face-to-face visit. It was all arranged for the last weekend in September. My dad couldn't go for some reason, so mom asked me to drive. I didn't have anything better to do, naturally, so I agreed.

"We got there about 9:00 o'clock on Friday night. The directions they provided were good, and we drove right to their house without any problems. Mom and Jo went nuts, of course, and talked all night long, I imagine. I spoke with Mr. Tollworth some, but there was little for us to talk about. Mainly, we just watched television and engaged in a little idle chit chat.

"He told me about Hanky, laughed about his rock and roll record, and talked about his possible opera career. He mentioned Susan was at a football game, playing in the school band, and would be home later. I didn't think much about it at the time."

"But that obviously changed," Jessica said softly.

"Yeah," he said, once again looking sad. "I don't know what I expected. In my mind, Susan was just a baby. Maybe I expected a baby to walk in the front door."

"But instead, a very pretty girl walked in and took you by surprise," Jessica said.

"You can say that again, Mrs. J," he said. "Susan is a pretty girl, especially without her glasses, and even more especially when she smiles. We talked for a few minutes getting better acquainted, but it was already late. Before long, she went off to her room, and Mr. Tollworth helped me get settled to sleep on the couch.

"In the morning, I was the second person awake. Mr. Tollworth came into the kitchen to make coffee, and couldn't help but wake me up. I got up and joined him. He was mostly interested in his newspaper and the morning news on TV, so I just sat around and waited for the others. Mrs. Tollworth came into the kitchen about an hour later and asked if anyone wanted breakfast."

"You're avoiding the point," Jessica said. "What happened with the girl?"

"I'm sorry," he said sadly. "I guess I *am* avoiding it." He sighed, and picked up the story at a later point in time. "Susan got up a little later and while she was eating her breakfast, her mom suggested she and I should go out, rather than spending the day couped up in the house. She suggested we go to *Six Flags Over Texas*, the theme park in Arlington. Susan had been there before and liked the idea; it sounded like an adventure to me. By midmorning, she and I were in the car and on our way."

He paused for a moment. "Have you ever had one of those days you wished would never end?" he asked, trying to keep the moisture in his eyes under control.

"Many times," Jessica smiled softly. "I understand what you're talking about. Julian and I spent a lot of days like that at Coney Island."

Larry nodded. "We rode all the rides, saw all the shows. We laughed together, and just ran around the park like neither of us had a care in the world. We stayed into the night until the park closed and they ran everybody out. It was like magic!"

"It sounds like you had a wonderful time," Jessica said.

"I did! But I let my guard down, Mrs. J," he said sadly. "I had such a good time, and it was so wonderful to have someone to share it all with, I forgot to keep my feelings under control. I had visions of having *more* days like that. The next morning, when I learned Mrs. Tollworth and Susan would be coming to visit us in Bryan in a couple of weeks, I was thrilled! I couldn't show her anything as fancy as *Six Flags*, but I was determined to make her visit as wonderful as I could."

"And she came to see you this weekend," Jessica noted.

"Yes, ma'am," he said sadly. "Susan and I went to a movie yesterday afternoon, but the highlight was to be the radio program last night."

"Susan seemed to have a good time last night," Julia said.

"She did," he said, "or at least, she told me she did."

"Something happened after the show?" Sam asked.

"Nothing dramatic," he shrugged. "I started talking about getting together more often. I told her I wanted to come to Dallas to see her, and asked if she could come down to Bryan once in a while. That's when it all crumbled, right before my eyes."

"Oh, no," Sam said. "I see it coming."

"Bingo!" he said looking at her, fighting the sting in his eyes. "Susan told me that wasn't what she wanted. She didn't want me as her boyfriend. She wanted me to be her just-friend, whatever the hell that is. I swear to God, if I hear that one more time, I'm going kill something!" He turned his face away, trying not to let anyone see the tears in his eyes. No one needed to see them to know they were there.

"When will I ever learn?" he asked, trying to wipe his eyes discreetly. "The biggest reason I feel so bad is I did all this to myself! I'm so stupid. That one day was magical to me, and I just assumed it was to her, also. After all these years, you'd think I'd know better by now."

"I'm so sorry," Jessica said.

"It's OK," he shrugged, "I'm not looking for any sympathy." He let out a chuckle before continuing, "Besides, if I really wanted it, I know exactly where I could find sympathy. It's been in the same place every single time I've ever looked."

"Where's that?" Jessica asked. She knew Larry well enough to expect an unusual answer, especially since she caught the tiny twinkle in his eye that always signaled he was up to something.

"In the dictionary, Mrs. J," he answered, "between *sylph* and *syphilis*."

Jessica grinned at him and shook her head. The fact he was nibbling on his lower lip told her a much different story than his outward smile. If only there was something she could do or say to relieve the pain he was fighting so desperately to contain. She decided the best thing would be to acknowledge his joke, show her appreciation for his witticism, and let the conversation move on its course. "In your free time, do you sit around and read the dictionary or something?"

"Well, John is actually the one who reads the dictionary, Mrs. J!" he smiled. "I'm more of a thesaurus guy. Do you know what a thesaurus is, John?"

"Of course I..." John began.

"A thesaurus is a dinosaur with a tremendous vocabulary!" Larry smiled.

"And what does that have to do with sympathy?" Jessica giggled.

"Nothing. I'd have said it came between *sylph* and *syzygy*, but then I'd have to explain what that word meant, and *syphilis* seemed funnier, doncha know."

"You can't fool me," Sam giggled. "If you didn't want someone to ask what it meant, then why did you even bring it up?"

"Good question, Sam," he replied.

"So what does it mean?" Julia asked.

"It's an astronomical term," he answered. "It's the point in an orbit at which the object is in conjunction or opposition."

"Hey!" John laughed. "I was trying to think of that very word just last week!"

"Joke about it all you want!" Larry grinned. "Someday, when all of the planets in the solar system happen to fall into a straight line of syzygy at the very same moment, and the gravitational forces cause the continental plates to shift producing gigantic earthquakes... Well, just don't go blaming me, OK?"

Monday, October 16, 1967
One Day Of Magic

It had not been easy for Larry to get to sleep in the first place. Not only was he heartbroken about losing yet another girlfriend, this time before it even got started, his mind was also troubled by thoughts of Julia. Her birthday was less than a week away. His dreams had been disturbed by her for a whole year, and he was no closer to understanding this now than he had been a year ago.

This night had been no exception. His dream began as a replay of that one day of magic at *Six Flags Over Texas*. Once again, he and his sweetheart strolled through the park, riding the rides, and watching the shows. Neither of them had a care in the world. It was a wonderful dream, in which he escaped the loneliness of his real life, enjoying one day of magic in a dream lifetime where he was happy, where he had finally made that special connection with someone, someone who cared about him as much as he cared about her.

The dream was a replay of his perception of that day of magic, which he knew was tainted by his desire to change reality. Yet something about it was different. At first, he did not grasp the difference, and the dream simply continued to replay the events as he remembered them. As dusk came, and the day slowly changed into evening, he and his sweetheart decided to ride through the Spelunker's Cave once again. Because there were not a lot of people in the park at that time, they were placed into their own private boat to be taken through the cave. They sat close together, enjoying the blast of cold air that helped build the illusion of an ice cave, and laughed at the animated characters lining the passageways. His dream deviated from the events of history when the girl turned her head towards him and kissed him. He gazed into her eyes following this kiss, and found himself lost in the vastness of the universe, falling weightlessly into two black holes surrounded by beautiful rings of deep green.

The image startled him out of his dream. Susan's eyes were brown, not green! He sat on the edge of his bed, rubbing his eyes in a vain attempt to stop the burning, wishing there was something, anything, he could do to stop that pain in his heart. Once again, she had filled his dreams, and once again, he was forced to recognize the extent to which he longed to be with her. *Just one day of magic,* he considered. *Is that so much to ask? Just one day, so I can learn what it is about her that calls to me so?* Just one real day of magic would end the worst of his torment. Perhaps it would be just the first day of a whole lifetime with magic. Or, if she was not the one he was searching for, then at least he would know, and that day could become a cherished memory providing him with a preview of the magic he would know when he finally did find the right girl. Either way, he would be at peace for a while.

Knowing it was pointless to try to get back to sleep, he walked over to his desk, and turned on his study lamp. He opened the notebook he used to keep notes about his music, and turned to a blank page. On the top line, he wrote *One Day Of Magic*. Below those words, he wrote a simple four verse poem. Over the next few days, he would refine that poem. He would work out a melody, then a complete arrangement. A few weeks later, he would show the finished work to John, and sing it for him to critique. It was his second original song.

> *One day of magic, one girl and one boy.*
> *One day of magic that filled us with joy.*
> *Only one day of magic, but magic is done,*
> *Just one day of magic, and now I have none.*
>
> *One day of magic and it was so right.*
> *One day of magic that turned into night.*
> *Only one day of magic, but that day is gone.*
> *Just one day of magic, and now I'm alone.*
>
> *One day of magic was all that we had.*
> *One day of magic, was it really so bad?*
> *Only one day of magic, and now we're apart.*
> *That one day magic has shattered my heart.*
>
> *One day of magic that I shared with you.*
> *One day of magic, I wish it were true!*
> *Only one day of magic, the magic supreme,*
> *But that one day of magic was only a dream.*

Sunday, October 22, 1967
I'll Get You

It is widely accepted around the area whenever an Aggie does something twice, it becomes a tradition. The first new tradition of the day was established when Mr. and Mrs. Jacobson provided a special birthday dinner for Julia and her current boyfriend, just as they had done the previous year by buying pizza for Julia and Jimmy. This year, they took Julia and Frank to the Pizza Hut so they could order and enjoy their pizza much hotter and fresher than after being carried all the way to Steep Hollow.

There was a fourth celebration to be added to the gang's repertoire this year. Now known widely among their peers as the *Four Musketeers*, there was a fourth birthday to add to their annual celebrations. After dinner, the gang gathered at Julia's house for this purpose. Larry and John established another new tradition that evening by entertaining at Julia's birthday party for the second time. The fact Larry and Sam were the only "official" Aggies at the time did not really matter as far as the establishment of traditions was concerned. They all knew these things were going to be repeated each year for quite some time to come.

Like the previous year, the Drug Company played for an hour to begin the party. At the appropriate moment, Jessica gave a signal to Larry. "OK, everyone!" he announced. "We're now going to do a song you all know, so please sing along with us!" He and John began to sing the simple song, and the rest of the guests joined in:

Happy birthday to you.
Happy birthday to you.
Happy birthday, dear Julia.
Happy birthday to you!

As they sang, Jessica carried out a large birthday cake, adorned with fifteen burning candles, and sat it in front of her smiling daughter. When the song finished, Julia closed her eyes, made a wish, and blew the candles out with ease, then made the traditional first cut into the cake. Larry could not help but wonder what she had wished for. While Jessica placed individual pieces of cake onto plates, and Julian dipped the ice cream into cups, he also could not help but make a wish of his own that somehow, he could be the one who might deliver on her wish someday.

His wishful thinking was interrupted when he was handed his own piece of cake and a cup of ice cream. Suddenly feeling a little out of place, he stepped into the background, away from the others, to sit alone on the low brick retaining wall surrounding the old willow tree. As he absentmindedly ate his cake and ice cream, staring up into the branches of the old tree, his thoughts were interrupted when Schotzy came up and placed two small feet on his knee. "Hello, boy!" he smiled to the dog. "Would you like a little ice cream?" A simple wag of his tail conveyed his response, and Larry allowed him to lick the remainder of the creamy sweetness from the cup.

When Julia began to open the gifts her friends brought her, Larry rejoined the group, standing in the background, trying to stay out of the way. It was not long before she pulled the wrapping paper from a box adorned with no card. When she peeked inside, she discovered a dainty little music box. Smiling, she looked at Larry, correctly guessing the gift was from him. That sweet smile was all the thanks he could ever ask for.

After some simple party games and a little dancing, it was time once again for the Drug Company to return to their stage. A few songs into their program, the boys changed pace by telling a story.

[John]	A burglar broke into an empty house and was rummaging through the belongings. Whenever he located something of value, he smiled to himself and placed the item into his knapsack. Imagine his surprise when he suddenly heard a soft voice speaking to him.
[Larry]	Jesus is watching you!
[John]	He swung around expecting to be confronted by an angry homeowner, but there was no one to be seen. Convinced he must have been hearing things, he continued his search for more booty. On the top of a dresser, he found a small jewelry box, and happily dumped its contents into his sack. Once again, he heard a voice.
[Larry]	Jesus is watching you!
[John]	As before, he could not locate the source of the voice. Even though he was worried he might be cracking up, he continued to

pillage everything he could find of value. Inside a hutch in the dining room, he located silverware and serving pieces, which he quickly placed into his sack.

[Larry]   Jesus is watching you!
[John]   The burglar pointed his flashlight in the direction of the voice and found a parrot sitting on a perch. "Did you say that?" he asked.
[Larry]   Yes, I did, and Jesus is still watching you!
[John]   What's your name?
[Larry]   Clarence, and Jesus is watching you.
[John]   You're pretty smart for a bird!
[Larry]   I've been told that before. And Jesus is still watching you!
[John]   Big deal! And just what is Jesus going to do about it?
[Larry]   I don't know, but Jesus is surely watching you!
[John]   I've never heard of a bird named Clarence. What kind of idiot would give a name like that to a parrot?
[Larry]   The same kind of idiot who would name a Doberman Jesus!

The guests laughed in appreciation of the little story, and the boys quickly launched into another song. At the conclusion of the song, Larry placed his guitar on its stand and stood in center stage with his hands tucked underneath his arms. "Since we seem to be in bird mode tonight," John announced casually, "we decided we want to pay tribute to a beautiful, yet little known bird. This bird, unfortunately, is on the endangered species list, and we thought we'd call your attention to its plight. I speak of the majestic and beautiful Ono bird!"

Larry flapped his shortened arms as if they were wings, and squawked at the guests, wearing a goofy, cross-eyed expression on his face, drawing a few expectant chuckles from the audience. "That's right," John continued. "As you can see, the majestic Ono bird is a large member of the stork family. Hunted nearly to extinction for the luxurious feathers on its back," John said as Larry turned his back to the audience, allowing them to examine for themselves the scrappy looking chicken feathers taped to the back of his shirt, "there are only a few hundred individuals remaining in the wild.

"Ordinarily, a simple hunting ban would allow the species to recover, but unfortunately, the Ono bird is not very prolific when it comes to breeding!" Larry quickly brought a small dropper bottle to his face and soaked both of his eyes with water, allowing the liquid to flow down his face in mock tears. A few of the guests expressed their sympathy by saying "aw" while others chuckled mercilessly.

"One characteristic trait of the majestic Ono bird is the length of its legs," John continued. "As you can see on this example of the species, its scrawny legs reach down from its body for a length of about three feet." Larry drew a laugh by giving John a dirty look and mouthing the word "scrawny" as if in a question, but carried on with the act by lifting one leg and then the other, allowing the audience to examine them.

"The problem," John smiled, "is the testicles of the male Ono bird will normally hang a good *four* feet below his body!" Larry made a show of alternating his glance between his own outspread legs and John's face, giving John a questioning look, drawing a few more chuckles from the audience. "This anatomical anomaly is not only the reason the majestic Ono bird is a very poor breeder, it also inspired the selection of its name. For after it has flown the hundreds of miles along its migration route into its traditional breeding grounds, who could ever forget the haunting call made by the male Ono bird as it comes in for its landing?"

Larry flapped his wings as he pretended to fly around for a moment, then prepared to make his landing. "Oh, no!" he squawked loudly as he tried to stretch his legs as long as he could. "Oh, no!"

When the laughter died down, the boys continued with their musical program. It ended with one of the early Beatles songs named *I'll Get You*. Larry found the lyrics to this song soothing when his mind was troubled over his thoughts of Julia, and he needed something to lift his spirit and determination. *"So I'm telling you, my friend, that I'll get you, I'll get you in the end."*

Friday, November 3, 1967
Louie Louie

It was the opening game of the season, and Frank expected to play most of the game. Now that Julia was fifteen, her parents allowed her to go on regular dates, but that seldom mattered. When the Broncos had a game, Frank and Julia frequently found themselves on a double date with Sally and her current boyfriend, Bill Foster, the same age as Sally and also a senior at Stephen F. Austin High School. This arrangement worked reasonably well. During the Friday night football games, while Frank was down on the field playing in the game and Sally was leading cheers, Bill and Julia would sit together and watch from the stands. After the game, the two couples reunited to enjoy whatever time was left to them for the evening.

On Saturday nights, the two couples usually went their separate ways. Frank and Julia liked to spend the evening working alongside her friends doing the *Top Forty Showcase* program. Sally decided this would create an uncomfortable situation not only for herself, but for Bill as well, so they always made other plans.

Frank was completely wrapped up in the athletics programs. Now in his junior year, he had been the starting wide receiver for the football team, was a starting guard for the basketball team, was expected to make a major contribution to the track team, and would most likely be the starting shortstop for the baseball team. If he could continue in this manner, during both this year and his senior year, he fully expected to be able to choose among several athletic scholarships from various major colleges. He wanted that more than anything he could imagine.

Since it seemed to be all he ever talked about, Julia was well aware of Frank's scholarship dreams. They used to see each other frequently and talk on the telephone almost daily. Once football practice started back in the summer, that was happening less and less frequently. Now, they saw each other only on Friday nights, for a few minutes before and after the game, and then on Saturday nights at the radio station.

Bill was dissatisfied with his relationship with Sally. They had been dating for several months now, yet she continued to decline his advances. The other guys who had dated Sally told him she would be a tough nut to crack. No one could establish a credible claim of having ever gotten inside those sweet little pants she wore beneath her cheerleader's skirt. Originally, he felt like he was up to the challenge, but was now starting to have doubts it was worth the effort. He wondered if she actually thought she could remain a virgin all the way through high school. He also wondered why she would want to.

So it was that Bill began to look for another target. At first, he started scanning through the bleachers during the games, looking to find girls sitting by themselves or in small groups, without any guys hovering around. If he found what he was looking for, he planned to move in on them and make some advances while Sally was occupied with her duties as cheerleader. When nothing seemed to catch his eye, it suddenly occurred to him he was already sitting next to a pretty little thing. Frank was a good looking guy, a star athlete who could probably have any girl he wanted. It occurred to Bill this girl Julia might be just the thing he was looking for.

"How did you meet Frank?" he asked. Even though he and Julia sat together during the entire football season, he realized he knew practically nothing about her.

"A friend introduced us almost a year ago," she replied. "He and Sally came out to my house one Sunday afternoon, and Frank happened to come along for the ride."

"Oh, yeah," Bill said, nodding his head. "I remember Sally saying something about the guy she used to go with to the radio station, and how he and his friends got together on Sunday afternoons."

"That's the one," she said. "His name is Larry. He and John and Sam are probably my best friends in the whole world. Frank and I also go to the radio station and still get together Sunday afternoons!"

"I don't guess I've ever met them," he replied.

"You probably know them," she said. "Larry and Sam graduated last year, but John is a senior, just like you and Sally."

"What's his last name?" Bill asked.

"Myers," she replied, "John Myers. Surely you've heard of the Drug Company."

"Now I know who you're talking about!" he grinned. "They sound pretty good!"

"I think so, too!" she said, returning his grin. "You and Sally ought to come with us to the radio station on Saturday nights, or maybe you could join us on a Sunday afternoon during one of their rehearsals. I'm sure they wouldn't mind."

"I don't know," he said slyly. "I'm not sure I want to take Sally someplace she could meet up with one of her former boyfriends."

"I don't think they were ever like that," she said, recalling the days when Larry and Sally had been dating. "They had a few dates, but they just sort of drifted apart about the same time Frank and I got together."

"I can understand that," he nodded. "Sally is a great girl, but she's really hard to get close to. I don't think she actually wants a steady boyfriend."

"You may be right," Julia said in a soft voice. "I think that's why my friend Larry stopped seeing her. I know he's been looking for a steady relationship ever since... Well, for a long time."

"Then he and I have something in common," Bill grinned. "I'm starting to doubt Sally and I will ever get together the way I want. I'm beginning to wonder how much longer it'll be before she sends me on my way, just like she did your friend Larry."

"I don't think it happened that way," she said. "She didn't send him on his way. I think maybe he lost interest in her for some reason. There are a lot of things about him I don't understand. I asked Frank about it, and that's what he told me."

"Yeah," he agreed. "What about you and Frank? Are you two getting along?"

"We're good," she replied. "I wish he didn't have to spend so much time with practice, but at least we have time together before and after the games, and on

Saturday nights."

Bill thought there was a little less enthusiasm in her reply than there should be. He saw opportunity knocking, and decided to start paying a little more attention to this girl. In spite of the braces that made her seem younger than she actually was, she looked pretty good. *She'll look even better once I get her pants off!*

Saturday, November 25, 1967
I've Got You Under My Skin

Julia came into the kitchen to help her mother prepare breakfast. "I wonder if the gang will be surprised when I show up with Bill tonight," she said casually.

"I would imagine," Jessica replied with a smile. "I take it you haven't mentioned the change to any of them yet?"

"Not yet," Julia replied. "I wasn't sure there *would* be a change until this week."

Jessica noted Julia was scratching her arms and stomach. "Have you got an itch?"

"I sure do, mom," Julia replied. "My back is driving me crazy! Could I get you to scratch it for me?"

"I'll try," Jessica smiled. She had Julia turn away from her and began to gently scratch her daughter's back. "How's that? Am I hitting the itchy spot?"

"It itches all over," Julia said. "Maybe I'm allergic to something."

"Really? Let me look at you." Jessica looked closely at her face, then her arms and hands. "Pull up your pajama top, so I can see your back and stomach." When her daughter complied, Jessica saw they were covered with tiny bumps. "You're covered with these! Do they itch?"

"Yes," Julia replied. "I hadn't noticed them before now."

"I think you might have a slight fever," Jessica said pressing her palm against Julia's forehead. "Let me get the thermometer and we'll test you."

"I don't feel bad," Julia tried to protest as her mother searched the medicine drawer for the oral thermometer, "just a little itchy."

"If you don't have a temperature, then maybe we'll chalk it up as some sort of allergy," Jessica said, removing the thermometer from its case and shaking to drive the mercury down into the bulb. "Put this under your tongue and be quiet for a moment." Julia sighed, but followed instructions, standing quietly with the thermometer under her tongue for sixty seconds. "Let's see what we have. Ninety-nine point seven."

"But I don't feel sick!" Julia protested again as she gently scratched her abdomen.

"Not yet, maybe," her mother replied, "but I think you may be coming down with something. Let's call the doctor and see if she wants to see you this morning."

"Oh, mom," Julia said unhappily, even as Jessica reached for the telephone.

"Now, you just hush," Jessica ordered while dialing the number. "If she says it's nothing to worry about, then we won't worry about it, but let's hear what she has to say first, OK?" She turned her attention to the telephone and spoke to the doctor's receptionist. "Yes, hello! This is Jessica Jacobson. I'm calling because I think my daughter might be coming down with something. She has a slight temperature, ninety-nine point seven, and it looks like her whole body is covered with tiny little bumps." "Yes, she says they're very itchy." "No, they just showed up this morning.

She says she feels just fine, but...." "It sounds like what?" "No, I'm quite sure she's never had..." "I see. So, what should we do? Should I bring her to the office?" "OK, fine. We'll be there at 10:30." "Thanks! We'll see you then. Goodbye!"

"What did they say?" Julia asked, knowing she was not going to hear good news.

"It sounds like something called 'chicken pox'. Apparently, it's a common childhood disease. The doctor wants to look at you to make sure, and we'll go from there. Oh, and she said they're highly contagious to anyone who's never had them before, so to stay away from small children and elderly people until they confirm it one way or another."

"At least *that* won't be a problem," Julia said, trying to scratch her back again.

"And she said you shouldn't scratch them too much, because they leave scars." Seeing the exasperation on her daughter's face, Jessica hugged her, and tried to comfort her. "I'm sorry, sugar. Try to relax. We'll have a nice breakfast, then go see the doctor, and hear what she says. Maybe it won't be all that bad."

Three of the *Four Musketeers* were at the station getting ready for the *Top Forty Showcase* program. Sam announced to the others Julia was not going to make it. "Mrs. J called me this afternoon. Julia is not feeling well, and has to stay home."

"What's wrong?" Larry asked, sounding more concerned than he should have.

"Nothing serious," Sam grinned. "She has chicken pox!"

"You're kidding!" John grinned. "At her age?"

"Apparently, she's never had them before," Sam continued. "Mrs. J says she's covered with little bumps from head to toe, and they itch like the dickens. It'd be funny, except we all know how uncomfortable it feels."

"Yeah," Larry said, wishing there was something he could do to help her.

"I know what you're thinking, Larry," Sam grinned, "and trust me when I tell you she's in good hands. They took her to the doctor this morning. She has all the medicine she needs. The doctor told her to stay home in a dark room, and not to scratch. So even if she *would* let you, you're not supposed to scratch them either!"

Larry growled, "I wasn't thinking about running out there so I could scratch her."

"No, but you are *now*, aren't you?" John teased.

"No!" Larry insisted, even though he realized they were both correct. He tried to change the subject. "Do you think Frank will be coming to help us out?"

"I don't know," Sam answered. "That subject didn't come up. Frankly, I doubt it. I don't think he'd come up here at all except she wants him to."

The remaining *Musketeers* dedicated most of the songs that night to their fallen comrade, issuing wish after wish that she get well soon.

Sunday, November 26, 1967
You Got It

When the doorbell rang, Schotzy barked at the unexpected intrusion and ran for the door. Moments later, Mr. Jacobson arrived. "Hello, Larry. This is a surprise."

"Hello, Mr. J," he replied. "Hi, Schotzy! How's the boy?" Returning his attention to Julian, he continued, "After John and I finished practice, I thought I'd check on Julie, see how she's feeling, and if there's anything I can get for her."

"It's nice of you to be concerned," Julian smiled. "I don't think she feels too bad, mainly just itchy and bored. The doctor says this is very contagious. Before I let you come inside, have you had chicken pox before?"

"Yes, sir," Larry smiled. "I had them when I was six."

"OK, come on in," Julian said. "Jessica can give you more details than I can."

"Thanks, Mr. J," Larry said as he stepped inside.

Julian led Larry through the foyer and into the family room, where Jessica was sitting comfortably, thumbing through a magazine. She looked up as the men entered. "Why, hello! What brings you all the way out here on a Sunday night?"

"It was my car," Larry replied with a grin.

"Oh, let's don't start that nonsense again," she snickered. "What's the reason for your visit? Let's see you twist the interpretation of *that* question!"

"I guess I can't," he chuckled. "You win. I just wanted to see how Julie was feeling, and if there was anything I could do to help."

"That's very sweet of you," she smiled. "You've had chicken pox before?" she asked, halfway accusing Julian of carelessness.

"I already asked him, Jessie," Julian said, almost defiantly.

"I had them when I was six years old," Larry replied. "My sister and I got them at the same time. I never felt sick. All I had was a slight fever and some aches and pains, but I was covered head to toe with little bumps that itched like the dickens!"

"Then you know how Julia feels," Jessica said with a slight grin. "The doctor told me to make her stay home, preferably in bed, in the dark if possible, and to try very hard to keep her from scratching."

"Yes, ma'am," Larry agreed. "I understand if you scratch them too much, they can leave scars. I remember hearing for every one of those little bumps on the outside, you have about ten more on the *inside!*"

"That's what the doctor told us," Jessica said. "It surprises me she doesn't feel any worse! But the doctor said this is a perfectly normal childhood disease, and there isn't anything to worry about as long as she takes care of herself."

"My mom told me sometimes older people can get the same disease, even if they've already had chicken pox," Larry said. "They don't break out on the surface so much, but it's actually a lot worse, and the pain can last for weeks! I think it has something to do with the virus attacking the nerve endings. They don't call it chicken pox when an older person gets it. I think they call it shingles."

"The doctor didn't mention that," Jessica said, "but I'll take your word for it."

"I'm surprised she's never had them before," Larry said.

"She never saw a live chicken until we moved here," Jessica snickered.

"I don't think you actually get it from chickens, Mrs. J," Larry smiled.

After a momentary silence, Julian continued the discussion, "I don't think you'll be able to see her tonight, Larry. She's already in bed, probably asleep by now."

"I understand," he said. "I just came to see if there was anything I could do."

"I think we have everything she needs," Jessica said. "The doctor prescribed some antihistamines, and also suggested she bathe in colloidal oatmeal."

"I've never heard of an oatmeal bath before," he grinned, "but it sounds like fun!"

"It's not like taking a bath in a bowl of oatmeal," Jessica grinned. "Julia says it helps, but it doesn't last very long, and she can't stay in the bathtub all day."

"What about calamine lotion?" he asked.

"Calamine lotion?" Jessica asked. "I remember the doctor saying something about some kind of lotion that might help the itching, but I don't recall the name. Do you think this would be better than the oatmeal baths?"

"I don't know," he said. "All I remember is how good it felt to pour calamine lotion all over me when I had the chicken pox! It stopped the itch for a little while, at least."

"Sounds useful," Jessica replied. "Thanks! I'll get her some in the morning."

"I'll go get it for her!" he suggested enthusiastically. "It'll only take a few minutes for me to run to the store!"

"You mean right now?" Jessica asked. "You don't need to go to any trouble!"

"It's no trouble!" he smiled. "I'm happy to do it! I'll be right back!" He opened the door and stepped outside. Julian and Jessica looked at each other, smiled, then settled back down, Julian watching television and Jessica returning to her magazine.

About twenty minutes later, the doorbell rang once again. "That was quick," Julian said. "I hope you weren't speeding!"

"Who, me?" he grinned. "Besides, this was a medical emergency. I'd be completely justified to exceed the speed limit a little."

"I suspect you mean a little more than you *normally* do!" Jessica snickered.

Larry blushed slightly and shrugged his shoulders. "Here's the calamine lotion," he said, handing over a paper bag clearly larger than necessary to hold a single bottle of lotion, even a gallon.

Jessica looked inside the bag. "That's heavy! What's this other stuff?"

"I got two bottles," he said bashfully, "just in case she runs out. You mentioned she was bored, so I picked up some books and magazines she might like to read."

"That was very thoughtful of you, Larry," Julian said. "I'm sure she'll appreciate it. Let me pay you back for the lotion, at least. How much did it cost?"

"Don't worry about it, Mr. J," he smiled. "My treat! Let me know if she wants help rubbing it on, and I'll... uh... Well, I guess she already has all the help she needs. Sorry, forget I said that," he said, completely embarrassed. "Don't worry about the lotion. It only cost a few pennies."

"Thank you very much, Larry," Jessica said, grinning at the boy's embarrassment. "I'm sure she'll want to thank you herself when she gets better."

"You're very welcome, Mrs. J! I should go," he added in his special coding. "Tell her I said hello, and hope she gets well soon."

"I'll tell her," Jessica smiled. "Goodnight, Larry." After exchanging goodnight wishes with Julian, Larry returned to his car and headed home. "What a sweet boy!" she said. "Even her new boyfriend doesn't show that much concern for her."

"He's only number two, Jessica," Julian chuckled. "He *has* to try harder!"

"What do you mean by that?" Jessica asked.

"Isn't it obvious?" Julian grinned. "He'd like to move up to number one!"

"Do you really think so?" she asked with a quizzical expression. "He had his chance a while back, but he didn't do anything about it. I wonder what's so different now?"

"Who knows?" Julian said. "Anyway, that's *her* business, Jessie. You should remain completely uninvolved when it comes to her romances. You have a good relationship with Julia. The surest way to ruin that relationship is for her to think you're trying to run her life. You can give her advice, especially when she asks for it, and answer any questions she might have from time to time, but otherwise, just step back and let her make her own decisions. Unless, of course, she starts heading down a path leading to something dangerous!"

"We've talked about this before," Jessica said, reminding him he was simply repeating her own advice to *him*. "But that doesn't mean I shouldn't be curious. Larry is a really sweet boy, Jules. I like him, and I happen to know you like him, too. Julia used to have quite a crush on him, and if you're right, I wonder why they aren't together already!"

"Wonder all you want," he said, "just don't try to push things in that direction."

"I won't, Jules," she answered with a scowl, "just like I know you won't try to push her towards some Jewish boy just because that's what *you* want!"

"Of course not, Jessie!" he said. After a brief pause, he added with a grin, "But if a nice Jewish boy just happened to come along, and if she just happened to like him, then I wouldn't do anything to stand in his way, and neither would you."

"The difference is I won't stand in the way of a boy who happens to be goy," Jessica said, mildly admonishing him. "Can you honestly say the same thing?"

"Yes, I think I can," he insisted. "All I want is for Julia to be safe, secure, and happy. Now, can you give me one good reason why she can't be safe, secure, and happy with some nice Jewish boy?"

"You're such a hypocrite!" she laughed, "but I love you anyway."

Monday, December 25, 1967
Blue Christmas

"Merry Christmas!" Larry shouted brightly. He was making his usual Christmas afternoon rounds, and started, as usual, at John's house.

"Merry Christmas!" John answered. "Come on in out of the cold."

"It's not that bad," Larry replied. "It's not a beautiful day like last year, but at least it's not raining and icy. It'd be a shame if Santa's helper was trapped inside on Christmas Day, doncha know." Once inside the house, he spotted Jimmy and their parents. "Merry Christmas, Jimmy! You, too, Mr. M, Mrs. M!"

"Merry Christmas, Larry!" they answered, practically in unison.

"Are you and Nora still a number, Jimmy?" he asked with a grin, already knowing the answer. He would not have asked the question without first confirming the answer would be a happy one. "What did you get her for Christmas?"

"I got her some perfume she likes," Jimmy answered with a smile. "She pointed out an advertisement in a magazine she was reading, and even nudged me when there was a commercial on television. With hints like that, what choice did I have?"

"Not much," Larry grinned. "I hope you like it, too!"

"It smells better on her than it does in the bottle," Jimmy smiled even more slyly.

"There's one way I know to make it smell even better than when she's wearing it, Jimmy," Larry said with a wink, "and that's the morning after you've had a date, and you wake up to discover you're wearing it, also!"

"Amen to that!" John agreed enthusiastically.

"OK, boys," Mr. Myers smirked. "Your mother and I have heard quite enough!"

"It's alright, Bill," Mary Myers said softly. "Our boys are growing up and aren't interested in the same sort of toys they used to play with on Christmas afternoon."

"Damn! Now *there's* a thought!" Larry sighed. With a faraway look on his face, he added, "What I wouldn't give to find *that* under the tree next year! How about you, John?"

"Amen!" John added with even more enthusiasm.

"You seem to be in a prayerful mood, John," Larry laughed. "You know what we should do? While we're thinking about it, let's get some paper and start working on next year's letter to Santa Claus! *I'm* going to be an *especially* good boy next year!"

"Me, too!" John said, as he and Jimmy joined their friend's laugher.

"It just might work at that, mother," Bill grinned, drawing a blush from his wife.

"In the meantime," Larry smiled, thinking it would be a good idea to change the subject, "I hope you'll enjoy this. I'm sorry it couldn't be what you and I both really want, but at least it's something, anyway." He reached into the large bag he was carrying, and brought out some packages. He handed one to John, another to Jimmy, and a third to their parents. "Merry Christmas!" he added with a bright smile.

"Thanks, Larry!" John said as he accepted the gift. "And Merry Christmas to you!" he replied, fetching a package for his friend from under the tree. "I'm willing to bet we won't have a repeat of last year! I hope you like it."

"Me, too!" Larry grinned. "I got you something you've never even mentioned!"

The boys opened their packages simultaneously and fell into hysterical laughter when they discovered the contents. Each of them had given the other a copy of the debut album from The Doors featuring their breakthrough single *Light My Fire*.

"I don't believe you guys!" Jimmy said, laughing along with them. "At least there's one thing I'm absolutely sure of, and that's that you didn't get me the same thing I got you!" he added handing Larry another package.

"I hope not!" Larry laughed, as he began to open his package. "Wow! Thanks, Jimmy!" he said when he saw the companion music book to the album. "I didn't even know this was out yet!"

"We were shopping in Houston a few weeks ago, and I saw it in the music store," Jimmy explained. "John already told me what he was getting, so I knew it had to be the perfect thing."

"It is," Larry smiled.

Jimmy finish opening his own gift, finding a rather smart looking collection of men's toiletry items, including a razor, shaving soap and cup, after shave, cologne, and deodorant. "Are you implying I stink?" Jimmy laughed.

"Not at all," Larry smiled, "but I think Nora might appreciate it if every now and then, you removed that peach fuzz that's starting to grow on your upper lip! In the past, you could probably just rub a little cream on your lip and have the cat lick them off, but I think you've about outgrown that. Besides, while nothing seems to work for me, Sam told me girls really like that cologne." He drew a blush from Jimmy, and general laughter from the whole Myers family by adding, "Maybe Nora would like finding that smell on her in the morning after a date with you."

"Maybe she would at that," Jimmy grinned as he blushed. "Thanks, Larry. I'll give it a try next time I see her."

"Let me know if it works out," he smiled. "If it does, I'll get some for myself!"

He then turned to Bill and Mary, urging them to open their package. "Go ahead and open yours. It's just a little something I thought you might like."

Mary opened the package for them, little more than an envelop, really, and found the card announcing they had been given a gift membership to the National Geographic Society, including a subscription to the National Geographic magazine. "Oh, thank you, Larry!" she exclaimed, delighted with the idea. "We'll all enjoy these so much!"

"We certainly will," Bill agreed. "I suspect the boys will even take a look now and then." Handing Larry another package, the last one underneath their tree, he smiled, "And we didn't forget you, either!"

"Thanks, Mr. M, Mrs. M!" he said accepting the gift. "You really didn't have to."

"We know," Bill replied. "We wanted to."

Larry opened the small package and grinned when he found a bottle of the same cologne he had given Jimmy. It was called "Top Brass" and had been popularized by advertisements featuring Barbara Feldon, pitching the cologne to the "tigers" in the audience while she stared into the camera with an almost unbearable sultriness.

"We hope it works for you," the Myers explained.

"Thanks! Sam told me this stuff couldn't miss!" Larry grinned. "If it doesn't work, then I guess the fault has to be with the one wearing it, not the cologne!"

"I hope you'll let me borrow a little of it from time to time," John chuckled.

"Get some from Jimmy," Larry laughed. "I need this stuff a lot more than either of you guys! In fact, I'm going to put some on right now. I'll find out how well it works when I get to Sam's house!"

"Or maybe when you get to Julia's house," Jimmy added innocently.

A wave of anguish swept across Larry's face, but he recovered quickly, knowing Jimmy was completely unaware of how much he wished that would be true. "Yeah, maybe," he forced a smile.

"I'll be waiting for your report," John said softly. "Merry Christmas, my friend!"

"Yes, Merry Christmas!" Jimmy and the adults echoed.

"Thanks," Larry said brightly, "and Merry Christmas to each of you!"

His second stop of the day was to see Sam and her mother. He pulled into the driveway, and paused before he got out of the car. As a joke, he splashed on a very small amount of the Top Brass cologne, just to see if Sam would notice. He suspected the only reason she had recommended it so highly was the fact Larry had made a lot of comments over the last few years about how much Sam looked like Barbara Feldon. Even though she denied it, and played it down as much as she could, Larry knew she felt complimented by the favorable comparison. As far as Larry was concerned, Barbara Feldon was the one who should feel complimented!

"Merry Christmas, Larry!" Sam smiled greeting him with a warm hug.

"Merry Christmas, Sam!" he replied, returning her hug. When they separated, he grinned to himself at the surprised look on her face. There was no doubt she smelled the cologne. The only question now was how long before she commented. "Merry Christmas, Mrs. K!" he shouted as they stepped inside and closed the door.

Gayle shouted her greeting from the kitchen. "Merry Christmas, Larry! I'll be right out. I'm just about to take another batch of Christmas cookies out of the oven."

"I hope some of them will be for me!" he called back to her.

"Since you get them so seldom," she laughed, "I didn't know you *liked* cookies!"

Larry looked at Sam and grinned wryly whispering, "By that same line of logic, she might not realize I like *girls*. You'll tell her I like girls, won't you, Sam?"

"I think she knows," Sam giggled. "Quit pretending to feel so sorry for yourself!"

"Who's pretending?" he laughed. In order to change the subject, he reached into his bag, brought out a small package, and handed it to his friend. "This is for you, Sam. Why don't you sit here on the sofa and open it. I want to see your eyes so I'll know whether you like it or not."

"Of course I'll like it," Sam smiled, sitting where he directed her. "I don't even have to open it to know that! Let me wait for mom to join us, OK?"

"Sure," he said, selecting a perfect position to see her face when she opened it.

"Hello, Larry," Gayle said, aglow with Christmas spirit.

"Why, Mrs. K! I've never seen you so radiant!"

"You sweet talker," she hugged him. "If only I was twenty-five years younger!"

"What difference would that make? I thought everybody knew I like older women. I find it hard to believe Sam never told you that!"

"The main difference is I wouldn't be trying to steal you away from my own daughter!" Gayle laughed. "Now cut out the nonsense, you silver-tongued devil! Has Sam given you your gift yet?"

"I'm getting a gift?" he feigned surprise. "Actually, Mrs. K, we were just waiting for you to arrive so Sam could open hers."

"Well, then go ahead," Gayle smiled.

Larry returned to his seat next to Sam, checked to make sure he would be able to see her eyes, then urged her to proceed. "It's not really a big deal, but I somehow think it's going to make you smile, Sam, and I just love to see you smile! Open it!"

Sam was already smiling as she began to pick at the tape holding the brightly colored paper surrounding the small box. After a few moments, she had removed the paper to find a small wooden box covered with intricate carvings. "It's lovely," she said to him.

"Open it!" he urged once again.

She unclipped the small metal clasp holding the box closed, and carefully lifted the lid on its hinge. Her eyes flashed with wonder at the crystalline figure of a small girl, nestled within the folds of the soft, velvety lining. She touched it with her fingers, then carefully lifted it out of the box. She smiled brightly as the figurine captured the light and returned it in a dazzling rainbow of color.

"I thought of you the moment I saw it," he said. "It goes with the unicorn I gave you last year. You're the lovely little girl who can capture the heart of the unicorn."

"Oh, Larry," Sam said softly, wiping a small tear from the corner of her eye. "How do you manage to keep finding a way to touch me like this?"

"You inspire me, Sam," he said simply. "How could anyone hope to find a better friend than you have been to me for all these years?"

"That's easy," she smiled through the tears continuing from her eyes. "I have a better friend than you'll ever know!" She put her arms around his neck and hugged him even more warmly.

"Not a chance," he said returning her hug. "Dry your eyes on my shoulder. I have plenty of experience with tears. I happen to know they won't stain." Gayle sat quietly and smiled at them.

"I feel so silly," Sam said as she released the hug and wiped her eyes. "I wish I could give you a gift that would mean as much as yours."

"Like the gift you gave me last year?" he smiled. "I wish I could've topped that!"

"Well, I'm afraid you're going to be disappointed this year," she said handing him a package. "At the time, I thought this would be just perfect, but all of a sudden..."

"If you thought it would be perfect, then it will be," he smiled. When the paper was removed and he could read the label on the box, he laughed brightly. "Top Brass cologne and after shave! Do you think I stink, Sam?"

"I certainly think you're a stinker!" she laughed along with him. "I thought maybe this would help you out when you meet your next girlfriend, but I can tell by my nose someone has already beat me to it! Or did you buy some for yourself?"

"Oh!" he laughed again. "Actually, based on your advise, I bought some for Jimmy to help him out with his girlfriend, Nora. The funny part is Mr. and Mrs. M turned around and gave me a bottle."

"So you don't need it anymore," Sam said, looking a little disappointed.

"I need all the help I can get, Sam!" he laughed. Seeing her disappointment, he quickly added, "Oh, Sam! You know what I want more than anything, and you have given to me something to help me find it. One of days, I'll find her, and when I do, I'll wear this for her. And when she tells me how much she likes it, I'll remember who gave me this gift, and I'll be even more grateful than I am right now! Thank you, my friend, from the very bottom of my heart!"

"How is it you always seem to know just the right thing to say?" she asked.

"Hardly," he smiled. "There are so many things I'd like to say, some to you, and some to someone else. If I only knew the right words, I assure you I'd say them."

There was a poignant pause as Larry and Sam looked at each other and nodded their heads in agreement. Gayle returned to the kitchen and returned shortly, interrupting the silence. "I have a package for you, also," she smiled handing Larry a box wrapped in colored foil.

"It's warm! I'll bet I can guess what's inside!" He pulled back the foil to find a tin box, decorated with Christmas scenes. Inside the box was a generous quantity of the Christmas cookies Gayle had been baking. "Thanks, Mrs. K!" he smiled.

"You're very welcome," Gayle said, returning his smile.

"I didn't forget you, of course," he said removing another package from his sack.

"Oh, you shouldn't bother," she grinned. She sat on the couch next to him and carefully unwrapped the gift, finding another cookie jar she could add to her collection. This one was shaped like a little Dutch windmill. "Oh, how nice! I think you just want me to bake more cookies!"

"Please do, Mrs. K!" he laughed. The threesome sat around in the living room enjoying some milk and cookies. After a while, he announced it was time for him to move on to his next stop. "Merry Christmas, Mrs. K! Merry Christmas, Sam! I'll see you again soon!"

"Merry Christmas, Larry," Gayle said, "and thanks once again for the cookie jar."

"You're welcome. I'll expect it to be filled soon with your wonderful cookies!"

Sam followed him to his car. "Are you going to her house next?" she asked as Larry opened his car door and slipped under the steering wheel.

"Yes," he said, trying to keep a blank expression on his face.

"Why do you torture yourself so?" she asked.

"Oh, Sam," he said sadly. "Every Christmas for the last few years, I've gone around in the afternoon and visited with my friends to play Santa Claus. That's just what I do. She's one of the *Four Musketeers* now; she's my *friend*, Sam. I shouldn't have to explain that, because you know it very well. I'm not torturing myself. I *want* to see her. I want to wish her a Merry Christmas."

"You haven't forgotten they don't celebrate Christmas, have you?" she asked.

"I haven't forgotten," he said simply. "I was a little worried about that last year, but not any more. They seemed to accept it quite readily. I think they were even moved a little. I wouldn't do it if I thought it offended them, Sam."

"Will Bill be there?" she asked.

"I don't know, but I hope not," he replied. "I doubt it. Maybe that's why I want to do this, Sam. It's one of the few times of the year when I have a good excuse to go see her, when there won't be a lot of others around, when I can talk to just her, even if it's only for a moment, and even if I can't say the things I want to say to her."

"And that's not torture?" she asked.

"No," he said sadly. "The torture doesn't come until New Year's Eve."

"Good luck, Larry," she whispered. "When I get inside, I'll make a wish things will be a little different for you next Christmas."

"Thanks, Sam," he said with a slight smile. "I need all the help I can get!"

Larry sighed heavily as he turned down the country lane leading to the Jacobson house in Steep Hollow. If he could change the circumstances of his visit, he would gladly do so. But like he told Sam, he was going to visit one of his best friends, to play Santa Claus, and to wish her a Merry Christmas. The same thing applied to Mr. and Mrs. Jacobson. They were friends as well, and he hoped the feeling was mutual.

As always, the house looked warm and inviting as he turned into the driveway. Pulling to a stop in front of the house, he reflected on his last Christmas visit, just one year ago. They had not expected him then. He wondered if they would be expecting him this year.

Would things go as well as before? When he came last year, she had just broken up with Jimmy. His own relationship with Linda was technically alive, but would last only a few more days. For the first time, he had seen her in tomboy mode. It was so cute the way she bounded from that old willow tree to greet him. *I wonder if she'll be up in that tree again? Not likely. It's much too cold for that this time.*

He gathered up his bag of gifts, along with all the courage he could muster, and walked up the sidewalk. Struggling to display an air of confidence he did not feel, he rang the doorbell. The familiar response this brought from Schotzy helped him to relax. He knew everything would work out fine, just like it had last Christmas.

Julian greeted the young man with a warm smile. The dog stood up on his hind legs to greet his friend with a wagging tail. "Hello, Larry. I can't say I'm totally surprised to see you. It occurred to me a little while ago we might get a visit from you today."

"I suppose I should have warned you," Larry said chuckling, "but I didn't think about it. I'm just so used to making the rounds to see my friends on this day I forgot you might not even know what day it is."

"It's a little hard *not* to know," Julian laughed. "They do tend to go on and on about it on television. Come on in out of the cold. The girls are in the family room."

"Thanks," Larry said as he stepped inside. "Oh, and Merry Christmas to you, sir."

Julian actually halted in mid-stride, and looked back at the boy. From his wry smile, Larry knew he was not offended, just playing his part in this odd little skit. "This way," he said simply.

In the family room, Jessica was the first to greet him. "Hello, Larry!" she said with a warm smile on her face. "How are you today?"

"I'm fine, Mrs. J," he replied. "I hope you're also doing well?"

"Very well," she said. "Thanks."

"Hi, Larry!" Julia said brightly.

"Hi, Julie," he said showing the brightest and bravest smile he could muster. "Just like last year, I came to wish you all a Merry Christmas. I hope you don't mind."

"Not at all," Jessica assured him. "It's very sweet of you to include us in your holiday celebrations."

"It surely is!" Julia agreed. "Chanukah doesn't start until tomorrow night, but we can go ahead and wish you a happy Chanukah anyway!"

"Thanks!" he said. "Happy Chanukah to you! Are you ready to get started?"

"Started with what?" Julia asked.

"I bear gifts!" he grinned.

"Oh, Larry," Jessica smiled, "You really shouldn't."

"But I want to, Mrs. J," he said simply. He reached into his bag and fetched a brightly wrapped package. "This is for you. Why don't you start this year?"

Jessica accepted the package and returned his smile. "Since you insist. It's rather heavy. I wonder what it could be?"

"It's a pony," he whispered to Julia, drawing a giggle from her which reverberated through his ears as if it was organ music inside a cathedral.

"I certainly hope not," Jessica grinned, also having heard the whisper, "or the poor thing will suffocate for sure!" She unwrapped the package, finding a box containing several jars of condiments and jellies. "These look interesting! What a strange assortment of flavors! There's some pickled jalapeño peppers, some sweet pickle relish containing habañero peppers, and two jars of jelly – some jalapeño pepper jelly and bluebonnet jelly? I didn't know you could make jelly from bluebonnets!"

"Neither did I," he laughed, "but apparently you can! Be careful with the peppers, especially the habañeros. They're very hot. The jalapeños aren't that bad, actually, and the jalapeño jelly isn't hot at all. I hope you'll all like them."

"I'm sure we will," Jessica smiled. "Thank you very much, Larry."

"You're very welcome, Mrs. J!" He reached into his sack again and produced another brightly wrapped package, and handed it to Julian. "You're next, Mr. J!"

Julian accepted the package, and from the size, shape, and weight, he knew it was going to be similar to the gift he received last year. Jessica caught his eye and winked, drawing a faint smile from him. "I wonder what this could be," he teased, pulling back the wrapping paper to reveal a bottle of Manishevitz kosher wine.

"I hope you'll like this one," Larry smiled. "I still can't buy it myself, of course, but the friend who bought it for me said this one is supposed to be a lot better than the one I got last year."

"Is that so?" Julian said without a trace of irony in his voice. "Well, thank you very much, Larry. I'm sure we'll be able to put it to good use." He returned the wink to Jessica, who covered her mouth to conceal her grin.

"You're very welcome," he said. Jessica's smile had not gone unnoticed, but he was unsure how to interpret it. He decided in future, he should do a little *personal* research on the subject of kosher wines, rather than relying on the recommendations of friends who might not know what they were talking about. It suddenly dawned on him he had no idea of what it meant for a wine to be kosher in the first place. *While I'm at it, I ought to do a little research on this* Chanukah *thing, also.*

Filing these notes away for later reference, he reached into his sack for a third time and drew out another small package. Trying to keep his hand from trembling, he offered it to the remaining party. "This one's for you, Julie," he said, simultaneously offering a silent prayer she would like it. Her smile as she accepted the package helped him relax. He knew there was no reason to worry. *Of course she will like it!*

Julia pulled on the tape holding the wrapping paper, and soon was working on the unmarked cardboard box underneath. This opened to reveal a small metal box. When she opened it, the little music box played the Beatles song, *A Hard Day's Night* that had been very popular a couple of years earlier. "Oh, thank you, Larry! At this rate, it won't be too long before half of the music boxes in my collection will have come from you! It seems the best ones came from you, already!"

"You're very welcome, Julie," he said, now able to relax. *Why was I so worried? Why was I concerned she wouldn't like it?* "Merry Christmas to you all!"

"Merry Christmas to you, also," the Jacobsons replied in near unison. "Larry," Jessica began, "it's not our tradition to exchange gifts during this season. Even for Chanukah, gifts are usually just small amounts of gelt, I mean money, parents might give their children. However, I was thinking I ought to make up a batch of latkes this afternoon. Would you like to join us?"

"Sounds intriguing, Mrs. J," he smiled, "but I don't want you to go to any trouble. Besides, I don't even know what a latkes is!"

"Jessie," Julian began, "it might be interesting to try some of that sweet pepper relish on the latkes. You've made them with bell peppers and we all liked them."

"That's a great idea, dad!" Julia grinned. "Or we might put some of the bluebonnet jelly on them to make Texas-style latkes!" This comment brought general laughter from them all. Larry joined in, though not really sure about the nature of the joke.

"Well, come on, Julia," Jessica laughed. "We'll go make latkes and leave the men to their own devices. Can you two keep out of mischief for a few minutes?"

"We'll manage," Julian replied. "Maybe Larry and I will open this wine."

"Julian, don't you dare!" Jessica warned. "Larry isn't old enough to be drinking."

"A small taste won't hurt him, Jessie," he said bluntly. "How about it, Larry? Do you think your parents would object to you having a taste of the wine you gave me?"

"I don't know, Mr. J," Larry replied, "but I don't think they'd mind too much. My father claims to be a complete tea-totaler, but I've seen him drink a very small glass of homemade wine before bed now and then. He says it helps his digestion."

"Homemade wine?" Julian asked. "Does he have a vineyard?"

"No, sir," he answered. "He just puts some extra sugar and yeast in a bottle of Welch's grape juice. I've tasted a sip of it. Frankly, I thought it was ghastly!"

"Um, hum," Julian grinned, as he nodded his head and glanced at the bottle of

Manishevitz wine. He led Larry into his study and produced two small cordial glasses. He opened the wine and poured a small amount into each glass, handing one of them to Larry and lifting the other for himself. "To life!"

Larry was surprised Julian offered any toast at all, and found himself repeating the toast as a reflex. "To life!" he repeated, holding his glass higher to match the motion of Julian. They then brought the glasses to their lips and took a tiny sample.

Julian watched Larry intently to gage his reaction. Not noticing Julian was watching him, Larry stared at the glass of wine in his hand and made a small frown. Somehow, he had expected something better than that. It wasn't the same as his father's homemade wine, but the similarity was unmistakable. It tasted very much like Welch's grape juice had been allowed to ferment. *That shouldn't be a surprise*, he thought. *After all, isn't that all wine really is – fermented grape juice?* On the other hand, he had tasted some other wines and found them to be markedly different than this. It suddenly dawned on him the reason there were so many different varieties of wine must be because there are so many different varieties of grapes! This was what wine made from concord grapes tasted like. He filed away another mental note to find out what kinds of grapes were used to make other kinds of wines.

"So, what do you think?" Julian asked, suppressing a grin.

"I'm no wine expert," he replied. "Besides, it's more important *you* like it."

"Larry, I appreciate the fact you went out of your way to find something you thought would please me," Julian replied honestly. "As far as the wine itself goes, to be honest with you, I have to tell you it's not my favorite. But the important thing about a gift is the thought behind it. I'm happy to tell you I'm very pleased with it."

"You're being kind, Mr. J," he said with a smile.

"Not at all!" Julian assured him. "I'm very pleased with your gift."

"I thank you for saying so," he smiled. "Next year, I'll find something better."

Once again, Julian raised his glass. "To friendship!" he smiled.

"Yes!" he said, returning that smile. "To friendship, Mr. J!"

Together, they tipped their glasses towards each other, drained what little wine still remained, and exchanged a smile affirming they were indeed friends. This simple gesture was the best gift he had received that Christmas. He had always been sure Julia and her mother accepted him. He now knew her father did, also.

"Let's go see how the girls are doing with the latkes," Julian suggested.

"Sounds great!" Larry agreed. At that moment, he felt a strong desire to let his eyes soak up the subject of so many of his dreams from the last year. Even though he knew none of those dreams would come to reality this day, he felt a powerful need to memorize every detail about her, so maybe his future dreams would seem that much more real. As he and her father walked towards the kitchen, he wondered, as he had done so many times since he had met her, what it was about this little girl that drew him so powerfully.

"How are they coming along?" Julian asked.

"We're just about to fry up the first batch," Julia replied.

"How did you like the wine, Larry?" Jessica asked.

"Uh," he said hesitantly, not really knowing how to proceed.

"We agreed it was an excellent gift," Julian offered.

He could not help but notice how Jessica pursed her lips and raised her eyebrows as she looked at her husband. He could easily see there was some form of silent communication between them, and wondered at the messages they were exchanging. But his eyes were soon drawn to another, and he found himself staring into those green circles surrounding infinity. He snapped back into reality by the aroma of the latkes beginning to cook. *How long was the gap in the space-time continuum this time?* he wondered. "Those smell wonderful, Mrs. J. You call them latkes?"

"Yes, I call them 'lat-kuhs', because that's the way my grandmother pronounced it. Julian calls them 'lat-keys' because that's the way *his* grandmother pronounced it. Julia does the same, because she's so close to her grandmother on Julian's side."

"I see," he grinned. "That makes sense. I'll probably pronounce them 'potato pancakes' because that's how I suspect *my* grandmother would pronounce it!"

"I imagine you're right about that," Jessica laughed. "So much for the big Jewish secret! They contain potatoes, onion, eggs, matzah meal, salt, and pepper."

"I don't know anything about matzah meal," he grinned. "Is that something my grandmother might pronounce 'flour'?"

"Probably," Jessica laughed again. "So I take it you've had latkes before?"

"So it appears," he grinned. "And you're very right about putting the pepper relish on them, Mr. J, and the bluebonnet jelly will be perfect on them, Julie! Or you can go the simple way and spread a little apple sauce on them, although I always preferred apple butter to apple sauce!"

"There's an interesting idea," Julian said. "Why have we never tried that?"

"Maybe it's because we seldom have any," Jessica replied. "I'll start buying it if you would like."

"I would!" Julia replied.

"Then it's settled!" Jessica laughed.

After enjoying latkes covered with sweet habañero relish, bluebonnet jelly, and jalapeño jelly, Larry once again wished all of them a merry Christmas, added a happy Chanukah for good measure, and departed. As he drove himself home, he reflected on his visit. It had been very worthwhile. The only thing it lacked was finding an answer to the question haunting his dreams for over a year now.

What is it about her? he asked himself. *Why didn't I do something about this last January when I had the chance?* No answers jumped at him from out of the blue. All he knew was he wanted to be with that girl. He enjoyed those moments, as she had done while he was leaving, when she would hug him. He wanted those hugs to come for a different reason. He wanted to hold her hand. He longed to taste her lips. They must surely be sweeter even than the wine he had tasted.

"Oh, please," he said aloud. "Let it be different next Christmas! Let these dreams I'm having come true." There was no acknowledgment of his wish, his hope, his prayer. Nothing to assure him it would granted. Nothing to indicate whether or not it would be denied. The worst part was there was nothing to indicate it had even been heard. Nothing at all – just the ongoing, ever-changing infinity of the universe.

Sunday, December 31, 1967
A Girl Like You

The guests began to arrive at 8:00, unaware the Jacobson family had held a private ceremony earlier in the evening, lighting six candles in celebration of Chanukah, the Festival of Lights. The Jacobsons were hosting a small New Year's Eve party for Julia and the other members of the *Four Musketeers*. The party was to be a small affair. Julia, of course, had invited Bill, her new boyfriend. John was bringing Daisy Drummond, his date for the weekend. Neither Larry nor Sam had elected to bring a date. It was not uncommon for outsiders to think Larry and Sam were together on such occasions, although the close circle knew this was not technically correct. Larry actually nurtured this misconception. In small gatherings such as this, he did not want it to be obvious Sam was there without a date. So when he learned John was bringing a date, he decided not to pursue finding a date of his own.

The youngsters were treated to a wide variety of snacks and nonalcoholic drinks, played games, and danced to the music provided by Julia's record collection. When everyone congregated around the clock in the family room a minute or so before the anticipated moment arrived, Larry casually stepped into the living room wanting to be away from the others, spending the moment in private reflection.

"Where's Larry?" Julia asked as the others gathered around to watch the clock.

Sam had seen him step away and tried to cover for him. "I think he stepped into the kitchen for a moment. I'll go get him. I don't suppose I could get you guys to wait for us, could I?" she added with a grin.

"Oh, sure!" Julia giggled. "Tell him to hurry!"

Sam walked into the living room after first taking a detour through the kitchen. When she saw the look in his eyes, she knew there was nothing she could say to him. She simply moved next to him and hugged him while they listened to the others counting down the final seconds of 1967.

"Ten... Nine... Eight..." they called. Larry reflected on the events of the previous year, almost as if he were replaying the entire year in his memory. There was no argument there had been some good moments. A beautiful girl named Sally had helped him recover from a devastating heartbreak. Having changed his image in a positive way, he felt he was now more accepted by the circle of society he still recognized as the "in" crowd. He had shared the experience of his Senior Prom with one of the most wonderful and beautiful girls he knew. He had received his high school diploma, enrolled in college, started working part time at the computer center, and made some wonderful new friends there. He had composed his second song, one he considered to be vastly superior to his first. Perhaps the most important event of 1967, however, was he had been freed from a promise binding his hands in what he considered the most titanic struggle in his life.

"Seven... Six..." they counted. On the other hand, there had also been plenty of moments that were not so good. While he had recovered from his broken heart, he had not found a new love to fill the void in his life. His one date with Sam had only made him reflect on the decision the two of them had made regarding their relationship, and wonder if they should reconsider. Since college life was a lot busier than he anticipated, he found his free time to pursue other interests was more limited than he wanted. His loneliness was more intense than it had ever been.

"Five... Four..." the countdown proceeded. He found himself wanting to step back into the family room just so he could look in her direction, to steal a glance of the girl who confused him so badly. There was one chance during the year when he might have done something about that. But while he felt constrained by a promise made to Jimmy, Frank came along and stole that chance away. Now, Frank had dropped out of sight for reasons Larry did not know, and Bill had come along before Larry was even aware Julia was without a steady boyfriend. He would have to stand by and wait awhile longer.

"Three... Two... One..." At the stroke of midnight, he once again felt an ache deep inside of him, one that haunted him every New Year's Eve since he had first heard of the silly superstition. At that moment, all he wanted was for his life to be a little different. He simply wished he could be the one who was about to welcome in the new year by kissing her. If that damn superstition held true, he would be repeating this wish over and over again during the coming year.

1968

Monday, January 1, 1968
Conspiracy Theory

"Happy New Year!" they all shouted as the clock struck midnight. Julian and Jessica turned to kiss each other, as did John and Daisy, and Bill and Julia. In the living room, Larry and Sam hugged each other while Larry attempted to regain his composure. When they sensed the kissing was over, they released each other, and the two of them returned to the family room to hug the others.

By 12:30, the party was winding down. "Goodnight, Daisy," Larry called while heading towards his car. "It was nice to see you again. Goodnight, John!" They returned his greeting, waving back to him as car doors closed and engines started. "Hey, Sam! Are you in a hurry to get home?"

"Not especially. Do you have something on your mind?"

"How would you like to go out in the woods with me?" he grinned.

"I might have known!" she laughed. "Is there anything *decent* on your mind?"

"We don't need to go out in the woods. All I want to do is ask a favor of you."

Sam could tell from the look in his eyes he was worried about something. "Just name it, Larry," she said seriously. "You know that I'd do anything for you."

"Obviously, you won't do just *anything*!" he laughed. "What if I really *did* want to go out in the woods with you?"

Sam read his eyes and saw while he was trying to make a joke, his heart was not really in it. Something was clearly bothering him. "I'd do anything, even that, if I thought it was the right thing to do. If I thought it was something you truly needed."

"I know," he said sadly, "just as I'd do anything for you, without qualifications."

"What do you need, Larry?" she asked. "What's on your twisted mind tonight?"

"I need your help, Sam."

"Let's go talk," she said. "Would a smoke help you relax and clear your head?"

"That's all I had in mind when I suggested we go out in the woods," he confessed.

Sam laughed and got into her car. Larry followed in his own, driving the short distance to the gravel road they knew so well. Sam hopped out and trotted over to jump into his car. It occurred to her something was very wrong with this picture. In a flash, she realized what that was. He had gone directly for the community stash instead of opening her door like he normally would. This was obviously serious!

He returned and handed a joint to Sam. "Ladies first," he said absently. She lit it, and handed it back to him as quickly as possible. He obviously needed this a lot more than she. He took a deep pull and handed it back, holding his breath a little longer than normal. "I have a problem," he said, finally indicating that he was ready to talk.

"We all have problems, Larry," Sam said as she drew a puff from the joint. "Which specific problem is bothering you tonight, and how can I help?" She handed the cigarette back to Larry.

He noted, "You know how I've been... bothered by a certain friend for a while."

"Yes, I know you have been."

"Do you think the others know?" he asked simply.

"John certainly knows," she said, handing the joint back to him, "but I don't think *she* knows, if that's what you mean. What others do you have in mind?"

"She's the main one," he said, absently drawing another toke. "What about everybody else, someone who might tell her? Do you think her mother knows?"

"She's a pretty shrewd detective," Sam smiled. "If she put her attention to it, I don't doubt for a minute she could figure it out."

"But do you think she already knows?" he asked pointedly, passing the joint back.

"My guess would be no," she said. "Last year at this time, after you broke up with Linda and Julia broke up with Jimmy, I'm sure she knew you wanted Julia. But when you didn't do anything about it..."

"That's all water under the bridge," he said sadly. "Maybe I should have taken your advice and broken my promise. But I didn't, and it's too late to change it now."

"I didn't mean to imply you were wrong about that," she said. "To tell the truth, I admire you sticking to your principles, even though it was painful for you to do so."

"I appreciate you saying that," he said sadly. "Would you say the only ones who know about my... little problem... are you, me, and John?"

"I think that's the case," she agreed, nodding her head in the affirmative.

"If only in one sense, I've been very lucky this year," he said. "If I'm ever going to have the chance to be with her, to correct my mistake if you will, then it's vital I keep my desire a secret until the right moment comes along. If she found out how much I want to be with her at a time when she's not ready to be with me, then she'd surely reject me, and all hope would be lost, probably forever."

"How do you know she's not ready to be with you right now?" Sam asked.

"Have you got any evidence to support that possibility, Sam?" he asked, almost begging. "From my perspective, I see there is another in the way. I don't see any evidence, but I'll freely admit I don't see things very clearly when it comes to her. I'd love to hear I'm blind!" Sam started to speak, but realizing she had nothing to offer other than encouragement, she kept quiet, and slowly shook her head. "I guess it's the fact we're starting a new year that got me thinking about this," he continued. "It's been a long and difficult year for me. What's worse is I don't see any end in sight. I'm afraid 1968 is going to be just as bad as last year, and maybe even worse."

"Do you have any evidence to support that conclusion?" she asked, almost mocking the question she could not answer moments earlier.

Recognizing that, Larry grinned at her before he answered. "Not really, unless you want to count the fact she's been dating Bill for a couple of months now, and I don't see any signs they're going to break up anytime soon. I'm going to need a lot of patience before the time is right."

"So how can I help?" Sam asked.

"Well, like I said a few minutes ago, I've been pretty lucky this year to keep my feelings a secret. I'm not sure I can rely on plain luck much longer. I'm hurting, Sam! It's eating me up inside! I can hardly look at her without having to fight back the tears. If I'm not careful, one of these days, I'm going to slip up, say something stupid, everyone will know, and my chance will be gone forever."

"I understand, Larry," she said. "So I ask you again, how can I help?"

"Let me throw out an idea. I won't be able to hide something is bothering me for long. I'm very lonely, everyone knows it, and there's nothing I can do to hide it. But maybe I can hide the reason. Do you know what the best camouflage can be? Do you know the best way to hide something, to keep a secret? Put it in plain sight! Put it right out there in front of the world where everyone can see it clearly."

"Your plan is to hide your feelings by letting everyone know?" she asked.

"Exactly," he said. "I can't hide the fact I'm lonely and hurting, so maybe I can trick them into thinking it's for a different reason. The easiest way to hide the truth is to point in a direction someone already wants to believe in the first place!"

"Make them think you want to be with someone else!" Sam said, seeing the essence of his plan. "If you can convince people you're interested in some other girl, they won't realize you're really interested in Julia. I have to admit I'm impressed, Larry! I never realized you could be so devious!" She considered the idea briefly, then put the rest of his plan together. "You want *me* to be that other girl, don't you?"

"I knew you'd catch on pretty quickly," he said. "My plan is to convince people I want to be with you. All you have to do is reject my advances. Laugh them off, like you already do. Treat me like the clown, like you don't take anything I say seriously. No one will question when I appear to be the clown with a broken heart. This shouldn't be much of a challenge to your acting abilities!"

"You're right about that!" Sam laughed. "Will we let John in on the game?"

Larry thought for a moment. "Let's wait on that. I hate to keep such a secret from him, but if we can fool him, then maybe we can fool the others. We'll know it's working if he ever says anything about it. But let's not overdo it! The idea is to use misdirection, just enough to convince them it's you I want, diverting attention away from her. As long as I'm in control and can keep my feelings hidden, I won't do much of anything. If I start feeling the pressure, then I'll start hitting on you. The higher the pressure goes, the more outrageous my offers will become."

"How is *your* acting ability?" she laughed.

"Don't you realize everything I do is an act?" he grinned. "All I have to do is act like I'm crazy about you. That won't be much of a challenge to my acting abilities. The truth is, I *am* crazy about you. I love you, Sam! Surely you know that by now."

"Yes, I know," she said seriously. "I love you, too, Larry."

"I know you do, Sam," he said with a grateful smile. "I still don't understand why you won't run off with me for real, but I accepted my fate a long time ago. I want to be with Julie more than anything, but I'd still be very happy to be with you." He paused for a moment, and Sam could see he was trying to think of the best words to say what he felt in his heart. "I'll make you a deal, Sam. Whenever I make an offer to you, no matter how outrageous it might seem, let me assure you the offer is genuine. I assume you'll reject it like you always do, but if by some miracle you change your mind someday, and decide you're willing to be with me after all, then all you have to do is accept one of my offers. We'll run off and be together, and I promise you I'll never, ever look back!"

"Oh, Larry," she whispered. "I think you really mean that."

"I *do* mean it," he said simply.

"I would just end up breaking your heart in the end," she said.

"You can break it all at once or a little at a time. What's the difference?"

"I don't want to break your heart at all!" she smiled. "I'll make *you* a deal. You have your dreams and I have mine. If I can, I'll help make your dreams come true. Perhaps you can help me with mine someday. If we're lucky, then maybe both our dreams will come true. But if they don't, then we'll reconsider our situation. Maybe we'll run off together after all, and I promise I'll never, ever look back, either!"

"I hope you mean that," he smiled warmly. "That just might be the best chance I'll ever have to find happiness."

Wednesday, February 14, 1968
Do You Want To Know A Secret?

The school bus lumbered away and Julia waved to her friends. It was a typical day in the dead of Texas winter, cold and wet, and as she walked along the driveway to her house, she opened her umbrella to shield herself against the light drizzle.

Valentine's Day was not as much fun as it used to be. In junior high, the kids decorated a paper bag and hung them in their homeroom so friends and would-be sweethearts could drop cards into them. This was not the practice at high school. Bill was sweet, of course. He gave her a nice card and a small box of candy. Even John sought her out to deliver the humorous card promising to become a tradition. Still, she missed the old days when everybody exchanged a little card with everybody else.

She reached the front door and stepped into the foyer. "Hi, mom!" she called, carefully wiping her shoes on the doormat. "Hi, boy!" she smiled at Schotzy who met her at the front door just like he always did, happily wagging his tail.

"Hi, sweetheart!" Jessica called back. "Did you have a nice day at school?"

"It was OK. I'll be right there." She headed for her room to drop off her coat and books before returning to the kitchen. "How were things around here?"

"Mostly normal," Jessica smiled. "You have a couple of Valentine's Day gifts on the table from your father and I, and there were also some cards in the mail."

"Oh, you guys didn't have to get me anything!" Julia smiled. "What are they?"

"Open them and see for yourself!" Jessica beamed back. "All I'll promise is *neither* of them contains a pony!"

Julia giggled at that reference, then closely examined the larger of the packages. Unable to guess what it might contain, she finally just tore into the wrapping paper to find a simple charm bracelet. "How did you guys know I wanted one of these!" she exclaimed with delight.

"Just a good guess," Jessica smiled. "Now open the other one!"

Julia returned the smile and then addressed the other, smaller package. Inside the wrapping paper she found a small box containing the first charm to add to her bracelet, a tiny figure of a dachshund. "Oh, how sweet! It looks just like Schotzy!" she said with obvious delight. Hearing his named called, Schotzy barked excitedly.

"I thought so, too," Jessica said hugging her daughter. "I just knew you'd like it."

"Oh, I do!" Julia smiled.

"Take a look at your cards," Jessica urged. "There's one in there I've been intrigued with since I brought in the mail. There's no return address on it. I almost steamed it open, but I was good! I forced myself to wait until you got home."

"Maybe I should get a post office box so I can have private mail!" Julia giggled. She examined the first envelope from her grandmother in New York. "This one's from Bobe," she announced, tearing open the seal to read the sweet and sentimental greeting. She handed the card to Jessica, adding, "Oh, I wish we could go see her!"

"We'll go this summer," Jessica said. "This is sweet! What else did you get?"

Julia looked at the return address on the next card. "This one's from Sam," she grinned, "probably something funny. Or knowing her like I do, it's probably something *dirty!*" She opened the envelope and pulled out the card. On the cover was a strange little poem:

> *The limerick form is complex.*
> *It's contents deal mainly with sex.*
> *It burgeons with virgeons*
> *And masculine urgeons,*
> *And a wealth of erotic effex.*

On the inside were several more in the same genre, which she began to read aloud. By the time she was done, Julia and her mother were rolling in stitches.

> *A remarkable race are the Persians,*
> *They do have so many diversions!*
> *They screw the whole day*
> *In the regular way,*
> *And save up the night for perversions.*
>
> *Anthropologists up with the Sioux*
> *Cabled home for two punts, one canoe.*
> *The answer next day*
> *Said, "Girls on their way,*
> *But what in the hell's a panoe?"*
>
> *A very young maid from Peru*
> *Had nothing whatever to do!*
> *So she sat on the stairs*
> *And counted cunt hairs:*
> *Six thousand, four hundred and two.*
>
> *An ambitious young woman in Reno*
> *Lost most of her money on keno.*
> *But she lay on her back*
> *And opened her crack,*
> *And now she owns all the casino!*
>
> *An innocent maid from Province*
> *Decided to take just one chance.*
> *So she let herself go*
> *In the lap of her beau,*
> *And now all of her sisters are aunts!*
>
> *An innocent maiden from Maine*
> *Declared she'd a man on her brain.*
> *But you knew from the view*
> *Of the way her waist grew,*
> *It was not on her brain he had lain.*

> *An insatiable lady from Spain*
> *Had multiple sex on her brain.*
> *She liked it again,*
> *And again, and again,*
> *And again, and again, and again!*

"What a naughty girl she is!" Jessica managed to say through the laughter and the tears. "I wonder where on earth she found that card?"

"I'll ask her!" Julia said, wiping her eyes.

"Now hurry up and open the one with no return address!" Jessica giggled.

"OK," Julia said, still snickering. She briefly looked at the envelope, noted it was postmarked in Bryan, and tore open the seal. Inside was a bright red card. She read aloud the message on the outside, "A good friendship is like a box of chocolate!" She opened the card and read the explanation, "Quality ingredients, nothing artificial, sweet, and always appreciated! Happy Valentine's Day! Love, Larry." Julia looked up at her mother and smiled. "He's so sweet!"

Before Jessica could respond, they were startled by the doorbell. Schotzy barked and ran to the front door, with Jessica and Julia close behind. Julia picked up the dog to stop him from running outside before Jessica answered the door.

"I have a delivery for Julia Jacobson," the boy announced.

"That's me," Julia said. Jessica took the dog as Julia accepted the box.

"Sign here, please," the boy requested, holding out his clipboard and a pen.

"Who is it from?" Julia asked.

"Don't know," the boy answered. "There's no card."

"No card?" Jessica asked.

"That's right, ma'am," the boy said. "I made sure of that before I left, because I didn't want anyone to accuse me of loosing it or something. It was specifically requested this be delivered with no card."

Julia signed the delivery form and thanked him. The delivery boy smiled, then hurried back to his truck, needing to make several other deliveries that afternoon.

"Well, what is it?" Jessica asked.

Julia opened the box finding a single, red rose wrapped in tissue paper. "It looks like I still have a secret admirer," she smiled, gently removing the rose from the box. She admired its simple beauty, sniffed its sweet, gentle fragrance. "Do you suppose it's from the same person as last year?"

"Probably. Same gift, same *modus operandi*," she said, thinking out loud. "There's no reason to doubt it came from the same person. We never did figure out who sent the last one, did we?"

"No, and he never revealed himself! Oh, mom! I wish I knew who he is!"

"Well, it certainly is someone you know," Jessica smiled, "someone who knows you, and is clearly very interested in you. We'll have to keep our eyes open!"

Saturday, February 17, 1968
Everybody Loves A Clown

The *Top Forty Showcase* program was on the air, with the *Four Musketeers* running things as usual. The only "outsider", the word Larry would choose though it would remain unspoken, was Julia's date and current boyfriend, Bill Foster. He and Julia were positioned in the side studio to take the telephone requests. Sam, John, and Larry sat in the main studio, working on the comedy bit for the show that night.

Sam announced the song, Diggs started the record, and killed the microphone, extinguishing the *"On the Air"* light. Julia delivered a set of song requests and dedications into the studio. "Here you go," she smiled, handing the pages to Larry.

"Hey, Julie!" Larry said. "Is that a new bracelet you're wearing?"

"It sure is!" she smiled again, showing it off for Larry and the others to examine. "My mom and dad gave it to me for Valentine's Day."

"It's nice," Larry said. "I guess the dachshund represents Schotzy?"

"Yeah!" she replied. "It's a start. I suppose they'll add more charms over time."

"Maybe others will also!" he grinned. "Do you want to get music boxes forever?"

"I don't mind," she grinned. "I'd better get back. See you guys in a bit!"

Larry smiled at her and watched as Julia turned away, left the main studio, and returned to her position sitting next to Bill in the side studio. When she disappeared from sight, Larry looked down at the papers and sighed softly. Suddenly aware of how quiet it was, he noticed Sam and John looking at him. "What?" he asked.

"Nothing," Sam replied. She and John exchanged a look, then got back to work.

At the beginning of the second segment, Diggs started the tape playback of the song recorded by the Drug Company for this week's show. It was a spirited little song called *Everybody Loves A Clown* popularized by Gary Lewis and the Playboys. The studio gang applauded vigorously in appreciation of the boys rendition of the song. John accepted their compliments on behalf of the band, since Larry had mysteriously disappeared for the moment. Later, having noticed Larry was being a little more moody that evening, John went looking for his friend. He found Larry sitting alone in the recording studio. "What's up, guy?" he asked casually.

"Nothing," Larry said softly. "I was just thinking, John. Was it my idea or yours to play that particular song?"

"I don't recall," John said. "I think it was just one of those songs we added by mutual agreement. It's a nice song, and it fits our style very well. Don't you agree?"

"I guess," Larry replied. "I hadn't thought about the words before tonight."

John knew what Larry had on his mind. "She still gets to you, doesn't she?"

Larry looked at John and chuckled. "Yeah, she still gets to me. Here it is, over a year later and I still don't know why. All I know is I get so tired of seeing her with other guys. Frank was bad enough, seeing I was the one who introduced them. That even got in the way of anything ever developing between Sally and me."

"I know," John said sympathetically.

"I don't know what to think about this one. He strikes me as bad news. Give me your honest opinion, John. Is it just me? What do you think of him?"

"It's hard to say, Larry," John replied. "I can't think of anything bad I could say about the guy. I can't think of anything good, either. He was just in the right place at the right time, I guess."

"Do you suppose I might be that lucky someday?" Larry asked rhetorically.

"I think you could make your own luck any time," John replied honestly.

"I wish I had your confidence, John," he sighed.

John could see the sadness in his friend's eyes, but there was nothing he could say to comfort his friend other than the words he had told him time and time again. "I can understand if you don't feel comfortable with telling her your feelings out of the blue. But if you want to be with her, then you'll have to tell her sometime. Jump on the first opportunity that comes along!"

Larry nodded his head and sighed once again. "I suppose you're right, John. Unfortunately, I don't think that opportunity will come along tonight." After a brief pause, he took a deep breath, then suggested, "I guess we'd better go give Sam a hand. She can't run this show all by herself, doncha know."

John grinned, "I wouldn't be too sure about that!"

Thursday, April 4, 1968
Eve Of Destruction

Larry was in a state of shock listening to the news on the television, wondering how this could happen in America. The only comfort he found came from the statement made by Bobby Kennedy.

Ladies and Gentlemen: I'm only going to talk to you just for a minute or so this evening, because I have some very sad news for all of you – Could you lower those signs, please? – I have some very sad news for all of you, and, I think, sad news for all of our fellow citizens, and people who love peace all over the world; and that is that Martin Luther King was shot and was killed tonight in Memphis, Tennessee.

Martin Luther King dedicated his life to love and to justice between fellow human beings. He died in the cause of that effort. In this difficult day, in this difficult time for the United States, it's perhaps well to ask what kind of a nation we are and what direction we want to move in.

For those of you who are black – considering the evidence evidently is that there were white people who were responsible – you can be filled with bitterness, and with hatred, and a desire for revenge. We can move in that direction as a country, in greater polarization – black people amongst blacks, and white amongst whites, filled with hatred toward one another. Or we can make an effort, as Martin Luther King did, to understand, and to comprehend, and replace that violence, that stain of bloodshed that has spread across our land, with an effort to understand, compassion and love.

For those of you who are black and are tempted to be filled with hatred and mistrust of the injustice of such an act, against all white people, I would only say that I can also feel in my own heart the same kind of feeling. I had a member of my family killed, but he was killed by a white man. But we have to make an effort in the United States, we have to make an effort to understand, to get beyond, or go beyond these rather difficult times.

My favorite poem, my favorite poet was Aeschylus. And he once wrote:

> *Even in our sleep, pain which cannot forget*
> *falls drop by drop upon the heart,*
> *until, in our own despair,*
> *against our will,*
> *comes wisdom*
> *through the awful grace of God.*

What we need in the United States is not division; what we need in the United States is not hatred; what we need in the United States is not violence and lawlessness, but is love and wisdom, and compassion toward one another, and a feeling of justice toward those who still suffer within our country, whether they be white or whether they be black.

So I ask you tonight to return home, to say a prayer for the family of Martin Luther King – yeah, it's true – but more importantly to say a prayer for our own country, which all of us love – a prayer for understanding and that compassion of which I spoke.

We can do well in this country. We will have difficult times. We've had difficult times in the past. And we will have difficult times in the future. It is not the end of violence; it is not the end of lawlessness; and it's not the end of disorder.

But the vast majority of white people and the vast majority of black people in this country want to live together, want to improve the quality of our life, and want justice for all human beings that abide in our land.

Let us dedicate ourselves to what the Greeks wrote so many years ago: to tame the savageness of man and make gentle the life of this world. Let us dedicate ourselves to that, and say a prayer for our country and for our people.

Thank you very much.

It was already getting late, but Larry knew he had to talk to his friends. He placed the calls to each of the other members of the *Four Musketeers*, finding them in much the same state of mind as he. They agreed this was not the time for them to talk. That time would come Saturday afternoon when they could get together, and give each other the comfort and reassurance they all needed. At least they knew they were not alone with their fears, uncertainties, and doubts. There were many troubled minds seeking the relief that sleep could bring only temporarily that night.

Monday, April 22, 1968
April Come She Will

John was not normally interested in school sports, but this was something different. His little brother, Jimmy, had surprised everyone by trying out for, and actually making the varsity baseball team. Now a sophomore at SFA, Jimmy was not expecting a lot of play time this season, probably seeing only spot duty as a pinch hitter or base runner, but he was on the team, and very excited about it! Naturally, his parents and big brother, John, were almost as excited as he was.

It took a lot of effort for John to talk his friends into coming that afternoon. While Sam did not have any conflicts, Larry normally worked at the computer center during the afternoon. But Larry recognized the significance of this event immediately upon seeing the look in Jimmy's face, and requested the time off from work.

Getting Julia to come had been slightly more difficult. Larry was the quickest to understand her problem. Her current boyfriend, Bill, was unable to come with her, and she was hesitant to attend an event where two former boyfriends were sure to see her. Jimmy would be there, as would Frank Sutherland, a star member of the baseball team. In the end, Larry had taken her aside and convinced her to come along with the gang. "Julie, you can't spend the rest of your life avoiding old boyfriends, doncha know."

"I just don't think I'll feel comfortable," she tried to argue. "I know each of them has a new girlfriend, but it might still be a little awkward, don't you think?"

"I understand a lot better than you think," he smiled. "Has it occurred to you Frank's sister, Sally, will undoubtedly be there, also? Can you imagine how awkward I'm going to feel when she doesn't even recognize me, much less remember we went out together a few times last year?"

"Don't be silly!" Julia giggled. "Of course she'll remember you!"

"Which one of us is being sillier?" he chuckled. "Come on, Julie. I need you to protect me from Sally. John, Sam, and I will protect you. I'll *always* be there to protect you whenever you need me – don't you ever forget that! Besides, there's even the possibility they won't notice you're there! It's spring, after all! Don't you know in the spring, a young man's fancy turns once again to thoughts of baseball?"

"Is that so?" she giggled. "I always heard it was something else. OK, I'll come."

"That's my girl!" he told her, wishing to himself there was more truth to that statement than reality wanted to support.

The *Four Musketeers* were sitting in the bleachers cheering Jimmy and the rest of the high school baseball team who took a lead in the first inning. "Hey, guys!" Larry said showing a little excitement. "I just noticed they're selling snow cones at the concession stand. I haven't had one in years! Would anyone like to join me?"

"Why?" Sam grinned. "Are you coming apart once again?"

"Cute, Sam," Larry snarled. "Do you want a snow cone or not?"

"No, thanks," she replied. When Julia started to speak, Larry noticed Sam intercepted her. "There's no need for you to buy a snow cone for us girls."

"Suit yourself," Larry said offhandedly, wondering what mischief Sam was up to.

"I'll go along with you," John said. "I've been trying to remember how long it's been since I had a snow cone. I think I was in Little League baseball at the time!"

"You're right," Larry grinned. "Maybe that's why I want one so bad. Let's go!"

Larry and John wandered off to the concession stand while Sam and Julia whispered to each other about something. When the boys returned, the girls were in a giggly mood. "What did I tell you, Julia?" Sam snickered. "Larry got a lime snow cone, and John's is cherry, the same flavors they always get."

"I happen to like lime snow cones," Larry frowned. "What's the big deal?"

"Me, too!" Sam grinned, "but I think I'd rather have cherry today. Are you guys going to share, or am I going to knock your blocks off like when we were kids?"

"You said you didn't want one!" Larry protested.

"So I changed my mind!" Sam laughed. "It's a girl's prerogative to change her mind, after all. Hand it over so I can get a bite!"

"Jeez!" Larry sighed, handing the snow cone to Sam.

Sam took a small bite out of Larry's snow cone and grinned at him. "What about you, Julia? Have you changed your mind, also?"

"They look better than I thought they would," Julia replied.

"Which do you prefer? Lime or cherry?" Sam asked.

"I think I want lime," Julia answered.

"You could have told us before we left to save us a trip!" Larry complained.

"Oh, there's no need for you to go back," Sam replied, handing Larry's snow cone to Julia. "I don't want a whole snow cone. I'll just share a little of the cherry one with John, and you and Julia can share the lime one. Is that OK with you, Julia?"

"Sure!" she giggled.

"But..." Larry tried to protest.

"Sit down and shut up," Sam ordered. "Come sit by me, John, and give me a bite of your snow cone unless you want me to beat you up like I used to do all the time."

"Girls!" John sighed.

"No shit!" Larry replied, acting disgusted, even though he was actually delighted with the prospect of sharing his snow cone with Julia. "You can't live with them..."

"Yeah, so get over it," Sam laughed.

The game was not even close. Bryan's star pitcher had an outstanding afternoon, giving up only three scattered singles in a complete game shutout. Jimmy made a brief game appearance, playing right field in the top of the last inning, catching a high fly ball for the final out of the game. The players on each team congratulated each other, then retired to their respective locker rooms to change into street clothes. The *Four Musketeers* remained in the stands to wait for Jimmy's triumphant return.

They were a little surprised when they were greeted by the familiar voice of Sally Sutherland. "Hi, guys! Long time, no see!"

Larry was the first to answer. "Hi, Sally. Nice to see you again."

"It's nice to see you, too, Larry," Sally smiled sweetly. "Hey, Julia! Hey, Sam! Hi, John! I guess the guys all came to see your little brother. I'm glad he got to play for a little while, anyway. You guys all know Betty, right?" She referred to the other senior class cheerleader, Betty Simpson.

"We're in choir together," John announced. "Hi, Betty!"

"Hi, John," Betty smiled. "Hi, Sam, Larry! Good to see you again. Hi, Julia!"

"Watch out for that one," Sally grinned. "She just might steal your boyfriend away while you're out there working your ass off as a cheerleader!" Seeing the shocked look on Julia's face, she quickly added, "I'm just teasing, Julia! How are you and Bill getting along these days?"

"We're doing OK," Julia answered sheepishly.

"I've been listening to you guys on the radio," Betty smiled. "You sound better and better all the time!"

"Thanks, Betty," Larry said. "We'll keep doing it as long as people appreciate it."

"Then you'll probably be doing it for a long time!" Betty said smiling brightly.

"You ought to get Larry to take you up to the radio station one of these nights," Sally said. "It's actually a lot of fun!"

"I remember you telling me how much fun it is," she said, looking at Larry expectantly.

"Hello!" Larry chuckled. "I may be dumb, but I'm not stupid! I certainly recognize a great opportunity when I see one! Betty, I'd be delighted to take you to the radio station if you happen to be free some Saturday night. And since there's no time like the present to start begging, let's go for the gold! Might I be so lucky you'd like to come with me this Saturday?" He made a grand bow before her as he asked this question, drawing a giggle from all of the girls.

But the best surprise of all was her one word answer. "Sure!" she said brightly.

Larry was so surprised, in fact, he was not prepared to proceed. "Uh, really? I mean... Wow, that's great! The show runs from 8:00 until 11:00. Should I pick you up around 7:00?"

"Sounds perfect!" Betty smiled.

"I hate to break this up, but we gotta run," Sally said. "It's great to see you guys!"

"Great to see you guys, too," the *Musketeers* agreed in unison.

Betty hung back for only a second when Sally moved away. "I'll be seeing you guys again this Saturday. See you later, Larry!" she added brightly before she trotted away to catch up with Sally.

There was a momentary silence while the gang watched the two cheerleaders depart. "Oh, shit," Sam said trying to sound disgusted. "He's got a date with another cheerleader. Stand back, Julia. You remember what happened last time. His head's going to start swelling any minute!"

"I think something else might start swelling first," John teased.

"Oh, thanks, John!" Larry said, trying to make it sound like a snarl. He tried to give Sam a dirty look as well, but could not maintain it when he saw Julia giggling at him. *Why does the sound of her laughter affect me so? Or is it the green stain on her lips she got from the snow cone we shared? It matches the color of her eyes!*

Thursday, May 30, 1968
School's Out

Larry was the first to confront John working his way through the crowd in search of his parents and friends. "Congratulations, my man!" he said hugging his friend without embarrassment.

"Thanks," John said simply. "Now I know how you felt last year. I never would have thought this would mean so much to me."

"I hear you," Larry smiled. "Come on and follow me. I know where your family

Thursday, May 30, 1968 – School's Out

and the rest are waiting." Larry worked his way through the crowd once more, with John in close pursuit. Moments later, they found the others searching the crowd in anticipation of John's arrival.

"There he is!" Mary Myers all but shouted. "Oh, congratulations, John. I'm so proud of you at this moment I think I might just burst!"

"Aw, mom," John hugged his mother. "It looks like the dams in your eyes have already burst. Take it easy, OK? It's not that big a deal. People graduate from high school every year."

"But our son doesn't graduate from high school every year," Bill Myers said with a laugh that did little to conceal the choke in his throat. "Congratulations, son!"

"Thanks, dad," John said sincerely. He and his father exchanged a handshake, followed by a hug.

"Congrats, Bubba," Jimmy grinned.

"Thanks, kid," John smiled. "Like I was telling Larry a moment ago, now I know how he felt last year. Today I am a man!"

"That's something you should have said on your thirteenth birthday," Mr. Jacobson chuckled. "Congratulations, John!" he said offering his hand. The handshake was quickly changed into a hug.

"Congratulations, John," Mrs. Jacobson smiled as she bypassed the handshake and went directly for the hug. "We're all very proud of you today."

"Congratulations, John," Julia smiled sweetly, the next in line to offer John a hug.

"Thanks, sugar," he grinned. "And thank you, too, Mr. J, Mrs. J!"

The Bristols were next in line. "Congratulations, John," Josh added.

"Thanks, Mr. B," John grinned as they shook hands.

"We're all very proud of you, John," Lena said hugging the young graduate.

"Thanks, Mrs. B," John said. "The best part about all this is it's finally over!"

"Until September, anyway," Gayle Kronkite laughed. "Congratulations, John!"

"Did you have to remind me?" John laughed. "Thanks, Mrs. K!"

"Congratulations, John," Sam added.

"Thanks, doll!" he grinned. "Do you guys think we could get out of here? I'd like to get this hot robe off!"

"Jeez, John," Larry exclaimed. "Didn't anyone explain you're not supposed to wear any clothes beneath your rope?"

"I recall seeing shoes, socks, and pants sticking out beneath *your* robe last year," John fired back.

"The shoes and socks were real," Larry grinned, checking out the grins on the faces of the others. "The pants were a complete fake, however, nothing but a few inches of material where I cut off the legs from an old pair of suit pants. Above that, I was naked as a jaybird! It was especially kinky when I walked across the stage to get my diploma. Didn't you notice how excited I was? I'm sure everyone else did!"

"Oh, bullshit!" John said as the others snickered. "I suppose Sam was naked under her robe, too!"

"I sure was!" Sam giggled, drawing even more snickers. "I was wearing nothing but a pair of shoes and some nylon stockings held up by a couple of garters!"

"Why do you think Sam and I hugged each other so many times?" Larry laughed. "And why do you think we hugged all the other graduates so much? We were all feeling each other up, man! I've never gotten to second base so many times in my whole life! Why don't you go hug some of your classmates and feel for yourself!"

"I think your little joke has gone far enough, guys," Bill grinned. "John, this is an old joke last year's graduates like to play on their younger friends. It's been going on since dirt was invented. They just want you to try and feel up one of your female classmates so they can watch her slap the crap out of you!"

Larry exclaimed, "No, we really *were* naked under our robes last year, right Sam?"

"That's right!" Sam grinned. "We're your *friends*, John! Would we lie to you?"

"Damn straight, you would!" John laughed.

Sunday, June 2, 1968
You're Going To Lose That Girl

It seemed to Bill this Sunday afternoon was *never* going to end! Sunday afternoons were a great time to drive out some lonely country road, find a nice private spot to park, and do some serious making out with your girlfriend. *But every Sunday afternoon is taken up by these damn guitar practices!* Bill could never get Julia to go out for more than a few minutes on Sunday night. Being a school night, there just wasn't enough time to get anything going! Saturday nights were almost as useless, with all but a few minutes eaten up by that damn radio program she insisted they go to. He would try to get in a little serious necking after the program, but time would always run out before things got hot enough to go for the good parts.

Thank God for Friday nights! On Fridays, Bill had the time he needed to make his moves. He had worked patiently for months, and a few weeks ago, his patience was finally rewarded! Now that he had cracked that nut open, he wanted to spend a lot more time doing the deed. School was finally out, summer was here, meaning he could spend a lot more time with his girl. There was no reason they could not go out *every* night. They could even go out every afternoon, for that matter! His plans were to start getting it on Monday, Tuesday, Wednesday, Thursday, *and* Friday. The arrival of summer meant Sunday night even loomed as a real possibility!

It was Sunday. *If only this damn guitar practice will ever come to an end!*

"What do you say we call it a wrap, John," Larry suggested around 6:00. "My fingers feel like they've been cut to shreds and are going to fall off any minute! I need to put on a fresh set of strings."

"Me, too," John agreed. "At least we're getting enough from the parties and other gigs to *pay* for all the strings we're going through!"

"They're not *that* expensive, are they?" Julia asked.

"Three to four bucks a set," John explained. "Larry, I wonder if some brands might last longer. I wouldn't mind paying five bucks if they lasted twice as long."

"We ought to check that out," Larry agreed. "I'll do a little independent research. Why don't you ask the guy at the music store. Maybe he'll tell us the true story, rather than some song and dance just to get us to buy the more expensive strings."

"Sounds like a plan!" John smiled. "Hey, guys! I'm thinking about stopping on the way home to celebrate my graduation a little more. Anyone want to join me?"

"Join you?" Sam giggled. "Why should we? Are you coming apart, too?"

"Cute, Sam," Larry grinned. "Count me in, John! How about it, girls?"

"You don't have to twist my arm!" Sam laughed. "What about you guys?"

"What do you think, Bill?" Julia smiled.

"I was kinda hoping we might spend a little private time together," Bill replied.

"Well, OK," Julia smiled to him. "But count me in for next time. OK, guys?"

"You're on, Julie," Larry smiled. The thought of her spending "private time" with Bill, or anyone else for that matter, cut him like a knife, but there was nothing he could do but soldier on, ignoring the pain. "I guess it's just the three of us, guys. Let me step inside to say goodnight to Mr. J and Mrs. J, and I'll be ready to leave."

"Don't you think we'll all want to do that on our way out?" Sam grinned.

Julia gently pushed Bill's hands away for the third time since they had parked the car and gotten comfortable. "What's the matter, doll?" he asked her.

"When you said you wanted to spend a little private time together," Julia replied, "I didn't realize this was what you had in mind. I thought maybe you were going to take me to a movie or something."

"You'd rather go to a movie than make out?" Bill asked.

"Sometimes," she replied. "Sometimes, all I want is to cuddle up and look at the moon and stars. Don't you like that?"

"Of course," Bill smiled. "I thought that was what we were doing!"

"We're not exactly looking at the stars," Julia giggled. "Can't you just hold me?"

"Oh, OK," Bill agreed.

Julia leaned back in the seat and looked through the windshield at the bright half moon shining down on this warm early summer night. Bill stopped pressing his advances momentarily and was looking at the stars with her. After a few moments, he turned his head back towards her, to nibble on her neck and fondle her ears with the tip of his tongue. "Stop that," she giggled.

"It sounds like you like it to me," he chuckled, pressing his attack a little further.

She actually did like the little tickling sensation on her neck and ears, and turned her head towards him to reward him with a kiss, hoping it might slow down his advance a little. His return kiss soon invited an open mouth response, which she granted. Moments later, she felt his left hand slip down from her shoulder to caress her breast. She quickly attempted to clasp his hand with her own. He eluded her grasp, and returned his caress to her breast.

"Can't we just cuddle tonight?" she pleaded gently.

"Oh, come on, baby doll," he said. "It's the first weekend of the summer, a beautiful night, and we're here all alone. Let's have some fun. Let's fool around, just like we did the other times. OK?"

Julia was not very happy about those "other times". She let Bill talk her into going parking during their Friday night dates, and his advances had slowly gotten more forward. Once she let him get to second base, it was much more difficult to stand her ground. It *was* exciting to feel his hands on her breasts, or caressing the cheeks of her backside as they wallowed together on the back seat of his car! It had been mostly curiosity when she let him unbutton her jeans, and especially when he encouraged her to unbutton his. When his fingers had found the gold between her legs, she was much too excited to protest very much, particularly since she was caressing his middle leg with her own fingers! It had been the first time she had ever seen a penis, much less touched one. She was fascinated, especially by how sensitive it seemed to be.

Their activities that first night had resulted only in some mutual masturbation. She saw with her own eyes what happened when a boy had an orgasm. Fortunately, the hot, sticky liquid he produced went all over his own jeans, rather than hers. But the next time, things quickly became a lot more intimate as she gave in to his repeated urging. They lay on the back seat of his car, and she allowed him to slip his swollen organ inside her. She was grateful it went in smoothly and painlessly. It was very exciting! Seconds later, when his passion exploded with the full force of its fury, she was grateful she insisted he wear one of those rubber things. Afterward, she was disappointed that he seemed to lose interest in her for the rest of the date.

They had repeated this activity twice more, once on each of the subsequent Friday nights. There was little difference between the first time and the last time. In fact, the only difference was he began pleading with her to let him put it in without wearing the rubber, "just for a moment or two". There was no way she was *ever* going to give in to *that* request! Here they were once more, and he obviously wanted to do it again. Undoubtedly, he would want to do it again and again all summer long. She wanted to know if there was any way to slow this all down a bit.

Is this all there is to it? she wondered. The buildup to the event was more exciting than the event itself, which never lasted more than a few seconds. It was exciting, but as far as pure physical pleasure went, it did not live up to her expectations. Julia had learned a lot from her friends, who giggled about such things during those slumber parties they used to have. Similarly, she had learned how to give herself pleasure when she really wanted it, and frankly, that was more pleasurable than actual sex had been! She considered asking her mom some questions. *Maybe I'm not doing it right.* Unfortunately, even though really close to her mom, she felt too embarrassed to ask her things like that! She had given up her virginity far too easily, and now had regrets. How could she ever explain to her mom? *Maybe I should talk to Sam. She's older and, no doubt, a lot more experienced in such things. Surely Sam could help me understand!* "But I don't feel like fooling around tonight," she said, thinking this sounded reasonable. "Do we have to do it every time?"

"Not every time," he countered. "We didn't do it last night, for instance."

"You wanted to. You told me so! The only reason we didn't was because there wasn't enough time!" Julia had been relieved the previous night, realizing she needed to think about this some more.

"Whatever the reason, the fact remains we didn't do it. Don't you know that guys *need* to do it more often than girls? That white stuff starts building up, and it gets more and more painful as the pressure grows. I made the sacrifice for you last night. Won't you make the sacrifice for me tonight?"

"I'll play with it if you want," she suggested. "I know you like that!"

"But that only helps for a little while! How about giving me a blow job?"

At first, she was sorry she had suggested anything at all. But as she thought about it, she realized maybe this was exactly what she was looking for – a way to get through this without allowing him to penetrate her again! Even though she had never tried it, she was not opposed to the idea of oral sex. In fact, the thought of it was somewhat intriguing to her. "Well... if it'll make you happy."

"Now you're talking!" he grinned. "Should I get it out for you?"

"I think I'd rather do it myself!" she grinned. *He certainly is eager enough!* Julia had enough basic knowledge of the technique to get started. From there, she figured she could watch his reactions to determine which things were good and which were not so good. Tentative at first, she began with some simple kisses. She found the taste a little unpleasant, imagining it similar to sweaty undergarments sprinkled with urine. She almost laughed to herself realizing *why* such undergarments might taste that way! She wondered how often a guy would wash it!

She was determined to go through with this. Fortunately, she found the taste did not linger nearly as much as she had feared. Becoming braver, she gently licked it, exploring different parts and noting which drew the biggest reaction from him. The biggest reaction of all came when she placed the tip of it in her mouth, sucking it gently like a lollipop, slowly stroking it to simulate the act of intercourse. Almost immediately, Bill let out a moan and grabbed her head, holding it in place while he thrust his hips in and out to enhance the pleasure of his climax.

Julia fought to suppress the gag reflex as he plunged more deeply than she wanted. On top of that, there was suddenly a new flavor. Her mouth was filled with a hot, thick liquid, undoubtedly the same liquid she had seen before. The flavor was not especially unpleasant, mostly salty with starch and protein. The primary source of her unhappiness was she had not been given any choice in the matter.

Bill was now content to take her home. They drove in near silence, in spite of her attempts to engage him in a meaningful dialog about sex or any other subject. The silence gave her time to think. There was a pattern to this. She realized his primary interest was in getting her to service his sexual desires. *Once he gets what he wants, he doesn't have much interest in me. And this is what he wants me to do all summer long?* When they arrived home, Julia opened her own door and slipped out of the car, as was her custom. They walked side-by-side up the sidewalk to her front door.

"Goodnight," he said, moving to kiss her goodnight. "I'll see you tomorrow."

"No, I don't think so," she said softly, not accepting the offered kiss.

"Is something going on tomorrow?" he asked.

"Nothing out of the ordinary," she answered.

"Then I'll see you tomorrow," he repeated.

"No, Bill," she said more directly. "You won't."

"I don't understand," he said.

"You won't see me tomorrow. I don't *want* to see you tomorrow. I also don't want to see you the day *after* tomorrow. I don't want to see you next weekend. To be honest, I don't want to see you again at *all*."

"What are you talking about?" he asked.

"I'm not stupid, Bill," she said calmly, "even though I've done some stupid things. I hope you're satisfied. You got what you wanted from me. I can't take it back, no matter how much I wish I could. There's one thing for sure – I don't have to give anymore. It's finished. Goodbye, Bill."

The last word she heard him say was an astonished, "But..."

Saturday, June 8, 1968
The Sound Of Silence

"Happy birthday, John," Larry said softly as he stepped into his friend's house.

"Thanks, man," John replied just as softly. "The others are in the living room."

The *Four Musketeers* sat and watched as events unfolded on the television screen. Only two months after the world had been plunged into madness by one murder, they suddenly learned the world had been plunged into that same madness yet again. On the screen, Ted Kennedy finished the eulogy for his brother, Bobby.

> *My brother need not be idealized, or enlarged in death beyond what he was in life, to be remembered simply as a good and decent man, who saw wrong and tried to right it, saw suffering and tried to heal it, saw war and tried to stop it.*
>
> *Those of us who loved him and who take him to his rest today, pray that what he was to us and what he wished for others will some day come to pass for all the world.*
>
> *As he said many times, in many parts of this nation, to those he touched and who sought to touch him: "Some men see things as they are and say why. I dream things that never were and say why not."*

Silence descended onto the room as the *Four Musketeers* fell into quiet, personal reflection. Sam was the first to break that silence. "I'm so sorry all the inhumanity and injustice inherent in the world has to spoil your birthday, John," she said sadly.

"That's just the way things are in this world," John replied softly. "The one thing I'm certain of is if he were here, he'd want us to carry on with our lives, with our hopes and dreams. There are still men of good will left in this world, even though that number has been reduced once again."

The foursome looked into each others' faces silently asking the question Julia voiced aloud, "What do you think is going to happen now?"

"There's going to be a lot of wheeling and dealing at the Democratic Convention," Larry replied. "I doubt any of us will be happy with the outcome. I imagine a lot of others are going to be unhappy, as well. Frankly, I'm scared shit-less!"

"I'm hip to that!" John said shaking his head.

After John's birthday party, the gang headed for their cars to split up temporarily. It would be only a couple of hours before they would gather once again to produce the next edition of the *Top Forty Showcase*. "See you guys tonight!" Larry waved slipping into his car and pulling away from the curb.

Sam and Julia waved to him. "Thanks for giving me a ride, Sam," Julia said when the girls got into the car and headed for Steep Hollow.

"Anytime," Sam smiled.

"Could I impose on you once again?" Julia asked.

"Of course, Julia! What can I do for you?"

"Could you give me a ride to the station tonight? Bill isn't going to get to come tonight." When she thought about it, the potential double meaning of that sentence tickled her. Her grin was a little more than she intended.

"No problem," Sam said casually. "I'll swing by at 6:30 and we'll go grab a bite."

"You'll hardly get home before you have to come right back out again," Julia noted. "I hate to be such a bother. Why don't you wait for me while I take a quick shower, and I'll just go with you now. It'll save you one trip, at least."

"OK," Sam smiled. "Say, why don't you grab your pajamas and a change a

Saturday, June 8, 1968 – The Sound Of Silence

clothes for tomorrow, and stay at my house tonight. We girls haven't had a chance to have a sleepover in a long time. It'll be fun!"

"That's a great idea!" Julia said enthusiastically. Even though she was content with the action she had taken on her own, she still wanted a chance to have a talk with Sam. This sounded like the perfect opportunity! "Are you sure your mom won't mind?"

"Are you kidding?" Sam laughed. "Mom will go nuts over the idea!"

"I don't want to be a bother," Julia smiled.

"It's settled," Sam stated flatly. "I'll call her from your house while you shower so she can vacuum the house, paint the front room, re-shingle the roof, and still have time to bake us some cookies!"

"You're a bad girl!" Julia giggled.

"It takes one to know one!" Sam giggled in return.

Larry noted Julia came to the station that night with Sam. When Julia gave the simple explanation Bill was "not going to come that night," he accepted it on face value, in spite of the curious grin Julia wore as she said it. When two of his three best friends explained they were planning to have a sleepover after the show, he was sorely tempted to start begging them to let him join! Discretion being the better part of valor, he resisted that temptation, not only since he knew they would flatly reject his offer, but because it would probably make his date, Betty, a little angry with him!

Sunday, June 9, 1968
The Birds And The Bees

Sam and Julia were having a great time. To their delight, they found one of the Houston television stations was running an all-night marathon of cheesy monster movies. Gayle Kronkite watched the movies with the younger girls as long as she could, but eventually grew so tired she could no longer keep her eyes open. She excused herself and retired for the night. The girls teased each other and laughed not only about the movies, but about any other subject that happened to come up.

All except one. Sam noted Julia would quickly change the subject whenever there was any mention of Bill. It was such an obvious exception Sam soon realized her younger friend wanted very much to talk about that particular subject, only she was not sure how to bring it up. Sam tried an indirect approach. "It sure is nice to see Larry with a girlfriend once again, even though it's just a casual relationship neither of them is taking very seriously. Don't you agree?"

"Yes," Julia agreed, "even though we *both* know the one he really wants is you."

"I wouldn't be too sure of that," Sam chuckled. "He's just lonely, and since we've been friends for such a long time, he thinks I'm the one who can cure his loneliness. But there are plenty of girls who could cure that loneliness if they just wanted to."

"Like Betty?" Julia suggested.

"Well, I don't know whether she's the cure he needs or not," Sam smiled, "but at least she keeps his mind occupied for now, so he doesn't think too much about other girls, like you and me!"

"Like you, anyway," Julia smiled. Sam was paying careful attention to see how Julia would react to her suggestion, but Julia obviously had other things on her mind tonight. "Sam, why is it you and Larry have never gotten together at all? I mean, the two of you just seem so natural together."

Sam had to let her suggestion slip by without further comment. In the end, Larry would have to find his own way to let Julia know his feelings for her. She hesitated to collect her thoughts before answering Julia's direct question. "I guess the main reason is for a little over three years now, I've been seeing someone else. I know it's easy for you to forget since none of you have met him."

"He's a real guy, right, Sam?" Julia asked. "I mean, he's not just some imaginary lover you use as an excuse to keep Larry and other guys at bay, is he?"

"No, Julia," Sam answered softly. "Donald is very real. Someday soon, I hope you'll all get the chance to meet him. He's a wonderful man, and I love him very dearly. So will you and the others. He has his own set of ideas, of course, some of which may not quite agree with mine and those of my friends, but he's very honest and sincere, and best of all, not judgmental of others who happen to see things differently than he does."

"He certainly sounds like a wonderful man, Sam," Julia agreed. "You're very lucky to know two wonderful men like that."

Sam was pleased to hear Julia say this. "Both of them would be thrilled to know you felt that way about them," Sam said softly, knowing one of those men would be more thrilled than the other. "Even though you and Donald have never met, I've told him all about you and my other friends. He'd be just as happy to hear you say that as Larry."

"So how is it you two never got together *before* you met Donald," Julia asked.

"In a very real sense," Sam explained, "we *did* get together. We're together now, and we love each other very much. We're just not *in* love with each other. Does that make any sense to you?"

"Not really," Julia admitted.

"I guess it's not easy for others to understand the true nature of our relationship," Sam sighed. "We share each others' secrets, each others' hopes, and each others' dreams. In fact, the only thing we don't share is our bodies. We're not lovers in the physical sense, yet our relationship is just as meaningful and intimate as that enjoyed by those who *do* share their bodies."

"But you and he have never..." Julia began.

Sam laughed. "He would tell you a gentleman doesn't talk about such things."

"I know!" Julia giggled nervously.

"But fortunately, I'm no gentleman!" Sam said with a giggle of her own. "I'm a very, very naughty girl, and I'll be happy to talk to you about such things! The sad part of this story is there's nothing to tell. Larry and I have never done the nasty!" She started laughing, then added, "What I mean to say is, we've never done the nasty with each other!"

Julia giggled at her joke, then hesitated before asking the obvious, "Why not?"

"I think we knew if we ever got started, we'd never want to stop," Sam giggled. "Now, I know what you're going to say even before you say it, Julie! What would have been so bad about that? Am I right?"

"Exactly!" Julia giggled.

"I'll never tell!" Sam laughed. "That's for me to know and you to find out!"

"You're a very naughty girl!" Julia said, joining in with her own laugh.

"Guilty as charged!" Sam grinned. "Let me remind you it takes one to know one."

"I guess you're right," Julia said, obviously lost in her own thoughts.

Sam could see Julia was still arguing within herself, trying to build up her courage to open a discussion of some other subject. The indirect approach was not working. After a moment of silence, she decided to take a very direct approach. "It's rather obvious to me you have something on your mind you want to talk about," Sam said softly. "Am I going to have to drag it out of you?"

Sam waited patiently as Julia hung her head, trying to hide her embarrassment. "Yes, there's something I'd like to talk with you about. It's very personal, but I could really use the benefit of your experience." Julia raised her head and looked Sam in the eye. "I've done a very stupid thing, Sam."

"We all do stupid things from time to time, Julia," Sam said reassuringly. "I wish I had a nickel for every stupid thing I've ever done!"

"Maybe not *this* stupid," Julia replied sadly. She hesitated before asking her question. "Sam, would you be willing to share some information with me? Would you be willing to tell me what it was like the first time you... Well, what I want to talk about... is sex."

Sam was suddenly overcome by a panic attack. "You've done something stupid and it has to do with sex? Please don't tell me you're pregnant! Are you late?"

"No! It's not that!" Julia exclaimed in her own panic attack.

"Are you sure?" Sam asked.

"Yes," Julia said confidently. "I started my period yesterday afternoon. That was the main reason I was so anxious to go home, take a shower, and change clothes."

"That's a relief!" Sam responded. After a moment, Sam began to smile again as her panic subsided. "So you want me to tell you about sex? OK, well first, the bee comes to the flower to collect some nectar," she explained holding up the index finger on her right hand. "When he gets to the flower," she continued, holding up her left hand, making a circle with her thumb and forefinger, "he puts his little stinger into the flower like this." She demonstrated by inserting her right forefinger into the circle on her left hand. "Then he rubs it in and out like this," she giggled as her actions matched her description, "and before you know it, he squirts a little honey out of his stinger, the flower drops seeds on the ground, and we get a bunch of baby flowers!"

"Cut it out, Sam!" Julia laughed. "I know all about the birds and the bees, and how you convince the stork to deliver a baby."

"Could you explain the stork bit?" Sam giggled. "I never quite understood that."

The girls shared their laughter for a few moments. Obviously a little more relaxed, Julia came to the point of her concerns. "Sam, I really don't have too many questions about sex as in reproduction."

"Ah! You're looking for pointers dealing with *technique!*" Sam grinned.

"Maybe," Julia said shyly. "What I want... What was it like your first time."

"You want to know about my first sexual experience?" Sam asked playfully. "Well, let's see. When I was a kid, about eight years old, I think, there was this boy I knew. He and I were about the same age, and we played together all the time.

"One day," she giggled, "we decided to play doctor, and I got a really good look at his little stinger. In fact, I examined it *very* thoroughly! In hindsight, I'd have to say it was really cute, although not actually extraordinary. Even before I touched it, it stood up tall and proud and I thought it was going to burst! Maybe it would have if I had touched it a little more, but I didn't know about that sort of thing at the time.

"He was just as curious about me, of course, wanting to know everything about the differences we could both see so clearly. Just as I had been delighted when my touches tickled him, he was equally delighted to discover the places that tickled me so nicely when he touched *them*. That's how I learned about the physical nature of a boy and his little friend, and how he learned about the physical nature of girls."

"It sounds kind of sweet," Julia smiled, "in a perverted sort of way, I guess."

"I don't think it was perverted," Sam smiled, "but I'd agree it was very sweet."

Julia's expression changed as she proceeded. "But that's not the sort of thing I meant. I want to know about the first time you actually did the deed."

"Oh, I see," Sam smiled. "That boy and I were too young to actually do the deed, as you say, but I've always thought of that as my first sexual experience." She decided it would be best for her to lay low for the moment, rather than pressing Julia why she was asking these questions. Seeing Julia wanted a serious discussion, she also resisted the temptation to make any more light-hearted responses. "OK, I'll come clean. I'd rather not name names, but other than that... What is it you really want to know about it?"

Julia hesitated to gather enough courage to proceed. "I guess to start with... Well, did you... Did you enjoy it? You know what I mean, don't you?"

"I know what you mean," Sam smiled, pausing for a moment. "The first time, I'd have to say yes and no. I didn't see fireworks, or feel the earth move, if you catch my meaning, but I did enjoy it, just not as much as I had expected."

"Have you always enjoyed it?" Julia asked quickly.

"I'll interpret that to mean you want to know if it got better the next time," Sam smiled. "To that question, I'd have to say yes. I can't say it's always been wonderful, but on the other hand, I can't say it's ever been bad, either. I think the amount of enjoyment you get depends on a lot of things, like the setting, your mood at the time, and of course, the mood of your partner."

"Did the boy enjoy it?" Julia pressed for more information.

"Boys *always* enjoy it!" Sam laughed. "It doesn't matter to them whether you're in the back seat of a car, in some romantic bungalow, or lying on the beach listening to the surf under the moonlight. As long as they get their cookies, they're happy." Both girls giggled a little, but Sam could see Julia was expecting more. "The truth is *some* guys care about those other things a great deal. The good ones are the guys who also want *you* to enjoy it, and at least try to make sure you get *your* cookies!"

Julia turned her head and looked at Sam sideways. "Really?" she asked.

"If they don't at least try, they're not worth keeping," Sam giggled. "Julia, I have to say you're starting to worry me a little. It sounds to me like you think I have a lot more experience than I really do. Sure, I talk dirty, and I tease about sex with my close friends, especially you, Larry, and John. But I don't go around boinking every guy I see, and I hope you don't think I'm the kind of girl who does!"

"Oh, I didn't mean to imply anything, Sam!" Julia explained quickly. "I just assume you have more experience than me, that's all."

"Maybe I do," Sam smiled, "and maybe I don't! I learned a long time ago the quiet little innocent types like you, the ones nobody would ever suspect, are the ones doing it the most! So why don't you tell me about *your* experiences. I can tell you have something on your mind, anyway. I'm willing to bet you're not asking these questions out of idle curiosity! Tell me about *your* first time. Did you enjoy it?"

Sam watched as Julia's face blushed with embarrassment. After a nervous laugh, she began to answer the question. "Did I enjoy it? I guess so, Sam, but it was nothing at all like what I expected. I mean, the lead up was exciting, but the actual deed itself left a lot to be desired."

"And probably didn't last very long," Sam smirked as she nodded her head, "like maybe thirty seconds?" When Julia shrugged, she attempted a different number. "Fifteen seconds?" Julia shrugged again. "Five seconds?" Sam asked.

"I couldn't exactly use a stop watch," Julia said shyly.

"That might be considered a little tacky!" Sam giggled. "Was it his first time?"

"I don't think so," Julia answered. "In fact, I'm pretty sure it wasn't. I take it from your reaction you'd expect it to last longer?"

"Absolutely!" Sam answered, perhaps too quickly. She paused momentarily to control her reactions before continuing. "Look, Julia, a guy without much prior experience is probably going to get a little overly excited, and might not last as long as he should. That's natural. Was there a second time, and did it last a little longer?"

"I didn't notice it lasted any longer," Julia answered, "and not the third time, either. Is it possible I'm just not doing it right, Sam?"

"Don't go blaming yourself. Do you think he's trying to make it last longer?"

"How could I tell, Sam?" Julia asked shyly.

"Do you talk about it after?" Sam asked. "Has he asked if you've enjoyed it?"

"He doesn't want to talk much afterwards," Julia said meekly.

"That's not uncommon either," Sam noted. "Have you tried different things?"

"What sort of things are you talking about?" Julia asked.

"Like maybe different positions," Sam suggested. She quickly realized this was unlikely. "Never mind that. I guess if you've only done it three times, you couldn't have tried very many different positions. Have you tried having oral sex?"

"Yes," Julia hesitated, "but I don't think I'm ever going to enjoy that very much."

"Really?" Sam asked. "I've *always* liked that. Why didn't you like it?"

"Well, it was OK at first," Julia replied, "but to tell the truth, it didn't last much longer than the regular way once he got going. I was just surprised when he held on to my head like that, and I almost gagged when he squirted that stuff in my mouth."

"I see," Sam said, shaking her head a little. "That's not exactly what I meant, Julia. What I was asking was if he tried giving oral stimulation to you!"

"Oh," Julia said, looking embarrassed again. "No, he didn't. I thought that was something girls who only like other girls did with each other."

"No, Julia, that's not something only girls do to each other," Sam said thoughtfully. "In fact, if guys did that more often, then there'd probably be a lot fewer girls who only liked other girls!"

"I see," Julia said. "To be honest, Sam, I did it just because he wanted to do it the regular way, and I wasn't in the mood."

Sam looked at her friend and shook her head a little stronger. "Julia..." she started, but then paused once again. After a moment, she worked up her courage. There were some things she needed to say to her young friend, but was afraid they might not be well received. After all, it could easily be construed as interfering in something that was none of her business. She soon convinced herself the things she needed to say were too important. "Look, Julia, I know we agreed we wouldn't be naming names, but surely you realize it's not too difficult for me to guess who you're talking about. You might not appreciate the things I'm about to say to you, but I hope you'll forgive me. You're too good a friend for me to keep quiet about this."

"Tell me what's on your mind, Sam," Julia said. "I really need your help to validate the things I've done, and confirm the things I think I should do."

Sam nodded her head. "Julia, there are only four reasons I can think of to cause it to be over that quickly, and not one of them would be your fault. It sounds to me like the reason you didn't enjoy this experience is completely *his* fault, not yours. Sex should always be enjoyable, and as long as each person sharing the experience cares about the feelings of the other, then it always will be.

"It's possible, but rather unlikely, he might have some sort of physical dysfunction, and should seek medical help. He could just be inexperienced and gets overly excited, but that would mean it should last a little longer the second time, and even a little longer the third. You seem to think he has some prior experience, so you'll have to decide that possibility for yourself. Now even if he does have prior experience, he might not know he should be trying to make it last longer for your benefit. Some boys don't even know girls have orgasms, and those who do might not know girls need more, or perhaps different stimulation than boys do. That's why it's important to talk about these things. Sex is a very intimate experience, and it should be easy to talk about it with someone you've experienced it with.

"To be honest with you, the story of your oral experience leads me to a very different conclusion. The most likely reason he hasn't tried to make you enjoy it more is he simply doesn't care whether you enjoy it or not. Unfortunately, there are boys out there who're interested only in their own pleasure. They figure they'll get theirs, and it's *your* responsibility if you want to get yours! I got the impression he held your head while he simply fucked your mouth, and unloaded his man goo without regard to what you wanted. That's not merely impolite, Julia, it's demeaning, and tells me he has no regard for your feelings at all. To him, you're nothing more than a receptacle he can stick his cock in for his own personal pleasure.

"You'll have to decide what you want to do for yourself," Sam looked directly into Julia's face, "but if a boy treated *me* that way, I'd get rid of him. If I was gracious enough to give him oral sex only to be treated like that, there's a good chance I'd cut his balls off, and I certainly wouldn't hang around to let him do it to me again!"

After a brief pause, Julia began to speak. "Thanks, Sam. Maybe my intuition was right. You have, at least, confirmed one thing for me. While I didn't cut his balls off, you'll be happy to know I broke off that relationship last Sunday night."

"Good for you!" Sam smiled. Her first thought was, *How am I going to pass this news to a certain someone I know who'll be interested without revealing too much?* While she knew he would be thrilled to learn Julia's relationship with Bill was over, she doubted he would be thrilled to learn the reason.

Julia's expression, however, told Sam the conversation was not over. "How did you feel about it a few days after your first sexual experience?" Julia asked next.

"I felt like I was ready to try it again," Sam smiled.

"Can I assume you eventually broke up with that boy?" Julia asked. "How did you feel about it then?"

"Ah!" Sam said, nodding her head. "I get the picture. You want to know how I felt after giving my cherry to some guy who was no longer in my future, am I right?" Julia's expression was almost as if she was pleading for an answer, although the nodding of her head was the only physical acknowledgment of Sam's question. "How do you think I felt? I was pretty confused. On one hand, I was happy to have taken a significant step in growing up. On the other hand, I felt ashamed, like I should have waited until Mr. Right came along so he could have been the one to pop my cherry."

"That's exactly how I feel!" Julia said sadly. "I feel so cheap, Sam. I feel like everyone is looking at me and whispering behind my back. I feel like everyone is going to start calling me names, and thinking I'm a bad girl!"

Sam could see Julia was now on the verge of tears. "Well, the first thing you need to do is relax and forget about that sort of thing! Giving up your virginity is a significant event in your life, but it doesn't signal the end of the world as you've known it. You'll find the world still goes on exactly as always. People won't start whispering about you behind your back, and they won't be showing your picture on the evening news. It's not like anyone will be able to tell you're no longer a virgin just by looking at you. In fact, you and he are the only ones who'll know, unless you decide to tell someone."

"What about when Mr. Right comes along?" Julia asked. "Isn't it obvious to a boy whether a girl is a virgin or not?"

Sam tried not to laugh. "No, at least not from anything physical. He might guess you're not a virgin if you act like a whore. On the other hand, there are whores who get paid extra because they can act like a virgin! How would he know?"

"I guess I knew that," Julia admitted. "I just wanted to make sure."

"Besides, Julia," Sam grinned, "I thought you were a liberated woman, like me. That old double standard doesn't apply! Should a guy expect his bride to be virgin when she can't expect the same of him? Do you expect Mr. Right to be a virgin?"

Julia shook her head and smiled, but clearly she was still worried. "I'm worried my mom can tell," she said softly. "I haven't been able to look her in the face for almost a month! She's going to be so disappointed in me!"

"You ought to talk to her about this, Julia," Sam repeated. "If you can't trust your own mom, then who *can* you trust? She may not be as disappointed as you think."

"It's not that I don't trust her, Sam," Julia said unhappily. "We've talked about sex before. I'm just ashamed! I don't know if I can face her and admit what I've done!"

"Then let's talk about that part of it. First, you shouldn't be ashamed. Sex is a natural biological function, just like breathing, eating, and drinking. You were going to try it eventually. Everyone does! Your experience isn't that different than others."

"Sex doesn't seem the same sort of thing to me," Julia argued. "If you don't eat, drink, or breath, you die! Have you ever heard of anyone dying from lack of sex?"

"No, I haven't," Sam giggled, "but I've known guys who *claimed* they would. On the other hand, while one can survive on nothing but bread and water, would anyone be happy with such a diet? Just like food and water, our minds and bodies are programmed for sex once we reach puberty. It's almost incredible how powerfully sex influences the way we live every moment of our lives. It affects who we are attracted to, who we fall in love with, who we'll share our lives with. Just look around you in the natural world, Julia. Sex is the primary driving force of life. Plants, animals, and humans are all driven by a powerful urge to merge. You've felt it yourself, so you know how powerful it is!"

"But there's a time and place for everything," Julia countered, "including sex."

"I definitely agree with that," Sam nodded, "but have you noticed people seem to have a whole lot of different ideas about the appropriate time and place for sex? Are you ashamed because you think you should have waited until you were married?"

Julia obviously stopped to think about her answer. "I remember asking my mom a very similar question once."

"And what did she tell you?" Sam asked simply.

"She put it back on me to decide for myself," Julia noted. "The one thing I remember the most was she said it'd be very difficult for her to find fault in two people expressing their love in that way, married or otherwise."

"I said something like that a little earlier tonight," Sam noted. "Sex is always best when the people truly care about each other. Doesn't her answer tell you something else? Doesn't it tell you this is strictly a personal decision? Doesn't it tell you your mom trusts you enough to know you'll make the right decision all on your own?"

"That's my problem!" Julia replied. "I don't think I *did* make the right decision!"

"Why is that?" Sam asked.

"Because I don't love him," Julia answered, "and he doesn't love me."

"But you liked him, right?" Sam asked.

"Yes," Julia said softly. "I liked him."

"OK, now we're getting somewhere," Sam smiled. "You're ashamed because the hormones in your body influenced you to do something your mind doesn't approve of, because days after the fact, your heart realizes you aren't going to stay with this guy for the rest of your life. Is that it in a nutshell?"

"I hadn't thought of it that way," Julia said, "but yes, I guess that's right."

"Can you remember what you were thinking at the moment?" Sam asked. "Just as he was about to slip it in the first time, your body was obviously screaming, *'Yes! Yes!'* What was your mind saying? What was your heart saying at that moment?"

Julia was lost in thought for a few moments. "Looking back on it now, everything seems to be blurred, but I remember thinking I cared about him a lot more than I previously thought. In my heart, I guess I blinded myself, thinking of him as the boy I see in my dreams all the time."

"So at the time," Sam concluded, "your body, your mind, and your heart all agreed it was the right thing to do?"

"I guess so," Julia said softly, "but they were wrong. I can certainly see that now."

"I'm not saying it was the right thing to do," Sam smiled. "I'm only trying to convince you not to be so ashamed of what you did. You thought it was right at the time. If you now think it was a mistake, the only thing you might rightly be accused of is a lapse in judgment. Think of it this way – it's like you missed one of the questions on an exam. That doesn't mean you flunk the whole course, does it?

"Chalk it up to experience, and try to make a better decision next time. That boy you see in all your dreams is still out there. Don't you think he also sees you in all his dreams? Everyone makes mistakes. He's probably made similar mistakes himself. Maybe he wants to find his dream girl so badly he fools himself into thinking he *has* found her." Sam smiled to herself knowing how much this statement applied to a certain someone she knew. "Hold on to your dreams! One of these days, you'll find each other." Her smile faded slightly as she realized this second statement was more of a hope and a wish than a solid fact.

Sunday, June 9, 1968 – The Birds And The Bees

"When he does find me," Julia said pointedly, "I won't be so pure anymore."

"He'll realize you've made mistakes while you looked for him," Sam assured her, "just as he'll see the mistakes he made looking for you. And because of all of the mistakes he made, he'll appreciate what a treasure he's finally found, and he'll love you all the more, just as you'll treasure him. The important question has *never* been who was the first. The only important question, Julie, is who will be the last!"

Sam had carefully chosen to call her by the nickname only one other person used. She was a romantic who believed in the power of suggestion. She hoped the realization she now saw in Julia's eyes included that suggestion. Regardless, she knew she had found the right words to help her dear friend. The thanks she would now receive were wonderful, but completely redundant. "Bless you, Sam!" Julia said as her tears began to flow. "You told me all the things I needed to know."

"You're welcome, Julia!" Sam smiled. "Do you know what's even better? Now that you've gotten rid of your problem, you're footloose and fancy free to go looking for that dream boy again!"

"Maybe I've even gotten a jump start on that!" Julia smiled softly. "For the last few months, this other guy has been calling me from time to time, wanting to take me out. I've always turned him down, but he happened to call me again last Monday, after I'd broken up with Bill. We went out Friday night for the first time."

"I see," Sam said forcing a smile to hide her disappointment. "What's his name?"

"Ed," Julia replied. "Ed Doggett. He even asked me out again next weekend."

"I'm happy for you, Julia," Sam smiled again. She now knew the actual news for her dearest friend was not the news she wanted to bring him after all. *It would be better not to take this news to him at all. He'll learn on his own soon enough.* She knew the disappointment would be very difficult for him to take, but at least she would be there to encourage him to keep faith in his hopes and dreams.

"He seems like a very sweet guy," Julia smiled, "and so far at least, he's been a perfect gentleman. That's good, because I'm not likely to let him or anyone else into my pants anytime soon! Not until I'm very sure of my own feelings as well as his!"

Tuesday, July 2, 1968
For No One

When Lena brought out the cake, John led the gang in song:
> *Happy birthday to you.*
> *Happy birthday to you.*
> *Happy birthday, dear Larry.*
> *Happy birthday to you!*

Larry smiled at each of his friends, then blew out the nineteen candles. "Thanks! I really don't know what I'd do without you guys."

"Well, for one thing," John laughed, "you'd eat a lot more of this cake!"

"I probably would at that!" he said as the others joined his laughter. The *Four Musketeers* were determined to make this a happy day. Other than John's graduation and a few other minor personal victories, the first half of 1968 had been a dismal year, and they all wanted to kick off the second half on a high note even though none of them held any great expectations the world was suddenly going to cure its ills.

They gathered at Larry's house without dates. John was not seeing anyone on a regular basis anyway, and Sam's boyfriend was, as always, mysteriously unavailable. They had previously met Julia's newest boyfriend, Ed, who was out of town for the upcoming Fourth of July weekend. The only response they got from Larry when asked about Betty was, "She couldn't make it. She had other plans."

After the "official" party at the Bristol house, the gang moved to their favorite site out in the country to continue their celebration with some traditional fireworks. They decided to save most of the big stuff until Thursday, so for today, the fireworks consisted mostly of a few firecrackers, some bottle rockets, and smoke generators. The smoke generators, of course, were of a homemade variety containing no gunpowder at all, intended to be inhaled, rather than admired visually.

Julia noted Larry seemed even more interested in the smoke generators than usual. "Are you trying to get yourself stoned today?" she grinned at him after he had taken a heavier than normal hit.

"Why not, Julie?" he laughed. "If a guy can't get stoned on his birthday surrounded by all his best friends, then when *can* he get stoned?"

"You have a good point!" she giggled. "OK, I'll make sure you get home safely."

"That's not really necessary," he said.

"But that's what friends are for," Julia added sweetly.

She was happy to see him react to her comment with such a smile. "Friends are also for singing to each other. I picked out your voice when you guys sang *Happy Birthday* to me. You sing very nicely, Julie!"

"Oh, I can't sing!" she giggled.

Larry shook his head and smiled at her. "Everyone can sing, Julie. Maybe some voices sound better than others, but a song comes from the heart, not from the throat. The more heart going into the song, the better it sounds in the throat, doncha know."

She could not miss the odd look in his eye as he seemed to stare at her. "Is something bothering you, Larry?"

He shook his head unconvincingly. "No," he said even more unconvincingly. With a smoke induced giggle, he added, "It's my birthday. I'm surrounded by my best friends, smoking some great weed. What could possibly be bothering me?"

Sam had been listening to this conversation on the sidelines and took this opportunity to jump in. "I don't suppose you could be disappointed Betty couldn't make it because she had other plans on your birthday, now could you?"

He nodded his head gently and grinned. "I suppose I could have been, but I'm not. I've gotten pretty used to that sort of thing, doncha know."

"What sort of plans did she have today, anyway?" Sam pressed.

"Come to think of it," he chuckled, "I don't think she ever actually told me."

Julia caught Sam's eye, thinking this sounded a little fishy, and could see Sam was having similar thoughts. "What was it she actually said to you?" she asked.

That odd looked returned to his eyes. "She said something about going to Galveston with Dick today."

"Who's Dick?" Julia wanted to know.

"Dick's," he grinned, looking around as if he had made a joke.

"Huh?" Julia asked giving Sam a bewildered look.

Sam flashed a grin at Julia, rolled her eyes, and clarified the confusion by rephrasing the question. "Larry, I think she wants to know who Dick is?"

"Oh!" he giggled. "Sorry, Julie, I misunderstood. I thought you wanted to know... Oh, never mind. Dick is this other guy she's been going out with. You guys knew our relationship wasn't exclusive, right?"

"I hadn't given that much thought," Julia replied. "Didn't she know today was your birthday? I mean, couldn't she have gone to Galveston with this Dick tomorrow?" As she thought about her own question, she saw the joke and started giggling. The smoke generators always made jokes a lot funnier than normal.

"It's about time you got the joke!" he laughed. "She knew it was my birthday, but this dick has been wanting an exclusive relationship with her, and she was afraid coming to my birthday party might make her dick mad. She's decided to have an exclusive relationship with this dick!"

"Clear enough," John grinned. "I have a question. What's this dick's name?"

"Dick," Larry laughed.

"So this Dick is now Betty's favorite dick?" John laughed.

"How could I possibly know that?" Larry asked as he fought to contain his laughter. "Anyway, John, we shouldn't talk about such things with ladies present, doncha know."

"Oh, please!" Sam giggled. "You don't have to talk about it, Mr. Lawrence Jackson Bristol. I know you very well, enough to know a lot about your relationship with her. For example, I can tell you never did her. If you'd dipped your stinger into that little flower, you'd be a lot more upset about this situation than you seem to be."

"I'll neither confirm nor..." Larry started but could not contain his laughter.

The rest of the gang joined in. Even as she laughed, Julia wondered, *Is Larry truly no more upset about this than he seems, or is he exercising that bravado of his, laughing it off as if it means nothing to him, trying to hide how hurt he is inside?* One look at Sam's face told her she was not the only one pondering this question.

"You don't have to be so bitter about it, Larry," Sam said. "Your friends are still here to help celebrate your birthday."

"I'm not bitter, Sam," he shrugged, "and I appreciate you guys more than you'll ever know. As far as Betty goes, I knew it was a temporary thing from the beginning. She and I had some good times, but she found someone she likes better, and it's over with us. I wish her the best."

Saturday, August 31, 1968
The House Of The Rising Sun

Just before the *Top Forty Showcase* went on the air, the gang got into a conversation about why one of their members was absent that night. "Don't you think Mr. J is overreacting to all this?" Sam asked.

"Yes," John replied angrily, "but on the other hand, I'm not sure I really blame him. To tell you the truth, after what we just saw in Chicago, I'm not sure *anyone* is safe on the streets of this country anymore, not even here in Bryan, Texas!"

"I think you're both overreacting," Larry nodded sadly. "It would be perfectly safe for Julie to join us tonight since no one around here is going to challenge the 'establishment' and give Mallory or any of the other local Nazis reason to go around cracking heads and arresting people. Bryan is probably a safe place for all the good little sheep being led around by their noses. There won't be any 'trouble' here."

"We could *do* something about that," John replied. "Have you noticed we're sitting in a radio station, and will soon have access to live microphones?"

"I understand what you're suggesting," Larry cautioned, "but I think it'd be very ill advised, John. For one thing, I suspect we'd get less than fifteen seconds before that red phone rang and Diggs would be forced to kill the microphones. We'd be off the air in a flash and never get a second chance. What could we say in fifteen seconds to wake these people up to what's happening in this country?"

"We have to do *something*!" John insisted.

"I know how you feel," Larry said as he shook his head, "but I think we can do better than that. As you've pointed out, we already have some influence over the others in our age group. I think we ought to hold onto that influence for another time, a time when we can make the most of it."

"He's right, John," Sam agreed. "I think we should just zip our lips and wait. What do you think will happen next, Larry?"

"God only knows, Sam!" he sighed. "There'll be more riots all over the country before anything gets resolved. Assuming a revolution doesn't cancel the election, I'll predict Tricky Dickie will win an overwhelming victory next November."

"Oh, Christ!" John exclaimed.

"Do either of you truly think it'd make any real difference if Humpty Dumpty won?" Larry asked, glancing back and forth between John and Sam. When neither of them responded, he continued with a chuckle, "Look on the bright side, John. At least we'll finally get to learn all about this 'secret plan' of his to end the war! I don't know about you, but I'm stoked just thinking about the possibilities!"

"You're so full of shit it makes me want to puke!" Sam chuckled.

"Trust me!" Larry said as he held up both hands in a "V" for victory sign. He shook his head to make his jowls flap as he added, "I am not a crook!"

Whenever someone called the station while the program was on the air requesting to speak directly with one of the key players, it was customary for such calls to be rejected. The helpers were asked to explain that person was not available while the show was on the air. If the caller wished, they could leave their name and number, and that person would call them back at their convenience. This policy attempted to discourage all the pointless calls from girls around the age of thirteen or fourteen, who wanted to speak to those dreamy boys in the Drug Company. Normally, it was enough to do so, and very few callback requests were actually taken.

When one of the helpers answering the phone lines handed Larry a note, he was quite surprised. "Who the hell is this? John, have you ever heard of Nichol Ball?"

"I don't think so," John replied. "Was one of our little groupies actually brave enough to leave her name and number?"

"More than that," Larry said. "It says she wants to invite us to a party."

"Just what we need!" John laughed. "A party where we're surrounded by little girls blowing kisses, mixed with bubblegum, and screaming their fool heads off while we try to make some music."

"What was that name again?" Sam asked.

"Nichol Ball," Larry shrugged, showing Sam the name on the piece of paper.

"Holy shit!" Sam said grinning from ear to ear. "I suggest you go call her back

Saturday, August 31, 1968 – The House Of The Rising Sun

right now! You'll *definitely* want to go to that party!"

"Why?" Larry asked with a blank expression. "Who is this Nichol Ball, anyway?"

"Nichol and her sister throw the hottest parties in town!" Sam replied. "They invite just about every girl on campus, especially all the incoming freshmen, and guys aren't allowed without an invitation. A girl can bring a date, but this is subtly discouraged. Instead, Nichol and her sister, Penny, send special invitations to all the hottest guys they know, and let me assure you they know them all! Most of the girls come to scope these studs out. And the guys get to meet just about every girl in school, especially the latest crop of coeds coming in for their freshmen year. You're being given a golden opportunity; most guys would *kill* for an invitation to those parties! More guys get laid at those parties than the rest of the year combined!"

"It sounds like something I might have a little interest in attending, unless I'm already busy that night," Larry grinned. "How about you, John?"

"I might be interested," John replied acting cool, "as long as I won't be out late."

"You guys are so full of shit it makes me sick," Sam laughed. "If you can't get yourself laid at one of *their* parties, then you might as well give up!"

"How do you know all this, Sam?" Larry asked.

If Sam had paid any attention, she would have seen the twinkle in his eye and known something was coming. "I went to the party they had last September. Incoming freshmen are essentially *expected* to go!"

"I see," he grinned. "And did you get laid or did you have to give up?"

At first, Sam was startled by this question, distracted by the excitement of telling the boys about these parties. She recovered quickly, however, and with her bright Agent 99 smile answered smoothly, "That's none of your business, buster!"

"What about poor Donald?" he fired back. "Is it any of his business?"

"Leave Donald out of this," Sam replied smartly.

"No, Sam, this is important," he smiled. "What I want to know is whether the girls are going to be saying, *'Oh, no, I already have a boyfriend!'* or if they might actually be open to someone new. You already had a boyfriend, but were you open to an advance from someone else?"

"I'm not going to tell you what I did at the party," she grinned, "but I'll tell you just about all the girls take *off* any rings they have when they get to the door. Whether or not they put them back on at the end of the night is another story."

"Thank you, Sam," Larry grinned. "That's exactly what I wanted to know. I'll go return her call and find out what this is all about. Wanna listen in, John?"

"He can't!" Sam stated. "We're shorthanded, and he's doing the next dedication."

"Then I'll be right back," Larry continued, still grinning. "Sorry, John!"

Larry went to a smaller, secondary studio where he could make the call in private. "Hello?" came the voice on the other end of the line.

"Hello!" he said with a friendly voice. "May I speak to Nichol Ball, please?"

"May I ask who's calling?" the voice requested.

"This is Larry Bristol. I'm returning her call."

"Oh! Hello, Larry!" came the response. "This is her sister, Penny. Thank you for calling us back so quickly. We've been very anxious to get in touch with you!"

"You're welcome, Penny," he said politely. "How can I help you?"

"As you might know, we're planning a party in a couple of weeks, welcoming all our friends back to school, and especially to welcome the incoming freshmen."

"Yes, I've heard of the parties you and your sister give," he said smoothly, neglecting to mention he had just heard about them a few minutes earlier.

"We're hoping we can talk you and your friend, John, into coming," she added.

"Why, thanks!" he said. "That's very nice of you. When is this party?"

"In two weeks, on the night of Friday the thirteenth," Penny giggled. "We're all hoping this won't bring anyone too much bad luck!"

"Friday the thirteenth has always been a *lucky* day for me, Penny," he chuckled. "Let me make sure I understand. I assume you're not inviting John and I to *attend* your party. You want the Drug Company to *play* for your party, am I right?"

"Both, actually," Penny giggled. "We've never met you guys, but you sound hot over the radio, so I bet you'd qualify! We're also looking for some entertainment, and we think you'd be perfect! You'll only have to play for a while. We'll pay for your musical performance, of course! The rest of the time, you're on your own, free to mingle with the other guests. As you know, there'll be lots of girls there, and I'm sure you'll make quite a hit! If anything happens, think of it as a fringe benefit!"

"I'll admit I'm intrigued," he chuckled. There was a brief conversation where Penny and Larry worked out the terms of the gig. The boys would entertain for a total of two hours, starting around 9:00. Penny offered a generous payment, which Larry accepted. "I'm curious. Where did you hear of us?"

"Nichol and I have listened on the radio for quite a while," Penny said. "Some of the local girls tell us you guys are hot! I'm looking forward to meeting you!"

"Well, I hope you won't be too disappointed," he laughed. "You know how sensitive we musicians can be at times!"

"I like sensitive guys," she giggled. "Don't be surprised if I pinch your ass!"

"I hope you'll wait until we aren't performing!" he laughed. "Otherwise, I'm liable to hit a high note I've never been able to reach before!"

"Ooh, now you've got *me* intrigued!" Penny giggled. "Listen, I know you need to get back to your program, and Penny and I have dates chomping at the bit to get going. Thank you for calling back so quickly. I'm looking forward to meeting you!"

"I'm looking forward to meeting you and your sister," he said, "and I'm also speaking for John. Thank you for inviting us. We'll see you on the thirteenth!"

"OK, Larry," she said. "Goodbye for now!"

"Goodbye!" He smiled to himself after hanging up the phone. This whole thing sounded like a dream come true, and he could hardly wait to tell John and Sam. He stopped off at the water cooler on the way back to the main studio, more because he wanted to collect his thoughts and appear cool when he told them. The red light indicating the microphones in the main studio were currently live was on, so he waited outside as the latest dedication was announced.

"It's about damn time!" Sam said when he returned. "What's the story?"

"No surprises," he said trying to be as cool as possible. "I talked to Penny rather than Nichol. I'm invited to their big party on the thirteenth." As an afterthought, he added, "You're invited, too, John."

"Cool!" John said suspiciously. "Tell me something, good buddy. Are we invited to attend the party, or are we invited to entertain at the party?"

"Both, actually," he smiled. "Apparently, there are some local girls who think we're hot!" He outlined the terms of the agreement, including the generous amount they would be paid. "In addition, John, we're invited to mingle among the guests. Penny mentioned we might be able to pick up some fringe benefits."

"I can dig it!" John smiled.

"Don't worry," Sam said. "I'll go along to protect you so you won't be molested by any horny women."

"That's quite alright, Sam," John assured her. "We're college guys now. We know how to protect ourselves from horny women."

"No, John," Sam insisted. "It's much too dangerous. You'll need someone to protect you from what's sure to be almost certain temptation. I don't think you're ready to handle horny women!"

"God knows *I* am!" Larry laughed. "I love to handle women, especially horny ones! But you're quite right, Sam. You should come along and keep John safe."

"Oh, please," Sam said with mock disgust. "You're no better than he is. I'll have to work my ass off to keep both of you from getting into trouble!"

Larry, John, and Sam looked at each other and grinned. They all knew this was going to be an exceptionally good time, and a great opportunity for them.

Sunday, September 1, 1968
From Me To You

Guitar practice was at Julia's house. The boys were especially excited about their upcoming gig for the *Gamma Alpha Sigma* sorority. It represented one of the largest audiences for whom they had ever performed. After Sam explained the main object of this party, Julia also knew it would provide them with a great opportunity to meet new girls. She knew how lonely both of her friends were, and wished them success. Subconsciously, she felt a little pang of jealousy. Even though she had been dating Ed for three months now, and had a good relationship with him, every now and then she would remember the crush she had on Larry.

They spent most of the afternoon on the patio. While it was still quite warm, the worst of the summer was beginning to loosen its tight grip in central Texas, with afternoon high temperatures barely managing to break into the low nineties. There was a gentle breeze to keep things bearable, especially since a lot of puffy clouds kept providing welcome shade. In the direct sunlight, however, it was still somewhat uncomfortable, even for those used to this climate.

The boys finished their practice session a little after 5:00. John and Sam bid everyone a quick goodbye and left to help out with their families' plans for tomorrow's Labor Day holiday. Larry held back for some reason, however, seemingly thinking about something. "What's your family planning for tomorrow?" Julia asked him to make conversation.

"Nothing special," he replied.

Julia followed his eyes to see he was staring at a small hummingbird feeder her mother hung from a hook outside the family room window, overlooking the patio. "Do you like hummingbirds?"

He chuckled, breaking his gaze from the feeder and the two small birds seemingly arguing over which of them controlled the treasure it contained. He looked at Julia more directly when he answered, "Yes. I like them a lot. Do you?"

"I think they're very sweet," Julia said, wondering at the glow seemingly radiating from his eyes that afternoon.

"I'm surprised there aren't more of them. Julie, we're sitting right in the middle of their main migration route, doncha know. There are literally thousands of them traveling south right now, planning to spend the winter down in Mexico. A lot of them go all the way down to Yucatan, even flying great distances across open water in the Gulf of Mexico to get there. It amazes me something so tiny, spending so much energy it almost needs to eat constantly, can make such a journey."

"I didn't know they migrated like other birds," Julia said.

"Oh, yes," he smiled. "Most of the hummingbirds spending the summer in the United States will fly through here each fall headed for south Texas and Mexico. Then in the spring, they'll all come back through here on their way north."

"Let me go get mom," Julia said. "I'm sure she'd like to hear about this!"

"While you do, I'll put my guitar in the car. I brought something to give you!"

She smiled at him as they stood to go their separate ways. But Julia watched him in silence as he stepped around the corner of the house, carrying his guitar to his car. She wondered what he was bringing her. Or did he mean "you" in the plural sense? She smiled to herself and stepped inside to get her mother, figuring she would learn the answer to that question soon enough.

Larry was already in the backyard when Julia returned with Jessica. "What are you doing?" Julia called to him stepping across the patio.

"I know your birthday is still three weeks away, Mrs. J," he said, "but I thought if I was going to show you this treat, I should give your present to you now."

"You don't need to buy me a birthday present," Jessica smiled.

"Oh, the gift isn't anything I could buy," he grinned. "Let me put these up now, and in a day or so, the gift will come to you on its own!"

Julia and her mother exchanged a puzzled look. "Go ahead," Jessica said. "What are you doing, anyway?"

"I have three shepherd's hooks," he explained as he stuck one of the metal poles into the ground just beyond the edge of the patio. "I'm going to put them into a triangular pattern, and then I'm going to hang two hummingbird feeders from each."

"I don't have enough hummingbird food to fill all those," Jessica chuckled.

"All you really need is sugar and water," he smiled. "Don't worry. I even brought you a bag of sugar in case you're running low. If you'd be kind enough to bring me a solution of six cups of sugar in six quarts of water, we'll be all set!"

Jessica and Julia exchanged another puzzled glance and shrugged their shoulders. "But Larry, there aren't more than two or three hummingbirds around here. That's all that come to the feeder I've already got. Why do you think you need so many?"

"You'll see," he replied, his smile growing even brighter. "You really shouldn't use the nectar that comes with the feeders. It contains red food coloring. It probably doesn't do them any harm, but it isn't necessary. You'll find plain sugar water works fine without any coloring, and so why risk it? I know they claim it has some extra vitamins and nutrients in it, but trust me on this. The birds will get everything they need from the real flowers they'll drink from. What they need more than anything right now is a lot of energy. They have a long way still to go on their journey south."

"I'll go make the sugar water, mom," Julia said. She grabbed the bag of sugar out of the paper bag, noticing there were also six hummingbird feeders, just as he said.

When she returned, he had placed all three of the shepherd's hooks into the ground, and was taking the feeders out of their boxes.

"Thanks, Julie!" he smiled brightly. He placed a small funnel into the first feeder, carefully filled it with the sugar solution, and hung it from the first hook, repeating the process five times. In the end, two feeders hung from each of three shepherd's hooks. "Now, all you have to do is sit back and watch. In the morning you should mix up six more quarts of sugar water. I think you'll need it by this time tomorrow."

"You're joking!" Jessica said.

"No, ma'am," he grinned. "I'm not. Would you mind if I came back tomorrow afternoon? I want to see how y'all like your gift!"

"You can come back anytime you want," Julia smiled.

"Well, I wouldn't want to wear out my welcome," he said softly.

"You obviously think more hummingbirds will come now that there are more feeders," Julia said. "What makes you think so?"

"Like I told you," he answered. "We're right in the middle of the main migration route hummingbirds take when they go south for the winter. They start their migration in late August and early September. There are thousands of hummingbirds all around. Some of them are going to find these feeders. You'll see!"

"Well, OK," Jessica said. "We get two or three with one feeder, so with six, we'll get maybe a dozen or two? That'll be fun to see!"

Larry laughed merrily. "I'll see you guys tomorrow!"

As the sun continued its journey into the western sky, or rather as the earth continued its rotation, the faintest idea of dusk began to form in the minds of all creatures viewing it. Julia stepped to the back door to take a quick look at the hummingbird feeders, and a smile washed across her face. "Mom, come see this!"

Jessica stepped from the kitchen where she was preparing dinner. "What is it?"

"There must be a dozen hummingbirds out there already!" she said excitedly.

"Already?" Jessica asked. Her smile broadened when she looked out the window towards the triangle of shepherd's hooks supporting the feeders. "We should have known he knew what he was talking about! It'll be dark soon. I wonder if any more will come in during the night?"

Monday, September 2, 1968
(They Long To Be) Close To You

Shortly before lunch, the telephone rang. Lena dried her hands on a dish towel, and picked up the receiver. "Hello? Yes, just a moment. I'll go get him." She sat down the handset, and stepped down the hall to Larry's room. She could hear him working out the details for a new song he was trying to learn. When he stopped, she knocked on the door and announced, "There's a telephone call for you, Larry!"

"OK, mom!" he replied. Two seconds later, his door opened. "Who is it?"

"I think it's your friend, Julia," she answered.

"Oh?" he said, unable to conceal the smile forcing its way onto his face. No matter how much he wished it would be different, it was not an everyday occurrence for her to call him. It surely must be something a little unusual. His smile broadened when it dawned on him what that probably was this Labor Day morning.

"Hello?" he said as casually as he could manage. "This is Larry."

"There must be fifty or sixty of them!" Julia said excitedly.

"Fifty or sixty of what?" he said with a grin he knew she could not see.

"Hummingbirds!" Julia practically shouted. "There are so many of them we can't even make a good estimate! We had to refill the six feeders you put up early this morning, and it looks like they'll have them emptied again by mid-afternoon!"

"Didn't I tell you there would be a lot them?" he chuckled.

"Yeah, but we never thought there'd be this many!" she laughed. "Mom has been sitting on the patio all morning with a pair of binoculars, and she won't share. Even dad keeps looking out the back window. He just smiles and shakes his head. I don't think he can believe what he sees!"

"Well, you see, Julie," he said trying not to laugh, "that's the difference between being in town and being out in the country. These little guys are pretty skittish, and they don't like all the people and noise in town. If I put those feeders in my backyard, I wouldn't see half that many. Out where you are, where it's quiet and they feel safe, those feeders will act like magnets bringing them in. There might be even more later this afternoon."

"You've got to be kidding!" she giggled.

"Not at all, Julie!" he laughed.

"You said you'd come back this afternoon. What time are you coming?"

"I don't want to wear out my welcome," he said. "What time do you want me?"

"Oh, come now!" she pleaded. "Don't you know you'll always be welcome?"

Even over the telephone, he could see her smile in his mind's eye. It made him feel wonderful inside to know how excited she was, to know he had done something to bring her joy. "I hope that'll always be true," he said, as if it were a prayer. "I'm not doing anything important. I'll see you in a few minutes, OK?"

"OK," she said. "Bye!"

Larry returned the handset to its cradle and stood there silently for a moment. He enjoyed how it felt to make her happy. OK, maybe it was not the way he wanted to make her happy, but it was something, anyway. It was like an investment. With any luck, maybe someday he would collect some dividends.

"What's going on?" his mom asked him.

"I put some hummingbird feeders in their backyard," he smiled. "They seemed to be a little excited about how many hummingbirds have come to visit. She wants me to come see for myself. I'll be back later, OK, mom?"

Jessica could not believe her eyes. She sat on the patio, watching the little birds fluttering from feeder to feeder. Occasionally, something would frighten them, and they would scatter in different directions, usually taking refuge in the nearby trees. This was especially true when she and Julia went to collect the empty feeders, and again when they returned after refilling them. But just a few moments after the disturbance passed, back they would come as if nothing had happened at all.

She heard a car pull to a stop in the driveway, heard the door open and close, and watched as first Schotzy barked, wagged his tail, then ran to greet whoever it was. Jessica was not surprised when Schotzy returned moments later, running circles around Larry. Even though he never got very close to them, many of the birds scattered at this intrusion, but returned quickly when they decided he was no danger to them, and was keeping his distance. "Did you know this was going to happen?" Jessica asked with a bright smile on her face.

"I suspected it would, Mrs. J," he answered shyly. Julia came out the back door, once again briefly disturbing the birds as she ran up to Larry and gave him a hug. "Hi, Julie! I invited several thousand of my little friends to come visit you for a few days. I hope you don't mind too much."

"Not at all!" Julia and Jessica said, almost in unison. "Larry, I've talked to several other ladies about hummingbirds. They suggested I put out a feeder. They talked about getting two or three at a time, but none of them hinted at anything like this!"

Larry smiled as he began to explain. "I figure this is the difference between town and being out in the country. Those other ladies probably live in town, right?"

"Mostly," Jessica agreed, "but not all."

"Maybe you should invite them out to see for themselves," he grinned. "The ones who live in the country could get this many if they wanted, and the ones who live in town can be jealous! A long time ago, I noticed a big difference in the number of birds coming to my grandparent's house out in the country, and those in town. I found some books about hummingbirds when I was working in the library, and started studying. Like I said yesterday, we're right in the middle of their migration path, so there are literally thousands of them around.

"I figure most of them must avoid the towns and cities. There are too many things to disturb them in town. But out here, where it's quiet, and there aren't too many things to threaten them, they're going to be very attracted to a plentiful source of food like this. I don't know if this is true or not, but I also suspect they are less enthusiastic about the domesticated flowers people tend to grow in town. I suspect they prefer the wild, native plants more prevalent out here in the country."

"Won't this interfere with their migration?" Jessica asked. "I mean, if they find a good source of food right here, won't it tempt them to stay for the winter, rather than moving further south, like they're supposed to?"

"No," he smiled. "Most of them will make only a brief stop before they move on. Many of the birds stopping here yesterday have probably moved on already. Some will stay for a few days to build up their reserves, but they'll all move on eventually. Because there are so many coming down the migration path at slightly different times, it just appears they're staying longer. I mean, honestly, can you identify one individual hummingbird you keep seeing over and over?"

"No," she laughed.

"Well, especially not from way over here!" he grinned. "Put down those opera glasses, pick up a chair, and come with me!"

"But we don't want to disturb them!" Jessica tried to protest.

"It'll be OK," he smiled. "Sure, they'll scatter when we approach, but if we all just sit quietly, they'll come right back. It's OK to talk quietly, just don't make any sudden or exaggerated movements. If you do, they'll scatter, but once we get quiet again, they'll come right back."

"Are you sure?" Julia asked.

"Positive!" he answered with a confident smile.

Each of them carried a chair across the patio towards the feeders. Jessica and Julia assumed they would stop some several feet away from the feeders, but Larry insisted they keep moving. Finally, he had them set their chairs right on the edge of the patio, no more than six feet away from the nearest feeders, bringing all three of the shepherd's hooks into their field of view.

"This is too close!" Julia said. "They won't come back while we're here!"

"Yes, they will," he smiled. "Just sit quietly and wait. It won't be long at all."

Sitting to either side of him, Jessica and her daughter exchanged a glance, shrugged to each other, but followed his instructions. The threesome sat quietly, the girls not moving at all. "You don't have to hold your breath," he chuckled quietly.

"Thank God for that!" Jessica whispered. "Oh, there's one now!"

"Try not to be surprised by all the noise," he said softly. "They make a lot more noise than you'd think, especially when hovering nearby. It's more like a buzz than a hum, but aren't you glad we don't call them 'buzzing-birds'?"

"Sh!" Julia said unnecessarily. Her eyes widened as a few more of the little birds returned to the feeders. They were wary of the new visitors to their feeders, and at first, tended to congregate on the farthest ones. But over time, as the threesome sat quietly, they returned in numbers. Before long, there were several dozen of them, buzzing loudly as they moved from feeder to feeder, and emitting the little chirping sounds more like the squeaks from a mouse than what one might expect from a bird.

"This is unbelievable," Jessica whispered, unable to contain her excitement.

"These are ruby throats," he whispered. "See the bright red patch on their necks?"

"Yes," Julia said softly. "It seems to glow when the sunlight hits it!"

"They also have an iridescent green color on their backs," Jessica whispered.

"Yes," he agreed quietly, "but their breast feathers are rather plain. See how they fan out their tail feathers as they hover? I think the black and white stripes are almost as attractive as their ruby throats."

"Some don't seem to have any color on their throats at all," Jessica whispered.

"I think those are girls," he smiled. "The *boys* are the pretty ones in *this* species."

Julia returned his look with a grin, but her attention quickly returned to the swarm of little birds. They flew in and out around the feeders, jostling each other for the best positions. At times, they seemed like they were standing, make that hovering, as if in a queue, each bird waiting to take its turn at the feeders. Occasionally, some birds would get too close to each other, and one could hear their wings beating together. Every now and then, a more aggressive individual would break in line, temporarily increasing the noise level as the other birds fussed at the intrusion. Sometimes, two birds seemed to face off with each other, hovering inches apart as if in some kind of Mexican standoff.

When one of the birds flew close to Julia's face, clearly challenging her in one of those Mexican standoffs, her excitement proved to be too much. The little squeal of delight she let escape did not sound normal to the hummingbirds, causing them to scatter for the trees. "I'm sorry," she said sheepishly to the others.

"Don't worry," he chuckled. "They'll be back."

"I'm going to take this opportunity to run inside," Jessica announced. "Watching these little birds drink so much is making me thirsty. How about you two?"

"Please," Julia smiled to her mother.

"Yes, please," Larry agreed.

"OK, I'll be right back," she smiled. "You two enjoy yourselves."

After Jessica departed, Larry and Julia sat watching quietly as the birds returned. Julia's eyes were practically glued to the feeders. Larry found it difficult to take his eyes away from the look of wonder and awe so clearly visible on her face. But he knew better than to stare at her, and forced himself to watch the birds, looking at Julia only now and then, when he could no longer bear not having her in his sight.

The two of them spent the afternoon that way, sitting on the patio, watching the hummingbirds, whispering to each other to look this way or that. Jessica joined them much of the time. Even Julian took a turn sitting by the feeders, smiling to himself as he watched the little birds dance their little dance. But for the most part, he stayed out of their way, and had this strange habit of asking Jessica to do this or that for him, taking her away from the birds, and leaving Julia and Larry alone.

Larry decided he had scored a tremendous victory in this small battle. There was still one more feat of magic he could perform, and was sorely tempted to press onward, to maximize his winnings. But in the end, he decided to save that magic for another day, for a time when the situation was more desperate, or perhaps for a time when a decisive and ultimate victory in the war was in view. Just as one needed patience to enjoy these hummingbirds at such close range, he needed patience to fight the war where victory would mean the achievement of his heart's desire.

Late in the afternoon, as long shadows began to creep over the countryside and the sun began to drift downward towards the horizon, Larry reluctantly made his unhappy announcement. "I should go," he said using his code phrase.

"Do you have to?" Julia asked.

"No," he replied hesitantly, "but I should. It's getting late, and your mom will prepare your dinner before long. So will mine, no doubt, and tomorrow is another working day for guys like me. There's no rest for the wicked, doncha know."

"I wish you could stay," she said.

Those words nearly tore his heart into pieces, but he fought to maintain self control. "I wish I could, too," he forced a smile. "But there'll be other days like this." *Was that a statement of fact*, he wondered, *or just another prayer?* "Come on. I want to say goodbye to your folks."

She followed him to the back door. "Larry's leaving, mom."

"Won't you stay and have dinner with us?" Jessica asked.

"I appreciate the offer, Mrs. J," he smiled, "but my folks are expecting me to have dinner with them. Maybe next time?"

"I understand," Jessica said warmly. "Tell them we said hello, won't you?"

"Of course!" he said.

"Oh, and Larry," Jessica continued, "thank you so much for the lovely gift. Now I understand what you meant yesterday when you said the gift was something you couldn't buy, but would come on its own."

"Yes, ma'am," he said shyly. "I'm glad you like it."

"We *all* like it," Jessica assured him.

Larry wondered if the smile on his face was as big as the one on his heart. "They'll keep coming back for a couple of weeks, but sooner than you'd like, their numbers will begin to decline. There'll still be some on your birthday, Mrs. J, but probably not by Julie's. I guess it all depends on the weather. Next spring, start putting the feeders out in late February or early March, as soon as you think there won't be another frost. They'll stop on their way back north, and come again in the late summer in an endless cycle. At least, I hope mother earth will see to it the cycle is endless, in spite of all the things we humans do to make it doubtful."

Friday, September 13, 1968
Norwegian Wood (This Bird Has Flown)

It was to be a pool party. Penny and Nichol Ball, identical twin sisters and self-appointed officers of the *Gamma Alpha Sigma* sorority, were throwing a bash to celebrate the beginning of their junior year at A&M, welcoming back old friends they had missed over the summer, and making new friends of the incoming freshmen and other students transferring into A&M from various junior colleges around the state. The Ball sisters were well known for the parties they threw. "Big Daddy" Jim Ball was never short of funds, and whenever his "precious angels" wanted something money could buy, he seldom denied their requests.

Few of the male students at A&M could deny their requests, either. The twins were attractive, vivacious, and precocious. Combined with daddy's money and the allure of an affair with identical twins, it was easy to see why the girls were always in high demand, and usually got whatever they wanted from the men they encountered.

The girls jokingly referred to their closest circle of friends as the *Gamma Alpha Sigma* sorority. It was not an official organization of any kind. The name was based on a common expression used by students at A&M. When a student got unhappy about how school was progressing, he or she expressed those feelings by claiming to have a "give a shit" attitude. Before long, someone shortened this expression by using the initials, G.A.S., which was quickly shortened further into the single word "gas". It was common to hear someone on campus say, "I've got the gas today!" The key to understanding this statement is the inclusion of the word "the". There was quite a difference between "having gas" and "having the gas"! You tended to avoid people making the first claim, whereas you wanted to party with people making the second.

The Ball sisters printed up fliers inviting all of the female students to their party. They were allowed to bring a date, but otherwise males were not allowed without a written invitation from one of the "sorority officials". When the *Gamma Alpha Sigma* sorority threw a party, it was the hottest ticket in town. Any male lucky enough to be invited would meet the hottest of the new crop of coeds. And the girls came, usually without boyfriends, knowing only the hottest guys would be there.

It was a hot September evening, without much of a breeze. It would get cooler once the sun went down, but in the meantime, the boys were very grateful the sisters had suggested they dress in swimming attire, like the other guests. The boys decided to wear matching swimming trunks, teeshirts, sunglasses, and sandals. They had managed to acquire two teeshirts advertising Tang, the instant breakfast drink being used by NASA for the moon program. The shirts were bright orange in color, with the Tang trademark over a breast pocket, and an image of the product adorning the back. They modified the shirts by adding some iron-on lettering, writing, "I love tang!" under the pocket, and "Tang – Breakfast of Champions" across the back.

They arrived early to set up their equipment, immediately challenged by the bouncers hired by the *Gamma Alpha Sigma* sorority to keep uninvited males away. Fortunately, one of the bouncers recognized them and they were directed to the main courtyard surrounding the swimming pool in the middle of the apartment complex.

Several people were already milling around the courtyard, almost exclusively attractive females in skimpy bikinis. Larry and John exchanged a few glances, acknowledging to each other the thought they had struck the mother lode! Before they could reach the pool, they were greeted by a beautiful brunette wearing a brilliant smile and a hot pink bikini barely covering anything. "Hi! I'm Penny. You must be Larry and John."

"Hi, Penny!" Larry answered, trying not to stare at the bodacious tatas on display before his eyes. "I'm Larry, and this is my partner, John. Thanks for having us!"

"I've been looking forward to it!" she smiled. "It's nice to actually meet you."

"Nice to meet you, too," John managed without stumbling over his tongue.

"Where would you like us to set up?" Larry asked, grinning at his friend's rather obvious fascination with the feasts in front of his eyes.

Penny also noticed, and smiled even brighter. "Anywhere you'd like!"

Larry spotted a small alcove set back a short distance from the pool, up against a blank wall. "That looks like a good spot. We can place our speakers to either side and project the sound over the entire courtyard without having to turn up the volume to ridiculous levels. People who want to watch us can do so, and anyone who doesn't like what we do can go to the other end of the courtyard and get away from it!" he added with a grin.

"I don't think there'll be much of that," she giggled. "Go ahead and get started. I'll let Nichol know you're here."

"Thanks!" Larry said when she turned to go. He looked at his friend John, now gawking at her backside as it wiggled away. "If you can get your tongue back in your mouth long enough, John, let's go carry in the rest of our stuff!"

"Damn!" John said. "I may not be able to sing if the place is going to be crawling with babes like that!"

"Nervous?" Larry asked with a grin.

"You bet I'm nervous!" John replied. "Aren't you?"

"Not any more than usual," Larry answered truthfully. "Just remember what Mr. Austin taught us a long time ago, and imagine the audience is naked." As John stared at Larry, a big grin swept across his face. Larry looked around once again, admiring the views. "I hear you! I'm *already* imagining what they look like naked. Maybe that's not such a good idea tonight. Let's try to imagine them all fully dressed! Maybe that'll keep our minds on what we're *supposed* to be doing."

"I don't think I have that much imagination!" John said with a little whistle.

"Then go back to the van and get a grip on yourself," Larry teased. "I may need to do the same thing myself. Leave me a clean tissue, will you?"

"Very funny," John chuckled. "OK, let's go unload our equipment for now. Maybe we'll get lucky and unload ourselves later!"

"Aren't you superstitious, John?" he asked as they walked back to the van. "It's Friday the thirteenth! Do you really think you're going to get lucky tonight?"

"Ouch!" John said. "I forgot about that. Then why are you still smiling?"

"I've always had *good* luck on Friday the thirteenth!" Larry laughed. "If either of us is going to get lucky tonight, it's going to be me!"

"Can I have sloppy seconds?" John grinned. "I know beggars can't be choosers!"

"Only if you'll make me the same deal," Larry laughed.

They were completely unloaded after three trips to van. As they were positioning the amplifiers, speakers, and microphones, a beautiful brunette in a skimpy hot pink bikini and a brilliant smile approached them and said, "Hi!"

"Hi, Penny!" Larry replied. "We're almost set up."

"I'm Nichol," the girl grinned at him.

"Oh, sorry!" he said. "I thought... Jeez, you guys really *are* identical!"

"Not completely," she giggled. "My guess is you're Larry, and the guy with his tongue hanging out is John. Am I right?"

"That's right," he snickered. "You'll have to forgive him. His parents don't let him out of the cellar very often, doncha know, and it's not easy for me to handle him." He turned towards John and pretended to beat him with a whip. "Down boy! Mustn't touch the pretty lady! Easy, now!"

John gave Larry a disgusted look and rolled his eyes. "I'm John," he said bashfully. "*He's* the one you need to watch out for!"

"Oh, I don't know. He looks harmless enough," Nichol grinned, looking both boys over from head to toe. "I *love* those teeshirts! They'll be a big hit with the girls who understand the joke! Where did you find them?"

"We made them," Larry blushed. "If you really like them, you can have mine. We try not to do a joke more than once. All I ask is you wait until after the show."

"Baby," she said with a wink and a smile, "if I come looking for you after the show, I'll want a lot more off of you than that teeshirt!" She giggled at how Larry gulped at that suggestion, and how John's eyes nearly popped out of their sockets. "Some guys will be setting up a couple of kegs by the pool in a few minutes. Help yourself. If you guys need anything else, just let either me or Penny know."

"We will," Larry smiled. He shivered watching Nichol depart, her bottom wiggling in a way no living male could ignore. It was John's turn to laugh.

They finished their setup, then tested the equipment and sound balance by playing one song to the delight of the handful of people gathered to listen. It was a current hit by Simon and Garfunkel called *Mrs. Robinson*, the theme song to the movie *The Graduate* starring Dustin Hoffman and Katharine Ross, released the previous year. Larry knew John could really show off his guitar skills with this song, and since they planned to play it later during the regular performance anyway, he got John relaxed and loosened up by playing it now, in front of a life, albeit smaller audience.

They were pleased with the sound, and acknowledged the response from the small audience. They set the master power switch into standby, placed their guitars on stands, and walked to the pool to collect on the promise of beer Nichol had given.

While standing around the pool sipping their beer, they were joined once again by the beautiful brunette twins in their skimpy hot pink bikinis. "That was wonderful!" Penny said. "You guys are going to be a real hit if you play like that all night!"

"Thanks, Nichol," Larry said, discretely checking out her bodacious tatas.

"Actually, I'm Penny," she giggled, purposely bouncing them a little.

"Sorry," Larry laughed, trying not to stare. "You're going to have to wear name tags for me to tell you guys apart!"

"That would spoil the fun!" Nichol giggled. "We like confusing people. When we were back in high school, we'd sometimes switch dates right in the middle of the night. I don't think any of the boys ever figured it out, either!"

"If I'd been lucky enough to have such a date," Larry smiled, "I'm not sure I'd have said anything even if I *had* figured it out! The only thing better than being with *one* of you would be the opportunity to be with *both* of you!" He immediately recognized his mistake. *I meant* each *of them!* His Freudian slip was showing.

Penny caught the subtle implication. "Ooh! We have a live one here, Penny!"

"I though you said *you* were Penny," Larry said, a little confused once again.

"She is," Nichol grinned.

"Are you sure?" Larry laughed. "I'm beginning to think maybe you've played your game so long even *you* are starting to get confused!"

The twins looked at each other and laughed. "Maybe," one of them said. "Maybe not," the other one added. "*We* know how to tell who's who." The other continued, "And every once in a while, we show someone *else* the secret."

"Now that sounds like a challenge," Larry smiled, "and I love challenges, especially one from a gorgeous doll. In this case, it's a *double* challenge! I'll have to put on my thinking cap!"

Penny giggled. "You'll have to get *lucky* to figure it out, right, Nichol?"

"Definitely," Nichol teased. "What a shame it's Friday the thirteenth!"

"Ah, ha!" he exclaimed with a bright smile, "What you don't realize is Friday the thirteenth has always been my lucky day, doncha know!"

The girls looked at him intently, then looked at each other. They exchanged a knowing smile as if passing some secret message between themselves, then looked back at Larry. "Maybe I *will* come looking for that teeshirt later," Nichol grinned.

"You guys have a good time tonight," Penny added as the twins were apparently about to move on. "Wow the crowd with your charms for now. Everyone should be here by 9:00, and then you can wow us with your music. At most of these parties, people start to pair off after midnight, so be sure to make yourselves available to your fans after your performance. You never know. This might actually *be* your lucky night, Larry!" she giggled. "That goes for you, too, John!"

"Thank you, ladies!" Larry smiled genuinely. "We'll do our best on *both* counts!"

The girls departed, while Larry and John watched their backsides wiggle away once again. After a moment, they looked at each other, and puffed their cheeks as they let out a breath. "Damn, John!" Larry said softly. "I've always had a fantasy about making it with identical twins. Those girls are hot! They're going to drive me nuts all night long!"

"Holy crap, man!" John laughed. "My fantasies are simple compared to yours! You'll need a shit load of good luck to pull off a double score like that! Myself, I'll be perfectly happy to make it with either one of them, or with any of the other chicks I've seen here."

"Me, too!" Larry assured him. "Still, what a fantasy that would be, eh?"

"I'll tell you what," John laughed. "I'll run out to the van in a minute and bring in another teeshirt. After the show, I'll change and give you this one. If either of them comes to claim your shirt, use mine as bait for the other! If you happen to make that double score, I want to hear all the details!"

"You're crazy, man!" Larry laughed. "But I'll take you up on it. I can't imagine being that lucky even in my wildest dreams!" After a pause, he asked, "What are you going to do if one of them comes for *my* shirt, and the other one comes for *yours*?"

"In that case," John grinned, "let me assure you I'll find you and get it back!"

A little after 8:00, Larry spotted Sam entering the courtyard. "Hey, Sam!" She waved and started walking toward them. "Sam's looking pretty hot herself! Would you rather tease her, or compliment her?"

"Let's go easy on her," John said. "Maybe if we're nice to her, she'll help out by sending some of this fine tang our way."

"Good thinking," Larry said. "Hi, doll! You look great tonight!"

"Thanks!" she said to both of them as John acknowledged agreement. She turned around in a full circle so they could see the entire package, a nice two piece swimsuit, somewhat more modest than the skimpy hot pink bikinis worn by the Ball sisters. "My mom helped me pick it out. Do you really like it?"

John whistled appreciatively while Larry smiled and nodded his approval. "It's fabulous! If you don't get any nibbles from these other jokers, look for me. I'll bite onto your line and you can reel me in at your leisure, with no resistance at all!"

"You guys are sweet," she smiled. "But what would Donald say about that?"

"Unless someone tells him about it," Larry laughed, "I doubt he'd have anything to say at all!" Sam smiled and gently shook her head. "Come on, doll!" he said seriously. "Loosen up and have some fun tonight. I figure this Donald character must really be something special for you to remain so faithful to him, but a beautiful girl like you should be free to go anywhere she wants, do anything she wants, and be with anyone she wants. I want to see you swapping some spit with one of these studs before the night is over. If that's as far as you want to take it, that's your business, but get in there and mix it up a little. Do it for me, won't you, doll?"

Sam smiled at him, then lowered her head shyly. After a second, she slipped her arm around Larry's neck and kissed him on the cheek. "OK," she whispered. "Just for you, but only if you'll do something for me!"

"Name it, babe!" he said brightly.

"You get in there and mix it up a little yourself. Tomorrow, I want to hear you and John talking about how you got lucky tonight."

"It's a deal," he grinned. "Just for you, Sam, I'll do my very best to get myself laid tonight! I wouldn't think about doing that ordinarily, doncha know, but if it'll make you happy, I'll make the sacrifice!"

"You're so full of shit, how do you manage to keep flies away?" Sam giggled.

"Hey! What about me?" John asked.

"You're full of shit, too, John," Larry laughed.

"Probably," Sam giggled, "but I want you to do the same. Get in there, get some tang, and tell me all about it tomorrow! By the way, I love those shirts!"

"Maybe you could pick out some of the better prospects and send that sweet tang our way," John suggested.

"Sugar, if you can't get it for yourself, there's not a thing I could do to help you," Sam laughed. "First you hit them with your music. When they see that music is coming from a couple of good looking guys like you, these girls will already be getting wet by the time you introduce yourselves and shake their hands!"

"Why, Sam!" Larry grinned. "I'm shocked and dismayed you'd talk that way in front of this boy child! You might scorch his virgin ears!"

"Oh, please!" Sam laughed. "Would one of you gentlemen get a lady a beer?"

John's eyes had been following a particularly hot bikini as its owner strolled over to the beer kegs. "I'll get it for you, Sam!" he offered.

Friday, September 13, 1968 – Norwegian Wood (This Bird Has Flown)

Larry and Sam watched John dash to the beer keg and intercept his target. They exchanged a grin as they watched John introduce himself and score a few points for his politeness and bright smile. When he started back with Sam's beer, he brought the hot little bikini number in tow.

John was beaming when he returned, "I want you to meet some friends of mine. This is Sam and Larry. Guys, I want you to meet Krystal."

"Hi, Krystal," Sam grinned. "It's nice to meet you!"

"It's nice to meet you, too," Krystal said. "Is Sam short for Samantha?"

"Do you think she looks like a witch?" Larry teased. "Hi, Krystal. It's very nice to meet one of John's newest friends!"

"Thanks," she said to Larry, "and no, I don't think she looks like a witch."

"My name is actually Susan," Sam grinned. "All my friends call me Sam, but I doubt any of them could tell you why. Have you been to one of these *Gamma Alpha Sigma* parties before?"

"No," Krystal giggled, "but from what I understand, they're very interesting!"

"They can be," Sam smiled. "Especially if you relax and let yourself get into the swing of things. The primary intent seems to be for people to get to know each other, especially the newcomers. And as you've already noticed, it's a great way to meet some good looking guys!"

"So I see!" Krystal said, returning her smile, and looking both John and Larry over from head to toe. "I'm one of those newcomers."

"Are you a new freshman?" John asked. "Where's home?"

"Yes," she replied. "I grew up in Hallettsville. Where are you guys from?"

"We're all locals," John replied. "I'm also a fish. Larry and Sam are piss heads."

"What?" Krystal asked.

"You have to understand we Aggies have our own way of doing everything," Larry snickered, "and even our own words for certain things. Freshmen are called 'fish', sophomores are 'piss heads', juniors are 'surge butts', and seniors are 'zips'. Welcome to A&M! Don't try to figure it out, just accept it."

"So I see!" Krystal giggled. "Are you and Sam an item, or just friends?"

Larry's face twitched a few times, but otherwise, he did not react. Sam jumped in quickly. "We're all friends. Larry and John are my best friends, along with another girl named Julia. She's still in high school, so she didn't get invited tonight."

"How can you have three best friends?" Krystal asked with a smile.

"We're just that good!" John suggested.

Sam giggled at his suggestion, but essentially agreed. "Maybe he's right! I've known Larry since we were in the third grade, so he's my longest best friend. I've known John since the sixth grade. My shortest term best friend is Julia, who I met about two years ago."

"That sums it up," Larry agreed with a twinkle in his eye. "Sam is absolutely correct when she says I'm her longest best friend. You do go along with that, don't you, John? And since Julia is a girl, I doubt anyone has ever measured how long she is. We can safely assume John's just a little longer than she is."

"Hey!" John protested as Sam and Krystal giggled appreciatively.

"Well," Krystal added, "I've always heard it's not the length of the rope that counts, anyway, but how well it pulls the bucket."

"Ooh!" Sam exclaimed delightedly. "Hallettsville must be pretty hot for a small town! You're going to make friends around here rather quickly!"

"Well, I hope I've already made three!" Krystal smiled. "I should probably go mingle some more and meet some others. It was great to meet you guys. Perhaps I'll see you a little later on." She looked at each of them, saving her brightest smile for John, then turned and walked away after the gang shared some parting words.

"You've got a live one there, good buddy," Larry said to John as they watched Krystal walk away, appreciating the wiggle in her walk.

"She wants me bad!" John grinned. "I can tell!"

"Did you ever get around to mentioning to her you and Larry are the featured entertainment for the evening?" Sam asked. She got her answer from the dumbfounded expression on his face. "I didn't think so. If you play your best for her tonight, and she notices how well you pull those guitar strings, perhaps she'll decide to see how well your rope pulls other things later on."

"Please don't make him nervous, Sam," Larry begged. "I need him playing his best to make *me* look good, so *I'll* have a chance to play a little jump rope!"

The gang mingled among the other guests for a while, meeting a lot of new and interesting people. Since all of the girls on campus had been invited, there was a wide range in their "quality", ranging from the breathtakingly beautiful "foxes" such as Penny, Nichol, Krystal, and Sam, all the way down to four legged beasts, affectionately known as "mooses". Since all the guys present were there by special invitation, they were all top shelf quality according to Sam, at least as far as their looks went. Regardless of their physical attractiveness, or lack thereof, the gang was pleased to associate with everyone showing any measure of friendliness. They all made several new friends during that first hour of the evening.

When 9:00 rolled around, the guys walked to the alcove where their equipment was set up. Knowing the drill, Sam waited as the boys strapped on their guitars. They made one final check to ensure they were still in tune, then signaled. She smiled at them, mouthed the words, "Break a leg," gave them a thumbs up, and hit the master power switch. "Ladies and gentlemen," she announced, drawing the attention of the guests, "The Drug Company!" The boys immediately sprang into their first number, *There's a Kind of Hush* as recorded by Herman's Hermits.

Larry was in good voice that night, and John was playing well. The opening number had been selected because it was simple to do, yet featured a nice melody for Larry to sing, while John added some close harmony. When the song was done, the boys felt relaxed, knowing they were in their groove, confirmed by the response from the crowd. It did not occur to them this was the largest live audience they had ever performed for.

At the risk of boring people who did not happen to like that style of music, the boys followed the opener with two other songs from Herman's Hermits. First, there was the title song from a recently released album called *Mrs. Brown You've Got a Lovely Daughter*, followed by *I'm Into Something Good*.

"Thank you!" Larry said acknowledging the response when they finished their third number. "As Sam told you, we're the Drug Company, and I promise you..." He waited for a moment as the applause started once again. "I promise you we won't be doing songs by Herman's Hermits all night." When this comment brought a round of applause and some snickers, he added, "I'm hip to that! In fact, I can safely say we won't be doing *any* more songs by Herman's Hermits tonight!" This drew some more laughter and another round of light applause.

"It's time for me to introduce the members of the band," he said. "First of all, on my extreme right," he paused for effect as even John turned and looked to his right, "is John Birch." Larry waited until the good reaction from the crowd died down a little. "We don't know what he's on, but on guitar and every other kind of stringed instrument you can name, is my good friend, John Myers." John played a short guitar riff, receiving an enthusiastic response from the audience. "He also does some vocals. I guess that takes care of the band. Did I leave anyone out, John?"

John looked around, shook his head, shrugged, then pointed back at Larry. "And on neither my right nor my left is me. I'm Larry Bristol. I do some vocals, and also play a little guitar." As the crowd applauded, he struck a single chord, and held his guitar away from his body, rocking it back and forth as if it needed to cool off from the hot lick he had just played.

"John," he smiled, "I'm not sure everyone gets the joke about Mr. John Birch."

"I'm not sure I do, either," John replied. "Who is he?"

"Beats me," Larry grinned. "But someone must like him, because they founded some sort of organization known as the John Birch Society."

"I see," John said. "Do you know any members of this organization?"

"I don't know any Birchers myself, but I know a lot of *sons* of Birchers!"

"I'm hip," John grinned.

As John switched from guitar to banjo, Larry made a suggestion. "Why don't we sing a little song and tell the good people about him?" John began playing a jaunty introduction to the next song, written by Michael Brown and performed by the Chad Mitchell Trio, entitled *The John Birch Society*.

With luck, there is a moment in every live performance when you know the audience is yours, you own them, and they will happily eat up everything you have to offer. From the response they were given to this song, Larry and John knew this moment had arrived. The rest of the first set rode on this wave of enthusiasm, as the boys played more serious songs by various authors.

A few minutes after 10:00, having played for just over an hour, John continued playing an instrumental to the previous number, and Larry announced, "We're going to take a short break, folks." To the voices calling out, "No, keep going!" he smiled, held up his empty beer cup, and pleaded, "I gotta go walkies!" When this drew a few snickers, he added an ad lib, "These days, the men's room is the only place left where a man can still hold his own, doncha know."

Most of the girls in the crowd put a hand over their mouth to hide the way they were giggling at this suggestive statement. "We'll be back in a few moments to sing some more songs. We might even have a few stories to tell in the second half of the show. Keep mingling. We'll be right back!" When John completed playing the instrumental, they put the master amplifier into standby, unstrapped their guitars, and stepped "offstage" to take a well deserved break.

It took a few moments for the boys to migrate through the crowd and get to the men's room. They didn't mind too much, however. It's a curious fact the male anatomy will suppress the urge to empty its bladder in favor of other urges arising from looking at attractive females, scantily clan in swimsuits. Apparently, it's a matter of priorities. "Whew!" Larry said as he stepped back from the urinal and pulled the handle. "We really shouldn't drink so much beer before a performance!"

"I agree!" John said. "But now the gig is half over, so let's go get some more!"

"Lead the way!" Larry laughed.

The boys walked briskly to the beer keg, drawing a crowd as they went. Krystal was among that crowd, and was paying John a lot more attention than previously. Larry saw this, and smiled to himself. Sam, hovering just outside the circle, also noticed. They grinned to each other. Then Larry noted two tall muscular looking guys hovering around Sam. He raised one questioning eyebrow in a Mr. Spock like manner. Sam laughed at his facial expression, then shrugged.

Someone asked Larry where they had found their teeshirts. Before he could answer, he heard the voice of Nichol Ball from behind. "Larry and I have already started negotiations over the disposition of those teeshirts, isn't that right, Larry?"

Larry raised that questioning eyebrow once again. "I seem to recall both you and your sister expressed some interest. I have some good news for you. John has agreed to give me his as soon as the show is over, so I now have two shirts to bargain with. Perhaps I could interest you ladies in a package deal?"

It was Nichol's turn to raise a questioning eyebrow. "You drive a hard bargain, but do you think you have what it takes to handle a package deal like that? Those negotiating sessions are likely to get physically taxing!"

"No doubt!" he grinned. "Sometimes a man's gotta do what a man's gotta do."

Nichol nodded her head and grinned. "I admit I'm intrigued by your proposal. I'll check with Penny to see what she thinks. Perhaps she'll also find it interesting."

Larry was glad none of the other girls listening to this conversation had a clue as to what it was really about. He considered it highly unlikely these sisters would really be that interested in him, especially with all the other guys around. To Larry, they all seemed to be taller, more muscular, and better looking than he. His best bet was to let the girls posture among themselves, filing their claims on all the other guys, and then maybe he could get lucky with whoever remained.

After a twenty minute break, the boys made their way back to the alcove, to continue with the second half of their performance. They opened with a refrain of the Paul Simon hit *Mrs. Robinson*, and continued with several other Paul Simon songs. They were all well received, but their rendition of *Scarborough Fair/Canticle* drew a particularly enthusiastic response.

About halfway through the second set, they diverted from the music. While John pretended to start another song, Larry interrupted him. The whole thing was completely staged, but the boys tried to make it appear as an impromptu diversion. "John, did I tell you about the Aggie who was so dumb when he found out his wife was having twins, he hired a detective to track down the father of the *other* one?"

"No, I don't think you have," John said as the audience laughed politely. Most of them had already heard this old Aggie joke. "So what happened?"

"It turns out the detective was an Aggie, also," Larry continued, "and after trying to catch the wife with someone else for about a month, he gave up and confessed *he* was the father of the other one." Since this was an original follow up to the old joke, it brought a better laugh from the audience.

It was John's turn. "Did I tell you about the Aggie who was so dumb he stayed up all night studying for a urine test?" Once again, the audience laughed politely at the old and well known joke.

"I can't say I remember that, John," Larry replied. "What happened?"

Friday, September 13, 1968 – Norwegian Wood (This Bird Has Flown)   -317-

"When morning arrived, he was finally able to hit the cup," John added, "but by then, he didn't have any more to give, so he got his sister to supply a urine sample for him. He secreted it into the clinic and turned it in. It created quite a stir in the clinic when they discovered he was six weeks pregnant!"

"I'm hip!" Larry said as the audience laughed. "I'm sure you've heard about the Aggie who took a couple of rolls of toilet paper to an all night crap game."

"During the game, someone asked if he wanted to buy some shit," John added.

"No shit?" Larry grinned.

"Since he didn't have any, he decided to buy some shit!" John continued. "When asked if he needed papers, he declined because he already had two whole rolls!"

Larry waited for the laughter to die down before continuing. "This all reminds me of the Aggie who was so dumb all the other Aggies *noticed!*"

"Wow!" John said. "What happened to him?"

"He transferred to TU," Larry smiled, "raising the average IQ score of *both* schools by some sixteen points!" The crowd erupted in laughter. Most of the older students let out the enthusiastic "whoop" yell the students were so famous for.

"Some Aggies aren't really dumb," John suggested, "they're just lazy. I knew an Aggie who was so lazy he went out and married a girl who was already pregnant!"

"Maybe you call that lazy, John," Larry shook his head, "but I call it dumb!" When the reaction quieted down a little, Larry asked another question. "Say, John, do you know what's the most useless thing ever found on a woman?"

John pretended to think carefully about the question. He held his cupped hands in front of his chest, looked at them, then shook his head. Then he put his hands behind him, rubbed his own butt, then shook his head once again. Next, he turned his back to the audience and acted like he was rubbing his pelvis, and once again shook his head. He turned back around and started to say something, but stopped, turned his back to the audience once more, and began rubbing his pelvis again. Slowly, when the sound of laughter started coming from the audience, Larry reached over, tapped John on the shoulder, and glared at him.

"Sorry," John said without explanation. "No, Larry, I don't know the answer. What's the most useless thing ever found on a woman?"

"An Aggie," Larry replied. After the laughter faded, he continued. "I suppose that must even be more useless than this new Chinese venereal disease going around called 'ping pong balls'. Have you heard of it, John?" By turning the old joke into this new form, the audience enjoyed it, just like the ones that followed in rapid fire.

"Ouch!" John said with a wince.

"I also know a guy who caught 'Moby Dick' from a mermaid!" Larry fired.

"What about the Russian variation called 'Rot-cha-crotch-ov' I heard about the other day?" John asked.

"Those foreign words are pretty weird," Larry said. "Do you know the Chinese word for a virgin?"

"No-yen-tu," John replied. "What about the German word for the same thing?"

"Gut-en-tite!" Larry answered. "The Germans also have an interesting word for a brassiere, doncha know?"

"Keeps-um-from-floppin," John said tentatively, stumbling a little over the pronunciation. "Damn, Larry, that's quite a mouthful!"

"If it ain't a mouthful, you don't need a keeps-um-from-floppin!" he suggested.

"Anything more than a mouthful is wasted, anyway," John observed.

"So I've heard, John," Larry agreed. "On the other hand, every now and then it's great to just put your head between them and do this!" He held his hands up to the sides of his face and shook his head vigorously, causing his cheeks to bounce from side to side. There was an enthusiastic response, especially from the male members of the audience. He followed with a question, "Do you know what every Aggie dreams about finding?"

"Some hot titties full of cold beer!" John answered, drawing another big response. "Say, Larry, did I ever tell you about the girl I was dating a while back? She was phenomenal! One breast tasted like vanilla and the other tasted like chocolate!"

"You've got to be kidding!" Larry said. "That's fantastic, John!"

"I thought so, too!" John said. "When I mentioned how much I liked it, she just smiled and said all the boys said the same thing, but her doctor said it was *cancer!*"

The reaction from the audience was a mixture of laughs and groans. "Oh, God, John!" Larry said, putting a shocked look on his face. "That's an awful joke! We should apologize right now! Better still, we should do some restitution. What should we do to get these nice ladies to forgive us for that awful joke?"

John handed Larry one side of a poster board they had made previously. They each held their half of the poster high over their heads so everyone in the audience could read, "Free breast examinations available at the conclusion of this performance!" The audience roared with laughter.

When things settled down, John announced a song. "From the name of our band, you might guess one of the people Larry and I admire is a certain PhD living on the west coast. This psychologist, teacher, philosopher, and eternal optimist is the incarnation of a revolutionary new way of thinking. We would like to dedicate this next song to him." They followed with their rendition of *Legend of a Mind* written by Ray Thomas, and most notably performed by The Moody Blues. This was followed by three other Moody Blues songs, all written by Justin Hayward, including *Nights in White Satin*, *Voices in the Sky*, and *Tuesday Afternoon (Forever Afternoon)*.

They had intended to close their performance with *Tuesday* but that was not allowed. For an encore, they played four Beatles classics. While he never did so with quite as much emotion as the version nearly two years ago, Larry found he could once again sing *Yesterday*. *And I Love Her* came next, and once again, people commented about how much Larry sounded like Paul McCartney. Next came *Michelle*. The show finally ended with *Norwegian Wood (This Bird Has Flown)*, setting the right sort of mood for the kinds of relationships most of the audience would be experiencing that evening.

Saturday, September 14, 1968
Hanky Panky

Now that the entertainment was over, one could almost see how the dynamics in the crowd were changing. Earlier, the crowd consisted mainly of individuals, migrating independently like free atoms. Now, compatible atoms were starting to combine into chemical compounds, as many of the individuals began to pair up.

As the clock struck midnight, several guys at the party, attracted to the number of girls hovering around John and Larry, joined their entourage. From time to time, a chemical reaction occurred between individuals, bonding two of the formerly free atoms into a new compound. After such a reaction, the newly coupled pair wandered off in its own direction, seeking privacy. Krystal reappeared and seemingly attached herself to John. From the amount of attention she gave him, and the responses he gave back to her, the other girls got a clear signal he was now spoken for.

Larry still had several options in front of him, and was in no hurry to make a selection. He was vicariously enjoying the amount of attention John was receiving from Krystal, and was delighted to see his friend eating that attention up. Larry also caught a glimpse of Sam, happily splashing around in the swimming pool, pursued vigorously by the same tall, muscular guys he had seen her with earlier. He was glad to see that, also, and smiled to himself wondering which she would eventually select.

His mental wanderings were interrupted by the reappearance of Penny and Nichol, who took up positions to either side of him, each placing an arm around his waist, and smiling at him brightly. "If you ladies will excuse us, we need to steal this good looking guy away a few moments. Our stars delivered a spectacular show tonight, and now we need to pay them for their services, and discuss a possible bonus."

"Sorry, ladies," Larry smiled to the others. "It looks like I need to take care of some business. I'll leave John with you, and be back as soon as Penny and Nichol are finished with me." The Ball sisters led Larry down the courtyard, into one of the ground floor apartments. Perhaps it was something in their eyes, or perhaps it was the way they kept rubbing his rear that told the other girls he would not return soon.

"This is our place," Nichol announced. The apartment and its furnishings were quite spectacular. The front door opened into a large living room featuring a huge rock fireplace on the back wall. To the right of the fireplace, a door opened into a bedroom. On the other side, a sliding glass door led out onto a private patio. To the left, another door opened into a second bedroom. Further to the left was the kitchen, dining area, and a wet bar. "Would you care for a drink?" she asked.

"No, thanks," he smiled. "I'm still fine with the beer."

"Let me pay you the money we agreed to," Nichol said, walking to a desk.

"There's no hurry," he said sincerely. "You can mail it to us later if you'd like. I'm sure I'm speaking for John when I say we enjoyed playing for you tonight. I hope you enjoyed the show as much as we did!"

"We certainly did!" Penny smiled. "That's why we want to discuss a bonus!"

Larry returned her smile. "That really isn't necessary," he said shyly.

"Maybe it's unnecessary," Nichol said, "but we want to do it, anyway. Besides, I still want to negotiate for that teeshirt. What will it take for me to get you out of it?"

"What about you, Penny?" he grinned. "Don't you want a teeshirt, also?"

"Oh, we don't really want the teeshirt," Penny giggled. "We just want to know how to get you *out* of it!"

"I see!" Larry said to her, chuckling at her directness. "All you have to do is ask nicely. I could never refuse a request from two beautiful girls such as yourselves."

"The first thing I'll request is we get into the hot tub!" Nichol laughed.

"You have a hot tub?" Larry asked.

Penny laughed as she took his hand and began pulling him onto the patio. He was stunned by the sight of a large hot tub, already bubbling away. From here, he could also get a better image of the layout of the girls' apartment. The patio was surrounded on three sides by glass walls. In addition to the sliding door from the living room, two others could be seen to either side, coming from each of the two bedrooms flanking the patio. The back was a tall brick wall offering complete privacy.

The most surprising feature, however, was a spiral staircase leading to a balcony covering approximately half of the patio. The layout of the exterior walls suggested the second floor apartment was arranged identically, with sliding doors leading out onto this balcony from each of two bedrooms.

Seeing his questioning stare, Penny explained, "Daddy also rents the apartment upstairs so he and mom have a place to stay when they visit. The staircase and hot tub didn't come with the apartment originally. Daddy installed them for us! And now that our little sister has come to school, she's living in the upstairs apartment."

"You have a little sister?" Larry asked, surprised by this bit of news.

"Yes," she laughed. "She'll probably be along in a little while, wanting to get in the hot tub with the good looking guy she's had her sights on all night. It's big enough for eight people, so space won't be a problem. Come on! Let's get in!"

Nichol was already stepping into the hot tub, and motioning for the others to follow. Larry placed one leg over the side of the tub before he stopped to take off his shirt. "I don't want to get this wet," he grinned at the girls.

"You're easy!" Penny giggled. "Will it be hard to get off your swimming trunks?"

"That'll depend on how hard it'll be to get *yours* off!" Larry laughed as he sat into the warm, bubbling water. "But that's not the way I like it. Rather than you taking them off, I'd rather you let *me* take them off – with my tongue!"

"Ooh!" the girls giggled. "I like your style. We'll just have to see how it goes!"

They snuggled up to Larry, one sitting on either side of him. He placed one arm around each girl's shoulder. They each slipped one arm around his waist, the other resting on his chest. While he kissed one on the mouth, the other kissed him on the shoulder, patiently waiting for him to alternate. Occasionally, one of the hands resting on his chest would rub his nipples, his stomach, or move down to his leg.

After a few moments of this quiet and pleasant stimulation, one of the girls stepped out of the tub to refresh all of their drinks. For the moment, Larry concentrated all his attention on the one remaining in the tub. The other returned quickly, however, demanding equal time. He could not believe his luck at having two beautiful girls, identical twins, paying so much attention to him. It also occurred to him it was now after midnight, no longer Friday the thirteenth, his lucky day.

"How is it I'm so lucky you girls decided to bless me with your attention tonight?" he asked, flashing a warm smile. "Surely you two have boyfriends."

Nichol grinned. "We're free to do what we want to do, just like they are. They probably think we each selected some guy to be with. But this time, rather than each of us picking out some ordinary guy, we decided to pick out one great guy and share him between us!"

"You're going to give me a swollen head!" he smiled.

"I certainly hope so!" Nichol giggled. "Besides, they're doing the same thing. They're paying all of *their* attention to Sam! That's where we got the idea!"

"Those two tall, muscular guys with Sam are your boyfriends?" he asked.

"Don't worry, sugar," Penny grinned. "We do this all the time. They aren't the jealous kind. They don't know the meaning of the word. To tell you the truth, they don't know the meaning of a *lot* of words! But they're pretty, so we keep them around to dress up the place, do the heavy lifting, and odd jobs from time to time."

They heard one of the sliding doors on the balcony open and close, and several giggles as someone came out of the upstairs apartment, and headed down the spiral staircase towards the hot tub. "That must be our little sister!" Nichol said.

Larry looked at the couple coming down the stairs and started laughing. "I must have been distracted by something. I should have guessed!" Standing at the foot of the stairs was Krystal, closely pursued by John.

"How you doing, good buddy?" John laughed. "You've already lost your shirt?"

"We're still deep in negotiations," Larry laughed. "This is your younger sister? Now that I'm not quite so distracted, I begin to see the resemblance. Assuming you all look like your mother, I'd have to say your father is a very lucky man!"

"Thank the man, sis," Penny said. "That's known as an indirect compliment." Larry started laughing again, obviously tickled by something. "What's so funny?"

"I just realized," he said, "your parents have a very interesting sense of humor!"

"Are you just now catching on to that?" Penny laughed.

"I caught on to the 'Penny Ball' name right away," Larry grinned, "but I assumed your real name is Penelope or something."

"No," she smiled, "it's actually on my birth certificate as Penny."

"The name 'Nichol Ball' did not sink in immediately," he confessed. "Like I said, I must have been distracted by something. I can't imagine what it could have been!" The girls snickered to each other. "But now here comes 'Krystal Ball', your younger sister! Your parents are too much!"

"It runs in the family," Krystal smiled. "We have a cousin in Bryan named..."

"Suellen Ball is your cousin?" Larry asked. "She was in my graduating class!"

"Get used to it," Penny giggled. "The whole family is made up of jokers."

"I'll give you another one," Larry grinned. "It's a good thing Krystal preferred John over me. Can you imagine how awful it'd be if she and I got together, and ended up getting married?"

"Oh, God!" Krystal laughed. "I'd be Krystal Bristol!"

"Now that I see how it works in your family," Larry added, "maybe I'll name my first daughter Krystal, assuming I ever have one. And if I ever have a boy, I'll call him Pistol! That's a good name for a son of a gun, don't you think?"

The five of them had a good laugh over the name game. John and Krystal got a drink from the bar, and joined the others in the hot tub. When they started swapping spit enthusiastically, Larry happily resumed his activities, alternating his attention back and forth between Penny and Nichol.

A few minutes later, the sliding glass door from the living room opened one more time. "I'm not surprised to find you guys here!" Sam said, laughing brightly. "My slaves told me they knew where we could find a hot tub. I should have asked them if they thought it would be occupied!"

"Come on in!" Penny grinned. "There's enough room for three more. If anyone else shows up, however, someone's going to have to move to the swimming pool!"

"Do you expect anyone else?" Krystal asked.

"I don't think so," Penny giggled.

Sam and her two attendants, Larry never did learn their names, hopped into the hot tub, and filled the remaining spaces. Larry grinned as he briefly watched Sam enjoying the attention she was getting. First, she would put her arms around the one on the right and kiss him emphatically, while the other one rubbed her back and kissed her neck. A few moments later, they would reverse positions. He could not watch this very long, however, as Penny and Nichol were soon demanding he return his attention to them.

Larry began to work on the problem of telling the girls apart. They told him if he was very lucky, he might be able to learn the secret. Since he had never felt so lucky before, he figured his prospects were good. He had not noticed any obvious differences between their faces, hair, or bodies, and he had been giving those bodies a lot of examination all night long! Their kisses were indistinguishable, their tongues equally delicious, as was their reaction to his stimulation. If their secret was a birthmark, or some other feature on their skin, then it was obviously still hidden beneath the skimpy bikinis they were wearing. Since Larry wanted to go exploring into those locations anyway...

While kissing the girl on his right, the one he assumed to be Penny, his hand rubbed her back. He found the string forming the back of her bikini top, and located the knot holding the two ends together. Realizing it was tied in a simple bow, he gently pulled on one of the ends, causing the knot to unravel. When Penny moaned softly, expressing her approval, he lifted the two triangles of cloth covering her breasts over her head, and laid them on the edge of the hot tub.

Moments later, he turned his attention to the girl on his left, assuming this one must be Nichol, and repeated the procedure. Both girls smiled at him with appreciation. Their nipples, floating gently on the surface of the bubbling water, were fully erect and inviting. He happily accepted those invitations, alternating his kisses from one girl to the other. Only now, when he turned his attention to one of them, she would raise her chest slightly so her breasts were just out of the water, inviting him to place his kisses there.

Larry took his time enjoying the shape, color, warmth, softness, and taste of these fine examples of the female form he had been admiring all night. He certainly was not disappointed to note there was still no discernible difference between the two girls. This meant he would be forced to continue his explorations, something he wanted to do very badly.

He stopped for a moment, looking carefully into each of the girl's eyes, smiling at them, silently communicating his desire to continue, and confirming their desire he do so. During this break, he glanced over to check on the progress being made by his friends. Since John was concentrating all his attention on only one girl, he and Krystal were much further along. Krystal was sitting on John's lap, facing him with her legs straddling his body. Her arms were around his neck, pulling his face to her bared breasts. *Good for you, John!* he thought to himself, and smiled at the two older sisters, who had also noticed this action.

Larry turned to look at Sam, and he saw she seemed to be lost in her own world. Her breasts were also bared, and each was being gently kissed and massaged by a different guy. *Enjoy yourself, my dear friend,* he thought to himself, then returned his full attention to the beautiful girls at his sides.

He observed the bottom part of the girls' bikinis consisted of two more triangles of cloth. One point from each triangle was stitched together with the other one forming the crotch. The opposite sides of the triangles were hemmed, containing a drawstring tied in a bow on each hip, securing the garment to the body.

His technique to attack this obstacle was a direct assault catching Penny by surprise! He started by kissing her on the mouth, and slowly worked his lips onto her neck and shoulders, then downward to her exposed breasts. As before, Penny raised out of the water to provide him with access to those delicious breasts. But this time, he did not stop, moving his lips even lower. She responded by raising her body a little more, granting him access to her abdomen. When he kissed her navel, she giggled, as did Nichol who was looking over his shoulder, watching this action intently. He continued moving his lips lower, and soon was kissing her waist along the top of the bikini. He could feel the drawstring under the cloth as he slowly moved his kisses to her right hip. When he located the bow, he took one end of the string between his teeth, and began raising his head, untying the knot. His kisses then moved to her left hip, where his repeated the procedure of untying the other bow. His head now continued upwards, returning to kiss her navel, then her breasts, and then her shoulders, neck, and finally back to her lips, while still holding the end of the drawstring between his teeth. Penny felt the pull on her bikini as he moved upward, and raised her body to let the triangles of cloth slip away freely.

When he next turned his attention to Nichol, she knew what to expect and was eager for him to proceed. He kissed her as he had Penny, but moved downward more quickly this time as she anticipated his moves. She moaned when he returned to kiss her lips with the drawstring still in his mouth, and hungrily pulled it out of his mouth with her own teeth. The hand she was using to rub his thigh rose to rub across his belly, where she felt his joy stick pressing against his swimming trunks, struggling in vain to free itself.

But it was not time for Mr. Happy to stand free and proud! Larry had two women, both of whom were ready and willing to have intercourse with him, and he desperately wanted to please them both. He would have to combine all the knowledge and techniques he knew to achieve that goal.

Larry and the twins stepped out of the hot tub, and retired to one of the master bedrooms. During their bedroom gymnastics, something unusual caught Larry's eye. Right next to a fold of skin forming the outer lips of Penny's flower, in a place no one could possibly see unless their face was buried in intimate contact such as his was at that moment, he saw a small mark. At first, he didn't think much of it, but as he examined it more carefully, he began to make out details. It was a tiny tattoo of a butterfly, with pink and red wings, no more than a half inch across. *What a delightful discovery!* he smiled to himself.

Moments later, he found himself in a similar position, only it was Nichol who was the object of all his attention. He was not surprised to find she also bore a small tattoo in exactly the same position. It could not possibly be seen by anyone unless their face was deep in this intimate position. But there was a difference! The wings on the butterfly of Nichol's tattoo were not pink and red like Penny's, but were yellow and gold. *What a wonderful and intimate secret I've discovered!* he smiled to himself. *This is indeed my lucky day, and it's not over yet!*

Concentrating his attention to first one then the other, resisting the urge to use anything more than his tongue, he managed to bring cries of ecstasy from each of them. Becoming more aggressive, the girls rolled him onto his back and pinned him down. At first, Penny straddled his hips while Nichol sat on his face. Moments later, they alternated positions, and continued to alternate them until Larry could no longer contain his excitement.

After finishing their exercises, Larry, Nichol, and Penny lay silently in the bed with their arms wrapped around each other for several minutes, enjoying the afterglow of their experience. Penny was the first to break the silence. "Damn, Larry! I'm glad we decided to invite you to join us. Neither of us really thought you, or any other guy, could take care of us at the same time!"

"Let me assure you it wasn't easy," he chuckled, "but my philosophy is sex is like a Chinese dinner. It ain't over until *everybody* gets their cookies!"

"What did *your* fortune cookie say?" Nichol asked, laughing at his joke.

"Same as always," he grinned. "Help! I'm a prisoner in a Chinese fortune cookie factory!" The girls laughed in appreciation. "I'm really glad you decided to invite me as well. My fantasy has always been to make love to beautiful, identical twin sisters. I figured it would remain nothing more than a fantasy for all of my life!"

"We're not really identical," Nichol giggled.

"So I noticed," he grinned. "For the record, which of you is pink and red, and which is yellow and gold?"

"Pink is for Penny," Nichol smiled.

"Gold is for Nichol," Penny giggled. "Even though nickels aren't made of gold, at least they're made of metal."

"Pennies are made of metal, also," Larry pointed out, causing the girls to giggle once again. "Oh, never mind. It'll be easy to remember pink is for Penny. I'll just have to remember to concentrate on the butterfly, because I saw plenty of pink on Nichol, as well!"

"I imagine you did!" Nichol laughed. "Now you know how to tell us apart!"

"So if I should see you on the street and want to know which is which, what should I do? Walk over, pull down your panties, and take a good look?" he laughed. "I have to admit I like the idea, but it sounds a little impractical to me!"

The girls laughed at the notion. "No," Penny grinned, "now that you know our little secret, all you have to do is ask our favorite color. We've promised each other, and everyone else who knows the secret, we'll always answer the question truthfully. The butterfly wings are our favorite colors. Mine is pink..."

"...and mine is yellow," Nichol said flashing a dazzling smile. "All we ask is you promise never to reveal our secret. If too many know, it won't be special anymore."

"A totally reasonable request! I promise I'll never reveal your secret!" After a moment's thought, he asked, "How many people now this secret, anyway?"

"Well, let's see," Nichol said. "There's Penny and me..."

"...and the guy who did the tattoos, of course," Penny added.

"What a lucky bastard!" he laughed. "I imagine he was a babbling basket case by the time he finished the job. I know I'd be!"

"I doubt he cared," Nichol giggled. "He was as queer as a three dollar bill! There's Bob, a guy I dated for a while in high school. Penny and I switched dates one weekend. It turns out Bob had great eyesight and a very good memory!"

"A guy doesn't tend to forget something like that!" Larry beamed.

"Really? Why not?" Penny asked trying to sound innocent. "Krystal knows, of course, and now there's you!"

"What about those two guys with Sam?" he asked. "Don't they know?"

"Tweedledee and Tweedledum?" Nichol laughed. "I doubt they've ever noticed the butterflies at all, and even if they did, they probably wouldn't notice there are two different colors!"

"So I'm one of a very privileged few," he said seriously. He smiled as he looked each of them in the face. "I'm truly honored, ladies."

"We're honored to have been treated by a real man like you!" Penny said sweetly.

"It was my pleasure!" he grinned. "Please don't keep *that* a secret. Tell *all* your friends what a great stud I am, and maybe I'll get a little more action!"

"I doubt you have much trouble," Nichol said. "Let's get a fresh drink and go back out to the hot tub. Do you smoke after sex, Larry?"

"Gee, Nichol, I know it gets hot, but I don't think I've ever noticed it actually smoking!" he laughed. "If it *is* smoking, could I get you to blow it out for me?"

"I'm game if you are!" she laughed.

After they stopped laughing, they fixed themselves a fresh drink. Larry laughed once again when Penny produced a couple of funny looking cigarettes they could share. With these in one hand and their drinks in another, they returned to the patio, still naked, and climbed back into the now strangely empty hot tub.

Seconds later, Penny fired up one of those cigarettes for them to pass around. "You said you'd get more action if we spread the word about you," she began. "That surprises me. Sam seems like a pretty hot little number to me. Isn't she giving you all the action you need?"

"Sam?" he grinned. "Sam and I aren't doing the dirty deed together."

"That surprises me!" Penny noted. "I'd think she'd put a smile on her boyfriend's face and keep it there!"

Larry snickered as he shrugged. "She probably does, but I'm not her boyfriend! She's dating some guy named Donald I've never even met. All I know is every now and then for the last few years, she's disappeared for a weekend, or perhaps longer. It's my assumption she runs off to be with him, but she won't talk about it."

"I assumed she was *your* girl," Nichol added.

"No," he smiled. "Sam and I are very good friends, but we've never had a romantic relationship. We used to play doctor when we were kids, but I never gave her a pelvic examination anywhere near as thorough as the one I just gave you!"

"That's too bad," Penny grinned. "If it's not Sam, who's the lucky girl getting all your attention?"

"I don't have a regular girlfriend," he said, trying to hide his sadness. "I date a lot of different girls, like a bee moving from flower to flower, gathering as much honey as I can find, doncha know."

"You don't strike me as the type of guy who'd like that, Larry," Nichol said thoughtfully. "Rather than moving from flower to flower, I suspect you'd much rather find yourself a sweet little honey pot to keep around all the time, so you could dip your stinger into her honey any time you wanted."

He laughed at the analogy. "You're right about me. In an ideal world, that's exactly what I'd like. But this is hardly an ideal world. I just go about my business, trying to keep my eyes and my options open. One of these days, if I'm lucky, maybe I'll find that sweet little honey pot."

"Do you have any hot prospects?" Penny grinned.

"There are these identical twin sisters I know," he grinned, "but somehow I don't think they're ready to settle down with anyone, much less an ordinary guy like me."

"You're anything but ordinary!" Nichol smiled.

"If only there were two of him!" Penny sighed. "You wouldn't happen to have a twin brother, would you?"

"I'm afraid not," he grinned.

"Pity," Nichol said. "We could get rid of Tweedledee and Tweedledum!"

Larry snickered at the suggestion. "That seems like a nasty thing to say about them. I thought those guys were your boyfriends!"

"Well, there are boyfriends, and then there are *boyfriends*," Penny said. "They're nice enough, and they're certainly pretty. We mainly keep them around for the heavy lifting and other services they perform, but they're not what we call keepers!"

"What are you girls actually looking for?" he asked.

They looked at each other and grinned. "I want a guy with a great heart and a good head on his shoulders," Penny said dreamily. "I don't care if he's tall, dark, or handsome. He doesn't have to be rich or even hung like a race horse. I just want him to worship me as much as I'll worship him."

From the way she closed her eyes and daydreamed, Larry knew Nichol shared this vision. A few moments after Penny finished, Nichol opened her eyes and looked in Larry's direction. "Are you positively sure you don't have a twin brother?"

"At this moment, I wish I did!" he said, returning her smile.

Nichol nodded her head. "What about you, Larry? What are you looking for?"

He chuckled as he looked out into the darkness. "I just want the same thing everybody wants. I want to find a girl who'll love me as much as I'll love her." Penny and Nichol watched as the expression on his face changed from a smile to one of FUD – fear, uncertainty, and doubt.

"It seems to me there's something you've left unsaid," Penny noted.

His forced smile did little to mask the unhappiness he was feeling. "I haven't been particularly lucky in this quest," he said, putting on a brave face to hide the FUD. "It seems I have this tendency to get ahead of the game. I start thinking I've found my little honey pot long before she feels the same about me."

"So you've gotten yourself hurt a few times, I take it?" Nichol asked.

"Now and then," he shrugged. "I'll get hurt a few more times before it's all over."

"We all will," Penny agreed. "But that's not what I meant when I said there was something you'd left unsaid. I get a distinct feeling you have someone in mind when you talk about that little honey pot you want so much."

Larry chuckled and marveled at her perception. "Not really. There is someone I'm... interested in. I don't really know why. There's just something about her... Well, it hardly matters. I doubt anything will ever come of it."

"Why don't you tell us about her?" Nichol suggested. "If it's not too personal."

"There's not much to tell," he said simply, once more looking into the distance. "I met her about two years ago. John and I sang at her fourteenth birthday party. It was our first actual gig, launching our musical careers! Ever since then, we've been getting more and more popular, doncha know."

"What about the girl?" Nichol asked, returning his attention to the subject.

He returned his gaze to their faces. "Her name is Julia," he said softly. "Something happened to me that night, the first moment I saw her. There she was, just a skinny little girl, really. A tomboy, with skinned up knees and a ponytail. She had a few pimples on her face, and braces on her teeth. I don't mean to say she was ugly, or anything like that. It's just she wasn't especially beautiful, like you girls are. I thought she was cute, OK? What really got to me were those big, beautiful green eyes of hers. You could stare into them and see to the edge of infinity, and man, let me tell you, that's exactly what I wanted to do! Ever since that day, I've been seeing those green eyes in my dreams, and even in my nightmares."

"Those eyes were the inspiration for your song *Green Eyes And Sam* weren't they?" Penny suggested, immediately making the obvious connection.

"Yeah," he admitted. "That's one of my secrets. Only Sam and John knew that."

"What happened between you and Julia?" Nichol asked.

"Nothing," he confessed. "She already had a boyfriend, John's little brother."

"And you couldn't sweep him out of your way?" Penny asked.

"I consider Jimmy to be my friend," he said simply, shaking his head. "Even if he wasn't my friend, I just don't work that way. Don't forget she was just fourteen at the time, and her parents weren't letting her go out on dates. I was seventeen. Her parents liked me well enough, but I suspect they would've thought she was a little too young for me. Or maybe I was a little too old for her."

"What about now?" Nichol asked. "Now she's sixteen and you're nineteen. Is John's little brother still in the picture?"

"She won't actually turn sixteen until next month," he corrected. "No, she broke up with Jimmy a couple of month's later, but she soon had another boyfriend, and then another. It seems like she *always* has a steady boyfriend. I've never had the opportunity to ask her out on a date, much less tell her the way I feel about her."

"How *do* you feel about her, Larry?" Penny asked softly.

"That's the problem, Penny," he said, looking at her and wishing she could provide him with the answer. "I don't *know* how I feel about her. Something about her calls out to me. I want to be with her for a while just so I can find out what it might be. Sometimes, I wonder if maybe she's the little honey pot I've been looking for all my life. But how will I ever know unless I can be with her for a little while?"

The sliding door to the other bedroom opened, and Sam stepped back onto the patio, as naked as the others. "Hi, Sam!" Penny called. "You ready to rejoin us?"

"I'm just looking for my swimming suit," Sam said with a nervous laugh.

"Oh, come on in and have a smoke with us, Sam," Larry said. "You can find your swimsuit later. Maybe it was a long time ago, but I've seen you naked before. Shall I go find my stethoscope?"

"I guess you have at that," Sam giggled. She walked over and slid into the hot tub, relaxing in the warm, bubbling water. "Ah, I've got to get me one of these!"

"Would you like me to get you a drink, Sam?" Larry asked.

"Why thanks, Larry!" Sam smiled at him. "You're much too good to me, like my personal slave! I may have to get one of those, also!"

Larry winked at her, slipped out of the tub and disappeared through the sliding door in the center, heading for the bar. Noting the way Sam watched him, Nichol grinned at her. "He's got a nice ass, doesn't he, Sam?"

Sam returned that grin. "I've always thought he was a good looking guy! From the smiles I see on your faces, I'd say he must have some other nice qualities."

"You won't hear any complaints from me!" Nichol giggled. "Not only does he have nice qualities, but he knows how to make the most of them!"

"Amen! Where did you leave Tweedledee and Tweedledum?" Penny giggled.

"Who?" Sam laughed before catching on. "They're conked out on the bed in there. I'm afraid I wore them out. I'm surprised Larry is still able to walk. You guys must have gone easy on him."

"Not a chance, girl," Nichol laughed, "We just might have another go with him before the night is over! Penny and I assumed you and he were together, Sam, but he tells us that's not the case. Is that your choice or his?"

"I guess it's mutual," Sam shrugged. "Part of it is neither of us wants to risk ruining our friendship. That's true enough, but it's really just an excuse. The real reason is each of us is pursuing other interests."

"He mentioned someone named Donald?" Nichol asked.

"Yes," Sam said. "That's my boyfriend. I hope you won't mind if I don't talk about him very much. I have my reasons."

"We don't mean to pry into your personal business," Penny said. She turned her head to admire Larry's naked form as he returned with Sam's drink. "I guess I'm more curious about him, wondering why he doesn't have a steady girlfriend."

"Oh, that's easy," Sam laughed. "His eyes have been fixed on one particular girl for the last two years, so he doesn't get involved with others." As Larry handed Sam her drink, and slipped back into the tub, she grinned, "Isn't it right, big boy?"

"Isn't what right?" he asked, not knowing the topic of the conversation.

"You don't have a steady girlfriend because there's one particular girl you want to be your girlfriend," Sam said, looking him in the eye.

He looked back at Sam and sighed. "Yeah, I'd like her to be my girlfriend, Sam, but she's not. She's a good friend, my best friend. There are three people I consider to be my best friends – Sam, John, and Julie."

"Is she the other girl we hear on the radio with you guys?" Nichol asked. When Larry nodded his head, still looking a little sad, she asked another question. "I don't understand the problem, Larry. If you want her to be your girlfriend, then why isn't she? A guy like you can have any girl he pleases!"

Larry smiled at her and shrugged. *At least she's never heard my old joke before.* "Apparently, I've never pleased one," he said, forcing an unconvincing smile.

"You surely pleased me!" Penny grinned.

A long silence followed as Larry smiled and looked at the girls. The unspoken question was clear to all of them, as was the answer. Yes, he had pleased these girls, but no, neither of them was now to become his girlfriend. They had all known from the beginning this was to be a brief encounter, a one-night stand if you will, unlikely ever to be repeated. Sam finally broke the silence. "He's never even told her he's interested in her," Sam said, practically scolding Larry.

"What would be the point?" he asked softly. "She already has a boyfriend."

"But Larry, surely you can have any girl you truly *want*," Penny added as a correction, "whether she temporarily has another boyfriend or not!"

"Oh?" Larry asked. "You've already admitted I pleased you, Penny. What if I were to tell you I wanted *you* to be my girlfriend? What would you say to that?" Penny merely looked at him, since the answer was obvious to both of them. He turned his attention to Nichol. "What about you? Didn't I please you as well. What if I wanted *you* to be my girl?" Once again, the answer did not need to be spoken.

To drive home his point, he turned to Sam. "Sam, we've known each other since

Saturday, September 14, 1968 – Hanky Panky

we were eight years old. Even though we don't have a romantic relationship, I feel closer to you than I've ever been with any girl. You know without question I love you, just as I know you love me. How many times have you turned me down when I've begged you just to go out on a date with me?"

"That's not fair, Larry," Sam protested. "Yes, we're wonderful friends. I *do* love you, and I know you also love me. But I already have a boyfriend, and..." She stopped in mid-sentence as she realized the point of his question.

"You all say I can have any girl I want," he said, looking from eye to eye. "I appreciate the thought, but clearly, your words aren't true. If I could have any girl I wanted, would I be spending my days and my nights wishing I wasn't so lonely?

"Perhaps I could have any girl I want as long as we stipulate she doesn't already have a boyfriend. But you show me a girl who doesn't already have a boyfriend, and I'll show you the reasons why, and it's probably not because she's some sort of four legged beast! In this town, there are five or six guys for every girl, so a girl who's pretty on the outside will have a boyfriend even if she's ugly on the inside. A girl who's pretty on the inside can overcome a whole lot of problems on the surface, and will also have a boyfriend. What does that leave? Do you really think I should go looking among those remaining? Ugly on the inside as well as on the outside?"

"So she has a boyfriend!" Sam insisted. "You have to fight for the girl you want!"

"I'm no fighter," Larry said calmly. "You know that, Sam."

"I don't mean you have to fight physically," Sam said.

"Do you really think I could win a girl's heart by beating her boyfriend in a game of chess or something?" he asked.

"Why are you being so ridiculous?" Sam demanded. "You know what I mean!"

"Yes, I know what you mean," he admitted, "but that's a fool's errand, Sam! Let me use you as an example, again. Tell me what I could possibly say or do that would make any difference with you, so you would dump this Donald character and be with me. There's nothing, because it isn't you don't like what you see in me, or I'm lacking in something. That's not the problem. The problem is you like what you see in *him*. That's why you want him to be your boyfriend in the first place. I'd be a fool to try to come between you and Donald. All I would end up doing is making both of you mad at me."

"But all boyfriends are not the same," Penny insisted. "Take Tweedledee and Tweedledum. They're really nothing but placeholders, while we wait for someone better to come along!"

"My assumption is if you found someone better," he said calmly, "you'd somehow let him know you're interested, wouldn't you? We all know I'm not going to take their place, either collectively or individually, but if you wanted me, then you'd let me know, wouldn't you?"

"Larry, we *are* interested in you," Nichol added. "The problem is there's only one of you. Maybe Penny and I would be content to share you for a little while, but sooner or later, one of us would want all of you. Surely you can see that."

"That's very kind of you to say, Nichol," he smiled, "but I think you see my point." He looked directly at Sam to announce the result of his analysis. "You've been wanting to know why I don't pursue Julie, or let her know I'm interested in her. The reason is simple – she doesn't say or do anything to make me think she has the slightest interest in anything other than my friendship. And I value her friendship far too much to risk losing it by chasing after some hopeless dream I don't understand in the first place."

"Has it occurred to you she doesn't show any romantic interest in you because you don't show any romantic interest in her?" Sam asked.

"But I *do*, Sam!" he said. "At least, I try to. OK, maybe I could try a little harder. You just have to realize I'm walking a pretty fine line, on one hand trying to let her know how much I'm interested in her, but at the same time trying not to put our friendship at risk. One of these days, I'll get my chance. One of these days, I'll be in just the right place at just the right time, and I'll have the chance to be more direct. In the meantime, I'll simply have to be patient."

"And in that meantime," Sam added, "you'll continue to be just as miserable and unhappy as you have been for the last two years."

"Do I look all that miserable to you?" he asked, smiling as brightly as he could manage. "I've just had a great time fulfilling a fantasy with two of the most gorgeous girls I've ever known! There are thousands of guys who'd jump at the chance to take my place right now!"

"Maybe you should try to get Ed to swap places with you," Sam suggested sarcastically. Larry would not have been more stunned had he been hit by a bullet in the heart. His eyes blinked as he stared back at Sam, fighting back the pain he felt, almost in disbelief she had said this thing. Sam saw her comment had scored a direct hit, inflicting much more damage than she intended. "I'm sorry, Larry," she said sincerely. She knew Larry would instantly change places with Ed if only he was given the opportunity.

"Who's Ed?" Penny whispered to her sister.

"Shh!" Nichol suggested. "My guess is that's the name of her current boyfriend."

The tension was broken by the sound of a sliding glass door opening and closing, a few footsteps across the second floor balcony, and the ringing of the metal in the spiral staircase, as John and Krystal bounced down, making their reappearance. "Hi, guys!" Krystal said brightly heading for the hot tub. Spotting all of the others were naked, she giggled, "Oh, I see we're getting more comfortable!" and began to remove the swimsuit she had just put back on moments before.

Larry relaxed and enjoyed the show, winking his approval at John. "Are you going to join us, John? I don't think any of these ladies have seen you naked. Perhaps they would like to see how your yoohootie measures up."

"I suppose that will depend on the stiffness of the competition!" John replied smoothly as he slipped out of his swimsuit and joined the others in the hot tub.

"You boys are nasty!" Sam giggled.

"You love it, and we all know it," John grinned in return. "So what have you guys been talking about?"

"We're talking about Larry and this girl he has the hots for," Penny answered. "He's been trying to explain why he hasn't swept away whatever competition there is, no matter how stiff it might be! We already know how well he measures up!"

"Oh, please," Larry said, shaking his head.

"Let's get John's opinion," Nichol said. "You're another guy, John. Do you understand what Larry has been saying to us? What do you think he should do?"

"I don't know exactly what he's been saying tonight," John began, "but if it's anything like what he's told me in the past, I have to admit I don't really understand it. I think he should just go to her and tell her he wants her, and see what she says. What's the worst that could happen?"

"That's easy," Larry answered. "I can tell you *exactly* what would happen. First, she would laugh at her funny clown friend, thinking it was all some kind of joke, and then wait for me to deliver the punchline. After a few moments, when she realized I wasn't joking, she would tell me she already has a boyfriend, maybe even getting angry with me for trying to come between them. In the end, she would tell me how sweet I am, but she doesn't want to be my girlfriend, and couldn't we be 'just-friends' instead? You know how I hate those words! And then, not only would I have lost any chance I might have at getting her to be my girl, I also would have lost her as my best friend."

"You don't know that would happen," Sam insisted. "Why can't you consider the possibility she wants to be with you just as badly as you want to be with her?"

"Things only work that way in fairy tales, Sam," he replied, becoming a little agitated. "They just don't happen that way in real life. At least, they don't happen that way in *my* real life. I need to wait until she doesn't already have a boyfriend."

"Too bad Julia wasn't at the party tonight," John said. "Most of the girls already had boyfriends, but were trying out new relationships without making a longterm commitment. You could have wowed her as much as you did Penny and Nichol!"

A multitude of conflicting thoughts passed through Larry's mind. A raging torrent of thought, swirling and churning into powerful currents and eddies, cascading like a waterfall over the rocks forming the foundation of his consciousness, mercilessly pounding against the walls guarding his sanity. "Oh, God!" he said, realizing he was losing his self-control. He needed to be alone for a moment, to get away from the others, to regroup. He used the first excuse flashing into his mind, "I gotta hit the can!" He literally jumped out of the hot tub and walked briskly through the sliding door into the apartment, and into the first bathroom he could find.

"Jesus, John," Sam said shaking her head. "Sometimes, I wish you'd stop and think before you say things to him about Julia."

"What did I say?" John said, alarmed.

"He may talk like he has modern, liberated ideas," Sam explained, "but he still has a lot of old fashion notions in his head. He has enough trouble dealing with the fact Julia has another boyfriend who holds her hand, puts his arms around her, and kisses her lips. You just reminded him there are *other* things she might be doing with those boyfriends. I don't think he's ready to deal with that."

"I'll go make sure he's OK, and apologize," John said, starting to get up.

"No, John," Sam said. "I'll go. You don't need to apologize."

"I have a better idea," Penny said. "*I'll* go. It sounds to me like he needs to vent his emotions and come to terms with himself. Perhaps the two of you are too close to his problem. He needs someone new, who doesn't already know the whole story, so he can explain it to them, and in so doing, clarify his own thoughts so he can better understand them himself."

Sam and John gave Penny a puzzled look as she stood to follow Larry into the apartment, then exchanged a look between themselves. Accepting the wisdom of her words, they eased back into the warm water and relaxed. Perhaps she was right. Perhaps Penny would be able to help him much better than they could.

Larry stood in front of the mirror and watched the flood of ideas in his head manifest themselves as rivulets of agony cascading from his eyes, down his cheeks, and falling into the sink. He could not exorcise the demon inside his head, tormenting him by ravaging and raping his sweet little Julie, a skinny little tomboy on her fourteenth birthday, staring at Larry with her big, green eyes, pleading with him to come rescue her! But there was nothing he could do.

"Are you alright, Larry?" Penny asked knocking softly on the bathroom door.

"I'm fine," he lied. "I'll be out in a minute."

"It's Penny," she whispered. "It's just me out here. Can I come in?"

"I'm not a very pretty sight right now, Penny," he replied.

"Please?" Penny pleaded softly.

In spite of the embarrassment it would bring, Larry knew instinctively he needed help. After a momentary hesitation, and without saying a word in response to her request, he reached down to the doorknob and turned it slightly, releasing the lock mechanism, allowing Penny to open the door if she wished to do so.

Penny head the faint click as the door unlocked. Tentatively, she turned the knob and cracked the door open. "Can I come in?" she asked again. When there was no response, she pushed the door open a little further, and stuck her head just inside.

Larry was washing his face, trying to remove the telltale evidence. Perhaps it hid the worst from her, but Penny could easily see the redness in his eyes, shining out like scars from deep wounds inflicted long ago, still refusing to heal. Rather than say anything, she simply stepped inside the bathroom, and put her arms around him, hugging him like a mother hugs a child who has broken his favorite toy.

He accepted her into his arms just as readily, almost instantly feeling the comforting warmth providing some relief from the images torturing his mind. Washing his face might have relieved some of the obvious symptoms, but it did nothing to stop the flood still streaking his face.

"What's wrong, sweet boy?" she asked him softly.

"I don't think I can explain," he replied.

"It's OK," she said. "If you don't want to talk about it, I'll understand, but maybe it'll help you to deal with these feelings if you talk about them. I'll be pleased to listen if you want to talk."

For several minutes, they stood silently, embracing. As promised, Penny said nothing and asked no questions. Strengthened by her support, he began to open up. "In my dreams, I always see Julie as a young woman, much like yourself, all grown up and strong, ready to take on the world. We're together, the way I want us to be, as free and happy as lovers are meant to be. When we make love, it's a symphony, where we make a beautiful melody lifted into the heavens as if on wings of gold.

"But when John said something about Julie coming to this party, I suddenly saw a different image. I saw the little girl I met two years ago, only she was being raped and ravaged by some terrible demon. She looked at me with those green eyes of hers, pleading with me to save her. All the while, the demon was laughing at me, knowing there was nothing I could do to stop him."

"It's never occurred to you she might have sex with one of her boyfriends, has it, Larry?" Penny asked softly.

"No," he whimpered. "To me, she's just a little girl. I guess I thought she'd remain that way until the day a miracle occurs, and she's mine. She'll suddenly turn into a woman who'll be mine forever."

"It's a lovely dream," Penny said softly, "but reality doesn't work that way."

"I know," he said in anguish. "That suddenly struck home a few moments ago."

"Do you expect her to remain a virgin until you come along to save her from all those dragons and demons roaming the world?" she asked.

"What if I'm already too late?" he asked.

"What if you are?" Penny replied. "Why do you expect something of her you're not willing to give yourself?"

Larry nodded his head in understanding. "I'm still obsessed with the old double standard, aren't I?" he asked, feeling ashamed of himself. "But I still can't bear to think of her being with another guy."

"Tell me something, Larry," Penny began. "Which would you rather be – the first guy to make love to her, or the last?"

The question actually brought a smile to Larry's face. "I'll assume that was meant as a rhetorical question. Penny, that sums up the real reason I'm so cautious about declaring myself to her. Yes, I want to be with her right now, today! But I know I'm only going to get one chance, and I want to give myself the best possible chance. What if she really *is* the little honey pot I've been looking for all my life? I can't afford to blow it because I don't have the patience to wait until the right opportunity comes along! Does it really matter if she has other boyfriends in the meantime? If she really *is* the right girl for me, then the important thing is not to be her very first boyfriend, or even her next. The important thing is to be her *last* boyfriend!"

"That's the spirit!" Penny said. "What do you really expect from this girl?"

"I don't know, Penny," he said sadly. "I really don't know. I don't know what I expect. I don't know how I feel. I don't know how to *tell* her the way I feel. I don't know what to do! I don't know *anything!*"

"Actually, you know quite a bit," Penny said softly. "You know she's a very special person to you. You know you want to be with her. And you know how to treat her when you do get together with her." She turned her head so she could look directly into his eyes. "Do you remember me telling you earlier about wanting to find a man with a great heart and a good mind? All I have is a dream. On the other hand, you're so lucky! You've *found* your dream! Your goal is in sight. You know where you want to go. All you need is a road map to guide you there."

"Yes!" he agreed, staring into her eyes. "But where can I find this road map?"

"Look into your heart," Penny said simply. "It may be a long journey, but when the time comes, you'll find your answer there."

Larry saw the truth in her words. In the stark reality of the world, little had changed. In fact, the only differences were in his attitude. He was no happier than he had been before. He had no more hope for happiness than he did before. His dreams were no closer to reality than they had been before. He had no more idea of how to make those dreams come true than he did before. But now, he realized he had a goal, and was committed to achieving that goal. He was now determined to use every ounce of his energy to answer one simple question. Was Julia Anne Jacobson the girl he saw in his dreams every night? Was she the girl with whom he wanted to spend the rest of his life?

But that question would not, could not be answered tonight. "Please don't take this the wrong way, Penny," he said with a soft smile, "but... I love you!"

"How could anyone take *that* the wrong way?" she laughed. She smiled sweetly looking into his eyes and saw the truth in his words. "I love you, too, sugar."

Still standing in the bathroom, still holding each other in a warm embrace, still naked from their earlier exercises, they began to kiss, once more caressing as lovers without a care in the world. Moments later, they found themselves lying on her bed, giving each other the physical delight and emotional comfort they both needed.

Outside, the others could hear the moans of pleasure coming from the bedroom. "It seems I was right, John," Sam grinned. "Penny is helping him a lot more than either of us could."

"A lot more than *I* could, anyway!" John agreed smiling. "I could use a little help like that myself. How would you like to run back upstairs for a minute, Krystal?"

"If it'll only take you a minute, then why bother going all the way upstairs?" Krystal laughed, swinging herself over to sit on John's lap. "I happen to know Nichol likes to watch almost as much as she likes to participate! If you don't like to watch, Sam, I suggest you close your eyes!"

"Check, please!" Sam laughed, calling for the non-existent waiter. Sam and Nichol watched the activities before them, and listened to those inside the apartment, finding them both to be fascinating. Minutes later, as the activity died down, they watched Krystal roll off of John's body, and cuddle up under his arm. She winked at the other girls, and they all laughed as John looked around sheepishly, not knowing what, if anything, he should say.

Fortunately, Larry and Penny soon reappeared through the sliding glass door, so John didn't have to say anything. As he stepped back into the hot tub, Sam noticed the smile had returned to Larry's face. "How do you feel, Larry?"

"He feels fantastic!" Nichol answered for him, drawing a laugh.

Larry and John exchanged a glance, wondering if they were the butt of some joke, but decided they really didn't care even if they were. "I feel much better, Sam," Larry answered for himself.

"I didn't mean to upset you, man," John said, making an unnecessary apology.

"Forget it," Larry smiled. "It wasn't your fault. My head just had a screw loose."

"I got it nice and tight for him," Penny bragged. The guys understood that joke.

Sunday, September 22, 1968
Somebody To Love

"Happy birthday, Mrs. J!" Larry beamed.

Jessica greeted him with a hug and a smile. "Thanks, Larry."

"I'd like you to meet some new friends of mine, Mrs. J. This is Penny, Nicole, and Krystal, otherwise known as the famous Ball sisters. Ladies, this is Mrs. Jacobson. And this little fellow trying to climb my leg is Schotzy!"

"It's nice to meet you girls," Jessica smiled.

The girls took turns introducing themselves both to her and to the dog. "Thank you for allowing us to come to your birthday party, Mrs. Jacobson," Penny said.

"Come on inside. We're happy to have you," Jessica assured them. "Friends of the famous *Four Musketeers* are always welcome here! I'm not actually having a party, anyway, just a gathering of a few friends."

"Isn't that what the best parties are?" Larry asked.

"I suppose you're right," Jessica smiled. "OK, girls! Welcome to my birthday party! Please call me Mrs. J, like the others, or simply Jessica if you prefer."

"Happy birthday, Mrs. J," Nicole said stepping inside, joined by her sisters.

"My goodness!" Jessica exclaimed. "I understood you were identical twins, but I wasn't prepared for this! I can guess which of you is Krystal, but how does anyone tell which is Penny and which is Nicole? You're even dressed exactly alike!"

"It's not easy," Penny and Nicole giggled, "unless you're one of the privileged few who knows our secret!"

Jessica chuckled along with them, carefully noting the way they glanced at Larry, and how it caused him to blush. She came to the conclusion this secret, whatever it might be, would not be revealed while the girls were fully dressed. Then she wondered whether they were teasing Larry because he wanted to know their secret, or because he did! "You're always full of surprises, Larry. Can *you* tell them apart?"

"Of course, Mrs. J," he beamed. "This is Nicole, and this is Penny."

"Are you sure?" Penny giggled. "Don't you want to ask anything first?"

"It's not necessary, Penny," he smiled.

"Is he right?" Jessica grinned. The little interplay told her he knew their secret, but was claiming he knew another way to tell them apart. The girls were certain to call his bluff before the day was over. That would provide even more entertainment!

"This time," Nicole grinned, "but he had a fifty-fifty chance of guessing!"

"You have a lovely home, Mrs. J," Krystal commented as Jessica led the group through the family room to the back door. "How do you like living in the country?"

"Thank you, Krystal," Jessica smiled. "We find it comfortable. We all like living in the country, especially when friends come to visit. The *Four Musketeers* spend a lot of time on the patio when the weather is as nice as today. The others are eagerly waiting for your arrival so the fun can start."

"She must be talking about some *other* group!" Larry laughed. "The *Four Musketeers* I know can have fun anywhere, anytime, whether I'm there or not!"

"But they have more fun when the whole group is together, now don't they, Mr. Smartypants?" Jessica teased. "Girls, this is my husband, Julian. Why don't we put him to the test again? Step on up, Larry, and introduce your friends properly."

"Hi, Mr. J! This is Penny," he said designating one of the girls.

Penny smiled at her sister. "It's very nice to meet you, Mr. Jacobson."

"Nice to meet you as well," Julian smiled. "Call me Julian. Oh, why do I bother? By the end of the day, you'll be calling me that 'Mr. J' nonsense like all the others!"

"This is her twin sister, Nicole," Larry grinned as he introduce the next girl.

"Welcome, Nicole," Julian smiled as they shook hands.

"Wonderful to meet you," Nicole smiled.

"And this is their sister, Krystal," Larry said, introducing the remaining girl.

Krystal offered her hand, "Pleased to meet you, Mr. J," she smiled.

"See what I mean?" Julian grinned. "It's a pleasure to meet you, Krystal."

When Larry turned his full attention to the one remaining member of the Jacobson family, Jessica sensed there was something more significant about the event than seen on the surface. "Girls, the other night, you met all of the *Four Musketeers* except one. This is Julia Jacobson, and her friend, Ed Doggett. You already know John and Sam. Guys, this is Penny, Nichol, and Krystal, the famous Ball sisters!"

As Julia and Ed greeted each of the sisters individually, Jessica wondered about the significance of this event. She was so distracted she almost missed the obvious exchange between John and Krystal. "Hi, John," Krystal said smiling brightly.

"Hi, Krystal," John replied softly. "You look as stunning as you did last week!"

"You're sweet!" she smiled. "Are you going to make some music this afternoon?"

"That's the plan!" John brightened. "What do you say, Larry? Are you ready?"

"Whenever the birthday girl is ready!" Larry grinned.

Larry and John had prepared a program of Jessica's favorite songs from Broadway plays and musicals. They began with songs from *South Pacific*, including *Bloody Mary*, *Younger Than Springtime*, and *This Nearly Was Mine*. They continued with *Oh, What a Beautiful Morning* and *People Will Say We're in Love* from *Oklahoma!* From *The Music Man* they added *Till There Was You*, followed by *With a Little Bit of Luck*, *Get Me To The Church On Time*, and *I've Grown Accustomed to Her Face* from *My Fair Lady*. From *Carousel*, Larry sang *You'll Never Walk Alone*, but avoided *If I Loved You*. During rehearsals, Larry never sang that song to completion without his voice breaking. From *Flower Drum Song*, Larry added *You Are Beautiful*, a song he had studied in the few private voice lessons he had ever taken.

Jessica's favorite musical was *Fiddler on the Roof*. The highlight of the program for her was when Larry put down his guitar and did a passable, but laughable dance singing *If I Were a Rich Man*. They ended her birthday performance with what many people thought was the most beautiful song from that show, *Sunrise, Sunset*. Unlike the original, where the various lines are sung by different characters in the play, Larry simply sang all of the verses himself.

No one noticed none of the songs from *The Sound of Music* were included. John and Sam assumed Larry was not interested, and did not want to drag up ghosts of the past. No one gave any thought that songs from *Oliver!* had been equally ignored. Frankly, because the program contained so many songs, no one even noticed these omissions.

Even when the program officially ended, however, there was still one more song to be sung. Just as the concert of show tunes concluded, Julia and her father sneaked into the house and signaled when they were ready. Larry got everyone to join him in singing *Happy Birthday* to Jessica while her family brought out the cake.

Larry started the drive back to the girls' apartment lost in silence. Krystal had come along for the ride that afternoon, happy to continue her acquaintance with John, but mainly interested in hearing the boys make more music. It was clear to both boys the romantic relationship between John and Krystal would not consist of more than the one-night they had already shared together. When John had offered to drive Krystal home himself, her response, that daddy had taught her "always go home with the one that brung ya," gently emphasized the point.

Larry's relationship with Penny and Nichol was no different. None of them thought this afternoon was a date in any true sense of the word. They were simply good friends, spending a little time with each other, just like the *Four Musketeers*. These particular friends had enjoyed the physical pleasures derived from sharing their bodies, and all of them agreed it had been a wonderful experience. Larry had a fabulous memory of a fantasy fulfilled he would cherish until the end of his days. But they would also agree this brief and shining moment was now in the past, unlikely to ever be repeated.

Penny broke the silence as they drove home. "She's a delightful girl, Larry. It's no wonder you're so much in love with her."

"I wish I knew for certain that's what this is all about," he sighed. "How can I be in love with her, Penny? It's true I love her as a dear friend, just as I love John and Sam. I've only known you a couple of weeks now, and I also love you. We've shared a few moments of intimacy together, enough to know our destiny isn't to share a future. I know I'm not *in* love with you, and you're not in love with me. On the other hand, Julie and I have had no such moments of intimacy, sexual or otherwise. We've never so much as held hands, looked into each others' eyes, or shared our innermost thoughts, hopes, and dreams. Don't you think you have to share at least a little of that before you fall in love with someone? Or do you actually believe in love at first sight?"

"I've never believed in love at first sight," Nichol answered. "I understand what you're saying, but I can see the love in your eyes when you look at her."

"I don't know how to explain it," Penny admitted. "But there's definitely something to this. You'll have to keep chasing this dream to find out what it is!"

"Maybe it's like the *Flower Drum Song* you sang for Mrs. J," Krystal suggested. "Maybe Julia is like the girl in the flower boat. All you really know about her is your eyes met briefly when her boat went drifting by one day. The day you first met her, you somehow knew at that moment, just like the last line of the song, *"You are the girl I will love someday."* Perhaps that's what love at first sight really means."

They rode along in silence again as Larry contemplated Krystal's wisdom. After a few moments, Penny broke the silence, "Nicole, I think our little sister has grown up a lot more than we thought, wouldn't you agree? Larry, you're only nineteen, and Julia isn't quite sixteen years old. You and she have a wonderful friendship. Perhaps the intimacy you seek to answer your questions is something the two of you aren't quite ready to share. Perhaps that lies ahead, somewhere in your future."

Larry nodded his head gently. "It's the best explanation I've heard yet. But I want her so! I need her so! What am I supposed to do in the meantime?"

"I suggest you treasure the friendship you share with her," Penny said, "and you treasure your dreams of how wonderful it'll be when the moment finally comes where you can hold her hand, look into her eyes, and share with her your innermost thoughts, your hopes, and your dreams."

"But I already treasure those things! How long must I have nothing but dreams?"

"Give that question some thought," Nichol said. "Perhaps someone smart enough to figure out a way to tell us apart without asking our favorite color is smart enough to come up with the answer on his own. Are you going to explain how you do it?"

"No," he smiled. "All I'll tell you is I'm sometimes able to sense what certain animals are thinking. After all, humans are animals, too!"

As was his custom, Larry opened the car doors and walked the girls to their front door. Krystal said goodnight and departed to her upstairs apartment, while the older sisters stood at the door for a few parting words. "Thanks for letting us meet her," Penny said. "I hope you'll let us know now and then how things are going."

"Yes, Larry," Nichol agreed. "Please let us know."

"I will," he assured them. "I'd also like to hear how you two are doing from time to time. I hope you can find suitable replacements for Tweedledee and Tweedledum. Jeez, this sounds so damn final, like we might never see each other again!"

"Our paths will cross again one of these days," the twins smiled in unison. "Goodnight, sugar!"

"Goodnight," he said softly.

On her way to retire for the evening, Jessica stopped by her daughter's room, as was her custom. Sometimes, when she knew there was no reason to think anything further was needed, she would simply stick her head in the bedroom door and wish Julia goodnight. Other times, such as tonight, she could sense there was a reason something more might be needed, and would give her daughter the opportunity to engage in a conversation. "Did you get all your homework done, sweetheart?"

"Yes, ma'am," came the unenthusiastic reply.

"So you're all set for another week of school?" Jessica asked calmly.

"As ready as I can be," Julia answered.

"OK, then bubee," Jessica smiled. "Goodnight, and sweet dreams."

"Goodnight, mom," Julia replied. "Oh, and happy birthday!"

"Thanks, sugar!" Jessica answered warmly, opening the door of opportunity for a conversation to begin. "And just think! Your own birthday is now just one month away. This year, you'll be turning sweet sixteen! Aren't you excited about that?"

"A little, I guess," Julia answered without much enthusiasm.

"Well, you *should* be!" Jessica smiled. "Sixteen is the age girls start to take more control of their own lives, becoming a little more independent from mom and dad. You're almost all grown up!"

"If you say so, mom," Julia shrugged.

"I though something might be bothering you," Jessica said. She sat on the edge of her daughter's bed. "Would you like to talk about it?"

"I don't know," Julia answered without answering.

"If you didn't want to talk about it, then you would have said so," Jessica smiled. "So what is this thing you want to talk about, but you don't know *how* to talk about? Are you worried about your next birthday?"

"Not really," Julia said, "although I admit I don't feel very grown up right now."

"Are you and Ed still getting along?" Jessica asked.

"Yeah, we're OK," Julia said.

"Something is troubling you," Jessica smiled, "something you don't understand."

"Maybe it's myself I don't understand," Julia said looking down at the floor. "At first, I thought I was just upset because of the way Ed gawked at the Ball sisters all afternoon."

"Very pretty girls have this ability to turn a man's head," Jessica smiled. "It's just something you have to accept and live with, because nothing will ever change it. Even an older man like your father is not completely immune, although I doubt he noticed himself how often he ogled them."

"What?" Julia asked, somewhat surprised by this bit of information.

"Oh, he'd never seriously entertain for a moment the thought he might actually do anything," Jessica grinned. "In fact, if they so much as looked at him cross-eyed, he would run away and hide so fast it would made your head spin!" The girls giggled to themselves at the incongruity of this image before Jessica continued. "It's just the way nature has made them, sugar. Deep in the male brain there's a place where they subconsciously evaluate their chances of spreading their genes with every female they encounter. Consciously, they're completely unaware of this activity."

"Unless they think their chances are real?" Julia grinned. "Or even fifty-fifty?"

"They don't even have to be that good!" Jessica said, returning her daughter's grin. "So don't be angry at Ed. He really couldn't help himself, no matter how hard he might have tried."

"I didn't know the reason," Julia sighed, "but I wasn't really angry. I guess I'm just jealous. I wish I could be one of those pretty girls who can turn a man's head."

"But you *are*, bubee," Jessica said giving her daughter a hug, "and you're getting prettier every day."

"Aw, mom," Julia said. "Don't try to fool me. I'm just a ugly, skinny little kid with a mouth full of metal. I'll never be able to turn a boy's head the way Penny, Nichol, and Krystal do."

"I won't try to fool you as long as you don't try to fool yourself," Jessica assured her. "You are most certainly not ugly! You have lovely facial features, with nice high cheek bones, an adorable little pug nose, and rich full lips. Don't you think for a moment those beautiful green eyes go unnoticed! You're certainly not skinny anymore, either. If you take a good look at yourself in the mirror, you'll see you've been filling out very nicely in all the right places for the last couple of years. You have a beautiful figure that's already capable of turning heads, and it's going to get even more capable in the near future.

"And sweetheart, I know you hate them, but please remember you won't have to wear those braces forever. You already have a very sweet smile, and when those braces come off, your beautiful, straight teeth are going to make that smile dazzling! When your features mature a little more, and your braces finally do come off, every boy you meet is going to notice you, just like they notice the Ball sisters, and that's a promise!"

"You're just saying that because you're my mom," Julia said sadly.

"No, bubee," Jessica assured her, "I'm saying these things because they are true."

"Do you think he'll notice me when my braces come off?" Julia whispered.

"Do I think *who* will notice you?" Jessica asked.

"You know who I mean," Julia said softly.

"You still have a crush on him?" Jessica asked, a little surprised by this revelation.

"Sometimes," Julia confessed. "Especially when I see him with beautiful girls like Penny, Nichol, and Krystal. I sometimes find myself wishing I could be the one who holds his hand, looks into his eyes, and shares secret hopes and dreams with him. But he wants to be with Sam, so what chance do I have?"

Jessica nodded her head to acknowledge her understanding, and spoke softly. "Does this crush create a problem with your friendship with either Sam or Larry?"

"I don't understand why she doesn't take what he's offering like I would," Julia sighed. "Sometimes I want to be both his friend *and* his girlfriend. Is that terrible?"

Jessica smiled warmly. "Hardly, sweetheart. That's the way I've always thought things should work. Two people start out as friends, and then one day, they find they have changed into lovers." Sensing that Julia was hanging on her next words, she thought carefully before proceeding. "I don't understand a lot of things about him. For example, I don't really understand his relationship with Sam. I know he noticed you, but I don't know why he didn't chase you when he had the chance. But he's known Sam for a very long time, and it's clear he has his sights firmly fixed on her."

"What should I do, mom?" Julia asked.

"I know it won't be easy, sugar," Jessica answered, "but all you can do is sit back and wait. The way she keeps resisting his advances, things might change someday, and his eyes might turn in your direction. If so, it'll be *his* responsibility to make the first move, and until he does, all you can do is wait. You should continue to be his friend, his best friend, just as you are now. Keep your options open. Like we talked about a few years ago, you have to look at a lot of possibilities before you know who's the right one, the one you'll share your life with."

"I know," Julia said. "I also said I hoped I wouldn't meet the right boy until I had enough experience to *know* he was the right one."

"You're still young, almost ready to turn sweet sixteen," Jessica smiled. "I promise you still have plenty of time. And when you *do* find the right one, you'll *know* he's the right one! Are you OK, sweetheart?"

"I'm OK, mom," Julia smiled. "I love you!"

"Goodnight, my daughter," Jessica said returning that smile. "I love you, too."

Tuesday, October 22, 1968
You're Sixteen

Early in the evening, her parents took Julia and Ed out for pizza, her favorite food and traditional birthday dinner. When they returned, the *Four Musketeers* and many other friends gathered at Julia's house for a simple party. There would be cake and ice cream, a few simple gifts for the birthday girl, and plenty of music and laughter. Once again, the Drug Company would provide entertainment for the party.

The boys more or less forced themselves to take on a positive attitude. So far, the year had been a mixture of very high highs and very low lows for them. It had been what people euphemistically refer to as an eventful year. Many of the personal events had been positive, but most of the world events were anything but. There was an ongoing war becoming increasingly unpopular, two horrible assassinations, and what the gang could only describe as a police riot in the streets of Chicago. In exactly two weeks, there would be a Presidential election in which the nation would be given the dubious choice between Richard Nixon and Hubert Humphrey. Before it even occurred, this election had destroyed what little faith the kids still had in the ability of the political process to resolve the many problems faced by the nation.

With all these things hanging over their heads, the *Four Musketeers* were determined to raise each others' spirits. What better time than when celebrating the birthday of their youngest member? After talking it over among themselves, they had come to an agreement. The jokes told by the Drug Company that night would be a lot more risqué than those from the previous years. While they had not been given much of a choice in the matter, Julia told her parents to expect this.

The party followed a familiar format. The Drug Company provided live music as the guests arrived, and continued playing for the first hour. The songs included the top four songs of the year, *Hey Jude* by the Beatles, *Young Girl* from Gary Puckett and the Union Gap, *People Got to be Free* by the Rascals, and *Mrs. Robinson* from Simon and Garfunkel. Upon a signal from Mrs. Jacobson, Larry led the group in singing the last song of the set, *Happy Birthday To You*. After enjoying the birthday cake and ice cream, the guests presented Julia with an assortment of small gag gifts.

Julia soon came upon a small box with no name card. "Who's this from?" she asked with a smile, looking around from face to face.

When no one confessed, Sam gave Larry a dubious look, and suggested, "Go ahead and open it, Julia. Maybe there'll be note or a clue on the inside."

"OK," Julia grinned. Under the wrapping paper was a small cardboard box. Inside this box was another, this one made of metal, and decorated with painted images of small dachshunds. "How sweet!" she smiled. When she opened the metal box, it played *(How Much Is That) Doggy in the Window*. She looked over at one of her dearest friends, who could not manage to hide the smile on his face, and said sweetly, "Thank you, Larry." He did not respond with words; his grin told everyone she had guessed correctly.

Moments later, an even smaller package appeared without a card. "This one doesn't have a card, either," Julia said. "Who's this one from?" This time, John, Sam, and several others simultaneously confessed they had each given it to her. "You ought to be ashamed of yourself!" she giggled. She pulled back the wrapping paper to find a small white cardboard box. Inside the box was a bit of cotton. Nestled on top of the cotton was a small silver charm – a hummingbird.

"What is it?" Ed asked her.

"It's a charm for my bracelet," Julia smiled examining it. After a moment, she raised her eyes and looked at him again. "You also gave me this, didn't you, Larry?"

He smiled and shrugged. Julia recalled the words he had told her on his own birthday, about how the most beautiful songs come from the heart and not the throat.

It was time for the Drug Company to take the stage again to perform their second set. After *San Francisco, Wear Some Flowers*, they broke into a conversational mode. John asked Larry a simple question. "Say, Larry," he began with a smile, "do you know the difference between the government and the Mafia?"

"Hmm," Larry said, rubbing his chin as if in thought. "Well, the main difference is that one of them is actually organized!"

The guests chuckled at the joke, generally agreeing that truth is actually funnier than fiction. The boys launched right into their next bit. "After a fabulous reception," John smiled, "the newly married couple retreated into their honeymoon suite. The bride was eager to consummate their marriage, and left for the bathroom to prepare for bed. She returned in minutes with great anticipation, in a beautiful sheer negligee, adorned in lace. Upon her return, she noticed her new husband was still sitting on the edge of the bed fully dressed."

"What's wrong, sweetheart?" Larry asked in a feminine voice imitating the bride.

Playing the roll of the husband, John replied, "I'm too embarrassed to undress."

"But sweetheart," the bride said, "I've been preparing for this moment all my life! Don't you want to get into bed with me?"

"Accepting the gravity of the situation," John explained, "the groom began to undress. Off came his shoes, shirt, and then his socks. As he pulled off his socks, she noticed his feet were all curled up."

Larry spoke again as the bride. "Oh, honey! What happened to your feet?"

"I had toe-lio as a child," John replied.

"You mean polio, right?" the bride asked.

"No," John insisted. "It was toe-lio."

"How dreadful!" Larry exclaimed. "It's OK. You don't need to be embarrassed."

"His pants came off next," John explained. "She stared at his disfigured legs."

"Oh, honey!" Larry put his hands to his face. "What happened to your knees?"

"I had knee-sels," John replied.

"Don't you mean measles?" Larry asked.

"No," came John's reply. "It was called knee-sels."

"Oh, sweetheart!" Larry exclaimed.

"The groom next stood, and shyly pulled off his underpants," John continued.

In an alarmed voice, Larry exclaimed, "Wait! Wait! Wait! Don't tell me! Did you also have smallcox?"

When the laughter subsided, Larry began playing a simple rhythm on the back of his guitar, emulating the sound made by a tom-tom. With this in the background, the boys entered into a solemn dialog. "Just a short distance from where I stand," Larry began, "are the hunting grounds of the famous Fukouwee Indians of East Texas."

"Widely known as the only *Pygmy* Indians in North America," John continued, "the stature of the proud Fukouwee warriors averaged a mere four feet, while the squaws stood at an average height three feet eight inches."

"Yet in spite of their diminutive size," Larry noted, "the Fukouwee Indians were renown for their fierce devotion to these hunting grounds, and for their skillful stand as they defiantly resisted the government's attempts to resettle them elsewhere."

John explained, "For they refused to give up their ancestral hunting grounds on the coastal plains of southeast Texas, where the salt grass grows to an average height of five feet." A few of the guests began to chuckle as they spotted the difference in the height of the Indians and that of the grass.

"Even today," Larry said, "years after the Fukouwee Indians were wiped out in the terrible battle known as the massacre at Burning Bush..."

"...fought between Grinning Beaver Ridge and Possum Bottoms..." John added.

"...if one stands very quietly within the five foot tall salt grass that continues to dominate those former hunting grounds," Larry said solemnly, as he stopped playing his impromptu tom-tom, "you can still sometimes hear their proud battle cry as the ghosts of those warriors from the past jump high into the air to raise their heads above the top of the grass, proclaiming their identity."

"We're the Fukouwee?" Larry and John exclaimed, both jumping into the air as high as they could. "We're the Fukouwee?"

The kids laughed merrily. Mr. and Mrs. Jacobson merely rolled their eyes exchanging a glance, trying not to snicker too obviously. But the boys quickly began another dialog.

"Hear ye! Hear ye! Hear ye!" John exclaimed. "All parties in the matter concerning Mouse vs. Mouse please step forward."

"Oh! Ha, ha, ha!" Larry responded in a Mickey Mouse imitation, "That's me!"

Now sounding like a judge, John instructed, "Mr. Mouse, please state your full name for the record."

"OK. Ha, ha, ha!" Larry continued. "My name is Mickey Mouse, your honor."

"Thank you, Mr. Mouse," John replied as the judge. "Now please state for the court the purpose of these proceedings."

"Well, your honor," Larry explained, "I want a divorce from my wife, Minnie. Ha, ha, ha!" Each time Mickey Mouse laughed, the guests responded stronger.

"Mr. Mouse," John continued as the judge, "I've read the motion you've prepared, but frankly, I have some serious questions about it. The main problem is you simply haven't listed any valid grounds I can use for granting you a divorce from your wife. Just because you claim your wife is insane doesn't give you grounds for a divorce."

"Oh! Ha, ha, ha!" Larry replied. "You don't understand, your honor. I don't want a divorce because I think she's insane."

John shook his head. "Then I really don't understand, Mr. Mouse!" he said sounding exasperated. "That seems to be exactly what your motion contends, even though you use a rather colorful way to describe her condition. If insanity isn't your reason, then please explain exactly how I'm supposed to interpret your request?"

"OK. Ha, ha, ha!" Larry said. "Your honor, it's not that Minnie is insane! She's fucking Goofy! You have to realize this isn't just colorful language. I mean it quite literally. She's been fucking Goofy for five years now!"

It took several minutes for the laughter to stop. Julia and the other girls laughed but covered their face to hide the embarrassing flush. Even Mr. Jacobson could not keep a stern face. The boys continued their program with more music. Just as he had done the previous year, Larry elected to conclude their concert with the old Beatles classic, *I'll Get You*. The song was a good summary of his feelings about the little girl with the green eyes who haunted his dreams, and his determination to discover the meaning behind those dreams. He would get her in the end.

Saturday, December 7, 1968
Hound Dog

Ed arrived to pick up Julia for their date shortly before 7:00. As usual, when he rang the doorbell, the dog barked excitedly. The bark changed to a low growl when the dog reached the door, looked through the sidelight window, and saw who was standing outside the front door. Ed and Julia's dog never got along very well.

Mr. Jacobson picked up Schotzy and held him. "Good evening, Ed. Come on into the living room. I'm sure Julia will be out shortly."

"Thanks, Mr. Jacobson," Ed said politely, giving the dog a dirty look.

Jessica stepped out of the kitchen to greet him. "Hello, Ed."

"Hello, Mrs. Jacobson," Ed echoed. "How are you this evening?"

"I'm just fine, thanks for asking." She took the dog from her husband, announcing, "I'll take Schotzy to Julia's room and see what's keeping her."

"What are your plans for this evening?" Julian asked, making light conversation.

"Nothing spectacular," Ed replied. "We're going to grab a bite to eat, then go to the station to help out with that radio show."

"I see," Julian said. He was relieved when Julia arrived from her room.

"Hi, sweetie!" Julia said brightly, giving him a quick peck on the mouth. "I hope I didn't keep you waiting too long. You're a little earlier than usual."

"Less traffic than usual," he replied. "Besides, I want enough time to eat before we get to the station, so those vultures won't have the chance to pick on our dinner!"

He grinned like it was a joke, but Julia knew it was actually one of his little pet peeves. "Then we'd better get moving!" she smiled. "Goodnight, mom! Goodnight, dad! Don't wait up for me!"

"Goodnight, dear," her parents said in unison.

"You kids have a good time," Jessica said. After Ed and Julia closed the door behind them, she added, "I guess I'll go let Schotzy back out now."

"I wonder what it is about that kid he doesn't like," Julian thought aloud.

Ed opened the door and Julia slid under the steering wheel. "I wonder what it is about you Schotzy doesn't like," she said as Ed slipped onto the seat beside her.

"Beats me," he said simply.

"Do you have a dog of your own?" she asked casually.

"Not any more!" he said.

"What kind was it?" she asked.

"Heinz 57," Ed replied.

"What was it's name?" she asked, trying to get him to talk more about it.

"Mom named him Tiger, but I called him Shit Head," he said with a laugh.

"So it was a boy dog," she asked rhetorically. It wasn't difficult for Julia to sense he was happy he no longer had this dog. "You don't particularly like dogs, do you?"

"They're alright, I guess," he replied with a shrug. "Maybe I got burned out on them. I got really tired of having to take care of the dog I used to have. All the time, my mom would get onto me. *'Feed the dog,'* she would say, *'Take the dog for a walk,'* do this, or do that. All the time, I always had to do something for that dog, and for what? The dog never did anything for *me!*"

"I imagine he gave you devotion and friendship," Julia said.

"Maybe, but who needs it?" Ed said with a chuckle. "Dogs are fine for little boys, but I'd much rather have the devotion and friendship from a girl like you!"

"Aw! You're so sweet," she smiled. "So what happened to your dog?"

"He just disappeared one day and never came back," Ed replied. "We assumed he ran off and got hit by a car or something. Or maybe he took up residence with someone else. I don't know, and frankly, I don't really care, either! All I have to say is good riddance!"

"That seems a little cold hearted," Julia said with a frown.

"Perhaps it is at that," Ed said, trying to soften his earlier statement. "But after all, Julia, it was just a dumb animal. It's not like we're talking about another human being, like my baby sister or something."

Sunday, December 8, 1968
Bless The Beasts And Children

That afternoon had been a good rehearsal session, and everyone was in a good mood. There were only two more weeks in the school semester, meaning there was still another week for everyone to get ready for final exams. This was not much of a concern for any of them, with one very minor exception. As the boys were packing up their instruments, and cutting up as usual, Julia interrupted their clowning with a slightly more serious question. "Larry, could I get you to do me a favor?"

"Sure thing, doll!" he responded. "What do you need? Blood? A liver transplant? Maybe a new kidney?"

"Nothing so dramatic," she laughed. "I've been having a little trouble with algebra. Every time I think I've gotten a handle on it, it seems to change on me. I was hoping you might be able to give me some pointers."

"You got it!" Larry replied happily. If there was anything in the world he liked to do, it was to help Julia in any way. Those chances came along rarely, it seemed, so he was eager to jump on every one of them. "When would you like to do this?"

"Is now a good time?" she asked hopefully.

"Now is perfect!" he answered with a bright smile.

"Let me get out of earshot first!" John pleaded. "The last thing I want to hear right now is anything that reminds me of the math course I'm taking this semester."

"I thought you were acing that class," Larry stated calmly, concerned his friend might not have been forthcoming with the truth when they talked about class work.

"I am," John assured him with a chuckle, "I just don't want to be reminded of it!"

"I'm with you, John," Sam grinned. "I remember high school algebra, but I'd happily forget it if they'd just let me!" Larry just shook his head and looked at her.

"I'm out of here!" John announced. "Goodnight, guys!"

"Me, too," Sam added, following closely behind him. The gang exchanged a goodnight wish as Sam and John hit the front door and ran for their cars, trying not to get too wet from the steady rain.

"One of these days I'm going to have to do a research study on this," Larry said, shaking his head as he watched them run to their cars. "I'm convinced you'd actually get less water on you if you simply *walked* in the rain, rather than running."

"That doesn't make any sense, Larry," Julia said to him.

"It does seem counter-intuitive, doesn't it?" he shrugged. "I'm not sure what makes me think walking would be better, but somehow it just seems right to me, and my own personal observations seem to bear this out. What I need is a scientific study, with controlled conditions. Then I could prove it one way or another."

"Maybe you should apply for a government grant," Jessica chuckled. "They seem to fund every other kind of study you can think of!"

Larry laughed at the suggestion. "You may be right, Mrs. J! Maybe I should check on that. Come to think of it, maybe I could get a government grant to study the types of things that qualify for government grants! Or something *really* mysterious, like why inmates want to break out of prison!"

"Or why men and women like to kiss each other!" Julia giggled.

"And *where* they like to kiss each other!" he laughed. It flashed through Larry's brain this could be interpreted in two very different ways. Rather than leaving well enough alone, he attempted to clarify, which in reality, only made the situation worse. "What I meant was where they *go* when they kiss each other, such as inside or outside, and what room they kiss in." He realized he needed to think about things before speaking. Seeing Jessica's grin, he decided it was time to shut up. "I'm making it worse, aren't I?"

"I wouldn't know, Larry," Jessica teased him.

Julia giggled at his embarrassment. "Maybe we should take a look at the algebra."

"An excellent suggestion," he agreed, grateful to change the subject. "What exactly are you having trouble with?"

"I'm not sure," she replied. "I'm able to do all the exercises, but it's not clear to me how I'm doing them. I don't understand *why* I get the right answer."

"Hmm," he said deep in thought. "Let's take a look at an actual problem. Maybe I can see where the difficulty is coming from."

He sat on a bench at the kitchen table while Julia got her notebook and algebra book. Schotzy took the opportunity to beg for attention. Larry picked up the dog and held him in his lap, even after Julia returned with her school work.

Julia showed him an example of an exercise giving her trouble. He had her work through the exercise and talk to him as she did, explaining every step she was taking and why. There never was a moment when Julia exclaimed "Eureka!" or anything like that, but after a few simple questions from her, and a few simple answers and other comments from Larry, Julia walked through all of the exercises in the book, was comfortable with the steps needed to solve the problems, and understood why she was taking those steps.

"Thanks, Larry!" she said finally. "Now I understand all this stuff."

"You're welcome, doll," he said, "but to tell you the truth, I'm not exactly sure what I did to help. It seemed to me like you knew what you were doing all along."

"Her dad and I both tried to help her," Jessica explained, "but I could tell she wasn't comfortable. You've been around teachers all your life. Maybe you picked up something from your parents, or perhaps you just have a knack for teaching."

"I guess it's possible," he said. He turned his attention to the dog in his lap, scratching his ears vigorously as he spoke with a big smile on his face, "But I couldn't teach *you* how to solve those algebra problems, could I, Schotzy? You're an old dog, and learning to solve algebra problems would be a new trick for you, doncha know!"

The way the dog looked at him would almost make one think he understood what Larry was saying. When he stopped scratching his ears, Schotzy looked in his face for a moment, then settled comfortably in his lap, and licked the back of his hand.

"He surely does like you," Julia smiled.

"I get along with most dogs," he said as he gently stroked the dog's back. "For that matter, I get along with most animals. Maybe they like the things I say when I talk to them. After all, I like the things they say to me, doncha know! Maybe it's because I think of them as my friends, and not just some dumb animal or something. Maybe that's why I get along with little kids so well. I treat them like they're real persons, and not like they're just little kids! W. C. Fields would not approve of me at all! *'Any man who hates dogs and kids can't be all bad!'* he would say, and I'm exactly the opposite. I don't think Will Rogers would approve of me, either. I also never met a man I didn't like... other than Will Rogers, that is!"

The girls snickered at his joke. "Do you have a dog of your own?" Julia asked.

Larry looked at her with a sad smile. "I used to," he said softly.

"What kind of dog was it?" she asked.

"A dachshund," he replied, "just like Schotzy. In fact, they'd look almost identical, I think, except Schotzy is somewhat older."

"What was his name?" Julia asked.

"We called him Dan Dee," he smiled. "Do you know that hamburger joint at the corner of Texas Avenue and Villa Maria Road called the *Dan Dee Dog*? The name came from those corn dogs on a stick. My mom loves those things, and since they reminded her of the dog, same shape, same color, the name just came naturally."

"That's a sweet name. What happened to him?" Julia asked softly.

"He died a couple of years ago," he said sadly. "I was fourteen. He was with me and my dad in the front yard. We were mowing the lawn, or something. Dan Dee decided to walk across the side street by our house. He knew better than to go into the busy street in front. Anyway, a man in a pickup happened to come down the street at that moment, and turned the corner." He fought to keep his eyes dry, but lost the battle. "He couldn't help it. He couldn't see the dog until it was too late."

"I'm sorry," Julia said to him.

"It's OK," he said, trying to dry his eyes. "It was a long time ago. I must look pretty silly right now."

"Don't worry about it," she said. "It's not easy to loose a dear friend."

"He was that," Larry agreed. "I think the worst part was seeing it happen before my eyes. I was looking right at him the moment he got hit." He stopped for a moment, trying desperately to control his emotions. "I'm sorry. It's not easy for me to remember all this. Dan Dee didn't die right away. He lingered on for several days. I convinced myself he was getting better; I wanted to believe it, but he wasn't. He eventually died of kidney failure. I just hope he didn't suffer too much!"

Neither Julia nor Jessica said anything. There was nothing either of them could have said. They remained silent while Larry regained his composure. "I'm sorry to be such a baby," he sighed. "We tried to get another dog a few months later. We originally got Dan Dee from our neighbors. They normally keep a female dachshund. They had a little female named Sally from the same litter, Dan Dee's sister. When she had her own litter, they offered us our choice. We actually took one for a while, a sweet little male with a crook on the end of his tail. It was either a birth defect, or maybe it just got broken during birth. But we weren't ready for another dog, because no matter how much we tried, no one ever bonded with him. We gave him back when another family wanted a dog. I'm sure he's happy now."

"That's a nice story, Larry," Jessica said. "Have you thought about trying again?"

"It's not a good time at my house right now since my sister moved back home with her baby. It seems to me animals must know a lot more than we humans give them credit. We know their senses are better than ours. Their eyes are better, ears are better, noses are better. I sometimes think they have other senses we don't have. They always seem to know who to trust, and who to keep away from.

"It's too bad no one paid any attention to Dan Dee's assessment of my sister's boyfriend! He hated that guy! Whenever he'd come to the house, I'd have to take Dan Dee to my room, or outside. He actually growled at him on more than one occasion, and I'm pretty sure he'd have bitten him if he'd been given the chance!"

Jessica and Julia exchanged a glance Larry did not understand. "I take it things didn't work out between this guy and your sister?" Jessica asked.

"No!" he said with a peculiar laugh. "They got married the summer after she graduated from high school. My parents didn't care much for him, either, but there was nothing they could do to stop it. She was eighteen, old enough to do whatever she wanted. I remember my father telling her just before they walked down the aisle it wasn't too late to change her mind. Maybe she would have backed out, but didn't think that was an option. She told him it was too late to back out, because all those people were sitting there in the chapel, waiting for the ceremony to start. I'd just turned thirteen at the time, so I didn't understand any of it. My job was to go light some candles to start the ceremony, so that's what I did.

"After lighting the candles, I remember walking over into an alcove on the side of the chapel, where no one could see me. I even cried when the ceremony started. I don't know why, and don't know why I'm telling you about it. I was just glad no one could see me, and I've never told anyone about this before. Maybe I knew something, also. Maybe I somehow understood why Dan Dee didn't like that guy!

"A few years later, after having his baby, my sister came back home to live with our parents again. He filed for divorce, she didn't contest it, and now all he's supposed to do is send some money each month for child support. Of course, he seldom bothers." Larry just sat there, silently looking off into the distance, shaking his head.

After a few moments, he was noticeably more cheerful. "I think dogs are a lot smarter than people. You agree with me, don't you boy?" he asked Schotzy, who stirred from his comfortable position, stood up on his hind legs in Larry's lap, and licked his face. Larry laughed happily as he exclaimed, "Ooh, wet doggy kisses! Get me some disinfectant!"

"Why do you let him do that?" Jessica asked with a grin.

Larry continued laughing and started his reply, "Because no one else..." He stopped in mid-sentence and shrugged. "It's OK. I like doggy kisses. At least I know they're honest and sincere."

"That's for sure!" Julia added, returning his grin.

"Well, if you're also sure of your algebra now, then I should go home." His code phrase was so ingrained into his psyche now he hardly even thought about how much he would rather stay.

"Thank you so much, Larry! I'm so lucky to have a friend like you!"

He smiled at her warmly. "I'm always happy to help. Whenever you need anything, you just let me know. I'll always be here for you." With that statement, he put the dog on the floor and stood up to leave, realizing he needed to get away quickly. *Maybe they understand the tears they've already seen in my eyes tonight, but how could I explain the ones that want to appear now?*

"Goodnight, Larry," Jessica said, smiling at him warmly.

"Goodnight, Mrs. J," he returned. At the front door, he stopped, looked at Julia once again and spoke softly as if it was an echo, "Goodnight, Julie."

"Goodnight, Larry," she said warmly. "Thanks, again!"

"Anytime," he said as he walked out the door. He could feel a burning sensation on his back, knowing those green eyes were watching him walk down the sidewalk. Perhaps she would think he was testing his theory about walking in the rain, rather than running. All he knew was he was grateful she could not see the tears on his cheeks. *Even if she could,* he thought, *perhaps she'd think they're nothing more than the rain.*

While Julian prepared himself, Jessica lay silently in their soft warm bed, staring at the ceiling, lost in thought. "You seem to be strangely quiet tonight, Jessie," Julian said crawling under the covers. "What are you thinking about?"

Jessica looked at him, smiled casually, then shrugged. "I've been thinking about what a remarkable boy he is."

"Which one are you talking about?" Julian asked even though fairly sure he knew the answer. He had learned over the years he got more information from her when he pretended complete ignorance. If she wanted him to know something, she would tell him, and if she did not want him to know, then it was pointless to ask anyway.

"I'm talking about John, of course," she said simply.

"Ah," Julian replied smoothly. Her answer surprised him, but he quickly realized she was pulling a double cross. "Yes, he's a remarkably gifted guitar player!"

"You hypocrite!" Jessica laughed. "You know damn well I wasn't talking about John! I was talking about Ed, of course!"

This time, Julian was even more surprised. "What in the name of hell is so remarkable about him?" he asked, not expecting her to give him a *triple* cross.

"That's better," Jessica grinned. "Do you think you'll ever find a man good enough to be with your little girl, Jules?"

"Maybe," he said, "but it damn sure isn't *that* one!"

"I don't think you'll get any argument from anyone else in the family, especially not Schotzy!" Jessica giggled. "And now that I've got your attention, maybe we can talk seriously, like adults sometimes do. You knew all along I was talking about Larry being quite a remarkable boy."

"That would have been my first guess," Julian confessed. "What has he done this time? Are you talking about how he helped Julia with her algebra?"

"Well, that's remarkable enough, don't you think?" she asked. "We both tried to help her. Maybe I'm not all that proficient in math, but *you* certainly are. She understood the mechanics, but just didn't quite grasp the process lying underneath. I listened to the whole thing, and I can't tell you what he said or did that changed anything at all. All I know is after he talked to her, explained to her the same things we had already explained, she suddenly understood what she'd been missing."

"Couldn't it simply be the third time is the charm?" Julian asked.

"We should include her teacher in the count," she smiled, "making him the *fourth* person to explain it to her." Jessica looked at Julian for a moment before she continued. "Jules, I really don't think it had anything to do with simple repetition. There was something subtly different in the way he explained it to her."

"But you didn't catch what that was," he said, completing the thought process.

"Not at all," Jessica sighed. "Most of the time, when someone learns something they'd been missing before, there's a moment of sudden insight, as if the curtains have suddenly been pulled back, and the truth is revealed."

"Yes, that's normal. It's usually quite evident when that moment arrives."

"That's what I've always thought, anyway," Jessica said, "but that's not the way it happened! It wasn't Julia who had the moment of insight, it was Larry! I remember seeing a sudden smile come over his face. He then backed up and restated some things he'd said earlier. It was like he simply started over. As far as I recall, he said exactly the same things as before, although not in the same words. From that moment on, Julia began to understand what he was telling her!"

"Indeed! That does sound remarkable." He contemplated this information for a moment. "There must have been something different in what he said the second time around, but you didn't notice any difference?" She shook her head and shrugged. "Perhaps you didn't notice because you already understood the answer."

"I see what you mean," Jessica said. "I understood what he said both times, because I understood how to do the exercises. She didn't quite grasp it until he explained it in a new and subtly different way!"

"That'd be my guess," Julian said, feeling happy with himself *he* had been the one to explain something to her!

But Jessica did not stop at this point. "So Larry had a moment of insight, saw what she was missing, and explained it in a different way she would understand?"

"Exactly!" Julian said confidently.

"But how?" Jessica asked. "How did he manage to see what she was missing? We hadn't done so, and obviously even her math teacher hadn't done so. How was this boy able to do this? Don't you find that remarkable?"

Julian was stunned by the question. Had Jessica been leading him along all this time, manipulating his thought patterns to this point, in the hope he could come up with the answer to this new question, the one she was wondering about all along? "Well, uh..." he stumbled. "Maybe it was pure luck. You know what I always say – even a blind squirrel will find a nut now and then!"

Jessica laughed in appreciation of his old joke. "I suppose it's possible, but somehow I don't think so. I saw him have that moment of insight just before this. He obviously figured out the problem, then took the steps necessary to correct it."

"But that's exactly what a good teacher tries to do," Julian said. "His parents are both teachers, and he's been exposed to academic thinking all his life. Maybe some of it has rubbed off on him."

"That would make sense," she agreed. "Perhaps there's nothing more to it than that, and I'm trying to read too much into this and other things."

Julian knew his wife well enough to know they had not reached the end of this conversation. Her last sentence had clearly left a new thought dangling. It was like finding a fumbled football lying on the ground. He was now expected to pick it up and run with it. "What other things are you talking about, Jessie?"

"Remarkable things," she said, again staring at the ceiling. "Something I heard him say tonight gave me some insight into his character, into his soul, if you will."

"What was that?" Julian asked. He was not merely playing the role he knew he was expected to play. He was genuinely curious about her insight into what he also considered to be a remarkable young man.

"You know how he seems to get along so well with animals?" she asked. "Julia told me the kids were once throwing some bread crumbs to the birds. The birds were coming surprisingly close to them. She told me Larry sat down on the ground, held out his hand offering them some bread crumbs, and two of the birds hopped over and ate directly out of his hand!"

"I've seen things like that happen before," Julian laughed.

"That's not the half of it!" Jessica continued. "I happened to be watching him one day, right out here on our patio. The other kids had run off for a moment, leaving him sitting there alone. A butterfly come fluttering by. Jules, he smiled at it, held out his hand, and the butterfly flew over and landed on it! I watched as he moved his hand up near his face to look closely at the butterfly. I swear to you I saw him whisper something to it! Then he held up his hand once again, and the butterfly flew off, continuing on its way."

"I know he gets along well with animals, Jessie, but what you're saying is bordering on the fantastic, don't you think?" Julian asked.

"Let's just call it remarkable," Jessica suggested. "Tonight, I heard him mention he talks to animals, and they sometimes talk back to him! And I've already told you he seems to be having a conversation with that old willow tree in the backyard."

"So what did he say tonight that relates to all this?" Julian asked.

"Julia was talking to him about how much Schotzy likes him," Jessica said. "He responded in his typical off-handed manner, but I remember his exact words. *'Maybe it's because I think of them as my friends, and not just some dumb animal or something.'* Later on, he said animals know a lot more than we humans give them credit. They always seem to know who to trust, and who to keep away from. Animals, even wild ones, somehow know they can trust him to be their friend. Jules, I don't know whether this is true or not, but I get the clear sense *he* believes it!"

"It would be nice to think he's right," Julian said, smiling at his wife.

Jessica snuggled up against her husband and sighed. They lay reflecting on this new insight they were sharing. "Something else he said struck me as significant," Jessica added. "After talking about animals, he also made a comment about why he gets along so well with small children. *'I treat them like they're real persons, and not like they're just little kids!'* Jules, we've talked about this subject before, and I'm sure he's right about children. Do you suppose it really is the same with animals?"

"I don't know, Jessie," he said thoughtfully. "It seems to me Larry possesses a certain quality of innocence about him. Maybe that's why animals and small children are attracted to him. Do you remember the legend of the unicorn? Wasn't it true an innocent little girl could ride a unicorn whenever she wanted, but once she lost her virginity, she could never ride them again?"

"I'm fairly certain Larry is not still a virgin, Jules," Jessica giggled.

"How would you know that?" he asked. When she gave him one of those *I know what I'm talking about* looks, he decided to drop the question. "Virgin or not, he still has that quality of innocence and wonder about him. If that's the secret, I hope he never loses it!"

"Me, too, Jules!" Jessica agreed. "Me, too!"

Wednesday, December 25, 1968
Jingle Bell Rock

Something about Christmas always made Larry joyful. It certainly had nothing to do with the supposed religious significance of the holiday. Whether the story of the first Christmas was true or not, he knew the twenty-fifth of December was clearly not the anniversary of the event. It also had nothing to do with the gifts he received. He enjoyed receiving gifts, of course. Everyone does, especially when one receives something special. But Larry was older now, and had a part time job. He earned enough money he could buy most of the things he wanted for himself. To him, the best gifts were those simple and personal things he had never thought about buying for himself.

No, the special thing about Christmas was the joy he felt in exchanging the simple and silly little gifts he and his friends would give each other. This was something truly special, something making this particular day different from every other day of the year. To him, it would be better if Christmas came everyday, at least in spirit. He did not enjoy the reality of the greedy commercial travesty Christmas had become.

He laughed to himself on his way to see John. There would be no repeat of the silly coincidences of their gifts to each other this year! He had made a special pilgrimage to Houston to shop. In the H & H Music store, he found the perfect gift for John. A *capo* is a device that presses all six strings to the fretboard of a guitar, allowing the player to change the musical key of the guitar without retuning. He and John had complained to each other for years about the *capos* they were using. An elastic strap went around the neck of the guitar to press a metal bar covered with soft vinyl against the fretboard. The problem with this design is that after a little usage, the strap loses elasticity. As a result, the bar is not held tightly across the strings, yielding a completely unplayable guitar! But the professional quality *capo* he found worked in a completely different manner. It would not wear out over time, and was even easier to use. To make this gift even better, there was one and only one in stock. When the store clerk made it clear they would not be receiving any more before Christmas, Larry bought it for John's Christmas present. While slightly envious he would not have one for himself, it virtually guaranteed his gift to John, for once at least, would be unique. That was a very special treasure indeed!

"Merry Christmas, John!" Larry announced as John greeted him at the door.

"Merry Christmas to you, Larry!" John grinned. "Come on in out of the cold."

Larry smiled brightly as he stepped over the threshold, carrying his sack full of goodies. He distributed his small gifts to John's parents, his little brother Jimmy, and accepted both their thanks and the small gifts they presented him. It was not difficult to show them the proper amount of appreciation, in spite of the fact he was itching to see the look on John's face when he opened this very special gift.

The moment finally arrived. "Here you are, my friend," he grinned, handing the small package to John. "Merry Christmas!"

"Thanks!" John said, returning a smug grin of his own. "And this one's for you. I can't wait to see the expression on your face when you open it!"

"Get on with it guys," Jimmy laughed. "I wanna see what you've *each* gotten each other *this* year!"

"Oh, it's not going to be that way this time," both boys said almost simultaneously. They looked at each other and laughed merrily, each one trying to get the other to go first. Finally, in the interest of making any progress at all, they agreed to open their packages simultaneously.

They watched each other open the packages, neither of them wanting to get ahead. Finally, they were down to the plain cardboard boxes, and even the cellophane tape had been cut. "On the count of three," John grinned. "One... Two... Three!"

Both boys pulled back the top of the box and reached inside, actually paying more attention to the other than to what they found inside their own box. Suddenly, they exchanged a funny look, then looked at the gifts they had just removed from those boxes. "Did I open the wrong one?" Larry asked.

"That's what *I* was wondering," John said, looking at the *capo* in his hand, identical to the *capo* Larry was holding in his *own* hand.

"Are you shitting me?" Larry asked in astonishment.

"I wouldn't shit you," John laughed. "You're my favorite turd!"

"Language, boys," Mr. Myers said trying not to laugh.

"But how?" Larry laughed. "When I bought this, the clerk assured me it was the last one in stock, and they wouldn't be getting any more until 1969!"

"I saw it in a catalog, and placed a special order with the local music store," John explained. "They supposedly got it from H & H in Houston. I wanted to get two of them, but they messed up the order and only shipped one, and by the time we discovered the error, the store in Houston was sold out!"

"Unbe-fucking-lievable!" Larry laughed, shaking his head.

"Boys!" Mr. Myers admonished, grinning once again.

"Sorry, Mr. M," Larry laughed.

Larry chuckled to himself as he drove to his next stop, thinking about what a special friendship John and he shared. The same was true of all of his friends. The special friendship Sam and he shared was beyond description, beyond any classification he had ever known. He even had a special friendship with Julia, of course, but that was one he wished he could change. Not improve, just change.

"Merry Christmas!" Sam said brightly when she answered the door.

"Merry Christmas, Sam," he smiled. The delicious aroma of cookies being baked greeted his nostrils as he stepped into the living room. "She does bake cookies more than once a year, doesn't she?" he asked Sam with a snicker.

"Oh, yes," Sam grinned, "but she knows you *expect* her to be baking cookies when you show up on Christmas afternoon."

"I hope she doesn't feel like she's obligated to do so," he chuckled.

"Would it matter?" Sam asked. "She does it because she likes to. It's as simple as that. Why don't we go to the kitchen and join her?"

"That's a great idea, Sam," he grinned. They walked through the living room and entered the kitchen, just as Gayle was removing a batch of cookies from the oven. "Merry Christmas, Mrs. K!" he said brightly. "Those smell absolutely wonderful!"

"I made shortbread cookies this year," she replied. "Merry Christmas, Larry!"

"I *love* shortbread!" he smiled, taking a deep breath to enjoy the aroma.

"You two sit down," she ordered, "and I'll pour us each a glass of milk."

They sat at the kitchen table, enjoying their cookies and milk, and chatting about the events of the last year, and their hopes for the year to come. Larry reached into his bag and brought out two gifts, handing one to Sam and the other to her mother. "I hope you'll like these. When I saw them, I just knew I had to get them for you."

Gayle opened hers first. No one was surprised it was another cookie jar for her collection, but they all laughed at what an unusual cookie jar it was. The jar itself was a ceramic frog in a magnificent green color, sitting on a bright green lily pad, and smiling brightly. The lid was a golden crown, as if to suggest the frog was in reality, a prince changed into a frog by some witch.

"It's adorable," Gayle said with a bright smile. "Thank you so very much! Why is it you just had to get this for me? Am I supposed to be the witch who turned the prince into a frog?"

"Hardly," he laughed. "Mrs. K, I'm not really sure. All I know is when I saw that little green frog sitting there with the golden crown on his head, he spoke to me, and I knew I had to buy him. Don't ask me to explain, because I can't."

Gayle handed Larry a box of his own to open, wrapped tightly in bright red foil. Still warm to the touch, he knew before opening it contained a generous quantity of the shortbread cookies he loved so much. "Thank you, Mrs. K! It looks like I'll have to start exercising a little more, at least until these are gone!"

"Don't you get exercise wiggling your fingers on the guitar?" Sam snickered.

"Sure," he replied, "as long as my fingers are the only things I need to keep thin! On the other hand, why should I worry about keeping my body in shape? After all, round is a shape, isn't it?"

"Boo!" Sam giggled.

"OK, Sam," he grinned. "It's your turn."

Sam examined the small box for a moment, then carefully unwrapped it. Just like last year, she found an intricately carved wooden box. Inside the box, carefully wrapped in soft velvet, was a crystalline figure. When she lifted it into the light, it worked like a prism to scatter the light into a dazzling rainbow. "What's with the frog theme this year?" she grinned. The figurine was a little frog sitting on a lily pad, and it was also wearing what appeared to be a crown on its head.

"Beats me," he shrugged, even as he returned her grin. "But somehow, when I saw him, I just knew it was the one to get you. It was just as if he looked up and said, *'Buy me!'* So I did! I hope you like it."

"I love it," she smiled. "Now I have a unicorn, a princess, and a little green frog. I'm already looking forward to next year. I can't wait to see what comes next!" She put her arms around his neck and hugged him warmly. "OK, so now you have to open yours!" she smiled, handing him yet another package.

Larry accepted the package with a smile on his face, then laughed heartily as he ripped the paper away in a single motion. Slowing down to a more casual pace, he winked at Gayle, and pulled back the tape holding the box closed. Inside, he found two bright coins, medallions, commemorating the launches of the Apollo 7 mission on October 11, and the Apollo 8 mission on December 21, just four days previously.

"Oh, wow, Sam!" he said with delight. "Thank you!"

"There's more," she grinned. "I've already ordered the medallions they'll make for all the Apollo launches next year, Apollos 9 through 12. You'll get them in the mail right after they're struck."

"That's wonderful, Sam!" he said excitedly. "This is going to be quite a year, doncha know! They're talking like they're going to move the moon landing up to next year so they can fulfill Kennedy's challenge of putting a man on the moon by the end of the decade. Oh, man! I wish I could be there!"

"So, why don't you become an astronaut?" Gayle asked.

"I'd think about it," he grinned, "except I'd probably have to join the Air Force first. No, thanks, if you catch my drift."

They shared a laugh about that, made a few other jokes about princes being turned into frogs, and before long, it was time for Larry to move on to his next stop. Sam stepped outside to say goodbye to him. As they walked towards his car, he surprised her with a question out of the blue. "Why has your mother never remarried, Sam? Surely she can find a man her age who would appreciate a fine woman like her!"

"I'm not so sure she can," Sam said thoughtfully. "She doesn't go out socially nearly as much as she should. I don't think she knows any single men her age!"

"We ought to do something about that. I'll give it some thought. Sam, I sometimes think we should also reconsider our *own* situation."

"I assume you mean the situation about our relationship," she replied.

"Naturally," he stated. "Sometimes I wish you'd tell me you've finally come to your senses, dumped this mysterious Donald you've supposedly been seeing so long, and you're ready to run away with me."

"Is that so?" she snickered. "You've had certain *other* wishes on your mind for some time now."

"Sometimes," he chuckled, "but other times I think about how lonely I am. I guess I'm getting a little impatient, Sam. I just wish things could be different."

"I understand, sugar. I remember last year I made a wish things would be different for you this Christmas. I'm sorry that wish didn't come true, but I'll keep wishing for you. You've always been superstitious about the number three. This is the third year you've known her. Maybe three is going to be your lucky number after all. Maybe this will be the year you've been waiting for, and your wishes will come true by next Christmas!"

"Keep wishing for me," he sighed. "I don't think the universe cares one way or the other whether my wishes come true, but you never know. It might not help, but surely it can't hurt."

"Merry Christmas, Larry," she said with a simple smile.

"Merry Christmas to you, Sam," he said, returning her smile. "See you later."

"Hello, Larry," Julian smiled. "We've actually been expecting you this year!"

"That's good, Mr. J!" Larry grinned. "And I'll keep coming back as long as you don't run me off."

"I'll keep that in mind," Julian grinned. "Well, come on in out of the cool air. The girls are sitting in front of the fire in the family room."

"Thanks, Mr. J," he said. "Merry Christmas, everybody!"

"Merry Christmas to you," they all replied. "What did you and John get each other this year?" Julia snickered.

"It's getting ridiculous," Larry smiled, shaking his head. "I was absolutely sure that wasn't going to happen again this year." He explained the story about how he had given John the last *capo* in stock, and how John had tried to buy the last *two* in stock, and how both their plans had been thwarted.

"That's funny," Jessica chuckled when he finished the story. "I was thinking some hot chocolate would be nice right about now. Would anyone else like to join me?"

"Why would we need to join you?" Larry smirked. "Are you coming apart?"

"Very funny," Jessica said with as much irony as she could muster. "You boys relax while Julia and I go to the kitchen. We'll be right back with the hot chocolate."

Larry watched as Julia and her mother stepped into the kitchen. *She's so pretty,* he thought. *Sweet little sixteen. Oh, how I wish she was my girl!*

"Did you see Sam and her mother?" Julian asked, interrupting his thoughts.

"Yes, sir. I just came from there," he replied. "They seem to be doing great. Mrs. K was baking cookies, as usual. She made a batch of shortbread butter cookies. I should run out and get them, so we can enjoy some with the hot chocolate!"

"Oh, don't bother," Julian grinned. "We already have plenty of cookies. Julia and her mother were baking cookies earlier this morning."

"I thought I smelled something baking when I came in," Larry smiled. "Did they bake some kind of special cookie I'll be trying for the first time?"

"Could be," Julian grinned. "Have you ever had kosher chocolate chip cookies?"

"I can't say that I have," Larry replied. "What makes them different?"

"Each chocolate chip has been inspected and blessed by a rabbi," Julian replied, "then individually wrapped in waxed paper made with beeswax from a hive in which that same rabbi personally circumcised each drone trying to mate with the queen."

"You've got to be kidding!" Larry said with astonishment.

"The chocolate chips are placed into the Ark of the Covenant, carried around the walls of Jericho seven times, then finally delivered here on Ezekiel's chariot while Jacob blows on his horn to announce their arrival," Julian added with a grin.

"Wow!" Larry said. "I wish I'd been here to see that! Did a pillar of fire lead the chariot on the way here?"

"The hardest thing was parting the Atlantic Ocean," Julian grinned.

"Personally," Larry added, as the girls returned with the hot chocolate, "I'd think parting the Atlantic Ocean would be trivial compared to circumcising a drone bee! I mean, just think about what kind of knife you'd have to have!"

"What in the world are you boys talking about?" Jessica asked.

"Oh, nothing," Julian replied casually.

"He was just telling me about how you made some kosher chocolate chip cookies, that's all," Larry said, trying to keep a straight face. "Is the recipe carved into tablets of stone, Mrs. J?"

"Oy vay!" Jessica said, shaking her head. "You see, Julia? You can't leave them alone for a minute without them getting into mischief of one kind or another."

Julia looked at Larry and giggled as she handed him a cup of hot chocolate. The sound of her laughter sent chills down his spine, almost as powerful as those he felt when she sat beside him on the love seat, offering to share with him a small plate of the now famous kosher chocolate chip cookies.

"Well, I guess it's your turn to go first this year, Julie," he said reaching for his bag of gifts. Fishing around inside, he located a small package and handed it to her. The universe stopped its motion momentarily when her hand touched his. "Merry Christmas," he said, practically in a whisper.

"Thanks," she said sweetly. "I think I can guess what this is!" Sure enough, upon opening the gift, she found another metal music box. She wound the mechanism and opened the lid to hear it play the Beatles song, *Hey Jude*, the number one song of the year. He could hear the words in his head as the melody played from the little box. *"Hey Jude, don't be afraid. You have found her, now go and get her."*

"Oh, how sweet!" she smiled. "Thank you so much, Larry!" Another gap appeared in the space-time continuum when she hugged him once again.

Larry did not know how much time had passed, only that it was necessary for him to move on. Reaching into his bag of gifts once again, he fetched another package and handed it to Julian. "This one is for you, Mr. J. Merry Christmas!"

Julian accepted the package, which looked very suspiciously like it might contain a bottle of wine. Realizing it must be difficult for a nineteen year old boy to acquire any wine at all, he braced himself with determination to appear both pleased and grateful. He was pleasantly surprised to find a bottle of Carmel King David Almog, imported from Israel. It was still a sweet red wine, not exactly his preference, but was definitely a step above Larry's previous gifts. It showed a great deal of thought and care had gone into its selection. "Thank you, Larry," he said sincerely.

"This is for you, Mrs. J," he smiled, lifting the last package. "Merry Christmas!"

"Thank you," she smiled. Thinking out loud, "I wonder what this could be..."

"It's a pony!" he snickered. He loved it when he was allowed to use that old joke.

"I think you've already given me two of those," Jessica snickered pulling back the wrapping paper. "Besides, how can one ride a pony shaped like a record album?" When the wrappings were removed, the jacket proclaimed it was the soundtrack of music from the movie *Funny Girl* released that year. "Oh, thank you, Larry! I love to listen to Barbara Streisand sing! Almost as much as I love listening to you!"

"Oh, Mrs. J," Larry blushed.

"Well, we aren't empty handed this year," Jessica said nodding to Julia.

Julia hopped up from the love seat, fetched a package from a nearby bookshelf, and handed it to him. "Merry Christmas, Larry, from all of us!"

"You didn't need to get me anything!" he tried to protest. "All I want is to see the smiles on your faces! That's the only gift I need."

"OK," Jessica said, "then think of it as a gift we're giving ourselves, because we like to see the smile on your face!"

Larry looked at the package, then smiled bashfully at each of them. "Well, OK," he said softly, then carefully pulled back the wrapping paper. He could tell it was some kind of book, and was delighted to see the package contained music books from three musicals he liked, *Kismet*, *Brigadoon*, and *Paint Your Wagon*.

"I expect you to learn to play these so you can sing them for us," Jessica smiled.

"I'll try, Mrs. J," he said brightly, "although I don't think it'll be easy to make a guitar arrangement for some of these songs." Without even looking through the index, he already knew the first song from each he would learn. Respectively, they were *Stranger In Paradise*, *Almost Like Being In Love*, and *I Talk to the Trees*. Each of these songs held a special message just for him. All he could say was a sincere, "Thank you very much for thinking of me!"

"Thank Julia," Jessica said. "She's the one who picked out the books."

He smiled at her. *I wonder if she could possibly know what these songs mean to me, and how much I want to sing them to her!*

Julia was relieved to see Larry was pleased with the music books. She was not sure whether he might have preferred rock and roll music. In the end, she selected these books because she had seen Larry was good at learning popular songs on his own, without the sheet music. From the smile her mother was giving her, Julia knew her mother also sensed Larry was pleased. She was not exactly sure how to read the expression on her father's face. He seemed to be looking directly at Larry, as if contemplating something deep and mysterious. Because of this, it did not come as a complete surprise to her when her father made a rather astonishing comment.

"Larry," Julian said, "I have to say that you seem to be... Well, how do I want to say this? You seem to be very different from other Christians I know."

"I'm not exactly sure how to take that!" Larry replied with a laugh.

"Oh, I didn't mean it quite the way it sounded," Julian said. Julia thought he looked a little flustered because what he meant as a compliment did not come out as intended. He decided to take a more direct approach. "I meant it as a compliment."

"Oh. Ah!" Larry smiled. "If you're trying to say I don't seem to fit into the same mold as most others do, then I'm pleased to accept your compliment!"

"Yes," Julian nodded. "That's what I meant. What makes you so different?"

"It's probably all these kosher foods you folks have introduced me to over the last couple of years," Larry laughed. "You know what they say! You are what you eat!"

"I don't think eating kosher foods will make you Jewish any more than eating sushi will make you turn Japanese," Jessica grinned.

"Maybe, maybe not, but it's interesting you should say that. John and I have been concerned we might be turning Japanese for a couple of years now," he chuckled.

"Ah, so!" Julia giggled brightly. She realized he probably doubted any of them would understand his little joke. But she had heard John and Larry laughing about "turning Japanese" before, and curiosity prompted her to ask Sam what the boys were talking about. Sam gave her a somewhat graphic explanation as to the meaning of that phrase, laughing she was ill-equipped to demonstrate the proper technique, but was quite certain either of the boys would be happy to volunteer their equipment, strictly for educational purposes, of course! She covered her mouth and blushed when both Larry and her father looked at her curiously before continuing.

"I don't think we should blame the food," Julian smiled. "This isn't a recent change in you, but something I've noticed ever since the day we first met."

"Well, I'm happy I'm different than most," Larry smiled. "Most Christians are interested in their religion only on Christmas and Easter Sunday. They show up in church twice a year, thinking these visits will somehow make them pure and holy."

"That sort of thinking is not unique to Christians," Julian grinned. "I know a lot of Jews who only practice Judaism twice a year – on Pesach and Yom Kippur!"

"Pesach?" Larry asked.

"You probably know it as Passover," Jessica explained.

"Oh," Larry nodded. "I guess people are just people, no matter what their religion, or lack thereof. There are a lot of what I call 'Sunday morning' Christians. They go out all week long, sowing wild oaks, then come to church on Sunday to pray for a crop failure!"

Julia giggled once again, only this time she was joined by her parents, neither of whom had any problem understanding Larry's joke. "I guess that goes along with the Jews I know who are quite diligent at keeping the Shabbat," Julian grinned, "but seem to have forgotten all about everything else in the Talmud."

"I'm not a Bible thumper, either," Larry continued, "but I've certainly had plenty of them thumped in *my* direction!"

"Amen!" Julian agreed.

"Mr. J," Larry smiled, "I seem to recall when I came out to wish you guys a Merry Christmas the first time, I mentioned something about there being different *kinds* of Christians. I imagine you were thinking in terms of such kinds as Catholics, Baptists, Methodists, and Church of Christ'ers, but what I was really talking about were the three kinds of Christians I just listed."

"You seem to be a little cynical about most Christians," Julian observed.

"I guess that's a fair assessment," he admitted. "I was brought up to believe we're supposed to do exactly what Jesus taught us to do. I was even pretty smug about that until I started to realize I was also being taught other things that had nothing to do with what Jesus taught. Some of that seemed rather trivial at first, but as I got older, and started to think more and more for myself, it started to bother me."

"What sort of things are you talking about?" Julian asked.

"The list just keeps getting longer and longer, I'm afraid," he sighed. "Mr. J, how much do you really know about the teachings of Jesus?"

"Not as much as you, I'm sure," Julian said. "Even among Jews, Jesus is generally recognized to be one of the prophets. We know about his message of peace and love."

"Then you know everything there is to know about him," Larry said. "But spend ten minutes in any Christian church, and you'd think his teachings must fill volumes! The truth is, his teachings fill only a few pages in what we call the New Testament. All he really taught us was to love one another. Over the last two thousand years, however, men have decided to embellish it with so many teachings of their own most people don't even remember the original message! I mean, think about people who say such things as *'Kill a commie for Christ!'* OK, maybe most people recognize that as some sort of a sick joke. Or do they? And how about the song that goes *'Onward Christian soldiers, marching as to war'*? How could someone who's heard his message of peace and love possibly think marching off to war has anything at all to do with Jesus?"

"You *are* cynical, Larry," Julian stated flatly.

Julia watched Larry sigh and shake his head. "I didn't mean to get myself so worked up. I'm just a silly, confused young man. I keep looking for answers, but all I seem to find are more questions." When he looked at her briefly before turning away, she thought his eyes could surely burn a hole clean through her.

"There's an aspect to Christianity I've never understood," Julian said thoughtfully. "I was always taught there is one and only one God. Perhaps you can help me understand this notion of *three* Gods?"

"I would if I could," Larry sighed.

"It occurs to me this is the fundamental difference between Christians and Jews," Julian said, "even more important than whether Jesus was the long awaited Messiah. A fundamental principle of Judaism is there is *one* God, not three."

"Really?" he asked. Something about the way he asked it, however, made Julia wonder if he was truly surprised, or simply furthering the conversation. "Then I really *do* wish I could explain the idea of the Trinity. The problem, Mr. J, is I don't understand it myself!"

"Does it bother you to talk about religion and philosophy?" Julian asked. "I know this isn't a subject a lot of young people feel comfortable discussing."

Julia noted how warmly Larry smiled. "Mr. J, I normally shy away from talking about religion and politics, but when I'm speaking with someone of good will, such as yourself, it doesn't bother me to talk about any subject."

"Thank you, Larry," Julian smiled. "That's a very nice thing to say. So how many Gods do you think there are – one or three?"

Once again, Julia noted Larry's expression was soft, as if he felt completely comfortable. "You may not like my answer, Mr. J. We've already established I'm not like others. Maybe it's the mathematical nature of my thinking, but I personally don't like *either* answer! Three just seems to be weird and arbitrary. Besides, I have a personal prejudice against the number 'three' because it always seems to be so unlucky for me. To me, it's like someone couldn't reconcile the differences they saw in the God of the old and new testaments, and so came up with this idea of three Gods to account for it. I should point out, Mr. J, most Christians don't believe in three Gods, either. It's more like three aspects of the same God."

"I've heard that before," Julian said. "So Christians believe in only one God?"

"Yes and no," Larry said, shaking his head.

"You said you don't like either answer," Julian noted. "What's wrong with the notion of one God?"

"Once again, it's a mathematical thing," Larry replied looking thoughtful. "There's something about the concept of unity that bothers me. The number 'one' makes me almost as uncomfortable as the number 'three'. Look around in the universe, and you won't find any examples of there being just one of anything."

"The earth seems to be one of a kind," Julian pointed out.

"Ah, but only as far as we know," Larry noted. "If we could see all of the billions of stars and planets out there, I don't think earth would be so unique after all!"

"I'll concede that," Julian agreed. "What's wrong with the idea God is unique?"

"Nothing, really," Larry admitted. "I just have a problem with the concept of unity. 'One' is what I call an imperfect number. It's far from infinite, yet it's not the exact opposite of infinity, either."

"Now you've lost me," Julian said. "What's the opposite of infinity?"

"Zero," Larry said simply.

"Are you saying there is no God?" Julian asked.

"Not at all!" he replied. "I'm just saying zero is the opposite of infinity, not one. But when we are looking for God, are we not trying to find the infinite, rather than its opposite?" Larry paused for a moment allowing Julian to catch up. "Numbers such as 'zero', 'one', and 'three' just don't feel right to me when thinking about God. I wonder if there might, in fact, be an *infinite* number of Gods, perhaps one God for every mind having the ability to contemplate the true nature of God."

"But surely the number of minds having the ability to contemplate the nature of God is not infinite!" Julian noted. "There are only some three billion humans alive. That might be a very large number, but it's hardly anything close to infinity."

"Very true," Larry agreed, "but I happen to believe there are a lot more than three billion minds. Mr. J, would you say you have a firm grasp on the nature of infinity?"

"Infinity is a difficult concept," Julian said, nodding his head. "Most people brush it aside by using words such as *'forever'* and *'eternity'*. In essence, these are nothing but synonyms, rather than definitions."

"I'm glad you see the difficulty with the whole concept," Larry said. "Infinity isn't something I take lightly. Have you ever read a book by the name of Flatland?"

"I don't think so," Julian replied.

"In a very interesting way, this book helped me begin to see the true nature of infinity. The full title is Flatland: A Romance of Many Dimensions. It was written back in the nineteenth century by a mathematician named Edwin A. Abbott. In it, he describes a vision of a universe in which there are only two dimensions, length and width, he calls Flatland. Now Flatland, it seems, is fully populated by beings in the form of various geometric figures, such as triangles, squares, hexagons, and circles. Indeed, the more sides a being has, assuming he isn't irregular in some manner, the higher his standing within society."

"Sounds pretty bizarre," Jessica noted.

"It is," Larry agreed, "but interesting. The main character in the story happens to be a square, not particularly high in the social order. A curious thing happens. The square has a vision of yet another universe he calls Lineland, consisting of only a single dimension. All of the inhabitants of that universe are lined up in single file, never meeting anyone other than their two immediate neighbors. In his vision, he attempts to explain to them about the second dimension, width, but since they can't conceive of anything outside the single line making up their entire universe, they can't comprehend this second dimension, how to measure it, or even in what direction it might run."

"I see his problem," Julian said thoughtfully. "How do you explain to someone a concept completely outside their experience? Indeed, outside their entire universe?"

"Exactly! Then he envisions another universe he calls Pointland, where there are no dimensions at all, just a single point with no length, width, or height! There's only one being within this universe, of course, and he fills the universe completely. The square can't explain to him the concepts of length and width, because the Pointland being doesn't even recognize the square exists at all! You see, unlike Lineland, where the square can at least project part of his body into that universe so he can be seen, there's no room within Pointland for any part of him. So the Pointland being thinks *he* is the one and only being that exists. He thinks he's the one true God, if you will!"

"Weird," Julia said.

"Yes, but if you think about it, it does make a certain amount of sense," Julian added. "How did this lead you to see the nature of infinity?"

"Well, Mr. J, a very strange thing happens to our poor Flatland square. It seems he gets visited by a being from the *three* dimensional universe, who attempts to explain the concept of *height* to him. Now it's perfectly clear to you and me what height is, but not to the poor square, who can't comprehend anything beyond the single plane that constitutes his entire universe. It's beyond his ability to envision this third dimension. Finally, in desperation, the visitor yanks the square out of his Flatland plane, into the three dimensional universe, where he sees and understands!"

"Smart move," Julian smiled.

"Maybe not," Larry smiled, "because it turns out the square begins to understand things even better than the visitor from the third dimension! For now, he demands to be shown the *fourth* dimension, even though the three dimensional being arrogantly claims there is no such thing!"

"A fourth dimension is beyond *his* capacity to understand!" Julian exclaims.

"And if someone were to show the square the fourth dimension..." Julia said, understanding the full nature of the problem.

"Then he would demand to see the *fifth* dimension," Larry smiled, "and so on."

"Interesting," Julian said thoughtfully.

Julia was fascinated by this story, and wanted to hear Larry tell more of it.

"Perhaps the most important point of the whole book," he stated, "is how easy it is to close our minds to things we can't comprehend, to things outside the boundaries of our own imagination. Yet just because something is outside the boundaries of our imagination doesn't mean it doesn't exist!"

Julian nodded his head in agreement. "I take it you believe there is something beyond the three dimensional universe we inhabit," he said casually.

"We have length, width, and height," Larry stated. "To that, let's add time as the fourth dimension. We can't control our movement along that dimension, but at least we recognize it exists. But envision a being who could. Imagine a being to which time is of no more consequence than length is to us."

"Like God," Julian said, nodding his head.

"He would surely seem like God to us," Larry smiled, "but what about a being who could move along some fifth dimension as easily as this God moves along the dimension of time? Would that not be an even greater God? And what about the sixth, seventh, and eight dimensions?"

"Do we really need that many dimensions?" Julian asked.

"Did our friend the Flatland square need more than two? I've heard it said if you possess a technology sufficiently advanced, it is indistinguishable from magic. Yes, Mr. J, I believe we need an *infinite* number of dimensions, so there can be a truly infinite God, so there is no possibility of a technology more advanced than that possessed by God. If there aren't an infinite number of dimensions, then there can't be a truly infinite God, whether there be one, three, or any number."

"A very good argument, Larry," Julian agreed, nodding his head.

"I can make things worse!" Larry smiled. "As you know, the matter in our universe is supposedly made up of tiny particles called atoms. At one time, they were thought to be the smallest unit of matter, something that couldn't be broken down into anything smaller. Then, of course, we discovered atoms were made up of even smaller particles, such as neutrons, protons, and electrons. For a while, these were considered to be the smallest units of matter, things that couldn't be broken down into anything smaller. But then something new came along called a quark, that can be used to build the other particles. You see where this is going, right?"

"Yes," Julian grinned. "No matter how small it gets, I assume your theory is it can always be broken down into something even smaller."

"Exactly!" Larry smiled. "Now atoms turn out to be mostly empty space. They are simply a few tiny particles making up something we call the nucleus, surrounded by electrons orbiting the nucleus. Then we find out each of those particles also turns out to be mostly empty space, essentially nothing but a few even tinier particles orbiting some other tiny particles, and so on, and so on, and so on, until guess what? The whole universe is nothing but empty space filled with bits of nothing but empty space, orbiting around still other bits of empty space! Think about it. There's nothing here at all, Mr. J! The universe we see around us doesn't actually exist! It's merely a figment of our imagination! Rene Descartes said, *'I think, therefore I am.'* I suspect that might be closer to the truth than even *he* realized!"

"I'm starting to get a little lost," Jessica said.

"And I'm not even done yet!" Larry giggled. "You've probably heard someone compare an atom to a solar system. Imagine the nucleus of every atom in our universe is actually a tiny star, and the electrons orbiting those stars are actually little planets, some of which contain intelligent life! There could be billions and billions of complete civilizations right here in this cookie crumb, going in and out of existence in the blink of an eye!"

"Please," Jessica giggled.

"And of course, every one of those stars is actually made up of smaller and smaller stars and planets and civilizations!" Larry chuckled. "In fact, since these bits of nothing keep getting smaller and smaller into infinity, we have to conclude there are an infinite number of people who live in an infinite number of universes!

"Stop it!" Julia laughed.

"And let's not forget to go in the *other* direction," Larry laughed. "Perhaps our solar system is really nothing more than a single atom within a universe so huge it defies our comprehension!" He took this moment to pause dramatically. "This is where it gets really interesting to me. Would you like to know my theory as to the meaning of life and the universe?" he asked with a grin.

Julia saw the twinkle in his eye, but could not resist the urge to hear his answer. "Yes," she grinned, "I would, whether mom and dad want to hear it or not."

"I think we ought to hear this, don't you, Jessie?" Julian asked with a smile.

"Go ahead, Larry," Jessica said, trying to keep a serious expression.

"Our solar system has nine planets, but I think of the asteroid belt as number ten."

"Well, I don't know about that," Julian stated, "but for sake of argument, let's accept that as given. What about it?"

Encouraged, Larry continued with, "Let's take a look at basic chemistry. A star with ten planets would be the same as a single atom with ten electrons in the next higher universe. We know such atoms as the element Neon. The asteroid belt, suggests to me this atom has been ionized by the infusion of energy. That's what ionization is; an atom gaining or losing electrons. In the next higher scale, it'd be the same as a star system gaining or losing planets!"

"Yeah, OK," Julian agreed. "I'll accept that."

"So, isn't it obvious?" Larry asked. "The Earth is nothing more than one of ten electrons orbiting the nucleus of an ionized Neon atom. Do you know where you find ionized Neon atoms? In neon signs, of course! All of us, and everything in our entire solar system, are nothing more than a single insignificant atom, part of an ugly neon sign hanging outside a cheap motel along some unfashionable back road lost in the nether reaches of a forgotten planet in the uncharted wilderness of some other universe. The sign probably reads, *'No vacancy'*, or *'Eat at Joe's!'* doncha know. It seems to me this is quite probably the best explanation of the meaning of life and the universe I'll ever receive in my lifetime."

They all shared a laugh. "Do you know what?" Julian chuckled. "I think you may be onto something!"

Julia looked at her dear friend, smiled, and saw him return her smile. She also saw the source of his smile was nothing more than this simple moment in time they were sharing together. When her eyes met his, even though she could clearly see the twinkle in his eye, she could also clearly see he believed the words he had spoken were true. And because he believed it, she knew she also believed.

Tuesday, December 31, 1968
Hey Jude

Larry and Sam rang the doorbell promptly at 8:00. They came together as part of the plan they had hatched one year ago. When he asked her to pretend to be his date for the evening, Sam did not find his request to be all that outrageous, and teased him about how his advances to her seemed to be lacking something lately.

He explained to her he was beginning to hate New Year's Eve. Maybe someday, things would be different for him, but for now, this day simply emphasized to him the extent of his loneliness, the depth of his despair. Julia would be at the party, of course, and he knew this simple factor alone was enough to make it a difficult evening for him, reminding him of his dreams. There she would be, paraded before his eyes, tantalizingly close, yet still separated from him by a huge gulf.

The Jacobsons were once again providing the *Four Musketeers* with another New Year's Eve party at their house, establishing a welcome tradition. Larry welcomed this new tradition in spite of his apprehension. In truth, it was the moment itself he dreaded, not its location. Regardless of where he might be when that key moment arrived, he knew she would be on his mind.

"Hi, Larry! Hi, Sam!" Julia greeted them brightly.

"Hi, Julie!" Larry returned, forcing himself to appear bright in spirit. While Sam and Julia hugged each other in greeting, Larry offered his hand to the other person in the room. "Hi, Ed. How are you guys tonight?"

"Doing fine," Ed replied as he shook Larry's hand. "How about yourself?"

"Fine," Larry answered.

To his relief, the lull in the conversation was broken by the arrival of John and his date, bringing on another round of greetings. Just as last year, Larry expected this to be a night of internal reflection. Once again, the Jacobsons treated the youngsters with a wide variety of snacks and nonalcoholic drinks. They all played games and danced to the music provided by Julia's record collection.

A few minutes before the stroke of midnight, Larry moved stealthily into the living room. Knowing he would do so, Sam also moved casually away from the others, a move noticed by Julia. She smiled at Sam and discretely waved to her as she made her "escape". The others watched the clock, counting down the final seconds of 1968.

"Ten... Nine... Eight..." they called. As Sam hugged him, Larry reflected on the events of the previous year, replaying the entire year in his memory. There had certainly been some good moments. While the relationship with Betty had been short, it had been pleasant while it lasted. And just how many young men his age could claim the incredible experience of a liaison with beautiful twin sisters? On more practical matters, his college career was proceeding on schedule, and he was truly enjoying his part time job at the computer center more and more. They had discovered his programming talents one day when there was more work to be done than there were programmers to do it. The other programmers were skeptical at first, but agreed to let him try as long as someone "qualified" checked over his work when he was done. When he successfully completed the task is less than half the time estimated for an experienced programmer, his programming talents started being utilized more and more frequently.

"Seven... Six..." they counted. But on the other hand, there had also been plenty of moments that were not so good. Two horrific murders had shaken his optimism the condition of the world was about to improve. Whatever hopes he clung to were shattered when Richard M. Nixon was elected President in November. Neither of his romantic relationships during the year had been fulfilling. They simply made him long for the day when he could finally make that certain connection with someone special, leading to a lasting and meaningful relationship. Even more than before, he questioned the decision he and Sam had made regarding their relationship, and wondered once again if they should reconsider.

"Five... Four..." the countdown proceeded. And, of course, *she* was there in the next room. He simply wanted to steal a glance of the girl who confused him even more now than she had a year ago. In theory, there had been one chance during the year when he might have done something about that. But in truth, that chance had never actually materialized. This new boyfriend, Ed, had come along before Larry even knew she had broken up with Bill. Larry would have to keep waiting.

"Three... Two... One..." At the stroke of midnight, Larry once again felt that ache deep inside of him as the result of a silly superstition. All he really wished for at that moment was he could be the one who was kissing her, welcoming in the new year. That damn superstition had held true for 1968. He dreaded the thought he would be repeating his wish over and over again during 1969.

1969

Wednesday, January 1, 1969
Crying

"Happy New Year!" they shouted when the clock struck midnight. Julian and Jessica turned to kiss each other, as did John and his date, and Ed and Julia.

In the living room, Larry and Sam were still hugging each other. "Happy New Year, Larry," Sam softly whispered to him.

"At least I hope yours is a happy one, Sam," he whispered back. "What were you thinking at the moment the clock struck midnight?"

Sam lay her head against his chest and sighed. "I was thinking about how much I'm looking forward to spending some time with Donald. He promised to send me some money so I can go visit him around Valentine's Day."

"Sounds happy to me," he whispered. "At least I know *you'll* have a happy year."

"What were you thinking at that moment?" she asked. When he did not make an immediate reply, she looked up at his face, seeing more sadness and loneliness in his eyes than she had ever seen before. Knowing there was nothing she could do to ease his unhappiness, she simply hugged him more closely than before, and fought back the tears that insisted on gathering.

When these caused her to sniffle, Larry released his embrace and looked into her eyes. "We'll have none of that," he said softly. "You're going to have a happy year. You know I can't stand to see you cry."

"I'm only crying because you refuse to cry for yourself," she whispered.

Larry flashed his patented half smile at her. "Then you needn't worry. I'll take care of that little detail later when no one can see me. And then I'll go out and face the new year. Surely 1969 will be better than 1968 was!"

"Forever the optimist?" Sam whispered.

"It's a tough job," he smiled, "but someone has to do it, doncha know."

They waited until Sam regained her composure before returning to the family room to join the others, hug each of them, and wish them a happy new year.

Friday, February 14, 1969
Only In Your Heart

Julia got home from school earlier than usual. Ed insisted she let him bring her home that day, rather than riding the school bus like normal. When they pulled into her driveway and stopped the car, he revealed the reason why. "I thought I'd go ahead and give this to you now," he said fetching a large box of candy from the backseat. "Happy Valentine's Day!"

"Thank you, Ed!" she smiled before leaning over and giving him a warm kiss. "You're so sweet to get me anything."

"Sweets for the sweet," he added with a laugh, collecting another kiss.

"Well, I hope you'll let me share them with mom," she grinned. "If I were to eat that whole box, I'd get as fat as a tick!"

"You'd still be a doll!" he smiled.

Julia doubted his sincerity, but returned his smile anyway. "I'd better run. What time are you picking me up tonight?"

"About 6:30," he answered. "We'll get some dinner before going to the dance."

"OK," she said sweetly. "Thanks for the candy. I'll see you in a little while."

Ed watched her stroll up the walkway to her front door. When she got to the steps, she turned and waved to him, flashing her smile once again. He honked his horn, turned the car around and headed back for the main road.

Jessica heard the horn honk and knew Julia was home. A few seconds later she heard the front door open, and listened to the familiar cry, "Hi, mom! I'm home!"

"Hi, sugar!" he called back. "Did you have a good day?"

"Yes, I did," Julia said stepping into the kitchen. "How was yours?"

"Quiet and relaxing," Jessica smiled. "What's that you have?"

"Candy," Julia smiled. "That's why Ed wanted to bring me home from school today. I guess he didn't feel like waiting until tonight to give it to me."

"That was very sweet of him," Jessica said. "There are a couple of things waiting for you here, also," she added, nodding towards the kitchen table. She watched her daughter's eyes move to the table, and saw how her bright smile at first faded for a moment, and then returned with a softer, somehow more elegant curve on her lips. When Julia looked back at her, Jessica returned that smile and simply shrugged. "It was delivered about an hour ago. Just as before, there was no card."

She watched Julia walk to the table and touch the rose gently, then lean forward to smell its delicate fragrance. "I wish I knew who he was," she whispered.

"At least he's persistent," Jessica said softly. "One thing for sure is he's not simply going to go away. One of these days he's going to let you know who he is."

"I hope so, mom," Julia said. "Do you have any ideas at all?"

"I've thought of three possibilities, but none of them seem likely," she replied. "They started after you broke up with Jimmy. Maybe he's still carrying a torch?"

"I don't think so," Julia said. "I see him everyday in my English class, but he hardly ever looks at me. Besides, he's had another girlfriend for quite a while."

"So you've told me," Jessica agreed. "I realize it seems unlikely, but it's still possible. This one may come as a shock, but have you considered they might be coming from his brother, John? After all, they've been coming ever since you and he met, you realize."

"No, I haven't considered that possibility!" Julia laughed. "John is a doll, but this wouldn't fit his style at all. If he was interested in anything other than friendship, I'm almost certain he'd come right out and say so. To tell you the truth, I'd say there's a better chance they come from *Sam* rather than John!"

"Now *there's* a possibility I hadn't even considered," Jessica grinned. "Do you think that's very likely?"

"No!" Julia laughed. "Have you noticed Sam has been away for the last week or so? The guys think she must have run off to be with that mystery guy again!"

"Good for her!" Jessica grinned. When the mirth settled, she continued, "The only other person I can think of is Larry. They've been coming ever since he met you. He'd seem to be the most likely possibility, except we both know he has his sights on

Sam. And even if that weren't the case, I can't imagine why he wouldn't let you know if he was interested in you as a girlfriend."

"He's awfully shy when it comes to girls," Julia said.

"Larry shy?" Jessica laughed. "Maybe he was shy a couple of years ago, when you first met him, but he certainly seems to have overcome his shyness now!"

"Maybe," Julia replied.

"Oh, sweetheart," Jessica smiled, "I know you still have a bit of a crush on him. I understand! If I were your age, I'd have a crush on him, too. Maybe he *is* sending these, but we need to gather more evidence before we jump to that conclusion."

"What do you think he'd say if I just went up and asked him if he was sending me a rose each Valentine's Day?" Julia wondered aloud.

"I don't know," Jessica smiled, "but I suspect it'd prove interesting. If he's the one, he'd probably deny it; if not, he'd definitely deny it. Either way, you'd know nothing more than you do right now. If it's him, you'd probably embarrass him, and maybe scare him if he's that shy; if it's not him, then he might decide you're chasing after him. You mustn't do that, Julia. Whoever this boy is, he'll let you know when he wants you to know, or maybe when he feels it's safe to let you know."

"I know," Julia sighed. "I'm just impatient. I want to know who he is now!"

"So do I," Jessica smiled giving her daughter a hug. "By the way, three envelopes came in the mail for you. One is from your grandmother, one is from Sam, and the other one has no return address. I can make a good guess who that one is from, and there's actually some evidence to back up that guess!"

At 6:30, Julian heard the doorbell. Schotzy was not pleased with this visitor, so Julian assumed correctly it must be Ed. He picked up the dog and handed him to Julia. "Good evening, Ed," Julian smiled as he opened the front door.

"Good evening to you, sir," Ed said, returning the smile.

There was something about that smile Julian did not like, but he never quite put his finger on it. "Come on in," he said.

"Hi, Julia," Ed said stepping inside.

"Hi, Ed," she replied. "Are you looking forward to the dance as much as I am?"

"Of course," he said.

Julian shook his head wondering how this boy could possibly know how much Julia was looking forward to the dance. "Goodnight, sugar. Let me take the dog."

"Mom is in the kitchen," she said. "Let me go say goodnight before we go."

"Sure," Ed agreed. "I'll come with you."

Ed walked behind Julia into the kitchen to say goodnight to her mother.

"Goodnight, sweetheart," Jessica replied. "Have a good time at the dance. Both a good evening and goodnight to you, Ed," she giggled. "Thanks for getting Julia the candy. I hope you don't mind if she shares some with me."

"No, ma'am," Ed said, distracted by the rose standing beside his box of candy.

Julia grinned when she saw the object of his attention. "That was delivered this afternoon." She winked discretely to her mother, adding, "There was no card. It seems I have a secret admirer."

"No card?" Ed replied. "It must have gotten lost. You don't know who sent this?"

Jessica opened her mouth to speak, but Julia cut her off. "We've been wondering all afternoon, but in the end, we decided we don't have enough evidence."

Ed saw a nice opportunity. "I'll have to complain to them about losing the card."

Julia and Jessica exchanged a glance. "Do you know something about it?"

"Well, of course!" Ed stated. "Who did you *think* sent it?" He was hedging his bet for the moment, making sure they really did not know who had sent this rose.

"I didn't guess," Julia looked at him strangely. "So my secret admirer is you?"

"Naturally," he said with confidence, now concluding no one would ever be able to challenge this claim. This was a lucky break for him, and a bad break for the poor bastard who was trying to make a move on his girl. "Are you ready to get going?"

"OK," Julia smiled. "Goodnight, mom! I'll talk to you later!"

"Goodnight, sweetheart," Jessica replied with a questioning look on her face.

After kissing Ed goodnight and stepping inside the foyer, Julia stood with her back to the front door, lost in thought. She heard the engine of his car engage, and saw his headlights come on. From the changes in the sounds and the reflections of the headlights, she knew he had turned around, driven down the driveway, returned to the country road, and started back to town.

After a moment, she stepped away from the door, and moved into the kitchen. Illuminated only by a soft night light under the kitchen cabinets, she looked at the rose sitting peacefully on the kitchen table. One more time, she touched it gently and sniffed its soft fragrance. "Who are you?" she whispered to herself.

She was startled by her mother's voice. "Maybe we can use the process of elimination." Jessica had been waiting in the family room for Julia to come home.

"You startled me!" Julia said nervously catching her breath.

"I'm sorry," Jessica said. "I assumed you'd be expecting me to wait up tonight."

"I was," Julia smiled. "What do you mean by the process of elimination?"

"First, we list everyone you know, then cross off the names of everyone who did *not* send the rose," Jessica said, "and then we can consider the names remaining. Let's see. Who do we know with absolute certainty did *not* send you this rose, since he clearly didn't send the one last year, nor the one the year before that?"

"Oh, mother," Julia said simply.

"Why did you let him get away with that?" Jessica asked.

"Does it really matter?" Julia asked. "*You* know he didn't send it, and *I* know he didn't send it. I'm not really interested in knowing who did *not* send me the rose."

"But..." Jessica tried to say.

"It doesn't matter, mom," Julia said. "If I didn't know it before, then I certainly know now Ed isn't the man I've been looking for. At least he's been nice to me, and he *did* buy me the candy, after all. But he lied to me, and we both know his days are now numbered. Pretty soon, someone else will come along and take his place. Maybe this time, it'll be the one who really *is* sending me these roses."

"I hope so, sweetheart," Jessica said.

Julia gently brushed her fingers over the rose once again and leaned over to inhale its fragrance. "Goodnight, mom," she said softly.

"Goodnight, sweetheart," Jessica whispered.

Sunday, March 16, 1969
You've Got A Friend

Larry discretely followed Julia home after guitar practice. She was not acting quite like normal, and he could see she was deeply troubled by something. She pulled into her driveway and parked her car in the back, just like she normally did. He arrived moments later, and waited a few more before going to the front door. The first thing he noticed was that Schotzy did not bark. Jessica answered the door, and it was obvious she had been crying. "This is a surprise," she said.

"I *thought* something was wrong, Mrs. J, and seeing you confirms it for me. I don't want to interfere in your business, but if there's anything I can do to help..."

"Maybe you can," she sniffed. "Come on in. Everyone is in the family room. Schotzy has been very sick the last few days. I'm afraid he's not doing very well." Larry found Julia on her hands and knees in front of Schotzy's bed, with Julian squatting nearby, attempting to comfort her.

He joined the others, kneeling down on the floor next to Julia. He smiled when the dog recognized him, and tried to stand up to greet him. "Just relax, old fellow," he said gently rubbing Schotzy's head. "What's troubling the boy?" The dog gave up on his struggle to stand. Larry leaned down close to let the dog lick his face the way he always wanted. Schotzy whimpered, but wagged his tail as best he could.

"The vet says he's injured his back," Julian said. "Apparently, it's a fairly common problem for dachshunds, especially as they get older."

"I see," Larry frowned, then looked back at the dog. "So that long back of yours has an ow-y, does it, boy? I'm sorry. Just lie still. It will all be OK." He looked back up at Julian to ask his next question. "What does the vet plan to do about it?"

"He's hoping it's just a strain," Julian answered. "If that's it, then he should get better soon. All he'll have to do is take it easy for awhile, so he doesn't re-injure it."

"And if it's not just a strain?" Larry asked, already afraid to hear the answer.

"Then it might be a ruptured disk," Julian replied unhappily.

"Oh. And in that case?" Larry inquired softly.

Julian looked at Larry and merely shook his head. Julia answered his question bitterly, "If he has a ruptured disk, the vet says he'll *never* get better!"

Larry looked at Julian and then Jessica, each nodding their head in confirmation of this bleak analysis. "That would be a shame, Julie. How old is Schotzy now?"

"Sixteen," she answered with tears in her eyes, "just like me. We got him as a puppy when I was still a baby. We've grown up together."

"That's a long time," he said calmly. "That's like being one hundred twelve in people years! Isn't that right, boy?" he said, trying to keep the dog calm and relaxed.

"I wish I knew what to do for him!" Julia said as tears ran down her cheeks. "It hurts to see a good friend in such pain!"

"I know it does," he agreed, feeling the pain not only from the dog, but from Julia and both her parents. He also remembered seeing his own dog, Dan Dee, hit by that pickup truck, and how he watched the little dog suffer for several days as he and his family all hoped he would get better. He looked up and saw not only was Jessica crying, but Julian was also losing his battle to fight back his tears. "Did the vet have any advice?" he asked, knowing what the answer would have to be.

"All we can do is wait and see how he progresses," Julian answered. "If it's just a strain, he'll get better as early as tomorrow. If it's a ruptured disk..."

"No!" Julia screamed. "I won't let them hurt him!" she said as her tears exploded.

"Of course not!" Larry said, even as his own eyes moistened. "Nobody is going to hurt Schotzy!" He paused for a few moments while everyone tried to regain control of their emotions. "There's something I want to tell you, all of you, especially Schotzy, and I can only think of one way to tell it. Can I go out to my car for a moment?"

When Julia nodded her head, Larry stood and walked through the front door to his car. He returned a moment later with his guitar, and sat down on the floor next to the dog. "Over the next few days, or anytime in the future, you might happen to need... Well, the song certainly says it a lot better than I can." He began to play the introduction to a song none of the Jacobsons had heard him sing before. It was *You've Got A Friend*, written by Carole King. After a few notes on the guitar, he looked from face to face as he sang. Even Julian had moisture in his eyes when the song was finished. Larry smiled as best as he could to each of them, telling them to be optimistic, to expect the best.

Julia put her arms around him and hugged him as she cried. "Schotzy has always liked you, Larry, better than anyone else who's ever come here. He knows you're his special friend. You may even have been a better friend to him than I have."

"Don't be silly, Julie," he said. "He loves you more than anyone."

Monday, March 17, 1969
That's What Friends Are For

Larry went directly to the Jacobson's house from work, arriving shortly after 5:00. When Julian answered the door, Larry knew there was no good news. "The vet is fairly convinced he has a ruptured disk," Julian explained. "He wants us to bring him into the clinic for an X-ray. We waited for you to get here before we left."

He followed Julian into the living room, where once again, Julia was sitting beside Schotzy's bed, softly crying and looking worried. He put his arm around her, and she leaned against him for support. Wordlessly, they walked out to the car and got into the backseat, with Julia in the middle. Julian carried Schotzy in his bed and handed the bundle to Larry who placed it gently onto Julia's lap.

When they arrived at the clinic, Julian told them to wait in the car while he went inside. He and the vet returned shortly with a small cart. The vet acknowledged each of them individually, including the dog. "Hello, Schotzy. You remember me, don't you, boy?" The dog wagged his tail painfully as the doctor reached in and petted him. "Will you help me take him inside?" Larry gently lifted the bundle from Julia's lap, and handed it to the vet who placed it on the cart. "It won't take but a moment to take the X-ray. Why don't you all have a seat in the waiting room?"

A few minutes later, he came to the waiting room with an X-ray picture in hand. "I'm afraid I don't have good news. There's definitely a ruptured disk. You can see the damage right here," he said to Julian, pointing to a spot on the X-ray. He even showed it to Larry and pointed out the problem area.

"What should we do, doctor?" Jessica asked.

"Mrs. Jacobson, I'm afraid there isn't very much that *can* be done," he said frankly. "If he was younger, I might be willing to risk surgery, if you wanted me to try. But it's a very difficult procedure, and at his age, I'm afraid it would be too much for him. Assuming he even survived the surgery, a long painful recovery period would follow. At best, there's only a marginal chance he'd ever return to normal. In all likelihood, his condition would be even worse than it is now."

"What's your recommendation, doctor?" Julian asked.

"We spoke about that the other day," the vet answered softly. "I think your family should consider euthanasia."

"No!" Julia screamed. "I won't let you kill my dog!" Larry took Julia into his arms and held her as she wept bitterly against his chest.

"Why don't you all come to the examination room and see him?" the vet suggested. "I'll go with you to answer any questions you may have." He led Julian and Jessica into one of the examination rooms. Larry practically carried Julia along behind them, and walked up to the table where Schotzy lay in his bed.

As he waited for Julia to calm down, Larry started to pet the dog, who occasionally whimpered from the pain in his back. *I will help you bear your pain*, Larry thought to himself as he rubbed the dog's back. *Give some of your pain to me so I can help you.* The dog whimpered again, but slowly relaxed and licked Larry's hand. "What a wonderful friend you've been, Schotzy! You've given them nothing but love your whole life. You've even given me your love for the last few years. You should know that we all love you, and all we want is what's best for you."

"I just want him to get better!" Julia said amidst her tears.

"Of course you do. We *all* want him to get better. We want him to be able to run and play again like always. Most of all, we want him to be happy, and free of pain."

"Yes," Julia agreed. "I want him to be happy."

"He's always done his best to make you happy, hasn't he? He's always wanted you to have the very best life could give, isn't that right, boy?" The dog licked Larry's hand as he spoke, as if he understood what Larry was saying. Then he started licking Julia's hand. "Do you see, Julia? Just as you love him, and want him to have the best, he loves you also, and wants *you* to be happy and to have the very best. When you fell out of that tree in the backyard, didn't he come to lick your wounds? That's how a dog knows to stop pain."

"Yes," Julia agreed. "I heard a dog's saliva has some kind of antiseptic and even a mild pain killer."

"I've heard that, too," he agreed. "And when you felt sick, or down in the dumps, didn't he lick your face or hands to cheer you up, to make your pain go away?"

"Yes," Julia said. "He's always been there for me when I needed a friend."

Larry looked at her and tried to smile. "He needs a friend right now, Julie. He needs someone who loves him to come and ease his pain. He's always been there for you, and now you're the only one who can be there for him."

"Don't you think I know that?" she said as her tears flowed freely once more.

"Yes," he said calmly. "Sometimes it's not easy to help the ones you love."

"I can't do it!" she wailed.

"You have to think of what's best for him right now, Julie," he said gently. "I can help make it easier for you. Would you like me to help you while you help him?"

"What do you have in mind?" she asked, as the tears rolled down her face.

"Shall we make the sacrifice needed to ease the pain of a good friend?" he asked her. He smiled as best he could, and held out his hand to her.

Julia looked at him for a moment, then took his hand, as her tears flowed even stronger. "I understand," she said. "I'm the only one who can ease his pain – the only one who can lick his wounds, and make him feel better."

"That's right, Julie," he said to her. "You have to become an empath. You will relieve his pain by taking it onto yourself. That's the sacrifice only you can make. But you won't have to bear that burden alone. I'll be here to help you. I'll bear some of the pain for you, and so will your mom and dad. Once we've taken his pain away, Schotzy can be happy once again. Are you ready to make that sacrifice?"

"Yes," she said through her tears. "I will ease his pain."

The vet looked at Larry with a bit of wonder in his eyes, then spoke in the manner he had been trained. "I know this isn't easy for any of you, but I think you're making a wise decision. He might live for several months like this, but he'll never be able to walk again. His quality of life would be terrible. As I understand, he's had a long and wonderful life. He's earned his rest."

"Can I be there with him when...?" Julia asked, unable to complete the question.

"Of course," the doctor said. "It'll comfort him to be with the people he knows and loves, and it usually helps the family, also. Schotzy won't feel any pain at all. He'll simply go to sleep like he always does. His pain will go away, and he'll be able to sleep peacefully. Let me know when you're ready."

They all looked at each other and nodded their agreement. The doctor prepared an injection, and first turned to Julian. Julian looked at Jessica with a dazed expression on his face. Jessica looked back at him, then turned to Julia. Julia's lips quivered. As she contemplated the unthinkable, she looked to Larry for an answer. He saw their hesitation and wondered, *Do I have the right to make such a decision? All I can do is ease their pain.* He looked into Julia's eyes and slowly nodded his head.

She held up her head and bravely looked at the doctor, nodding her head for him to proceed. The doctor gave Schotzy the injection, then whispered, "I'll be back in a few moments." He left the room so they could be alone with their friend and family member. Julian, Jessica, Julia, and Larry petted Schotzy. He wagged his tail weakly, licked each hand, then slowly and painlessly, went to sleep.

A few moments later, the doctor returned and examined the dog briefly. "He no longer feels any pain," he said softly. Julian and Jessica hugged each other, unable to fight back their tears, and offered to share the hug with their daughter. Julia refused that offer, running out of the room, out the front door of the clinic, and into the parking lot. Larry followed immediately.

Julian and Jessica looked at each other. "I should go to her," Jessica said.

"She'll be fine," Julian assured her.

The vet nodded his head and added, "Your daughter's boyfriend is a very interesting young man. It's obvious he cares about her a great deal."

"They are exceptionally good friends, and they do indeed care about each other very much," Jessica stated, "but he's not actually her boyfriend."

The vet gave Julian a curious and questioning glance.

Julia sat on the curb, resting her head on her knees, and wept unashamedly. Larry caught up with her and sat next to her without saying a word. Even though his back was now a little sore, he knew he would be able to bear this ache, and that it would soon depart. After a few moments, he began to rub her neck and shoulders with his hands. *Let me bear this pain for you*, he thought to himself. *Give me your pain so I can ease your burden!*

Moments later, she put her head on his shoulder. "Why? Why? Why?"

He thought carefully before saying a word. "Because," he said gently. "That's the only answer there is." She continued to weep while he did his best to comfort her.

Several minutes later, Julian and Jessica came outside and found them sitting on the curb. "Is she alright?" Jessica asked Larry when he looked up.

"Yes," he said softly. "She's just grieving the loss of a dear friend."

"Julia," her father asked, "what would you like to have done with... the remains. Would you like to bury him on the property, have him cremated, or something else? It's entirely up to you, sweetheart. We'll do whatever you want."

"I don't know," she said without looking up. "Whatever you think is best."

Larry could see she was in no condition to make such a choice. "If he were *my* dog, I'd want to have him buried on my property, near the place he called home so I could visit anytime I wanted, and remember him."

Julia looked at him and agreed. "Yes, I want to have him nearby."

Julian went back inside and made arrangements to pick up the body the next day. When he returned, Jessica, Julia, and Larry were waiting in the backseat of the car, just as they had been on the ride there. Without a word, Julian climbed behind the wheel and started home. They rode in silence most of the way. That silence was interrupted when Julia asked a simple question, "Do dogs go to heaven, daddy?"

"I don't know, sweetheart," Julian answered. "They supposedly don't have a soul like humans do, so it's hard for me to see how they could."

"I hope they do," Julia said as more tears flowed down her face.

"I'll share a bit of wisdom my father told me when I asked the same question," Larry said. "At first, his answer was much the same as yours, Mr. J, but when he saw how unhappy I was with that answer, he explained it to me in a slightly different manner. He told me in heaven, your happiness is unconditional. You'll be able to have anything and everything your heart desires, no matter what that might be. So when you get to heaven, Julie, if it will make you happy for Schotzy to be there, whether dogs have a soul or not, there's one thing you can count on with absolute certainty. He'll *be* there!"

They continued on in silence for a while. Julian spoke just as the car turned into the driveway. "That's a wonderful thought, Larry. Your father is a very wise man to think of heaven that way. I don't doubt this wisdom in the least."

Back in the house they sat in the family room, each trying to find a way to dry the tears in their eyes. Trying to comfort her, Larry rubbed Julia's neck and shoulders again, whispering, "Use my shirt to dry your eyes, Julie. I have plenty of experience with tears. I know they don't leave stains."

She clung to him even stronger than before, wiping her tears on his shirtsleeve. Her nose was also filled with tears, and when she sniffled, he extended his invitation. "Blow your nose on my shirt if you need to, Julie. I'm not worried about getting your boogers all over me. I've never been afraid of cooties, either."

"What?" she said. She looked up at him with surprise on her face and saw his soft smile. "You must be crazy!" she chuckled even through her tears. "Thank you, Larry. How is it you always seem to know just the right thing to say to me?"

"Hardly," he said, thinking of other things he wanted to say so badly, "but whenever I can think of something to make you laugh, or even just smile a little, I promise I'll say it. I cannot bear to see you cry, Julie." He looked into her eyes once again, wishing he had the courage to tell her what was in his heart, but knew even if he had that courage, this was not the right time. "Are you going to be alright?"

"I guess so," she answered softly. "Thank you for helping me. Thank you for being my friend. I don't think I would have been able to do this without your help. I'm sure Schotzy would thank you himself, if he only were here to do so."

"Your thanks is all I need," he smiled. After a pause, he added, "I should leave," immediately recognizing his code phrase. "This is a time for family to be together. You don't need an outsider like me getting in your way."

"Stay as long as you like," Jessica said. "Tonight, you *are* part of this family."

"I appreciate that, Mrs. J," he said, "but I think my usefulness for the evening has come to an end. I'll leave you in peace."

"Will you come back tomorrow evening?" Julian asked. "We'll need to select a good site to put Schotzy, and I'm sure I could use your help one more time."

"I'll accept that as an honor," Larry said. "What time should I be here?"

"Can you come at 5:00?" Julian asked, looking at Jessica and Julia for agreement.

"I'll be here." They each hugged him warmly, starting with Julia. He walked away with his heart aching. The knowledge he had been useful in helping to ease her pain lifted his spirit a little. But he knew her pain was far from over, and no matter how much he wanted, or how hard he tried, he could not take all of it away from her.

Tuesday, March 18, 1969
Rainbow Bridge

Larry arrived promptly at 5:00, greeted at the door by Julian, who suggested they take a walk around the property to find a good burial site. "What do you have in mind, Mr. J?" he asked. "Will you put any kind of marker on it later?"

"I don't think so," Julian answered. "We talked about that, and Julia seems to think it'd be better to put him somewhere special, but out of the way, where she can go to remember him whenever she wants, but not have it as a constant reminder."

"I know just the spot," Larry said. He took Julian around to the backyard, down a little path leading to the stock pond. Not far from the base of the dam was a cool, shady spot in a grove of trees, a place someone might go for some private reflection.

"Yes, this is perfect," Julian agreed. "Do you think the girls should watch, or should we complete the burial before bringing them out."

"What sort of condition is he in?" Larry asked.

"He looks normal, but very lifeless, of course," Julian answered. "There seems to be a bit of rigor mortise setting in."

"Perhaps it would be best if they didn't see that," Larry said. "Let them remember him the way they saw him last – sleeping peacefully."

"That was my thinking," Julian agreed, "but I wanted a second opinion."

"Why don't we confirm they agree," Larry said. "If you'd like, I'll come back down here and take care of the details while you keep them occupied. When it's done, I'll come get you and show them where he's been placed."

After Larry finished the burial, he went to the garage to return the shovel and to get his shirt. He went to the bathroom in the back of the garage to clean himself up, surprised to find someone had thoughtfully placed a fresh towel there, along with a comb and a can of spray deodorant. He washed his face and hands, brushed the dirt off his shoes, freshened himself with the deodorant, put his shirt back on, and combed his hair. He returned to the house looking at least as fresh as when he first arrived.

He knocked at the back door and waited. "Everything is ready. Would you all follow me?" As dusk began to gather in the gently rolling hills in central Texas, Larry escorted Julia down the little path to the grave site, with Julian and Jessica following close behind. When the girls saw the grave, they started crying again, although they managed to agree it was a wonderful location.

They stood solemnly near the grave. Julian spoke only three words, "Chazak! Chazak! Venitchazek!" While Larry did not understand these words, he expressed his agreement with a clear "Amen", using the old fashioned pronunciation. Later, he learned Julian's words asked for strength.

"Would anyone like to say something?" Julian asked.

When neither Jessica or Julia wanted to speak, Larry stepped forward. "A few years ago, when I lost another friend of mine, I heard a beautiful story about dogs and heaven. It meant a lot to me then and has ever since. I would like to share it with you. It's guaranteed to make even the most cynical person cry, but since everyone is crying already, I don't see how it can make things worse. The story is called *Rainbow Bridge*.

"Just this side of heaven is a place called *Rainbow Bridge*. When animals who have been especially close to someone here on earth dies, they go to the *Rainbow Bridge*. Here, they find meadows and hills where they can run and play together. They have plenty of food, water and sunshine, and they are warm and comfortable.

"Those who were old are restored to youth. Those who were sick are made healthy. Those who were injured are made whole and strong again, just as we remember them in our dreams of times gone by. They are happy and content as they all run and play together, except for one tiny detail – they each miss someone very special to them – someone they had left behind.

"Every now and then, one of them suddenly stops. He looks into the distance, down the road leading to the *Rainbow Bridge*. His bright eyes are intent, and his body begins to quiver with excitement. Suddenly, he bolts from the others, flying over the green grass as fast as his legs can carry him!

"For he has seen *you* coming down that road. You and your special friend cling together in joyous reunion, never to be parted again. His happy kisses rain down upon your face. Your hands again caress his beloved head, and once again you can look into his trusting eyes, so long missing from your life but never from your heart. And then you cross the *Rainbow Bridge* together."

No one was immune to the tears this story brought to them, but they were all happy to think such a place could actually exist, and Schotzy was even now running and playing with some new friends as he waited for them at that bridge. As twilight grew deeper, they stood under the trees together, each of them searching for his or her own way to say goodbye to the little dog they loved so much.

Just before going to bed, Julian stepped out to the garage to collect the items he had placed there. Even though he tried to be casual, he could not escape Jessica's watchful eyes when he returned the toiletry items to their normal places, and dropped the used towel into the hamper. "Where did those come from?" she asked.

"The garage," he answered simply.

Exactly as he expected she would, Jessica quickly put the pieces together. "You took him a towel and some other items so he could himself clean up? That was very thoughtful of you, Julian," she smiled.

Julian nodded his head. "It was the least I could do for him, Jessie."

Saturday, March 22, 1969
Are You Sitting Comfortably?

Larry wanted to make sure Sam and John were aware of the circumstances. "We should plan to do the show with just the three of us. I don't expect Julie will show up tonight. Even if she does, I don't think she's going to be the same as normal."

"Why is that, Larry?" Sam asked.

"I sensed something was bothering her," he explained, "so I followed her home after guitar practice. Schotzy had injured his back and wasn't doing very well."

"That's a common problem for dachshunds, isn't it?" John asked.

"Yeah," Larry nodded. "I guess that long spine isn't as strong as it needs to be. All three of them were really worried about him. The vet told them it might be just a back sprain, in which case it'd get better in a few days, or it might be a ruptured disk, in which case he was unlikely to get better at all."

"I have this horrible feeling it didn't turn out to be just a sprain," Sam said sadly.

"You're right," he said. "I went back Monday and helped them take him to the vet for X-rays. That's when they found out he was in serious pain and a lot of trouble."

"Poor boy," John said.

"Poor all of them!" Sam added.

"Yeah, they were pretty devastated," Larry nodded. "The vet told them Schotzy was too old for surgery, and there was no real hope he would ever recover. He recommended they... put him to sleep."

"Oh, no!" John said. "How did they take it?"

"Like you'd expect," Larry answered. "I don't think any of them wanted to be the one to make the decision. I know how hard such a decision would be for me! But she ended up making the choice. She managed to call up the strength and courage she needed to set him free." Larry sniffled as he added, "I was so proud of her!"

"She's a very brave little girl," Sam added.

"Yeah," Larry said softly. "I went back Tuesday evening to help bury him. Do you remember that little grove of trees near the base of the dam for the stock pond? That's were we put him. There's no marker to be a constant reminder, but she knows the spot, and she can go there to remember him whenever she feels like it."

"I wish I had known, Larry," Sam said softly. "I'm glad you were there, but she's also our friend. I'd have been there for her as well, and so would John."

"I probably should have told you," he admitted. "I don't know. I guess I thought it better to keep everything simple as possible, something just for the family. If they could have handled it without my help, I wouldn't have intruded at all. I left just as soon as I could. This was something her family needed to share together in private."

"Perhaps you're right," Sam said. "We would have been intruding."

"Well, I don't know," Larry said, "but I doubt she'll come to the station tonight, and we probably won't see her tomorrow, either. Maybe next week."

"I'll call her during the week and check on her," Sam volunteered.

"Would you do that for me, Sam?" he asked. "I really would appreciate it!"

"You can call her, too, Larry," Sam noted softly. "You might earn a few points."

"I'm not looking to score points from this," he whispered. "You know that, Sam."

"Good evening, Mr. J," Ed smiled when Julian answered the front door.

"Hello, Ed," Julian said, wondering to himself how Ed could appear to be so normal. It occurred to him Ed was not aware of the news. "Come on in. You may have to wait a moment. I don't think Julia is quite ready just yet. None of us are moving very fast. This has been a rather difficult week for us."

"I'm sorry to hear that," Ed replied as he stepped inside.

Soon, Julia followed Jessica into the living room. "Hi, Ed," she said flatly.

"Hi, sugar! Are you OK?" Ed asked. "You don't look so good."

"I'm OK," she sighed. "I'm not sure I really want to go out tonight. Would you mind terribly if we just stayed here, and maybe watched some TV or something?"

"If that's what you want," he answered. "What's wrong? Are you sick?"

"No, I'm not sick," she said as a tear appeared on her cheek. Julia turned to her mother for a comforting hug, and Jessica stoked her daughter's hair.

When Ed appeared to be mystified, Julian attempted to explain the situation. "We lost a family member this week, Ed," he said softly, trying not to upset Julia any more than necessary, even though he was feeling his own depression returning.

"Oh, I'm sorry to hear that!" Ed replied. "Was it some sort of accident?"

"It was old age," Julian answered. "At least he had a long and happy life."

"How old was he?" Ed asked softly.

"Sixteen," Julian replied.

"Sixteen?" Ed exclaimed. "Who dies of old age at sixteen?"

"It was Schotzy!" Julia explained, exasperated by Ed's misunderstanding.

"*That's* why he didn't bark when I arrived tonight!" Ed chuckled thoughtlessly. "What a relief! I thought your grandfather had passed away or something! Come on, sugar! The best thing to do right now is to get out, have some fun, and get your mind off of this!"

"I don't feel like going out and having fun, Ed," Julia said.

"Oh, come on, Julie," Ed urged. "He was just a dog!"

"He was part of the family!" Julia argued. "I've known Schotzy all my life! We got him while I was just a baby! OK, so maybe he wasn't a member of the family by blood, but he was still just as much a part of my family as mom or dad or my grandmother. Just because he was adopted doesn't make him anything less. My sister, Sarah, is a member of this family even though she was adopted!"

"That's crazy!" Ed replied. "It's just an animal, a pet. How can you possibly compare him to your parents, your sister, or your grandfather?"

"I'm *not* comparing him to my grandfather!" she insisted, even as her tears began to flow more profusely. "How can you be so insensitive? Just because you never cared anything about your own dog doesn't mean I shouldn't love mine!"

"No, but can't you see how much trouble he's causing you now?" Ed tried. "If you didn't care so much about this... this animal, then you wouldn't be so upset! Come on, Julie! Let me help you forget about him!"

"I don't *want* to forget him!" Julia said forcefully. "And stop calling me that! Don't you *dare* call me that ever again! My name is *Julia*! Only people I truly *love* are allowed to call me Julie!" With that, she marched out of the living room, turned down the hallway, and slammed her bedroom door behind her.

Ed stood in the living room dumbfounded. "Jeez, I've never seen her so upset!"

"I take it you never lost a pet you cared very much about," Julian said softly.

"Not *that* much!" he replied. "I guess I should leave her alone for now. Will you tell her I'm sorry, Mr. J?"

"I'll tell her," Julian replied softly.

"Tell me something before you go," Jessica asked calmly. "What exactly are you sorry about? I'm sure that'll be the first question out of her lips."

"Tell her I'm sorry... she's upset because her dog died," he answered hesitantly.

"We'll tell her," Julian said. He followed Ed to the front door and opened it for him. "Goodnight, Ed," he said casually, even though he was fairly sure the word "goodnight" did not exactly cover the situation accurately.

"Goodnight, Mr. J," Ed said softly, shaking his head. "Goodnight, Mrs. J."

"Goodnight," Jessica repeated, watching Ed return to his car.

Julian exchanged a glance with his wife. "Interesting," he said simply.

He always suspected Jessica could read his mind. That suspicion was further amplified when Jessica replied, "Very interesting, indeed! When I talk to *Julie*, I'll be sure to tell her both her father and I love her very, very much!" She had obviously picked up on the same trivial little subtlety he had.

Saturday, June 14, 1969
I Talk To The Trees

Since it was the night before Father's Day, John and Larry decided to sing a song about their fathers, inspired by a comedy routine they had heard performed by the Smothers Brothers. After a jaunty introduction, Larry sang the first verse of an old traditional song.

[Larry]	*My old man's a sailor. What do you think about that?*
	He wears a sailor's collar. He wears a sailor's hat.
	He wears a sailor's raincoat. He wears a sailor's shoes.
	And every Saturday evening he reads the Sunday news.
[Both]	*And someday if I can*
[Larry]	*I'm gonna be a sailor, the same as my old man.*

"Very nice," John stated, as they continued to play their guitars.

"Thanks, John," Larry replied. "Why don't you tell us about your dad?" John quickly followed with his own solo verse, one the boys had written themselves.

Saturday, June 14, 1969 – I Talk To The Trees

[John] *My old man's a psychologist. What do you think about that?*
He wears a psychologist's collar. He wears a psychologist's hat.
He wears a psychologist's raincoat. He earns a psychologist's pay.
And every Saturday evening he reads "Psychology Today".
[Both] *And someday if I can*
[John] *I'm gonna be a psychologist, the same as my old man.*

"Very impressive!" Larry said as they continued playing. "But John, I didn't know your father was a psychologist. Isn't that what you plan to do yourself?"

"So what?" John countered. "I happen to know your dad isn't a sailor, either."

"He was during the war," Larry replied. "But you're right. Let me fix that."

[Larry] *My old man's a preacher. What do you think about that?*
He wears a preacher's collar. He wears a preacher's hat.
He wears a preacher's raincoat. He wears a preacher's shoes.
And every Saturday evening he reads the Gospel news.
[Both] *And someday if I can*
[Larry] *I'm gonna be a preacher, the same as my old man.*

"Nice," John said, "but I thought he actually was a school teacher."

"He's both," Larry explained. "OK, John. It's your turn."

The interesting thing was John's father ran an appliance repair service, and was a perfect fit for the verse originated by the Smothers Brothers. *"My old man's a refrigerator repairman. What do you think about that?"*

"You're very glib today, John," Larry grinned.

"It sure does," John replied before completing the verse. "Let's see you top that!"

"OK, John," Larry said. "I'll give it a try. Check this out! *My old man's a cotton pickin' finger lickin' chicken plucker. What do you think about that?"*

"I think you'd better not make a mistake!" John snickered. "This is live radio!"

"I'm very aware of that, John," he replied. "I'll be careful." To the relief of all, especially the station owner, he completed the tongue twisting verse without incident.

When the program resumed after the final commercial break, Larry and John played the musical introduction to a song, which Larry then began to sing. It was called *I Talk To The Trees*, written by Alan Jay Lerner and Fredrick Loewe for the Broadway Musical *Paint Your Wagon* released as a movie that same year. *"I talk to the trees, but they don't listen to me. I talk to the stars..."*

John started snickering during the first line. Larry, pretending to be irritated, stopped in the middle of the verse and demanded, "What's your problem, John?" This routine had been inspired by yet another comedy bit performed by the Smothers Brothers on their television program.

"You talk to trees?" John asked, still snickering.

"Sometimes," Larry replied simply.

"Do they ever talk back to you?" John snickered once again.

"Well, not literally," Larry replied. "It's a metaphor, John. I go out among the trees and talk about my troubles, and I look up to the stars and explain my dreams. But, of course, they don't make any response. That's the whole point of the song."

"It's a pretty stupid song, if you ask me!" John laughed. "Imagine, going out and talking to a tree! Hi there, tree! Read any good books lately? Hello, stars! What do you think about my new haircut?"

"OK, John," Larry said with clear signs of disgust. "It's not meant to be taken so literally. I don't actually go around talking to trees and stars. It's just a metaphor, but to me, the song expresses some very personal and poignant ideas."

"Poignant?" John said. "There you go again, Larry, making up another word."

"It's not a word I made up, John," Larry explained. "It's a very common word, actually. Poignant – it expresses something pointed, keen, satirical. Something pregnant with feeling."

John laughed. "I might have known the song was dirty!"

"Not at all, John!" Larry tried to correct. "It's about a young man who has very strong feelings for a girl, but since he's too shy to tell her, the only thing he can do is express his feelings to the trees and the stars. I think it's very moving and tender, myself, and I wish you'd be more serious about it. Now can I go ahead and sing the rest of the song with any further interference?"

"OK," John agreed, continuing to snicker. "And now, ladies and gentlemen, Larry would like to sing a song about a girl he dreams about getting poignant." Without further ado, John began playing the musical introduction once again. After a very audible sigh, Larry joined in with his own guitar, then sang the song straight.

Nearly three months ago, yet another door had opened and then closed for Larry before he had even known about it. He wanted to give her some space after the death of Schotzy, and fate played another trick on him. During that time, she broke up with Ed, and a new boyfriend appeared almost immediately. This one was named Steve.

But there was nothing Larry could do about that now. Another potential opportunity had come and gone. All he knew at the moment was he really did find this song moving and tender. How often had he found himself talking to trees, in particular that old willow tree in her backyard, and to the stars in just this way? The song gave him a little hope that someday, fate would quick playing such tricks on him, and he might suddenly see his dreams coming true.

Wednesday, July 2, 1969
Mr. Lonely

Larry was determined to keep the tradition he did not work on his birthday. He hated it when his birthday fell on a Wednesday like this year, because that meant the Fourth would fall on a Friday. Friday, of course, would be a holiday, and with some luck, he might even find Thursday the Third was listed on the holiday schedule. But no amount of luck would ever result in getting a holiday on Wednesday, his birthday.

Getting the day off from work was no problem, other than the simple fact hours not worked were hours not paid. Getting the day off from class, however, was another story. If his birthday was within a regular spring or fall semester, he might simply cut classes that day. Cutting a class during one of these hectic summer semesters, unfortunately, was the equivalent of being absent for a whole week of a regular semester, certain to have an unacceptable impact on his grade, even for a good student like Larry.

He had been forced to accept a compromise. He would take the day off from work, but not from class. Fortunately, his only class was early in the morning. So he begrudgingly got up that morning like any ordinary day and went to his class. He then returned home to enjoy a birthday lunch with his family. Now, about mid-afternoon, he was on his way to Julia's house to meet his friends for a second birthday celebration. After sunset, they would have another of the traditional impromptu fireworks displays.

In spite of the unfortunate circumstances of his life, he was not in a bad mood on this, his twentieth birthday. He understood why Julia was attracted to Steve. After all, Steve was a good looking guy who would attract *any* girl. He was tall, and because he had been an athlete in high school, he had a muscular frame. Steve had been a member of the "in" crowd in high school, and that popularity rolled over upon his arrival at college. While his family was not rich by general standards, they had enough resources to give him a new car as a graduation present. In Larry's mind, Steve was essentially everything he was not – attractive, athletic, popular, and rich. Not only did Steve have a steady girlfriend, something Larry only dreamed about, the worst part was he had Julia, the girl Larry saw as the standard by which all girls were measured.

He pulled into the Jacobsons' driveway and parked in his usual spot. He got out of his car and headed to the front door, determined he would not let any of these circumstances bring him down. It was his birthday, and he would spend the better part of it with his best friends, the *Four Musketeers!* If he felt lonely, he could commiserate with his friends John and Sam, both of whom were also alone this day.

As expected, Mr. Jacobson greeted him. "Happy birthday, Larry!" he said brightly. "Come on through. The girls are out back on the patio."

"Thanks, Mr. J," Larry smiled as he stepped inside. "How are things going with you today?" he asked, making polite conversation.

"I'm fine, now," Julian replied.

When Larry's eyes adjusted from the glare of the midday sun to the conditions inside the house, he noticed something unusual. "Mr. J, did you know you have a big red blotch on the back of your neck?"

"Yeah, and another one here on my right arm," Julian replied, showing Larry the spot on his arm that was red and a little swollen. "I had a little run-in with some wasps this morning. We noticed they'd built a nest in the backyard, under the eave of the house, so I decided I needed to get rid of it before someone got stung."

"So you went ahead and got all the stinging taken care of this morning," Larry said, trying not to snicker. "That's good thinking, Mr. J!"

"Go ahead and laugh," Julian said with a wry smile as they stepped out onto the patio. "One of these days, you'll have a house of your own and will have to face the same sort of problem. This kind of thing just goes with the territory."

"Hi, Larry! Happy birthday!" Julia called. She and Steve were sitting on the brick retaining wall surrounding the old willow tree.

"Thanks, guys!" he said, returning their greeting. "I really don't mean to laugh, Mr. J," he snickered as they walked to the picnic table where Jessica was sitting. "I don't even own a house, but I've still had a few encounters with wasps in my life. What kind of wasps were they?"

"The kind that sting!" Julian said grumpily. "I didn't ask them for an ID card."

"Happy birthday, Larry," Jessica smiled. "I see you've heard about Julian's little adventure this morning."

"Thanks!" Larry grinned. "I'm sorry he got stung. What color were they?"

"Yellow and black," Julian answered. "Does it really matter?"

"I just wanted to know what you were dealing with," Larry said. "It sounds like you encountered some of my old friends, the Yellow Jacket. Or maybe I should say my old nemeses rather than friends. I've had *more* than my share of encounters with them! Mr. J, this is one of the few creatures on this planet I don't get along with."

"Indeed," Julian said, not sounding particularly interested.

"Yes," Larry continued unperturbed. "I know they're actually beneficial, eating other insects you don't want around, but I simply can't tolerate how aggressive they are! It's one thing when they're just guarding their nest. Maybe you have to forgive them for that, but I've been stung by Yellow Jackets for no particular reason at all! As a result, whenever I see one of their nests, I also tend to see red, if you catch my drift. Texas is simply not big enough for even one Yellow Jacket and me!"

"Then it's too bad you weren't here this morning," Julian grumbled. "You'd have been welcome to chase these away!"

"I hear you," Larry grinned. "Their stings really hurt! Just be glad you didn't have an allergic reaction! The best way to handle Yellow Jackets is to discourage them from nesting on your home, rather than constantly knocking those nests down."

"How can you do that?" Jessica asked.

"Well, they normally build their nests at ground level, such as in heavy brush, or hollow logs," Larry explained, "but they'll also build nests in sheltered places, like the eaves and overhangs around your house. If you understand what they're looking for when they select a nest site, you can make your house less attractive to them."

"Really?" Jessica said. "What are they looking for?"

"Food and shelter for the most part. They want to build their nests near a source of food, and in a place where they can be out of the hot sun and the rain. The food source is not hard to control. They mostly eat other insects. You'll see a lot of them flying around your flowers and shrubs, and because of their color, you might think they're bees. While the adults sometimes eat nectar just like a bee, they're usually more interested in catching the other insects attracted to the flowers, so they can munch them up and feed them to their larvae. If you spray your plants, like you probably want to do anyway, then you'll tend to discourage them from gathering around the house!"

"That makes sense," Julian said. "OK, I'll start spraying the shrubs and other flowering plants next to the house."

"Have you noticed they're also attracted to human food left outside?" Larry asked. "Some people think it's fun to leave a bit of meat on a plate and watch them tear it up and carry it back to their nests. Not me! Personally, I'd rather see them starve! But they'll probably come around this afternoon to investigate our food, like my birthday cake. They like human food, so if you aren't being diligent about it already, be sure to keep your garbage can well covered."

"That's not a problem," Julian said.

"Just doing those things will go a long way," Larry nodded, "but there's another thing you can do. You're probably going to laugh at me, because I'm sure you'll think it sounds like an old wives' tale!"

Jessica grinned. "Sometimes there's a lot of truth in those old sayings."

"Just paint all the eaves, overhangs, and soffits, a pale blue color," Larry grinned.

"What?" Julian asked in surprise.

Wednesday, July 2, 1969 – Mr. Lonely

"You're joking, right?" Jessica asked.

"No, I'm not!" Larry smiled. "It's based on the idea they want to build their nests in a place that's sheltered from the sun and the rain."

"Oh, come on, Larry," Julian scoffed. "Painting the overhangs blue isn't going to affect the amount of shelter."

"No," Larry agreed, "but it affects their perception of the shelter they'll provide! It's like this, Mr. J. For the best shelter, they're programmed to think they shouldn't be able to see the sky above them. Open sky means exposure. So if the overhangs are painted pale blue, resembling the color of the sky as closely as possible, they won't build their nest there!"

"What a load of crap!" Steve laughed.

Julian joined the laughter, "This may be the biggest bobemayse I've ever heard!"

"I knew you'd laugh," Larry said smugly, "but you know what? It works! I've seen it with my own eyes. It wasn't an old wife who told me about it, it was my grandfather! He keeps the overhangs on his house and garage painted pale blue, and I've never seen a wasp nest of any kind on his house. Try it for yourself, Mr. J."

Julian shook his head. "I don't buy this. You're just trying to trick me into doing a bunch of unnecessary work so you can sit back and laugh at me while you watch."

"I understand. Maybe I deserve that," Larry smiled. "I'll make a deal with you. I'll help you paint the overhangs on one side of your garage a pale blue color, and we'll leave the other side alone. Then you can see the difference for yourself. If any wasps build their nests on the blue side, I'll personally come back out here, knock them down, and repaint your entire garage for you."

"You got a deal!" Julian laughed.

Sam arrived a few minutes later. "Happy birthday, Larry!" she said.

"Thanks, doll!" he replied.

Sam knew Larry would try to enjoy this day as much as humanly possible. He and John would sing cheerful songs. Later that afternoon, he would smile when they brought him his birthday cake. She already knew what he would wish for when he blew out the candles. He would laugh merrily as he opened the gag gifts they would give him. He would make the appropriate "ooh" and "ah" sounds while they set off their fireworks. To everyone else, he would be the prototypical version of a young man happily celebrating his twentieth birthday. But in spite of the upbeat mood he wore as a mask, Sam could see the traces of the lonely sadness that always seemed to reside in the corners of his eyes.

John arrived next, and the gang got busy celebrating Larry's birthday. They told funny stories and laughed together. They especially had a good laugh at Larry's expense when Steve related to Sam and John the deal Larry had made with Julian about painting the garage. Sam even joined in as they all teased him, although she knew better. She had seen this sort of thing too many times in the past. Larry undoubtedly knew what he was talking about. She was quite sure he would not end up having to repaint that garage.

As expected, Larry and John played their guitars and sang for a while. Sam enjoyed listening to her friends make their music. Already popular to the local community as a talented and entertaining little two-man band, they seemed to be improving continually as they expanded their repertoire and displayed a unique style of their own. She noted that even Mr. and Mrs. J enjoyed listening to them.

More importantly, Sam noticed how much Julia enjoyed listening. Perhaps someday soon, Larry's music would help open a certain door for him. If only she could convince him to simply go bang on that door for himself! But he was too shy, too insecure, too critical of himself. He did not think himself a worthy adversary, especially when pitted against someone like Steve. She looked at Steve casually, once more sizing up his qualities. He certainly had his charms, but in Sam's eyes, Larry made him look like a chump. *Is that because I know so well the inner qualities Larry possesses?* she asked herself.

When the boys took a break for a while, Sam wanted to talk to her friend. "I feel like taking a little stroll down by the stock pond. Feel like being my escort, Larry?"

"I'd be happy to, Sam," he smiled. "Not that I think you need such an escort. If the bogeyman jumps out at us, I assume you'll protect me, OK?"

"You got a deal," Sam grinned. As they stepped away from the patio, she lowered her voice to speak more privately. "I just wanted to know if you're feeling OK."

"I'm fine, Sam," he smiled. "Thanks for worrying about me. How about you?"

Sam looked around at the beautiful countryside and sighed. "I'm great, Larry," she said. "I wish I could explain how happy I feel at this moment. In fact, the only thing wrong is Donald isn't here to share this beautiful day with me."

"I understand," he said. "Will you tell me more about this Donald of yours? I wish just once you'd bring him around so I could meet him. Anybody you care about as much as you obviously care about him is bound to be someone I'd like!"

"I'll bring him around one of these days," she said. "I promise. Even though the two of you will have some strong differences of opinion about some things, I'm also sure you'll like each other, just as I'm sure he and John will like each other."

"Sounds like maybe he'll soon become the fifth *Musketeer*!" Larry grinned. "Where is he, Sam? Why doesn't he come visit you?"

"He just can't right now," she answered. "That's all. But sometimes he sends me money so I can go visit him."

"And when he does, you sneak off without letting your friends know about it!"

"I know," Sam admitted. "I'm sorry. It's not that I like keeping secrets. I'll explain it one of these days. Please don't ask me to tell you more. Trust me, OK?"

Larry stopped in his tracks. "Sam, I would trust you with my very life!"

"I know you would," she said seriously. "I also trust you with my life! It makes me feel so terrible I'm keeping so many secrets from you. Believe me, Larry, it's not a matter of a lack of trust. It has to do with certain promises I've made. I know you can understand about the power of promises!"

"I certainly do, Sam," he smiled nodding his head. "I won't pressure you to reveal those secrets. I'll be here for you if you ever need anything, secrets or no secrets."

"Stop that," Sam said softly squeezing his hands. "You're going to make me cry!"

"Don't you dare!" he chuckled. "Not unless you want me to cry, as well! You know I can't stand to see you cry!"

"And I can't stand to see you so very lonely," she said.

"Unless you're ready to dump this Donald and be my girl," he grinned, "then I don't suppose there's much you can do about that, now is there! Oh, Sam, sure I'm lonely, but I'll be OK. I'm sort of used to it, doncha know. One of these days, things will be different. I'll either get the chance to be with Julie and learn what it is about her that calls to me so, or I'll find someone else just like her. You'll see!"

"It's good to see you so confident," Sam smiled. "I most certainly agree with you. One of these days, things are going to be very different. Personally, I think I'll be just as happy to see that day arrive as you will!"

"I doubt that very seriously!" he laughed. "Come on, Sam! Let's go back and join the others. I won't deny I'm lonely, but I'll cope with it. What else can I do?"

Sunday, July 20, 1969
Man On The Moon

John and Larry could not concentrate on music that afternoon. There was simply too much going on in the world, demonstrating what a thin line exists between imagination and reality. To Larry, at least, that seemed to be the case for all the mundane things in the universe. When it came to all of his most important dreams, unfortunately, it was more like a gulf rather than a thin line that separated his imagination from reality.

That was not to say the Apollo 11 mission was unimportant to him. The truth of the matter was he saw this day as potentially the most significant one in all of human history. Mankind must reach for the stars to find its destiny. One of Larry's dreams was that he could somehow be a part of that journey. The only problem was, he did not want to make that journey alone, anymore than he wanted to stay on earth alone. Solving that trivial little problem was the key item on the critical path to the stars.

At the Jacobson house, Julian, Jessica, Larry, John, Sam, and Julia sat in the family room. Six pairs of eyes were glued to the television set, transfixed by the voices and images reporting the events in minute detail. The fact there were few details to report didn't alter anything. As long as it had something, *anything* to do with journey, those six pairs of eyes, like millions of other eyes around the world, absorbed it eagerly.

If possible, six pairs of eyes became even more intensely glued to the television as the first critical moment of the day approached. Astronaut Michael Collins was alone in the Command Module; Neil Armstrong and Buzz Aldrin were in the Lunar Module preparing for the undocking, the next critical step for the actual landing. A few seconds after the spacecraft emerged from the far side of the moon, Collins would fire the engines on the Service Module to pull away from the Lunar Module. He would remain in lunar orbit as Armstrong and Aldrin began the great adventure.

[Capcom]	Hello, Eagle, Houston. We're standing by. Over. Eagle, Houston. We see you on the steerable. Over.
[Eagle]	Roger. Eagle. Stand by.
[Capcom]	Roger. Eagle. How does it look?
[Armstrong]	The Eagle has wings.
[Columbia]	I think you've got a fine looking flying machine out there, Eagle, despite the fact you're upside down.
[Eagle]	Somebody's upside down.
[Columbia]	OK Eagle, one minute to T. You guys take care.
[Eagle]	See you later.
[Eagle]	Going right down U.S. 1, Mike.

Moments later, as the television coverage continued, Larry sat upright with an observation. "Hey, you guys! Did you notice Schirra's lapel pins? A few minutes ago, they showed the Command Module and Lunar Module in a docked position. Now, they're separated!"

"No kidding?" Sam said. "That's neat!"

The Eagle's orbit once again carried it to the back side of the moon. Anticipation grew to tremendous levels with the knowledge that when the Lunar Module reappeared, it would be at an altitude of some ten miles, with its orbit still carrying it downward towards the lunar surface.

[Capcom]	Eagle, Houston. You're a go for powered descent. Over.
[Columbia]	Eagle, this is Columbia. They just gave you a go for powered descent.
[Capcom]	Columbia, Houston. We've lost them on the high gain antennae again. Would you please – we recommend that they yaw right ten degrees and try the high gain again.
[Columbia]	Eagle, you read Columbia?
[Eagle]	Roger, read you.
[Houston]	Coming up one minute to ignition.
[Capcom]	Eagle, Houston. Everything is looking good here. Over.
[Capcom]	Eagle, Houston. You are go. Take it all at four minutes. Roger you are go – you are go to continue power descent. You are to continue power descent. Altitude 40,000 feet. We've got data dropout. You're still looking good.
[Eagle]	And the earth right out our front window.
[Houston]	We're still go. Altitude 27,000 feet.
[Eagle]	Throttles down better than the simulator.
[Capcom]	Rog.
[Houston]	21,000 feet, still looking very good.
[Capcom]	Altitude 13,500. Eagle, you're looking great at eight minutes. Correction on that velocity, now reading 760 feet per second.
[Capcom]	We're go. Altitude 9200 feet. You're looking great. Descent rate 129 feet per second.
[Capcom]	Eagle, you're looking great, coming up on nine minutes. We're now in the approach phase, everything looking good. Altitude 5200 feet.
[Eagle]	Manual altitude control is good.
[Capcom]	Roger. We copy. Altitude 4200 and you're go for landing. Over.
[Eagle]	Roger, understand. Go for landing. 3000 feet. Second alarm.
[Eagle]	Roger. 1201 alarm. We're go. Hang tight. We're go. 2000 feet. 2000 feet, into the AGS. 47 degrees.
[Capcom]	Eagle looking great. You're go.
[Houston]	Altitude 1600. 1400 feet. Still looking very good.
[Eagle]	35 degrees. 35 degrees. 750, coming down at 23. 700 feet, 21 down. 33 degrees. 600 feet, down at 19. 540 feet down at 30 – down at 15... 400 feet down at 9... 8 forward... 350 feet down at 4... 300 feet, down 3½... 47 forward... 1½ down... 70... got the shadow out there... 50, down at 2½, 19 forward... altitude-velocity lights... 3½ down... 220 feet... 13 forward... 11 forward, coming down nicely... 200 feet, 4½ down... 5½ down... 160, 6½ down... 5½ down, 9 forward... 5 percent... quantity light 75 feet. Things

Sunday, July 20, 1969 – Man On The Moon

	still looking good, down a half... 6 forward... lights on... down 2½... forward... 40 feet, down 2½, kicking up some dust... 30 feet, 2½ down... faint shadow... 4 forward... 4 forward, drifting to the right a little... 6... drifting right...
[Capcom]	30 seconds.
[Eagle]	Contact light. OK, Engine stopped... decent engine command override off...
[Eagle]	Houston, Tranquility Base here. The Eagle has landed!
[Capcom]	Roger, Tranquility. We copy you on the ground. You've got a bunch of guys about to turn blue. We're breathing again. Thanks a lot.
[Tranquility]	Thank you.
[Capcom]	You're looking good here.
[Capcom]	Roger, Eagle. And you're stay for T-1. Over. You're stay for T-1.
[Tranquility]	Roger. We're stay for T-1.
[Capcom]	Roger. And we see you getting the ox.
[Capcom]	Roger, we read you Columbia. He has landed. Tranquility Base. Eagle is at Tranquility. Over.

Six pairs of eyes in the Jacobson family room stared at each other in silence. The only noise in the room came from the television. Two pairs of those eyes looked at each other and contemplated the true distance between imagination and reality. In reality, nothing had changed at all. Yet as the thin line between imagination and reality on one plane of existence disappeared in a small cloud of lunar dust, surely the gulf dividing imagination and reality on that other plane grew a little smaller itself. Whenever important experiences are shared, the participants are inexorably drawn closer together.

Larry had one very special thought that evening. *If a man can cross this quarter of a million miles that separate the earth and the moon, then surely I can find a way to close the gap between us. This is my quest. I promise I will never abandon this pursuit. Someday, she and I will walk down the road of life together, hand-in-hand, sharing our joys as well as our tears.*

Monday, August 18, 1969
Woodstock

Sam, John, and Larry were tired from the long journey, but they made it, and that was all that counted. Thirty-six hours of non-stop driving was divided into nine shifts of four hours each. From Bryan, they drove north to Dallas, then turned more eastward to Texarkana, and onward though Little Rock, Memphis, and Nashville. Northward once again, they passed through Louisville, Cincinnati, and Columbus, then almost due east to Akron before crossing into Pennsylvania. Continuing east, they passed through Hazelton, then veered northeast to Honesdale. They turned north once again to Rileyville, then east through West Damascus, Tyler Hill, and Damascus. Crossing into the state of New York, they passed through Cochecton, East Cochecton, and Fosterdale. Finally, early on Friday, the fifteenth of August, they reached their destination – the small town of Bethel, in Sullivan County, New York. They arrived, more or less, at the same time as a half million others!

The first day alone made the trip worthwhile. They listened to Ritchie Havens,

Sweetwater, Bert Sommer, and Tim Hardin. They floated to the music of Ravi Shankar, then grooved along with Melanie, and Arlo Guthrie. They joined in with Joan Baez as she sang *We Shall Overcome*. After the end of that day's concert, they tried to sleep in John's van, but were far too excited to get much rest. And of course, there was much more to come.

The second day seemed to be even better than the first! Quill was followed by Country Joe McDonald, where a half million voices joined in the *Fish Cheer*. John B. Sebastian came next, followed by the Keef Hartley Band, Carlos Santana, and the Incredible String Band. Then they listened to Canned Heat, the Grateful Dead, and Creedence Clearwater Revival. They were blown away by the incredible voice of Janis Joplin, then relaxed a little to the sounds of Sly and the Family Stone. Next, they were driven to new heights as The Who essentially performed the rock opera *Tommy* in its entirety. Jefferson Airplane rounded out the most incredible day of music they ever heard, ending with *White Rabbit*. How does one sleep after that?

Yet still it did not stop. The third day raised the bar to a whole new level, starting with Joe Cocker, Country Joe and the Fish, Leslie West/Mountain, then Ten Years After. Next came The Band, Jimmy Winter, then Blood Sweat and Tears. The day was rounded out by an incredible performance by David Crosby, Stephen Stills, and Graham Nash, who were joined by Neil Young. After midnight, came the Paul Butterfield Blues Band, Sha-Na-Na, and the simply unbelievable Jimi Hendrix.

All good things must come to an end. The kids decided they simply had to sleep a little before starting back to Texas. Later that morning, John woke up to take the first shift, letting Sam and Larry sleep awhile longer, knowing that one of them would take over in four hours, allowing him to get more rest.

Almost as if on queue, Larry crawled into the passenger seat from the back of the van. "How are you doing, John?" he asked, immediately followed by a huge yawn.

"I'm doing fine," John replied. "How's Sam?"

"Sleeping like a baby," Larry answered. "I don't think she slept as much as five minutes the whole time." He took a deep breath and sighed, watching the countryside pass by. "This has got to be the best adventure of my entire life."

"You can say that again!" John agreed.

"This has got to be the best adventure of my entire life," Larry restated.

John saw the huge grin on the face of his friend. He returned a half grin, half scowl. "Why do you have to take everything I say so literally?" he chuckled.

"Do I? Sorry, John. It's just the way I am, I guess."

John could see that Larry was in a soulful mood. "What was the best part?"

"I don't think I could pick any one thing and call it the best," Larry replied. "It was the combination of everything! I loved the music, of course, but the oneness I felt with all those people sharing the experience was just as important. I especially liked all the new friends we made, and how they appreciated the little impromptu mini-concerts we played while they set up the stage for the next big band."

"I'm with you," John agreed. "So if you can't pick out the best part, what was the worst part?" he asked with a chuckle.

"You probably expect me to say it was either the rain, the traffic, the lack of food, the lack of restrooms, or something like that, right?" Larry grinned. John returned his grin and waited, knowing his friend had something else in mind. "All of those things were minor inconveniences," Larry smiled. "It was none of those, John. The worse thing about it was that only *three* of the *Four Musketeers* could be there."

John was a little surprised at first, but quickly realized he should not have been. Julia had been invited to come with them, of course, and she clearly wanted to do so. But Mr. J and Mrs. J would not budge. "Do you really think it's appropriate for a sixteen year old girl to run off for a week or more with another girl and two older boys?" Mr. J asked them flatly. Mrs. J softened it by assuring the boys she knew they could be trusted, but it just was not the right thing to do. The boys understood, but none of the foursome could hide their disappointment.

The boys' parents had not raised that much of an issue. John was nineteen, Larry was twenty. There was little their parents could have done to stop them other than setting all their possessions out on the lawn and telling them not to come back. John knew that would not have stopped him, and was fairly sure it would not have stopped Larry, either. Sam's situation was completely different. Mrs. K thought it was a great idea, and even considered coming along with them! John assumed Sam talked her out it, even though it would not have been all that bad if she had come.

John agreed Larry was right. The worst part was that Julia had not come with them. He also knew Larry's feelings were a little different in that regard than his own. "You really care about her," he said, stating the obvious.

He was only a little surprised by Larry's response. "Of course I do, John," he stated. "She's my friend, just like you and Sam."

"I know," John said. "It truly is a shame she couldn't come with us."

"John," Larry sighed, "this was something extraordinary. People are going to be talking about this for years to come. I feel privileged to have been a part of it. I wish she could have been here to share it with us."

"You want her to be something more than a friend," John said softly.

"*More* than a friend?" Larry asked. "You know better than that, John. I just want her to be something different. At least, that's what I think I want. Sometimes I'm not sure what I really want at all. Not about her. Not about anything."

"I know you want to play around with those computing machines," John said.

"Most of the time," Larry agreed. "On the other hand, there are times like right now, when I wonder if I shouldn't pursue a different career. Just think what it must be like to go to events like this all the time, and see it from the inside. I know we're not nearly as good as those guys, but if we really worked at it, maybe we could be."

"Well, ain't this quaint?" John chuckled. They had talked about this subject before. John was the one who normally suggested this possibility. Obviously, his friend was deeply moved by the events of the last few days. "You always argue with me when I suggest that. Why the sudden change?"

"Shouldn't that be *'Isn't this quisn't,'* John?" Larry grinned. He paused before addressing John's question. "Maybe the excitement of the last few days has made me rethink some things. Why don't you pull over and let me drive a while, John?"

It was time for the shift change, so John obliged his request. "It'd be an exciting lifestyle!" he stated, returning to the subject of turning pro.

"That's for sure!" Larry grinned, driving the van back onto the highway. "Is that what you want, John?"

"Sometimes," he replied thoughtfully. "Most of the time, I'm like you, though. I just want to finish school, settle down, and live a normal life. It'd be fun to run all over the country, making music all the time, and partying with the groupies all night long. But I really think I'd get tired of that after a while."

"I'd *never* get tired of partying with sweet young things all night long!"

"Yes, you would," John grinned. "I know you very well, my friend. You'd rather find one girl you can really care about, and who'd really care about you, than to have a new squeeze every night, no matter how hot they all might be."

John saw Larry look at him for a moment, then return his eyes to the road. "You're right, John," he said softly. "If I could have anything I wanted, I'd finish school, get a great job working with computers, find someone to love who'd love me, and settle down to live happily ever after, just like in a fairy tale. Although things wouldn't necessarily have to happen in that order. And I'm no city boy. I think if I had my choice, I'd build a house on a few acres out in the country so I could keep in touch with nature. I like watching the deer, the hummingbirds, and all that sort of thing."

"Like the Jacobson house?" John asked.

"Exactly," he answered. "Julie isn't the only thing that draws me to that place."

"I know how you feel," John agreed. "I like being there, as well. Is it the place that makes them seem so special, or is it they that make the place special?"

"That's a very profound question," Larry smiled. "Maybe it's the combination. I'll have to give it some thought."

"Well, try to keep your mind on the road, won't you?" John teased. "I'm going to catch some Z's. If Sam isn't awake in four hours, I'll take over again, OK?"

"OK, John," Larry smiled.

John crawled out of the passenger seat, moving into the back to get some sleep. After thirty-six hours of driving, divided into some nine shifts, they would all be home in Bryan, Texas, bubbling from an experience none of them would ever forget.

Tuesday, August 26, 1969
Learn How To Fall

Larry led the small group in a familiar chorus:
>*Happy birthday to you.*
>*Happy birthday to you.*
>*Happy birthday dear Sam!*
>*Happy birthday to you.*

Sam smiled as they sang, and as soon as it ended, she leaned over and blew out the twenty candles on the birthday cake Jessica made with help from Julia. "Thanks, everybody!" she said happily. After the wonderful adventure she and her friends had just returned from, she was in what might almost be described as a euphoric state of mind, tempered only by the disappointment that *all* of her best friends did not get to share the adventure. But they were together again, and Julia enjoyed the stories they told, allowing her to participate in the great adventure vicariously.

Julia had something of an adventure of her own while they were away! After wearing them for years, her orthodontist made a surprise move by removing her braces. Her new smile was dazzling, and everyone agreed she looked more mature and even prettier than before. Steve strutted around the patio like a peacock, as if he had anything to do with it at all. It was more than clear he was especially happy about the change in his girlfriend.

But not everyone was as pleased as Steve. Sam noticed that one individual seemed to be troubled by it. While he was participating in the birthday party as enthusiastically as anyone, playing his guitar and singing along with John, there was something about the expression in his eyes that told her things were not exactly as they appeared to be.

She sought out an opportunity to speak to him privately. "Are you feeling alright, Larry?" Sam asked softly when no one was paying any attention to them. "Your face looks a little green."

"I'm OK, Sam," he said softly. "Don't let me spoil the party."

"Something is bothering you," she said, looking around to make sure no one was eavesdropping. "What's the problem?"

"Nothing, Sam!" he insisted.

Sam knew instinctively something was bothering him. "OK, fine," she said calmly. "I'm going to take a little walk down by the pond, just to get away from all the noise and bother for a couple of minutes. If you know anyone who'd like to come along, let them know." With that, she stood up and started walking casually towards the little path that would lead her down to the stock pond. About halfway across the patio, she looked back. Slowly, Larry stood up and followed, joining her at the edge of the patio, where she calmly waited for him.

"What's wrong, sugar?" she asked once they were far enough away to be out of earshot. "I know that look on your face, and something is troubling you." Larry just shook his head and looked into the distance. Sam let it go for the moment. She knew he would speak when he was ready to do so, and not until then.

They reached the pond and stopped. Larry looked around for a stone he could skip across the water. Sam helped, pointing out some stones for him. He tossed the first and they watched it skip four times before sinking into the murky depths.

"Nice throw," she said softly.

"Thanks," he said sadly. He looked at Sam and apologized. "I'm sorry to be this way on your birthday, Sam. I don't want to bum you out just because I feel so..." His voice trailed off as he left the explanation dangling in mid-sentence.

"What's troubling you, Larry?" she asked again. "Julia?"

"What else would it be?" he said sadly. "My God, Sam, she's beautiful! Why does she have to be so beautiful?"

"Don't you want her to be beautiful?" she asked softly, not understanding what was troubling him.

"No!" Larry said.

"Oh, come on," Sam said. "We both know better than that!"

Larry looked down at the ground, as if searching for another stone. "Sam, I've known her since she was just a skinny little tomboy with pimples on her face, braces on her teeth, skinned up knees, and a ponytail. None of that ever mattered to me. I've always wanted to be with her, and it's never had anything to do with her physical appearance."

"Yes, I know that," Sam said patiently.

"It's not physical beauty I'm interested in. When I look at her, I see her beautiful soul, her beautiful heart, her beautiful mind. That's why I want to be with her!"

"I know," Sam agreed, still being patient.

"Now look at her! She's all grown up. The pimples are gone, the braces are gone, the knees are intact, and her hair is... Oh, Sam! Now she has a beautiful face and body to go along with everything else, and every guy in the world will want to be with her. I haven't been good enough for her before! What possible chance will I have now, against that competition? Why couldn't she be just a little less beautiful?"

"My dear, sweet boy!" Sam said, feeling his anguish. "Do you really think the guys only interested in her face and body are going to be any competition to you?"

"They've done a damn good job so far!" he said bitterly. "Is she throwing herself at me? No, she's up there with that pretty boy, Steve. He's not interested in her soul, her heart, or her mind. She's just a tchatchke to him, an ornament, something he can show off to the other guys. And now she's even prettier than before!"

"Don't you think she knows what he wants?" Sam asked. "Don't you think Steve's days are numbered?"

"Sometimes I wonder," he said sadly. "I don't know, Sam. Maybe she's not the girl I think she is. All I know is that I've never been good enough for her, even when she wasn't so beautiful."

"That's simply not true, Larry," she argued. "I know for a fact she had a crush on you a couple of years ago. She wanted to be with you after she broke up with Jimmy, but you..." Sam let her voice trail off. She knew this was a bad time to remind him of those days, but it was already too late.

"Thanks for reminding me," he snarled. "I've been regretting that mistake for over two years now, Sam. I've been watching and waiting for a chance to correct it, but I don't think it'll ever happen, especially not now."

"All I wanted to point out was that you're wrong about things," she insisted. "You were good enough for her then, and you're good enough for her now. You're not exactly what I would call a slug, yourself! You've grown up, too, Larry! Take a good look at yourself sometime! You're a great looking guy, even hot enough to attract the famous Ball sisters last year. And when you combine that with the beautiful soul, beautiful heart, and beautiful mind you have, you really *could* have just about any girl you choose!"

Larry sighed. He knew intellectually Sam was right, to some extent. So why was it that this just didn't seem to matter? "I appreciate you trying to build up my confidence, but let's be a little more realistic, OK? I know who and what I am. I'm just an average sort of guy. I accept that. There's nothing wrong with being average. Let's assume for the moment that you're right when you say I could have just about any girl I choose. It's that *'just about'* part that's killing me. What if I chose to be with *you*?"

"Oh, Larry," she said sadly. "I already have someone else, someone really special to me. That's not a fair test!"

"So you say," he agreed, nodding his head. "She already has someone else, too. What good is it to say I can have any girl I choose, if I have to choose one who doesn't already have a boyfriend? You might as well say I can be a millionaire – all I have to do is find a million dollars that doesn't already belong to someone else."

"You're just discouraged, Larry," she added, "and who can blame you? All I can tell you is that this guy won't last forever. One of these days, he'll be gone, and you'll get the opportunity to be with her."

"Like the opportunity I had after Frank was gone?" he asked. "Like the one I had after Bill? Or do you mean the one I had after Ed?"

"All I'm saying is that you need to have a little more faith in yourself," Sam urged. "So maybe it won't be easy, but nothing worthwhile ever comes easy, does it? You're a great guy! All you have to do is step up to the plate and show her what a great guy you are! You'll get that chance one of these days!"

"And so will a million other guys, Sam," he said sadly.

"Maybe," Sam smiled, "but after all, you're one in a million. If I can see that, don't you think she can, also?"

"What if she can't?" Larry asked.

"How could a beautiful girl with a beautiful soul, a beautiful heart, and a beautiful mind fail to notice a great looking guy with a beautiful soul, a beautiful heart, and a beautiful mind of his own?" she asked with a smile.

He stared at his friend for a moment, then chuckled to himself and shrugged. With a slight grin on his face, he whispered, "Thanks, Sam. Maybe I just needed a pep talk today. I've waited this long. I guess I can wait a little while longer."

"That's the spirit!" she smiled. She stepped over and gave her friend a hug and kissed him on the cheek.

"Sam," he smiled back, "we're down here all alone and it's a beautiful warm afternoon. We could do anything we wanted and no one could see us, doncha know. Why don't you let me give you a special birthday present! Why don't you let me show you that, all by my little lonesome, I can be even more interesting than Tweedledee and Tweedledum ever were?"

"You're incorrigible!" Sam laughed.

"All I need is a little 'incorrigment' and I'm good to go!" he smiled.

"Well, then good," Sam grinned. "Let's go!"

"Do you mean it?" he asked with a bright smile.

"Of course I mean it!" she laughed. "Let's go – back to the *house!*"

When he playfully reached for her, she wiggled out of his grasp, and ran back up the path, laughing merrily as he chased after her, pacing himself just enough so he wouldn't quite catch up to her.

Saturday, August 30, 1969
The End

Promptly at 8:00 o'clock, Diggs played the prerecorded tape, one of the old *Rocky and Bullwinkle* bits the boys had done in the past. Most of the show, in fact, consisted of a nostalgic replay of the comedy bits the gang had done over the years. Most of the serious songs were recordings the boys had made, selected by popular demand. The majority of the dedications called in requested that songs be played for the *Four Musketeers*: Larry, Sam, John, and Julia.

None of them knew why the show was being canceled. It certainly was not a lack of popularity; the show had steadily increased in popularity ever since the gang took over its production. Nor was it due to a lack of sponsorship; there was a waiting list of local businesses wanting their commercial message aired during this popular time slot. Mr. James Krueger, the station owner, normally known by less formal names by the gang, had decided to turn the Saturday night time slot over to a network broadcast. Listeners would still hear popular rock songs. Turning it over to the network would make it simpler, cheaper, and much less risky for the local station.

"It looks like it's nearly 11:00," Larry said. "You know what that means!"

"No," John answered. "What does it mean?"

"It means the show is almost over, and it's time for us to go," Larry replied.

"Where are we going?" John asked, sounding concerned.

"Say goodbye to the boys and girls, John," Larry said calmly.

"I don't want to say goodbye!" John blubbered. "I don't want to go anywhere!"

"Everything will be OK, John," Larry said.

"No!" John said, wailing as if in agony.

"There, there," Larry said, pretending to give John some reassurance.

"I know exactly how he feels," Julia announced. "I don't want to go, either. These last couple of years have been a wonderful experience. I'm going to miss it a lot, and I want to extend a heartfelt thanks to all the people who've listened in and supported us all this time. And I want to thank my dear friends, John, Larry, and Sam for letting me join them, showing me the ropes, and for putting up with me."

"You helped make it special, Julia, so thanks go to you as well," John added, now in a more serious tone. "I especially want to thank everyone who encouraged us. It's been a lot of fun, but we couldn't have done it without you guys. I also couldn't have done it without Larry and Sam. Thank you for letting me be a part of this."

"What would we have done without you, John?" Larry asked softly. "Or without you, Julie? I certainly thank you both, and like you've already said, I especially want to thank the fans who've made it such a pleasure. When Sam asked me to join her on this program back when, I never thought it would become what it has. I should have known better. I know whenever Sam puts her mind to something, it's going to turn out special. The person I want to thank the most is Sam, the creative genius who brought us together and held us together. You're the best, Sam!"

"Those are kind words, indeed," Sam said in a relaxed tone, "but I'm hardly worthy of such praise. We did it together! If we did good, then the praise goes to the *Four Musketeers* as a whole, and not to any one individual. We've been serious; we've been silly. There have been a few anxious moments over the years, but I have to say it's been quite a thrill for me to be part of this program. To all our fans, I just want to say, *'Thanks!'* You're the ones I'll miss most of all!" She paused for a moment, then asked a question that was obviously directed to John and Larry. "So, did you guys put together something worthy of our final moment on the air?"

"Remains to be seen," Larry chuckled. "So long, everybody!" At his signal, Diggs started the final tape. As the gang shouted their final farewells, Diggs faded their voices into the background, bringing the music forward. For the last moments of the last *Top Forty Showcase* program, the Drug Company had prerecorded a rendition of the last verse of a Beatles song called *The End:*

And, in the end, the love you take
Is equal to the love you make.

The song ended. After thirty seconds of dead air time, practically an eternity for broadcast radio, Diggs came on, announced that news would be coming at the top of the hour, and then went to a commercial.

The *Four Musketeers* looked at each other with mixed feelings. It was time to clean up the studio, return the records to the racks, document and file the tapes away, and leave the studio for what they assumed was to be the last time. A lot of memories of other nights and other programs came flooding back into their heads. The boys were determined they would tough it out and not show their emotions. The girls were not quite so brave, allowing little unwelcome tears to appear in the corners of their eyes.

"Hey!" Larry said as they gathered in the main studio one last time to ensure their work was completed. "It's been a great run, but it's time to move on. Sure, we'll miss coming up here, but look on the bright side! At least we'll be free on Saturday nights to do anything we want to do!" He fought back a choke on the last few words, realizing a free Saturday night meant he would be sitting at home, alone. *This* was what he wanted to do. If nothing else, it was a chance to see her. Even though she was always with someone else, wasn't it better to see her than to not? He knew he would continue to see her even without the show, of course. The gang would go on as strong as ever. They did not need the radio program to keep their friendship alive.

Once the network news began, Diggs was free to leave the control room, and he joined the kids in the studio. "I just wanted to tell you what a pleasure it's been to work with all of you guys these last few years. I'm really going to miss you."

"We're going to miss you, too!" Sam said, tears breaking through once again as she gave him a hug. "Don't you think for a moment we don't know how many times you went to bat for us with old Mr. Fussbudget!"

"None of that, now," Diggs smiled. "This isn't goodbye. It's more like *'Hasta la vista!'* and you know it!" He turned to Julia who immediately gave him a hug of her own. "Take care of yourself, Julia."

"I will," she replied. "You take care, as well!"

"Don't I always?" he grinned. Turning to the boys, he added, "I have this feeling I'll be seeing you guys sooner than anyone expects. Keep your music alive. Feel free to come back any time and use the studio to make recordings. I don't care what old Mr. Fussbudget might think about it."

"Thanks, Diggs," Larry grinned. At first, they merely shook hands, but they quickly broke down and hugged each other like the old friends they really were. "I plan to keep in touch with you. There are still a few things you can teach me."

"You got *that* right!" Diggs laughed. "For one thing, you still need to learn how to get your honky ass *down* and get funky!"

"I'll teach him," John volunteered, taking his turn at hugging Diggs.

"Uh, huh!" Diggs smirked. "I've seen you get a little funky with that guitar in your hands, John, but can you get funky without it?"

"Sometimes," John replied with a grin.

"Well, so long, my friends," Diggs said. "Drop in and see me from time to time."

"We will," Larry assured him, the others joining in unison. "Let's get out of the man's hair, shall we? Let's go see what new thing the cold, cruel world has to offer us." He smiled at Diggs and said his parting word, "Peace!" As the gang headed for the door leading to the lobby, the others joined in that final word as well.

The best thrill of the evening came when the gang stepped out the front door. The parking lot was packed with cars, as many of their faithful listeners had driven up to the station to express their appreciation for all the fun the *Four Musketeers* had brought them over the years. From the studios on Villa Maria Road, the gang was escorted by these fans around the local drag circuit. They drove up Texas Avenue into Bryan, back down College Avenue past Hensel Park into College Station, turning around on University Drive to close the loop by returning to Texas Avenue, then circling through the A&W drive-in for several turns. All during the drive, the *Four Musketeers* were greeted by flashing car lights, horns, and by friends yelling out their thanks.

Friday, September 12, 1969
Sweet Sir Galahad

The boys spun around when they heard their names called. "Hi, John! Hi, Larry!" Krystal yelled from across the patio, smiling brightly as she waved. They looked at each other and grinned, sharing the knowledge of the thoughts passing through each others' minds. Dressed in yet another skimpy swimsuit, she was one of the most delightful sights any young man could hope to behold.

They maneuvered the short distance across the patio to stand beside her. This year's *Gamma Alpha Sigma* party was in full swing, and the place was hopping, just like it always was. "Hi, girl!" John smiled brightly, greeting her with a big hug.

"Hi, baby!" she beamed. Her hug was just as warm greeting Larry. "Hi, sugar!"

"You look fantastic, Krystal!" Larry smiled. "Gosh, I haven't seen you since last September! How have the fabulous Ball sisters been getting along?"

"Same old same old," Krystal grinned. "I'm glad you could make it tonight. It's great to see you guys again!"

"We wouldn't have missed it for the world!" John laughed.

"White man speak heap truth!" Larry chuckled. "Thank you for inviting me, Krystal. It was a wonderful surprise when I opened the envelop with the invitation."

Krystal grinned at him. "After the hit you guys made last year? How could you be surprised? You may be the two hottest guys on campus right now!"

"Oh, sure!" John laughed. "I certainly appreciate the compliment, anyway. I saw some guys setting up their equipment over there. Who's the band tonight?"

"Some guys out of Houston," Krystal reported. "I wanted to have you guys back, but Penny and Nichol said they never do the same thing two years in a row."

"Oops!" Larry laughed even stronger. "I don't know about you, John, but I'm devastated! I guess it's just as well we didn't make up another fancy teeshirt for tonight! Are Penny and Nichol around, Krystal, or have they already found their prey and dragged them back to their cave for the evening?"

"I saw them a few minutes ago," Krystal grinned, looking into the crowd for her two older sisters. "There they are!" she pointed to the other side of the pool. "Why don't you guys go say hi. Right now, I've got lots of mingling to do if I'm going to find something better than last year! Maybe I'll catch up with you later, OK?"

"Later!" John smiled. The boys watched her walk away, staring unashamedly at the way her backside wiggled. They laughed to each other when their eyes met, returning their attention to the real world instead of the world of fantasies. "God knows I'm also going to have to do some mingling if I want to top last year!"

"I'm not even going to *try* to top last year," Larry chuckled. "Come on, John. Let's go say hi to Penny and Nichol."

"Can you really tell which is which?" John asked when they started working their way in the direction of the older Ball sisters.

"Yep," Larry said grinning.

"Could you teach me how?" John asked.

"Nope," Larry replied with an even bigger grin.

"Aw, come on!" John pleaded.

"Not a chance," Larry grinned. "There's one easy way to tell them apart, but I promised not to reveal that secret, and you know how I feel about promises! I also figured out another way on my own, but I don't think I could teach you or anyone else. There's something different about the aura I see surrounding each of them."

"Huh?" John asked.

"Forget it," Larry answered. They arrived at their destination in the vicinity of Penny, Nichol, and an entourage of young men, all vying for the girls' attentions. Rather than drawing attention to himself, Larry merely looked in their direction, smiled, and waved his hand in greeting.

Penny was the first to see them. "Hi, Larry!" she said pleasantly, stepping around the others to greet him with a hug. "Hi, John! I'm glad you guys could make it."

"Hi, Penny," Larry smiled. "I wouldn't have missed it for anything!"

"Hi, sugar," Nichol grinned as she delivered her own greetings. "If you're just guessing she's Penny, then you're having a great run of luck. Hi, John! It's great to see both of you guys again."

Larry's glance briefly passed through the gathering of young men surrounding the beautiful sisters. His smile abruptly disappeared as recognition struck, stunning him into silence. The two eyes staring back at him were even more surprised. Sensing the tension in the air, Penny spoke up. "Have you guys met before?" she asked. "If not, let me introduce you. Larry, this is Steve Scott. Steve, this is Larry Bristol."

"We've met," Larry said.

"Who invited *you* here?" Steve asked pointedly.

"*We* did," Nichol answered before Larry could respond.

"Larry and John will *always* be invited to our parties," Penny added, "especially after the spectacular performance they gave us last year!" She was not exactly sure what the deal was with these two, but she did not appreciate the insulting way Steve had asked his question. Steve should already know about the public performance provided by the Drug Company. Her answer was worded and expressed in such a way to make him wonder if she might be referring to a different, more private performance, planting a strong hint in the direction of reality.

When Larry did not respond, John decided to break the silence. "I think we should take that as a compliment, how about you, Larry?"

Larry continued to stare at Steve as he replied, "Definitely, John." After another moment of silence, he asked his own question, "What are *you* doing here, Steve?"

"I was invited, also," Steve replied arrogantly. Recovering from his momentary surprise, and sensing he was not going to make any points with the Ball sisters, he decided to make a strategic retreat. "I think I should be mingling with all the other guests right now. It's been nice to meet you, Penny, Nichol. Perhaps we'll bump into each other a little later. Good to see you, Larry. You too, John." Larry said nothing as he watched Steve disappear into the crowd.

Penny wanted to make some sense out of this. "What was *that* all about?"

When Larry showed no sign of answering, John provided the information to fill the missing gap. "Do you girls remember last year how we talked about a girl Larry was interested in, a girl you met a few days later?"

"Julia?" Penny asked softly, hoping that only John could hear.

"Steve is Julia's current boyfriend," John answered just as softly.

There was another period of silence, finally broken by Nichol. "Do you guys know if Sam is coming tonight?"

"She didn't come with us," John answered.

Larry's concentration was temporarily broken by this new topic. "I tried to get her to come with us, but she told me she wasn't going to make it. She did ask me to say hi to you guys."

"Too bad," Penny giggled. "I was hoping she could babysit Tweedledee and Tweedledum to keep them occupied again."

"I thought you guys never do the same thing twice?" John asked with a grin.

"We don't," Penny giggled.

"But they do," Nichol added. "That's one of the many reasons we keep looking!"

Larry was losing his concentration again, and began staring out into the crowd looking for Steve. Penny noted his distraction. "What are you thinking?" she asked.

He broke his stare and looked back at her. "Nothing. Nothing at all."

"It looks like something to me," Nichol added. "Why are you so upset he's here? Would you rather he was out with Julia?"

"I guess not," he sighed. "It just bothers me to think he's cheating on her."

"You know, Larry," Penny said, "that happens to be one of the traps at these parties. Some of the attendees get quite a surprise when they see their regular boyfriend or girlfriend here. It's only cheating if your partner doesn't know what you're up to. We don't think of it as cheating on Tweedledee and Tweedledum, and they aren't cheating on us. We all know what the others are doing, and it's OK."

"I doubt very seriously *she* knows what he's doing," Larry said. After a pause, he shook his head and looked at Penny. "This is none of my business," he declared. "If either one of them wants to explore other potential relationships, then that's their business, not mine. I just wish she was the one doing the exploring."

"Are you going to tell her you saw him here?" John asked.

"Hell, no!" Larry answered forcefully, "And neither will you, John!"

"Isn't it my business what I might decide to do?" John asked.

Larry looked at his friend and sighed. "You're right, John. I apologize. But I sincerely hope you'll decide not to say anything to her about this."

"Why is that?" John asked.

Larry looked once again in the direction Steve had gone and shook his head. "It just doesn't feel right. My chance will come when the time is right. It would be a mistake to try to speed things along. If she finds out from you or me, I'd like to think she'd defend him. That's what I'd want her to do if she were my girl. I want a girl who'll be loyal to me as long as I'm loyal to her, who'll give me the benefit of the doubt if someone came along accusing me of something."

"I like the way you think, Larry," Penny smiled.

Even though Steve saw that Larry and John were not hovering around them, he purposely avoided making any further contact with the Ball sisters, taking his pursuits in other directions. Those beautiful girls were confusing him. What did they see in this guy? *Larry is nothing more than an ordinary local jerk. He's not good looking, doesn't run in the right social circles, isn't athletic, doesn't have money, or have any other virtue I can see.* He would concede Larry and John were decent entertainers, but certainly nothing spectacular.

Yet that was the very word the Ball sisters had used, saying he had given a spectacular performance last year. He made a couple of inquiries and learned the Drug Company had entertained at last year's *Gamma Alpha Sigma* party. If their performance was so spectacular, why hadn't he heard about it before? Why was it that a few of the girls he had been hitting on that evening had looked at each other, pointed at Larry and John as they happened by, whispered secrets to each other, and giggled. There was clearly more going on than met the eye.

What bothered Steve the most was the way Larry had stared at him, as if accusing him of something. He had always suspected Larry's interest in Julia extended beyond that of mere friendship. It was the way he looked at her that aroused Steve's suspicions, especially the way he looked at her while singing those songs of his. Was it just his imagination that Julia seemed to be encouraging him? Did she also harbor some secret interest in this guy?

Steve laughed at the thought. Julia was a very beautiful girl, even more so now that her braces had been removed. He realized this was utter nonsense! Clearly she would have no romantic interest in a nobody like him. He was simply one of her special friends. If there had been any romantic interest between any of these *Four Musketeers*, it would have come out a long time ago. *All for one and one for all!* he chuckled to himself. *D'Artagnan is simply a romantic fool who doesn't think a guy should be out looking for more pussy when his girlfriend already puts out. I wonder if he's ever managed to get himself laid? What a laugh! What kind of chick would be desperate enough to spread her legs for a nobody like that?*

Wednesday, September 24, 1969
This Magic Moment

The flight carrying Joseph and Sarah Silverman, along with their two children, was scheduled to arrive at the Houston Intercontinental airport late that evening. Julian was not familiar with the new airport in Houston, and was happy to accept Larry's offer to navigate for them. There was plenty of room in their GMC Suburban for all of them.

They arrived at the airport without incident just after 9:00, and parked near the international terminal. After checking the display screens for information, seeing the arriving flight listed as "on time", they settled into the waiting area where one could greet arriving passengers after they were cleared though customs. The flight arrived a few minutes later, and before long, weary passengers began to trickle through.

"There they are!" Jessica said excitedly spotting Sarah carrying an infant child, sound asleep in his mother's arms. Sarah was closely followed by a three year old girl looking around in wonder at the strange new world she was seeing for the first time. This small girl was followed by a man struggling with several large suitcases.

"Mom!" Sarah shouted when she saw Jessica, beginning the tearful reunion. Sarah had not seen her stepparents in several years, having attended college in Israel, followed by a tour in Africa as a member of the Peace Corps. No one in her family had ever seen either her children or her husband except in photographs.

A progression of hugs and introductions followed, starting with Ruth. The three year old girl was picked up by Jessica and hugged while Sarah tried to explain to the confused little girl this was her grandmother. After a few moments, Jessica passed Ruth to Julian so she could hold the baby, Judah, for a while. Eventually, she passed Judah to Julian in order to officially meet Joseph, her son-in-law, for the first time.

After hugging his stepdaughter, Julian received Ruth in his arms, explaining he was her grandfather. After more hugs, he passed her to Julia's arms so he could hold his grandson. Finally, he handed the baby to Julia to meet Joseph, his son-in-law.

"I'm Julia, your tanta," she explained to the little girl as they hugged each other. In her excitement at seeing her stepsister and meeting her family, when it was her turn to hold the baby, she handed the little girl to Larry.

Larry, who had been standing back enjoying the show, was surprised to find himself holding a three year old girl, looking at him with eyes filled with wonder. "I'm Larry," he said. Seeing she was not sure what this was supposed to mean, he added, "I'm a friend, and I hope you'll also be my very special friend!"

"Lahwe?" Ruth asked, trying to say his name.

"That's right, Princess," he smiled at her. "Larry."

"I'm not a princess!" the little girl giggled. "I'm Ruthie."

"You look like a princess to me," he said, continuing to smile. "A very special and very beautiful princess!" Julia then wanted to hand the baby to him, so Larry sat the little girl down to stand beside him on her own feet. Larry stood there sheepishly, holding the baby boy, while Julia met her brother-in-law.

"Oh, for goodness sakes!" Jessica laughed when she looked at him. "Sarah, this young man taking care of your children is Larry Bristol, a good friend of the family. Larry, this is our other daughter, Sarah."

"I'm pleased to meet you, Sarah," Larry said pleasantly as Jessica took the baby back from him. Ruth felt uneasy surrounded by so many strangers, and since Larry was the closest person to her, she grabbed his left hand when it became free.

"Nice to meet you, too, Larry," Sarah smiled. "I see you have already met Ruthie and Judah. This is my husband, Joseph."

"Hello, Larry," Joseph said warmly, offering his hand.

Larry and Joseph gripped hands as Larry completed the introduction. "Nice to meet you, Joseph. I hope you've all had a pleasant trip."

"It wasn't too bad," Joseph said to all of them. "It was probably harder on the children than on us, but at least the worst is over."

"You still have a two hour car ride ahead of you," Julian grinned. "Is that all the luggage you've brought?"

"We just have some of our clothes with us," Joseph explained, "and a few essentials for the children. Everything else has been crated up and left in storage in Africa. We'll have it shipped to us as soon as we figure out where we'll be living."

"You could have it shipped here," Julian suggested.

"It seemed to make sense to leave it until we know where we'll be going," Joseph explained. "That way, it only has to be shipped once. I have some job interviews scattered all over the place – one in Chicago, another in St. Louis, one in Los Angeles, and one in Atlanta. We don't know where we might eventually end up!"

"Well, for now," Jessica smiled, "you'll be living with us."

Joseph and Sarah looked at each other and smiled. Joseph thanked them, "I really appreciate you're willing to open up your home and let us stay with you. It is very comforting to know Sarah and the kids will be safe while I'm out looking for a job."

"Of course," Jessica smiled. "You're family, and family is always welcome!"

"I still appreciate it," Joseph smiled. "We'll try not to be too much of a burden."

"Nonsense!" Jessica grinned. "Why don't you boys gather up the luggage and we'll get started home?"

Julian grabbed two of the suitcases. When Larry attempted to get one, Joseph waved him off. "It looks like you have a more important responsibility," he smiled, noting his daughter had attached herself to the young man. "I can handle these two suitcases. You just make sure Ruthie doesn't get lost!"

Larry looked at the little girl clutching his hand and grinned. He looked back at her father, grinned once again, and nodded his head. "Thank you for entrusting me with such a treasure. I'll do everything in my power to see that I deserve such an honor." Joseph looked back at him and smiled.

Sarah, Julia, and Jessica (carrying the baby) led the entourage, followed closely by Larry and Ruth, Julian and Joseph. They wandered the corridors of the terminal, then out into the parking area to their vehicle. After the luggage was placed in the very back, the human cargo was loaded. Julian took the driver's seat, with Joseph riding shotgun. Jessica and Sarah took the second seat, Jessica still holding the baby boy in her arms, while Julia, Ruthie, and Larry climbed into the rear seat.

During the ride back to Bryan, Julian and Joseph talked and got acquainted, while Jessica and Sarah tried to catch up on all the experiences they had enjoyed since last seeing each other. Julia grinned at Larry when Ruthie insisted on sitting in his lap. They played some simple games for a while to keep her entertained.

But it had been a very long and exhausting day for all of the Silvermans, and Ruthie, like her baby brother, soon grew tired. She put her head on Larry's chest and fell asleep even before they reached the Houston city limits, and headed up the highway back to Bryan.

Larry and Julia smiled at each other when Ruthie fell asleep, and settled down to relax for the duration of the trip. It had also been a long and exhausting day for Julia. She leaned over, closed her eyes, and placed her head against Larry's shoulder. A huge gap opened in the space-time continuum because of this magic moment. He stared out his window, watching the countryside pass by, dreaming of a time when it would be a normal, natural occurrence for Julia to put her head on his shoulder. He dreamed she would lift her face from his shoulder and look into his eyes, inviting him to kiss her!

But he knew this was *not* a normal, natural occurrence, and even if she did lift her face and look at him, there would be no such invitation. It was not his time. If there ever would be such a time, it was not going to happen this night. As he stared out of his window watching the darkened countryside slip past, a small tear formed in his right eye, the one farthest from Julia. He refused to let one form in the left eye for fear she might see it! The tear rolled down his cheek and, upon reaching his jaw, took the plunge from his face to his collar.

Casually, he raised his free hand to wipe the moisture from his cheek. As he did so, his eyes were caught by Sarah's, who was looking into the back seat to check on her daughter. He wondered if she had seen that tear. He doubted it. *Would it matter if she had? How could she possibly understand the reason behind that tear?*

Just before midnight, some two hours after they left the airport, the car arrived back at the Jacobsons' home. "We're home," Julian announced unnecessarily, parking the vehicle near the garage and turning off the engine. While he and Joseph opened the rear door and started carrying the luggage inside, Jessica and Sarah carefully slipped out of the side door, trying not to wake the baby.

Sarah looked into the rear seat and smiled at the sight of her daughter sleeping peacefully in the lap of this young man Jessica had introduced as a "good friend of the family". Larry returned her smile and shrugged his shoulders, indicating he did not think there was any way they could get Ruthie out of the car without waking her. "Wake up, Ruthie," Sarah said softly, trying not to startle her.

"Wake up, Princess," Larry added as she began to stir. "You're home." She opened her eyes and looked around sleepily. She sat up, put her arms around Larry's neck, and held on, refusing to let go even at the urging of her mother. "Princess, we can't get out of the car unless you let go of me," he chuckled.

"OK, Lahwe," she said letting go of his neck. "Will you carry me inside?"

"OK, Princess," he laughed. "Go to your mom. When I get out, I'll carry you."

"Promise?" she asked.

"Promise!" he grinned. "And I would *never* break a promise to a beautiful princess like you!" Satisfied, Ruthie let go of his neck, and crawled into her mother's arms.

When Larry did not immediately follow, Jessica stuck her head into the car door to see if there was a problem. There she saw Larry looking back at her, not having moved an inch. Even though he was fighting to hide it, she could not help but note the look in his eyes. She wondered if it had something to do with Julia leaning up against him, clearly asleep. Jessica shook her head slowly, and broke into a soft smile. "You're going to have to wake her if you want to keep your promise to Ruthie," she whispered.

Larry contemplated his options. It did not take him too long to realize she was right. *I should wake her up,* he thought, instinctively using his code phrase even to himself. He did the last thing in the world he wanted to do, and nudged her gently. "Julie, it's time to wake up." He repeated this whisper a little louder, nudging her gently again, and she began to stir. "You're home, Julie. It's time to wake up."

Julia opened her eyes and looked around. Larry was looking at her with a soft smile on his face that did not bother her, but she felt a little embarrassed when she saw the grin on her mother's face. "We're home?" she asked as she sat herself up.

"You're home, and I have a promise to keep," he said with a smile as he began to crawl forward to get out of the car, "then I have to get home myself."

"What promise is that?" Julia asked sleepily.

"I promised to carry a beautiful princess inside the house," he replied looking back at her, as if that should explain everything.

"And I don't think he means you," Jessica teased. She noted the same sad expression on Larry's face once again, although it quickly changed into a smile.

"Hop up onto my shoulders, Princess," Larry said squatting down. "I'll be your prancing pony and carry you into your bright new shining castle!" She giggled slightly. After climbing onto Larry's shoulders, he whisked her away. She laughed merrily as he bounced her into the house, being very careful when they passed through the back door, and then stood proudly in the family room.

"OK, Ruthie," Sarah said as she entered the house, "It's time for you to go to bed, and let your pony return to his stable for the night."

"No!" she tried to argue. "I want to play horsey with Lahwe some more!"

"We'll play horsey some other time, Princess," Larry said to her.

"Promise?" she asked once again.

"Absolutely!" he laughed merrily. Seeing she was satisfied with his promise, he turned to Jessica and grinned, "Where do you want me to deposit my cargo?"

"Follow me, Mister Lahwe!" Jessica laughed, and headed down the hallway towards the bedrooms. "We figured Ruthie would sleep in Julia's room," she explained to Sarah, "while you and Joseph take the guest room. We've rented a crib and set it up for you in there. I hope this is all OK with you."

"It sounds fine," Sarah replied, "but even if it wasn't, I'm too tired to argue."

When they reached Julia's room, Larry lifted Ruthie off his shoulders and tossed her onto the bed playfully. She laughed with delight bouncing on the soft mattress, then stood up and held out her arms to him. "Goodnight, Lahwe!" she said.

"Goodnight, Princess," he replied giving her a hug. Ruthie wrapped her arms around his neck and planted a goodnight kiss. When he turned to leave the room, he felt embarrassed encountering Jessica, Sarah, and Julia, all grinning at him. "What's the matter?" he asked with a sheepish grin. "Haven't you ever seen a boy kiss his girlfriend goodnight?"

"Not in her bedroom," Jessica replied with a rich laugh.

Wordlessly, Larry looked back at her. His eyes then shifted to see Sarah grinning at him, and then Julia. The color of his face changed to match that of a male cardinal, a bird common to the area. "I should go home," he said trying to appear dignified. "Goodnight, Sarah. It's been wonderful meeting you." As he headed out the bedroom door and down the hall towards the living room, he added, "I'm sure I'll see you again very soon. Goodnight, Mrs. J. Goodnight, Julie."

"Goodnight, Larry," they called after him with giggles in their voices.

Larry said a quick goodnight to a puzzled Julian and Joseph on his way out the back door. When he got outside, he remembered his car was parked in the front. He decided his best course was to walk around, rather than going back through.

On his way home, Larry reflected on the events of the evening. He loved every opportunity he got to be near her, especially when *he* was not around. *How many "he's" have there been now?* There had been Jimmy, Frank, Bill, Ed, and now Steve. He knew that was not the important question. The important question was, *How many more "he's" will there be before* this *he gets his chance?*

When he got home and began to undress for bed, he realized he could still smell the soft sweetness of Julia's hair on his shirt, where she had laid her head against his shoulder. Held to his face all night long, the aroma stimulated his dreams. This magic moment only made him long for more.

Julia went to bed right after Larry left. She smiled to herself as she looked at her niece, the sweet little three year old girl laying beside her. She smiled again when she thought about how Larry had won her confidence so quickly. He seemed to have a knack for doing that, especially when it came to small children and animals. What a wonderful friend he was to her!

Jessica and Sarah sat up for a while after their husbands retired to their respective beds. It had been years since they had enjoyed a simple mother and daughter chat. Even though they were both tired, it just seemed like the thing they wanted to do. Sarah told her mother of the adventures they had while working in Africa. There had been some good times, of course, but there had also been horrible times, when there was nothing they could do to ease the misery and suffering they saw.

Jessica finally got to hear the sweet details of how Sarah and Joseph had met, fallen in love, and come to be married. They laughed together at the adventure it had been to have her first baby. "Joseph and our doctor went to work in a different village for a couple of days," she explained, "but they assured me they'd be back at least a week before the baby was due. Ruthie, of course, wasn't impressed with such assurances, and decided to be born early. She's always been very independent."

"So Joseph was gone when you went into labor?" Jessica asked.

"Yes," Sarah laughed. "There I was, about to have a baby, all alone in deepest Africa, with no husband and no doctor around! I was terrified at first, but the women in our village weren't concerned, and assured me everything would be just fine. They managed to get me to relax, and sure enough, everything happened naturally, just like it's supposed to. We sent word to Joseph, who rushed back the next day with the doctor, but there was nothing they needed to do. The doctor just grinned, and went back to the other village to continue his work. Joseph, of course, stayed right there!"

"He seems like a wonderful man," Jessica said warmly. "I'm very happy for you."

"Thanks, mom," Sarah said softly. "I feel like I've been very blessed to find a man like him. I would say sis seems to be doing pretty well for herself, as well!"

"You mean, Larry?" Jessica grinned. "He really is something special, that's for sure, but they're not together in that way."

"Really?" Sarah said, somewhat astonished. "I would have sworn..."

"I understand what you mean," Jessica interrupted. "I used to think that myself, but things have never worked out that way."

"So what's the story?" Sarah asked.

"They met about three years ago, on her fourteenth birthday," Jessica said. "He and his friend John came to her party to play their guitars, sing, and entertain."

"Really?" Sarah grinned. "Are they any good?"

"They're *very* good!" Jessica smiled. "You'll get to hear for yourself this Sunday. The gang usually gets together on Sunday afternoons. Larry and John practice, and all of them clown around and have a good time together. There are four of them: Julia, Larry, John, and another girl they call Sam. They're practically inseparable, and we call them the *Four Musketeers*. I'll let you see this for yourself and you'll know why!"

"So if Larry isn't her boyfriend..." Sarah began.

"You'll get to meet him on Saturday," Jessica explained. "His name is Steve. They've been dating about six months now."

"He must *really* be something!" Sarah laughed.

"He seems to be a nice enough boy," Jessica agreed, "and *very* good looking. The only problem I see is that he *knows* it."

"Is their relationship serious?" Sarah asked.

"Difficult to say," Jessica answered. "I'm not sure how Steve feels about her, but I can tell she's enamored by him. He's a good looking young man. I should tell you Steve is very suspicious of Larry. He thinks Julia spends way too much time with him, and does everything he can to make sure he's around anytime Larry is nearby."

"That's funny!" Sarah laughed. "So does he have reason to be suspicious?"

"None that I can see," Jessica grinned. "Julia did have a crush on Larry a while back, and to tell you the truth, I think she still does to some extent. But he's never made a move towards her, so I don't think Steve should be concerned."

"He doesn't want to get with Julia?" Sarah asked, sounding incredulous. "Then I assume he must have some other girlfriend."

"Apparently, that's not the case," Jessica answered. "It looks to me like he has his eyes on this girl Sam I mentioned before, but she has another boyfriend, and isn't interested in him! It's all very complicated!"

Sarah remembered seeing that tear in Larry's eye, but now figured she must have misinterpreted it. She knew her mother was very adept at seeing things like that and interpreting their meaning. She decided not to mention it.

Sunday, September 28, 1969
All The Pretty Little Horses

Sarah saw for herself why her sister and friends were known as the *Four Musketeers*. The previous evening, she met Steve, and exactly as Jessica had predicted, here he was again this afternoon, obviously keeping an eye on someone he considered to be a rival. She also observed that Larry's eyes would sneak a peek in Julia's direction whenever he thought no one would see, and those eyes had that unmistakable look about them. Sarah had seen that look before! Had Jessica missed that look in his eyes?

She was now hearing for herself that Larry and John were as good as her mother had described them. As the boys practiced, they thoroughly entertained their audience, Sam, Steve and Julia, her parents, and her husband. Judah was too young to appreciate the music, but this was certainly not true of little Ruthie. Sarah could only laugh at how her three year old daughter was captivated by her new boyfriend.

None of this was lost on Larry, who seemed to be selecting the songs they played to emphasize this fact. Songs such as Bobby Sherman's *Little Woman*, Gary Puckett's *Young Girl*, and *Yummy Yummy Yummy* popularized by The Ohio Express were performed, delighting not only Ruthie, but Julia, Sarah, and Jessica, as well.

Sarah had learned from her mother that Larry loved children. Maybe that was the primary reason he paid so much attention to little Ruthie, playing little games with her, teasing her, laughing with her. She could not help but believe, however, that another big factor was that he really wanted to do these things with Julia, and since he could not do so, Ruthie was the best substitute available. Even when the practice session ended, and everyone sat around enjoying the cold cuts Jessica provided, Ruthie could not be coaxed away from Larry's side. The sweet part of it all was Larry did not seem to mind.

After dinner, Larry, John, and Sam began to pack their instruments and collect their things to leave. Predictably, Ruthie was hanging onto Larry for all she was worth, begging him to stay and play, "just one more song, Lahwe!" even though Sarah was struggling to prepare Ruthie for bed. Just as predictably, Larry promised he would play her another song, a special song just for her, if she would be a good girl and let mommy get her ready for bed. Not so predictable was her response. She hugged his neck, and then allowed her mother to take her away for a bath, and to change into her pajamas.

John and Sam took the opportunity to excuse themselves, but not before teasing Larry just a little. "Goodnight, Lahwe!" they giggled as they headed for the front door. Julia giggled at Larry also, while Steve merely smirked.

"Very funny, guys," Larry replied, trying to look disgusted. Nevertheless, he unpacked his guitar and started getting ready for the special performance.

Moments later, Ruthie ran back into the family room and climbed onto the sofa to sit beside her boyfriend. "Give everyone a hug and a goodnight kiss, Ruthie," Sarah urged. "It's time for you to go to bed."

"But Lahwe promised to sing me another song!" she protested.

"And I *will* sing you a song, sugar," he smiled to her, "just as soon as you get into bed and let mommy tuck you in. OK?"

"OK," she said to him softly, then went around the room hugging everyone and kissing them goodnight. Even Steve got a hug and a kiss, causing Julia to giggle with delight. But she quickly returned to Larry, and all but jumped into his arms. "Come on, Lahwe!" she squealed. "Let's play horsey again!"

"OK, Princess," he laughed. "Sarah, if I could impose on you to carry my guitar..." Larry whinnied like a pony, and carried the little girl down the hallway into Julia's bedroom, careful not to bump her head as they went through the doorway. Like he had done previously, he tossed her off his shoulders and bounced her on the soft bed, bringing squeals of delightful laughter.

She immediately hopped up and begged him, "Do it again, Lahwe!"

"It's your bedtime, Princess," he smiled, "but we'll play horsey again next time."

"Promise?" she asked.

"I promise," he smiled. "Now get into the bed and let mommy tuck you in."

The little girl followed his instructions to the letter. Sarah grinned at Larry as she returned his guitar, then turned her attention to her daughter, getting her all settled and comfortable. Larry began to play a soft melody on his guitar, and then, as the rest of the household stood listening from the hallway, he sang her the special song he had promised, called *All The Pretty Little Horses*.

"Night night, buttercup," he whispered as he turned to the door.

"Night night, Lahwe," she said softly.

"Goodnight, angel," Sarah said as she kissed her daughter.

Wednesday, October 22, 1969
Old Friends

Early in the evening, Julian and Jessica treated Julia and Steve to her traditional birthday dinner. Sarah and the children stayed home, partly to keep out of the way, but mainly to wait by the telephone. She was expecting a call from Joseph, and was afraid she would miss the call if she left the house. Joseph had returned to Chicago for a second interview with one of the employers there, and the Silvermans were eagerly anticipating his job search would soon come to a successful conclusion.

Sarah was bubbling with excitement when her stepparents got home. "He got the job!" she all but shouted, running to give her family a hug.

"That's wonderful!" Jessica smiled. "This is the one he really wanted, isn't it?"

"Yes!" Sarah said.

"What are the details?" Julian asked. "Do you know when he'll start, and how much he'll be making?"

"All I really know is that he got the job," Sarah answered, "and that they want him to start next month, on the first, I suppose."

Julian glanced at a calendar hanging on the kitchen wall. "Probably not," he said. "That's a Saturday. Perhaps he'll start the following Monday, November 3."

"Congratulations, Sarah!" Julia said excitedly.

"Thanks, sis!" Sarah replied.

"Oh, I just thought of something," Jessica said. "This means you'll be moving away, just as I was getting used to having you living with us again!"

"Ah, mom!" Sarah chuckled, hugging her stepmother once again. "Let's not spend the rest of the evening talking about Joseph and me. It's Julia's birthday. Tonight, she should be the star of the show!"

The *Four Musketeers* and other friends gathered at Julia's house to celebrate her seventeenth birthday. As usual, the Drug Company entertained the guests as they arrived, and continued to play until all of the preparations were complete. Around 8:00, Jessica signaled to Larry they were ready, and he led the assembly in a chorus of *Happy Birthday To You* while the cake was delivered to the birthday girl.

After enjoying their cake and ice cream, her friends urged her to open the presents that had been gathered nearby. She soon came to one with a familiar pattern – a small box wrapped in brightly colored paper without a name tag to announce from whom it had come. After examining the box, she looked up to find Larry, smiled at him warmly, then opened the present, knowing she would soon have another music box to add to her collection. "Thank you, Larry," she said with a sweet smile.

"You're very welcome, sugar," he said returning her smile. Other than Steve, everyone smiled as Julia made a point to stand up from her seat, and give Larry a warm hug. She then returned to the pleasant task of opening the remaining gifts.

Later, the Drug Company returned to center stage to continue their program. After singing several songs, another familiar pattern arose. While Larry tried to introduce the next song, John interrupted, "That last song is one I'm really proud of!"

"John," Larry sighed, "I really wish I could get you to improve your grammar. I realize that dangling participles are now in common use, but all it takes is a little effort to avoid them."

"So instead of saying, *'That last song was one I'm really proud of!'* you think I should say, *'That last song was one of which I'm really proud!'* Is that right?"

"It would be nice," Larry replied.

"This is something I'll have a lot of trouble dealing with," John said sadly.

"No, no, no!" Larry said. "You did it again! You should say, *'This is something with which I'll have a lot of trouble dealing.'* It really isn't that hard, John. Sir Winston Churchill used to chastise people about dangling participles. He would say, *'A dangling participle is something up with which I simply shall not put!'* You have to admire the way he spoke the English language." John hung his head as if in shame, and Larry attempted to announce the next song once again.

"Say, Larry," John said, interrupting him again. "Have I ever told you about the time my friend, a famous Cajun lawyer, journeyed to Boston to present a case?"

"I don't think so," Larry replied, obviously annoyed he had been interrupted again. "Do I know this friend of yours?"

"Probably not," John answered. "His name is Jean Claude Pierre, the famous Cajun lawyer from Baton Rouge, Louisiana."

"You say he traveled up to Boston?" Larry asked.

"Yes!" John replied. "He was very excited about it. The first thing he did, of course, was to take care of his business. He went to the courthouse, presented his legal argument, and won the case quickly and easily."

"He must be a good lawyer!" Larry said, sounding impressed.

"Indeed he is!" John agreed. "Since he won the case so quickly, he found he had a lot of free time on his hands. So he decided to walk around in Boston to visit all of the famous historical sights he had heard about all his life."

"Makes sense to me," Larry noted, nodding his head.

"As he walked around town, he happened upon the Boston Public Library," John continued. "Realizing it probably contained more law books than he had ever seen in his entire life, he quickly dashed inside, filled with anticipation, and spoke to the gentleman at the information desk."

Larry picked up the story, speaking with a thick Cajun accent. "Hello dare. My name is Jean Claude Pierre, da famous Cajun lawyer from Baton Rouge, Louisiana. It sure looks like you gotta mighty fine li-berry here! I wonda if you could point me to da place where you keep your law books at."

John replied in a thick Bostonian accent. "Sir, I will have you know that here in Boston, a well educated and refined gentleman will use the English language in a proper fashion. One simply does not end a sentence with a preposition."

"Oh, I do apologize for dat, sir," Larry continued with his thick Cajun accent. "Please allow me to rephrase my request. I was wondrin if you could point me to da place where you keep your law books at... asshole!"

When the laughter died down, Larry continued. "I know that grammar isn't an easy thing to master. Did I tell you about the time *I* made a trip to Boston, John?"

"Did you go to the li-berry?" John grinned.

"No," Larry chuckled, "but I certainly learned something new about grammar!"

"So what happened?" John asked in his role as the perfect straight-man.

"Well," Larry began, "I've always heard good things about New England seafood. It's not the same as the Gulf Coast seafood we get all the time, doncha know."

"So I've heard," John prompted.

"On my first night in Boston, I waved at a taxi," he said, acting out the process.

"Where to?" John asked in his taxi-driver voice imitation.

"I've been thinking about this all day!" Larry said excitedly. "Surely you know all of the best places in the Boston area someone from out of town wouldn't know. Take me to the best place in Boston to get scrod!"

John looked at Larry and shook his head. "I've heard it used as a verb and even as a noun. I've heard it in the past tense, the present tense, and even the future tense. But this is the first time I've ever heard it in the pluperfect subjunctive!"

It took a few seconds for everyone to catch on, but once they had, the joke was well received. Larry announced the next song, and the boys continued with the musical part of their program. Like he had done for the last two years, Larry elected to conclude the program with the old Beatles classic, *I'll Get You*.

Sunday, October 26, 1969
The Great Pretender

About 6:00 o'clock, the boys decided they had practiced enough for the day. As they were packing their instruments, Jessica announced she had prepared a tray of cold cuts, and invited everyone to make a plate. The whole entourage moved into the kitchen to attack the feast she had prepared.

Julian was almost out of breath when he rushed into the kitchen. "I just got off the phone with mother," he said excitedly. "She's planning to come visit us in December. Maybe it'll be during the holidays!" He walked over to a calendar hanging on the wall and began to flip the pages. "Does anyone know what day Chanukah starts this year?"

When no one else provided an immediate answer, Larry chimed in, "I'd imagine it starts on the twenty-fifth of Kislev, Mr. J, just like always." He pretended to return his full attention to the music book he had brought into the kitchen with him. John, Sam, and Steve exchanged a glance, but having no clue to the meaning of what Larry had just said, they merely shrugged and returned their attention to the feast.

On the other hand, Julia's jaw hung open as she stared at her friend. She raised her eyes to look into those of her father, who was also gazing at Larry in stunned silence. Almost simultaneously, they both turned to look at Jessica, who returned their stare with a puzzled grin on her face. In unison, they all turned to look at Sarah and Joseph, who were each displaying a similar look of astonishment. Finally, they all stared back at Larry as if waiting for some kind of explanation.

Larry was fighting very hard to keep a straight face, but he could not hide the slight grin forming as he began to lose that battle. He continued his pretense, intensely studying the music book, but the grin grew wider and wider. Without raising his head, he lifted his eyes in their sockets, trying to sneak a peek at the others in the room. Finding five pairs of eyes staring back at him intently, he finally lost control completely, and broke into general laughter.

"How do you know that?" Julia asked with a smile, a bit of wonder in her voice.

"I'm omniscient," Larry said with a grin.

"Omniscient, my ass!" Julian laughed. "Sorry for the language, ladies, but I'm not going to stand here and let him get away with this sort of thing any longer. How do you know about the Hebrew calendar?"

"It really shouldn't be all that mysterious," Larry confessed. "I've been curious about some things, so over the last few years, I've been going to the library and doing a little research from time to time. I found out about the story of Chanukah a long time ago. Eventually, that led me to learn about the Hebrew calendar. I've been learning about many of the Jewish traditions, so you're going to have a hard time keeping such secrets from me. Unless you speak in Hebrew, that is. I haven't learned any of *that* language, but I *am* learning to speak some Yiddish. So far, I'm afraid most of the words I've learned are ones I shouldn't use in mixed company."

Julia, Jessica, Sarah, and Joseph laughed, thinking this was a delightful surprise. Julian also laughed, but was secretly impressed a young boy like Larry would go to so much trouble to learn about their traditions and beliefs. "This goy thinks he's a chochem!" Julian said with a chuckle.

"I prefer to think of myself as a badhkin!" Larry laughed.

"More like a kibbitzer!" Julia giggled.

"Alright, alright! Genug shoyn!" Julian said smiling. "Let's stop now before this gets out of hand, shall we? I still need to know what day Chanukah starts... on the *Gregorian* calendar, if you please. Do you happen to know the answer, Larry?"

"Not off the top of my head," Larry confessed with a grin.

"December 5," Jessica said, scanning the wall calendar. "That's a Friday."

"That's perfect!" Julian said excitedly. "Mother said she was hoping to come down sometime near the beginning of December, and thinks she'll be with us for two weeks or so. With any luck, she'll be here during all eight nights of Chanukah!"

Steve, who always tried to be present whenever Larry was around, was wearing a scowl on his face during the whole incident. John and Sam exchanged another glance and grinned at each other, especially when they noted Steve's expression.

The youngsters sat around a patio table, enjoying their sandwiches and joking with each other. Little Ruthie took up her position on Larry's lap. When they finished eating, Steve convinced Julia to move. They sat on the brick retaining wall surrounding the old willow tree. Larry tried to maintain a smile, but the more he stared into the branches of that old tree, and noted how closely Julia sat next to Steve, the harder that task became.

"Come on, John," Sam suggested as she began picking up the empty plates, "Let's pick up the dishes and carry them inside for Mrs. J."

"I'll help you, Sam," Larry said, beginning to lift the little girl off his lap.

"We got it," Sam insisted. "You stay here and entertain your sweetheart!"

At this suggestion, Larry's face became a mixture of a grin and a frown. Sam had meant the statement as a happy thought, overlooking the fact that the girl he wanted to be his sweetheart so badly was otherwise occupied. She instantly recognized the source of Larry's frown. The look in her eyes silently transmitted her apology to him; there was no need for it to be expressed audibly.

"Why don't we go for a walk, Ruthie," Larry asked the little girl.

"OK, Lahwe," she replied. She climbed off his lap and waited for him to stand. As soon as he did, she grabbed his hand and began to lead him down the little path that led from the patio down to the stock pond.

Larry tried to be bright and cheerful as they walked down the path. He did not want to worry the little girl, but he could not hold back the heartache that began to seep from his eyes when they reached the pond. "What's wrong, Lahwe?" the little girl asked when she saw the tear on his cheek.

He wiped the tear from his face and smiled as best he could. "It's nothing, Princess," he lied. "I'm just sad because you'll be leaving tomorrow, and I'm already starting to miss you!" He held out his arms and when the little girl practically jumped into them, he could not help but laugh. "Oh, how I wish you were a little older. I'd marry you and keep you with me all the time so I wouldn't be so lonely," he teased while tickling her.

"I'm too little!" she giggled.

"I know," he grinned. "It's just silly of me to wish such things, isn't it?"

He was startled by a voice from behind him. "It's not all *that* silly, Larry. No one likes to be lonely. Why shouldn't you wish for the things you really want?"

Larry turned to see Sarah's smiling face, and returned her smile. "Making wishes is fine as far as it goes, but wishful thinking doesn't get anything accomplished."

"That's true," Sarah agreed. "Ruthie, would you like some ice cream? I bet if you asked your zayde to dip some ice cream that he'd be more than happy to do so!"

"Oh, boy!" she shouted. "Ice cream! Do you want some ice cream, Lahwe?"

"I surely do, pumpkin!" Larry grinned. "You run on ahead and get zayde started, and your mom and I will join you in a minute, OK?"

"OK," she said happily. For the first time since they began their walk, she let go of his hand, and ran up the little path, back to the house to the promise of ice cream.

"It looks like ice cream is all it takes to satisfy *her* wishes," Larry smiled. "Do you ever wish that you could be a child again, so life could be so simple?"

"I guess everybody does, Larry," Sarah agreed.

He knew from the moment of silence that followed her statement something more was on Sarah's mind. "You didn't walk all the way down here merely to offer your daughter some ice cream," he began. "What else do you have on your mind?"

Sarah looked at him intently, then smiled at his perception. "No. We'll be leaving tomorrow. I guess I just wanted to talk to you about wishes."

"I don't have the power to grant wishes," he laughed. "God knows how I wish I did! What would you ask me to grant if only I had such power?"

"I'm not here to talk about *my* wishes," Sarah said softly, "but about yours."

"*My* wishes?" he asked, a little surprised.

"Yes," Sarah replied. "I don't have the power to grant wishes, either, but I'd like to know what wish *you* would make if only I had the power to grant it."

Larry smiled to her and shook his head. "I want the same things everybody else wants," he said. "I'd simply wish I could find happiness."

"You'd wish to find happiness even though you already seem to be happy?" Sarah asked. When he merely looked at her and smiled, she added, "You and I both know you aren't happy at all. You're simply playing a part in a story you didn't write, desperately trying to find a way to change your part in that story."

Larry shook his head once again. "I assume by this you mean there are things about my life I'd change if I could. I don't deny that. Isn't that true of everybody?"

"You'd change your life so you wouldn't be so lonely." She said this as if it were a matter of fact, and not as a question.

That arrow struck right into the heart of the matter and took Larry a little by surprise. He quickly recovered, however, and attempted to deny the truth. "I have wonderful friends and a wonderful family. I'm constantly surrounded by people who care about me. Most people have only *one* best friend. I'm truly blessed in that I have *three* best friends! It seems a little strange that you would think I'm lonely."

"You'd change one of those best friends into something different," she followed, once more as a matter of fact.

Larry felt that arrow was now being twisted. How badly the truth could hurt at times, especially when one has been denying it for so long. He fell into his standard defense mechanism. "Well, that's obvious to the casual observer. She's been my best friend for a very long time. Yes, I'd change that. I'd have her be both my best friend and my lover. But she's convinced this is not our destiny, and won't give me the chance to prove her wrong. And besides, there's someone standing in my way."

"All you have to do is sweep him aside," Sarah suggested. "There's nothing between them with any permanence to it."

How could she make such a statement? Sam rarely spoke about Donald, and he certainly had not been around during the past few weeks. "Well, I've always thought that only a fool would try to steal another man's girlfriend. This is certain to make him angry at you, and will probably make her angry as well! If their relationship is solid, then you aren't going to make any progress. On the other hand, if there's nothing permanent about it, as you say, then your best course is to sit back and wait. When it falls apart, you can swoop in and pick up the pieces."

"Is that your plan?" Sarah asked. "To swoop in and pick up the pieces when the relationship falls apart? Why haven't you done so when you've had the chance?"

That question had troubled Larry almost unmercifully over the last three years. It bothered him, but at least he understood why he had missed on his first opportunity. After all, a promise was a promise. There had been other chances, but he had always somehow seemed to miss them, allowing another to step in before he even realized the door had been opened. But that was reality, and it did not fit the facts of his cover story. "There have not *been* any opportunities like that," Larry said calmly. "She's been with Donald for a very long time."

"Donald isn't the one standing in your way," Sarah said in that matter of fact manner that was so disturbing to him.

"Of course he is!" Larry tried to protest. "Who else could it possibly be?"

"Sam is not the best friend you would have become your lover," she said simply. While Larry stared at her, she continued, "You have three best friends. It isn't Sam you want to be your lover, and unless I've misread you very badly, it's also not John. Why is it, I wonder, that you call my little sister Julie when her name is Julia?"

"It's just a nickname," he said, denying the truth. "Just like Sam is a nickname!"

"Yes," Sarah agreed, "but *everybody* calls her Sam. On the other hand, you're the *only* one who calls my sister Julie. You're the only one she *lets* call her Julie."

"It's just a coincidence," Larry tried.

Sarah looked at him and smiled, hoping to get him to relax. "I remember the night you picked us up at the airport. On the way home, Julia leaned her head against your shoulder and went to sleep. Is it just a coincidence you had a tear in your eye when I looked at you? What were you wishing for at that moment? Earlier, you said you wished you could find happiness. What would have made you happy at that moment? What did you want so badly it brought a tear to your eye?"

Larry knew from the look in her eyes it was pointless to continue his deception. She had seen too much and knew the truth. First, he looked at the ground. As a tightness fell across his lips, he shook his head sadly. Finally, he looked up at her and made his confession, "I was wishing right then, as I wish now, the moment would arrive when I could simply have a chance, just one chance, to try to make her become my girl."

Sarah nodded her head and smiled at him. "Surely you can make any moment be that moment, Larry. All you have to do is go to her and tell her how you feel!"

"No, Sarah," he said shaking his head, "I cannot do so. I won't attempt to steal her away from another guy. Like I said before, only a fool would do that. My chance will come along one of these days. I just have to be patient.

"I can't just walk up to her and tell her I want her to be my girlfriend. I can see exactly what would happen. First, she'd think I was making a joke. She'd look at me with a smile, waiting for the punchline. When she realized it wasn't a joke, she'd be shocked, maybe even angry with me, or simply disgusted that an ordinary guy like me would have the audacity to think she'd want to be with him. Finally, she'd pat me on the head, tell me I was her best friend, and that was all she wanted from me. I couldn't live with that, Sarah. So I would end up loosing everything, including my best friend."

"You don't know that's what would happen!" Sarah argued.

"I can't take that chance until I have reason to hope she might want to be with me, also," he said sadly. "Part of the problem, Sarah, is I don't really know how I feel about her! I know I want her, and that I need her. But how could I be in love with her? We've never dated, never kissed, never so much as held hands. The only thing I know for sure is she's my best friend. That's reason enough to love her. How could I risk our friendship without knowing the answer to so many questions?"

"How can you know the answers unless you take a chance?" Sarah asked simply.

They looked at each other for a moment, then Larry slowly nodded his head. "A very good question. There seems to be a paradox. I'll have to give it some thought."

"Please do!" Sarah urged. "It's my little sister I'm really thinking about. I happen to think you and she belong together. I can't really tell you why, I just do."

"I wish I knew whether that was true or not," he said simply. "It seems to me there would be a lot of strikes against us in the long run, and it *is* the long run I'm interested in." There was a long pause before he continued. "Sarah, I've gone to a lot of trouble trying to hide my thoughts and feelings. Obviously, you've seen through that disguise. I need to know – who else knows about this?"

"No one, Larry," she assured him. "Well, perhaps I should qualify that. All I can tell you is that I haven't spoken about this to anyone other than yourself."

"So as far as you know," he asked, "Julie is not aware of these things?"

"Not that I know of," Sarah answered.

"How about Mrs. J?" he asked, thinking this was the key player in the game.

"No," she replied with a smile.

"Sarah, I'll beg something of you. Please don't tell them! Help me keep my secret just a little while longer. Someday, I hope I'll get the chance to tell her myself. I really want to have that chance, but it has to come at just the right moment, when maybe... Sarah, in fairy tales, wishes sometimes *do* get granted, and dreams really *do* come true."

Sarah nodded her head. "I understand, Larry. I won't tell them."

"Will you make that a promise?" he asked hopefully.

"Yes," she said softly, "I promise to keep your secret."

Larry examined her eyes and saw she spoke from her heart. "Thank you," he smiled, both to acknowledge her promise, and to express his gratitude.

"I'll also wish you luck, Larry," she added. After a moment, she smiled and asked, "What do you say we go get some of that ice cream?"

After enjoying a bowl of ice cream, John and Sam were prepared to leave. "It's been a pleasure meeting you folks," John said to Joseph and Sarah. "Good luck in your new job, Joseph! I hope you'll all enjoy living in Chicago."

"Thank you, John!" Joseph said. "It's been a pleasure to meet you. If you should find yourself in Chicago, please give us a call. We'd be delighted to see you!"

"I'll remember you said that!" John smiled, "though I imagine you'll be back down here before I have reason to visit Chicago."

Sam stepped in to say goodbye. "It's been great meeting you, Sarah! You too, Joseph! Take good care of those beautiful children. I wish you the best!"

"Oh, Sam," Sarah said, "even though I've only known you for a few short weeks, I feel like I'm leaving a lifelong friend! The same goes for you – if you should come to Chicago, please be sure to look us up!"

"I will," Sam smiled, "but I agree with John. You'll probably come back down here before I get up that way." She bent down and opened up her arms to Ruthie, who had a very sad look on her face. "How about giving me a bye-bye hug?"

"Bye, Sam!" Ruthie said as they hugged each other.

"Goodbye, sweetie!" Sam said. She stood up, said a final goodbye to Joseph and Sarah, goodnight to the rest of the Jacobsons and to Larry. Perhaps she was making a silent statement, or perhaps it was just an oversight, but she said nothing to Steve.

John also said goodnight to the Jacobsons. As he turned to walk to his car, he added, "I'll see you later in the week, Larry."

"Goodnight, John," Larry replied. "Goodnight, Sam! I should leave, also," he said softly, recognizing the code phrase he seemed to use every time he left the Jacobson house. It was pointless for him to stay any longer. The others needed to get to bed so they could get an early start in the morning. His navigation services would not be needed again. He also knew the later he stayed, the later *Steve* would be staying. It would be easier on everybody, especially himself, to leave sooner, rather than later.

"It's been a pleasure to meet you, Larry," Joseph said sincerely. "I'm sure you know you're also very welcome to come stay with us if you're ever in Chicago."

"The pleasure has been mine, Joseph," Larry smiled. "I'll certainly keep your offer in mind. Good luck to you in your new job. Take good care of yourself and your wonderful family. I'm sure our paths will cross again someday!"

"Perhaps you're right," Joseph smiled back.

"I'm absolutely *certain* they will!" Sarah smiled. "At least, that's something I wish for very, very much! And, Larry, it's not *only* in fairy tales that wishes come true. You be sure to keep all of your hopes and dreams alive!"

"Thank you, Sarah!" he said with the most sincere smile he had felt in a long time.

"I plan to do exactly that! And since my hopes and dreams may well involve marrying your daughter," he grinned swooping Ruthie into his arms and tickling her, "our paths may cross a lot sooner than you expect!"

"Stop it, Lahwe!" Ruthie giggled while the others grinned.

"Goodbye, Princess!" Larry said to her as he kissed both her cheeks. "Will you hurry and grow up, then come back and marry me?"

"OK!" she giggled as she returned his kisses. "Bye, Lahwe!"

"Bye, sugar," he said softly, handing the little girl to her mother. Sarah winked at him and smiled. "Goodnight Mr. J, Mrs. J!" Larry said brightly to them. "Be careful driving to Houston tomorrow."

"Goodnight, Larry," they said, practically in unison.

Finally, Larry turned his attention to Julia. For the first time all day, he looked deeply into her eyes, gazing into infinity. Even though he held her eyes for only a moment, to him it could have been eternity. "Goodnight, Julie," he said softly. Even as he held her gaze, without changing the expression on his face in the slightest, and without so much as looking in his direction, Larry both acknowledged and dismissed his rival with an effortless statement, "You too, Steve."

"Goodnight, Larry," Julia said just as softly. If Larry was right, that the eyes truly are the window on the soul, then he had just looked deeply inside her. Windows, however, are transparent in *both* directions. *I wonder what she sees in* my *eyes?*

Monday, October 27, 1969
He's A Good Lad

Joseph sat in the front seat as Julian drove the Suburban to the Houston Airport. Jessica and Sarah sat in the second seat chatting while the children slept peacefully during the drive. "It's been so wonderful to see all of you," Jessica said, trying to hold back her tears realizing they were leaving once again.

"Oh, mother," Sarah smiled. "Don't get all weepy on me! Chicago is a lot closer to you than Africa. In fact, Chicago is even closer to you than New York! We'll be back to visit you soon, and the three of you can come visit us anytime you want!"

"I know, Sarah," Jessica said, "but you'll be all the way up there, and we'll be way down here! It's not like I can hop in the car and see you just any time I want to."

"Well, no, but guess what?" Sarah teased. "They even have *telephones* in Chicago! You can pick up the phone and talk to me anytime you want to!"

"But I don't know your number!" Jessica said in alarm.

"That's because we don't have one yet!" Sarah giggled. "That's another of the many things we have to get done this week. Mom, I promise the minute the phone's connected, I'll call and give you our number! And just so you'll relax, let me remind you that I'm just as good at keeping promises as a certain boy we know!"

Jessica smiled and nodded her head. "Yes, I remember you used to be good at keeping promises. Oh, Sarah! I'm just so grateful you've finally come back home. It seems like you've been gone forever!"

Sarah smiled. "Africa was an adventure, but it won't be long before these babies start school. I want them to have the very best, just like you and dad gave me."

"We tried our best, Sarah," Jessica said modestly. "I only wish we had moved down here to Texas while you were still small. Maybe if you had lived down here, instead of New York, you wouldn't have felt it was necessary to run off to Africa!"

"Oh, mom," Sarah laughed. "I didn't go to Africa to escape from the city. I went there because it was the right thing to do. I would have felt the same no matter where I was living. I'm glad you moved! It's obvious you're all very happy here."

"Yes," Jessica agreed, "we're happy. We've met some wonderful people in Texas. I know there are wonderful people everywhere, but somehow..."

"I'm particularly impressed with Larry, John, and Sam," Sarah smiled.

"I can tell," Jessica agreed. "I'm happy Julia has found such wonderful friends."

"Mom, could I ask your confidential opinion about something?"

"Well, of course, dear," Jessica assured her.

"We talked about this a little the first night I got here," Sarah began. "I know Julia and Larry are very good friends, but I find it hard to believe that's all there is to it!"

"Maybe you should ask *her* about it, Sarah," Jessica confessed. "She had a crush on him right after they met, but he didn't make a move for her. Over time, their relationship has grown quite a bit, but as far as I can see, it's completely platonic. But I wouldn't be at all surprised to learn she's still harboring that crush."

"What about him?" Sarah asked.

"It seems rather clear his interests are aimed at Sam," Jessica replied. "They've known each other for many years, and are exceptionally close friends. He wants to change that, but she rejects his advances, claiming she has a serious boyfriend living elsewhere. I sometimes wonder if that's nothing but a ruse, however. I think she's afraid they'd ruin their friendship if they tried to become lovers."

"He has more than one best friend," Sarah said. "I wonder if he'd like to change the relationship with more than one of them."

"I'll assume you aren't including John," Jessica grinned. "I don't know, Sarah. It's possible, I suppose, but if that's the case, I really don't understand why he hasn't done anything about it. He's certainly had the opportunity to do so."

"Maybe *he's* the one afraid to ruin a friendship," Sarah suggested.

"That's an interesting idea, Sarah," Jessica admitted. "I'll have to give that some thought. Perhaps I'm too close to the situation to see the reality. For one thing, that would certainly provide an explanation for that rose she gets every Valentine's Day."

"What rose?" Sarah asked.

"She has a secret admirer," Jessica smiled. "For three years, she's received one red rose on Valentine's Day. There's never a card, and no one claims responsibility."

"How romantic! Do you think Larry might be the one responsible?"

"It's possible," Jessica shrugged. "They started coming on the first Valentine's Day after they met. But, like I said, his interests are clearly in Sam."

Sarah had no doubts at all about who was sending those roses, recognizing the full extent of Larry's hopes and dreams. Maybe he did not want to admit it to himself, maybe he was afraid of ruining their friendship, or maybe he was just too shy to tell her, but it was clear Larry was deeply in love with Julia, even though he denied it even to himself.

Now she faced a dilemma. She had promised Larry she would not tell anyone of his feelings. *Would I be breaking my promise by nudging Jessica in the right direction?* Technically, she did not think so, but what about the spirit of that promise? What did Larry say he wanted? He wanted to tell her about his feelings himself, when he was sure he knew what those feelings were, and when the right moment had finally arrived. Sarah knew if Jessica was on his side, she would see to it he got that chance someday.

"It's *very* romantic," Jessica smiled. "One of these days, I'm going to figure out who he is, and I'll make him tell her how he feels with words, not just with deeds!"

Sarah returned her mother's smile. *So much for that dilemma!*

Monday, December 1, 1969
Draft Dodger Rag

Sam and John were in the front seat of her car, while Larry and Julia sat in back. They were parked in the place they called their smoking room, but their interest was not on smoking. Instead, they were glued to the radio, as faceless voices described the events at the Selective Service National Headquarters in Washington. For the first time since 1942, a lottery drawing was being held to determine the order of call for induction into the armed forces during calendar year 1970. It would apply to those born between January 1, 1944 and December 31, 1950. Larry and John both fell within this range.

"What would you do if you were called up?" Sam asked.

"I don't really know," John answered. "I've been thinking I might go to Canada. One thing's for sure – I'm not going to participate in any of this madness."

"What about you, Larry?" Julia asked.

Unsure of his actions, Larry shrugged and sighed. "I should tell you guys something. When I registered for the draft, I checked the box indicating I have a conscientious objection to serving in the military. I just wanted to go on record, doncha know."

"I hear you," John said. "I saw that box, but I figured it was pointless."

"I thought so, too," Larry said, "but I checked it anyway. The strangest thing happened. A few weeks later, I got a letter from the local draft board asking me to come and explain. So I went in and told them I didn't believe in fighting. They asked me to tell them things that had happened in my life to demonstrate what I meant. I told them about the time that creep cornered me in the boys' locker room at Lamar and beat the crap out of me while I just stood there. Then they wanted to know the names of some people who'd known me a long time who might confirm my beliefs. So I gave them names of some teachers and people from church. A few weeks later, I got a new draft card in the mail, reclassifying me as 1-A-O."

"Are you kidding?" John asked. "You're classified as a conscientious objector?"

"Yes, although it's not as wonderful as it sounds, John. 1-A-O means I can still be called up for military duty, but only as a non-combatant."

"Like a truck driver, cook, or something like that?" Sam asked.

"With my computer training, it'd be logical to give me a job in logistics, but since the phrase 'military intelligence' is an oxymoron, I'd probably become a medic."

"Oh, shit!" John said.

"You got it," Larry agreed, shaking his head.

"What's wrong with that?" Julia asked.

"The first guys shot are the ones with brass on their collars or a red cross on their helmet!" John explained.

"Why do you say that?" Sam asked, suddenly looking concerned.

"Kill the officers and the grunts will be unorganized," John explained. "Kill the medics and the wounded will die."

"I understand the officers don't wear their insignia in combat," Larry noted. "The men know who they are, and don't need to see brass on their collar to know who to obey. I hear the medics don't wear those red cross helmets anymore, either! Some are even carrying rifles, without ammunition, to disguise themselves from Charlie."

"Hang on," John said. "They're drawing the first capsule." The radio announced the lottery had begun. The first date drawn was September 14. "Whew!" John laughed nervously. "I had visions of being called up tomorrow morning!"

"Me, too! Number two isn't likely to be any better," Larry added. "I wonder how deep the draft will go, anyway?"

"A guy I know told me they'd probably be calling up guys with numbers as high as two hundred," John said. "We have a long way to go!"

"I won't feel safe unless I get three sixty-five, and maybe not even then!"

The next dates drawn were April 24, December 30, and February 14. "It figures," Sam said. "Valentine's Day is fourth. I suppose Jesus' birthday will be next."

The fifth selection was October 18. "You may be right!" Larry laughed nervously. "Who knows when He was born, anyway? Does you know Moses' birthday, Julia?" he asked rhetorically. The next selections were September 6, October 26, September 7, November 22, and December 6.

"At least we escaped the top ten!" John chuckled.

"I hope we can escape the top two hundred," Larry said seriously.

The boys were nervous about this whole process. Their plans for the future depended on the random selection of blue beads from a glass bowl. If it was not so serious, it would have been ludicrously funny!

The lottery continued with August 31 and December 7, "a date which will live in infamy," Sam joked, also feeling nervous – not for personal reasons, but for the sake of her best friends. The next numbers were July 8, April 11, July 12, December 29, January 15, September 26, November 1, and June 4.

Larry flinched each time a day in July was called. John did the same with days in June. The twenty-first date was August 10, followed by June 26, July 24, October 5, February 19, December 14, July 21, June 5, March 2, and March 31. On and on, capsules were drawn and dates announced. The one hundred seventeenth capsule was October 22. "I guess Julia will get called up sometime next year," John laughed.

"No," Larry chuckled, "she was born in 1952. This lottery only applies to people born up to 1950. You're safe for now, sugar."

"Do you suppose it might also matter that I'm a girl?" Julia giggled.

"It damn sure matters to me!" Larry laughed. Sam saw a sad look pass over his face, as if to say he *wished* it mattered, anyway, and smiled at Larry reassuringly.

The tension mounted as more and more capsules were drawn and the selected dates came and went. They all breathed a sigh of relief when March 19 was announced as number two hundred, and neither of their birth dates had been called. They became more and more relaxed as more and more capsules were drawn, more and more dates were called out, and still their birth dates had not been mentioned.

Finally, when the lottery reached number two hundred forty-five, the radio announced the drawing of the capsule containing August 26. "It looks like you'll be the next to go, Sam," Larry laughed. "You *were* born before 1950!"

"Does it matter that *I'm* a girl?" Sam asked teasingly.

"Prove it!" Larry demanded. "Show me some physical evidence of that claim!"

"I should have known you'd say something like that!" Sam laughed.

More and more capsules were drawn. They reached number three hundred, and still neither of the boys' birth dates had been selected. The lottery went past selection number three hundred ten, three hundred twenty, then three hundred thirty, and *still* they had not been drawn. "Do you think maybe they forgot us?" Larry asked. They passed number three hundred forty. "I hope mine comes up before they get to the end! I'd hate to find out I missed hearing it somewhere back around number forty-two or something!"

"You didn't miss it," Sam insisted. "Keep listening."

The announcement declared the three hundred fiftieth date selected was July 2. "That's me!" Larry exclaimed with a mixture of relief and joy. "At least I know I didn't miss it earlier. Now we just need to hear John's birth date!"

Three hundred fifty-one was April 25, followed by August 27, June 29, March 14, January 27, June 14, May 26, June 24, and October 1. "Good grief!" John said. "I'm convinced I missed my *own* birth date!" Number three hundred sixty was June 20, three hundred sixty-one was May 25, three hundred sixty-two was March 29.

"I'm betting you get number three sixty-five, John!" Larry laughed. Three hundred sixty-three was February 21, three hundred sixty-four was May 5. "Here it comes!" he said smugly. Number three hundred sixty-five was February 26. "Huh? Now *I'm* worried! How could we have missed it?" The radio announced the final date, number three hundred sixty-*six*, was June 8.

"You forgot about leap years!" Julia laughed.

"Holy shit!" John yelled. "Three sixty-six – I must be living right!"

"Congratulations, John," Larry said sincerely, giving his friend a high five.

"You, too," John replied. "Three fifty and three sixty-six! We're *good*, dude!"

"This is even better than winning the Irish Sweepstakes!" Larry laughed.

"This calls for a celebration!" Sam announced. "I have a surprise for you guys. I figured we'd either need to celebrate or drown our worries, so I called in a favor from this guy I know and scored a pint of Jack. I've also got some weed, all safely hidden away in the trunk. Who's ready to join me?"

"You took a big risk, Sam," Larry chuckled, "but I'm *always* ready to join you!"

"I know you are," Sam giggled, "but not tonight, big boy. Sometimes I wonder what you'd do if I suddenly accepted one of your indecent proposals."

"You know, Sam, I wonder about that, also," Larry said pretending to be serious. "Why don't we find out!" he grinned, reaching out like he was going to grab her.

"Eek!" she screamed playfully, easily jumping out of his reach. When she opened the trunk of her car, as promised, she produced a small ice chest containing ice, one small bottle of Jack Daniels Kentucky Bourbon, and a few plastic cups.

The boys grabbed the four cups and added a little ice to each. Sam opened the bottle and poured about two ounces into each cup. They lifted their cups and looked at each other, thinking someone should say something.

Beginning to feel a little more serious about the matter, Larry was the first to speak up. "I feel like a tremendous weight has been lifted off my shoulders, guys. Not only do I feel better personally, but I also know my best friend won't face making a terrible choice. John, I would have supported whatever choice you made. Thank God you won't be forced to make one!"

"Hear! Hear!" Sam agreed, lifting her cup.

"To the future!" John said with a smile.

"Le Chaim!" Larry and Julia said enthusiastically.

They each drank a significant portion of the liquid from their cups. "What does that mean, anyway?" John asked. "It's a Jewish expression, isn't it?"

"It means, *'To Life!'* I can't think of anything more appropriate at this moment!"

"Me, either," John agreed. "Le chaim!" he said, joined immediately by Sam.

"To life!" Larry and Julia agreed.

The boys felt like singing. "John, I know the perfect song for us to play right now!" Larry laughed. He played a few chords, John smiled with recognition and soon joined in, singing *Draft Dodger Rag*, written by Phil Ochs. After the song, the foursome drained their cups and looked at each other with smiles on their faces. Sam poured a second round, killing the bottle. "Are you planning on getting us pissed so you can have your way with us later, Sam?"

"I don't mind you getting pissed," Sam laughed, "but I don't plan on having my way or anyone else's way with either or both of you at this time!"

"Damn! I was hoping to get booze, drugs, and sex at the same time!"

"Two out of three ain't bad," John snickered.

"As long as I get to pick which two I get!" Larry chuckled.

"Well, *I* picked which two you can have tonight," Sam said. "You've had booze, and now you can have some grass. Take it or leave it!"

"I'll take it!" Larry sighed.

The foursome shared several joints and a lot of laughs. Eventually, they agreed it was time to let themselves sober up so they could drive home.

Julia's house, of course, was the first stop. As was his custom, Larry walked her to the front door. "So you won't get lost on the way," he explained if she asked why.

"My grandmother is coming Wednesday," she said. "Do you want to meet her?"

"Of course," Larry replied, "but I don't want to interfere with family time."

"You won't," she smiled. "She'll be here before I get home from school. If there's anything special planned for that night I'll let you know, but unless you hear from me, why don't you come over about 6:00 and you can have dinner with us."

"I'd be honored! Make sure it's OK. I don't want to impose or be a burden."

"I'll check," she smiled, "but when have you ever been a burden out here?"

"I don't know," he grinned. "Maybe I've been a terrible burden and you and your folks are just too nice to tell me!"

"See you Wednesday," she said, subtly calling his suggestion complete nonsense.

"Goodnight, Julie," he said. He wished he could say that more intimately.

She reached over and gave him a warm hug. "Goodnight, and congratulations on having such a good birth date. Tell John I said the same for him, also, will you?"

"I will," he said. He watched her open the front door, step inside, and turn back to look at him. They waved to each other. As Larry turned to walk back to the car, he heard the door close softly behind him. He sighed once, gently shook his head, and forced himself to once again take that first step that he disliked so much.

He sat in silence during the ride home, staring out the car window. John and Sam both knew what was on his mind, and decided not to disturb him. They simply exchanged a single glance and a sad shrug.

Sam pulled up to Larry's house and stopped. "Goodnight, Larry. Congratulations on winning the lottery!"

"Thanks, Sam," he said softly. "Congratulations to you as well, John. I'll see you guys later, OK?"

"Goodnight, Larry," John said. "Take it easy, man!" Larry nodded his head in agreement, then turned and silently walked away. "Man, he's got it bad!"

"Over three years now," Sam said. She turned the car towards John's house.

"Do you think she knows how he feels about her?" John asked.

"I doubt it," Sam said. "I guess it's what they call selective vision. I know she used to have a big crush on him, but when he didn't make any moves for her, she decided he wasn't interested. Now she has lots of boyfriends to divert her attention."

"It's a real shame," John said. "I feel a little guilty myself, since it was the promise he made to my little brother that caused such a problem."

"Not to mention his refusal to break that promise," Sam said.

"Do you think they'll ever get together?" John asked.

"I hope so," Sam said simply. "Not only for his sake, but for hers! I don't know if you've been paying much attention, but she's not very happy, either. She has all the boyfriends a girl could want, but she doesn't really care for any of them."

"I didn't know that," he said, shaking his head. "As long as she has a boyfriend, he's going to just sit on his hands. He doesn't have enough confidence in himself to make a move, to tell her how he feels."

"And as long as he seems to ignore her," Sam continued, "she'll have a boyfriend, and whenever she gets so tired she can't stand him anymore, she'll pick a new one."

"Can you think of anything we could do to break this vicious cycle?" John asked.

"Maybe," Sam said thoughtfully, "but you know what *he'd* say about that! He'd tell us to leave it alone, saying it'll happen all on its own if it's meant to be. He believes if anyone tries to intervene, it'd only cause more problems, and ruin his chances forever."

"Do you believe that?" John asked.

Sam looked at him. "Are you willing to take the risk that he might be right?"

Wednesday, December 3, 1969
A Most Peculiar Man

"Bobe!" Julia squealed, running across the room to give her grandmother a hug.

Ruth Jacobson was one of the happiest, most loving souls one could ever hope to meet. Some said she radiated as much warmth and love as the sun itself. Others claimed that would be a terrible understatement, giving far too much credit to the sun. "Hello, bubee!" Ruth answered as she joyfully accepted and returned Julia's hugs. "How you have grown! And such a beauty! Oy, how you must be breaking all the boys' hearts!"

"Oh, bobe," Julia smiled. "I don't want to break anyone's heart."

"Look at this girl and tell me how she could help but break their hearts!"

"She's broken a few," Jessica grinned.

"Listen to that," Ruth said to the ceiling as she held up her hands in a shrug. "A beautiful girl like this has only broken a few hearts? What's the matter with these Texas boys? Are they blind?"

"Maybe they just have stronger hearts," Julia suggested with a giggle.

"I should live so long to find a man with a heart so strong!" Ruth chuckled. Underneath her bright face was a sad memory of her beloved Benjamin who died of a broken heart the day he learned his oldest son had been killed in the war.

"How was your trip, bobe?" Julia asked. "Did you like flying in a jet airplane?"

"What an adventure!" Ruth laughed. "I asked myself, how is it possible for this furshlugginer contraption to get off the ground? So much tummel! Faster and faster it went. We made a good jump, I guess. How it could jump all the way from New York to Texas is anyone's guess, but thank heaven we made it.

"What, I should tell you about this nice man who sat next to me on the plane," she continued. "Such chutzpa! His name was Jim Ball, a big Texas oil man returning home after giving some schpeel, and let me tell you, he was dripping with gelt. We schmoozed all the way from New York. He kept ordering schnapps for me and we laughed all the way. Oy, I was so vashnukad I could plotz! If he hadn't helped me find the gate for Trans-Texas Airlines, I'd still be looking for it!"

"Good old TTA!" Julia giggled. "We call it Tree Top Airlines around here."

"I'm still shaking like a leaf!" Ruth exclaimed. "I was the only person on the plane other than the pilot. It's just as well, because they couldn't have gotten more than eight people in it, anyway. He asked me to sit in the front seat so I could see better. Oy, what I could see didn't make me relax, let me tell you! He drove this tiny plane across the airport, around all those other big planes. It was worse than the taxi ride in New York! Then we started racing down the runway, swerving from side to side. We hit a big bump or something, bounced into the air and didn't come back down until we landed here. After a few minutes in the air, he leaned back in his seat, lit up a cigarette, and asked me to take over! Like I should know how to fly that furshlugginer thing!"

"He probably put it on autopilot or something, Ruth," Jessica laughed.

"So now the planes fly themselves?" Ruth asked. "Oy, if I had known they could do that, I would have walked all the way from New York!"

"It sounds like you had a good time to me!" Julia giggled.

"It was OK," Ruth grinned. "So now tell me, bubee, how is it you should have broken only a few hearts?"

"I don't like to break someone's heart," Julia said seriously.

"So how many boyfriends have you had?" Ruth asked.

Julia thought for a moment and counted the list in her head. "I'm on boyfriend number six," she said. "His name is Steve. You'll get to meet him Saturday night."

"So you've broken five hearts," Ruth chuckled. "You could do better."

"Actually, it's seven broken by my count," Jessica giggled. "There's a little boy up the road who used to have a big crush on her. You'll meet the other one tonight."

"Oh, mom," Julia said almost pleading. "I've never broken his heart."

Wednesday, December 3, 1969 – A Most Peculiar Man

"What, she should break someone's heart and not even know it?" Ruth asked. "Now that's more like it. A lot of hearts she has broken this way I would bet!"

"He's one of my best friends," Julia said, "but he's never been my boyfriend!"

"He should want to be your boyfriend," Ruth said.

"I don't think so," Julia said a little sadly. "He could have asked me out, but he never has, so I don't think he likes me that way. We're very good friends, but he's not my boyfriend, and he doesn't want me to be his girlfriend."

"A boy who doesn't want you to be his girlfriend I don't want to meet," Ruth said.

"Oh, bobe," Julia sighed. "I promise you'll like him."

"I agree with that, Ruth," Jessica smiled. "I think you'll like this boy."

"We'll see," Ruth chuckled.

Larry rang the doorbell just after 6:00 o'clock. He was pleased Julia had invited him to meet her grandmother, but felt a little awkward to be intruding on the very first day of her visit. "Hello, Larry," Julian said. "Right on time, as always, I see."

"Good evening, Mr. J," he said. "I try to be punctual. I know I don't like to wait for someone, so I try not to make anyone wait on me."

"Come on in out of the chill," Julian said. "The girls are out in the family room, sitting around the fire."

"Thanks! I appreciate you allowing me to interfere with your family time. I hope you don't feel like I'm intruding."

"Nonsense," Julian said. "Come with me. I want you to meet my mother." Larry followed Julian into the family room and looked sheepishly at the women as Julian spoke. "Mameh, I'd like you to meet one of Julia's friends. Well, actually, I should say he's a friend to all of us. This is Larry Bristol." Turning to Larry, he completed the introduction, "Larry, this is my mother, Ruth Jacobson."

"It's very nice to meet you, Mrs. Jacobson," Larry said politely. "I hope you had a pleasant trip."

"Such things I could tell you!" she smiled. "It's nice to meet you, young man. And don't be so formal with that furshlugginer Mrs. Jacobson nonsense. Please call me Ruth!"

"Oh, I couldn't possibly do that, Mrs. Jacobson!" Larry blushed.

Ruth laughed. "There are two Mrs. Jacobson's here, so how will we know who's supposed to answer you? What do you call her?" she asked, indicating Jessica.

"I couldn't persuade him to call me by my first name, either," Jessica laughed, "so he calls me Mrs. J, and calls Julian, Mr. J. All of Julia's friends do the same."

"And what does he call Julia?" Ruth laughed. "Miss J?"

"No, ma'am," Larry smiled. "I call her Julie."

"Such a sweet little nickname," Ruth said, returning his smile.

"And Larry is the only one she lets call her that," Jessica teased. "One of her boyfriends tried to call her Julie once and she nearly bit his head off!"

"Oh, mother," she said, "you exaggerate. John and Sam call me Julie sometimes."

"I've never heard either of them call you that," Jessica said, still teasing.

Larry decided it was time to intervene. "Would it be OK if I called you Mama J?"

"Mama J," Ruth considered. "I have to admit I like that! OK, young man, you can call me Mama J if that's what you like. So tell me about yourself."

"There's not much to tell," he said shyly. "I'm just an ordinary guy." He paused, hoping he might be excused from filling in additional details, but the smile on Ruth's face told him she was waiting for more. "Well, OK, if you insist. I'll tell you the story of my life.

"I started as a child. I was born in a small town in south Texas by the name of Raymondville. Now Raymondville happens to be the first bit of civilization, if one could call it that, one encounters driving south from the town of Kingsville across the King Ranch. That drive is a truly marvelous experience, Mama J. Why down there, they have miles and miles and miles of nothing but miles and miles and miles!

"Right about now, I imagine you're probably asking yourself, *'Self,'* you're asking, *'why would someone obviously as suave and sophisticated as this allow himself to born in such an humble location?'* Well, to tell the truth, I was terribly young and immature at the time, and wanted to stay close to my mother for protection.

"Eventually, I became a little more independent. When I was four, I moved my parents here to Bryan, and got them jobs teaching at a private military school so they could support me. But when I was seven, while I wasn't paying enough attention, they picked me up and moved me to a little town in south Texas called Harlingen! I quickly regained control and moved us back to Bryan by the time I was eight.

"I received a first rate education as the hands (and some would say the knees) of the Bryan Independent School system, graduating in 1967. There was little they could have done to prevent it, actually, but they didn't know that at the time. After graduation, my parents made me one of those offers that cannot be refused. They offered to pay for my tuition and books at any state supported college I wanted to attend. Any other expenses, such as room and board, would be my own responsibility. I could, of course, choose to continue living at home for free.

"Now, Mama J, since my parents hadn't raised a fool..." He paused for a moment. "Well, perhaps they did. I *do* have an older sister." Shaking his head as if to clear his thoughts, he proceeded, "Anyway, I accepted that offer and have been attending college here at Texas A&M University ever since. I'm now in my junior year, studying computer science. I have a part time job at the computer center on campus. Oh, and I'm also the head of a super secret spy organization known as *Spectre*."

"What?" Jessica asked, surprised by the last statement.

"Nothing!" he smiled. "I was making a little joke. I'm not the head of any secret spy organization at all! Just forget I said anything, so I won't have to kill you all."

Ruth glanced around the room to see Julian and Jessica looking at her with grins on their faces. Julia was sitting on the sofa giggling. Ruth looked back at this strange young man and smiled. "Did you leave anything out?" she asked simply.

"One or two minor details, I guess," he shrugged. "Oh! I've been known to fumble around with a guitar and sing a little from time to time."

"Did you bring your guitar with you?" Julia asked enthusiastically. "Maybe you could play and sing something for us after dinner!"

"I didn't think to bring it, Julie," Larry said. "I'm sorry. But she can hear John and me on Sunday afternoon if you think she can stand it."

"He really is very good, mameh," Julian said. "A true badhkin!"

"Well, he certainly has the ability to schmooze!" Ruth laughed. "But where is your accent, young man? You say you've lived in Texas all of your life yet I can't hear any of that charming Texas drawl in your voice."

"Ya mean, lahke the-is, ma'am?" he said with as much accent as he could muster. "Shucks, ma'am, ah guess they musta juhs plain ol rund owt uh dem accents afore dey got to me. But ah-ma fixin' to git me a big un soon as dey git em back in stock. I dohn want y'all ta be disappointed, doncha know?"

"He does it better than Jim Ball!" Ruth burst out laughing.

"Ball? Did you say Jim Ball?" Larry asked. "How do you know him?"

"I met him on the airplane from New York," Ruth replied. "Do you now him?"

"I think I know *of* him," Larry smiled. "That's quite a coincidence!"

"Let's start dinner before the bovine excrement gets any deeper," Julian grinned.

"Hey, that sounds great! I'm famished!" Larry snickered. "What are we having, Mrs. J? I could sure go for some nice pork sausage covered with melted cheese!"

"Oy vay!" Jessica chuckled. "Will you behave yourself? You're starting to make me wish I'd told Julia not to invite you, Mr. Smartypants!"

"I'm being as *'have'* as I can!" Larry said with false meekness.

Julian shook his head and grinned, "There's one thing you have to get used to about these Texans, mameh. They never run out of BS it seems."

"Neither did your father, Julian," Ruth smiled, taking her son's arm. Julian returned his mother's smile and escorted her into the dining room.

Julia stepped up to Larry, winked at him, and took his arm, as well. Larry returned her smile and escorted the girl he cherished above all things into the dining room, wishing it was something he was expected to do more often.

Dinner was a simple affair, consisting of baked fish, baked potatoes, a green salad, and some freshly baked bread. Larry had never eaten a baked potato without drowning it in butter, but found it was very good anyway, especially in combination with the fish. Before long, the conversation turned to the upcoming celebration of Chanukah.

"I have to tell you about a funny incident, mameh," Julian said. "Last October, when you told me you were coming to visit, I came running into the kitchen to tell the girls. It occurred to me you might be here during the holidays, so I asked if anyone knew what day Chanukah started this year. Larry was sitting at the table studying one of his music books. Without even looking up, he said, *'I imagine it starts on the twenty-fifth of Kislev, Mr. J, just like always.'* I thought we were all going to die laughing!"

"How would a goy know that?" Ruth asked, looking at Larry with interest. "Oh, I'm sorry, Larry. That just means someone who isn't Jewish. It's not derogatory."

"No offense taken, Mama J," he smiled. "I was curious about some things, so I did a little research at the library. I read the story of Chanukah and from there, I learned a little about the Hebrew calendar."

"For what did you go to so much trouble?" Ruth asked.

"Oh, it wasn't really any trouble, Mama J," he smiled again. "I think it's interesting to know things about my friends."

"Larry, I should warn you that everything you read about Judaism may not actually apply to us," Jessica said. "There are a lot of different movements within the Jewish religion that have some different views of things."

"I saw some stuff about that," he nodded. "I guess it's like the many different kinds of Christians there are?"

"Something like that," Julian responded. "To tell the truth, we Jacobsons are pretty liberal in our views. We try to keep the Shabbat, celebrate the holidays, and even try to eat kosher, but we're not particularly fanatical about it. I've always believed the way you conduct your life is more important than keeping rituals."

"I'm the same way, Mr. J," Larry said. "Frankly, all the rituals I see in Christian religions strike me as being close to idolatry. The church I was raised in only has a few rituals, and I was never very happy about them. I just try to be a good person."

When Jessica and Julia began to clear the table, Larry jumped up to help. Jessica tried to stop him, saying guests should not have to clean the dishes, but Larry would have none of that. "It's the least I can do to thank you for inviting me, Mrs. J!"

As Larry was busy helping with the cleanup, Ruth whispered a question to her son. He nodded his head and smiled before he spoke. "Larry, I'd like to extend an invitation for you to celebrate Chanukah with us. If you're interested, it starts on Friday night, and goes on for eight days."

"I wouldn't know what to do!" Larry said.

"You don't have to do anything if you don't want," Julian smiled. "Chanukah isn't a particularly important holiday. It's more like a festival. In fact, it's often called the Festival of Lights. If you want to see what it's all about, you're welcome to join us."

"Oh, please join us, Larry," Julia said enthusiastically. "It'd be fun to have you here!" Ruth made a mental note of the enthusiasm Julia showed for this invitation.

If there had been any resistance to the idea, her plea would have changed everything. Larry would do anything to see Julia smile or to hear her laugh. "How could I possibly refuse an offer as generous as that?" he asked. He received his reward when Julia smiled brightly, sending a warm glowing sensation up his spine. Ruth nodded to herself noting how the expression in Larry's eyes changed when he saw Julia's smile.

"You can't refuse it," Jessica chuckled, "so plan to be here a little before sunset each night. The ceremony will only take a few moments, but you're welcome to stay afterward for as long as you like, and to join us for dinner."

"Could I bring anything?" Larry offered.

"You could bring your guitar!" Julia exclaimed.

"Just bring yourself," Ruth suggested. "That should be gift enough." She looked at Julia and saw her granddaughter nodding in agreement.

Friday, December 5, 1969
Dream Baby (How Long Must I Dream)

Larry rang the doorbell as the sun was sinking low. "Hello, Larry, and happy Chanukah!" Julian said when he opened the door. "I'm glad you could make it."

"Thanks, Mr. J," Larry said brightly. "And happy Chanukah to you as well." He stepped into the foyer and smiled admiring the bright decorations. "Very festive!"

"Come into the family room to join us," Julian suggested. "We'll relax a moment before we begin. We need to wait until a few minutes after the sun goes down."

Larry followed Julian into the family room and was greeted by welcomes and cries of "Happy Chanukah!" He responded in kind. He felt the genuine warmth of his welcome and was grateful his friends did not consider him an intruder.

"I see you remembered to bring your guitar!" Julia said happily.

"Whatever my princess commands," he chuckled placing the guitar in an out-of-the-way location.

"I thank thee, Sir Galahad," Julia teased.

"I found this for you," Julian said, handing Larry a piece of paper containing some printed symbols arranged in three sets. He recognized the first set as Hebrew characters, but that was all he could tell about them. The second set contained familiar characters, but the words were in another language unintelligible to him. The final set contained lines of English he could read easily. "These are the Chanukah blessings," Julian explained. "We recite these blessings during the ceremony of lighting the candles. Then we let the candles burn themselves out, and that's all there is to it. The most important part is sharing the time together."

"I can't even pronounce these words!" Larry chuckled.

"Don't worry," Julian smiled. "I'll say the blessing in Hebrew, and everyone else can repeat them in English. We've done it that way many times before. You can join the recital if you want. No one will be offended if you choose not to."

A few minutes after the sun set, Julian suggested they all move into the living room to begin the ceremony. In the living room was a large candle holder called a menorah with places for nine candles. Larry watched Jessica select a candle from a box and place it into the rightmost position on the menorah.

Julian selected another candle and lit it. He stood in front of the others, holding the burning candle, and recited the first blessing. "Barukh atah Adonai, Elohaynu, melekh ha-olam asher keed'shanu b'meetzvotav v'tzeevanu l'had'lik neir shel Chanukah. (Amein)"

Larry joined in as the others repeated the blessing in English, "Blessed are you, Lord, our God, king of the universe who has sanctified us with His commandments and commanded us to light the candles of Chanukah. (Amen)"

Julian added the second blessing. "Barukh atah Adonai, Elohaynu, melekh ha-olam she-asah neeseem la-avotaynu ba-yameem ha-heim ba-z'man ha-zeh. (Amein)"

Larry and the others repeated, "Blessed are you, Lord, our God, king of the universe who performed miracles for our ancestors in those days at this time. (Amen)"

On the first night of the festival, Julian continued with the third blessing. "Barukh atah Adonai, Elohaynu, melekh ha-olam she-hecheeyanu v'keey'manu v'heegeeyanu la-z'man ha-zeh. (Amein)"

The others repeated, "Blessed are you, Lord, our God, king of the universe who has kept us alive, sustained us, and enabled us to reach this season. (Amen)"

Julian handed the burning candle to Jessica. She went to the menorah, used it to light the candle she had previously positioned there, and placed the new candle into the center position, slightly elevated above the others.

After this brief ceremony, they sat in the living room and talked while the candles burned down. Ruth told stories how she and her brothers and sisters played dreidel trying to win the most candy. Julian and Jessica recalled similar stories about Chanukah's from the past. Julia told how she and Sarah used to play dreidel. She blatantly cheated Sarah out of the candy, but her older sister never said a word.

About an hour later, after the candles had burned out, Ruth, Jessica, and Julia went to put dinner on the table. Ruth found her interest in this boy increasing, especially when he offered to help. "Sit down and relax, young man," she smiled. "You're a guest, and guests do not help serve dinner in a Jacobson household."

"In that case," Jessica smiled, "you sit yourself right there beside him. You're a guest in *this* Jacobson household!"

"I'm no guest," Ruth laughed. "I'm family!"

"Family or not," Jessica insisted, "You sit!"

Julian laughed out loud. "You'd better do what she says, mameh," he chuckled. "When she gets that look in her eye, there's just no reasoning with her."

Ruth started to protest, but decided to yield to Jessica's directive. After all, this was Jessica's household, and Jessica had long ago won Ruth's respect. She sat at the table next to this interesting young man, and discretely observed his behavior as they all talked pleasantly and enjoyed dinner. She noted how shyly he bowed his head whenever he noticed anyone, especially Julia, was looking at him. His attention moved around the table to look at whoever happened to be speaking. Whenever there was a lull in the conversation, his eyes would inevitably be drawn to Julia, sitting at his side.

After dinner, Larry tried once again to make himself useful by carrying his dirty plate and utensils to the sink. "Thank you, Larry," Jessica smiled at him.

"It's no trouble, Mrs. J," he replied. "Let me help with the others!"

"I'll get them," Jessica assured him. "The rest of you go relax."

"Yeah!" Julia added. "It's time for you to sing us some songs!"

Ruth noted how Larry smiled. "Do you see how it really is, Mama J?" he asked mischievously. "*You* may be a guest, but I'm expected to *sing* for my supper!"

"Get out of here," Jessica chuckled, shooing the others back into the living room.

Ruth positioned herself in a comfortable chair, while Julian sat on a sofa, leaving room for Jessica to sit beside him. Larry brought his guitar out of its case, sat on the floor, and began to tune up and get his fingers limber. Julia sat on the floor nearby, and started thumbing through music books to pick out songs she wanted him to sing.

After a few moments of thought, Larry pointed out a book of songs performed by Roy Orbison. "I think you might recognize some of these, Mama J. I wish John were here. He's a much better guitarist than I am."

Ruth could sense he was nervous. "I'm sure you'll be just fine without him," she said warmly. As Julia turned from page to page, he began to play *Blue Bayou*.

Ruth was pleasantly surprised by his performance, and wondered why he seemed so nervous before. During the song, Julia looked at her to see how she was reacting. Ruth returned her smile, nodded her head, and winked at her, signaling her approval. After the song, she signaled her approval to Larry by her applause and compliments.

He followed with a couple of other songs, then surprised Julia by singing a song that was not in the book at all, *Dream Baby (How Long Must I Dream)*. The song is commonly associated with Roy Orbison, but was actually written by Cindy Walker. Ruth sensed there was something different about the way he sang, and his decision to sing it was no accident.

She observed how Julia kept him busy by requesting song after song, and that he never refused to play any song she requested. It was obvious her granddaughter liked to listen to him. That was certainly no surprise. She enjoyed listening to him, as well. It was equally obvious that he enjoyed playing for them just as much.

When the grandfather clock struck ten times, Larry began to excuse himself. "I should go and let you people have some family time together," he said shyly. "Thank you for inviting me to join you tonight. I've been given a very special privilege."

"We were privileged to have you," Julian assured him.

"Are you coming back tomorrow night?" Julia asked.

"If I'm still invited," he said hopefully.

"What do you think of him?" Julia asked her grandmother after Larry departed.

"I like him a lot, bubee," Ruth declared. "Where did you find him?"

"I met him on my fourteenth birthday," Julia answered with a smile. "He and his friend John entertained at my party."

"She thought she'd seen him someplace before," Jessica added, "but we never *did* figure out where that might have been, did we, Julia?"

"Why did he and his friend come to your party if you had never met?" Ruth asked.

"One of Julia's first boyfriends was John's little brother," Jessica explained with a little more detail. "When we were making plans for her party, Jimmy practically begged us to have his older brother, John, come entertain. John and Larry were just starting a little two-man band at the time, and so they both came."

"He is pretty good all by himself," Ruth said.

"Larry's a better singer," Julia clarified, "but John's a better guitar player. They are really good when they get together. You'll hear them together Sunday afternoon when they come here to practice. You can also meet my other friend, Sam."

"Three boyfriends!" Ruth exclaimed. "That's my bubee! What's Sam like?"

"She's a girl," Julia giggled. "Her real name is Susan, but we all call her Sam."

"She's one of the sweetest girls you'll ever meet!" Jessica explained. "She and Larry are the same age, and have been friends since the third grade. They're three years older than Julia, by the way. John is two years older."

"Ah," Ruth said, drawing an incorrect conclusion. "So *Sam* is Larry's girlfriend."

"No," Julia corrected, "but he'd like her to be. It's hard to describe their relationship. They're extremely good friends, extremely close. They constantly tease each other about dating and even about sex. They went to their senior prom together, but as far as I know, that was the only time they've gone on a date."

"Romance begins with friendship," Ruth smiled. "So if *Sam* is not his girlfriend, and *you* are not his girlfriend, bubee, then who *is* his girlfriend?"

"I don't think he has one," Julia said thoughtfully, "at least, not a serious one. He dates a lot of different girls, but hasn't had a steady girlfriend for a long time. He says he doesn't have much luck when it comes to finding and keeping girlfriends."

"Which is something he wants very much," Jessica added. "It seems to me like he's had a run of bad luck. He reminds me of a moth flying around an open flame. He sees the flame and it draws him to it. He thinks it's wonderful and beautiful, but every time he reaches out to touch that flame, he gets burned."

"Bubee," Ruth asked, "what do you think he'd do if he found another flame, one more wonderful and beautiful to him than anything he's ever seen, one that drew him so powerfully he wanted not only to touch it, but to throw himself right into the middle of it?"

"Since he's been burned a few times, I imagine he'd be very, very wary," Julia replied. "Why do you ask?"

"No particular reason," Ruth smiled.

Saturday, December 6, 1969
Turn Around, Look At Me

The second night began much the same as the first. Larry arrived just before sunset, and the group relaxed in the family room. "Julie, haven't you changed something about the way you fix your hair?" he asked.

"A little," she smiled. "I thought the ends were getting a little ragged, so I trimmed them up a bit. Do you like it?"

"Yes," he said shyly. "Your hair used to all fall behind your shoulders, but now some of it comes forward and sort of frames your face. It's very pretty!"

"You're so sweet!" Julia said with a bright smile. "Thanks!"

A few minutes after the sun completely disappeared, they moved into the living room to enjoy the Chanukah festival. Once again, Jessica selected a candle and placed it into the rightmost position on the menorah. Ruth selected a second candle, and placed it into the next position to the left of Jessica's candle.

Julian selected a candle, lit it, and recited the blessing as before. "Barukh atah Adonai, Elohaynu, melekh ha-olam asher keed'shanu b'meetzvotav v'tzeevanu l'had'lik neir shel Chanukah. (Amein)"

The others repeated, "Blessed are you, Lord, our God, king of the universe who has sanctified us with His commandments and commanded us to light the candles of Chanukah. (Amen)"

Julian continued, "Barukh atah Adonai, Elohaynu, melekh ha-olam she-asah neeseem la-avotaynu ba-yameem ha-heim ba-z'man ha-zeh. (Amein)"

The others repeated, "Blessed are you, Lord, our God, king of the universe who performed miracles for our ancestors in those days at this time. (Amen)"

There was no third blessing this time. Julian handed the lit candle to Ruth, who used it to light the leftmost candle in the menorah, followed by the one to the right. She then placed the original candle in the center position.

Following this brief ceremony, they sat around in the living room talking. Larry found it relaxing. He enjoyed hearing the stories Ruth told about the old days, and the stories Julian and Jessica told from when they were children. Most of all, he enjoyed the stories Julia told. He told a story about being a small boy and going to visit his grandparents. His paternal grandfather was still living near the town of Raymondville. His maternal grandmother lived in the west Texas town of Abilene.

But this night was different than the first. Once the candles burned themselves out, Larry used his now familiar code talk, "I should leave."

"Do you have to go before dinner?" Jessica asked.

"I think it would be best," he said sadly. "I appreciate your kind offer, Mrs. J."

Knowing what the problem was, Jessica decided not to press the issue. "I understand. I hope you'll come back tomorrow, and continue to celebrate with us."

"If you're willing to put up with me once again," he said standing to leave, "I'd be pleased to do so. Goodnight, everybody. I hope you all have a pleasant evening."

Julia excused herself to prepare for her date. "Why did he leave?" Ruth asked.

"He knows what will happen next," Jessica said softly. "Julia's boyfriend, Steve, will be showing up in a little while, to take her out on their date."

"Oh," Ruth nodded. "I forgot he's not her boyfriend. Larry doesn't like Steve?"

"I wouldn't say that," Jessica said. "Steve and Larry get along well enough when they are together. It's just that Steve doesn't like it when Larry is hanging around."

"So why hasn't Steve been here these last two nights?" Ruth asked.

"I doubt Steve knows that Larry has been here," Jessica said. "If he did, I imagine he'd have been here, also. Julia and her friends always get together on Sunday afternoon, and you watch. Steve will be here. And when he finds out Larry is celebrating Chanukah with us, he'll probably want to join in himself!"

"I'm looking forward to meeting this Steve," Ruth said. "If Julia likes him more than Larry, he must be something special!"

The doorbell rang a few minutes after 8:00 o'clock. As always, Julian answered the door and welcomed him. "Good evening, Steve. Julia will be out shortly. Come into the family room for a moment. I'd like you to meet my mother."

"Thanks, Mr. Jacobson," Steve replied politely. "Julia told me her grandmother was coming to visit."

"She arrived Wednesday," Julian said casually. "It's nice to have family together for the holidays. Mameh, I'd like you to meet Steve Scott. Steve, this is my mother, Ruth Jacobson."

"It's nice to meet you, Mrs. Jacobson," Steve said pleasantly.

"Nice to meet you, also, young man," Ruth replied brightly. "There's no need to be so formal. Please call me Ruth."

"OK, Ruth" he said. "I understand you live in New York?"

"That's right, if you could call that living! So many people, I tell you it's a nightmare. I certainly understand why my little Jules brought his family way down here. So much room to grow!"

"Yes, ma'am," Steve said politely. "That's one thing we certainly have plenty of."

"So tell me about yourself!" Ruth requested.

"I'm a sophomore at A&M," Steve stated proudly. "I grew up in Corpus Christi. I used to play a little football in high school, but I wasn't good enough to win a scholarship or anything."

The awkward silence that followed this brief history was interrupted by Jessica. "What do you and Julia have planned for this evening?"

"We're going to a party some of my friends are throwing," he said.

"I hope there won't be any alcohol involved, Steve," Julian said. "I don't want Julia exposed to a bunch of drunken behavior."

"Oh, there won't be any alcohol, Mr. Jacobson," Steve said with a straight face. "None of my friends are old enough yet."

"When I was that age," Ruth said with a wink, "all the boys knew how to get alcohol when there was to be a party."

"Mameh!" Julian exclaimed.

"What?" Ruth asked with a look of innocence. "You want I should lie? And don't you try to tell me you didn't do the same! I could see that the levels in the bottles in your father's liquor cabinet kept going down faster than they should. So what am I going to think, that the mice must be drinking it?"

Steve grinned at Julian's obvious discomfort. In his eyes, Ruth was mothering her son. Julian's true discomfort was her suggestion there would be alcohol at this party.

Julia entered the room. "Hi, Steve," she said, then gave him a small kiss. "Do you see anything new?" she asked, fishing.

"Is that a new dress?" Steve guessed.

"No," Julia said. "I cut my hair a little shorter!"

"Oh, yes, I saw that," Steve lied. "I thought you meant you had some new clothes or something."

"So do you like it?" Julia asked.

"Yes!" Steve said. "I like it very much! You didn't cut very much, did you?"

"It was just a trim," she said, now doubting he had noticed any difference at all. "I just needed to straighten up some ragged ends."

"We should get going," Steve suggested. "We're already late. Mr. Jacobson, since we're getting started a little late tonight for some reason, would it be OK if she stayed out a little later than usual?"

"Steve, you have almost four hours," Julian said calmly. "I think midnight is late enough for a girl her age."

"Yes, sir," Steve said disappointedly.

"Come on!" Julia giggled. "Goodnight, mom, dad! Goodnight, bobe!"

"Goodnight, bubee," Ruth said. "It was very nice to meet you, Steve."

"Have a good time," Jessica added.

"We will," Julia said cheerfully.

With that announcement, Julia and Steve walked through the front door and departed, leaving the adults alone. None of the them spoke for a few moments. "I don't know about the rest of you," Jessica said, breaking the silence, "but I'm hungry. Are either of you ready for some dinner?"

Sunday, December 7, 1969
Something

Larry was first to arrive. He parked in his regular spot, retrieved his guitar and music case from the trunk, and headed for the front door. He stopped halfway up the walk when Sam's car turned into the driveway, and waited for her to catch up.

"Hi, babe!" he called as Sam hopped out of her car. She returned his greeting, and walked briskly up the sidewalk. "I dig that new sweater of yours," he grinned. "It shows off what nice Bristols you have!"

"Go ahead and look all you want, pervert," Sam giggled, "but if you reach out to touch anything, you'll bring back a nub where your hand used to be!"

"Damn it, Sam," he pretended to pout, "you never let me have any fun!" They saw John's car pulling into the driveway. "We might as well wait for John to join us. Or would you like to go one at a time and make Mr. J answer the doorbell three times?"

"Let's wait," Sam grinned. "As I understand it, poor Mr. J has been answering the doorbell a lot this week."

"I think he likes it," Larry grinned. "Hey, John! How are you feeling today?"

"Feeling fine," John smiled. "How about you guys?" he asked, fetching his guitar case from the trunk and heading up the walk.

"I'm OK," Larry said. "What do you think of Sam's Bristols?"

"Her what?" John asked, looking a little perplexed.

"Her *Bristols!*" Larry repeated. "Haven't you heard the old sailor's expression about something being *'ship shape and Bristol fashion'*? It came from the reputation the port of Bristol had for preparing the sailing ships in such good order."

"And what does that have to do with Sam?" John asked innocently.

"Wouldn't you agree that she's ship shape and Bristol fashion?" Larry grinned.

"Yes!" John chuckled.

"It's a rhyming thing," Larry explained. "The nickname for the soccer team in Bristol is *'Bristol City's'*, which rhymes, of course, with 'titties'. Everybody knows if you want to find the girls with the *biggest* Bristols, you go to Bristol, England!"

"I see," John grinned at Sam. "I've always admired Sam's Bristols!"

"One of these days I'm going to knock your blocks off," Sam growled. "Come on! Let's go meet Julia's grandmother."

"You're going to love Mama J!" Larry smiled.

"Is that what you're calling her?" Sam asked. "I might have known that Mrs. Jacobson or Grandmother Jacobson wouldn't be good enough for you."

"She asked me to call her Ruth," Larry said when they reached the front door. "I suppose that's her name, but you know, it suddenly occurs to me that might be wrong. Maybe she just likes the name for some reason."

"Oh, please," Sam giggled, ringing the bell.

"No, wait!" Larry said. "I remember Mr. J introduced her as Ruth Jacobson. I guess we should assume that really is her name after all."

"I'm glad we've that cleared up," John said.

As usual, Julian answered the door. "Hello, kids. Come on in."

"Thanks, Mr. J," Sam said as she greeted him with a hug. "It's nice to be around a gentleman for a change." Larry and John looked at each other as if mortally injured.

Julian stopped the boys and grinned. "I don't want to know what you've done to cause her to say that, but you better cut it out before you get to the family room."

"We haven't done anything!" Larry insisted. "We're completely innocent!"

"You'll *never* convince me you're completely innocent," Jessica laughed, hearing the tail end of this conversation. "What have they done this time, Sam?"

"I complemented her on how nice her sweater fits!" Larry claimed. "Sam has a great personality, and that sweater shows off two of the nicest parts of her personality. She seems to have taken offense for some reason!"

"I wonder!" Jessica snickered. "Behave yourself or I'll put you in the backyard."

"I *am* being *'have'!*" Larry pouted.

Julian shook his head. "Mameh, I'd like to introduce two more of Julia's friends, Susan Kronkite and John Myers. This is my mother, Ruth Jacobson."

"It's very nice to meet you, Mrs. Jacobson," Sam said with a bright smile.

"Nice to meet you also, Susan," Ruth said. "Please call me Ruth."

"My friends call me Sam. I understand Larry calls you Mama J. If it's OK with you, I'd like to do the same to cut down on confusion."

"That will be fine, dear," Ruth said pleasantly. "It's a pleasure to meet you, also, John. I've heard a lot about you. Do you play that guitar as well as everyone says?"

"I do my best," John said modestly. "It's very nice to meet you, Mama J."

"Well, now that all of the formalities are out of the way, why don't you boys bring out those guitars and start playing so I can judge for myself!" Ruth smiled.

"I'll go make everyone a glass of lemonade while you get started," Jessica said. "Would you give me a hand, Jules?" Julian and Jessica departed for the kitchen, leaving Ruth alone with the youngsters. Larry and John brought out the guitars and began to tune up, while Sam and Julia settled in to listen.

After a few moments of tuning and seemingly nothing but fumbling around, the music slowly settled into an introduction to a song Sam and Julia recognized as one of the more recent released by the Beatles called *Get Back*.

"That's very nice, boys," Ruth said. "I can tell from the girl's reaction this must be a popular song these days."

"Yes, ma'am," Larry nodded. "It's by one of our favorite songwriting teams – John Lennon and Paul McCartney. You might know them as the Beatles."

"Well, at least I've heard of them!" Ruth laughed. "Play some more."

"This is another song by the Beatles, written by George Harrison. It's called *Something*. It's one of my favorites. I think you'll like it." Ruth made a note of the way Larry had a hard time keeping his eyes off of Julia as he sang.

The doorbell rang, and Julian got up to answer. He returned moments later with Steve, who had come to listen to the boys play, but mostly to keep an eye on Larry.

They next played several songs from *Hair*, the cult opera Larry had adapted for a two-man band. The easiest of these to adapt was *Good Morning Starshine*. The adaptation of *Aquarius/Let the Sunshine In* still needed some work, as did the theme song *Hair*, since they sounded better with more than two voices.

"I know a song about New York you might like, Mama J," Larry said. "It's called *The Boxer* by Paul Simon, another of my favorite songwriters."

The remainder of the afternoon went normally, as the boys worked through various songs, some new and some old, preparing for a future engagement. Around 4:00, Jessica served up some cold cuts so everyone could make a sandwich. After the break, they returned to their guitars and continued to practice for another hour.

Sam whispered in John's ear a reminder they needed to leave before sunset. "I'm ready to call it a day, Larry," John said. "I think we'll be ready in time, don't you?"

"I think so, John. We have more than enough material ready, even if we aren't comfortable with the new songs yet. We'll work on them some more next week."

John finished packing his guitar and stood up to leave. "Thanks for having us once again, Mr. J, Mrs. J." he smiled. "It was wonderful to meet you, Mama J. I understand you'll be here next weekend. If you can endure it, we'll play some more for you then."

"I'd like that," Ruth smiled. "You boys are very good, just like everyone said."

"Thanks!" John said as he waited for the others.

"It was nice to meet you, Mama J!" Sam added. "I'll see you next weekend as well. I hope you have a nice visit with your family."

"Thank you, dear," Ruth said. "You have a nice week."

John and Sam exchanged goodbyes with the others and headed for the front door, followed by Larry. "Are you leaving too, Larry?" Julia asked.

"Not just yet. I thought I'd go ahead and put my stuff in the car. Be back in a minute." The threesome walked outside to their cars. They discussed some subject for a moment, then exchanged their goodbyes. John and Sam got in their respective vehicles. They honked their horns and waved at Larry as they started down the driveway and departed. Larry returned their waves and smiles before he started back to the front door.

Inside, the most interesting conversation was the one between Steve and Julia. "Is he staying for this Chanukah business?" Steve asked a little roughly.

"Yes," Julia replied. "My parents invited him to join us."

"You're welcome to join us, also," Julian said calmly. "This will be the third night of the festival. There are five more nights after this one."

"I'll stay tonight, at least," Steve said. "I'm not sure I can come tomorrow night."

"Will you try?" Julia asked.

"Yes," Steve said a little shortly.

Larry returned from his car and joined the others in the family room. Julia announced that Steve would be joining them for the festival that night. "Great!" Larry said sincerely. "I think you'll enjoy it, Steve. It's a good chance for friends and family to share some time together. Do you know the story of Chanukah?"

"No," Steve said, fighting a scowl on his face. "Why don't you explain it to me."

"OK," Larry said, responding to the challenge. "You've heard of Alexander the Great. He conquered all the known world, including Israel. He wasn't so bad, but about a hundred years later, one of his successors was rather nasty. He started suppressing the Jews severely, and defiled the Temple in Jerusalem. They revolted, recaptured the Temple, and wanted to rededicate it. There's supposed to be a flame that burns continuously, but they only had enough oil for one night. Miraculously, the flame lasted for eight days. They celebrate this miracle with the holiday called Chanukah, also known as the Festival of Lights. Did I get it right, Mr. J?"

"Close enough for government work, as I've heard you say," Julian snickered. "You really did do your homework, didn't you?"

Larry smiled. "I'm just glad you aren't asking me to name of the Greek ruler, and the names of the guys who led the revolt. I only remember Judah Maccabee."

"It never occurred to me Alexander the Great had anything to do with it," Julia giggled. Steve looked at Larry with a satisfied sneer.

"He got his history right," Julian said. "It *was* Alexander the Great who captured Israel, although he was dead by the time of the Chanukah story." He handed Steve a copy of the text he had given Larry previously. "If everyone is ready, why don't we move into the living room?"

Shortly after the sun disappeared, they moved into the living room to enjoy the Chanukah festival once again. Jessica selected a candle and placed it into the rightmost position on the menorah. Ruth followed by selecting a candle, placing it into the next position to the left. Julia selected another candle and placed it into the third position.

Julian selected a fourth candle, lit it, and held it as he spoke the first blessing in Hebrew, "Barukh atah Adonai, Elohaynu, melekh ha-olam asher keed'shanu b'meetzvotav v'tzeevanu l'had'lik neir shel Chanukah. (Amein)"

Larry and the others repeated in English, "Blessed are you, Lord, our God, king of the universe who has sanctified us with His commandments and commanded us to light the candles of Chanukah. (Amen)" Steve did not participate.

Julian then spoke the second blessing, "Barukh atah Adonai, Elohaynu, melekh ha-olam she-asah neeseem la-avotaynu ba-yameem ha-heim ba-z'man ha-zeh. (Amein)"

The others followed, "Blessed are you, Lord, our God, king of the universe who performed miracles for our ancestors in those days at this time. (Amen)"

Julia accepted the candle from her father, and used it to light the leftmost candle in the menorah, followed by the next one to the right, and finally, the rightmost candle. When all three were lit, she placed the original candle into the center position.

Following this brief ceremony, they sat around in the living room talking. Larry told them a story about the first time he had ever seen snow, during a family trip to Abilene to visit his grandmother during the Christmas holidays. They all laughed as he described building his first snowman, and how he had pelted his older sister with a bunch of snowballs he had prepared for when she came out of the house to see it.

Julia could not recall the first time she had seen snow, but remembered her first Chanukah *without* snow. It was the year the Jacobsons had moved to Texas, and they spent their first Chanukah season in the south.

According to Steve, the first time he had seen snow was on a skiing trip with his parents as a small boy. He described the strange feeling it was to strap a couple of boards to his feet and try to stand on them as he slid downhill.

After about an hour, the candles burned out, and Jessica suggested they move back into the family room. Larry decided this was a good opportunity, and announced his intention to bow out. The sight of Julia and Steve together made him depressed, and since he knew Steve would not leave first, he decided it would be less stressful on everyone if he left. He smiled bravely, but Ruth noted the sadness in his eyes.

Monday, December 8, 1969
The Fool On The Hill

Larry went to Julia's house directly after work. Waiting for sunset, Julian asked Larry if he would like to participate in the ceremony. "Are you sure it's allowed?"

"It's allowed," Julian smiled. "Do you want to?"

"I wouldn't know what to do!" Larry protested mildly.

"There's nothing complicated about it," Julian assured him. "You've seen how it goes. All you have to do is select the fourth candle, place it into the next position on the menorah, and after the blessings, you simply light them all from left to right."

"You add the candles from right to left, but light from left to right?" Larry asked.

"That's right," Julian answered. "We light them in the opposite order because it's proper to honor the newer things first. Would you like to participate?"

Larry smiled and nodded his head. "I'd be honored," he said softly.

Shortly after the sun had disappeared, they moved once more into the living room to enjoy the Chanukah festival. Jessica began by selecting a candle, placing it into the rightmost position. Ruth selected the next and Julia selected the third candle. Larry selected the fourth candle and placed it on the menorah.

Julian selected a candle, lit it, and recited the first blessing holding the burning candle. "Barukh atah Adonai, Elohaynu, melekh ha-olam asher keed'shanu b'meetzvotav v'tzeevanu l'had'lik neir shel Chanukah. (Amein)"

The others repeated in English, "Blessed are you, Lord, our God, king of the universe who has sanctified us with His commandments and commanded us to light the candles of Chanukah. (Amen)"

Julian continued with the second blessing, "Barukh atah Adonai, Elohaynu, melekh ha-olam she-asah neeseem la-avotaynu ba-yameem ha-heim ba-z'man ha-zeh. (Amein)"

The others repeated, "Blessed are you, Lord, our God, king of the universe who performed miracles for our ancestors in those days at this time. (Amen)"

Julian handed the burning candle to Larry, who proceeded to light the four candles on the menorah from left to right, ending the ceremony by placing the original candle into the center position on the menorah.

They sat in the living room and talked as the candles slowly burned down. Ruth wanted to hear about these strange thinking machines Larry worked with. "They don't really think at all," he smiled. "In fact, you couldn't really classify them as intelligent in any way. All they can do is blindly follow instructions. They just happen to be very good at following instructions, and never get bored doing the same thing over and over. They're especially good when the instructions involve numbers, although the only numbers they truly understand are zero and one."

Julian asked, "I thought they could handle huge numbers and text data as well!"

"It's all done with mirrors!" Larry grinned. "Actually, Mr. J, they don't even understand zero and one in the same way we do. Their understanding, if you really want to call it that, is more like a light switch than anything else. They understand the difference between on and off, and there's no middle ground. Either a wire has voltage or it doesn't – on and off – and that's all computers can handle. Everything else they do is based on our interpretation. For example, when a wire has voltage on it, we call it one, and when it doesn't, we call it zero."

"So how does it handle other numbers?" Julian asked. "I assumed it used different voltages to represent other numbers, the bigger the voltage, the bigger the number."

"That's sort of the basis for what they call *analog* computers," Larry explained. "I'm not very familiar with them. These days, almost everything is done with digital computers. All they really know is on and off, which we treat as zero and one.

"To get bigger numbers, we just use more digits! Take a look at the way we humans handle large numbers in the Arabic system. We only have ten digits, zero through nine, yet we can represent large numbers by stringing digits together. We call the rightmost digit the 'ones' position, the next digit to the left represents 'tens', the next represents 'hundreds' and so on. By stringing the same ten digits together like that, we can represent any arbitrary number, including very large ones.

"Computers do the same thing, except they only have two digits – zero and one.

But we can also string them together to get bigger numbers. The rightmost digit represents the 'ones' position, just like in the Arabic system. Since there are only two digits instead of ten, the next digit represents the 'twos' position. The next digit represents 'fours', then 'eights', then 'sixteens', and so on. String enough digits together, and you can also represent any arbitrary number, no matter how large."

"I get it!" Julia said. "So the number 'two' is represented by the digits '10'. 'Three' would be '11', 'four' would be '100", and 'five' would be '101'. Wild!"

"That's right, Julie!" Larry smiled, impressed by how quickly she caught on. "It's just another way of representing numbers. The Arabic system is sometimes known as 'base ten' arithmetic, because it uses ten digits. We call that the 'decimal system'. We humans feel comfortable with this system because we happen to have ten fingers. Why do you think we call them 'digits'?

"But you could take any number of digits and create a new numbering system. If you used the letters of the alphabet as digits, for example, you could have a base twenty-six arithmetic system. When there are only two digits, we call it 'base two' arithmetic, although it's better known as the 'binary system'. The nice thing about binary is it makes the electronic circuitry a lot less complicated than decimal. How high can you count on your fingers, Mr. J?"

"One, two, three, four, five, six, seven, eight, nine, ten," Julian replied.

"Well check this out!" Larry laughed. "I can count to one thousand twenty-three on my fingers!" Using each of his fingers (and thumbs) as a binary digit, he demonstrated the process to the delight of Julia. "Now, it's awfully tedious for humans to write out a large number in binary, so computer people typically use another number system called 'hexadecimal' that uses sixteen digits, zero through nine followed by the letters 'A' though 'F'. It's funny listening to people read off hexadecimal numbers because we don't use the actual letters in speech. We say 'Apple', 'Baker', 'Charlie', 'Dog', 'Easy', and 'Fox'."

"Now I'm confused again," Julia said.

"Don't think you're alone!" Larry laughed. "Hexadecimal is just a shorthand way of combining a group of four binary digits into a single digit." He then asked a question with a sly smile. "Would you like to hear a slightly vulgar computer joke?"

"I might have known you could make a vulgar joke even when it came to computers," Julia laughed. "Go ahead if you dare. I won't be embarrassed!"

Ruth and Jessica looked at each other, grinned, then turned to Julian. "Go ahead," he said reluctantly.

"As you probably know, we use abbreviations, and shorthand notations for everything when we talk about computer stuff. For example, we never use the term 'binary digit'. Instead, we take the 'b' from the beginning of 'binary', and the 'it' from the ending of 'digit', put them together, and call it a 'bit'. A binary digit represents the tiniest bit of information you can have. Got it?"

"I get it," Julia agreed. "What's vulgar about that?"

"There's more," Larry grinned at her. "We organize the computer memory into groups of eight bits we call a 'byte'. I'm not sure what the derivation of that word is. I just assume someone changed the short 'i' in 'bit' into a long 'i' sound, and came up with a word that represents a bigger unit of information – a byte."

"Go on," Julia grinned.

"I also told you about hexadecimal," he continued. "It turns out each hexadecimal digit is the same as four binary digits, so we needed a name. We call it a 'nibble'. A nibble is half of a byte, you see?"

"I'm with you," Julia smiled, nodding her head.

"Sometimes," he continued, "we refer to a unit containing two bits. We call this a 'twit', as in 'twin bit', doncha know."

"A twit?" Julia giggled. "That's not quite the same definition *I* use for a twit!"

"I understand," Larry grinned. "So now I've told you about a bits, bytes, nibbles, and twits. See if you can guess what a 'twat' is!"

Julia covered her mouth and giggled, while the others rolled their eyes and shook their heads. Ruth was the one who demonstrated her bravery. "We give up, Larry," she said with a smile, "What is a twat?"

"I don't know," he smiled, "but I hear it's a hell of a lot more than two bits!"

The room was filled with slightly embarrassed laughter. "You ought to be ashamed of yourself!" Jessica snickered.

"Let me assure you, I am!" Larry grinned.

Tuesday, December 9, 1969
I Will

For the fifth night, Larry went directly to her house from work. "Did you bring your guitar tonight like I asked you to?" Julia asked as he stepped into the foyer.

"Of course, Julie," he smiled. "I left it in the car."

"Why don't you go ahead and bring it in now?" she suggested.

Shortly after the sun disappeared, they moved into the living room to enjoy the Chanukah festival. Jessica began by selecting a candle and placing it into the rightmost position. Ruth selected the next candle and placed it to the left. Julia selected the third candle, placing it into the next position, and Larry selected the fourth. Now Jessica picked a fifth candle, placing it onto the menorah just left of center.

Julian lit his candle and recited the blessing in Hebrew, "Barukh atah Adonai, Elohaynu, melekh ha-olam asher keed'shanu b'meetzvotav v'tzeevanu l'had'lik neir shel Chanukah. (Amein)"

The others repeated the same blessing in English, "Blessed are you, Lord, our God, king of the universe who has sanctified us with His commandments and commanded us to light the candles of Chanukah. (Amen)"

The second blessing was given, "Barukh atah Adonai, Elohaynu, melekh ha-olam she-asah neeseem la-avotaynu ba-yameem ha-heim ba-z'man ha-zeh (Amein)"

This was followed once again by the others repeating in English, "Blessed are you, Lord, our God, king of the universe who performed miracles for our ancestors in those days at this time. (Amen)"

It was Jessica's turn to light the candles on the menorah. She took the candle from Julian, lit the other five from left to right, and then placed the last candle into the center position. The group settled back to relax and talk.

Before the candles had burned down, Julia voiced a request. "Sing us a song!"

"Now?" Larry asked.

"Why not?" she countered.

"OK," he replied. "Is there anything in particular you want me to play?"

"Not really," she said. "Play something new. I know you and John go off and practice some songs in secret before we ever hear them on Sunday afternoons. Play us something you guys are working on we haven't heard before."

"That sounds dangerous!" Larry chuckled. "You want me to play something I haven't practiced very much? You're in a strange mood tonight, Julie!"

"I'll take my chances," she grinned.

"If you insist," he replied. He took his guitar out of the case and thought for a moment while making sure it was in tune. He looked at Julia and nodded his head. "I know just the song," he smiled. He played *Daydream Believer*, written by John Stewart, and popularized by The Monkees on their television program. It was a simple song, but it held some meaning to him, as he truly believed his daydreams would come true someday.

He had hardly finished before Julia was after him once again. "Sing another!"

He smiled to himself and to the others, knowing he could never deny her anything she wanted. "There's a Beatles song we have been working on lately. Would you like to hear that one?" When Julia nodded her head, he returned her smile and began to play *I Will*. So many songs hold so much meaning to him it was not easy to choose among them.

"I love that song!" Julia smiled brightly. "Sing another, Larry!"

"Just one more tonight, OK, Julie?" he begged. "It looks like the candles are almost out, and I really should go do some homework." There was no homework, but he was afraid if he kept singing songs like the last one, he might blow his cover, and did not want to have to explain anything. In spite of this anxiety, he elected to sing a dangerous song. It was by Hal David and Burt Bacharach entitled *(They Long To Be) Close To You*. After all, the song explained the reason he was in that particular place at that particular time.

"What a sweet song," Jessica smiled. Ruth nodded her head in agreement. She had quietly enjoyed the songs, noting how Larry could not keep his eyes off Julia as he sang, no matter how hard he tried.

"I thought you'd like it," Larry said softly with a satisfied smile on his face. There was only one word within the song he did not like. One of these days, he hoped to modify the second line of the chorus so that he could change the color of her eyes from blue to green. "And now, I really should go," he said in code as he packed his guitar, trying not to show he wanted to stay and be close to her just a while longer.

"You're coming back again tomorrow, aren't you?" Julia asked.

"If you want me to, I will," Larry said, smiling to himself with the realization he was quoting a line from the Beatles song he had sung earlier. *If she wants me to, I'll wait a lonely lifetime, believing in my daydreams of the time I can be close to her.* "Goodnight, Julie," he said as he showed his smile visibly. "Goodnight, everybody!" he repeated, picking up his guitar and heading for the front door.

"Goodnight, Larry," they all called to him. Julia followed him to the front door and watched him stroll down the sidewalk, get into his car, and start home.

Wednesday, December 10, 1969
You Didn't Have To Be So Nice

On the sixth evening, the ceremony was repeated in the same manner as before. Jessica placed the first candle, followed by Ruth, Julia, and Larry. Jessica placed the fifth candle and Ruth placed the sixth.

Once again, Julian spoke the blessing in Hebrew while holding a lighted candle, "Barukh atah Adonai, Elohaynu, melekh ha-olam asher keed'shanu b'meetzvotav v'tzeevanu l'had'lik neir shel Chanukah. (Amein)"

"Blessed are you, Lord, our God, king of the universe who has sanctified us with His commandments and commanded us to light the candles of Chanukah. (Amen)"

"Barukh atah Adonai, Elohaynu, melekh ha-olam she-asah neeseem la-avotaynu ba-yameem ha-heim ba-z'man ha-zeh. (Amein)"

"Blessed are you, Lord, our God, king of the universe who performed miracles for our ancestors in those days at this time. (Amen)"

Ruth took the candle from Julian and used it to light the candles on the menorah, from left to right, then placed that candle into the center position. The group settled down to chat and enjoy each others' company as the candles burned down.

They talked about various subjects for a while. As the candles were burning close to the menorah, Ruth asked a key question. "Where is Steve tonight, Julia?"

"It's getting close to finals and he needs to stay on top of his books," Julia said.

"I'm sorry Steve hasn't been able to join us," Larry said sincerely. "I don't think he understands me very well, and it seemed like a good opportunity for us to get to know each other a little better."

"Yes," Julia said simply.

"Why don't *you* need to study like that?" Ruth asked.

"I *do!*" he laughed. After letting this set in for a moment, he added, "Since I'm also working part time, I have a lighter class load than most students. This keeps me busier than most during the semester, but fewer classes means I also have fewer finals. My work load doesn't get a lot worse just because of final exams."

"I'd never thought of that," Julia said. "That makes sense when you mention it."

"That made sense?" Larry snickered. "Something must be terribly wrong! Nothing is ever supposed to make sense at A&M, doncha know."

"Har, har, har," Julia chortled. "You must feel right at home then!"

"I do most of the time," he grinned. "But that's because so little in life has ever made any sense to me. It turns out to be a real advantage now that I'm in college. I don't have to unlearn all the sensible things others have learned over the years."

"You are so full of crap," Julia giggled.

"That's why my eyes are brown," he snickered. "I need to make sure you know what to do in case they ever turn blue. You know what that means, right?"

"I'd rather not guess," Julia smiled. "What does it mean if your eyes turn blue?"

"It means I'm a quart low," he said, "and someone needs to top off the tank."

"This has happened many times in the past, hasn't it, Larry?" Ruth grinned.

"Ooh!" he laughed. "That was a good one, Mama J!"

"Do you ever take anything seriously?" Ruth asked.

"Yes, but I try not to think much about things I take seriously," he smiled. "Those things hurt too much, and frankly, I'd rather stay in a good mood, especially when I'm around good friends, doncha know?"

"You're *always* in a good mood," Julia said pleasantly.

"I wish *that* were true!" he said. "I assure you I'm not. Maybe you just never happen to be around when I'm in bad mood." Ruth smiled to herself, thinking the truth was likely to be the converse. He was never in a bad mood whenever she was around. "You've been here for a week now, Mama J. What do you think of Texas?"

"I'm beginning to understand a lot of the things I've heard about Texas," she said with a smile. "Texas may be the biggest state in the union..."

"Second biggest for now," Larry corrected, "but most of us are just waiting for the ice to melt, and then we'll see for ourselves which is really the biggest."

Ruth shook her head as she grinned. "OK, second biggest, but that's only accounting for the size of the land, not the size of the hearts of the people who live here. Any place that would take in a crazy old Jewish woman from New York City and make her feel as welcome as I feel is alright in my book!"

"Aw, Mama J," he said, "you're neither crazy nor old."

"And just look what Texas has done for my son and his wonderful family," Ruth continued as if she had not heard. "I'm so proud of you, Julian, for having the good sense it took to move your family down here. It's not at all difficult for your mameh to see how happy you are, how happy you *all* are. It's also not difficult to figure out a lot of that happiness comes from the wonderful friends you've made here, not the least of whom must be this fine young man who's gone out of his way to entertain us, to learn our ways and customs, and to share them with us, even as he shares his own ways and customs with us. I can't begin to tell you how much this means to me."

The look in Larry's eyes and the blush on his face was all the thanks Ruth needed. Julian and Jessica looked at each other, then at Larry, silently expressing their agreement as they smiled warmly. The smile on Julia's face meant the most to him, but he knew all he could do was accept those smiles with gratitude. "If you're going to speak about me in this manner, then I'm afraid I shall have to leave," he said. "The candles have gone out, anyway. I should go before I wear out my welcome."

"That won't happen any time soon," Julia grinned.

"I sincerely hope not," he said softly, almost under his breath. "If you're willing to put up with my nonsense one more time, I'll see you all again tomorrow night."

Ruth stood and was the first to give him a hug. "Goodnight, young man!"

"Thanks, Mama J," he said. "Goodnight to you." Jessica also hugged him goodnight. Even Julian offered his hand as Larry headed for the door.

"What about me?" Julia asked as his hand reached for the doorknob.

Larry looked back at her and smiled. "Goodnight, Julie," he said softly.

Julia wrapped her arms around his waist and hugged him warmly. "Goodnight, Larry. Please bring your guitar again tomorrow, OK?"

"Anything you want, you got it," he said honestly. "Sweet dreams to you, Julie."

Thursday, December 11, 1969
Boy From The Country

The ceremony on the seventh evening followed the familiar pattern. Jessica placed the first candle, followed by Ruth, Julia, and Larry. Jessica placed the fifth candle, followed by Ruth and Julia.

Julian spoke the blessing, "Barukh atah Adonai, Elohaynu, melekh ha-olam asher keed'shanu b'meetzvotav v'tzeevanu l'had'lik neir shel Chanukah. (Amein)"

"Blessed are you, Lord, our God, king of the universe who has sanctified us with His commandments and commanded us to light the candles of Chanukah. (Amen)"

"Barukh atah Adonai, Elohaynu, melekh ha-olam she-asah neeseem la-avotaynu ba-yameem ha-heim ba-z'man ha-zeh. (Amein)"

"Blessed are you, Lord, our God, king of the universe who performed miracles for our ancestors in those days at this time. (Amen)"

Julia took the candle from her father, lit the seven candles, and placed the final candle into the center of the menorah. They chatted while the candles burned down, then Julia voiced the expected request, "Larry, please sing us a song or two."

Larry always felt compelled to comply with any request she made. It was, of course, never a chore for him to sing for her! As expected, he fetched his guitar from its case, loosened his fingers with some warm up exercises, then began to play the introduction to one of his favorite Beatles songs, *Mother Nature's Son*.

He smiled softly as he accepted their appreciation. Perhaps that song had put him in a mood to think about the outdoors. Whatever the reason, another song came into his mind. Without a word, he started playing a gentle guitar introduction to his next song, *Boy From The Country*.

"I've never heard you sing that before," Julia said. "Is it something you wrote?"

The question made Larry laugh, breaking the softly sad mood he always felt after singing this particular song. "That's probably the nicest compliment anyone has ever given me!" he said sincerely. "No, Julie, I only *wish* I could write something that good. It was written by Michael Murphey. It's a very special song to me."

"Do you know him?" Julia asked. "He must have written it about you. Surely *you* are that boy from the country!"

"Why on earth would you say a thing like that?" he asked with amazement.

"Don't you see that it fits you perfectly?" Jessica said. "We all know how you feel about nature and the natural world in general. We know you really *do* think of the forest as your brother, and of the earth as your mother."

"And I swear I've seen you talk to animals!" Julia said. "I watched you speak to Schotzy when he needed you..."

"And I've seen you talking to that old willow tree in the backyard," Jessica smiled, "not to mention the way you brought in all those hummingbirds last year."

"Nonsense," Larry smiled, "anyone could do that! I'm certainly not Dr. Doolittle! OK, so I like nature, but the only line that really applies to me is the one where people said the boy from the country was insane! And if you think I really can talk to animals and trees, then maybe that line applies to you as much as it does me!"

"Come on," Julia grinned. "Admit it!"

"You're all even crazier than I am!" he laughed.

Friday, December 12, 1969
Lost In The Stars

On the eighth and final evening, the menorah would be filled with candles. They followed the same order as before. Jessica was first, followed by Ruth, Julia, and Larry. Jessica then placed the fifth candle, followed again by Ruth, Julia, and Larry.

"Barukh atah Adonai, Elohaynu, melekh ha-olam asher keed'shanu b'meetzvotav v'tzeevanu l'had'lik neir shel Chanukah. (Amein)"

"Blessed are you, Lord, our God, king of the universe who has sanctified us with His commandments and commanded us to light the candles of Chanukah. (Amen)"

"Barukh atah Adonai, Elohaynu, melekh ha-olam she-asah neeseem la-avotaynu ba-yameem ha-heim ba-z'man ha-zeh. (Amein)"

"Blessed are you, Lord, our God, king of the universe who performed miracles for our ancestors in those days at this time. (Amen)"

Larry was pleased to take the burning candle. He lit all eight candles on the menorah from left to right, then placed the final candle into the center position. As they had done for seven nights, they talked about various things that interested them.

Larry was a little more depressed than usual that night, and it showed. Perhaps it was the dismal weather. Perhaps it was because this was the last night of Chanukah, and he had enjoyed the opportunity to share it with Julia and the Jacobsons. Perhaps it was because it was Friday night, and he was keenly aware someone else would soon arrive. After a brief appearance, he would carry away the one Jacobson Larry wanted to carry away himself. Perhaps it was a little bit of all these things.

When it came time for him to play a song, his selection was a little more melancholy than normal, even though no one could argue it was inappropriate. He sang *Lost in The Stars* almost A Capella, merely strumming a few chords on his guitar as he went. When he finished the song, he sat in quiet contemplation, as lost in his thoughts as he had been lost in the stars while singing. The Jacobsons, *all* of the Jacobsons, also sat in quiet contemplation. At least one of the Jacobsons also considered the thoughts that might be going through the head of this very unique and perhaps peculiar young man.

After a few moments, Larry seemed to reanimate, and returned to his more normal and jovial self. The tempo raised as he performed a medley of Neil Diamond songs, including *Sweet Caroline*, *Red, Red Wine*, and *Cherry, Cherry*. Sensing that it was almost time for Steve to arrive, he smiled to everyone and excused himself.

After Steve and Julia departed on their date, Julian retired to the family room to relax and watch television. Jessica and Ruth spent a few moments cleaning up the kitchen and chatting. "Jessica, there's something I'd like to ask you," Ruth began.

"Go ahead, Mama J," Jessica said.

This brought a smile to Ruth's face. "Isn't it interesting you should call me that?"

At first, Jessica was not sure what she meant, but after a moment, the point of the question sank home. "He does seem to have quite an effect on people, doesn't he?"

"Yes, he certainly does," Ruth agreed. "That's exactly what I want to talk about. I'd like to hear more about this boy. There's more going on than meets the eye."

"You sense something, too, do you?" Jessica replied. "Sarah also believed that."

"And what do you think?" Ruth asked, knowing Jessica should have a much better handle on these things than either she or Sarah.

"To tell you the truth," Jessica sighed, "I don't know what to think. Maybe I'm too close to the situation. Most of the time, I think I have him figured out, but once in a while, I wonder a little. He is something of an enigma to me. I can sense he has a few secrets, but unlike most people, he's very good at keeping them to himself."

"Tell me everything you know," Ruth said. "Start with how you met him."

"Well, like I mentioned earlier, we met him on Julia's fourteenth birthday. He and John came to the party to play their guitars and sing..."

"And how did Julia meet him?" Ruth interrupted.

"She met him that same night," Jessica noted, "although she thought at the time she had seen him previously. She had a little boyfriend named Jimmy at the time, John's little brother. When we started planning Julia's birthday party, Jimmy all but begged us to have John and his friend come entertain at the party. Larry and John were just getting started with their little two-man band back then."

"What happened when they met?" Ruth asked.

"Nothing," Jessica said. "Julia thought she had seen him someplace before, but we've never figured out where it could have been. It was probably a coincidence."

"Did anything happened between her and Jimmy?" Ruth asked.

"Not right away," Jessica answered thoughtfully. "She and Jimmy stayed together for about two more months. I could tell she was enamored with Larry. Jimmy was really just a little boy, and I think Julia was starting to develop more mature interests. Perhaps she saw Larry as the mysterious older man. I don't really know. After she broke up with Jimmy, she met another boy, his name was Frank, and they dated for several months. Then there was a boy named Bill, one named Ed, and now Steve."

"Has there ever been a time when she didn't have a boyfriend at all?" Ruth asked.

"Yes," Jessica nodded. "Right after she broke up with Jimmy, there were a couple of months. She usually has a steady boyfriend. I'm sure you can see the reason!"

"Yes, she's a lovely girl," Ruth smiled. "What do you know about his girlfriends."

"There's not much to tell, I'm afraid," Jessica began. "From some of the conversations I've heard, I gather Larry has never had very good luck when it comes to finding and keeping a girlfriend."

"That's hard to understand. A nice boy like that could have any girl he pleased!"

"I've said that to him myself," Jessica giggled, "and you should hear his answer! He knows he can have any girl he pleases, but he just hasn't pleased one yet!"

"That sounds like something I'd expect from him," Ruth smiled. "How is it he hasn't pleased one? Why hasn't Sam or one of these other Texas girls grabbed him? Tell me about the girlfriends he *has* had, at least the ones since he met Julia."

"The night they met at her birthday party, Larry and John paired up with a couple of Julia's girlfriends," Jessica explained. "Larry really cared for that little girl. Her name was Linda, and they dated for about two months. I have it on pretty good authority that she introduced him to the delights of being a man!" Jessica giggled. She turned more serious as she continued, "He was so terribly hurt when she broke up with him! Soon after that, he started dating a very pretty girl for a while, one of the school cheerleaders. Her name was Sally. Now that I remember, that was how Julia met her next boyfriend. Frank was Sally's little brother."

"Let me see if I understand," Ruth said. "When they met, Julia had a boyfriend named Jimmy, and Larry started dating a girl named Linda. Larry and Linda broke up at about the same time Julia broke up with Jimmy."

"That's right," Jessica confirmed.

Ruth shook her head. "But they didn't get together?"

"No," Jessica said thoughtfully, "and to tell you the truth, that's always puzzled me. She had a big crush on Larry back then, and I was quite sure he was interested in her, but nothing came of it. That's why I told you he was the seventh broken heart she has caused. After a while, she started seeing another boy, and that could easily have been the end of the story, except that Larry and Julia went on to become very good friends, along with John and Sam. There's no doubt at all, however, that Larry wants Sam to be his girlfriend, and has wanted that for a very long time."

"I see," Ruth said, deep in thought.

"Why are you so interested in him, Ruth?" Jessica asked.

"It's the way he looks at Julia," Ruth replied. "I can see in his eyes that he's very interested in her, Jessica. He tries to hide it, but I can tell. Does Julia still have that crush on him?" she asked.

"I sometimes think so, but she's so occupied with other boys it's hard to tell."

"It's pretty clear to me she's interested in him at some level," Ruth said, "whether she knows it or not. I can also see it in *her* eyes! Did you notice how she practically begged him to join our Chanukah celebrations, and how she keeps begging him to sing songs? Didn't you tell me it was her idea for him to come meet me that first night?"

"Yes," Jessica said. "I noticed."

"Why didn't she invite her boyfriend, what's his name, if she's so interested in him, and not in Larry?" Ruth asked.

"Steve," Jessica answered absently. "I don't know the answer to that, Ruth, but I don't think there's anything too mysterious going on. Steve really is her boyfriend. She goes out with him just about every Friday and Saturday night. Larry is her best friend, and she spends the rest of her time with him, along with John and Sam."

"Something just doesn't sound kosher to me," Ruth said. "I'll think on it."

Sunday, December 14, 1969
Can't Take My Eyes Off Of You

The boys took a break from practice. The gang had gone inside to grab some food, apparently leaving Larry alone for a few moments. He sat on the brick retaining wall surrounding the old willow tree, gazing up into its bare branches, his conscious mind lost in thought. Subconsciously, he considered the three small doe watching him from a thicket of heavy brush some twenty-five yards away.

Occasionally, his conscious and subconscious would reverse. Subconsciously, he wished the tree would speak to him, and give him some answers to the questions troubling his mind. Consciously, he wondered why the deer were being so timid. If he sat quietly and remained very still, they would sometimes approach a little closer. "What are you afraid of today, ladies?" he asked with a calm voice. One of them stepped out of the brush as if she was going to approach, but hesitated.

"Hello, my brave little friend," he said softly, smiling at her. "I'm sorry I don't have any special treats to give you today." The doe stared at him silently. The only motion he saw was the flicking of her tail, an alarm signal she was giving the others. Suddenly, the three of them bolted away at top speed.

"You really *do* talk to animals," Ruth said, startling Larry almost as much as she had startled the deer.

Larry recovered from his surprise quickly, looking over his shoulder to see Ruth smiling at him warmly. "Talking with the animals is no trick, Mama J," he chuckled. "Anyone can do that. The hard part is getting them to understand what you say, and understanding what they say back to you."

"If they were to speak to you, what do you think they would say?" Ruth asked.

"I don't really know," he said with a soft smile. "Perhaps they'd tell me they're hungry, a little frightened, or maybe a little lonely." Larry turned to look once more at the thicket where the deer had been standing.

"A penny for your thoughts," Ruth smiled as she sat next to him.

Larry chuckled, then looked to see her smiling face. "Oh, Mama J," he said, returning that smile, "I was just sitting here thinking about how nice it would be if someone came along and gave me a shiny new penny!"

"I doubt that, you kibbitzer," Ruth laughed. "Are you ever serious?"

"Sometimes," he said, trying to appear cheerful, "but I try not to be serious very often. When I think seriously about things, it tends to make me feel a little sad."

"Why would such a nice young man be sad?" Ruth asked. "Are you like the deer? Frightened, a little hungry, a little lonely?" He looked at the ground and shrugged. "What you need is a sweet little meydele to keep you from feeling those things!"

"God knows I'm trying," he chuckled as he looked back at her. "But I've never had very much luck in that regard, I'm afraid, and I don't see any reason to think things are going to change for the better any time soon."

"Why not?" Ruth asked. "Why, a nice young man like you could have..."

"Please don't say I could have any girl I please, Mama J," he said before she could complete her sentence. "That simply isn't true. If I could, why would I be sitting here all alone, underneath this willow tree, asking it to help me figure out what I need to do?"

"This tree, it also talks to you, does it?" she smiled.

"Sometimes," he sighed. "Well, not really, of course. But sometimes, I'm able to find answers to some of my questions when I sit underneath its branches and think about them. I have a lot of questions, it seems."

"Would the advice of a crazy old Jewish woman from New York City be more useful than the advice of an old willow tree?" Ruth asked him.

"It might at that," he smiled. "Do you know where I could find one?"

"I know plenty of crazy old Jewish women back in New York," she laughed, "and one who has come to Texas to visit her zun and his family."

"You're not old, Mama J," he smiled. "You'll *never* be old. People are only as old as they let themselves be, and you'll always be young in your heart. And you aren't crazy, either! At least, not half as crazy as I am. So if there's a young and sane Jewish woman from New York who wants to give some advise to a poor, lonely goy from Texas, I'm sure he'd find a way to put it to some good use."

Ruth looked at her young friend and smiled. "You're surrounded by your friends, people who care a great deal about you. How is it you should feel lonely?"

"I've asked myself that question many times, Mama J," he replied, trying to smile.

"My advise would be for you to get up off your tuchus, march right into that house, and tell those friends exactly how you feel about them. What do you think that zun of mine would say to you?"

"I have to admit that's the best advice I've been given all day!" he grinned. "I don't know how Mr. J would react. I like to think of him as my friend. I hope he thinks of me as a friend, also."

"Of course he does," Ruth smiled. "And what about Jessica?"

"Mrs. J is the classiest lady I've ever met in my life," he said instantly. After only the slightest pause, he grinned and added, "until I met you, of course, Mama J!"

"How is it none of these Texas girls have gotten their hooks into a sweet talker like you?" she sighed. "Surely I don't need to tell you how highly the Lady Jessica thinks of you!"

"I like to think she's also my friend," he said softly.

"What would John say to you?" Ruth asked.

"John is my best friend," he smiled. "I don't know what I'd do without John! He and I are closer than most brothers!"

"Of course you are," Ruth agreed. "And what would Sam have to say to you if you told her exactly how you feel about her?"

"Mama J, a long time ago, I lost count of the number of times I've told Sam how I feel about her," he replied sincerely. "I'd be completely lost without her around to keep me pointed in the proper direction. Even if no one else in the world understands, she knows exactly how I feel about her, just as I know precisely how she feels about me."

"I have seen that the two of you have a very special relationship," Ruth said.

He nodded his head and pointedly sighed. "And Julie is my other very best friend," he said confidently. "I probably should tell them how I feel more often, but I really think they know how I feel without me having to remind them all the time."

"Perhaps there's one who doesn't know exactly how you feel," Ruth suggested.

Alarm bells went off in Larry's head. He played a neutral card. "I've told Sam how I feel about her many times, Mama J, but it doesn't help."

"I'm not talking about Sam," Ruth answered calmly. "Don't you think Julia would be shocked to know how you really feel about her?"

"What makes you say that?" A wave of anguish passed over Larry's face as he realized from the look in her eyes that she could see through his disguise. "Is it really that obvious?" he asked as his eyes fell to the ground, afraid his little ruse might be falling apart completely.

"No," Ruth said trying to reassure him, "it's not that obvious, except maybe to a crazy old Jewish woman from New York. I can see it in your eyes when you look at her, especially since you seem to have so much trouble taking your eyes off of her. I can hear it in your voice when you sing to her. I hear it in the words of the songs you choose to sing to her. Rather than beating around the bush so much, why don't you simply go to her and tell her directly how you feel?"

"How can I tell her what I don't know myself, Mama J?" he asked.

"Don't you love her, Larry?" she asked him directly.

"Of course I love her, Mama J!" he said sadly. "She's my best friend."

"You want her to be something more than that," Ruth suggested.

He looked into the branches of the old willow tree. "I wouldn't use the word *'more'*. I want her to be something... different than she is right now. I really don't know what it is I want, Mama J. That night I met her, right here under this old tree, I knew there was something special about her. It reached out to me and touched something deep inside me. It still touches me every time I look into her eyes. But I neither know what it is, nor what it means. All I know is I want to find out. I *need* to find out!"

"Why don't you do something so you can?" Ruth asked. "There's a really easy way to do so. All you have to do is tell her that you want her to be your girlfriend."

"What have I got to offer her?" he asked sadly. "I'm not like the other guys who call on her. They're tall, dark, and handsome, popular at school, heroes in various kinds of sports. Their families are high in the social circles. They're outright rich by comparison. I'm not like that! Why would she want to be with me?"

"You're selling yourself short," Ruth suggested. "What have you got to lose?"

"Oh, just everything!" he replied a little too strongly. "I can tell you exactly what would happen, Mama J. First of all, she'd probably think her best friend, the funny clown, was making some kind of joke. She would laugh, and then sit back and wait for the punchline. But there wouldn't be a punchline this time, Mama J, and when she realized I was serious, she'd be frightened, or maybe a little disgusted that I dared have the audacity to think she would want to be my girl. But since she's my best friend, she'd pat me the head, and go easy on me. She'd tell me what a wonderful friend I am, and how that's all she wants from me. *'Can't we be just friends?'* she would ask."

Larry tried to stop the tears, but could not do so. "I've heard those words far too many times, Mama J. I couldn't *bear* to hear her say that to me! Not only would I have lost what little chance I'll ever have to be with her, I would inevitably lose my best friend as well. You ask what I have to lose? Just everything! That's all!"

"I understand your fear," Ruth said softly. "You do realize, don't you, you'll have to take that chance someday. Wouldn't it be better if it was sooner rather than later?"

"Go ahead and get it over with, is that your advice?" he asked. "Mama J, maybe you're right. Maybe it would be better for me to just get this over with once and for all so I can forget all about my silly little dream, and get on with what I laughingly refer to as my life. Is that what you're suggesting?"

Ruth was taken aback by this response. She knew this boy had feelings for her granddaughter, but was surprised to see their intensity. "I guess I'm not sure... anymore," she answered truthfully, "but surely you can see you can't continue this way forever. Do you have a better plan?"

He sighed and wiped his eyes as best he could. "Not really. That's what I keep asking of this old willow tree. The last thing it said was to wait, because the time is not yet right for me to have my chance. OK, so I'll wait. I'll wait and watch as all the other guys come along, giving it their best shot. Maybe I can learn from their mistakes. Maybe it will give me a better chance someday when my turn finally does come. I'll wait as long as I have to. I'll wait forever, if necessary."

"You will suffer much *tsuris*," Ruth said.

"I already have, Mama J," he said softly. "I already have."

"This crazy old Jewish woman from New York should have left you alone," Ruth said. "I'm sorry I have brought this sadness upon you. Please forgive me."

"There's nothing to forgive," he said looking up at her. "Mama J, could I beg a favor of you?"

"Of course," she said softly.

"Please keep my secret a little while longer," he begged. "I know that in the long run, my chances aren't very good. But what little chance I have is to wait, and hope that someday, the right moment will arrive. Surely you can see even that chance would be lost forever if she already knew how I feel about her."

"Your secret is safe with me, Larry," Ruth whispered, "but you must not wait forever, because there are other eyes that can easily discover the truth."

"I know," he said. "It's a miracle Mrs. J hasn't figured it out already."

"Yes, she'll figure it out eventually," Ruth said softly. "There are other eyes, as well, including some that might come as a surprise to you. Some that understand your problem far better than you realize. Some you might not have considered."

"Well, I don't know about the rest of you guys," Sam said, "but I have a busy day tomorrow. Monday is my heaviest class day, and I need to get my beauty sleep."

"Is *that* how you keep passing those courses without studying?" Larry teased.

"Jealous?" Sam teased in return.

"Hell, yes!" he chuckled.

"Too bad!" Sam grinned. "Goodnight everybody. I won't get to see you again before you go back to New York, Mama J. It's been a real pleasure to meet you. I hope you have a pleasant trip home, and that you'll come back to visit again soon."

"Thank you, dear," Ruth said. "It's been wonderful to meet you as well. It's nice to know Julia has such good friends. Keep an eye on her for me, won't you? If anyone can keep those two hooligans in line, it'd have to be you."

"I'll try, Mama J," Sam said, giving her a hug, "but I can't make any promises."

"I'm not a hooligan," John protested. "Am I? What's a hooligan, anyway?"

"Look in the dictionary," Larry grinned. "You'll see your picture by the word."

"Right underneath yours, I'll bet," John laughed. "Goodbye, Mama J. Come back to Texas soon and visit us again, OK?"

"I'll do that, John, just so I can hear you play the guitar some more!" Ruth turned her attention to Larry. "And what are *you* going to say to me, young man?"

"I've already said too much, I suspect," Larry smiled. "I'll just say I'm going to miss you a great deal. Please come back and see us soon."

"Maybe the next time I come," Ruth said, "you will have found some answers to your questions. Zol zion mit mazel, boytchik."

"A sheynem dank," Larry replied, "from the very bottom of my heart." He turned his attention to the others. "Goodnight, Mr. J, Mrs. J." They echoed his words. He looked into those green eyes that haunted his dreams so much and said softly, "Goodnight, Julie. Sweet dreams to you. I hope you have a good week." She smiled to him, but said nothing. Once again, he turned to Ruth and gave his final goodbye, "Biz hundert un tsvantsik. We'll meet again."

Wednesday, December 17, 1969
The Rainbow Connection

Julia sat at the kitchen table eating her breakfast, engaged in some wishful thinking. "Daddy, can I play hooky today so I can go with you when to take bobe to the airport?"

"Don't you have some important tests this week?" Julian asked.

"A few," Julia answered weakly.

"School is where you should be, bubee," Ruth smiled. "I'm sure your father can get your old bobe to the airport just fine!"

"I miss you already, bobe," Julia said sadly.

"We'll have none of that, you silly girl," Ruth said warmly. "As soon as you and your friends get together again, you'll forget I was even here."

"No way!" Julia protested.

"I agree with her, mameh," Julian added. "We're all going to miss you!"

"If you miss me so much, why don't you ever call?" Ruth asked, one of her standard complaints. "I looked at your cockamamie Texas telephone, Julian, and I was surprised to find it has the same sort of dial as the ones in New York!"

"I'll start calling you more often," Julian said, trying to appease her.

"Oy, that I should raise a zun who would lie to his own mameh!" Ruth lamented.

"I mean it, mameh!" he protested. "I promise I'll start calling you more often!"

"If only you were as good at keeping your promises as a certain mentsh bekovedik I met recently," she teased, piling on as much guilt as she could muster, "then maybe I could expect to hear from you by Pesach!"

"Oh, mameh!" Julian said in exasperation.

"Don't worry, Mama J," Jessica inserted just to tease him even more, "I'll remind him to call you from time to time."

"And so will I!" Julia giggled.

"A zun shouldn't have to be reminded to call his own mameh," Ruth replied, piling on another helping of guilt.

Julian merely grunted, and attempted to regain control. "Finish your breakfast and get yourself moving, young lady," he commanded. "I don't want to hear you were late for school this morning!"

"OK, daddy," Julia said. She wolfed down the last bite of breakfast and put her dishes in the sink. She hugged her grandmother warmly. "Bye, bobe! It was wonderful to see you. Please come back soon!"

"I'll try, bubee," Ruth promised. "Don't forget you can also come see me now and then. Now help your mother to keep your father in line after I'm gone. And please tell those wonderful friends of yours I'll never forget how they made a crazy old Jewish woman from New York City feel so welcome!"

"I will," Julia grinned. "Oh, I wish I didn't have to go to school today!"

"Go!" Julian said sternly, even as he grinned at her.

"Bye, bobe," Julia said once again. "Have a good trip home!"

"Bye, bubee," Ruth waved as Julia rushed out the back door on her way to school.

The sun rose to mid-morning, and after Jessica bid her final farewells to Ruth, it was time for Julian to make the short drive to Easterwood Airport so his mother could catch her commuter flight into Houston, where she would connect with the larger service back to New York City. Ruth wanted to speak privately with her son about a few matters, and this ride provided the best opportunity she would have. "This has been a wonderful visit, Julian," she said to induce the conversation as her son began the drive.

"I'm glad you enjoyed it, mameh," Julian smiled. "I hope you'll take Julia's words to heart and come back to visit us again soon."

"I'd like that," she agreed, "but at my age, it's hard to travel far from home."

Julian looked at her scornfully. "What do you mean by that 'at my age' nonsense? You're not old, mameh! You'll *never* be old. People are only as old as they let themselves be, and you'll always be young in your heart."

"Someone else said exactly the same thing to me just the other day!" Ruth laughed. "Thank you, Julian. I'll admit I feel a lot younger now than I did before I left home. I think it must have done me some good to be around you and Jessica, not to mention Julia and all of her young friends. She's such a lovely girl, Julian! I'm sure I don't have to tell you how proud you and Jessica should be of her!"

"We're very proud," he smiled. "Our little girl is a ray of sunshine in our lives!"

"She surely is," Ruth said returning his smile. "I don't know if you've noticed, Julian, but she's not such a little girl anymore. She's rapidly becoming a beautiful young lady!"

"Just like her mother," Julian said, still beaming with pride.

"Exactly! She's a senior in high school, right?" Ruth asked. "Does she have plans after graduation?"

"Nothing too definite," Julian replied, "but I know she wants to go to college. To tell you the truth, mameh, that's something I was hoping to ask you about. I think it might be good for her to get away from home, to get out and see other parts of the world. But I'd also like her to stay close to someone within the family, so they can keep an eye on her. I was thinking maybe she could go to college in Chicago, where she'd be close to Sarah, or in New York, close to you. What do you think?"

"Oh, Julian," Ruth smiled, "I would, of course, be delighted for her to come live in New York. But I couldn't keep an eye on her unless she actually came to live with me, and I hardly think a young college girl would want to live with her old bobe!"

"I wouldn't be too sure," Julian grinned. "I think she'd enjoy living with you."

"She might for a while, I suppose," Ruth said. "And I'm sure she'd enjoy living with Sarah for a while. But Julian, if you really want her to get out and see other parts of the world, like you said, then it might be best if she truly went out on her own, rather than living with a relative. Perhaps she'd like to go to school in Israel, like her sister did. Why don't you ask her how she feels about that?"

"I have, mameh," Julian admitted. "She said she'd rather stay home and go to A&M, the local university. I'm not sure going to Israel is a good idea these days. There's too much turmoil! That's why I'm thinking about Chicago or New York."

"You might be right about that," Ruth nodded. "Her idea sounds sensible to me, Julian. It certainly would be a lot less expensive for her to go to school right here!"

"I'm not worried about the costs," Julian noted. "I think it might be good for her to get away from home, see other parts of the world, and meet other people."

"She has a whole lifetime to see the world," Ruth smiled. She saw an opportunity to turn the conversation to the topic in which she was interested. "I doubt she could ever meet people any nicer than the ones she's already met right here!"

"She's met some nice people," Julian agreed. "We've all met nice people in Texas. But as you pointed out, she's not such a little girl anymore. I think it might be time for her to meet *other* people."

"Ah!" Ruth smiled. "As in marriageable young men. Is that what you mean?"

"Well, yes," Julian said. "Mameh, the only complaint I have about living in this small Texas town is that the Jewish community is also rather small. I'm afraid she doesn't have nearly as many choices as she ought to have."

"Are there no young men at the local synagogue?" Ruth asked.

"Not too many," Julian explained. "It seems the ones who live here are either too young or much too old. I did meet a very nice young man earlier this year who has come from Israel to study, but neither of them showed much interest. I suppose he's too busy with his studies, and she's too distracted by this Steve she's dating."

"You don't care too much for him, do you, Jules?" Ruth asked.

"Do you?" he countered.

"He's a nice boy, I suppose," Ruth replied casually, "but Julia could certainly do better. I don't think you need to worry about him, anyway. Jessica tells me their relationship isn't serious, and she's starting to get tired of him."

"That's good, as far as it goes," Julian said, "but should she break up with Steve, then all it means is that yet another will come along shortly thereafter. I need to get her into an environment where she has a better chance to meet the right young man."

"I don't doubt another would come along!" Ruth chuckled. "She's a very lovely girl, Jules. A boy would have to be blind not to notice her! I happen to know a nice young man who'd be *very* interested in being the next one in line!"

"So you've noticed him, too, have you?" Julian asked.

"How could I miss it?" Ruth laughed merrily. "It wasn't that long ago. I remember another young man, perhaps a little older than this one, who had the same look in his eyes whenever he was around the beautiful girl who had captured his heart and soul. About the only difference between these young men, other than their age, is that one of them can't sing nearly as well as the other. They're both very sweet, but also very shy."

"One of them received a mazel and his dreams came true," Julian said softly.

"Perhaps the other will also have *his* dreams come true," Ruth countered.

"I'm afraid this boy doesn't have the same chance," Julian said seriously.

"Is that the reason you want to send Julia to college in Chicago or New York?" she asked. "To get her away from this boy before she notices he wants to be with her?"

"Not at all," Julian protested, "I just want her to go where she can meet some nice marriageable young men. Don't you think this is something I owe her?"

Ruth looked at him and smiled. "What you owe her, Jules, is your love. As far as matters of the heart go, let your old mameh give you some advice. If you truly love her as much as I know you do, you must not attempt to impose upon her your notions about the young men with whom she spends her time, with whom she falls in love, or with whom she might marry. God will lead her to the man He has chosen. You, me, Jessica, and anyone else would be best advised to stay out of His way."

"Amen!" Julian agreed.

"Mrs. Jacobson!" Tom Garrett said brightly. He had noted her name on the passenger manifest and remembered her from the earlier flight he had piloted.

"Hello, Captain Garrett," Ruth said. "Julian, this is the nice young man who flies that furshlugginer contraption from here to Houston. Captain, this is my son, Julian."

"Nice to meet you, Captain," Julian smiled and offered his hand.

"No need for such formalities, Julian," Tom grinned as he accepted the handshake. "Just call me Tom. It's very nice to meet you, as well. Your mother was such a delightful copilot during our last flight together that I wanted to make sure she'd join me in the cockpit once again. How about it, Mrs. Jacobson?"

"Oh, please call me Mama J," she gushed.

"Mama J?" Tom grinned. "Sounds like I'm becoming a friend of the family!"

"Oh, how silly of me," Ruth giggled. "My name is Ruth."

"Ruth is a very special name," Tom smiled, "but unless you object, I think I'd rather call you Mama J! It sounds so much more friendly and intimate, somehow."

"I agree!" Julian grinned.

"The only thing wrong with calling me Mama J is that it might make you think I'm an old woman," she grinned. "I'm not so old I don't appreciate attention from a handsome young man like you!"

"You'll never be old, Mama J!" Tom laughed. "We can board the aircraft anytime you wish. I plan to give you another flying lesson today! Would you rather handle the takeoff or the landing?"

"Oy vay!" Ruth exclaimed.

"Goodbye, mameh," Julian laughed, giving his mother a hug. "Tom, please let me apologize in advance for any trouble she may cause you."

"I assure you that she'll be no trouble at all," Tom said to him with a wink.

"Goodbye, zun," Ruth said. "I'll call you when I get home to let you know I arrived safely. But after that, it'll be your turn to call me, just like you promised."

"I will, mameh," he said just before they exchanged a kiss. "Have a safe trip!"

Ruth Jacobson allowed her newest friend, Tom Garrett, to escort her through the terminal building, out the exit doors, and onto the tarmac. At the top of the stairway into the aircraft, she turned one last time, waved goodbye, then disappeared through the door. At Tom's insistence, she took her position in the copilot seat. Moments later, the other three passengers boarded the aircraft and the twin engines started. The plane taxied to the end of the runway, stopped momentarily before the engines roared to full power. The small aircraft hurled itself down the runway, climbed smartly, banked as it turned to the southeast, and disappeared over the treetops lining the horizon.

Thursday, December 25, 1969
Rockin' Around The Christmas Tree

Larry woke on Christmas morning, noting it started out much the same as always. The tradition in his family was to open their gifts to each other the night before, on Christmas Eve. During the night, they would sneak back into the living room to distribute a few more items. Christmas morning, they returned to see what goodies had been left in their stockings. Those stockings typically contained simple food items, such as fruit, nuts, and candy, but there would also be small gifts, usually gag gifts. It was the best part of Christmas! His family had often talked about abolishing the Christmas Eve extravaganza with its bigger and more expensive gifts. They generally enjoyed opening their stockings much more than all the gifts on the night before. Perhaps they never performed this simplification because they assumed the stocking gifts would quickly become more and more "significant", moving the commercial aspect of Christmas none of them liked from Christmas Eve to Christmas morning, defeating the whole idea. Larry thought to himself that someday, when he had a family of his own, he would make this change.

After opening their stockings, the Bristols enjoyed a large country breakfast, just as they had done for as long as he could remember. It might be something as simple as biscuits and gravy, or as special as a stack of buttermilk pancakes drenched in some of his father's homemade syrup. This particular Christmas morning, it was to be biscuits covered with an unbelievable concoction, a family secret known as egg butter, a thick, viscous mass consisting mostly of eggs, butter, and a lot of caramelized sugar. Larry tried to explain it once as the gooey part of a pecan pie, without the pecans or pie crust.

After breakfast, in earlier years when he was a small boy, the rest of the day was spent playing with his friends, everyone showing off their new toys. Now that he was older, there were fewer and fewer "toys" to be played with. The toys he *really* wanted would not fit inside a Christmas stocking. He smiled, however, thinking the toys he wanted the most might be found wearing stockings. So much for Christmas dreams.

For all intents and purposes, when the family breakfast was over, so was Christmas. He even coined a phrase to describe the feeling he had after Christmas breakfast: "There's nothing so over as Christmas when it's over." When he became old enough to drive, he started his own tradition to extend the joy of Christmas a while longer. As he had done many times in the past, early Christmas afternoon, he gathered the gifts he was giving to his friends, and drove from house to house to play Santa Claus.

On his way to his first stop, he chuckled to himself about the odd coincidences that seemed to occur when he and John exchanged their Christmas gifts. Three years ago, they bought each other the same music book; two years ago, they each bought the same record album; last year was the incident with the *capos*. Determined not to allow that to happen again, Larry noted a common thread running among those gifts. This year, his gift to John had nothing to do with music! Problem solved.

"Merry Christmas!" Larry announced as soon as John answered the front door.

"Merry Christmas, Larry!" John replied. Their friendly handshake escalated into a boy-boy hug, faces turned in opposite directions, and the requisite back slapping.

The rest of the Myers family quickly arrived to greet Larry as well. They were fully aware of this Christmas tradition and had come to enjoy it as much as their oldest son and his friend. The ritual began with Larry distributing the gifts he had for Jimmy and the parents, followed by those they had for Larry. The highlight of the event came when it was time for Larry and John to exchange the gifts they had for each other.

"So what did you guys get each other this year?" Jimmy teased.

"I figured out Jimmy has been your spy all these years," John laughed, "telling you what I was getting you so you could get the same thing for me. So this year, I made sure he didn't know. Mom and dad don't even know what I got you!"

"Why would I want to get you the same thing you get me?" Larry laughed. "Oh, well. It was still a good plan, John, but we don't have to worry this year."

"Rats," Jimmy said, disappointed there would be no repeat of the coincidences.

Larry reached into his sack for John's gift while John fetched his gift from under the Christmas tree. The boys looked at each other and laughed when they saw their gifts were approximately the same size and shape. After exchanging the packages, they laughed again noting their similarity in weight. When Jimmy and the Myers started laughing as well, the boys grinned at each other and shrugged.

"There is no chance in hell!" Larry chuckled confidently. "Go ahead, John!"

"Shall we open them simultaneously, Larry?" John suggested.

"Fine!" Larry grinned.

The boys pulled back the wrapping paper, revealing the inner boxes containing the gifts. These were obviously different. Each of the boys had taken a larger box and cut it down in size to be a better fit for the gift within. After a few cuts on the tape holding the boxes closed, the boys saw a similarity in the gifts. They were obviously receiving a book of some kind. They slipped their respective book from the box and looked at each other in utter disbelief as the others roared with laughter. The books were boxed editions, sporting a red leather-like jacket embossed with gold, blue, and green symbols, collector's editions of <u>The Lord of the Rings</u> by J. R. R. Tolkien.

"This is not fucking possible!" John exclaimed.

"Language, John," Bill Myers scolded, even as he laughed openly.

"Why didn't you get me a gift having to do with music?" Larry asked.

"Because I figured *you'd* do that," John explained, "and I wanted to get you something different at least once in my life!"

"Well, well, well," Larry said shaking his head and smiling. "You know what? I love this book, John. As I understand it, people mostly buy gifts they'd like to have for themselves. Next year, why don't we save some time, and go together to buy our gifts to each other?"

"That's not a bad idea!" John chuckled. "I also love the book. Merry Christmas!"

"Merry Christmas, John," he smiled.

"Merry Christmas, Sam!" Larry exclaimed when she met him at the door.

Sam let him inside and greeted him with a hug. He noted the air was filled with the traditional aroma of cookies. "Merry Christmas," she whispered into his ear.

He wondered how many times they had hugged each other like that. "Oh, Sam," he whispered. "Sometimes I wonder why we don't grow up and run off together so we can live happily ever after."

"We both know the answer," she smiled as they looked each other in the face.

"Do we, Sam?" he said gently. "Sometimes I wonder."

"Hang on to your dreams, Larry," she said calmly, "just like I'll hang on to mine."

"I will," he said with a warm smile.

"Merry Christmas, Larry," Gayle said brightly stepping from the kitchen.

Larry and Sam released their hug. "Merry Christmas, Mrs. K!" Larry replied embracing her with a hug of her own. "Do I smell fresh cookies baking in there?"

"Gosh, I hope so!" Gayle giggled. "I'd hate to think I've been wasting my time all afternoon! I'm making your favorite again this year."

"Shortbread?" he grinned. "Oh, boy! I guess I'll have to start exercising again if I want to maintain my boyish figure!"

"Me, too," Sam giggled.

"Why would you want to have a boyish figure?" he smirked. "I like you the way you are, Sam!" Before she could respond, he directed them both to the sofa. "Well, come on, you two. Sit yourselves down on that sofa. I came here to play Santa Claus, and it's time to get started." He knelt on the floor in front of the sofa, reached into his sack of gifts, brought out the first box and handed it to Gayle. "Merry Christmas, Mrs. K!"

"You didn't have to get me a gift," Gayle smiled.

"Yes, I did!" Larry chuckled. "I have to stay on your good side in case you become my mother-in-law one of these days! Would you please talk some sense into this daughter of yours so she'll run off to Vegas with me?"

"I keep trying, Larry," Gayle giggled.

"Mother!" Sam said pretending to be shocked. "I thought you liked Donald!"

"I like both these men," Gayle teased. "You know what they say about having a bird in the hand. This one is here at hand, while the other is off in the bush somewhere."

"Maybe you've found the key, Mrs. K!" Larry said excitedly. "Sam, do you prefer birds in the bush? Sugar, you can take my bird in your hand and lead me off into the bushes anytime you want. I promise I won't resist!"

"Get away from me, you pervert!" Sam laughed.

"Maybe I should open this just to change the subject," Gayle snickered.

Larry pretended to pout. "I guess so, Mrs. K," he said winking at her.

Gayle carefully unwrapped the gift Larry handed her, and peeked into the box. "Oh, how pretty!" she exclaimed. It was his traditional gift of a ceramic cookie jar, this one shaped in the form of a castle with tall towers, looking like it belonged in a fairy tale. "Thank you, Larry!" She hugged his neck and kissed his cheek.

"You're very welcome, Mrs. K," he smiled. "I was hoping you'd like it."

"I do like it!" she repeated. "So what did you get Sam this year?"

"Two tickets to Vegas," he said pretending to pout again, "but she doesn't want it."

"Behave yourself," Sam grinned, "or I'll break your arm!"

"Can you feel the love, Mrs. K?" he laughed. Sam grabbed his wrist and began to twist. "Ow! OK! OK! I'm being 'have'! Now let go so I can get your gift out of my sack!" She twisted his arm a little more before releasing him. He looked into her face as if mortally wounded, then reached into his sack to fetch another gift box. "This is your real gift," he smiled warmly. "Merry Christmas, Sam!"

"Thanks, Larry," she said returning his smile. She began to pick at the cellophane tape holding the wrapping paper in place. The box this year was much larger than usual, and she was very curious as to what it might contain. The cardboard box was marked, "Fragile! Handle with care!" Underneath what seemed to be a ton of packing material was a crystal castle. "It's beautiful!" she said, her eyes filled with wonder.

"You needed a place for the princess to live," he explained, "so the unicorn and the little frog prince will know where to find her." Before he could even complete this explanation, she carefully handed the crystal castle to her mother and put her arms around his neck to hug him once again. He considered teasing her about running off together again, but in the end, he decided he had teased her enough today. Sometimes, he realized, it wasn't really teasing, anyway.

While her daughter hugged their dearest friend, Gayle placed the castle onto the shelf next to the crystal princess, unicorn, and frog prince, then fetched the boxes containing their gifts to him. She placed them on the floor next to him, then returned to her seat on the sofa, waiting patiently for the hug to end. Larry and Sam sat looking at each other, exchanging silent messages along with their smiles.

After a few moments, they broke eye contact. He looked at Gayle and exchanged a smile with her, and then noticed the two packages on the floor beside him. "What's this?" he said pointlessly.

"Open them and see," Sam and Gayle said almost simultaneously.

"Well, OK," he grinned. One of them was a large box wrapped in colored foil, still warm to the touch. He opened it first, delighted with the thought of what it surely contained. "Thanks, Mrs. K!" he said happily at the sight of a large mound of the buttery shortbread he loved so much.

"You're welcome. That's for you to take with you, so don't go eating any just yet. There's more in the kitchen, and we'll have some with milk after you open Sam's gift."

Larry picked up the other gift, examined it, but could not guess its contents. He pulled back the wrapping paper to find a cardboard box, apparently cut down from some larger box in order to better fit around whatever was inside. He pulled away the tape holding this box closed, and pulled out the gift itself. It was another boxed collector's edition book, this one with a green leather-like jacket embossed with gold and red symbols, The Hobbit by J. R. R. Tolkien.

"I love it, but I'm a little confused, Sam," he said. "You were with me when I bought John's gift. Why didn't you give this to him to complete the set?"

"I *did* give one to him, you dumb ass!" she laughed. "I was also shopping with him the day before when he bought *your* gift! It was all I could do to keep from laughing when you picked out your gift to him. I went back the next day and bought two copies of this book, one for each of you!"

"Merry Christmas, Mr. J!" Larry smiled brightly.

Julian flashed Larry a warm smile. "Merry Christmas, Larry. Come on in. The girls are in the family room. We've been expecting you."

When Julian escorted Larry into the family room, Jessica and Julia greeted him before he could say a word. "Merry Christmas, Larry!" they said in perfect unison, as if they had rehearsed it. Larry suspected they actually *had!*

"Merry Christmas, Mrs. J!" he grinned. "Merry Christmas, Julie!" he said turning his eyes to gaze at her. How he enjoyed the feeling that ran down his spine whenever he saw her for the first time on any given day. The second feeling that ran down his spine was always one of pain, brought on by the realization all he could do was look at her and wish it could be different. But the joy of that first feeling was worth the pain of the second, so he knew he would never stop looking at her.

"Have you read any good books lately?" Julia snickered.

"So you were in on the joke, too?" Larry asked.

"Sam told me all about it," Julia giggled, "and I told mom, of course!"

"Naturally," Larry said with a mock scowl. "I'm beginning to think the only way I'll ever give him a unique Christmas gift will be to make it myself."

"Are you even sure that would work?" Jessica teased.

"Not really!" Larry laughed. "Did I smell something baking when I came in? Did you make some more of those wonderful kosher chocolate chip cookies, Mrs. J?"

"Julia and I made some cookies," Jessica smiled, "but Ezekiel's Chariot was overbooked this year, so I'm afraid they're just ordinary chocolate chip cookies. I hope you won't mind too much."

"Well..." Larry said as if terribly disappointed.

"Why don't we eat some while Larry plays his Santa game?" Julia suggested.

"An excellent idea! Come along, mother," Julian said offering Jessica his arm.

"Ooh!" Jessica smiled. She took her husband's arm, heading for the kitchen.

Larry looked at Julia and trembled at the simple beauty of her smile. "Will you allow me to escort you to the kitchen, Julie?" If anyone had read his mind, they would have known it was the most vital question he had asked anyone the entire day.

"Sure!" she smiled. She took the arm he offered, and they followed her parents.

Once the foursome was seated at the kitchen table, Santa went to work, pulling the gifts from his knapsack. "Who wants to be first this year?" he asked brightly.

Julia reached under the table and collected the gift she had secreted there previously. "I think *you* should be first this year," she giggled.

"Santa Claus shouldn't get the first gift!" he tried to protest.

"Santa shmanta!" Julian added while Jessica and Julia laughed. "Just open it."

Larry joined the laughter. Realizing he was sure to be outvoted, he decided to go along. "OK, OK! I'll go first this year." He accepted the gift box, thinking to himself, *I wish it would contain the beautiful smile she's wearing*, and began to pull back the wrapping paper. Under the paper was a copy of The Silmarillion, a collection of notes and stories by J. R. R. Tolkien. "Wow! Thanks, guys!"

"You're very welcome," Julia replied, still wearing that same smile he had hoped to find inside the box. Forcing himself to take his eyes off of her, he looked at Jessica and Julian, noting the warmth of their smiles, and conveying his gratitude by his own smile.

"OK, who's second?" Without waiting for discussion, he made his own selection. "It's your turn, Mrs. J!" He handed her a package of a familiar size and shape.

"Another pony?" she giggled. After a chorus of "boo's" from the others, she unwrapped the package, happy to find the soundtrack album to the movie version of *Hello, Dolly!* starring Barbra Streisand released that year. "Oh, thank you so much! I love listening to her sing!"

"To tell the truth," he smiled, "I thought she was much too young for that role, but I also love to hear her sing!" After a short pause, he picked up the next package and handed it to Julian. "It's your turn, Mr. J!"

Julian accepted the box with a smile but without comment. There was little doubt as to what it contained. Larry knew his wine selections had gotten better over the years, but he was not sure about the sort of wines Mr. Jacobson actually liked. This year, still staying with a kosher wine, he had gotten something a little different. He could see that Julian was pleasantly surprised to find a bottle of Carmel Cabernet Sauvignon, a kosher wine imported from Israel, but not a sweet wine like the ones he had given previously. "Thank you, Larry," Julian said.

"I hope you'll enjoy it," Larry smiled softly. Eagerly, his eyes turned to look at the girl he saw so often in his dreams. He picked up the remaining gift and handed it to her. "And this one is for you, Julie," he added timidly. "I hope you'll like it."

"I'm sure I'll like it," she said sweetly as their eyes met and locked.

"Well, go ahead and open it!" he urged, wanting to break away from that terrible gaze that burned right through him, even as he simultaneously longed to stare into those green eyes that had haunted his life so long.

Julia smiled once again, and then turned her attention to the small package. She carefully pulled back the tape holding the brightly colored paper in place, to find the small pasteboard box within. From this box she removed the small metallic box inside, and admired the ornate designs covering its surface. Making sure the mechanism was wound, she opened the little box to hear the tune it would play, and smiled when she recognized the Beatles classic *All You Need Is Love*.

He would do anything to see her smile like that. "I hope you still like to collect these things, Julie," he said softly.

"Of course I do!" she said, her smile even warmer than before. "Thank you so much. You know, I think most of the music boxes in my collection have come from you, and I treasure each and every one of them."

"I'm glad," he replied, returning the warmth he saw in her smile and in her eyes.

Wednesday, December 31, 1969
Voices In The Sky

Once again, the Jacobsons offered their house for the *Four Musketeers* to have their traditional New Year's Eve party. Larry and Sam were the last to arrive, greeted warmly by John and his date, and by Julia and Steve. Just as always, the Jacobsons treated the youngsters to a wide variety of snacks and nonalcoholic drinks. They all played games and danced to the music provided by Julia's record collection.

A few minutes before the stroke of midnight, Larry and Sam quietly excused themselves, moving away from the others to spend the special moment alone. They listened as the others watched the clock, counting down the final seconds of 1969.

"Ten... Nine... Eight..." they called. As before, Larry reflected on the events of the previous year, replaying the year in his memory. The highlights of the year had been the excitement they shared during the moon landing, and the joyous expedition to the Woodstock festival. Also important was the way he and John had won the draft lottery! Romantically speaking, the year had pretty much been a bust. Julia had dominated his thoughts all year, making it difficult for him to appreciate other girls. There had been one very special moment that was now a recurring theme in his dreams. It had been a pleasure to meet Sarah and her family, and of course, Mama J, just as it had been a special treat to join in their holiday celebrations!

"Seven... Six..." they counted in the next room. Of course, one has to take the bad along with what little good there is. He truly missed doing the *Top Forty Showcase* program, and still could not understand why it had been canceled. Maybe it was just the universe's way of telling him to move on. Perhaps the worse event of the year had been Schotzy's death. It broke his heart to see her so unhappy, but at least he had comforted her in her hour of need.

"Five... Four..." the countdown proceeded. And, just as always, she was right there in the next room. He could steal a glance of her any time he wanted, but all that seemed to do was make him want her even more than before. Somehow, although he did not know the details, Ed had been a casualty from Schotzy's death. Larry figured it was natural for the universe to see that Larry was not given an opportunity to make his move before this Steve came along. Now that Julia had blossomed into such a beautiful girl, good looking guys like Steve would always be hanging around. On top of it all, the cover story he and Sam had concocted to hide his feelings seemed to be failing.

Sam suddenly cried out, "Oh, God! No!"

"What's the matter, Sam?" he asked, his concentration broken.

"Three... Two... One..." Just before the clock struck midnight, Larry forgot his own troubles completely, more concerned about his dear friend than anything else.

End of Crossroads Part I: One Day Of Magic

The story of the *Four Musketeers* - Larry, Sam, John, and Julia - continues in <u>Crossroads Part II: Heaven In Her Eyes</u>, as the teenagers grow into young adults.

Other plans are put on hold when a tragedy befalls them. They are forced to come even closer together than ever before, not only to take care of each other, but to take a stand against the injustice and insanity that holds the world in its ugly grip.

The harsh reality of the universe confronts Larry personally. The dream he has been nurturing for over four years moves hopelessly beyond his reach. The only option left to him is to let it go, for the secret of happiness is not the pursuit of the things one wants, but the satisfaction derived from the things one has. He must transform himself from the boy seeking his own selfish interests and desires, into the man who selflessly places the wellbeing of those he loves ahead of his own.

Yet how can he simply walk away from everything he cherishes? He knows what he has seen and what it means. He must find a way to reach the *Heaven In Her Eyes*.

Yiddish for Goyim

The following is a simple glossary of Yiddish (and Hebrew) terms and expressions used within this work. It is intended to be neither authoritative nor exhaustive, and quite probably contains terrible errors and numerous omissions. Many of these words are also presented with tongue firmly in cheek! The English spellings of these words is purely an approximation based upon their pronunciation, which makes the whole thing rather bopkes when one considers that I personally have difficulty pronouncing most of these words in the first place!

At best, this is merely a guide for goyim (just in case you are *particularly* dense, this includes myself), hopefully allowing them to correctly "interpret" the intended meaning when such words and phrases are used within the story. I have carefully chosen the word "interpret" rather than "translate". Like the words "anxious" and "eager", if you do not understand the difference, then this furshlugginer glossary is probably of no use to you anyway. Mishugas! Such chutzpa this goy has!

Oy, how I could have used a good English to Yiddish dictionary while writing this! Of course, producing such a thing would be just about the same level of difficulty as producing a good Texan to English dictionary. For example, how do you define the word "rat"? No, I don't mean the nasty rodent pest. I mean the word "rat" as in the sentence, "Ima fixin' tago down yonner and git me a shit load rat now!" This sentence also illustrates why Texas will never convert to the metric system. There is simply no metric equivalent to a shit load!

So, without further tsimmes, here goes.

Adar	twelfth month of the Hebrew calendar.
Adar II	thirteenth month of the Hebrew calendar.
aicht	eight.
akhim	brothers; brethren.
alter kakher	old fart.
Av	fifth month of the Hebrew calendar.
azoi	as; in the same way; like; as in; such as.
b'suleh	virgin.
badhkin	comedian; entertainer.
bahaltn	to hide.
baleboosteh	(feminine) an excellent and praiseworthy homemaker.
baleboss	(masculine) the head of the household; owner of a store; one who assumes authority.
bashert	soul mate; predestined; fated.
bedekin	the ceremony in which the groom covers the face the bride with a veil before the formal marriage ceremony begins.
bekovedik	upright; honorable; decent; admirable.
belev same'akh	with a cheerful heart.
bentshn	to bless; bless.
bin	am (first person singular).
bissele	a little bit.

bist	are (second person singular).
biteh	please.
Biz hundert azoi ve tsvantsik	You should live to be one hundred like a twenty year old.
Biz hundert un tsvantsik	You should live to be one hundred and twenty; Long life to you.
bobe	grandmother.
bobegum	candy your mother gives her grandchildren that she never gave to you!
bobemayse	old wives tale; nonsense; something patently silly and untrue. (example: <u>Crossroads</u> by Larry J. Bristol)
bopkes	something trivial; worthless; absurd; foolish; nonsensical. (see also bubkes)
boytchik	boy. (affectionate)
brocha	blessing; a prayer of thanksgiving and praise.
bubee	affectionate term of endearment, is widely used for darling, dear child, honey, sweetheart, good friend. (see also bubeleh)
bubeleh	affectionate term of endearment, is widely used for darling, dear child, honey, sweetheart, good friend. (see also bubee)
bubkes	something trivial; worthless; absurd; foolish; nonsensical. (see also bopkes)

Chanukah	Jewish holiday, also known as the Festival of Lights.
chatan	groom.
chazak	be strong.
Cheshvan	eighth month of the Hebrew calendar.
chochem	genius, usually meant sarcastically, as in a man who argues with a policeman.
chuppah	the canopy under which a marriage ceremony is conducted.
chutzpa	brazen nerve; gall; self-centered boldness; incredible guts; moxie.
chutzpapa	a father who wakes his wife at 4:00 in the morning so she can change the baby's diaper.
cockamamie	crazy; ludicrous.

dayn	your. (familiar, singular)
dayneer	yours. (familiar, plural)
deja nu	the feeling you've seen the same exasperated look on your mother's face, but not knowing exactly when.
der	the (masculine, singular).
di	the (feminine, singular); the (plural, regardless of gender); these; those.
dos	the (neuter, singular); this.

dray	three.
dreck	crap; shit.
dreidel	a child's toy, similar to a top, used to play a traditional Chanukah game. It has four sides, each with a symbol from the Hebrew alphabet: Nun, Gimmel, Heh, and Shin. These stand for the Yiddish words nit (none), gantz (all), halb (half), and shtell (put).
driter	the third. (as in: first, second, third).
du	you. (familiar, singular)
Elul	sixth month of the Hebrew calendar.
eppes	a little something; a somebody.
er	he.
es	it.
eyner	the first. (as in: first, second, third)
eynss	one.
farmisht	confused; befuddled.
feh	an exclamation of disgust.
feter	uncle.
finf	five.
firh	four.
flanken	1) a strip of beef from the chuck end of the short ribs. 2) a Jewish dish using this cut of beef, which is boiled and usually served with horseradish.
foter	father.
frosh	frog.
froy	wife.
furshlugginer	wacky.
gai	go. (imperative)
gantse magillah	a whole big story.
gantz	all; everything.
gelt	money.
genug	enough.
genug shoyn	enough already!
getrank	a drink; beverage.
gevalt	a cry of fear, astonishment, trouble; a cry for help.
geyn	to go.
gezen	seen.
gezunt	health; healthy.
gimmel	one of the letters in the Hebrew alphabet.
goot gezugt	well said.
Got	God.

goy	a person, place, or thing that is non-Jewish. (*plural:* goyim)
goyim	persons, places, or things that are non-Jewish. (*singular:* goy)
goyster	The author of this book is a perfect example. (see also oyster) (Lighten up! It's a joke!)
grin	green.
grober yung	crude youth.
gut	good.
halb	half.
haltn	grab; halt; stop.
hamentaschen	triangular fruit-filled cookies commonly served during the holiday of Purim.
Hava nagila	Let us rejoice.
Hava narenena	Let us sing.
heh	one of the letters in the Hebrew alphabet.
hint	dogs.
hintl	puppy.
hobn	to have.
hundert	hundred.
hunt	dog.
Hus du gezen in dayn lebn?	Have you ever seen anything like this in your life?

ich	I.
im	him.
ir	you. (formal, singular or plural)
Iyar	second month of the Hebrew calendar.
iz	is.

jewdo	a traditional form of self-defense, based on the idea that one should be able to talk their way out of a tight spot.

knish	1) a baked dumpling usually filled with potato, meat, or barley. 2) vagina.
kallah	bride.
kalt	cold. (weather)
ketuvah	marriage contract.
kibbitz	to chat; to joke; light conversation.
kibbitzer	joker.
kiddushin	marriage ceremony; sanctification; dedication.
kind	child.
kinder	children.
kinderlach	little children.

kippah	a thin, usually slightly rounded cloth cap worn by Jews. (*plural:* kippot) (see also yarmulke)
Kislev	ninth month of the Hebrew calendar.
kittel	a long white robe worn to symbolize cleanliness and purity, such as that worn by the chatan during the kiddushin, or during Yom Kippur.
kleyn	little; small.
klutz	a clumsy, graceless person.
kop	head. (the one on top of your shoulders)
kosher	legitimate; right; honest.
kranken	sick.
kurveh	whore; prostitute.
kvetch	to complain; a chronic complainer; fuss; fret.
latkes	a traditional food served during Chanukah. It is pronounced either as "lot-kuhs" or "lot-keys" depending on where your bobe comes from. If your grandmother is goy, then you probably pronounce it "potato pancakes".
Le chaim	To life!
lebn	life. (as in your life)
Lozn geyn	Let them go.
macher	big shot.
mameh	mother.
mamzer	illegitimate child; bastard. (*plural:* mamzerim)
mamzerim	illegitimate children. (*singular:* mamzer)
man	husband.
matzah	unleavened bread.
mayn	my. (possessive, singular)
mazel	luck.
mazel tov	congratulations.
menorah	a candelabrum with nine branches used during the Chanukah festival; a candelabrum with seven branches used to symbolize the seven days of creation.
mentsh	a person; a human being. (*plural:* mentshn)
mentshn	people. (*singular:* mentsh)
meydele	girl.
mikh	me.
mir	we.
mishpocheh	family, including relatives.
mishuganah	just plain crazy.
mishugas	craziness.
mit	with.
mitzvot	commandments.

naches	proud pleasure; special joy particularly from the achievement of a child.
nas	wet. (weather)
nayn	nine.
nebech	a person who suffers because he makes other people's problems his own. (A schlemiel spills his soup, it falls on the schlemazel, and the nebech cleans it up!)
Nissan	first month of the Hebrew calendar.
nit	not; none; nothing.
nosh	to eat a little something; to snack.
nosher	someone who eats; a nibbler.
nudge	to bother; make a nuisance of yourself.
nun	one of the letters in the Hebrew alphabet.
oy	pain; a lament; a protest; a cry of dismay; a reflex of delight. The most expressive exclamation in Yiddish.
oy vay	"oh pain", but it's an all purpose expression from minor irritation to abysmal woe.
Oy Vayder	a Jewish Sith?
oyster	someone who sprinkles Yiddish expressions into an English conversation. (see also goyster)
Pesach	Passover.
plotz	to burst; to explode; to be aggravated beyond bearing.
potch	a slap; a smack and insult; a blow to one's pride; a setback to one's hopes.
ptcha	a thick, gelatinous soup.
Purim	one of the most joyous and fun holidays on the Jewish calendar, commemorating a time when Jewish people living in Persia were saved from extinction.
pushke	the little can or container kept in the home in which money is to be donated. Usually, a charitable organization would provide its own pushke.
putz	penis (see also schmekel); sometimes used as an endearing term for one's male in-laws.
putznosher	someone who nibbles on a penis. (Can you say "cocksucker"? Oy!)
Rosh Hashanah	holiday commonly known as the Jewish New Year. (literally: the head of the year)
rugalach	bite-sized crescent-shaped cookies with a rich cream cheese dough, with a variety of fillings including fruit, nuts, poppy seeds, or jam.

Santa shmanta	the story Jewish children are given to explain why they celebrate Chanukah while the rest of humanity celebrates Christmas.
schlemazel	a person who suffers through no fault of his own; an unlucky person. (A schlemiel spills his soup, it falls on the schlemazel, and the nebech cleans it up!)
schlemiel	a person who suffers due to his own poor choices or actions; a fool. (A schlemiel spills his soup, it falls on the schlemazel, and the nebech cleans it up!)
schlep	to drag; to pull.
schmaltz	1) cooking fat – usually chicken. 2) overly emotional; mush; luxury; wealth; fancy.
schmekel	penis, usually of the small variety. (see also putz)
schmooze	friendly talk; heart-to-heart prolonged talk.
schmuck	asshole.
schmutz	dirt, as in when your Jewish mother says to you, "Oy, *you've got some* schmutz *on your face! Stay still while I clean it off!*" as she takes a tissue, moistens it in her mouth and proceeds to scrub your face.
schmutzig	dirty.
schnapps	booze.
schpeel	selling job, pitch.
schtupn	to push; to shove; to have sex; to fuck. (Surely you knew it would be here somewhere! What good is a glossary for *any* language that doesn't give you the "F" word?)
seychel	common sense; wisdom; good judgment.
Shabbat	Sabbath.
shalom	peace. (a greeting)
Shevat	eleventh month of the Hebrew calendar.
sheynem dank	Thank you very much!
shikker	a drunk.
shin	one of the letters in the Hebrew alphabet.
shney	snow.
shpaltn	to stab.
shpritsn	to squirt.
shtarker	thug; hoodlum.
shteln	to put.
shul	Synagogue or school.
shygetz	a non-Jewish male, as in "she's going out with a shygetz".
shykse	a non-Jewish female, as in "he's going out with a shykse".
simkhah	celebration.
Sivan	third month of the Hebrew calendar.

Talmud	the most significant collection of the Jewish oral tradition interpreting the Torah.
Tammuz	fourth month of the Hebrew calendar.
tanta	aunt.
tateh	father.
tchatchke	1) little toys; knickknacks. 2) a pretty young thing, like a trophy wife.
tefillah	a leather pouch containing scrolls with passages of scripture, used to bind the words to the wearer's hands and between their eyes. (*plural:* tefillin)
Tevet	tenth month of the Hebrew calendar.
Tishri	seventh month of the Hebrew calendar.
Torah	the Jewish bible; to goyim, the Old Testament.
trogedik	pregnant.
tsenn	ten.
tsimmes	1) a side dish of mixed cooked vegetables slightly sweetened, usually carrots, prunes, sweet potatoes. 2) A prolonged procedure, involved business, a mix-up, troubles.
tsu	to.
tsu gezunt	Gesundheit! (literally: to health!)
tsuris	problems; trouble; grief; aggravation; heartache.
tsvantsik	twenty.
tsvey	two.
tsveyter	the second. (as in: first, second, third)
tuchus	your bottom, buttocks. (By the 1940's, a slang version in use was "tushee", which later was shortened to "tush", now in regular use throughout American culture, thanks to Jewish film makers.)
tummel	noise; commotion; noisy disorder.
un	and.
unz	us.
uru	wake up; awaken.
varem	warm. (weather)
vaser	water.
vashnukad	intoxicated; drunk. ("I was so vashnukad I could plotz!")
ve	and.
venis'mekha	and be glad.
venitchazek	may we be strengthened.
yarmulke	a thin, usually slightly rounded cloth cap worn by Jews. (see also kippah)

About the Author

My name is Larry J. Bristol – the *head honcho* at the Double Luck (http://www.doubleluck.com). That (plus one dollar and fifty cents) will buy me a cup of coffee at almost any airport in this country. Being *head honcho* is not the same as it used to be. As *head honcho*, I make *all* of the important decisions – what should be done to end wars, disease, and hunger – what should be done about taxes and social security – what should be done about global warming and deforestation – what should be done to prevent El Niño weather patterns. Trivial matters – what we eat – when we eat – what we buy – where we go – what we do when we get there – I leave to my wife, Marsha.

I started as a child, born in 1949 in a small town in south Texas by the name of Raymondville. There is nothing distinguished about Raymondville, unless you think being the first bit of civilization encountered driving south across the King Ranch is distinguished. You are probably wondering why someone as important as me would choose to be born in such an humble location. The reason is I was quite young at the time, and being rather immature, wanted to stay close to my mother.

Before I knew what had happened, I was whisked off to another small town in central Texas, known as Bryan. There, I received a first rate free public education at the hands (and knees) of the Bryan school system, eventually graduating from Stephen F. Austin High School. Actually, there was little they could do to prevent it.

At this point, my parents made one of those offers that cannot be refused. I could attend any institution of higher learning I desired. As long as it was a state supported school, they would pay for tuition and books. I could live anywhere I wanted, with free room and board, but only if I lived at their house. Any other financial needs were to be my own responsibility.

Fortunately, a state supported institution, Texas A&M University, happened to be located just down the road in an even smaller town called College Station. Since my parents had not raised a fool, I decided this university was perfect for my needs. Before one could wink, blink, or turn on the lights, I received a degree in Industrial Engineering, graduating in 1972 with a BAL of 4.3!

That means "Blood Alcohol Level", and has nothing to do with grades. Later in life, this fact would serve me quite well! For in one of my most important current roles, I am the brewmeister for the Double Luck Brewery.

I studied to become an engineer because I had always been fascinated with trains. Imagine my surprise when the professors kept droning on and on about vectors and tolerances and something called *thermodynamics!* None of these things had any influence on my life, although my love of trains continues to serve me well. In another of my most important roles, I am the chief gandy dancer for the Double Luck Railroad.

Why would one want to get a college degree in anything *useful?* Playing the classic game of "And Now for Something Completely Different," I soon found I could earn a decent living by arranging zeros and ones into esthetically pleasing patterns. In my spare time, I am a systems software architect, having played in the computer industry since 1967. (Did I not say I started as a child?)

The rest, as they say, is history.

Printed in the United States
48315LVS00003B/3